OWEN GLEN

Books by Ben Ames Williams

SPLENDOR

THE STRUMPET SEA

THREAD OF SCARLET

COME SPRING

THE STRANGE WOMAN

TIME OF PEACE

AMATEURS AT WAR (Editor)

LEAVE HER TO HEAVEN

IT'S A FREE COUNTRY

HOUSE DIVIDED

FRATERNITY VILLAGE

A DIARY FROM DIXIE (Editor)

OWEN GLEN

OWEN GLEN

BEN AMES WILLIAMS

19 50

HOUGHTON MIFFLIN COMPANY BOSTON

The Riverside Press Cambridge

The characters in this novel; with the exception of BB Beecham and his family, are purely fictional; their resemblance to human beings is intentional, but any likeness to an actual individual is accidental.

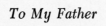

To My Father

"That is the most perfect government in which an injury to one is the concern of all."

Legend encircling the great seal of the Knights of Labor.

OWEN GLEN

1

January 1890

BREAKFAST was buckwheat cakes, and plenty of them. Sally Beecham had set a batch of batter a week or ten days before, and each evening the replenished mixture, covered with a damp dish-towel, was left on the hearth to rise overnight and to be stirred down in the morning while the soapstone griddle reached the proper temperature. The griddle held three cakes, each the size of a small plate. While Sally cooked, the heat of the stove tinted her cheeks, and little moist curls formed above her forehead. BB ate with a quiet efficiency, never seeming to hurry. When she deposited three beautiful brown cakes on his plate, he tilted the topmost with his fork and slid under it a slice of butter about two inches square and a quarter-inch thick; he lifted the next and repeated the process. Then he laid another slice of butter atop the pile, spreading it as it softened, so that it was for a moment a golden-brown liquid before it settled into the cake and disappeared. Over the pile he poured dark molasses till it overflowed on all sides; then, in the last instant before the molasses spilled off the plate itself, he cut a triangular section an inch and a half on a side and an inch thick, deliciously dripping butter and molasses, and delivered it to its ultimate destination.

While cakes were cooking, Sally liked to stand in the doorway from dining room to kitchen, watching her happy husband. Across the room, BB's sister Jane pinned a dry diaper on Bertie. She had lived with them since before the baby was born, shared now with Sally the happiness of taking care of BB and the baby and the house. Jane was a cheerful, round-faced young woman, older than Sally and younger than BB, as jolly as Santa Claus and with twinkling

1

eyes that seemed — behind her thick-lensed spectacles — larger
than they were. She was one of those divinely generous individuals
who by preference serve others rather than themselves, and who
are better content to give pleasure than to receive it. Now as BB
reached repletion, she brought Bertie for him to mind, while she
cooked cakes for Sally and for herself. BB stood the baby on the
floor, and the little boy, holding fast to BB's hands, bounced up
and down, chortling with delight, till gently BB took his hands
away and left the baby standing in precarious balance.

"Look, Sally." She turned to watch, and he extended his hands
till they were almost, but not quite, within the baby's reach.
"Come on, Bertie. Come to papa."

Bertie panted, his mouth open; he tried with one hand to reach
BB's extended fingers. The effort put him off balance, and to catch
himself he took with one foot one short step.

BB snatched him up with proud ejaculations. "See that! He
took a step! And he's only ten months old! Ten and a half!"

Sally smiled. "It wasn't much of a step!"

"A step, all the same." Jane called a question from the kitchen,
and BB told her: "Bertie's walking!" Sally laughed at him, and
Jane came in with a heaped plate, and they argued the question,
BB yielding never an inch.

After breakfast and before going to town, BB had proofs to read,
and Sally held the copy. For six or seven months now BB had
been the owner, and therefore the editor, of the Hardiston *Journal.*
The proofs which he read this morning, Sally speaking only when
a mistake must be corrected, made up a four- or five-column sketch
of Hardiston. It was headed:

HARDISTON

IN

1890

" 'At the beginning of a new decade,' " BB read, " 'it is only
proper that we take a survey of Hardiston and her industries, both
for the edification of the living as well as for the benefit of pos-
terity.' " He read in a rapid monotone, hurrying through a familiar
task. Sally thought the word "both" was unnecessary, but it was
in the copy so she did not speak. BB's father and mother had been
Welsh, as were most of the men and women in Hardiston County,

so he spoke and read Welsh before he knew any English; yet at sixteen he passed the examinations for a teacher's certificate, and two years later he began to teach a school in the hill country near Adams Furnace, ten miles south of Hardiston. His father had died while he was still a baby, and a considerable proportion of BB's earnings went to help support his mother; but he saved enough to be able to go, at intervals over a period of years, for half a dozen terms, to the University at Athens. There he supplemented his savings by working in the college library; and one day Sally went to draw out a book and his still persisting Welsh accent at first amused and then attracted her. They took long walks together in the Asylum grounds, a favorite promenade of the period; and she invited him to Mississippi for Christmas and to meet her family. A few days after Christmas they were married. He was twenty-four and she was nineteen. He began to read law in her father's office, but after her father's death two years later they decided to return to Ohio and here make their home; and, waiting only till their son was born and she was ready to travel, they did so.

BB's toneless voice raced down the columns. He held the proofs folded over a copy of the *Atlantic Monthly*, his pencil ready to make any needed changes. " 'Founded in 1817, Hardiston in 1860 was at the geographical center of population of the United States; ten years later that distinction passed to Wilmington, and in 1880 to Cincinnati. Now, with the official disappearance of the frontier, and with increasing settlement in the West, the new census will doubtless shift the center to Indiana.' "

Sally was strictly attentive to the copy. Names and dates and figures must be right. Population "about 5000." Railroads, three. Telephone system, established 1882, " 'first used on August 11 of that year. The number of instruments at first was 44 but in a short time it had increased to 83. At present, however, the number is only 36. Our electric light system was begun on March 21st, 1888. There are 26 arc lights in use now, and 550 incandescent lights.' "

The Fire Department, two banks, three newspapers. " 'The third paper is known as the *Star*. It was established under peculiar circumstances. On July 29th, 1889, Mr. Frank C. Towne was nominated for Auditor by the democrats of this county.' "

Sally interrupted. "You have 'democrats' with a small 'd.' "

"I want it that way," he assured her. "The noun 'democrat' as now used is the commonest kind of a common noun. There is not a man in the party who knows what the word means." And he read: " 'On the 5th of the following month, Mrs. Towne lent $550 to James Studley to start a paper. Although the name of James Studley appears as that of editor, yet it is not known that he has ever written an editorial.' "

BB's voice hardened as he read, and Sally's eyes for a moment lighted with amused affection. He had bought the *Journal* from James Studley, Mr. Studley agreeing not to start a new paper for two years; now BB had a pending damage suit against Mr. Studley for his violation of that agreement, and he lost no opportunity to remind the readers of the *Journal* of Mr. Studley's perfidy. His voice raced on: ten churches, four schools, two halls, three hotels, three livery stables, a band, four iron furnaces, a nail mill, a foundry, two flour mills, three planing mills, a tannery, three brick-yards, a carriage factory, six blacksmiths, a gunsmith, four shoe-makers, four building and loan companies; and under each heading, names and names and names. " 'There are probably a hundred and fifty coal mines, large and small, in the county. The largest operator is Mr. Herbert Canter, who either owns outright or has an interest in well over a score of mines. Mr. Canter still owns his home in Hardiston, but his residence is now in Columbus, and he has large interests in Cincinnati, Cleveland and New York. Among other leading operators . . .' " Names and names and names.

When he finished and folded the proofs, Sally reminded him: "You haven't said anything about the saloons. There are more saloons than anything else."

"Fifteen," he admitted. "But neither men nor communities parade their sins, Sally! The less said about saloons, the better." He rose, stuffing proofs and copy into his pockets. "I must go." He kissed her cheek, and — their arms entwined — they stepped out on the front porch. "My, smell that air!" The morning was fine, sunny and warm. "It's more like April than January. Why don't you walk to town with me and enjoy it?"

"Oh, I have the breakfast things to clean up."

Jane had come to the door behind them with the baby in her arms. "You go along, Sally," she said. "I'll have Bertie put to bed in a minute, and I'll do the kitchen."

So Sally went to find hat and cape, and BB said to Jane: "Wish I could take a tramp in the country. I will tomorrow, if it's as fine as this." Today was Wednesday, press day for the *Journal*. The inside, boiler plate except for a few columns of editorials, was always printed on Saturday; the outside Wednesday afternoon. So on Thursdays, BB's time was relatively free.

Jane agreed that the day was fine and followed Sally indoors, and BB strolled around the corner of the house, looking off across the open land in the rear where a few cows and horses were at pasture. The morning was so warm he half-expected to hear a robin sing; but the robins seldom came before early March.

When Sally called from the front porch that she was ready, he returned to join her and they went down the steps — the house was a dozen feet above the grade of the street — and turned toward town. He was two inches less than six feet tall, yet a little over the two-hundred-pound mark; but he was stocky rather than fat, thick-chested and erect, with strong legs. She was slender, and a few inches shorter than he, and she needed to hurry to keep pace with his quick strides. As they descended the steps, a wagon passed with a load of ore for Union Furnace, and horses and wheels raised a thin dust from the powdered slag and cinders with which the street was surfaced.

At the corner by Hodson's store, Evan Jenkins was lowering the arc light to put in fresh carbons; and they paused to watch while he removed the burned-down stubs of carbon, tossed them aside and replaced them. BB picked up one of the discards. "Here's a treasure for some boy," he said; and Evan, a lank, red-haired man with a remarkable Adam's apple, nodded, hauling the arc light up into place again.

"Saturdays when there's no school, they follow me around, scrambling for 'em."

"If this weather holds, you'll soon be plowing," BB remarked. The other, though he worked all day and every day at the electric light plant, had a farm on the Pike just outside the corporation limits.

Evan made a grumbling sound. "Don't know as I'll take the trouble. I don't raise only enough to feed my cattle anyway, and there's no money in beef nowadays. I sold a good yearling to Hughie Morgan yesterday, weighted close to five hundred, and all

I got was fifteen dollars. Three cents a pound! Keeps on, I'll sell the farm."

"A farmer never has to go hungry," BB reminded him; and he and Sally went on, BB idly handling the bit of carbon. Sally asked why boys wanted these stubs. "They use them as crayons to draw pictures on sidewalks, or to mark out a hop-scotch game," he explained. "I wonder why they call it hop-scotch. Maybe because hopping on one foot might save shoe-leather for a thrifty Scotchman."

Sally smiled as one smiles at the familiar, for this abiding interest in words and their sources was a part of him. As they went on, he spoke to everyone they met, usually by name. "You know half the people in town already," she remarked, proud of him. "And we've hardly been here six months. I don't see how you remember."

"I'm interested in them. Perhaps that's why. We always remember things that interest us."

Mrs. Arthur, a neighbor a few years older than Sally, quick as a wren in all her movements and with a ready smile, paused to talk with them. Prices, she declared, were a scandal. "When Charlie and I were married, I could get four pounds of steak for a quarter. Now Hughie Morgan asks eight cents a pound, and even roasting beef is seven cents." She smiled at herself. "Well, I just won't pay such prices! If a quarter's worth of steak isn't enough for me and Mr. Arthur and the young ones, that's not my fault! That's all I'll buy."

Sally agreed that eight cents was high, and BB said the real trouble was that the farmers who raised the beef were paid less than their due. He quoted what Evan had said, but Mrs. Arthur retorted that three cents a pound was enough for the farmers. "All they do is let the critters eat their pasture! Sally, you didn't come to the Chautauqua Circle last night."

"Bertie was cutting a tooth. I hated to leave him. Was it a good meeting?"

"Well, a lot of the members were behind on their reading!" Mrs. Arthur tossed her pretty head. "Now you be sure and come next month!"

She went her way, and so did they. At the Broad Street corner, where Moses Evans had put in along the front of his lot a sidewalk of stone slabs, they saw Mr. Evans himself — a stubby, bearded man who operated half a dozen coal mines up the creek — staring angrily at a cabalistic set of marks on one of the slabs. He pointed indignantly. "Here! Look at this!" They saw a rectangle drawn in white chalk, and within it a muddle of meaningless lines, with five stars like a signature.

"What is it?" Sally asked.

BB was about to answer, but Mr. Evans said hotly:

"Knights of Labor! This is the way they call one of their —— " He hesitated, checking a profane adjective just in time. "One of their secret meetings. I'd like to find out where it's going to be! I'd teach them a lesson!"

BB asked: "Your men talking strike?"

"They know better! I'd let 'em strike and let 'em starve."

They left him still fuming; and Sally, her cheeks hot with anger, exclaimed: "I'd like to see him starve awhile! But do the Knights of Labor have secret meetings? They had a ball at the Rink, New Year's Eve! That was public enough!"

BB smiled. "Well, as a matter of fact, their meetings aren't secret now. I think boys like to chalk up Mr. Evans's flagstones just to make him mad. In the old days, of course, the Knights had passwords, and a grip; they used to meet at night, slip out of their houses after dark and walk miles, sometimes, to the meeting place. For years, anyone known to be in their organization was likely to be discharged and blacklisted. But there was never so much feeling in Hardiston County as in Illinois and Iowa."

Before they came to the first stores, BB had stopped to talk with a dozen people; he had more than once scribbled a hasty line in his notebook. They saw Will Dine, the druggist, who had been accidentally shot by some boys using a Flobert rifle a week before, sweeping the sidewalk in front of his store. Outside Hughie Morgan's butcher shop, BB spoke to someone, shaking hands, saying: "Well, what's new up the creek?" This was a generic term for the coal fields north of Hardiston and for the three villages of Slacktown, Glendale and Belton; and since Sally had no interest in the news up the creek, and wished to buy a piece of liver for dinner, she caught BB's eye with a smile of farewell and turned into the butcher shop.

BB, presently proceeding toward Main Street and the *Journal* office, saw in front of the Court House two strangers with a muzzled bear on a chain. The center of a circle of men and boys, they were offering ten dollars to any man who cared to wrestle the bear. BB exchanged with them a word or two, then went on to the office.

He took the corrected proofs of his sketch of Hardiston back to the pressroom and gave them to Will Davis, the foreman who set type, ran the job press, made up the paper, fed the big press, built the fires, swept out, and did every other mechanical and physical task that needed doing. Will was a lean young man about BB's age, who never seemed to hurry, yet accomplished miracles. He took the proofs now and said:

"I left a jar or two of sausage on top of the safe. We killed the other pig last week."

"Fine!" BB was delighted, for Mrs. Davis made famous sausage. "We're having buckwheat cakes every morning, and sausage is just what they need. Is she well?"

"Same as always."

"A wonderful woman."

Will grinned with quiet pride. "I've got so I think so myself."

Back in the front office BB sat down at his rolltop desk — never closed, since it was so full of exchanges, books of account, letters and curios that to close it would have required a considerable house-cleaning — and wrote up the three or four locals he had collected on the way to town. Of the men with the bear, since he missed no opportunity to gibe at the opposition party, he wrote:

> *Two men with a chained bear came through Hardiston*
> *Wednesday offering ten dollars to any man who would*
> *wrestle their bear. Since they met no democrats they*
> *found no one foolish enough to take their offer.*

He left the items on his desk and went to Bob Henson's barbershop to be shaved. Usually BB planned to be shaved on Tuesdays, Thursdays, and Saturdays; but tonight he and Sally were going to see *The Last Days of Pompey* at the Rink, and she had suggested he make an exception. Bob Henson was not in the barbershop when BB entered; but he arrived a moment later, an impressive black-hatted figure wearing a wide mustache and a goatee. He was the town marshal, and before attacking BB's beard he laid aside his black coat and unbuckled his revolver belt and put it and his revolver on the shelf below the shaving mugs. There were three or four dozen of these mugs, one for each of his regular customers. Some had the customer's name or initials in gilt letters. While he was lathering BB's chin, Bob spoke approvingly of the editor's speech at the Court House Saturday night, when at the meeting of the Hardiston Debating Society, BB took the affirmative of the proposition: "Resolved, that Canada should be annexed to the United States."

The talk in the barbershop gave BB two more locals for the paper. On the way back to the *Journal* office, he picked up his mail, four letters and the morning papers from Columbus and Cincinnati. Governor Foraker, defeated for re-election and now a private citizen, wrote to thank BB for his support. Since the Ohio Legislature was Democratic, Foraker and Major McKinley had declined to be candidates for the Senatorship. BB thought either one of them could have been elected on a popular vote, and he wrote a short editorial urging that Senators be elected by the people. The Legislature had elected Mr. Brice, and there were rumors of corruption, and BB concluded:

> *A Brice has not enough money to buy the people of Ohio. Give the people a chance.*

He added the locals he had heard in the barbershop, and took this copy back through the file room to the foot of the stairs that led up to the type loft. An endless tape with two hooks fixed in it ran over wheels at the top and the bottom of the stairs. BB hung his copy on the lower hook and turned the wheel to carry it up to the stair head where the girls who set type could reach it.

2

The day was so warm that in the front office BB opened the door to the street. He was at his desk, his back to the door, when behind him someone said: "Good morning, teacher."

BB swung around and saw a pretty girl of sixteen or seventeen standing in the doorway. Her face was pleasantly familiar, but her name for the moment eluded him. He rose, extending his hand, saying: "Come in! Come in!"

She said smilingly: "You haven't the faintest notion who I am, I know."

But BB, as he came to greet her, had seen on the sidewalk behind her Evan Williams of Adams Township, talking with John Vaughn, who was cashier of the Citizens' Bank; and the sight of Evan helped him recognize this pretty girl as Evan's daughter who had been in the first school he taught, years ago.

"Of course I do! You're Marged Williams. I remember the day you learned to spell 'cat.'"

"Oh, you saw papa here behind me," she protested, laughing yet pleased. "You couldn't remember me! You haven't seen me since I was six years old!"

BB did not argue the point. "Sit down," he suggested. Half a dozen chairs were ranged along the wall opposite his desk and she took one of them and looked curiously all around. BB followed her eyes, taking his cue from her glances. "That squash on the safe, shaped like a setting hen; Dave Walters gave me that, last November. The round thing beside it is a witch ball." He brought this to let Marged examine it. It was as big as a baseball, as smooth as though it were enamelled, with a hole cut in the side through which could be seen a mass of tight-packed hair. "Ned Howell brought me that."

"Our Ned Howell? Keeps the Furnace store?" she asked; and as he assented: "Sammy Howell is in my school."

"Ned found that ball in the stomach of a steer he butchered," BB explained. "When they lick their flanks, hair sticks to their tongues and gets into their insides and balls up like that. In the old days, witches used these balls for charms." He showed her a small bottle of alcohol in which was preserved a baby hummingbird no larger than a bumblebee, and naked of feathers. "I found that under the nest. It had fallen out on a rock and the fall killed it."

"I found a hummingbird's nest once, with two eggs in it. The mother bird used to dart at me when I came near it."

"As though she were swinging in a hammock?" BB suggested, "swooping and turning and swooping again?"

"Yes. And once I found a sick hummingbird. That was when I was little. It was sitting on a fence rail and it let me pick it up. I took it in the house and gave it sweet warm water, but in the morning it was dead, with its wings and its tail all spread wide. It was so beautiful, I cried and cried!" She smiled as she spoke, but her eyes misted at the memory.

Her father came in to join them, and BB rose to grip his hand, and asked for news. Evan said Adams Furnace would blow out in March. "Throw a lot of men out of work, but the flat's covered with piles of pig iron and no sale for it."

"I heard something about trouble with the men."

"Well, the ore-diggers were talking that they wanted a dollar and a half a day, instead of a dollar. They got up a petition. But the furnace was going to blow out anyway."

"I brought some items for the *Journal*," Marged said, and produced a folded paper and handed it to BB. His eyes ran down the paragraphs. David Lewis and Amy Glen were to be married when school closed. The Literary Meeting at Sardis Church had been a success. Mrs. Lloyd Davis had gone to visit her sister in Gallia County. Thomas Evans was able to be about again, his broken leg well healed. Sammy Howell had trapped two mink. Representative Samuel Llewellyn spent Sunday with relatives in Sycamore Hill.

While BB read, Marged watched him, coloring. "I guess you'll have to fix them up."

"Not at all. We'll put them in the paper just the way they are."

"Marged teaches Redfern School this term," her father said proudly. "She writes good."

"Redfern?" BB echoed. "That was the first school I ever taught, and Marged was in my first class. I was only sixteen or seventeen, and I didn't know much more than the pupils."

"I'm seventeen," Marged said. "But Mr. Masters had Redfern School till this year. Amy Glen — " She nodded toward the sheet of paper in his hand. "She's the one getting married to Dave Lewis as soon as school lets out; the one I wrote about there — she teaches Oak School. She's my best friend. Her brother's the smartest boy in my school."

"Glen? I don't know the Glens. They must be since my time. I went to Mississippi three years ago, and I haven't been out to the furnace since before that."

"Tom Glen's folks settled in Gallia County," Evan explained. "After the War, Tom went coal-mining out in Indiana, but he joined the Knights of Labor and the operators blacklisted him, so he came back here four-five years ago and went to digging ore for the furnace."

"It's his son Owen in my school," said Marged. "I give him books to read, and he reads them. He's only ten, but he's a fine boy."

BB, watching her, thinking she had a finely intelligent countenance, asked absently: "What do they pay teachers in Adams Township now?"

"Twenty-five dollars a month if you're a woman, thirty if you're a man." And Marged said: "I've got a three-year certificate, but I'm going to take the examinations again this spring. That's why I came with papa today. Our *Journal* got burned up, two weeks ago, the one that always has the old examinations in it, and I wanted to get one." The Board of School Examiners of Hardiston County gave examinations to aspiring teachers on the first Friday of each month, and BB regularly printed in the *Journal* the set of questions they had used. He found a copy of the old paper for Marged, and she thanked him, explaining: "If I can get a five-year certificate, maybe I can get a better school, here in Hardiston, or up the creek."

BB liked her, and when they were gone, he turned to his desk and wrote:

> *When will the time come that a teacher's salary will not be rated too low, just because the teacher happens to be an enterprising young woman? If an attractive, intelligent and amiable young woman is fit to teach at all, she should receive the same wages as one of the more exalted beings who take their hats off in church. Give the girls a chance.*

Certainly girls as pleasant and as intelligent as Marged Williams should be given a chance. He decided to write and ask her to send him weekly items from the Adams Furnace neighborhood. He might even go down there, toward the end of March, for a day's tramp through those hills once so familiar. The world would by that time be full of birds, with spring flowers blooming. Suppose he went to Redfern School, to hear the exercises on the last day, to see Miss Williams again. He set a dash below the paragraph just written and began another.

There is a class of people in our county who are the most influential class among us. We refer to our teachers. Our children come under their care at the tender age of six years; consequently they have almost as much to do with the formation of their characters as the parents themselves. We believe that teachers as a class are not valued highly enough, and we take advantage of this opportunity to call attention to them.

It occurred to him that he might prepare and publish a list of all the teachers in the county, with their age, qualifications and salary; but that must wait for a later issue. The paper would go to press tonight, and while boiler plate did well enough for the inside — the four-column sermon by Doctor Talmage, which BB published every week, was popular with his subscribers — he always tried to fill with local news and editorials as much of the outside as was not needed for the advertising of Hardiston merchants. He was writing locals when Will Davis brought proofs of the week's advertisements for him to read. Howell's shoe store advertised nailed brogans, miner's shoes, for $1.45. BB decided to buy a pair to wear on his weekly walks, to save wear and tear on his best shoes. When the advertisements were corrected, he turned to the weekly exchanges, clipping and pasting up a paragraph here and there, with due credit to the paper from which he borrowed. Occasional callers were an interruption; but from each he garnered an item or two. At noon he walked home to dinner and it was not till late afternoon that he found time to go through the dailies. Nellie Bly had finished her trip around the world in 72 days, 6 hours and 10 minutes. "So 'Around the World in Eighty Days' is out of date," BB wrote. "Miss Bisland, who started around the world in the opposite direction, has not yet reached New York, but she is on the Atlantic, and she too will certainly break the record of Phileas Fogg. Fact is stranger than fiction."

BB added a paragraph predicting that Nellie Bly would be remembered, but that Miss Bisland would be forgotten, since no one ever remembered who came in second; and — his thoughts returning to Miss Williams — he wrote another paragraph on the importance of teaching geography in the schools.

*The proper way to teach geography is to start by teach-
ing the geography of the immediate neighborhood, then
of the county, then of the state, then of the United States
and so finally of the world. Thus the pupil is led gently
onward, a step at a time. This is the only true education,
to lead out, to lead on from the known into the unknown.*

In mid-afternoon Will Davis reported that there was copy
enough on the hook to fill the outside; but at early dark BB, turning through the dailies, found another piece of news whuch must
be reported. He wrote:

WITH THE MINERS

*Hardiston County, with its 150 or more mines and its
thousands of miners, is vitally interested in the proceedings of the joint convention of the National Progressive
Union and National District Assembly 135 of the Knights
of Labor. This convention convened at Columbus last
week and continued over until this week.*

*The result has been that the two Orders have been con-
solidated, and the new Order has been named "The
United Mine Workers of America."*

*We hope the new Order will be successful in securing
to the miners all their rights.*

II

March 1890

Owen Glen's first lasting memory was of the day his brother Tom was killed by a fall of slate, in the mine where he and Owen's father and his brother Evan were all employed. Owen was at the time between two and three years old. His mother, sitting down for a moment's rest after finishing the week's washing, caught up little Owen and began laughing play with him, tickling him till he screamed at the delicious torment, hugging him tight and kissing him. She smelled of steam and of wet clothes, a sharp delightful smell; and she and Owen were having a fine romp together when suddenly he felt her arms tighten, and he looked up into her face and saw that she was staring through the window, and he squirmed around to look that way. A wagon had stopped in front of the house; and Owen's father and his brother Evan were standing on the plank that served as sidewalk, while the man driving the wagon swung his horses to cramp the wheels, and backed the wagon till the tailgate was at the walk. There was something in the wagon, something flat and shapeless and covered with an old piece of canvas. Brother Evan and the driver of the wagon pulled this something out through the tailgate. It rested on a wide board, and they carried this burden up the walk toward the house, bowed under the weight. Owen's father, black-faced with coal dust as he always was at day's end, came ahead of them and opened the door.

Owen always remembered his father's tall black figure silhouetted there in the open door; but most of all he remembered his mother, her wiry arms straining him close against her warm breast, her whole body shaken by waves of shuddering tremors, convulsive, beginning feebly, becoming stronger till he too was shaken by

15

them, then slacking for an instant only to begin again. Looking up — she held him so close against her breast he could not move except to raise his eyes — he saw tears on her cheeks, saw new tears form and trickle down her cheeks and follow the line of her jaw to her chin and grow larger there till they dropped on his own brow and trickled into his eyes, so that he had to wipe them away while his own tears joined hers. He always remembered the keen thin smell of her tears, and the soundless sobs that shook her, so terrible and frightening. He climbed up to stand in her lap and hugged her head close against his chest; and he too was crying with terror and grieving tenderness, but he did not remember this. His mother, her warm body, her tears wetting his cheeks, her tight-clasping arms; these were his memory. As long as he lived he never forgot this moment, never forgot his all-surrendering love for her.

2

Owen had no other memory of Tom than this, and after Tom's death, Evan and his father meant little to Owen. They were up and away to work before daylight in the winter and at first dawn in summer, while he still slept or stayed in bed. His day began after they were gone, and after his sister Amy had been sent off to school. Then his mother took him up, and dressed him and gave him breakfast.

He and she were alone together all day long, till the night when the others returned; for he and Evan and Amy were, after Tom's death, the only children. There had been others, two boys and a girl. All three died within a week, of diphtheria, while Amy was still a baby and before Owen himself was born. Amy was ill at the same time, but she recovered, and Tom and Evan escaped the disease.

Tom was nineteen when he was killed. Soon after, Evan married and moved into a house like their own, one of the company houses built along the valley below the mine. Till then, Owen had slept with his sister Amy on a mattress stuffed with corn husks in a bed built of boards against the wall; but after Evan married, Amy had the bed which Evan and Tom had shared, and Owen was as lonesome as a puppy taken from its litter-mates. Bedded together, he and Amy had been warm on the coldest winter nights; alone he was cold. Sometimes Amy let him come and sleep with her again, and sometimes he got into bed with his father and mother, curling close in his mother's arms, but he learned to wait till his father was asleep before creeping secretly into that sweet haven.

A little while after Evan was married, a loaded coal car ran over his foot and he lost all the toes on that foot and walked with a limp thereafter. At about the same time, there were weeks when Owen's father stayed much at home, silent and angry; and at night other men came secretly to see him. Though their words were to him meaningless, Owen heard the bitter, hopeless anger in their tones; and sometimes after they were gone Owen's mother would lament:

"Eh, Tom man, it's such talk as that takes the bread out of our mouths. Will you never learn to hold your tongue?"

Once Owen heard his mother say it was a bitter day when his father joined the nights, and his father silenced her in stern and righteous anger, and Owen wondered how anyone could join a night, and why what she had said was wrong; and again and again he heard his mother say like a wail: "Eh, Tom, I'd not have you be so. The worst of men is too good to wear Cain's curse today, and dig and delve in the pits of darkness for his daily bread." The boy heard enough to know it was somehow a victory for her when at last they left their home in Indiana — travelling by train, to Owen's wonder and delight — and came to Ohio. They said goodbye to Evan and his young wife, and it would be thirty-one years before Owen saw his brother again. Then it was Evan's limp that told Owen who he was.

3

When they returned to Ohio, they went at first to visit relatives in Gallia County. Owen's father had come from Wales in 1849, with his father and mother and many brothers and sisters, on a sailing vessel chartered to bring some two hundred Welshmen to the United States. A hundred and eighty-three men, women and children embarked; but measles broke out on board, and during the six-week crossing seventeen children died. The last, a year-old

sister of Owen's father, died while the vessel was coming up
Chesapeake Bay to Baltimore; and, for fear the quarantine officers
might throw them all in prison, her small body was dropped over
the side at dead of night. From Baltimore, the Welshmen came
west by rail, by canal boat and by oxcart, and they floated down
the Ohio River on huge rafts and landed at Marietta and made
their way through what in those days was still half a wilderness
toward the settlements already established by the Welsh folk who
had come before.

During his stay in Gallia County — he was not yet five years old
— Owen heard the tale of that tragic and terrible voyage told and
retold. Usually it was Welsh the narrator spoke, but though
Owen's mother always spoke English to him, and though except
for family prayers all their talk at home was in English, he understood the Welsh well enough to follow the familiar narrative.

When they had been two or three weeks in Gallia County, Tom
Glen found work digging ore for Adams Furnace, eight or ten
miles away. Their new home was a two-room house on the flat
below the furnace — one of a dozen, all very much alike, which
stood either on the flat or on the hills around. The furnace itself
was a monstrous, growling beast. At night its roar, a sobbing,
throbbing sound never to be forgotten, at first kept Owen awake
and then filled his dreams. The stack was built against the face of
a sandstone bluff, and a bridge led from its top to the stock yard on
the bluff, where charcoal and limestone and iron ore were piled
till they were wanted. The charcoal buggy and the cart full of
limestone and iron ore crossed by the bridge to the top of the furnace
to dump the charge into the bell. When the bell tipped its contents
into the fires below, flames soared high; and Owen thought of the
pillar of smoke by day and of fire by night that guided the Hebrews
on their flight from Egypt. At such moments, the roar of the
furnace for a moment hushed, while the upward-reaching flame
floated like a flag above the stack; but otherwise the roar was never
silenced except on Sundays, when God forbade man to work. When
the furnace cast, the glow of molten iron turned the sooty pot-
house into a bower of golden beauty, and Owen liked to creep
near enough to watch the red stream flow into the molds, guided
through the sow and into the pigs by the sweating, black-faced
men. There were men everywhere to serve the monster; the stock

men loaded the charcoal buggy, the fillers charged the stack, the engineers and keepers and the pot-house men were pigmies around its foot. Owen watched them at their tasks.

All across the flat below the furnace, pig iron was piled to await a market. The flat was criss-crossed by ruts where oxcarts had hauled loads of iron, and it was sprinkled with soot from the furnace, and grown to tall weeds. Along the further margin, a little creek was its boundary, and in the spring the creek overflowed the flat and left it a sticky quagmire of red and yellow clay. The house in which they lived, and the others set along either side of the creek like beads on a necklace, were built high off the ground to avoid this flood water; and pigs and chickens slept under the houses on hot summer days, or took shelter there against winter storms.

Their house, like the others on the flat, had cracks in the floor and cracks in the walls, but these could be stuffed with rags or paper, or daubed with clay, to keep out winter winds. Of the two rooms, one was kitchen, laundry, sitting room and dining room; the other was the bedroom where Owen's father and mother slept. Owen and Amy lodged in the attic that was reached by a ladder nailed against the wall of the kitchen. Amy slept in a narrow bed, Owen on a pallet of husks laid along the floor; but on rainy nights a leak in the roof let water drip on his bed, and in winter his single blanket did not keep him warm, so even after he was nine or ten years old, just as he used to do when he was a baby, he often slept with Amy. He looked forward to these occasions, for Amy smelled like his mother. Pressed close to her he slept soundly.

Owen never thought that their home was a miserable place, because the other houses on the flat were no better. Some, in fact, were worse. There was land enough so that those who cared to do so could make a garden, or keep a cow tethered in good grass and move it to fresh pasture every day. Across the road behind the store, a good spring came out of the conglomerate; and the springhouse was big enough to accommodate many crocks and pans, and open for anyone to use. It was part of Owen's routine each day to carry needed water from the spring.

In the house nearest theirs lived a widow woman named Roberts, and her son Bobby. Bobby was ten years older than Owen, but Owen liked him from the first, because Bobby knew so many remarkable things. He knew where to find calamus root, and slippery elm bark; he made Owen a pair of stilts and taught him how to use them; he showed Owen how to catch catfish and sunfish and suckers in the creek, and gave him a fishhook and sinker and a line; and he knew how to make whistles out of a willow or a hazel twig, tapping the bark with the butt of his knife to loosen it, sliding it off, notching the white wood of the twig and then sliding the bark back on again. He and Owen sometimes splashed in the deepest pool in the creek and he taught Owen to swim dog paddle.

Bobby worked at the furnace and made a garden, and kept a cow and two pigs and he planned some day to buy a farm. He had a class of little children, Owen among them, in the Sunday School at Sardis Church; and on warm summer Sundays he might take his class out among the gravestones in the cemetery behind the church, and find a shady spot; and when the week's lesson was done he would read aloud to them passages from the Bible, grand and stirring narratives of battle and massacre, of fire and sword.

Pete Radford was another boy who lived on the flat, and if Bobby was Owen's first friend, Pete was his first enemy. Pete was two or three years older than Owen. He and Sammy Howell, the storekeeper's son, were much together, and they sometimes admitted Owen to their fellowship. Owen liked Sammy, who in winter set mink traps along the creek and allowed Owen to help him; but Pete took every opportunity to make Owen miserable. Owen was puzzled by the fact that when they were all together, Sammy was as mean as Pete, inflicting such small torments as a Dutch scrub or a twisted arm, or — worse still — running away from Owen when he wished to play with them; but when Owen and Sammy were alone, they had congenial hours.

When Owen was old enough to go to school, his mother sent him off each morning with bright dreams in her happy eyes. She had already begun to teach him to read, using as a textbook the English Bible. He went at first with Amy to the Redfern School not far from their home. There were fourteen children in the school, boys and girls, some as old as Amy, some as young as Owen. The teacher was a man — Owen thought him an old man, though he was no more than thirty-five or forty — and his name was Masters. He seemed to be half-sick all the time, and kept in his desk a bottle of medicine from which he took an occasional sip; and he was lean, and sly, and thin, and quick with the switch and paddle. Owen thought the only good thing about Mr. Masters was that he frequently whipped Pete Radford; but he whipped other boys too, and sometimes he switched even the older girls. Once he switched Amy, and Owen told his father, and Tom Glen stalked up to the school with a set jaw and burning eyes, and Mr. Masters never touched Amy again.

To Owen during these first years his father, though he was a buckler against the world, was rather feared than loved; and when Owen learned that he must never creep into bed with his parents as long as his father was awake, something like hatred mingled with that fear. He knew that once upon a time his father had gone away to war, for Tom Glen could tell terrible stories of bloody battles, of bitter cold and baking heat and stinging flies and merciless mosquitoes and men spilling their lives away in disease-ridden camps; but this did not make Tom, in Owen's eyes, any more approachable. To the boy, though his mother was close and dear, his father seemed remote and far away.

4

During his three years under Mr. Masters, Owen hated going to school; and this was especially true after Amy took the examination and earned a one-year certificate and began to teach, so that he went to Redfern School alone. But just before Christmas the year Owen was nine years old, he and the other children, under the leadership of Sammy Howell, locked Mr. Masters out; and though he soon battered in the door, the school committeemen agreed that a new teacher was needed.

Marged Williams took Mr. Masters's place. Her father's farm was halfway to Sycamore Hill, but she and her father and mother — and Aunt Molly, who lived with them — came to Sardis Church; and Owen had watched her there with a breathless wonder. He thought her as beautiful as his mother. Although Marged and Amy were friends, Marged had never come to the house, so Owen had seen her only at church; but now she was at school every day, and sometimes, if it were raining, she spent the night with Amy. On these occasions she and Amy shared the bed in the attic, and Owen from his pallet on the floor heard their soft whispering laughter in the darkness, and thought how warm they must be, close together in the narrow bed.

In school, Marged found that Owen read as well as most grown people, and once, when she spent the night with Amy, she spoke of this to his mother. Mrs. Glen's eyes shone with pride. "He's read the English Bible through."

Marged looked at Owen and smiled, and he felt hot and miserable and yet happy too; and she asked: "Why don't you read other things, Owen?"

"It's all the English book we've got," Mrs. Glen explained.

"I've books at home," Marged said. "Books I've studied for my examinations. You can read them, Owen."

More because he wished to heighten his stature in her eyes than from any deep hunger for knowledge, Owen nodded; and next day she brought him a textbook of American history. He read with a slow diligence, engrossed in every page; and having finished the book, he turned back to the beginning and read it again. When Marged one day asked him whether he was done with it, he said: "No, ma'am, I've read it, but I ain't through with it."

"Am not, Owen," she suggested gently.

"Am not through with it," he echoed. Owen, without being tall, was nevertheless big for his age, with a deep chest and heavy shoulders. His head was large and he had the white skin and the dark hair of the black Welsh. He was a sober boy, deadly serious, seldom smiling. "I am not through with it," he repeated carefully.

"Well, you keep it as long as you want to, and then I'll lend you something else."

Thus he had from her presently a geography, and after that a history of Greece and Rome. He read more and more rapidly, fixing his mind on what he read, remembering and remembering.

5

Owen that fall began to wonder why Dave Lewis, son of a farmer who lived beyond Sardis Church, liked to walk home from church with Amy. Owen and his father and mother and Amy went to church every Sunday, and spent the day there. The three-hour service lasted all morning; then the women made hot coffee in the

Ty Bach, the little house beside the church, and everyone had
brought food. After they had eaten, there was Sunday School, and
the long afternoon droned by. The church was small; the seats
were hard and narrow and only a few inches wide, and the backs
were so straight up and down that they seemed to tilt a little
forward; so though the sermons might last two hours or more, no
one ever went to sleep.

For Dave to walk home with Amy, only to turn around and re-
trace the long way past the church to his father's house, seemed to
Owen puzzling. When he learned that Dave and Amy were going
to be married, he guessed that their walking together had been
some sort of preparation for marriage, but he could not guess why.
He had observed that as they followed a few paces behind him and
his father and mother, they seldom spoke to one another; they just
walked. One day he questioned his mother.

"Mama, did you and papa walk together before you got married?"

"Yes, Owen. Of course."

"Why?"

She laughed in amused confusion. "Just — keeping company."

"But why?"

"Well, to find out if we liked being together."

"Is it anything about keeping step?"

She considered. "Well, maybe, yes, like soldiers, Owen. They
learn to keep step, and that makes them — feel close to one another.
It's because people want to keep close always that they marry."

Dave and Amy would be married toward the end of March. Two
weeks before, since there was no market for iron, the furnace blew
out; so Owen's father was left idle. Owen had heard Tom Glen
talking with other men, urging that they should be paid a dollar
and a half for a day's work instead of a dollar; and Owen's mother
now blamed her husband, saying the furnace had closed down to
teach him and the others a lesson. Tom Glen stormed at her with such
violence that Owen, with the instinctive understanding of children,
knew his father felt guilty and ashamed.

"But work or no work, Amy's going to be nice for her wedding,"
Owen's mother declared.

She planned that Amy should be married in the church. Tom
Glen said a girl ought to get married at home; but Mrs. Glen,
though she never complained about their small house, overruled

him. "There'll be too many people, Tom. Everyone likes Amy; and then all Dave's friends."

She and Dave's mother agreed that for the same reason the wedding dinner would be at Dave's home; and when Tom Glen urged that everybody could as well come here, even if they had to picnic along the creek bank, Mrs. Glen said kindly: "Now, Tom, you let the womenfolks manage things. It's their job." Tom surrendered in a shamed submission, and Mrs. Glen kissed him — that was so rare an occurrence that Owen stared in wonder — and said: "Never mind, man dear. You've done the best you could."

Long before the wedding, Mrs. Glen and Amy lost themselves in a passion of preparation. They went to Sycamore Hill and came home with treasured parcels; and thereafter Mrs. Glen was sewing all day long, and Amy after each day's teaching hurried breathless home to sew with her mother.

Owen thought he saw something new in Amy's voice and in her eyes. It had never occurred to him to think of his sister as pretty, but he thought she was mighty pretty now; and he began to feel toward Dave Lewis dislike mixed with envy. When Amy married Dave, she would go to Dave's house to live. Owen wanted her to stay here and just be his sister; but he knew it was useless to tell her so. Probably she'd go away and never come to see them again. One night when she and his mother were sewing in the kitchen, thinking about this made him so lonely and miserable that he climbed down the ladder.

His mother was startled. "Why, Owen, whatever's the matter?"

"I want to kiss Amy goodnight." He felt like crying.

Amy laughed in a warm happy way, and hugged him, and he hugged her and kissed her over and over, till his mother rapped his head sharply with her thimbled finger.

"There, Owen, that's enough! Get you back to bed." When he still clung to Amy, his mother pinched his arm hard enough to hurt him. "Get you back to bed!" she said sternly.

So he climbed the ladder again and crept to his pallet, but he was still completely wide awake. He began in a whisper to recite *Custer's Last Fight,* which he was to declaim on the last day of school. Every boy and girl in school would have a part in the program, acting in dialogues, reading compositions or selections, singing or declaiming. Miss Williams had suggested *Custer's Last*

Fight to Owen, and had heard him recite it, showing him the gestures he should use. Lying on his pallet, remembering the gestures, carefully moving one hand or the other as he whispered the words, he became so absorbed that he spoke aloud; and his mother called up to him from the kitchen:

"Owen, you stop talking to yourself and go to sleep!"

6

Tom Glen had drawn the petition asking higher pay for the ore-diggers; but Lloyd Davis, the manager of the Furnace, said that to pay more was impossible. Then the annual meeting of the Furnace voted a rich dividend to the stockholders; and when he heard that, Owen's father swore he would never work for such men again. Ten days before Dave and Amy were to be married, he tramped away to Sycamore Hill and took the train to Hardiston; and he came back in time for supper with word that they would move to town. "There's a job in Erie Mine," he told them. Owen heard the ring in his strong tones, and saw that he was glad.

"Back to the coal?" Owen's mother spoke in sorrow. "Eh, Tom, I wish you hadn't to. Working in the light of day you've had none of the rheumatism that was so bad before. Now you'll be down in the dark again. Oh Tom, man dear!"

"It's my work," Owen's father said in deep pride. "And fit work for a man, and it needs a man to do it."

"Not till Amy's married, then." Her voice was firm.

He said awkwardly: "Aye, we'll stay here till the child's wed."

During these last days before the wedding, since Amy and her mother were busy with feminine affairs, Owen had learned to feel himself in the way; and when next morning after breakfast his father turned out-of-doors, the boy, with a sudden hunger for comradeship, followed. They walked idly toward the creek. Tom sat down on the trunk of a fallen sycamore, and Owen picked up a small flat stone and sent it skittering across the water.

"Pretty good," said Tom Glen. Owen looked for another likely stone, and his father asked: "What's this piece you're going to speak, last day of school, Owen? I met Miss Williams on my way back from Sycamore Hill and she was telling me. Go ahead and speak it to me. I've spoke some pieces myself, in my time."

So Owen recited for his father *Custer's Last Fight,* with gestures, and Tom Glen sat on the old sycamore and nodded and nodded. "You know it good," he said when Owen was done. "But you're over-young to praise death and failure. It's living and working and helping others that ought to take up the mind of a boy — or a man." He hesitated. "Listen now a bit to me. All this that I'll recite to you was secret once; but now, even in the newspapers, the holy name is printed day on day. Eh, yes, and the name will be forgotten too, and there'll be no more Knights to get out the coal, but only this new thing. United Mine Workers they'll be now; and the fine secret work forgotten."

And while Owen stood attentive, he began to speak. " 'In the beginning of creation, it was ordained that all things tangible should have certain qualities. In some, form and size. In others, strength, weight, density and ductility. In others, color, flavor, nutrition and warmth. In all, purity and plenty in their order. These qualities determine their fitness for the use of man, and by them he can decide, with the certainty of nature's laws, their intrinsic value.' "
Owen, bewildered by many unfamiliar words, trying to guess what each new one meant, was for a moment lost in his own perplexities; till his father rose to stand erect, his words ringing. " 'To pause in his toil, to devote time to his own interest, to gain a knowledge of the world's commerce, to unite, combine and co-operate in the great army of peace and industry, to nourish and cherish, to build and develop the temple he lives in, is the highest and noblest duty of man to himself, to his fellowman, and to his Creator.' "

His words echoed in the silence, and as he went on, his voice rose till it was a great cry, and Owen listened breathlessly. " 'We welcome you to the army of peace . . . render useless the mere handler or jobber, and save the extortion of the speculator, the drone, or the non-producer.' " Words were often meaningless, but from the fire in his father's eyes and the ardor in his voice Owen took fire. " 'We shall use the five elements of nature. . . . The God-given wealth of the world, to produce the materials that promote the happiness of all. . . . We affirm that five days of the week are sufficient for industrial pursuits, and shall therefore labor to bring the time when there shall be five days in the week for labor, and two days for rest — one for God, and the other for humanity.' "

Tom Glen finished in a hushed reverence, and looked at his son with burning eyes, and then in faint embarrassment at his own fervor, he sat down upon the log again. Owen watched him for a moment, and at last he said:

"What is that, papa?"

Tom grunted. "Did you never hear tell of the Knights of Labor, son?" Owen shook his head; and Tom looked at him thoughtfully. "Sit down and listen. It's a thing you ought to know."

There beside the yellow waters of the creek, Tom spoke of his youth to his son. He was a soldier home on leave when he and Annie Evans were married, and after the War he worked on farms, and at making charcoal, and the children came, six of them; but then three died in a week of diphtheria, and about that time Tom heard rumors of steady work and good pay in the Illinois coal fields, and Annie Glen wished to leave the little house so full of sorry memories, so they went to live in Illinois.

But the fine promises proved to be a delusion. "I got a job all right, but pay was scrip that you had to spend at the company store, same as here; and the store prices were high, and rent too; and if you wanted to trade somewhere else besides the store, they'd hold up your pay a month after you'd earned it — once it was two months — so you'd have to go to the store or starve.

"I was young and high-headed, and I said what I thought, not caring who heard me. Then one day old Morgan Morgan — he died two years after — spoke to me by myself. It was little he said, and no reason he gave; but he asked me to meet him, come full dark, at the crossroad a mile north of the mine.

"Well, I did. He was there before me, but when I would have asked a question, he hushed me. Then he took me off along the road two-three miles, till we came to a house that showed no light. He knocked, and the door opened and we went into a pitch-black room, and the door shut behind us. Then there was a waiting, and I could feel men in the blackness all around, and hear the thud of my heart against my ribs." Owen felt his own heart pound as Tom went on. "Then a voice came at us, asking questions. 'Do you believe in God, the Creator and Universal Father of us all?' Mr. Morgan squeezed my arm, so I knew I was supposed to answer, so I said I did. Then came the next question. 'Do you obey the Universal Ordinance of God, in gaining your bread by the sweat of your brow?' I said I did, and then the voice asked: 'Are you willing to take a solemn vow binding you to secrecy, obedience, and mutual assistance?' I said I was."

Owen, sitting on the ground at his father's feet, looking up at his father's grave eyes, asked breathlessly: "Weren't you scared?"

"You might say so. Yes. But I was in earnest, too. Dead earnest.

"So that was the night I was initiated into the Noble and Holy Order. Now everyone knows the name, the Knights of Labor; but then you weren't supposed ever to write the name down, or say it aloud. If you had to write it, you just put five stars. Everything about it was secret. After that day, I was a proud man, knowing I was united with fine men in a holy purpose of helping each other."

He hesitated, summoning memories. "Well, awhile after that — 1882, I think it was — the operators decided to use a larger screen."

"What's that?"

"Why, it's an iron screen with holes in it. Your car of coal is dumped to slide down the screen, and whatever goes through the holes you don't get paid for. So making the holes larger, the way they aimed to, we'd be paid less. So we struck.

"It was the Knights that started the strike, and I did some talking to the men; but the operators beat us; and after we went back to work, the mine boss told me I was through."

"Why?" There was passion in Owen's cry.

"I asked him. He said it was because I talked too much. I told him there was other mines around, and he said: 'Go try them.'

"Well, I did, but nobody would hire me. There were eleven of us on the blacklist. The operators had found out somehow we were in the Knights of Labor, and that was enough. But I didn't give up till I'd tried all around.

"So then I decided to move to Indiana, and Tom and Evan — they were working in the mine, but they quit to stick to me — they went to Indiana with us." His voice roughened with tears. "Tom got killed there. If he'd stayed in Illinois he might not have been, but he stuck to me."

"I remember the day you and Evan brought him home."

"Do you so? Well. But outside of Tom's getting killed, we got along. The Knights were in Indiana, too. One of them made me a sign, so I knew them; but then the operators got a spy into the Knights and I was on the blacklist again."

"I remember that time. I remember your going off all day hunting work." Owen laughed breathlessly. "One night you came home late and I heard mama say it was a bitter day you joined the nights, and I thought she meant — " he hesitated. "Well, you know, nights instead of days."

"The Knights of Labor." His father's voice was gentle. "They were the noblest society ever conceived in the hearts of men."

"Papa, will you teach me that that you recited. I want to recite it, at last day of school."

"Why, son, it's secret; it's part of the secret words of the order."

"But it's all true, papa. Everyone ought to know it." Owen was warm with high delight. Until today he had always been afraid of his father, but this hour together had brushed aside all fears; he felt himself one with this brave and gentle man, bound in mutual understanding and in love.

Tom Glen hesitated. "There's hundreds of thousands have heard it, to be sure," he admitted. "It's no secret now; aye, and no harm if children learn the noble words." He spoke in proud decision. "Yes, I'll teach it to you, Owen. It's a fit gospel for a miner's son to know."

So for an hour or two, there beside the creek, they were prompter and pupil, Owen repeating after his father phrase by phrase. Till Amy's wedding, father and son each day escaped from the confusion at home to this fine comradeship, and Owen each day more deeply loved and cherished this fine man.

7

Last day of school was also Amy's wedding day. Marged borrowed for the day her father's surrey, and on her way to school left it at Amy's home, so Amy and her father and mother need not walk to Sardis Church for her wedding. She reached the schoolhouse an hour before the exercises would begin, and put on an apron and tied a handkerchief around her hair and fell to work. The morning was fine and sunny; but she built a fire in the stove, and then took her broom, and when the sweeping was done, the dustcloth. A step outside made her look toward the open door, and she saw BB Beecham rapping on the lintel.

"May I come in?" he asked, and she gave him a delighted welcome. "I came down to Sycamore Hill on the Mail and hired a livery to bring me this far," he explained. "Can I stay for the exercises?"

"Of course," she said. "And you must speak to the pupils. Sit down, do. I'll be through in a minute now."

She and BB talked together while she worked; and before the first arrivals, she was done with her housekeeping, her apron laid aside. She greeted the mothers and settled the children, while BB and the fathers talked together in a group near the door. They spoke of the weather, of this fine March day, of the snowfall three weeks ago that had turned the roads to mud. "Mud so deep it took a six-mule team to haul the stockholders from Sycamore Hill for the Furnace meeting," said Lloyd Davis, the Furnace manager. They told BB the neighborhood news. There was to be a Literary Meeting at Sardis Church next week. With the furnace blown out, some of the ore-diggers and the other workmen would be moving away. Samuel Llewellyn, who represented the county in the lower house of the Ohio Legislature, had been in Sycamore Hill last week, and he said times were hard all over the state. This winter and last winter had been so warm that people burned less coal than usual, so the operators had to lower the price of coal to sell it at all, and that meant lower pay for the miners. It was only the lucky ones who earned twenty dollars in a month, and Mr. Llewellyn had seen no hope of higher pay; but twenty dollars was not enough to let a man pay rent and feed his family. Someone spoke of the great colliery explosion in Glamorganshire two weeks before, when a hundred and fifty miners died. Two of the men in the little group here had relatives working in that Welsh colliery. Ned Howell, who kept the furnace store, said his father had escaped the other disaster in Monmouthshire a month ago. "But a hundred and ninety men were killed there," he said. "And four of them I knew." For the miners of coal throughout the world, death, whether singly or wholesale, was a commonplace; to work as they did, in daily peril, deep underground, bound them together as those are bound who sail the sea.

Marged, standing near the door to greet newcomers, listened with one ear to the talk of the men. They spoke in Welsh, but that was her tongue too. David Thomas, the brakeman, had lost his hand yesterday at Sycamore Hill, coupling cars at the brickyard; but such accidents were frequent. When cars were coupled, the brakeman had to hold the coupling link level as the cars came together, and drop the coupling pin in place at precisely the right moment. If he were an instant too late in snatching his hand away, he was caught. The railroads, in this and other ways, maimed or killed scores every year. There was diphtheria in Sycamore Hill, and BB told them how the disease had wiped out, within the month, the entire family of John McGregor of Zanesville. "He was reading clerk of the Ohio House," he said. "He and his wife and their eight children all took sick, and they all died." The listening men nodded with sober unction, and Marged thought Welsh people found a gloomy satisfaction in such tragic happenings. It was as though their own immunity gave reassuring evidence of a certain purity and virtue in themselves; there was always the suggestion that those who died were destroyed because their sins had found them out.

When the children, scrubbed and shiny, were at last all in their places, Marged went to the platform and bade the grownups find seats, and there was brief confusion and then order. Her eye fell on Owen Glen, in the second row on the side; the boy's face was set and white with a breathless waiting, and she wondered why Owen seemed to her to be so different from the other boys in her school, why she so often thought of him.

She began to speak. "We're very glad to see you all here today, and we're all glad, I'm sure" — her smiling eyes ran along the rows of young faces — "that this is the last day of school." Appreciative giggles rewarded her jest. "I know I was always glad, when I used to come to school in this very schoolhouse, when it came last day of school." She looked toward BB Beecham, in the rear. "My first teacher is here today, Mr. Beecham, the editor of the Hardiston *Journal*. I'm going to ask him to speak to you, to open our exercises."

BB came to join her on the platform, a beaming, quick-striding man, short legs and sturdy body. He stood smiling, his hands clasped in front of him. "Your teacher told you I was her first teacher," he began. "But she did not tell you that she — and the others — were my first pupils; for this was the first school I ever taught." He smiled. "You know it's a good deal more difficult to teach than to be taught. Your teacher has to study much harder than you."

He hesitated, then went on: "Books seem to you now just chores you have to do. But actually, books are wealth. Everything men have learned in ten thousand years has been preserved in a book somewhere; so if you want to find the accumulated wisdom of the ages, you hunt in books. Once upon a time, books were few, and only the very rich could own them, because each book had to be written out a letter at a time and a word at a time. So poor people, and even people with plenty of money, couldn't always afford to buy them. Then the printing press was invented, and movable type; and so now books can be made cheaply, and anyone can own one, or can own many.

"Of course some people have never learned to read, so books are of no use to them. But you are learning that here, so your teacher has been giving you the key to all the treasures of the world. You children here are already better educated than almost anyone who was alive a thousand years ago; you are that much richer than even the kings in the old days. Some of you, I expect, have already read more books than even the wisest men had read in Christ's time. There were only a few books in the world then. There are more books in the world today than there were letters in all the books that existed then.

"So by learning to read, you open the door to all the wealth of the world; for wisdom is the greatest wealth. By reading you can make that wealth your own. So you must thank your teacher."

He turned to Marged and bowed and stepped down to go back to his seat; and Marged said: "Well, children, I'm sure we're glad Mr. Beecham could be here today. Now we'll begin our exercises by singing: *Bringing in the Golden Sheaves*."

As the minutes dragged away, Marged, anxious to be done and to go to Amy, thought it was too bad to have such a long program; but unless every child in school did something, there would be not only disappointed children but resentful parents. When the song was done, three of the girls like three parrots recited the lines of a dialogue, "How we will spend vacation," written by themselves. Then Sam Howell declaimed, with gestures, *I'll Be a Man*, and Edith Blanchard recited *Sheridan's Ride*, and they all sang *Have You Sown?* and Hetty Morgan declaimed *Little Midget*.

Marged announced each new number on the program; she rose when it was done to wait for the brief applause, vigorous on the part of parents of the performer, polite on the part of others eager for their own offspring to have their turn. When she came to Owen Glen, she felt a certain curiosity. He had asked permission to discard *Custer's Last Fight* in favor of something his father was teaching him; but she did not know what this was and Owen said it had no name. So she only said: "The next number is a recitation by Owen Glen."

Owen trudged to the platform, his heavy shoes clumping. He and most of the boys were already going barefoot; but for this occasion all were shod. When Owen made his jerky bow to her and to the audience, she was attentive, wondering what was to come.

The first words were completely unfamiliar. " 'In the beginning of creation it was ordained — ' " She frowned, puzzled and suddenly uneasy, listening as he went on, till suddenly his voice rose strongly. " 'But ignorance and greed have established other standards in the world. While nature and industry may create in plenty, false distribution withholds, and causes artificial scarcity and famine. Greed adulterates, and idleness gambles in the products of toil and grows rich off the necessities of the producers.' "

Marged, in real dismay, saw men in the audience look at one another, saw feminine glances interchanged. Last day of school was not the place for such words as Owen was speaking. Ignorance and greed? Whose ignorance? Whose greed? Teachers had been deprived of their positions for less than this!

" 'While machinery should be the only slave of man,' " said Owen in sonorous tones, " 'to do his work and lighten his toil, capital can and does monopolize machinery, thereby depriving labor of its God-ordained increase, dictating its remuneration, riveting more firmly the chains of oppression — ' " Marged saw faces pale with astonishment, or stern with understanding, or uneasy at hearing familiar phrases that should be spoken only in hushed secrecy thus vociferated on the peaceful morning air. Except for Lloyd Davis and Ned Howell, every man in the room was either a laborer or a farmer — and some were both, for many of the farmers made charcoal for the furnace. Half a dozen of the men here depended on their jobs at the furnace — jobs which Lloyd Davis could give or withhold as he chose — to support their families. She wished Owen had stuck to *Custer's Last Fight*. That, at least, would have been harmless!

Owen's voice broke into her consciousness again — "'. . . promote the happiness of all. We shall assert our right to the five mechanical powers. . . .'" Would he never finish? "'We affirm that five days in the week are sufficient for industrial pursuits, and we shall therefore labor . . .'" The furnace, when it was in blast, worked six days, and so did every man here, though on Sundays the furnace banked its fires. The children of these godly families were not even permitted to pick an apple or to gather nuts on the Lord's Day. "' . . . and keep two days,'" said Owen reverently, "'one for God, and the other for humanity.'"

He bowed to the audience, and then to her, and stumped back to his seat. Tom Glen was clapping his hands, and Lloyd Davis turned to glower at Tom, and then other men began defiantly to applaud. Marged, standing, waiting to announce that Peter Radford would now recite *Old District School House*, wished they would stop. There were only five men clapping, banging their hard hands together; but wives furtively tugged at the elbows of their husbands, till one by one they all were silenced. Marged could see that Lloyd Davis was furious, and he was chairman of the committee that had selected her to teach Redfern School; but after all, she would not teach here again, not if she did well on the Teacher's Examination next week in Hardiston.

For two hours the exercises dragged along. Marged thought that all over Ohio — yes, and all over the United States — other last days of school at this season of the year were being held; and everywhere children were declaiming, or singing, or acting dialogues, and proud parents were listening, dreaming of the great deeds their children would do when they grew up to be men and women. But how few of all these hopes and dreams would really come true!

Her glance once more touched Owen Glen. That boy might do some great thing, some day; he seemed now so much older than his years, so quiet and controlled, yet with a capacity to feel that passion of earnestness which had rung in his tones awhile ago. Was not the capacity for deep feeling at the root of greatness? Yet how few were capable of passionate conviction. She thought, in a sudden flashing certainty, that there were too many calm people in the world, too much tolerance, too great a willingness to forgive idleness and greed. Those were Owen's words, and she recognized them; he had given her something that would always hereafter be a part of her thinking. Yes, there was too much tolerance of idleness and greed. Instead of tolerance, men should be intolerant; they should be angry, be filled with a hot hard rage at all that was evil and base and greedy. When men ceased to be so supinely tolerant of wrongs, then wrongs would at last be righted. Owen Glen seemed calm enough, but there had been passion in his tones awhile ago; she thought that he would not grow up to be a tolerant man.

The last piece was recited, the last song sung; the little crowd began to disperse. Marged stood at the door to bid each family goodbye. Some had come in buggies or in teams, their homes too far for easy walking. The horses were hitched along the road, and one by one the vehicles filled and moved away. Some, who had come afoot, departed as they had come. Marged saw Tom Glen and other men — the same men who had applauded Owen's declamation — gather by the corner of the schoolhouse in earnest talk together, some heads nodding, some shaking in dissent. BB Beecham was standing with Owen, leaning against the ledge of puddingstone by the roadside. He was talking, Owen listening; and she wondered what BB was telling the boy. When almost everyone had drifted toward the road and departed in their several ways, she moved down to join them; and BB said to her:

"I've been telling Owen what a fine name he has, telling him about Owen Glendower."

"I've heard of him," Marged agreed. "I know he was the great Welsh hero."

BB said: "It's a name every Welshman honors. Owen Glyndwyr, really; Owain Glyndyvrdwy before that; Owen Glendower on English tongues. It was he who rallied the Welsh to fight for their independence, and the King of France called him Prince of Wales, and sent twelve thousand troops to Milford Haven to fight under him. He fought for a free Welsh parliament and a free Welsh church, and free Welsh colleges. The Welsh, you know, Owen, are the only unconquered people. The Romans came to conquer them, and the English armies; but though the very language the Romans spoke is dead now, the Welsh tongue lives on; and the memory of Owen Glendower, who fought for freedom when most men were

slaves, keeps the minds of Welshmen free today. Like as not some
of your ancestors were called Glyndwyr before they were Glendower, or Glen." He rested his hand on Owen's shoulder. "So
you've a great name to live up to, Owen."

Owen nodded. "Yes sir," he said, and Marged wondered whether
BB felt, as she did, strength and promise in the boy.

"First time you're in Hardiston, come in to see me," BB suggested. "Come and see how we set type and print the paper. As
long as men can print what they want to, they'll always be free.
You come and see me."

"Papa's going to move to Hardiston, now the furnace has blown
out. He's going to work in Erie Mine."

"Why, then I'll see you soon."

Marged asked: "Can you come to the wedding this afternoon,
Mr. Beecham?"

"I can't stay. I'll have dinner at Uncle Josh Evans's, but then
I'll take a tramp over the hills, and catch the up train. See here,
will you write a piece for the *Journal* about the wedding?" She
protested that she could never do that, but he was sure she could,
and in the end she agreed.

Tom and Mrs. Glen joined them, and since Marged would help
Amy dress for her wedding, she and Mrs. Glen went ahead, leaving Owen and his father with BB; and Marged asked: "Weren't
you proud of Owen this morning?"

Owen's mother tossed her head. "It was some of his father's nonsense he recited!" Marged smiled at the older woman's pretended
wrath. "Tom's forever talking himself into trouble, and like as not
the boy will be as bad as his father!"

"If he's as good a man as his father, you'll be pleased."

"Oh, aye," Mrs. Glen admitted. "Tom Glen's not so bad, if he'd
ever learn to hold his tongue. But that he'll never do."

They walked on in silence, Marged in her thoughts composing
the opening sentences of the piece about the wedding which she
would write for the *Journal*. "Never in the month of March was
a more beautiful day than the 27th. The sun shone in all its glory,
and its rays fell upon us as warm as in the balmy month of May.
The birds chirped from tree to tree, singing their gleeful songs,
and their songs seemed to be more gleeful and sweeter on that
morning than usual. Even the frogs in the creek greeted our ears
with their constant, cheerful chorus as if to say that for them too

the day was all that they desired. . . . " She must describe the crowd at Sardis Church, and the supper afterward. Tomorrow would be time enough to make a list of who brought presents, and what they brought, and to write up everything that happened. She could mail the piece to BB in plenty of time for next week's *Journal.*

8

When he came home from the schoolhouse, Owen wished to be with Amy, to stay by her side. To know that he was about to lose her forever left him all one hollow emptiness, but she and Mrs. Glen were in the bedroom, the door closed. He lingered near till his mother came out, but when she saw him she cried: "There, Owen, you're always underfoot! And with all we've got to do! Get along with you now! Wash your face, and for goodness' sake don't get your boots muddy, and go on to the church! Don't stay mooning here!"

"Won't there be any dinner? I'm hungry."

"Dinner, my foot! As if we didn't have enough to do. You can wait till supper time."

"I'm awful hungry." Grief at losing Amy, sorrow because she would leave them and go to live with Dave, these were a pain like hunger.

"Well, there's fresh-baked bread in the crock, and jelly on the table. Fix yourself a piece." She caught up her sewing basket and vanished into the bedroom again. Tom Glen, sitting in the corner out of the way, said in comfort:

"Don't worry, Owen. Women go crazy when there's a wedding. Eat some bread and jelly."

But Owen decided he was not hungry. "Besides, the butter's way over at the spring house. It's too much trouble. I guess I'll go ahead."

So he drifted away up the road toward Sardis Church and crept into a thicket by the roadside and waited there till he saw the surrey pass. His father and mother were in the front seat, Amy and Miss Williams in the back. He followed, and when he reached the church, he circled around to the cemetery and stayed there, whetting his unhappiness by telling himself Amy would not want

him in the church, not now when she was going to leave them for
good. Or maybe she would refuse to get married unless he was
there; he clung to that straw till the organ stopped and he knew
the ceremony had begun.

He saw half a dozen boys busy about Dave's buggy in the carriage shed, and moved nearer and watched them tie ribbons to the
wheels and a string of old tin cans to the axle; and then Dave's
father came out and the boys scattered, and Mr. Lewis, grinning
a little at what they had done, unhitched the horse and led it near
the open door of the church.

Owen, lurking by the steps, could hear the murmur of the
preacher's voice; and then the wheezy organ began to play, and
people came hurriedly out of the church, forming uneven lines on
either side of the steps, shouting and laughing. Then in the doorway Dave and Amy appeared, and everyone threw rice and things
at them, and they held hands and ran to the buggy. Owen ran
with them, thrusting his way through the smiling throng, crying:
"Goodbye, Amy! Amy, goodbye!" She heard him, and turned, and
caught him and kissed him; and then someone thrust him aside —
young Morgan Jones, a friend of Dave's — and shouted: "Everybody kiss the bride!" Morgan caught Amy and kissed her, and
others tried to do the same, but Dave pulled her up into the
buggy, and whipped his horse, and they drove away; and Morgan
Jones caught Owen by the arm and shook him, and said angrily:
"Hey, stop kicking me, Owen! What's the matter with you?"

Owen wrenched free and turned and fled, biting his lip to keep
back sobs. Everybody kissing Amy! He wanted to kick them all!

But then Marged called his name, and he saw her with his
father and mother over by the surrey in which they had come to
the church. "Want a ride?" she asked, and he went to join them.
His mother was crying, scrubbing at her eyes; she sat in front
with his father, he and Marged behind, and Marged said: "Wasn't
it wonderful?"

Mrs. Glen sobbed happily. "Every bit of it," she agreed. "Tom,
you looked real grand."

Owen realized, with a new pang, that he had not been missed.
It was bad enough that Amy had not missed him; he had imagined
her crying: "Wait, where's Owen? I won't be married unless Owen's
here." But she had gone ahead and got married anyway. That
was bad enough; but that his mother had not missed him was

worse, a bitter grief. He sat in gloomy silence while Marged and his mother sighed in deep content at each new tender memory.

But early supper at Dave's house was fun; fried chickens by the panful, and ice cream, and pie. Afterward — it was still bright daylight — they went out-of-doors and played *Tucker* and *Going to the Mill*, till at dusk everyone crowded indoors to give Dave and Amy their presents. That took a long time, and everyone cracked jokes, and Dave made a speech to thank them all, and Mrs. Lloyd Davis announced that the infair would be at her house next day, and everyone cheered.

So at last people began to leave, and again his loneliness seized Owen. When his father and mother came out-of-doors and his mother called him and he knew they were going home, he sidled away into the darkness; to their repeated calls he gave no answer. Let them go without him! He would stay near Amy as long as he could. He watched from the darkness till except for them and some nearer neighbors everyone was gone, and he heard his father say over and over: "He's got a ride home is all. He's all right, mama." Dave and Mr. Lewis spoke in equal assurance; and at last they drove away.

Owen watched till the lantern that was hung under the front axle passed out of sight; then he moved off across the meadow above the road to the edge of the woodlot. He imagined himself staying there all night; yes, and all next day too, and the next night, and the next, till probably he would just starve to death, and they would find him and weep; and he relished the delicious anguish of their sadness.

The last goodbyes were called, the last guests gone, and Owen sat in the wood above the house, watching the lighted windows, wondering why Dave's family did not go to bed. Amy, he guessed, would sleep in the spare room; and Owen wished he knew which it was, so he could creep near and crouch below her window. Perhaps, when everyone else was asleep, he could tap on the glass and whisper her name, and she would hear and come and find him and be sorry she had left them all forever. He wanted her to be sorry.

After a long time — or a time that seemed long — he heard fur- tive sounds from the road; the stir of feet, and low voices, and a chuckle of mirth, and a clank as though someone had touched a tin pan with a spoon. On hands and knees, heedless of the soft muddy ground and his best pants and his boots, he moved nearer, near enough to see many dark figures in the road. In sudden understanding he realized that these people were come to give Dave and Amy a belling, and sure enough, as they reached the house a terrific din arose. They had tin pails and old powder cans, and horns, and sleighbells, and noise-makers of a hundred sorts; and they pounded and clanged and shouted and whistled and hooted, and laughed and uttered shrill cries. Owen drew nearer, with clenched teeth, in a raging anger.

Then the door opened, and Dave came out on the porch with a lantern in one hand and a box in the other. When he held up the lantern, Owen by its light recognized some of those here around him. Pete Radford and Sammy Howell were at his shoulder. Dave passed cigars, holding out the open box for those who wished to help themselves; and Amy came to stand by Dave's side, clinging to his arm, smiling proudly. Everyone shouted congratulations and good wishes, and began to call goodnights, and Dave kept saying: "Thanks, boys," and Amy cried happily: "Oh, thank you! Thank you!" She stood on tiptoe to kiss Dave's cheek, and everyone cheered, and then she and Dave went back indoors.

In that first moment's hush as the door closed upon them, Owen heard Pete Radford say jeeringly to Sammy: "Look at her kiss him! Bullish heifer, ain't she?"

Owen knew what that meant; he had once helped lead a bulling cow to Lloyd Davis's bull and watched what happened. But that was animals! He drove at Pete with such headlong violence that the older boy, unwarned, was thrust over sidewise; and Owen fell on top of him and beat and clawed at him in a sobbing silence till someone pulled Owen off, and held him tight and said in a friendly tone:

"Stop that, now! Stop it!"

Pete climbed unsteadily to his feet. "I didn't do anything," he protested. "He just jumped on me. He made my nose bleed." He put his hand to the back of his head and said in frightened tones: "Yes, and my head's cut, too!"

Owen, finding himself helpless, gave over his struggles. It was Bobby Roberts who held him, and Bobby asked: "What started it, Owen?"

"None of your business!" Owen hated even Bobby Roberts in this hour.

That made them laugh, and someone said: "Well, next time, pick on someone your size."

"I can lick him, no matter how big he is."

Pete, snuffling his bloody nose, repeated in that plaintive tone: "I didn't do anything!"

"All right for you," Owen told him bleakly. "I'll get you alone some day."

They all laughed again; and Bobby Roberts said gently: "Not tonight you won't, young rooster! You come along home with me."

Owen knew himself helpless, and his rage was dying, and he was trembling. He and Bobby and a dozen or so others set out along the road toward the church and the furnace beyond; and when he and Bobby were alone, the young man asked in a quiet sympathy: "What got you started, Owen?"

"Nothing."

"Must have been something."

"Nothing, I said!"

Bobby chuckled. "Well, you gave Pete quite a going-over for nothing. But I guess I know what it was. Don't pay any attention to Pete. Pete's dirty. The only thing to do with boys like him is keep away from them." Owen looked up at the tall young man beside him in the darkness, wondering whether Bobby too had heard; but he did not speak, and Bobby said mildly: "A dirty boy sees dirt in everything, Owen; even in a wedding. But a wedding's the cleanest, nicest thing there is." They were at home, and Bobby saw the lighted window. "Guess your mother's waiting up for you. Owen, you'll have to learn to look out for that temper of yours, or you'll hurt somebody bad, some day. Goodnight, now."

Owen's mother, when she saw him, cried: "Owen, wherever have you been? And what's happened to you? You're covered with dirt, and you've tore your pants, the only nice pair you had. Of all things to do!"

"I went to the belling," Owen said. "And — I fell down." He wished he could talk to her, or to someone; but some things you could never talk about.

Yet he lay long awake that night, thinking of what Pete had said. The unacknowledged realization that somewhere behind Pete's word lay truth, truth more mysterious than any lie, only made him set his jaw, the more determined to give Pete a good licking one of these days.

III

April to Christmas 1890

Owen, except on the trains coming from Indiana to Ohio, had never seen any town larger than Sycamore Hill; but Hardiston, now to be their home, was almost a city. The town was set on high ground with the valleys of Salt Creek on one side, of Erie Creek on the other. Peach Street, Ridge and Main bounded the compact heart of the community, forming a right-angled triangle with Peach as the perpendicular, Main as the hypotenuse. South of Peach Street, except for the Fair Grounds, lay for the most part open fields; but southwest of town, around Erie Mine and Erie Furnace, a few small houses clustered. Northeast of Main and its extensions, the railroad yards, the Nail Mill, Moon Furnace and Union Furnace, and most of the industrial life of the town sprawled along the meandering course of Salt Creek.

Pearl Street, two long blocks north of Peach, crossed Ridge Street and proceeded into the country, becoming the Pike. A fine oak grove lay north of the Pike for a quarter-mile beyond Ridge Street, to where a little wet-weather run crossed the road and proceeded furtively toward Salt Creek. At one point this stream had kept open its channel through the heart of a tremendous slack pile, above which in many places small plumes of smoke rose from spontaneous fires. This slack pile was refuse from the old Morgan Mine, now worked out and abandoned. West of the slack pile, a dozen small houses once occupied by the men who had worked the mine straggled toward the Pike. All but two or three, since they were no longer occupied, approached collapse; but the one nearest the Pike was precariously livable.

This house Tom Glen rented from Moses Evans, who had owned

42

the mine and who still owned the houses, the slack pile, and the land. The house was a mile or more from Erie Mine, where Tom worked; but it was cheaper than houses nearer Erie. The rent was four dollars a month.

To this house, a few days after Amy's wedding, they brought their household goods. Dave, Amy's husband, helped them load everything into his father's hay wagon and drove them to Hardiston. Their possessions included two beds, a bureau and a wardrobe, a cooking stove, a coal bucket, four kitchen chairs, a big rocker and a small one, three pails, a box half full of dishes and kitchenware and left-over groceries, two washtubs and a washboard, two coal-oil lamps, a box full of bedding into which had been folded their two Bibles and both mirrors, a home-made wooden chest containing their clothes, five pictures in frames and wrapped in newspapers, a barrel into which a varied assortment of small objects had been dumped, and a crate of hens. Another crate contained a small, complaining pig; and tethered behind the wagon trailed a fretful and reluctant cow soon to come fresh.

They left Adams Furnace at first light, and it was not yet midmorning when they arrived. While Owen staked the cow and his father and Dave began to unload, Mrs. Glen went to inspect their new home. The kitchen was larger than in the house they had left; there were two bedrooms instead of one; and what might at a pinch serve as another bedroom had been converted into a shed for storing kindling, coal, washtubs, garden tools, and anything else too big or too dirty to be kept in the kitchen.

Before she would let the furniture be carried indoors, Mrs. Glen insisted the floors must be scrubbed. Tom and Owen built a fire by the stream side and heated water, and Owen helped his mother while Tom climbed into the attic to look for leaks in the roof. The other houses between them and the old entry a hundred yards down the slope furnished an abundance of material which could be used for repairs, and before dark that first day Tom had the roof tight, and Owen and his mother had the floors clean. The walls were almost as dirty as the floors had been, but Mrs. Glen said they would have to wait. "There'll be time enough after we get settled down."

Owen, awake for a while in these new surroundings, heard far away at the other end of town the roar of Union Furnace, and that was familiar, like the voice of the furnace at home. It was his lullaby.

During the weeks that followed, Tom and Owen put the house in better repair. Since Erie Mine only operated when coal was needed at Union Furnace, Tom had many free days; and on these days he made the patched roof secure, nailed odd boards over the worst cracks in the walls, and replaced broken window panes. Owen's part was to supply the materials his father needed. Moses Evans had given Tom permission to use whatever he could find in the other houses, now well gone to ruin; and Owen searched them all, finding not only sound boards, useful bricks, hinges and latches, a door or two in good condition, and whole panes of glass, but two window sashes with every pane intact.

Their water came from a never-failing spring, about fifty yards from their house, which had been walled with stones to a depth of six or eight feet. Owen and his father bailed it out and cleaned it, and when it filled again, the overflow made a persistent small stream that trickled down to the run. At his father's suggestion and with his father's advice Owen built a spring house, digging away the earth to a depth of two or three feet, laying a pavement of broken bricks big enough to accommodate three or four milk-pans, roofing the place with boards on top of which he placed good sod, and contriving a door to keep out wandering cats and dogs.

2

When there were no tasks for him to do at home, Owen went exploring. His first excursion led him down past the slack pile to the Ohio Southern yards. Usually full of coal cars, the yards were a favorite gleaning ground for small boys with home-made carts or hand-barrows or empty short sacks. Owen on his first venture saw two or three thus engaged, picking up coal fallen from the cars; and next time he brought a sack and easily garnered as much coal as he could carry home.

He took only coal that was already on the ground, but he saw other boys climb into the cars and throw coal down; and one day two boys climbed on a moving freight train, tossing off lumps of coal as the train rolled out of the yards. When the train began to gather speed, they jumped off; but one of the boys fell between the cars, and Owen saw the severed legs roll over and over down the embankment beside the moving train. He ran home, sobbing as he ran, and it was a long time before he went near the tracks again.

But there were many other things to see. Sometimes he went to Erie Mine to wait for his father and walk home with Tom and carry his dinner pail. Often they had for a while companions, men like his father with blackened faces and pale eye-sockets and in coal-black garments so that they looked like shadows. Four or five or six of them would leave the mine together, and the others turned aside by ones and twos as they passed near their homes. Owen came to know some of them. Little Mat Steel was not much bigger than Owen himself, despite the pretty wife who often came to the gate to meet him, with a baby in her arms and two other youngsters at her heels. Isaac Williams, if he were in the group, walked with them as far as Pearl Street, where he went one way while they went the other. He had gray hair and seemed older than Tom Glen, and he was an elder in the church, passing the contribution box on Sundays. Owen saw his father's respect for Isaac Williams, and he too felt a certain weight and judgment in this man. John Carver sometimes walked as far as Peach Street with them; he was younger than the others, so he might drop back with Owen, talking with him on even terms, as though their ages were the same. One of the trap boys, Chet Masters, sometimes joined Owen, following the older men. Owen told Chet one day: "I had a school teacher named Masters, down in Adams Township, till we locked him out." Chet said that Mr. Masters was his uncle, sick now with something wrong in his stomach. "He's in a hospital in Columbus." Owen was briefly sorry for the pedagogue.

There were others near his own age whom Owen came to know, boys who worked as trappers in the mine. Tom Powell was one of them, his cousin Jenkin another. Tom's father was John Powell, the mine boss, whom Owen knew from a distance as a casual and cheerful man who seemed never in a hurry or for any reason anxious or concerned. Tom and Jenkin were a year or two older than Owen, proud of their status as workers; but Tom explained to Owen that he worked here only in the summer, went to school in winter. "And I'm going to college when I'm old enough, too."

Jenkin's father was a farmer, his home a mile or two out the Liberty road. Tom was tall for his age, with a careless friendliness; Jenkin was smaller, and there was something sly about him. Owen decided he liked the one, but not the other.

Among the men who for one reason or another attracted Owen was Evan Harned. Owen's attention was drawn to Harned because he and Isaac Williams often came out of the mine together; and though Harned was the younger, Owen felt some bond between them. Evan's brother Jim was as old as Mr. Williams, and Jim and his son — whom Owen guessed to be at least twenty years old — likewise worked in Erie, and usually left the mine with Evan. Father and son were unusual in that they worked the same room in the mine, while most experienced miners preferred to have a room of their own. Owen heard his father discuss this one day with Isaac Williams, and they agreed that the bigger the room, the harder it was to keep the roof secure. He asked his father why Isaac Williams and Evan Harned were so much together, and Tom explained that they were president and vice-president of the Erie local; and Jim Harned was the secretary-treasurer.

Owen enjoyed walking home with his father and the others. His mother had exacted a promise that he would not go into the mine, and he never did so; but it was fun to wait by the dark portal, to hear far away underground the muffled thud of shots, to hear hoofbeats as a mule approached with its train of loaded cars, to peer into the darkness and see stars of brightness from the lamps the men wore in their caps, to see suddenly the mule's forefeet and then its nose and head and body and then the wheels of the cars and then the cars. Sometimes men and boys rode out on the loaded cars, their day done; and Owen came to know them and they to know him. He laid envious eyes on the trap boys, only a few years older than himself, whose task it was to wait by the doors placed at intervals through the mine to control the circulation of air, opening the doors to let cars or men through, closing them afterward. Some older boys worked as miners, and Owen dreamed of the day he would be one of them.

One day he told this dream. He and John Carver had become friends. John was only sixteen, so Owen felt no great gulf between them. They were walking homeward together, following

Tom Glen and Isaac Williams, and Owen said proudly: "I'm going to be a miner, too, as soon as I'm old enough."

To his surprise, John gripped his arm. "Don't you do it!" he protested. "Not unless you just have to."

"I want to. I want to earn some money." Since coming to Hardiston, Owen had discovered that his father and mother were poor. Back at Adams Furnace, the other houses on the flat had been very much like the one in which they lived, and even Ned Howell's over by the store, was only a little bigger; but here in Hardiston, just about everybody had a nicer house than theirs. Some even had houses two stories high! So he knew his father and mother were poor, and wanted to help them.

"Well, if you want to, all right," John conceded. "But I won't. I'm saving money, and I study every night at home; and some day I'm going to get to be a school teacher, and then I'm going to teach school and save money till I can go to college, and then I'm going to be a lawyer."

Owen was impressed, but he thought he would rather be a coal miner than a lawyer, and he wished he could start in as a trapper boy now. He could surely open a door as well as anybody; but he knew it was useless to suggest this. His mother would never, while she could help it, let him go to work in the mine.

But his desire to earn money persisted, and one day he discovered a source of income. He saw, stopped before a house on Pearl Street near Mr. McAuliffe's store, a cart with a spring scale hanging at the tail, and a man was weighing in the scale a heap of old rags. Owen questioned him and found that the man would buy rags, bones, scraps of iron or zinc or tin, and even empty bottles. After that day Owen's wanderings were no longer aimless. Alleys became his hunting ground; each heap of rubbish was a potential gold mine, and daily he carried home small treasures. When his hoard assumed respectable proportions, he led the junk man to their house and sold his accumulation for nineteen cents.

Even his father was impressed. "That's the pay for half a day's work, a boy of your age," he said. "Or pretty near."

Owen found another way to earn money. One day Tom Glen forgot his dinner pail, and Owen took it to the mine. On his way home, he diverged from the shortest route in order to pass the mine stables, which had for him a strong fascination. When he left the stables and climbed the hill toward Peach Street, he heard a strange, metallic, rattling sound; and when he came to Peach Street, he saw in the yard across the street a man pushing the machine which made the sound.

Owen crossed to watch at closer range and recognized Mr. Beecham, who had come to last day of school and had talked to them about books. Mr. Beecham, in his shirt sleeves, red-faced and perspiring, became conscious of the boy's scrutiny, and stopped to mop his brow, and Owen said:

"Howdo, Mr. Beecham."

"Hello, there." BB was puzzled, then remembered. "You're Owen Glendower, aren't you. No, Owen Glen. Well, where did you come from?"

"We live here now. I took papa his dinner pail, down to Erie Mine." He was looking at the machine. "What's that?"

"Didn't you ever see a lawnmower?"

"No sir." Owen was on the sidewalk, from which a double terrace rose to the level where BB stood.

"Today's the first time I've tackled my lawn this year. Grass hasn't started to grow, yet. Come up and see how it works." And when Owen reached his side, BB explained: "These blades, whirling around, scrape along this sharp edge here, like a pair of scissors. Try it." Owen pushed the lawnmower a few feet, and grinned with delight; and BB said: "See here, how'd you like to cut my grass today? I'll pay you a quarter."

To be paid for doing what he was so eager to do was dazzling. "Yes sir," said Owen.

"All right, it's a bargain." Owen set to work, and BB watched him for a moment and said approvingly: "That's fine." He went into the house, leaving Owen to his task.

The level lawn was easy enough, but Owen found that the steeply sloping terraces required all his strength and all his patience too. He labored till his back and his shoulders and his legs were shaking with fatigue. When he finished, BB came out to pay him the quarter.

"I expect you feel you earned it," he suggested.

"I'd like to do this right along."

"All right, I'll give you the job. I mow it about every two weeks, but if we have much rain it can stand to be done oftener. Come around to the back porch. Mrs. Beecham has made some pretty good lemonade." So Owen went with him, and Sally Beecham brought out a squat silver pitcher dewy with moisture and full of the delicious draft, and BB said: "Sally, this is Owen Glen. He's going to cut our grass this summer."

Mrs. Beecham shook hands with Owen. She looked so clean and cool and sweet that he was ashamed to have her touch his sweaty hand, and wiped it on his pants too late; but she seemed not to mind. He gulped the lemonade thirstily, and BB asked:

"When did you move to town?"

"Right after the wedding, the next Monday."

"Whose wedding?"

"My sister's. The day you were down there."

"Well, you've been here quite a while. You haven't come in to see how we print the paper." The lemonade pitcher was still well-filled. "Have another glass?" Owen hesitated, and BB filled his glass again. "Come in some day. Wednesday's the best, or Saturday. And you keep an eye on the lawn, mow it when it needs it. If I'm not here to pay you, you'll usually find me at the office."

Owen went proudly home to give the coin to his mother, and he found thereafter other lawns to mow. Usually he was paid only ten cents, or fifteen, for few of the lawns were as large or as difficult as BB's. A pretty woman named Mrs. Paxley was, after BB, his best customer. She always paid him a quarter — though her lawn was small — and usually she gave him lemonade, or cookies, or both. She seemed to be lonesome, sometimes keeping him a long time in the kitchen after his task was done, asking questions about other people for whom he worked. He suspected that she did not know many people in Hardiston. Mr. Paxley never seemed to be at home.

Owen found jobs by asking for them, but he was not always successful. Once he saw a pretty woman mowing her own lawn, while a grotesque dog watched her from the nearest shade. He spoke to her and offered to mow her lawn for a dime, but she shook her head. "It will be a long day before I pay anyone to mow my lawn. What's your name, boy?"

"Owen Glen."

"Well, I'm Mrs. Arthur. Take my advice and never pay anyone to do a thing you can do yourself."

"Yes'm. What kind of a dog is that?"

Her face broke into a charming smile. "He's a pug. His name's Major. Named after Mr. Arthur's father, because they look so much alike." Major, recognizing his name, came waddling to her side, to be caressed. "Isn't he handsome? He won't bite." Owen grinned and she put the lawnmower once more in motion and he walked on.

He had other experiences which like this were more educational than profitable. Mr. Ames, who lived next door to Mr. Beecham, was a big man who always wore a long black coat, and talked very loudly, and smoked evil-smelling stogies. Owen never saw Mrs. Ames, but there were two children in the family. The thin little sandy-haired boy, two years older than Owen, was Freddie; the girl named Celia, a year or so younger, seemed to hold Owen and her brother in an equal contempt.

Mr. Ames one day saw Owen cutting Mr. Beecham's lawn, and came to the fence between the yards and called: "Here, boy. When you get through, come over and do mine too."

Mr. Ames's lawn was badly kept, the grass was already too long for easy cutting, and there were some weeds in it; nevertheless, Owen welcomed a new customer, so he agreed. But Mr. Ames proved to be slow pay, so he never again cut the big man's grass.

However, there were other lawns, and Owen made that summer a considerable contribution to the family purse. He had no thought, nor had his father and mother, that he might keep the money for his own.

3

Owen during these first months in Hardiston saw a thousand things new to him and strange. He saw boys playing marbles on Sunday, though he had been taught it was wrong even to whistle on the Sabbath day. He saw a tank on a wagon drawn by two stout horses sprinkle water on the dusty streets, to convert the dust briefly into mud. He made friends with big John Morgan, who

drove the dray that met all trains and who allowed Owen to ride
with him. This was in itself an adventure. The dray was flat-
bodied, sloping slightly toward the rear, with holes bored con-
veniently so that by setting staves in holes where they were
needed, even a barrel on its side on the sloping bed of the dray
could be made secure.

But the best part was that the dray had no seat for driver or
passenger; you rode standing up, and after a little patience you
no longer needed to hold on to the staves to keep your balance,
but stood secure and easy, swaying to the movement of the dray.

Mr. Morgan's son Tommy sometimes rode the dray with his
father. Tommy was Owen's age, and it was hard to believe that
so frail a youngster could be stalwart John Morgan's son. Tommy
was pale and thin and small, with a persistent cough; and his
mother and father, even in hot summer weather, made him wear a
light wool comforter around his throat. Mr. Morgan's brother
Charles lived in a pleasant house at the corner of Ridge and Pearl
Streets, a short quarter-mile from Owen's home; and all summer
that house swarmed with visiting grandchildren. Little Tommy
regularly came to play with them, so Owen was drawn into their
pleasant company. Charles Morgan was a coal miner, coming
home each afternoon well begrimed; but on days when he did not
work, he spent much time with his grandchildren, and Owen
learned to know him and to like him. Mr. Morgan had the pleasant
habit of treating children as his equals.

Big John Morgan, his brother, seldom volunteered anything more
than a word or two; but he would answer questions. When Owen
rode the dray to the station to see the trains come in and the
passengers alight, he wondered where the men and women all
came from, and where they went, and whether the cowcatcher on
the engine ever really caught a cow. When they met the down
train in the afternoon, a woman strangely clad, and whose lips
forever moved in soundless speech, was always among those waiting on the platform. She wore a rusty black silk dress, spotted
and stained, and an outlandish old-fashioned hat, and a black lace
shawl around her shoulders. Her hair, so black Owen thought she
must dip it in ink, hung in oily ringlets; her face was white as
though plastered with flour, and her cheeks were splotched with
red. When the train came in, she always waved, lifting a thin

hand in a black lace mitt which left the ends of her skinny yellow fingers bare; and she watched each passenger descend, pressing nearer to peer into each masculine countenance. After the train had gone, she trudged back uptown, whispering to herself, shaking her head or nodding it, smiling upward over her shoulder as though to some tall man beside her. Owen asked John Morgan who she was. Her name, said the drayman, was Adelina Fortune, and she was crazy. For a long time, that was all Owen knew about her; but he felt for her a wondering pity, and an impulse to be kind, yet never dared to speak to her at all.

He saturated himself in new sights and scenes. He saw saloons, and he saw men staggering with drink, and he heard that a drunk man in Slacktown up the creek had killed three men. He learned to dodge out of sight whenever he saw Marshal Henson, not because he himself had committed any crime, but because one day down by the railroad yards he heard the Marshal threaten three coal-stealing boys with something mysterious called the "cala-boose." A caboose was a car at the end of a freight train, but a calaboose was, obviously, something else, and frightening. Eventually Owen learned that the calaboose was a room with a barred door in the back part of the fire-engine house. He had stopped in the open door of the engine house to stare at the engine with its gleaming pear-shaped dome, when a tall man with a small beard, wearing a fireman's helmet labelled "Chief," came out of that barred door and strolled toward him. Owen could see the horses in their stalls, but there were no bars on their stalls, so he asked the man:

"What do you keep in the room with the bars?"

"That? That's the calaboose, the lockup." The Chief seemed a friendly man, and there were many things about the fire engine which Owen wished to know. The polished dome, the Chief assured him, was to help them find fires. "Wasn't for that dome, we'd get an alarm and wouldn't know where to go! As 'tis, soon as the engine's out in the street we c'n see the smoke, or if it's night, the glare, reflected in that dome."

Owen believed him, and the place entranced him. He dreamed that some day he might discover a fire and come running to ring the bell, and then watch the sleek horses leap from their stalls and stop under the harness hanging ready to drop on their backs, and when the harness was snapped on, at a stirring gallop race away.

4

While Owen wandered at will, his father and mother made new friends. Mrs. Glen met at Mr. McAuliffe's grocery on Pearl Street Mrs. Freeman Lewis, whose husband was a conductor on the Ohio Southern and who lived down Ridge Street near the railroad yards. They were at once congenial and soon began to spend an occasional afternoon together. When Mrs. Lewis came to the house, she was as apt as not to bring a bag of red drops, or a stick of licorice or of white chewing gum for Owen; he felt affection in her and returned it, but he asked his mother one day:

"Why does she look so sad all the time when she's laughing and joking with me?"

"She had a baby boy that died and he'd be about your age," his mother explained. "And that was the only baby they ever had."

Then there were the Evan Jenkinses, their nearest neighbors out the Pike. Evan worked in the electric light plant, and Mrs. Jenkins, a day or two after they were established in their new home, came bustling over to pay a friendly call, bringing a basket of eggs and a pound of butter. The first Sunday, she and Evan stopped to escort the Glens to the Welsh church at the other end of town where they presented their letters. Mrs. Jenkins and Evan had three daughters, young women in their early twenties who, since Evan was all day at the light plant, did much of the farm work, hoeing corn, knocking off potato bugs, weeding, harvesting, haying; and they milked the cows, fed the chickens, gathered the eggs, made butter and slopped the pigs. They were a buxom and a jolly trio. All three sang in the church choir and so did Evan himself, in a deep bass that came strangely from his lean neck. When Evan sang, Owen watched in fascination the mysterious movements of his Adam's apple. Sometimes the choir came to have supper at Evan's farm and practice afterward; and on these occasions Owen and his father and mother were always invited. The sisters discovered that Owen had a true soprano, and tried to persuade him to join the choir, but he refused, in a red embarrassment. He liked them, but they had a frightening exuberance, forever laughing, fond of teasing, plump and rosy. Their names were Betty and Mary and Allie, but they looked and acted so much

alike that Owen thought their names did not matter very much.
He heard Mrs. Jenkins tell his mother that Betty had been married
a year or two before to a young miner named Edwards, who was
killed by a fall of slate a month after their marriage, but Owen
thought she seemed as cheerful as her sisters. Usually the choir
practices at their house were fun, but once someone named Miss
Means was there, and she was so severe and sarcastic and generally disapproving that she spoiled the evening for everyone. On
the way to church the following Sunday, Owen asked Allie Jenkins
who Miss Means was, and Allie laughed much harder than the
question seemed to justify.

"She's mama's stepsister," Allie explained. "We call her Aunt
Wormwood — behind her back, of course. She's awful, isn't she.
She teaches school." Alice jabbed Owen in the ribs and shrieked
with mirth. "Maybe she'll be your teacher some day."

"What's the matter with her?"

"Oh, just because Betty —— " Allie clapped her hand over her
mouth. "Oh, she just thinks we're awful, and says we'll all come
to a bad end. When Betty's baby died, she said it was a judgment
on us all, and what did we expect." She squeezed his arm: "I
know what she is! She's an I-told-you-so-er! Waiting around for
things to happen to us so she can say she told us so." Owen
thought the prospect of going to school to Miss Means gravely
unattractive.

Just as Mrs. Glen made new friends, so did Owen's father. On
days when the mine did not work, one or two men might come to
sit with Tom in the shade beside the house; and their talk touched
everything that happened, or that had happened, in the county.
Some farmers out along the Pike had been victimized by strangers
who persuaded them to sign what they thought was an agreement
to serve as agents for a newly invented patent fence, only to find
when it was too late that they had signed promissory notes. The
gallows which had been used to hang the Jones boys, seven years
before, had been sold to a county in Pennsylvania; but Owen's
father had never heard of the Jones boys, so the men told the tale
of their crime and described how they were hanged in the yard
beside the Court House. Owen, who always listened to the talk,
dreamed bad dreams that night. A colored man in the Ohio Legislature, a man named Greene, had introduced a law to make September 1 a legal holiday and call it Labor Day. The farmers were

talking about forming an Alliance, to go into politics; and Tom Glen predicted that some day men would be able to vote without letting their employers see the ballots. Then farmers and laboring men together would rule the country.

Listening to them, and listening to his mother and her friends, Owen began to be interested in the things which interested grown people: in the fact that Mr. and Mrs. David Morgan — Mr. Morgan was an elder of the church — had gone to visit their son in Denver; in the fact that there were 46,214 Ohio members of the Grand Army of the Republic; in the fact that Mr. McAuliffe's grocery just down the street had been broken into by burglars; in the death of the Reverend D. T. Evans of Sycamore Hill — Owen had heard him preach, more than once, at Sardis Church — who was killed by a train when his horse balked at a crossing; in the sad affair down in Gallia County where the wife of a farmer whom Tom Glen as a boy had known went insane and threw her two-year-old daughter down a well; in the guesses about what the census then being taken would determine Hardiston's population to be.

But Owen liked best of all to hear his father and the other men talk of mines and of mining. There were tales from the old country, tales of men penned by hundreds in the deep Welsh pits to be suffocated by the fouling air, and tales of explosions when the fire damp rolled like a billow of flame from end to end of the mine and cooked the flesh off a man's face as it passed. Isaac Williams told them of the Avondale catastrophe, twenty-odd years ago, when a hundred and nine men were suffocated by smoke and gas.

"But they died to save the rest of us, as truly as Christ did," said Isaac reverently. "For it was because they died that the first mine safety laws came to be passed in the old country, and then in Ohio after."

There were tales of the February day at Braidwood, in Illinois, when a weight of surface water broke through into the mine and drowned sixty-nine men; of the similar tragedy two years later on the Nanticoke slope in Pennsylvania when twenty-six men died; of the Pocahontas explosion which killed every man underground. Owen began to realize that the men spoke of these tragedies in tones not of terror but of pride. It was as though they boasted that while they toiled, death was always at their side; and he began to share this pride, to honor them as heroes, to long with

an even keener yearning for the time when he might join their
dauntless ranks.

But their slow talk together was not always of danger and
death. Tom Glen in particular was apt to speak of the Knights
of Labor, and of John Siney and Terence Powderly and other
great men alive and dead. He had joined the Erie local as soon as
he went to work there, and he was a loyal union man, but his
deepest loyalty was to the older organization. The Knights of
Labor were to have a celebration on the Fourth, and for weeks
past Tom had promised to take Owen to watch the parade, and
listen to the band, and see all there was to see.

In these idle hours when two or three or half a dozen men
gathered for slow talk in the shade beside the house, anything Tom
said was apt to come back to the same beloved topic. One day he
grumbled because Mr. and Mrs. Herbert Canter — Mr. Canter
owned many coal mines in the county — were gone off to Europe
for the summer. Tom said hotly that Mr. Canter was paying his
way to Europe with dollars he had taken out of the pockets of his
miners.

"And as long as he's let do it, who's to blame him? If a dog
bites a man once, it's the dog's fault; but the second time, it's the
man's fault. The only way to stop a burglar is to stop him." There
was always, when Tom spoke of such matters, violence in his
words and his tone. "The worst thing coal miners ever did was
quit the Knights of Labor for this United Mine Workers. The
Knights, give them time, would have got us somewhere."

Isaac Williams said mildly: "Nothing gets done in a hurry, Tom.
You've only been a miner maybe fifteen years. We've come a ways
in that time; but wait till you can look back forty years, like I
can."

Tom did not argue the point, and this silence was eloquent of
his respect for the older man. Owen knew this, and the knowledge
increased Isaac Williams's stature in his eyes.

5

Mr. Beecham had more than once urged Owen to come and
watch the paper being run off; and eventually Owen overcame his

diffidence and did so. BB took him in charge, explaining the operation of the press; he pointed out how the type on its steel bed, after making contact with the sheets of paper on the revolving cylinder, slid back under the rollers to be inked again. Will Davis, standing on a high platform, feeding each sheet into the press with smoothly rhythmic movements, held a worn old brass key in his right hand; and after each sheet was caught by the clips and drawn away, Will stroked the top of the remaining pile of paper with this key. Owen asked why, and BB explained:

"He does that to slide the top sheet down a little, so he can catch hold of it." Will gripped each sheet, then flipped it lightly, before he led it down against the guides, and BB said that little flip was to release the top sheet from the others. "If he didn't do that, the sheets would stick together. He has to let air in between them."

That day was Saturday, and they were printing the outside, but at BB's invitation Owen came again on Wednesday night, when not only the press but the folder was working. This machine first folded each sheet in the middle, then trimmed the edges of that fold so that there were two sheets instead of one, then folded these again, and again, and again. Once a tape in the folder broke, and Will stopped the press and pulled out the wadded papers and threw them away before he mended the broken tape, lacing it together as though he were lacing shoes.

BB gave one of the rumpled papers to Owen to take home. "We always spoil a few," he explained. "Any time you're here, you can have one."

That was the paper for July 9. There was a piece about the Fourth of July celebration which Owen and his father had seen and heard, and he read it with the keen interest everyone feels in reading about something familiar. He read about the baseball game on the afternoon of the Fourth between Hardiston and Chillicothe — Hardiston won by nine to nothing — and he read the many paragraphs about Hardiston people, and the advertisements of the Hardiston stores, and the patent medicine advertisements and testimonials. Syrup of Figs was pleasant and refreshing to the taste and acted gently but promptly on the Kidneys, Liver, and Bowels. Bradfield's Female Regulator was a boon to women. H. B. Pool of Pearl Street, New York, knew how to cure fits; and

weak men would be well advised to write Professor Knowles of
Moodus, Connecticut. Owen read that there was a new state
named Idaho; and BB had written:

> *Idaho is the last link in a line of states reaching from
> the Atlantic to the Pacific. The United States is now pro-
> tected from Canada's advances by thirteen states, the
> leading states of the Union.*

Owen could not understand the columns of political notes, but
he read that Stanley's own book, *In Darkest Africa,* would soon
be printed. Hugh Barnum of Hardiston was the sole agent for the
county, and he wished to engage canvassers, to whom he promised
exclusive territory; and Owen wondered whether he could be a
canvasser. There was a sermon, four columns long, preached by
Doctor T. DeWitt Talmage at Beatrice, Nebraska, and a reminder
that one of Doctor Talmage's inspiring sermons was published in
the *Journal* every week; but Owen skipped the sermon. He was
shaken by the fact that thirty-one miners had been killed in an
explosion in Dunbar, Pennsylvania; and he read that since January
1, five persons had been killed by railroads in the county, and two
by lightning. He himself had seen one boy killed by a train.
Swift's Specific would positively cure consumption and cancer; and
Doctor France, whose photograph, two columns wide, showed him
to be a handsome, bearded man with piercing eyes, would be at
the Flagg House on Saturday to treat, in strictest confidence, all
chronic diseases, with special attention to young men, middle-aged
men, and suffering women. Owen found half a column of items
from Adams Furnace. Miss Marged Williams would teach next
winter in Glendale, one of the towns up the creek, and she would
board with her uncle Isaac Williams in Hardiston. That must be
the same Isaac Williams who worked in Erie Mine, so Owen
thought he would sometimes see Miss Williams, and the possibility
made him happy. Dr. Haines's Golden Specific was a positive cure
for the liquor habit. The census takers reported that Hardiston's
population was 4300, and BB said that was five hundred below the
lowest guess he had heard. Flux could be avoided by refraining
from drinking foul water, or from eating stale vegetables; to
sprinkle lime in damp cellars and gutters and remove filth and
garbage from back yards would reduce sickness in the family.

Owen went to the *Journal* office again the following week, and again brought home a paper that had been rumpled by the folder; and this became a regular procedure. The *Journal* reported that Wyoming, the new state admitted a few days after Idaho, had given women the right to vote. Tom Glen, whose eyes were weak, had asked Owen to read the paper to him; and when he heard of Wyoming's folly, Tom exploded angrily. Women did not know anything about politics! Of course, you couldn't vote the way you wanted to, anyway, as long as your employer could see your ballot and know how you voted. The Knights of Labor had always fought for a secret ballot, and some day they would get it, and then men could vote as they chose. You would see a lot of things changed in the world when that came to pass; you wouldn't see Mr. Canter going off to Europe, for instance, with money stolen from his men.

Tom said all these things like a man making a speech, and without interruption; for Owen only listened, and Mrs. Glen, busy with the dishes after supper, seemed to pay no attention. After a while, his father bade Owen read on, and Owen did so. There were, according to the *Journal*, twenty thousand miners in Ohio. They had worked last year an average of 167 days apiece, and had averaged to earn less than $350 in the year. Tom Glen grumbled that miners were no better than slaves; but he sounded so sleepy that Owen stopped reading to see what would happen, and Tom's head drooped and he was asleep in his chair.

6

Except for long dislike of Pete Radford, culminating in a brief hot rage and sudden violence, Owen had never hated anyone till this first summer in Hardiston. Their rent was due on the first of each month, and it was payable in advance. Once or twice Tom had sent Owen with the money to pay it. Moses Evans, their landlord, had a second-floor office on Main Street, across from the *Journal* office; and although he was usually away, and only his secretary — an angular middle-aged woman with a sharp voice and a kindly eye — was there to receive the money, Owen had once or twice seen Mr. Evans and remembered him.

On a Saturday in August, he was helping his father in the garden when a buggy came down the hill from Ridge Street and pulled up at the head of the path above the house. Owen recognized Mr. Evans in the buggy, and Mr. Evans raised his whip in a peremptory gesture. Tom Glen muttered something and went up the path to the roadside. Owen was loosening a row of cabbages, lifting each one just enough to break a few roots so that the heads would not grow too rapidly and split. He moved up the row toward the road till he was near enough to hear what passed between them.

Mr. Evans said: "Looks like a mighty comfortable house you've got here, Glen."

Tom looked down the path to their home and nodded proudly. "It was ready to fall down when we moved in, but I fixed it up pretty good."

"Your garden's on my land, and your pig pen too."

"Why, I figure I'm renting the land along with the house."

Mr. Evans shook his head. "Your rent's too low for a house as snug as that one, and for the land besides. Call it six dollars from now on."

Owen saw his father's spine stiffen. "The house wasn't worth a dollar till I fixed it up!"

Mr. Evans gathered the reins. "Six dollars," he said, and drove on down the Pike.

Tom stood looking after him, and Owen saw his father's lips move and heard no words; and when Tom turned back toward the house, his face frightened Owen. That fright translated itself into hatred of Mr. Evans. He wanted to run after the buggy, to shout, to throw rocks, to do something; but because he was frightened, when he saw his father going toward the house, he followed, trembling.

Indoors, Tom sat down, slumping in his chair. "Well, Annie," he said. "We've got to move." She stared at him, and he told her what had happened. "We've had to scrape to pay four dollars, and the house ain't worth that, only for what I've done to it. We can't pay six."

Mrs. Glen came to his side, and for a moment her hand touched his shoulder. "We'll get along, Tom. We'll get along."

"I don't see how we can."

"We will! We always have."

So — though once or twice Tom thought he had discovered a cheaper house that would serve — they did not move; but after that day Owen's mother found a way to earn a little money. Whenever Owen or his father wore out socks or mittens, she had always unravelled them and dyed the wool in strong coffee and wound it on a ball. In the same way, every bit of twine that came into the house was laboriously freed of knots and wound on another ball, which was preserved as jealously as her ball of yarn. The two balls, one of yarn and one of twine, which his mother always kept on the high shelf behind the stove, were among Owen's earliest memories. When twine was needed, it was there; whenever she knitted, the ball of yarn was in her lap. Sometimes the ball was as big as Owen's head, sometimes smaller than his fist.

She began now to knit socks not only for Tom and Owen, but for the men at the mine. They brought her their worn-out socks, and she ravelled out the yarn and dyed it and added it to the ball, and presently she was ready with a new pair of socks. She charged five cents a pair, and she could knit four or five pairs a week. With what she earned, added to Tom's wages and to the small sums Owen brought home, they paid the two dollars Mr. Evans had added to their rent.

Owen was proud of her, but this did not modify his hatred of Mr. Evans.

7

One Thursday morning, Owen came home with an armful of sticks picked up in the grove across the run and found Mr. Beecham talking with his mother beside her small flower garden. As Owen joined them, Mr. Beecham was saying: "I'm off for a tramp in the country. I like to get out in the hills when I can." And he added, surprisingly: "Owen, why don't you come along? Unless your mother needs you."

Owen looked eagerly at his mother; and Mrs. Glen saw his eyes and smiled. "I can manage. You go if you want to, Owen."

That was a rich day in the boy's life. They went past the house

and down toward the railroad and across to the creek, and Mr.
Beecham told Owen that Indians used to come here long ago to
make salt. "There's salt in the creek water," he explained. "The
Indians dug deep pans in the soft sandstone beside the creek to
catch water in the spring when the creek was high, and that
water would get salty as it evaporated. Then they came every
summer, and the squaws would keep filling the pans and then
rolling hot rocks into the water to make it boil away. Then
finally they'd let the pans dry and scrape up every grain of salt."

"They went to a lot of trouble just to get salt!"

"Salt was scarce in those days. Even after the whites came, it
was worth five and six dollars a bushel. The whites boiled salt
here, and in 1803, when the first capital of Ohio was established
in Chillicothe, the state took over the salt works."

They crossed the creek at Buzzard's Rocks, an overhanging sandstone shelf beneath which a deep bank of dark sandy soil stretched
from end to end. "That pile is mostly ashes of Indian campfires,"
BB said. "Did you ever hear of Daniel Boone?" Owen had not,
and the editor explained: "He was a famous Indian fighter. The
Indians once captured him and brought him here and made him
help the squaws boil salt, but he got away from them when they
started home."

Each mile of their walk suggested to BB some anecdote of the
past; of the Indians, and of those unknown people who before the
Indians built mounds on these hills; of the early settlers; of the
day during the War, less than thirty years before, when Morgan's
raiders came this way and spent the night in Hardiston. He took
Owen a mile out of their way to meet a farmer whose horses the
raiders had taken; and when they went on, BB told Owen how his
father went to Portsmouth to help fight off the raiders if they
attacked the town; and he told how the raiders in Hardiston
wrecked the office of the *Journal,* throwing the press and the type
out of an upstairs window and pouring tar over the type so that
it was months before the paper could be printed again.

"Did they kill anybody?" Owen asked.

"They killed a farmer named Harvey Burris, because when they
caught him they found a pistol in his pocket; and they shot at
William McGhee and killed his horse. Union troops were hot on
their heels and in Hardiston the Union soldiers destroyed the

office of the *Express*, the Copperhead paper here, to revenge the
damage done the *Journal*. The *Journal* was the Union paper."

"I've seen copperhead snakes."

"So have I. But in those days, Southern sympathizers were
called Copperheads, because the copperhead gives no warning
before it strikes." To speak of snakes led him to talk about the
beaver and bear and elk and deer and buffalo which once roamed
these hills: "I'll show you a buffalo wallow, a mile or two farther
on. There were bear here till the 1830's, and deer when I was a
baby, and panthers and wildcats. And of course there were millions
of birds, from wild turkeys down, and many pigeon roosts. There
was one roost near Buffalo Skull that covered four acres, and the
birds filled the trees so thickly that men and boys used to knock
them down with sticks by the hundreds."

"I had a collection of birds' eggs," Owen said. "But they got
broken when we moved up here."

"Well, collecting eggs does no harm, if you're careful. Never
take but one from a nest, or the mother will desert the nest." And
BB added agreeably: "I'm glad you're interested in birds. So am
I. In so many ways they're ahead of us. They work only long
enough to get the food they want, they migrate rather than stay in
an unpleasant climate, they have as much government as they
need but no more, and the females have the final vote!"

Owen remembered his father's scorn because Wyoming let
women vote. "Do you think that's a good way?"

"Yes, if women will take the trouble to learn how to vote. There
are enough good women in the country to keep all the bad men
out of office."

"What happened to all the birds that used to be around here?"

"You mean the wild turkeys, and the passenger pigeons?" Owen
nodded, and BB said: "Men killed them off. The little birds
around here now aren't worth the price of powder to kill them, so
men let them alone." And then he added: "To be little and unimportant is the way to be safe, but who wants to be safe? The only
real happiness in life comes from trying, risking."

"Trying to do what?"

"Trying to do something you can't quite do. I'm not talking
about success. No one ever succeeds, for we all die, and death is
the ultimate failure. But to keep trying is to be happy. When you

hear a man grumble, you can be sure it's because he's been too lazy to try."

BB had lunch in his pockets and at noon they built a fire and spitted bacon on switches and cooked it in the flames; and while they ate, BB talked of many things, till Owen asked: "How did you get to know so much?"

BB looked at him as though in surprise. "I don't know much, Owen; but I understand what you mean. Yet it's a hard question to answer. I was teaching school when I was sixteen. I saved enough money to go to the University at Athens for the spring term, and there I found out how little I knew; so that fall I bought Webster's Unabridged Dictionary, for nine dollars and a half, and that winter I read it through."

"Gollies!"

"I know, I can't imagine doing such a thing today. But I did. Then I taught school for two years, and went back to Athens for four terms. Then in Mississippi, I studied law for two years." He hesitated, smiled. "But this isn't answering your questions. What I know, I've learned mostly by asking questions; usually by asking myself the questions and then working out the answers."

"I always kind of hate to ask questions."

"Mm-hm!" BB made a curious sound of disapproval. "That's a mistake. Asking questions is not only a good way to learn things, it's also one of the best ways to win friends. Some day you'll want to read Ben Franklin's essay on that subject. You know who he was?"

"I read about him in a history Miss Williams lent me."

"Well, of course, you can't always believe histories; they're colored by the author's opinions, and you have to allow for that when you read them. But they all agree that Ben Franklin was a great man. He used to say that the way to persuade people was to ask them questions, and then to ask questions about their answers, till you led them to think they were trying to persuade you. If you can make people believe they're suggesting a new idea to you, you've got them." He went on: "And in any case, you'll be learning things. Curiosity is to the brain what appetite is to the stomach. Babies are born curious; that's why they develop so rapidly. As soon as a man stops being curious, he begins to die. So — ask questions. If you're sufficiently interested to ask, you'll probably remember the answers. And think. That's what your brain's for. Keep it exercised. To argue is good mental exercise, as long as you remember that proving someone else is wrong doesn't prove you are right. So argue enough to keep your brain in a mild sweat much of the time. Ask, and think, and read."

"I like to read. Miss Williams lent me some books. But I haven't got any to read now."

"If you want books, I've plenty. Come over and borrow whenever you like."

"I'm going to buy a book, sometime, when I earn some money mama don't have to have."

"You needn't buy books. The man who reads a book owns it, just as the man who sees beauty, and appreciates it, makes it his own." They were lunching in a deep valley by a little run, among great trees. "For instance, look around us. I own this valley. No one else ever comes here. In the spring, there's a carpet of blue and white and dogtooth violets all around, but it's muddy in this low land in the spring, so I don't suppose anyone has ever seen those violets but me. They're mine because I see them and enjoy them. If you devour a book or a landscape or a tree or a flower or a hill with your eyes and your mind, no one can take it away from you. That's the proper business of youth, Owen, the accumulation of memories you'll be glad to remember."

"It's things that happen to you that you hate to remember."

BB nodded gravely. "It's a pretty good world — all men who see clearly are optimists — it's a good world, but there are still a lot of things wrong with it, things that can be cured. There's a lot to be done in the world by boys your age, Owen."

"How?"

"Well, start by making yourself into a fine man. The better man you make of yourself, the more you'll be able to do for others." He spoke slowly, as his thoughts took form. "And also, the more you do for others, the richer you'll be." He chuckled. "We're all in this together, you know; that's one thing the rich man hasn't yet discovered. He grew rich by keeping laboring men poor; but when laboring men are richer, so will rich men be. In the long run, an injury to one man is an injury to all men."

"My father says that!" Owen's tone was eager.

"It's a truth all men will one day accept." BB rose from the log on which he had been sitting. "Well, time for us to go."

When on their homeward way they came again to Buzzard's Rocks, two boys were digging in the great heap of ashes under the overhang. BB said they were looking for Indian relics. "There are lots of shards, fragments of pottery, in the ashes." He turned aside, and began to climb the mound, and picked up something half-embedded in the soft mixture of sand and ashes. "Here's a bit of pottery."

Owen took it in his hand. "It looks like a piece of bone."

"Oh, no, that's pottery. Here's another piece."

Owen compared them. "No, Mr. Beecham," he insisted. "They ain't — are not — the same. This one has little holes in the edge of it. See?"

BB took back the first fragment and examined the edge where Owen pointed. "I see what you mean," he admitted. His tone quickened. "Let's dig a little deeper here."

They dug for an hour or two, and in a shared excitement found more skull fragments, part of a jawbone with some teeth in place, a few ribs, some arm and leg bones. They found, too, a barbed arrowhead. BB was delighted. He packed the bones — loosely, for they were ready to fall to bits — in an old newspaper, to carry them home. "This was a great find, Owen, and you get the credit for it," he said. "It was you who recognized that piece of skull for what it was. How did you know?"

"I'd seen little holes like that in a piece of a dead horse's skull, down near the furnace."

BB nodded approvingly. "You know how to keep your eyes open, and to reason from the familiar to the unfamiliar." For a while he did not speak, but as they neared Owen's home he asked: "How much schooling have you had?"

"Ever since I was six years old."

"I suppose you'd be in the fourth grade in school here; but you're a lot more grown up than most fourth-grade boys. I think I'll speak to Mr. Atkinson about you."

Owen wondered who Mr. Atkinson was, but he did not ask. Obviously he would some day know without asking, so he held his tongue.

Reading the next issue of the *Journal* he discovered, in a sudden thrilling excitement, his own name. BB had written:

Owen Glen, ten-year-old son of Thomas Glen who is employed in Erie Mine, took a walk with us last Thursday, and on the ash heap at Buzzard's Rocks he recognized what we took to be a shard of pottery as a fragment of human skull. We dug up together enough bones to make a fairly complete skeleton. The Indian brave had been killed by an arrow which penetrated his chest and we found the barbed arrowhead among the ribs. He had been buried in a sitting position, in a shallow grave. Doubtless his friends built a fire over his grave to hide it and save his scalp from the enemies.

Owen showed the paragraph to his mother, and Mrs. Glen carefully cut it out and put it away in the English Bible which was always kept on the high shelf with the ball of yarn and the ball of twine and her other treasures.

8

Owen made friends more easily with men — John Morgan the drayman, or his brother Charles who lived up on the corner of Ridge Street and worked in Miss Ellen Mine up the creek, or Mr. Beecham — than with boys his own age. In his explorations that summer he met many boys — Tommy Morgan and Freddie Ames and Tom Powell and Jenkin Powell and others — but in only a single instance did a friendship develop. Whenever he went to Erie Mine, he liked to return past the stable where the mules were housed; the shadowed interior, the rich fragrance of hay and sweat and manure, the steady grind of teeth on hay or oats or corn, the occasional human voice — these held for him a stirring charm. One day when he stopped there and stood for a moment in the doorway, a man and a boy came into the stable from the door at the other end. The man turned into one of the stalls, but the boy saw Owen and slowly approached, stopping a few feet away.

For a moment they eyed each other, and then the boy said with a proprietary air: "My father works here. That's him cleaning out the stall."

"My father works in the mine," said Owen.

"What's your name?"

"Owen Glen."

"Mine's Willie Tutson." Willie came nearer. "I've got a secret cave," he said, in a low, impressive tone.

"Whereabouts?"

"Promise cross your heart not to tell!" Owen crossed his heart in due form, and Willie whispered: "Come on! Stay ten feet behind me, so no one will know we're going any place."

Owen, as ready as any boy — or man — to be initiated into a mystery, obeyed. Willie, whistling in an elaborately casual fashion, strolled out of the stable and away, Owen at a respectful distance to the rear. After they passed the nearest house, Willie led the way into a weedy field, and they crawled through the weeds back toward the barn again, till they could dart across a narrow open space to the pig pens under the barn floor. They climbed on the fence that enclosed the pens and walked it till they came under an open trap down which manure from the stalls could be shovelled; they swung up through this trap, Willie enjoining silence with many whispers and warning gestures, into an empty stall. Thence Willie climbed on the manger and scrambled up through the hole above it into the mow; he scaled an upright timber to which pieces of wood had been nailed like a ladder, and — first making sure no one below could see him — walked a beam to the opposite mow. The beam was a dizzy height above the barn floor; and Owen, dutifully following the leader, had to be careful, as he crossed, not to look down.

They came among mountains of baled hay; but at one end, behind the bales, loose hay rose almost to the roof. Willie crawled across the top of the bales and across this loose hay to the farther corner; there, in the angle of the walls, he slid down into a sort of well, and when Owen followed and stood beside him, Willie pointed into a low tunnel dug through the hay against the wall.

"That's my cave. I dug it myself."

They knelt together and Owen peered in. "It's not very big," he suggested.

"It ain't finished yet. We'll make it bigger."

They set to work, pulling out the hard-packed hay with their hands till they had made a chamber where if they kept their heads bowed they could sit side by side. The day was warm, the toil had

left them hot and sticky, and hayseed inside their shirts scratched
and tickled; but they were happy.

Willie pointed out the advantages of this secret retreat. Through
cracks in the wall they could see out toward the mine and furnace
beyond. "We can spy on everybody from here," he said, and Owen,
flattered by that "we" nodded. "I'm going to start a club and this
will be our secret meeting place. Want to join my club?"

Owen, though he had an uneasy suspicion that he was too old
for such games, nevertheless welcomed Willie's friendliness; and
again and again that summer they sought the cave together. Willie
insisted that they approach the stable by stealthy ways, so to reach
the cave at all was an adventure; but to be there was an anticlimax,
for except at last to depart as secretly as they had come, there was
nothing to do. To remedy this lack, they brought apples and ate
them in the cave; and Willie decided that under certain vague con-
tingencies they might have to hide here for days and days, and so
should stock the retreat with provisions. "Things that will keep,"
he specified. But it was not the season for nuts, and bread molded,
and edible vegetables like carrots and turnips soon softened and
spoiled, so they decided the cave would never stand a siege.

But it would still serve as a base from which profitable forays
could be made. Once Willie led Owen to where he had hidden in
a weedy ditch a watermelon, and laboriously they transported it to
the cave and ate it there, using Willie's broken-bladed pocket knife
to hack it open. It was not quite ripe, but they assured each other
that it was just about the best watermelon they had ever tasted.
Owen was pretty sick that night, but his mother gave him a liberal
dose of castor oil and he recovered.

They decided they could hide their treasures in the cave, and
Owen brought a top with no point — he had found it while prowling
the alleys in search of junk — and a forked piece of hickory which
would be just the right shape to make a slingshot as soon as he
could get some rubber bands; but rubber bands of the right size
cost a nickel a pair. Willie brought a ring made out of a horseshoe
nail, and when Owen admired it, Willie promised to persuade the
blacksmith who shod the mules to make another, and was as good
as his word, and they decided to make the rings a secret badge
which only members of the club could wear. Also, Willie brought
his collection of tin tags; and when Owen asked what they were

good for, Willie explained that when you had enough, of the right kinds, you could get premiums, just the way you could with covers off Arbuckle coffee. And it was easier to get tin tags. Willie explained the technique of the collector. You just walked along the gutters up town and kept your eyes open. The men who chewed tobacco threw the tags away, and whoever swept the sidewalk whisked them into the gutters. The best time to look for them was after a shower, which washed the tin tags clean and made them easier to see.

Owen became an ardent collector, and they pooled their assets. They kept all their tags in a cigar box in the cave, well hidden in the hay; and with Owen's additions the hoard swelled day by day.

They had other uses for the cave. Willie's father liked to read dime novels, and Willie brought three or four which his father had discarded, and Owen read them aloud. This was difficult, because in the cave they never spoke above a whisper; but if Willie kept his ear close to Owen's mouth he could hear. Once Willie brought a piece of the rattan handle of a buggy whip and proposed that they smoke it, but Owen thought the hay might catch fire, so they abandoned that idea. Instead, they tried chewing tobacco; but after a few minutes, Owen decided to go home, and he reached the open air before the catastrophe occurred.

The cave was fun, till one day when Owen was reading aloud — in a whisper — a particularly exciting dime novel. The hero was tied to a tree and the Indians had piled sticks about him and were just about to set fire to them; but one of the Indians was friendly, and if he could ever get a revolver into the hero's hands, the situation would be saved. Suddenly Willie caught Owen's hand and hissed for silence; and Owen listened and heard from the open mow above them a sound like a giggle. Willie crawled out of the cave to look up, and Owen after him; and Willie challenged in a whisper:

"Who goes there?"

For answer, a girl slid down off the hay and toppled in a heap at their feet. She looked up at them with laughing eyes and said demurely: "H'lo!"

But she had no clothes on! Owen backed hurriedly away and scrambled up to the level above, in headlong flight. Willie called after him: "Hey, Owen don't go! It ain't nobody but Nellie! I told her to come. Come on back. We're going to play a new game."

But Owen did not hesitate. Too frightened to take the usual way, he jumped down to the barn floor and ran. He never came back to Willie's cave again, and he never saw Willie after that day till Willie was dead.

9

On a day in September — it happened to be a day when Erie Mine did not run, so both Owen and his father were at home — somebody knocked on the door; and when Mrs. Glen opened it, Marged Williams stood there with a heavy basket on her arm, pink-cheeked and panting. "Hello," she cried, smiling in the pretty way she had. "Here are some things Amy sent you."

"Come in, come in," Mrs. Glen cried. "Give me that great basket." The day was raw with a threat of rain. "Come in and warm yourself."

Marged laughed. "Whew! I'm hot enough! That basket's heavy. I tried to find Morgan to carry it for me, but he was gone somewhere. Hello, Mr. Glen. Hello, Owen. You know Morgan, don't you, Owen?"

"Yes'm." Morgan was Isaac Williams's son, and they were in the same class in Sunday School; but their acquaintance was on a severely formal basis.

"I think you and he will be in the same room in school," Miss Williams predicted, laying aside her shawl, taking the rocker Tom Glen yielded to her. "He's a year older than you, but you're ahead of most boys your age. I spoke to Mr. Atkinson about you." BB had mentioned Mr. Atkinson. "He's superintendent of schools." She asked Mrs. Glen, "Well, how are you all?"

"The way you see us. You going to teach school here?"

"No, in Glendale up the creek. I'll board with Uncle Isaac, and go up and back on the train."

Mrs. Glen had finished unpacking Amy's basket — jars of jellies and preserves, ears of sweet corn, a ham — and she and Marged settled down to an exchange of news. For half an hour they chatted happily, but when Marged rose to go, she said to Owen: "Morgan will come and take you to school the first day, and he'll take you to Mr. Atkinson. You must come and see me sometime."

She smiled, head a little on one side. "Will you?"

"Well, prob'ly." He was flushed and miserably happy.

"Don't forget me. I won't forget you. Goodbye now."

Mrs. Glen stood in the doorway to watch her depart, then closed the door and returned to them. "She's a real nice young woman, Tom."

"She is so."

"Friendly," said Mrs. Glen. "Owen, she sets a pile of store by you. She didn't say when school starts. Pretty soon, I guess."

When the time came, Mrs. Glen made Owen dress in his Sunday suit. "For the first day, anyway." She saw to it that his finger nails were clean, and his hair slicked into place; and he was ready long before Morgan Williams came down the hill from Ridge Street and shouted from the road above the house:

"Hi, Owen! Come on."

Mrs. Glen watched them set off together. Owen would be eleven years old in another two months, and in no time now he would be in his 'teens; and something that was half-pride, half-sadness, made her eyes sting. When the boys were out of sight, she went indoors and sat down, staring at her clasped hands on her bony knees; but after a little she stirred and stood up, sniffling away the taste of tears.

"Can't just sit here," she muttered. "Not with all there is to do."

Owen and Morgan walked at first in silence, but then Morgan began to step on cracks in the pavement, and when the slabs gave way to bricks he tried to step on all the cracks, and tripped over his own feet, and they both laughed. Then Morgan produced from his hip pocket a slingshot, and he scuffed along the edge of the road looking for small stones suitable as missiles. He found one and loaded the slingshot and fired at a sparrow and missed. Owen remembered that fine hickory fork which he had meant to use for a slingshot when he could get some rubber bands, but he had left it in Willie's cave, to which he would never return. To make what show he could against Morgan's slingshot, he said:

"I've got a zooner."

"Let's see it."

The zooner was a round piece of tin which had been soldered on the end of a tin can as a seal. Owen had melted it off — surprised to find how hot a fire was required to melt solder — and pierced it

with two holes, through which now ran a looped string. He hooked
the string over the middle finger of each hand, rotated the piece
of tin with a rolling motion of his hands till the string was twisted
on itself, and then by alternately pulling his hands apart and letting
them come nearer together again he made the tin disk whirl like a
top, with a satisfying, zooning sound.

Morgan begged to try it, and Owen let him. "But look out it don't
cut you," he warned. "It's awful sharp." He gave Morgan instructions until the other mastered the art and returned the zooner.

"I can throw apples on a stick," he announced, and produced a
knife and from an overhanging bough cut a stick and pointed it.
"Have to look out for this knife," he said. "It's about as sharp as a
razor, I guess."

"I'm going to buy me a knife some day," Owen declared.

When the throwing stick was ready for use, they could see no
convenient apple tree. They were nearing the schoolhouse, a
two-story red-brick building on Broad Street, and the bell in the
tower above the front door began to ring; so Morgan hid the stick
under a fence and they went in. The hall and the stairs were full
of boys and girls; and Owen felt big and clumsy, and he thought
everyone was looking at him. Morgan led the way upstairs to
Mr. Atkinson's office. The Superintendent, a tall man, red-haired
and red-faced and extravagantly thin, was talking to one of the
teachers and to a woman who held by the arm a boy somewhat
younger than Owen. He saw Owen and Morgan at the door and
called: "Come in, boys." They edged into the room and backed
against the wall, and Owen's ears were ringing and his eyes would
not focus.

Mr. Atkinson ushered the others out, and when they were gone
he turned to the two boys, recognizing Morgan. "You're Morgan
Williams."

"Yes sir. And this here is Owen Glen. My cousin Marged
Williams told you about him."

Mr. Atkinson shook Owen's hand. "Yes, I remember. How old
are you, Owen?"

"Ten, going on eleven."

"Miss Williams says you're a pretty good scholar." This seemed
to be a question; but Owen did not answer it. He knew that he
was smarter than Pete Radford, or Evan Davis, or Tom Owens, or

even Sammy Howell; but they were the only boys in Redfern School, and there must be hundreds of boys in this school, and probably they were all smarter than he. So he held his tongue. Mr. Atkinson asked: "How many terms of school have you had?"

"Since I was six years old. Four years."

"But your school let out in March," Mr. Atkinson reflected. "So you've only had eight terms. We have three terms each year. I think you'd better start in the fourth room. Miss Dine's your teacher. We'll see how you get along. Morgan, you show him where it is."

In the hall, Morgan said under his breath, "That Old Skinny! Cousin Marged said you ought to start in the fifth room with me, and I guess she knows. She told him so, too!"

Owen was disappointed, but when he saw Miss Dine his disappointment vanished; she was so pretty, and so nice. She was at the door, greeting each newcomer; and she said to Owen: "Just sit down anywhere, that's a good boy," and patted his shoulder as he passed her. Owen stood still for a moment, feeling that touch on his shoulder, and surveying the room ahead of him in some confusion. There seemed to be a great many children already here, boys and girls, some standing up and talking together, some sitting down. The seats were different from those in Redfern School. There, the children sat side by side on benches, facing a long table on which they laid pads and books; but here the seats were separate, and each one was not only a seat but a desk, the back of the seat supporting the flat-topped desk. Probably you could lift up the top and put books and pencils and things in the place under it. Owen went toward the back of the room and sat down. A girl at the other end of the room waved to him, but he was sure he had never seen her before, so he flushed and looked away.

When it was time to begin, Miss Dine made a little speech, smiling at them all. "Now, boys and girls, I'm sure we're going to have lots of fun this year. You'll really be the teachers, as much as I am; because, you know, I'll tell you a secret. This is the very first time I ever taught school in my life. So you'll be teaching me just as much as I'll be teaching you; and you must be nice and help me all you can and keep me from making any very terrible mistakes."

She looked along the rows. "I think the first thing is to get you all

seated properly. The way you are now, the girls are all together
down front and the boys in back; but a boy and a girl and a boy and
a girl is lots nicer, more sociable. You and you!" she pointed. "I
don't know your names yet, but I'll take names in a minute. You
two change places." With giggles and tittering, the designated two
obeyed her. "And you and you! And you and you!"

Owen found himself seated in the second row, behind a girl with
long yellow pigtails; and there was a red-haired girl with freckles
on his right, and an extravagantly small girl with black hair and
dancing black eyes on his left.

When the long confusion of these rearrangements was over, Miss
Dine said: "There, now those are your regular seats. Don't forget
them. Now I'll take down your names."

She began in the front row, at the left-hand end. She wrote
down each name in a notebook; but since she was standing, this
was awkward, so when she came to the boy diagonally in front of
Owen, she put one foot up on the empty seat in the front row,
and rested her notebook on her knee. This lifted her skirt so that
Owen could see her other leg almost to the knee. He had never
before seen a grown woman's leg, and this glimpse was a brief
one, for almost at once Miss Dine took her foot down and moved
on; but his eyes followed her, and his thoughts too.

Then at the farther end of the room he heard a girl giving Miss
Dine her name. The name was Nellie Tutson! The girl was Willie's
sister, who in that instant in the haymow had driven him into headlong flight. To know that she was now to be in the same room with
him was frightening. Hoping he was mistaken, he leaned forward
to look along the row. He did not recognize her as the girl in the
haymow, but she was the girl who had waved to him when he
came in.

Yet he still hoped he was mistaken, till as they filed out for recess
that first day she spoke to him. "H'lo, Owen."

"H'lo." He burned brick red.

"I bet you don't know who I am."

"Yes I do too! You're Willie's sister. Where's he?"

"He goes to Erie School."

They emerged into the open air and he said hastily: "Well, g'bye."
He escaped her for the moment, but her daily presence was to be

the only blemish on that winter, when just to be able to see Miss
Dine, morning and afternoon, every day except Saturday and
Sunday, was a long delight.

10

School was hardly begun when the first frosts, like an artist
setting up his palette before he begins to paint, spattered tentative
spots of color across the wooded hills. Owen had an October day
with Mr. Beecham and they sampled persimmons well frosted and
delicious, and found a pawpaw tree, and collected a bag of hickory
nuts. With the first morning that was not only crisp but cold, Mrs.
Glen hung around Owen's neck the little bag of asafoetida which
would keep him safe till spring against the common ills of the flesh.

A few days later, Tom Glen had a touch of rheumatism, and
late in November, a severe attack kept him for days at home, and
he lay groaning while Owen's mother ironed his back with a hot
iron to ease the pain. Every evening Owen read aloud to him,
usually from the *Journal*. To read the paper through might take
a week, for Tom was a gluttonous listener and not even Doctor
Talmage's sermons could be skipped. A vein of fire clay fifteen
inches thick had been discovered near Belton. Eleven Hardiston
young men organized an Independent Drum Corps, and held a
social to raise money to buy drums. The fancy dress party given by
the Halma Club proved to be a hilariously amusing affair. *A Cold
Day*, the famous farce comedy, played at the Rink; and Ezra
Kendall would presently appear in *A Pair of Kids*. In a mine up
the creek, a man named Ransom was killed by a fall of slate. Near
Sycamore Hill a tramp sleeping in a haystack set fire to the stack
and burned to death. The postmaster in Glendale absconded with
twelve hundred dollars, and tried to conceal his thefts by a pretended burglary.

Just before the Christmas holidays, with Tom still lame, yet
working when he could, Miss Dine told her room they would for
next term need two new schoolbooks. When Owen reported this
at home, his father and mother fell into a frightening and angry
argument. His mother insisted that Owen must have the books,
his father retorted that there was no money to pay for them.

"There will be!"

He snorted angrily. "When, I'd like to know! With the scrip I've drawn, and me laid up so I can't work half the time, there's no pay coming."

"Tom Glen, you listen to me! Pay or no pay, Owen's going to have those books."

Tom stormed to his feet. "Don't talk to me, woman! What can't be, can't be, and that's all there is to it."

Owen, frightened at the anger between these two who were his world, said hopefully: "Mama, Miss Dine said if anyone couldn't buy the books, the school would furnish them."

"Oh she did, did she? Well, you just tell her that Tom Glen's son's no pauper! You hear that, Tom! You going to let folks think that of you, and shame your son before them all?"

"He don't have to have the books. Let him do without, or quit school!"

"He will not! Owen's going to have his schooling if I have to work my fingers to the bone. If you can't support your family, I will, somehow!"

They threw words like missiles to and fro, and Owen, frightened by the storm he had provoked, slipped away. This was a Saturday morning. He wandered aimlessly, trying to think how he could earn enough to buy the books. During the summer there were lawns to mow, but grass did not grow in winter. He could discover no other source of income; but he remembered that Mr. Beecham had given him his first job, and the thought led him toward the *Journal* office.

There were two men with Mr. Beecham when Owen opened the door, so he went through to the pressroom to wait there till BB was free. Will Davis was making up the inside, and Owen watched with never-failing interest. It was wonderful to see Will dip a sponge into the inky water in the pail beside the stone and slosh water on a galley of type and then lift great masses into place without mishap.

"I don't see how you do it and never drop any," Owen said admiringly.

"I pied many a galley learning. When you've got to do a thing right or do it over, you do it right." Will adjusted the quoins and locked them, and then BB came to put some copy on the hook, and Owen seized his chance.

"Mr. Beecham, I wanted to — to see you."

BB stopped and turned. "Oh, hello, Owen."

"I want to — well, do you know any way I can earn some money?"

The other nodded understandingly. "No lawns to mow in winter, are there? You need money for something special?"

"Yes sir, to buy some schoolbooks Miss Dine says we've got to have, next term."

The editor hesitated, turning half away. He said soberly: "Teachers could win a lot of friends among parents if they stuck to the same schoolbooks every year. The heaviest tax a poor man with a large family has to pay is the schoolbook tax, buying books for his children to use. Book publishers persuade the teachers and the school board to change textbooks every year or two, so instead of using the same arithmetic, or the same geography, or the same history or physiology or algebra that his older brothers and sisters used, each boy has to buy new ones. If the teachers stopped that, parents would be more willing to pay them higher salaries." He had been talking to himself, thinking aloud, but now he remembered Owen, and smiled and said: "But that wouldn't do you any good, with no older brothers and sisters in school, would it?"

"No sir."

"What are the books?"

"A new speller, and a botany."

"Botany? You take a walk with me some day next spring and I'll teach you more botany than you can learn from a book." He looked at Owen thoughtfully. "You're interested in things here in the office, aren't you?"

"Yes sir."

"We could find plenty for you to do here. You'd have to get here by seven o'clock or earlier, build the fires in winter, sweep out the office and the file room, do all you could before school. Then you could come back after school and run errands and deliver packages and carry in coal. And you'd have to work all day Saturdays."

Owen's eyes had grown big, his face was white. "Yes sir," he said.

"I'll pay you a dollar a week," BB proposed. "Maybe you can learn to set type, feed the presses. Would you like that?"

"Yes sir."

"Want to start today?"

"Yes, I do."

BB hesitated. "Well, suppose you walk down to the bookstore

with me right now, and we'll buy the books you need. I'll pay for them and take it out of your pay, a quarter a week. Is that all right?"

"Yes sir."

They returned a little later with the books, well wrapped, tucked under Owen's arm. Then BB took Owen back to Will Davis. "Will," he said, "Owen wants to learn the newspaper business. Can you find something for him to do?"

Will nodded. "I can for a fact," he said. "He can run an errand for me right away. I've mislaid my left-handed monkey wrench. Owen, you trot down to the *Star* office and ask Joe Tinker to lend me theirs."

Owen looked at Will in open suspicion. "There's no such thing," he said positively. "Monkey wrenches are the same on both sides."

BB chuckled and turned away, and Will drawled: "Why, you don't say. It's going to be real handy, Owen, having someone around here as smart as you." He went on with his work, lifting a wet fist of type into the form. He was about to turn back to the galley when, as though something had attracted his attention, he paused, inserted his composing rule between two lines of type, and leaned down to peer into the crevice. "Hm-m!" he said, and pushed the lines together again and stepped to the galley.

"What was it?" Owen asked.

"Nest of type lice," Will said abstractedly. "First I've seen this winter."

"Can I see?"

"Why, I guess so, if I can find them again." Will tried the composing rule in three or four different places, peeping between the lines, shaking his head. Then at last, triumphantly: "Here it is!" He pointed with the rule. "Here! Right down in here!"

Owen leaned close to peer down into the crack, and Will pushed the loosened lines of type smartly together. Inky water spurted up into Owen's face and eyes; he sprang back and wiped his eyes and heard Will's loud guffaw and swung furiously toward the man.

But then he caught himself. He did not laugh, but he said steadily: "That's a pretty good joke on me, all right."

Will stopped laughing. He offered Owen his own handkerchief. "Here, wipe your face," he said. "You're all right. You'll do to take along."

IV

Christmas 1890 — June 1891

O WEN'S MOTHER, when he came home to dinner at noon and told her he was working in the *Journal* office, caught him in her arms and held him tight. "Oh son, son!"

"Aren't you glad, mama?"

"You ought to have a chance to play, like other boys!" She hugged him harder. "But yes, yes, I'm glad, Owen. Now maybe you'll be an editor some day, like Mr. Beecham, and not have to go working in the coal."

Tom Glen made a scornful sound. "Editor! When I was your age, Owen, I was cutting charcoal wood at two bits a cord; yes, and I could cut and work up three cords a day, summertime, when there was long light. It's a soft-handed job you've got; but one day soon I'll take you into the mines with me."

"That you'll not!" cried Owen's mother, but Owen said, almost wistfully:

"I've never been in a mine yet."

"Nor you never will," his mother insisted. "With the slate ready to fall and mash you like a bug!" But Owen's eyes met his father's and something passed between these two. Men were men; there were things women could never understand.

They had a happy Christmas. Owen cut a small tree in the woods beyond Evan Jenkins's pasture, and he and his mother strung popcorn and red cranberries to festoon it, and set small candles in tin holders among the branches. Mrs. Glen had knitted mittens for Owen and for his father; and Owen, to whom BB gave his first week's salary intact without deduction for the schoolbooks, bought a bag full of candy and another of nuts for his mother, and a corncob pipe for his father. Tom Glen proudly produced a new dress for Mrs. Glen, and she scolded him tenderly for the extravagance, particularly when he admitted he had borrowed the money from Evan Harned. They had a fine rib-roast of pork cooked in a pot of beans, and a merry time together.

The best part of Christmas came two days later, when Dave drove up from the farm with word that Amy had a baby, a son, born Christmas night, and named David after his father. He brought a barrel of potatoes, and another of apples to eat with the pork from their own pig which Owen and Tom had butchered two weeks before, and three huge pumpkins, and many happy messages from Amy to them all.

"She says I'm to come up and get you, Mrs. Glen, first fine day in the spring, and fetch you down to see your grandson."

"So do," Mrs. Glen agreed. "He'll be the first grandchild I've ever laid eyes on. Evan had a boy and girl, by the letter we had last Christmas; but they're away off in Indiana. Soon's the frost is gone and the roads dry out, I'll come."

To see her so happy at Dave's news and at the prospect of going to visit Amy awoke in Owen a secret faint resentment; it was as though he felt himself supplanted. Dave had taken Amy away from them; why couldn't he be satisfied, and not try to take mama too?

2

Owen, with a regular job — to be sure, it was part time, but it was a regular job, all the same — felt in himself a new maturity. He rose before day, and he and his father had their breakfast together; then Tom Glen went off to the mine, and Owen walked uptown to the *Journal* office. There, letting himself in with the key BB had given him, he kindled the fires; the pot-bellied stove in BB's office, the big iron stove in the pressroom, another almost as large in the type loft upstairs. After that, there were floors to sweep. Will Davis taught him first to sprinkle the floors with wet sawdust. "And always draw the broom toward you. You go swishing it around the way a woman does, and you scatter sawdust and dirt all over everywhere. Like this." He took the broom and gave so

ridiculous an imitation of a woman at her house-cleaning that Owen
had to laugh; and when he did so, Will stopped and said in a
comical tone: "Why, you're laughing. Didn't know as you ever did.
Most times you wear a face as long as your arm."

Owen grinned. "I laugh when there's anything to laugh at." He
quickly came to feel a quiet affection for the foreman, who without
hurry got a great many things done, and in whom mirth was always
near the surface. Edna, one of the girls who set type in the loft,
seemed to Owen to be forever making up to Will, coming to show
him a piece of copy or to ask him to read a word for her, or to
advise her which font to use. Something about her made Owen
uncomfortable and uneasy, she was at once so prim and in a disturbing way so pretty.

There were two girls in the type loft, and on his first Saturday in
the office Will introduced Owen to them. Bets — it was some time
before Owen knew their last names — was a plump young woman
in her late twenties, who kept a paper bag of gumdrops always
within reach. When Will brought Owen to meet her, she extended
the bag to him; but it was dirty where her hand had touched it and
Owen declined. She guessed his reason, laughed.

"Dirt'll never hurt you, sonny, not if it's the kind you can wash
off!" She had a jolly laugh, and in spite of her grimy hands he
liked her; so he took a gumdrop and thanked her politely.

"Don't mention it. Help yourself any time. Always some here."

Owen thought he would go right on liking Bets, but not Edna.
She was thin where Bets was plump, solemn where Bets was full
of easy laughter, neat and clean where Bets was soiled and blowsy.
Edna had a curiously pointed nose, and she wore white paper cuffs
to protect her sleeves while she was at work, and she was forever
washing her hands, soiled by the inky type. She acknowledged
Owen's presence by a brief glance which made him think his face
must be dirty, then resumed her work. She seemed to be working
fast, her fingers flying, while Bets never appeared to be busy at all;
but Owen was to find that Bets actually set more type, and set it
more accurately, than Edna.

Owen sometimes spent all Saturday morning in the type loft,
since, when there was no immediate task in the pressroom, Will set
him to learn the case, to memorize each compartment's location so
that his hand went without hesitation to the needed letter. "Time

you learn the case," Will promised, "I'll let you set some type; and
when you get good at that, you can learn to throw in." Redistribut-
ing used type, he explained, was much more difficult than setting it;
for when you set type, you could see your mistakes, but when you
threw a letter into the wrong box, you did not find out you had
done so till your mistake eventually made trouble for you — or for
someone else.

Owen found that there was more to his job than the work itself.
"You must read the paper," BB told him. "Read everything in it,
till you understand what newspapers try to print and what people
want to read. I don't mean the advertisements, nor the boiler plate;
but read the news and the editorials."

"I already do. I read it aloud to papa."

"Good. Keep it up. It's part of your education, just as important
as your school work."

Owen obeyed. Much that he read interested him not at all, but
there was meat enough. The Seventh Cavalry had trouble with
Indians in Nebraska, and a former Sycamore Hill man named
William Sell, who now lived out there, wrote in a letter to the
Journal:

> *General Brooks sent a dispatch for all settlers to get*
> *together; and by Tuesday, Gordon and Rushville were*
> *full; Court House, churches, and all places where people*
> *could get shelter. Colonel Summer was sent out to get*
> *the guns from the Indians, and found some hidden guns,*
> *and the Indians started the fight; but they were all killed*
> *except four bucks and fifteen squaws. We have lost 50*
> *killed and 33 wounded; the Indian loss is between 400*
> *and 500. The best of all was the killing of Sitting Bull by*
> *Indian police, four volunteers.*

It was hard to realize that somewhere out West soldiers were
still killing Indians, and being killed by them. But the *Journal*
reported tragedy — and sometimes comedy — nearer home. A hun-
dred and twenty-seven men were killed in a mine explosion in
Pennsylvania. Two little children, brother and sister, playing in the
Ohio Southern yards, were run over by freight cars being shifted.
Lilian Kennedy and Alfred Kelcy were the star performers in
Casey's Troubles at the Rink. A Gallia County man eighty-three

years old who had lost all his teeth was reported to be growing new ones. The United States led the world in iron production, with Ohio second only to Pennsylvania. Eleven candidates took the examination for teachers, and nine passed. Among those who passed, Owen saw the name of Sammy Howell, who was only two years his senior, and who had been with him in Redfern School. Owen knew himself a better student than Sammy; and the thought that in two years he too might know enough to teach school was suddenly a spur.

He read the *Journal* conscientiously, but this was often a wearying task. So much of the paper was filled with editorials against something called Free Silver, and against the Democratic gerrymander of Ohio then in progress. One day BB asked Owen what his father thought about the Australian ballot. Owen had never heard the phrase, and BB explained: "At the polling places now, a man marks his ballot at a table where everyone can see him. The Australian ballot is a system that lets a man mark his ballot in secret, so no one knows how he voted."

"I know papa wants that to be the way. The Knights of Labor have always wanted that. Don't you?"

BB hesitated. "Well, I don't know. If a man's ashamed of his vote, he ought not to have voted the way he did. I've seen men sit down and mark their ballot and then put it in their pocket while they walk across to the ballot box. When they drop a ballot in, you're never sure it's the same one. I don't believe in vest-pocket voting. I like to see a man mark his ballot and then hold it up over his head where everyone can see it. An honest man ought to be proud to mark his ballot publicly."

"Papa says if you vote the way you want to, and the boss sees you, you're apt to lose your job."

"Well, a man ought to be willing, when he believes in a thing, to stand up and be counted." BB hesitated. "Yet I can understand that a miner, or a laborer with a wife and children to support, might hesitate to mark a ballot against his boss if the boss were looking on."

Owen was interested in political questions only as they interested his father, and Tom Glen was interested only as politics touched the mining industry. When the United Mine Workers in convention in Columbus proposed that operators should weigh coal before

screening it, Tom Glen approved. The convention urged, too, an
eight-hour day; but a week later the Association of Ohio Coal Operators voted to refuse both demands. Mr. Herbert Canter of
Hardiston, said BB in the *Journal*, dominated the meeting; and it
was his firm insistence which led the Association to refuse all con-
cessions to the miners.

BB headed the *Journal's* report of that refusal:

THIS MEANS STRIKE!

When Owen read this to his father, Mrs. Glen said wearily:
"Oh, Tom, do you think they will?"

"Might as well!" Tom spoke in a harsh tone. "Work's slacking off
anyway, till a man can't earn enough to live on. An open winter
like this one, people don't have to buy coal, so there's no sense in
mining it. What the coal business needs is an old-fashioned winter."

But the mild weather continued. Owen and his father went to the
memorial meeting at the Rink in honor of General Sherman, under
whom Tom Glen had briefly served. In Columbus the editors of
rival newspapers exchanged shots on the street, and one of the
editors and a passer-by who was hit by a chance bullet were killed.
In a cocking main between Hardiston and Belton fanciers, Belton
won seven out of the nine fights. The Rutledge Dramatic Company presented *Michael Strogoff* at the Rink.

One Wednesday afternoon when the outside was being run,
Owen read the paper as it came from the press; and he found an
item that tightened his throat and made his heart pound. Willie
Tutson was dead. Willie's father, cleaning one of the stalls, tossed
a forkful of soiled straw out through the door just as Willie ran
past, and the tines of the fork struck Willie in the face. One went
through his eye into his brain.

3

Owen had not seen Willie since the day Nellie surprised them in
the haymow. When he read this paragraph, he remembered that
she had not been in school yesterday or today; but she was as
irregular in attendance as she was backward in her studies, so her
absence had not made him wonder.

He felt no grief for Willie. In fact he knew a certain relief, because he had always been afraid Willie would tell someone about that day in the haymow, but when he reached home that night and heard that Mrs. Tutson had come to ask him to be one of Willie's pallbearers, he was flattered and proud. "She says Willie always talked about you," his mother explained. "She says he liked you a lot. I told her you would."

On the day of the funeral, dressed in his Sunday suit and big with a pleasant sense of his own importance, he walked out Ridge Street and down to Willie's home. It was raining hard, so he carried his mother's umbrella. She did not go to the funeral, nor — since that was a work day at the mine — did Tom Glen. When Owen arrived, fifteen or twenty people were gathered in the parlor of the small house; and he recognized men and boys from the mine. While he still stood uncertainly in the doorway, John Carver came in with Edna, the girl who set type in the *Journal* office; and Mr. Moury, the undertaker, subtly guided them all past the open casket. Owen looked in pale curiosity at Willie lying there. Mr. Moury had been able to conceal the torn eyeball through which the pitch-fork penetrated; but another tine had pierced Willie's cheek and Owen saw that small wound.

Beyond the casket Edna somehow disappeared, and Mr. Moury swept John and Owen before him toward two empty chairs beyond which Jenkin Powell and a boy Owen did not recognize were already seated. They all waited for a while, and the small room was steamy with the smell of moist garments and of people, and the rain slashed the windows, and from somewhere in the back of the house came low wailing cries. Then a squeaky organ with two or three silent notes began to play very softly, and a minister whom Owen did not know, standing in the doorway between two rooms, prayed, and then he told them what a good boy Willie had been, and then he called for *Jerusalem the Golden*.

While that was being sung, Owen and the other pallbearers, under Mr. Moury's whispered instructions, carried the casket out to the waiting hearse. It was raining harder than ever, so they were half-drenched in the process. The pallbearers had their own carriage for the long ride to the cemetery, and while they waited for the other carriages to be filled, Owen saw Will Davis come out of the house with a pretty little woman who used a cane and who was

so lame she could hardly walk at all, clinging to his arm. They did
not get into a carriage, but turned away toward Ridge Street. Owen
remembered the happy sweetness in her face. She must be Mrs.
Davis, and he thought how hard for Will to have a lame wife; but
perhaps she was just Will's sister or something.

As their carriage presently began to move, he noticed that John
Carver was crying, and that surprised him. Owen had no desire to
cry. His senses were unnaturally acute, but he felt no grief, nor any
other emotion except a pleasant sense of his own conspicuous part
in what was happening.

Before they reached the cemetery, the carriage dropped two
wheels into a mudhole and tipped half-over; and they all stepped
out into the mire and helped to right the carriage again. In the
cemetery, they bore the small casket to the grave; and when the
burial service reached the appropriate stage, Owen held one of the
stout tapes by which the coffin was lowered into the earth. During
what followed, staring down at the coffin, he wondered whether
the worms were already eating Willie. He had seen the fly-blown
carcasses of dead dogs and pigs and cattle, so he knew what worms
looked like; and he was glad when clods began to fall on the
casket, glad when it was hidden from sight.

When it was time to leave the grave, he for the first time lifted
his eyes to look around. He saw Willie's father, and he wondered
how Mr. Tutson was feeling. It must be pretty bad for a man to
know he had killed his little boy. Owen for a moment shared Mr.
Tutson's agony, and winced with pity and pain, and then he began
to wonder whether Mr. Tutson would after this be different. Would
he work harder or work less, be nicer to Nellie and to Willie's
mother, or worse than in the past?

He watched Mr. Tutson and Willie's mother go toward their
carriage. Nellie and Edna walked just behind them, so Edna must
be some relation. John Carver went to overtake them and came
between Nellie and Edna; he put his arm around Nellie, and she
clung to him, pressing her face against his coat, pressing herself
against him while Edna held fast to his other arm. Owen thought
that was no way to act with Willie just buried. Nellie looked all
lumpy and bulgy, and Owen remembered that day in the haymow.
Then she was certainly pretty thin, but she was getting fat now.

John walked with Nellie and Edna to the family carriage, then came to ride back to town with the other pallbearers.

The next time Owen went to the *Journal* office, seeing Will reminded him of that lame woman who was at the same time so beautiful and who had come with Will to the funeral, and he wanted to ask who she was; but some diffidence restrained him. He did tell Mr. Beecham about the carriage tipping over, and BB wrote an editorial urging the building of better roads.

4

If Owen's hours in the *Journal* office were a steady delight, so were his days in school. He worshipped pretty little Miss Dine — as did most of the other boys in the class, and all the girls. Teacher was so pretty, and so nice. Other teachers sometimes sent misbehaving youngsters to Mr. Atkinson; and Mr. Atkinson had a famous paddle. "He pulls your pants tight on your butt and whacks you good." To be sent up to Mr. Atkinson was the direst punishment; and when youthful howls of pain came from behind the closed door of the Superintendent's office, a shiver went through every boy within hearing. But Miss Dine never sent anyone to Mr. Atkinson. When a boy threw paper wads, or committed some similar misdemeanor, Miss Dine just pretended not to notice. Louie Peters one day made a miniature slingshot by stretching a rubber band between two fingers and hooking over it a bent pin. When the band was drawn back and then released, the pin flew like a bullet. The first one Louie tried struck point first on the back of Tommy Morgan's head and stuck in Tommy's scalp; and Tommy yelped, and slapped his hand to the spot and felt the pin embedded there and began to scream — more in terror than pain — and Miss Dine hurried to pull out the pin, and sat in Tommy's seat with him, holding Tommy in her arms and comforting him. Any boy in the room would have allowed his head to be converted into a pincushion for that.

When Tommy was quiet, Miss Dine made them a sorrowful little speech. "I want us all to have a good time this year together, so it makes me sad when we're mean to each other. I could report the boy who did this to Mr. Atkinson, but I think corporal punishment brutalizes boys, so I won't do it. But let's all try to enjoy this year

and not be unkind to each other." She had been at first so serious
that Owen thought she might be going to cry; but now she smiled
beautifully. "There, now we'll forget all about it, shall we?"

Owen knew, of course, that by "corporal punishment" she meant
a paddling from Mr. Atkinson; but the word "corporal" was new
to him. There was a dictionary in Mr. Beecham's office, and that
afternoon Owen looked up the word. BB asked what it was he
wished to know, and Owen told him. "It says 'corporal' means
'bodily,'" he reported, and BB nodded.

"Yes. The word comes from 'corpus.' That's the Latin word for
body. Latin is the language the Romans used to speak and write.
Many of our common words have a Latin root." He asked where
Owen heard the word.

"Miss Dine made a speech in school today," Owen explained. "She
said it brutalized boys. Does that mean make them like animals?"

"Something of the sort." BB asked curiously: "Was it a good
speech?"

"Yes sir."

"That's one of the things you'll want to learn, as you grow older,
how to make a good speech."

"How do you learn it?"

"Acquire the tools, and then practice using them. You'll need to
build up a vocabulary, and to store your mind with eloquent
phrases. Bible phrases are best. When you use a Bible phrase,
your audience will recognize it and be proud of themselves and
therefore grateful to you."

"What's a vocabulary?"

"Your vocabulary is the words you know and use. It isn't enough
to know them, you must use them, too. They say when a man has
used a word three times, it becomes his own." And he remarked, as
though it were a question: "You like Miss Dine, don't you."

Owen, faintly conscious of criticism implicit in Mr. Beecham's
tone, spoke strongly. "Yes, I do. She's awful nice."

"As nice as Miss Williams?"

Owen hesitated, trying to decide. He had seen Miss Williams
occasionally this winter — she was always at church — and he liked
her smile and her friendly ways. She was nice, no doubt of that;
but Miss Dine was somehow more exciting.

"Well, I see Miss Dine more."

BB did not pursue the inquiry, turning to his desk; but some editorial paragraphs in that week's *Journal* awoke in Owen the disturbing suspicion that Mr. Beecham did not like Miss Dine.

> *The Board of School Examiners has had occasion to reprimand one of our teachers for playing cards on Sunday. We presume that they will be more severe if the offense is repeated.*

> *The most demoralizing thing that can happen to a school is to have among the girls a coquet. She thinks she is pretty, and is sure she can fascinate any boy she chooses. If she is about sixteen, and her teacher is a young man, she plies her charms on him. If she is ignored, she sows the seeds of trouble; if not, she may lead the teacher to forget his position. In the country school, the coquet is more dangerous than the rowdy boy. It sometimes happens that the teacher herself, if she is young, may in all innocence coquet with the boys in school. That way lies disaster.*

The word "coquet" sent Owen to the dictionary. A coquet, he found, was a man who practiced coquetry; a "coquette" was a woman who did so. But clearly Mr. Beecham by "coquet" meant a girl, or a woman, so Owen read the definition of coquetry. "An action intended to attract admiration, gallantry or affection without responsive feeling; trifling in love."

But if Miss Dine were a coquet, her apparent affection for her pupils was pretense; and Owen did not for a moment believe that. He turned back to the *Journal*, read the next paragraph.

> *Dancing has been made the subject of much comment in our city within the last three weeks. It has been much discussed, as well as the propriety of dancing by a teacher of young boys and girls, who should be molding their character as well as their minds, helping them by example as well as by precept. Dancing will never be popular except among the giddy and the gay.*

That too might mean Miss Dine; but Owen, though he had a high respect for Mr. Beecham, was sure that if the editor disliked her, he was wrong.

5

As spring came flowing north across the Ohio hills, BB wrote several editorials about the shortage of work, using the word "depression," which Owen looked up and made his own. The editor's prediction that the hard times would be worse before they were better did not frighten Owen. Depressions, hard times, such abstractions were the concern of grownups, not of boys; but BB said one thing which set Owen thinking. Mr. Beecham thought one cause of the depression was an oversupply of labor, and he wrote:

> *When six men want one job, the employer chooses the one who will work for the lowest pay. Foreign labor in the coal fields of Pennsylvania and colored labor in West Virginia works for low wages, and Hardiston coal mines have to compete with the cheap coal they produce and so have to pay our miners wages almost equally low.*

BB added a suggestion, offering what seemed to him at least a partial remedy.

> *Some of the idle laboring men in the country might be put to work on our roads. The policy of temporary patching means a continuing expense, but a well-built macadam road, like the Pike, costs very little in repairs. Money spent in building good roads benefits the county and helps keep men at work. The Roman roads, built almost two thousand years ago, are in some places in England and Wales still in use. The secret is good foundations. A house built upon sand will not stand, and neither will a road.*

Most of BB's editorials had a tincture of politics, and in this case he argued that the Cleveland administration had left economic wounds not yet healed. He urged the nomination of Bellamy Storer for Governor, of Major McKinley for Senator; and he quoted prices to show the advantages of the McKinley Tariff. "Last week sugar sold at 13 pounds for $1.00. This week a dollar buys 20 pounds. Credit the tariff."

Owen each week read the *Journal* to his father, while Tom

drowsed in his chair. Colonel J. P. Sanford lectured at the Rink on "New Times and Old." A new bridge was being built over Salt Creek on the Chillicothe road; the first bridge there was built in 1820 at a cost of $67. The Legislature passed the Australian Ballot Law. Of seventy-two who took the examination for certificates as teachers, forty-nine passed; and Marged Williams wrote the best examination and received a five-year certificate. Mr. Jewell, the aptly named jeweller, was in Philadelphia buying stock for his store. Professor J. C. Webb, an expert penman who wrote equally well with either hand, had a desk in the lobby of the Flagg House and was kept busy writing visiting cards. Wallace and Company's circus would come to Hardiston in May.

Through such paragraphs as these, Tom Glen seemed to sleep, but if Owen read anything about mines and miners he was quick to rouse. Mr. Beecham had predicted that a strike would begin on the first of May; but late in April the United Mine Workers decided against striking, and Mr. Beecham said they were to be congratulated.

Owen's father, when he heard this, exploded. "Congratulated my foot!" he cried. "The miners at Erie ought to strike, even if the Union don't. Our day men only get a dollar twenty-three, and they ought all to get a dollar and a half anyway, and maybe two dollars, and I say we ought all to go out till they do. If we can get it for them, then we can get more pay ourselves. I've said so to Isaac Williams; yes, and to Charles Morgan too."

"What's he got to do with it?" Mrs. Glen asked in surprise. "He don't work at Erie."

"No, but he's president of the biggest local in the county. He's a big man, and a brainy man. If I could get him to give Isaac Williams a prod, we'd get somewhere."

"Oh Tom, you're forever trying to start trouble. As if we didn't have troubles enough as it is."

"You're wrong there, Annie. I'm not starting trouble; I'm trying to get rid of some of the troubles we've got. Maybe trying won't do us any good, but if we keep trying, time Owen here's a man things will be some different." His tone was calm. "You and me, folks our age, we can't do much to help ourselves. It's too late. But what I do might help Owen, and what he does might help his young ones."

"Oh, you make big talk; but all ever comes of it, you're out of a job and we have to move, or starve or something."

"Times are changing, Annie," he insisted. "With the secret ballot now, so a man can vote any way he wants, and the Farmers' Alliance and the Knights of Labor going to get together and start a new party, we'll change a lot of things."

She made a scornful sound. "Talk, talk, talk," and when next day Tom was late returning from the mine she said resentfully: "Like as not he's talking to someone, wanting them to strike. I wish he'd come home when he's supposed to, 'stead of letting me stay here and worry myself sick."

"I can go find him, mama," Owen suggested.

"No, no, you'd just upset him. It always makes him mad to have me worry."

When Tom belatedly appeared, Owen knew at once that something had gone wrong. He asked a question, and Tom shook his head, but Mrs. Glen said sharply: "You can't fool me, Tom Glen. What happened?"

So he told her. Jim Harned and his son John worked a room in the mine together; and at their first shot today, the roof came down. They were crushed under twenty tons of slate. "I stayed to help dig 'em out," he said.

When he began, she had dropped into a chair; she sat motionless, limp hands lying in her lap, till he was done and for a moment longer. Then she brushed her forehead with the back of her hand. "Have a wife, did he?"

"Jim didn't, no. She's dead. His boy was married, had a little girl. Lulu, her name is. His wife and the little girl were there today when we got him out. I guess she's expecting. Lulu's seven or eight years old. Right pretty."

Mrs. Glen rose to put supper on the table. "Go wash up," she said. "Things have been getting cold. Here's the kettle."

He took the hot water and went through to the shed to change his clothes and wash away the coal dust which made him black-faced as a minstrel. Owen saw his mother's shoulders heave with a deep sigh, and he went to her and put his arm around her waist, and she looked down at him with haggard eyes and hugged his head against her bosom.

"It might have been you and me, Owen," she murmured. "Wait-

ing for them to get the slate off Tom Glen and carry him out and
bring him to us."

He tightened his arm around her. "Don't you worry. Nothing
will ever happen to papa."

"No, no, I know, son. No, nothing ever will."

For a day or two after the tragedy, the mine did not run, and
Tom and Owen went to the double funeral; but next day Tom
came home with a new light in his eye. He did not wait to tell his
news. "Annie, Jim Harned was secretary-treasurer of the local.
Isaac Williams wants me to take the job — till they can elect a new
one, or maybe elect me, at the next meeting."

She looked at him with a shrewd eye. "When will that be?"

"June, I think."

"You want to do it, don't you, Tom."

"Well, I told him I would."

"I know you, Tom Glen. You and Isaac Williams are cooking up
some trouble between you."

He denied this so violently that Owen suspected it was true;
and he was not surprised to hear at the mine during the days that
followed new talk of the grievance of the day men. In mid-May,
the hundred and eleven men at Erie, and sixty or seventy others at
two smaller mines just outside the corporation limits of Hardiston,
went out on strike, and Tom came home exultant.

"We're out, Annie!" he cried, as he flung open the door.

"More fools you! Men have to have a fight every so often or they
ain't satisfied. You strike, and I have to manage the best I can."
She brushed her eyes with her knuckle. "But that's the way it goes.
The roosters crow, but it's the hens that lay the eggs."

"You wait! I'm going uptown in the morning, send a telegram to
Columbus, get the Union to send a man down here."

"What can he do?"

"Talk to the furnace men. Union Furnace owns Erie Mine, and
Moon Furnace owns the other two."

She nodded, said wearily: "You'll do as you're a mind to, I guess,
spite of anything I say or do."

Mr. Beecham reported the strike in the *Journal*, but his only
comment was: "We hope the trouble will be adjusted before Union
Furnace has to shut down for lack of coal. The striking mines provide all the furnace's coal, and a shutdown would throw four
hundred men out of work."

As a result of the telegraphed request, John Nugent, vice-president of the Ohio District of the United Mine Workers, came to Hardiston; and Tom went to Isaac Williams's home to meet him. Owen, in school all day and at the *Journal* office after school, did not see the great man; but he imagined Mr. Nugent as tall and strong, with a broad brow and a warm beard and something God-like in his bearing. Tom that night reported that Mr. Nugent had endorsed the strike, and his tone suggested that the endorsement made victory sure. Owen believed this, and when next day the men at one of the smaller mines which had struck with Erie accepted defeat and returned to work, he felt scorn for their weakness.

A day or two later, a man named Malone was killed by a fall of slate in Miss Ellen, up the creek. This was one of Moses Evans's mines, and the other miners there struck, demanding better timber to use as props to support the slate. That was on Tuesday, but Friday they surrendered; and Saturday Owen, at work in the file room just behind the *Journal* office, saw Mr. Evans come in and heard him say exultantly to Mr. Beecham:

"Yes, they've gone back to work — and they'll get the same timber they always had! I'll shut down sooner than give in to them."

Something like a welling spring of rage surged in Owen, and he started that way. Mr. Beecham saw him, and as though he guessed the boy's anger, he made a reassuring gesture, and Owen heard him say:

"Used to dig coal yourself, didn't you?"

"Started when I was fifteen years old!" Mr. Evans said proudly. "And we didn't ask anyone to baby us in those days, either. That was before Andrew Dale got his fool ideas through the legislature." He made a furious, scornful, spitting sound. "Two entries to every mine! Ventilate! A hundred cubic feet of air per man per minute! We didn't have any such fool notions! We dug coal!"

He threw up his hands. "But now all I get from the men is whine, whine, whine — and I lose money on every ton of coal they dig." He laughed bitterly. "Strike? I wish they'd strike and stay struck! If they'd stay out long enough, I'd save enough money to make me a rich man."

Owen heard him rise and stamp out of the office; and BB caught Owen's eye, beckoned him, said smilingly: "Mose has a hot temper!"

"I hate him." Owen's fists were clenched.

"He's not as bad as he sounds, but he enjoys getting mad. He

was so red here a minute ago, I thought he'd have an apoplectic
stroke." BB added quietly: "Don't let him upset you. It never
pays to get mad."

Yet Owen remembered, and he told his father that night what
Mr. Evans had said. Tom paid little attention, and Owen saw he
was troubled, and asked why.

"I've been telling your mother," Tom explained. "Mr. Nugent
put in a report that we're working below scale. The Union might
call our strike illegal."

"Would that mean you'd have to go back to work, or something?"

Tom nodded helplessly. "Just about." But after supper he got
out pad and pen and ink and settled at the table, the lamp at his
elbow, and began laboriously to write. Mrs. Glen asked:

"What you doing, Tom?"

"Isaac Williams wanted me to write them a letter, give them the
straight of it." He took off his spectacles and rubbed his eyes, and
peered through the lenses. "My eyes get worse all the time, Annie.
Next thing I know, Owen, I'll have to get you to do my writing for
me." He bent to his work again, and he was still at the table when
Owen went to bed. In the morning he gave Owen the letter and
two pennies, and Owen mailed the letter when he left the *Journal*
office and before going to school.

The letter failed of its purpose, for a few days later Mr. Penna
of the United Mine Workers came from Columbus and told Tom
and the other miners at Erie that their strike was illegal. Since they
had no hope of victory without the support of the Union, they
surrendered. Tom Glen at home that night sat in brooding anger.
"He told us we had to be sensible, says there's no use striking when
times are hard. He says we'll have to wait till the operators are
making money, so they can't afford to shut down."

"He's got something in his skull besides straw," Mrs. Glen approvingly declared. "I wish I could say the same for you. What's
the sense in starting a fight when you're bound to be licked?"

Tom did not answer, shook his weary head; but Owen thought his
father more nearly right than his mother. There was something
finely valorous about fighting a brave battle you were sure to lose.

6

When the Wallace circus came to town, BB gave Owen passes for himself and his father and mother. Tom Glen worked that day, but Owen and his mother went together. They were early enough to watch the balloon being inflated. The big bag was laid out on the ground beside a trench covered with a sheet of iron, under which a man built a fire. He poured coal oil on the fire, and all the smoke went through a stovepipe into the balloon, which swelled till it stood erect, pear-shaped, tugging at its ropes. Then a man made a speech, and another man in tights took hold of a trapeze handle that was fastened to the long white parachute attached to the balloon; and then suddenly the ropes were let go, and the balloon surged upward, the parachute and the man in tights swaying below it. The man did tricks, hanging by his hands, then swinging his feet up over the bar to hang by his knees and then by his feet. He skinned the cat, hanging by his arms and swinging his body through between his arms so that he hung upside down, then swinging his body back through his arms again. By that time the balloon was so high you could hardly see the man at all, and then suddenly he was falling, the parachute trailing after him like an empty white stocking; and then the parachute opened, the balloon high above him turning upside down, pouring out black smoke till it seemed to be on fire, and then like a thin rag falling faster and faster.

Owen raced to be near when he reached the ground; and he saw the man bundling the parachute up in his arms, and then two of the circus men came to help him and Owen heard the man say: "That God-damned rope God-damned near cut me in two when she opened!" Owen, ashamed to have heard the oath, went quietly back to find his mother.

The circus was fine. Owen wished he could hang a trapeze to one of the trees in the grove beyond the slack pile and learn to do some of the tricks the show people did; but even though he earned a dollar a week, it went into the family purse, and rope was expensive, so he could only wish.

There was a revival meeting in Hardiston that spring, and some of the boys and girls in Miss Dine's room went to hear the shouting,

but Owen respected the opinion of his father and mother that
making a show of yourself in public was not true godliness and
stayed away. A committee of ladies called upon Mr. Beecham to
ask him to advocate an election on the saloon question, but BB
declined. "Votes for temperance," he remarked in the *Journal*, "can
best be won at the mother's knee"; and he reminded the ladies
that Glendale, up the creek, where for some years there had been
no saloons, had held an election a month before and voted to allow
them.

Among the Glendale items that week was one about a baby bitten
by a blacksnake. "But he was put under the influence of whiskey,
and by next day he was well."

That was a dry spring, and the sprinkling cart was busy laying
the dust. On the way to school, barefoot boys followed the sprinkler, playing tag in the slippery footing, laughing when a boy fell
and smeared his clothes. Owen did not join in this play, because his
one suit must serve for school and church; but one day Louie
Peters, stamping in a puddle, splashed muddy water on him.
Owen tried to catch Louie and inflict suitable punishment; but the
other for the time escaped. Owen cleaned his clothes as well as he
could, and removed his celluloid collar and wiped off the mud; but
his shirt and his coat and pants still showed the drying stains. At
recess he cornered Louie and sent him in weeping flight back to the
sanctuary of the schoolroom. Miss Dine helped Louie stop his
nosebleed, and scolded Owen; but since Louie was bigger than he,
Owen felt more pride than remorse.

As soon as the grass began to grow, Owen, in addition to working
before and after school and all day Saturday in the *Journal* office, cut
some lawns during the noon hour. This meant going without dinner,
but there were palliations. Mrs. Paxley lived only a block or two from
the schoolhouse, and her cookies or gingerbread — or perhaps it
was a jam or jelly sandwich which she gave him — helped him
forget he was hungry. He was grateful to her, and glad of the
work and of the quarter he earned so easily; but he began to be
ill at ease with Mrs. Paxley. She was apt to pat his head, and once
when she paid him she squeezed his arm. Usually, he hated being
touched. Edna Tutson seemed to go out of her way to brush
against him in the *Journal* office, and in school Nellie never passed
within reach without poking him.

But though he resented these contacts, he was never happier than when Miss Dine laid her hand on his shoulder, supporting herself as she leaned down to look at his work. Sometimes the side of her pompadour even touched his cheek.

His hours in school were completely contenting, though he began to be sure that Miss Dine, nice as she was, was not very smart. Mr. Atkinson, the Superintendent, occasionally came to listen to one of her classes; and so did Mr. Freeland, the principal. Sometimes, the visitor asked the class questions: "Who can tell me — " this or that. Then from among the many raised hands, he selected one to answer.

On such occasions, Owen never raised his hand, but one day Mr. Atkinson singled him out, called his name. The class had been spelling in unison as Miss Dine called each word. Mr. Atkinson said: "Owen! Owen Glen!" Owen stood up, and Mr. Atkinson asked: "Owen, how do you pronounce p-e-o-n-y?"

Owen hesitated, not because he did not know, but because Miss Dine had just given the word to be spelled and had pronounced it "piny." He hated to disagree with her, but he knew she was wrong. "Peony," he said.

"And a-r-c-t-i-c?" Mr. Atkinson spelled out the word. Miss Dine always pronounced it "Artic."

"Arctic," said Owen.

The Superintendent tugged at his mustache, and after an awkward moment, Miss Dine said in a pretty confusion: "Owen has his own ideas about some things, Mr. Atkinson. Sometimes he's right, too; but of course none of us are always right." Owen knew she was embarrassed, and he blamed Mr. Atkinson, trying thus to forget his own complicity in that embarrassment. He did not like Mr. Atkinson. The Superintendent, when he spoke to Miss Dine, always seemed severe.

On the other hand, Owen liked Mr. Freeland, the principal. This was largely because Miss Dine so obviously welcomed his visits. When Mr. Atkinson was in the room, she never seemed natural; but she and Mr. Freeland laughed together, and sometimes whispered a word or two together, and when he left she was likely to slip her hand through his arm as they walked together to the door.

Last day of school came at the end of May, and Miss Dine arranged a program, not as long as the program at Redfern School but satisfying all the children; she made a little speech about the happy year they had had together, and she said she wished they could all be in her room next year, and they all echoed the wish. She stood at the door to say goodbye to them and to shake hands as they passed out, and Owen felt so keenly the tragic drama of this parting that he squeezed her hand too hard, and she cried out in pain, and he flushed with embarrassment and with grief; but she said she did not really mind because they had come to be such good friends.

A week after school closed, Owen read a paragraph in the *Journal*:

> *Miss Alice Dine, who taught in Hardiston schools last winter, has gone to Columbus to attend Normal School. Her place will be taken next year by Miss Marged Williams, who this year taught the Ryan School at Glendale.*

He was sorry Miss Dine was going away, and only mildly interested in the fact that Miss Williams would take her place; but the day after that item appeared, on his way to Mr. McAuliffe's store to buy twenty cents worth of side meat for his mother, he saw approaching the store from the opposite direction a man carrying a buggy whip. He recognized the man, on closer view, as Miss Dine's father.

Mr. Freeland lived in the second house beyond the store. He was mowing his lawn. Mr. Dine turned in at Mr. Freeland's front gate, and without a word began to slash Mr. Freeland with the buggy whip. Mr. Freeland shouted, and tried to come to grips, and the older man backed away, hitting Mr. Freeland across the face and arms and body. Then Mrs. Freeland ran out of the house and jerked the buggy whip away from Mr. Dine, and screamed something, and Mr. Dine shouted:

"Because he's got my girl in trouble, that's why!"

At that, Mrs. Freeland turned on her husband, screaming with rage, and slashed at him with the whip; and he dodged away and ran into the house, his wife pursuing him with cries and blows.

Mr. Dine, when they had disappeared, came out of the yard and stalked away, and Owen abruptly realized that he was not the only spectator. Mr. McAuliffe and Mrs. Lewis had come up beside him, and on the sidewalk beyond Mr. Freeland's, two women whom Owen did not know, and a strange little boy, had watched the incident with avid eyes. Mr. McAuliffe and Mrs. Lewis went back into the store, and the two women moved aside to let Mr. Dine pass, and they whispered there together till Mrs. Freeland threw up a window and screamed at them:

"Go on! Get out of here!"

The little boy ran, the women wrapped themselves in dignity and departed, and Owen followed Mrs. Lewis and Mr. McAuliffe into the store to do his errand. He was trying to understand. Mr. Freeland liked Miss Dine, so why would he do anything to cause her trouble? When Owen entered the store, Mrs. Lewis and Mr. McAuliffe were talking together in excited tones; but they stopped, and Mrs. Lewis said: "Good morning, Owen. How's your mother?"

He knew his mother and Mrs. Lewis had been together yesterday afternoon, so the question was the silly sort of thing grownups were forever asking children. He told Mrs. Lewis his mother was fine, and she bade Mr. McAuliffe wait on Owen, insisting she was in no hurry, so Owen knew she wanted to stay behind with Mr. McAuliffe and discuss what had happened. He went home with the side meat and asked his mother:

"Mama, how does a man get a woman in trouble?"

She looked at him in sharp surprise. "What talk have you been hearing, Owen?"

"Mr. Dine said Mr. Freeland has got Miss Dine in trouble!"

"Well, my land o' Goshen!" She hesitated, as though about to ask another question, then reddened angrily. "Don't bother your head about such things at your age!"

So Owen was silenced, but the dictionary in the *Journal* office gave him a hint. "Trouble" meant pain, or distress, or things like that; but at the last of many definitions, Owen read, "Dial. Eng. Pain in childbirth."

That might mean that Miss Dine had had a baby, but something happened a day or two later which made Owen sure that having a baby was not trouble but great happiness. The paper went to press Wednesday night, and next day Mr. Beecham did not come to the office at all; but Friday morning he appeared fairly radiant; and he told them proudly:

"Well, we have a new little baby at our house. A little girl!" Will congratulated him, and asked how Mrs. Beecham was, and Mr. Beecham said: "Fine, they're both fine!"

He was so happy that he infected the whole office. Obviously, Mr. Beecham did not feel that having a baby was "trouble," so this could not have been what Mr. Dine meant.

That mystery remained for the time unsolved, yet Owen found what he thought might be the answer. Reading the *Journal* to his father, he came to the news that Mrs. James Harned, whose husband had been killed in Erie Mine a month ago, was dead; and Owen's mother, busy with the dishes, said over her shoulder:

"You didn't tell me that, Tom. The poor thing."

"The baby died too," he said. "Evan Harned's taking Lulu to live with them from now on."

Owen knew that animals sometimes died in giving birth, and he guessed this was what had happened to Mrs. Harned. If Miss Dine was going to have a baby, perhaps dying was the "trouble" Mr. Dine meant.

The following week, the *Journal* reported that Mr. and Mrs. Freeland were moving to Washington Court House; that Mr. Freeland had resigned as principal and in Washington Court House would go into the furniture business. Then suddenly everyone was talking about Miss Dine and Mr. Freeland. A part of Mr. Freeland's work had been to visit country schools around Hardiston, driving out and back the same day; and people began to say that Miss Dine had used to meet Mr. Freeland secretly outside of town, and ride into the country with him. Owen could see no harm in this, but since Miss Dine did it secretly and furtively, it must be something of which she was ashamed; yet he clung to his faith in her.

Coming home one afternoon he heard through the open door as he approached the house his mother say to his father: "— rid of that hussy, and a good thing too." As he appeared in the door, she fell silent, but he asked:

"What's a hussy, mama?"

Mrs. Glen tossed her head. "Nothing for you to bother your head about! You wash up for supper now."

Owen guessed his mother was speaking of Miss Dine. The dictionary told him that a hussy was "a worthless woman or girl, a jade." He looked up "jade," but a jade, too, was a worthless woman, so he got nowhere. Yet surely Miss Dine, so nice, and loving them all, was not worthless.

Full enlightenment, when it came, was shattering. Owen's father sometimes drew scrip against wages earned but not due till the fortnightly payday. The scrip could only be spent at the company store, and one day Mrs. Glen sent Owen with scrip to buy five pounds of sugar with which to preserve some blackberries she and Owen had picked, out along the Pike. Nellie Tutson was in the store.

"H'lo, Owen," she said. He made some wordless sound, and asked the storekeeper for the sugar, turning his back on her; and to his relief she went out. But when he emerged with his package under his arm, she appeared from around the corner of the store and walked along with him.

"I've fixed up the cave again, Owen," she announced. "It's lots nicer now. Come on over and see it."

"I've got to take this home to mama." His voice trembled as much with alarm as with anger.

"You don't have to go right away. Come on. Jenkin Powell helped me fix it. We have lots of fun there. You come and I'll show you." Owen hurried his steps in a rising panic, not knowing what to say, and she jeered at him. "Fraidy cat! You're scared."

"I'm not either! I don't want to, that's all."

"Yah! I guess you think you're one of Miss Dine's nice little boys! She wasn't so much!"

"She was too!" He walked faster, but Nellie kept pace with him; he wished to run, but he might fall down and burst the bag of sugar. "She was too! You let her alone!"

"She was bad! You ask Jenkin Powell! He saw her go into the woods one day, her and Mr. Freeland, out past his father's farm; and he sneaked up and saw them a-hugging and a-kissing and everything!"

"He did not!"

"You just ask him, if you don't believe me!"

"You're a — you're an old liar, that's all! You leave me alone!" Owen suddenly began to run.

To his relief, she did not pursue him, but she called after him: "Fraidy-cat! Fraidy-cat! Owen Glen's a fraidy-cat!"

When he had put her safely behind him, he slowed to a walk

again; but he was trembling and half-sobbing. His formless thoughts put on no words to make them recognizable; he knew without knowing what it was he knew. Halfway home, passing an open field grown up to sumac and sassafras, he plunged into the thicket and pressed on till he was hidden from any chance passer-by; and he threw himself headlong, his face buried in his arms, and wept in woeful grief, in the hopeless grief of childhood when all catastrophes are irretrievable.

V

June 1891 — *March* 1892

AFTER SCHOOL let out for the summer, Owen, unless he could find a lawn that needed mowing, spent most of his time in the *Journal* office. He set type till he knew the case with his eyes shut, and he learned to feed the presses. He and Will had long since become good friends. That pretty little lame woman whom Owen had seen with Will at the funeral was Mrs. Davis. She came one day to the office, and Will, proud as a young father, introduced Owen to her. When she was gone, he explained her lameness. Two or three weeks after their marriage, she seemed to catch cold, and she was feverish, and had a stiff neck. The doctor thought she had *La Grippe* and put her to bed, and she got better, but then something went wrong with her legs.

"Like they were paralyzed," Will explained. "So the doctor put her in splints, and he wanted to keep her in bed, but she said she had too much to do to stay in bed, so she got around on crutches for a while. Before Annie was born she could manage on canes, and since Bill came, last winter, she gets along fine." Will laughed proudly. "She claims that after she has a couple more, she'll be as well as ever. She works in the garden as it is, besides doing the house and the babies and the washing and all. And hog-killing time she makes the best sausage in the county. Folks bring her their sausage meat for her to put up for them."

Owen thought she must be pretty wonderful, and because Will was her husband, Will's stature was increased. Will, for his part, liked the boy's eager interest in his work; and he must have praised Owen to BB, because the editor suggested that Owen during the summer work all day Wednesday as well as Saturday — since on

105

those two days the paper was printed and Will had more need of help — and raised Owen's pay to a dollar and a half.

"We'll reduce it to a dollar again after school starts, when you can't work Wednesdays," he explained.

Owen would have been glad to work all day every day for no pay at all. Everything delighted him, from the big press to the wash basin on its low bench and the ink-soiled roller-towel that hung above it. The first time he tried to feed the job press, he inked the tympan; but Will showed him how, if he failed to place the card that was to be printed accurately on the clips, he could throw his weight on the treadle and stop the press before the jaws closed. Owen practiced that feat till he perfected it.

When there was no work for him in the pressroom, he set type with the girls. The loft, reached by an outside stair as well as by the stairway from the pressroom, was even on the hottest day reasonably cool. Bets — Elizabeth Tilden was her full name — sat nearest the window, Edna at the case by the head of the stairs. Owen normally worked at the case between them. His first impressions of the two girls persisted. He liked Bets, because she seemed to like him. Edna did not seem to like anyone, not even John Carver, who on days when the mine did not work sometimes came up the outside stairs to speak to her.

One Wednesday evening when the paper had been put to bed, BB suggested that Owen go with him next day for a walk into the country. They took the Liberty road, and they stopped now and then while BB identified a flower, or a bird song. They stopped, too, to speak to an occasional farmer. One, a big man with a loud blaring voice, told them profanely that dogs had killed six of his sheep three nights before, and BB sympathized with him. They had paused for a drink of water from his well, and stayed in talk awhile. Owen saw a little old woman looking out at them from the kitchen door, and he caught glimpses of at least one other woman in the kitchen. The man's big voice pounded at them, and Owen had never heard a man swear so much. He was glad when they moved on, and he asked BB who the man was.

"His name's Frye, Nate Frye." BB chuckled. "And he talks louder and says less than any man in the county."

"His mother was watching us."

"That's his wife, not his mother." The editor added: "She looks old enough to be his mother. I suppose that big voice of his has thumped the youth out of her." After a moment he said reflectively: "But it's too bad about his sheep. Farming here in Hardiston County is about done. The soil is worked out, or gullied and washed away. Our farmers ought to stop raising grain and put in orchards; grow apples and peaches, and raise stock and poultry. But a man can't raise sheep with dogs running wild."

Owen thought this was probably true. Hardiston was full of dogs which seemed to have no master, cross-bred mongrels skilled in the art of taking care of themselves, raiding slop pails, killing chickens, snarling at every human. Now and then one went mad and ran through the streets at a shaky trot, with hanging head and white flecks of saliva around its muzzle; and once Owen saw Marshal Henson shoot such a dog. Foraging dogs frequently circled Owen's home, looking for scraps; and Mrs. Glen, like most other housewives, kept a kettle ready on the stove so that if the chance offered she could throw boiling water on an offending beast. There were many lean mongrels in Hardiston with spots on their bodies naked of hair where they had been thus scarred. The dogcatcher was the constable, a lean, sick-looking, middle-aged man named Marks, and when dogs were a too-persistent annoyance, house-wives sent for him. Everyone called him Doggy Marks; and he could seduce into captivity dogs that would let no other human being approach.

Mr. Frye had said he was going to put out poison baits for the sheep-killing dogs. Now and then there was an epidemic of poison-ing these stray and ownerless creatures, and several times Owen had seen stark, contorted bodies, fly-blown and decaying, in the alleys of the town; and once he saw a poisoned dog go into con-vulsions on Main Street and froth and snap its teeth at nothing and try to stand up and then fall down again and kick awhile and die. Remembering Mr. Frye's threat, he told Mr. Beecham about the incident. "It was awful," he said.

"A man who would poison someone else's dog would murder a child; but ownerless dogs should be mercifully put out of the way."

"I never had a dog; but if I did and anyone poisoned him, I'd kill them."

BB smiled. "What you mean is you'd feel like it. But of course you wouldn't."

They had a fine day together. BB talked to Owen as he would
have talked to a man, and many of the things the editor said would
always be a part of Owen's thinking. They ate lunch in a cool glen
where a spring came out of a waist-high crevice in the conglomerate, and a stream of water as thick as Owen's wrist cascaded to
the ground; and they came home past Erie Mine, parting at the
corner of Peach Street a block from BB's home. Owen had a stone
bruise that troubled him as he limped along Ridge Street, but when
he came in sight of the house he forgot it; for his father, dressed in
his Sunday clothes, was standing by the open door. Owen knew
something must have happened; he began to run.

Tom Glen told him quietly: "Little David's dead, Owen. Amy's
baby. Bobby Roberts came up in Dave's father's carriage to take
us down there. Go get into your clothes."

Owen saw his mother in the kitchen, sitting quietly in her low
rocker, her hands crossed in her lap. She did not seem to be crying, for her face was set in a stony calm; but there were tears on
her cheeks. At the sight, grief for her swept him, and he came close
to her, wanting to hug her and comfort her yet helpless in the face
of her silent sorrow. She said: "I didn't get to see him, Owen.
Dave never came to take me down. He said he would, but he
never came. I never saw my grandson."

Owen looked to his father for some word to comfort her; but
Tom Glen shook his head. "Get your clothes on, Owen. Bobby'll
be back any minute. He's only gone to tell Marged Williams.
He'll be here right away."

2

It was long past dark when they reached Dave's father's house,
and Owen remembered the last time he had seen this doorway, the
night of Amy's wedding. They stayed that night and Friday night,
and returned to Hardiston Saturday, after the funeral. Mrs. Glen
had wished she need not leave so soon, but Tom Glen said: "Now,
Annie, Amy's got her husband to comfort her best he can, and
you've got Owen and me to take care of. The world don't stop
turning, just because a baby's died." Dave drove them in to
Sycamore Hill to catch the Accommodation, the northbound train.

There were two trains each way, six days a week; the Accommodation was so called because it sometimes carried a freight car or
two, as well as passengers. The Mail, though like the Accommodation it stopped at every station, never condescended to haul
freight.

During their first days at home again, Owen watched his mother
fearfully, grieving for her, afraid she would never be happy again; but
as the summer days drifted across the shimmering hills their lives
soon returned to normal.   The *Journal,* under the heading,
"Additional Locals," recorded a procession of events always differ-
ing yet always the same. Owen asked Will one day: "Why do you
call them 'Additional Locals'? Additional to what? They're on
every page in the paper."

"Well, they're additional to the ones on the other pages."

"The locals on page one aren't additional to anything?"

"Course they are! They're all additional to each other."

Certainly, every week, there were dozens of these short paragraphs, news, editorials, advertisements. The cantata, *Esther,* was
presented at the Rink to benefit the Methodist Church Parsonage
Fund; the Presbyterian Woman's Missionary Society held a children's meeting. Mr. William Dine, the well-known druggist, sold
out and moved to Columbus. Two stores were burglarized in
Sycamore Hill and $115 was stolen from one, $40 from the other;
but the burglars, both boys, John Sauer and Peter Radford, were
caught and sent to the Reform School. The fact that Pete was now
in the Reform School lent him for Owen fearful importance. When
John Robinson's Exposition showed in Hardiston, the Ohio Southern
ran special trains from Belton and Sycamore Hill. Several hundred
people attended the camp meeting at Webb's Grove. Immigrants
pouring into the United States, said BB, kept wages down. "They
come from impoverished countries, so wages that seem low to us
seem high to them; and our laboring men are trampled into poverty
by the stampede of cheap labor from Europe, just as stampeding
cattle trample everything in their way." When Major McKinley
was nominated for Governor, BB predicted that if he were elected,
he would go on to the White House. In mid-July, three babies,
none of them four years old, playing under the freight cars in the
C. D. and I. yards, were run over; two of them were killed, the
other lost a foot. The new Populist Party was basically a revolt

against the Democratic ring. Blaine, said BB, was the most popular man in the United States, the most popular American since Washington; but Cleveland, since he had come out against Free Silver, might be re-elected. A saloonkeeper was murdered at McArthur; and a man was killed by falling slate in the Peebles Mine. Of the proposed system of city waterworks, BB said: "It is not worth while to take a stand on the question, since everyone has either a well or a cistern, so except for a few individuals everyone is opposed to the idea."

3

Marged Williams, after closing her school in Glendale and passing the examination which won her a five-year certificate, went home for a few weeks. Owen saw her at the baby's funeral. In July she returned to Hardiston, and a day or two later she came to find Owen. Since little David's death, he spent more time at home, thinking that by doing so he might help his mother forget her grief. They were together in the kitchen, Mrs. Glen peeling potatoes, Owen preparing to slop the pig, when Marged appeared in the open door.

Owen thought she was prettier than ever. He saw that she was happy about something; her eyes were dancing, her cheeks pink. She kissed Mrs. Glen, and shook Owen's hand, and said rapidly: "I had to come right away, couldn't wait! Owen, I've just been to see Mr. Atkinson, and what do you think? I'm going to teach the sixth room this winter."

Owen would be in the fifth room, and he felt an instant regret that Miss Williams would not be his teacher. Mrs. Glen said: "Why, there, now, Marged; I sh'd think you'd be real pleased."

"Oh, I am," Marged assured her. "But that isn't all of it! You know, Mrs. Glen — I don't need to tell you — Owen's a fine scholar. Well, I want him to be in my room. And Mr. Atkinson has had his eye on you, Owen. I talked to him today, and he says if you'll study this summer, learn some of the things you'll miss by not being in the fifth grade, he'll give you a double promotion. Then you'll be in my room. Would you like that?"

Owen grinned with delight, and Mrs. Glen laughed and said:

"Look at him! 'Course he would. I take that real nice of you, Marged."

Marged was watching Owen. "You haven't said," she reminded him, smiling, challenging him. "Speak up! Cat got your tongue?"

"Yes'm. I'd like it. But I don't know what to study."

She nodded cheerfully. "Of course you don't. The nice part of it is, I'll be studying too. The same things. You come to Uncle Isaac's every morning and we'll study together."

"I have to work in the *Journal* office Wednesdays and Saturdays."

"That's fine. We can do lots, the other four days. Probably I'll have to work pretty hard to keep up with you. We can have races, make it a game. Want to start tomorrow?"

"Yes'm. Do I have to get any books?"

"I'll borrow some for both of us, from school. Come about half-past eight, can you?"

That night, drowsy before he slept, he thought how wonderful it would have been to study every day with Miss Dine, and then he remembered about Miss Dine and was ashamed. Miss Williams was not at all like Miss Dine; he never felt ashamed of liking her.

Through the weeks till school opened, Owen found it true that Miss Williams studied as hard as he did; and once he spoke of this.

"It's the same with everyone, Owen," she assured him. "You never get old enough to stop studying. There's always something more to learn, but ordinary men don't bother." She smiled, affection in her eyes. "You know, it's quite easy to be an ordinary man, or an ordinary boy, Owen; but you'll never be ordinary, so you might as well brace yourself. You'll have to work harder and harder every year of your life. It's like climbing a slippery hill; if you stop to rest, you slide back — and you'll never let yourself do that."

Owen under her guidance learned to attack the tasks she set him with a steady concentration. As he progressed more and more rapidly, she increased her demands, and by the time school opened, she was able to say: "You're ready to go on. You've done as much work this last month as you would have done in the whole school year." Yet she warned him: "But now that you've learned to study, you'll find work this winter pretty easy. The whole class can't go ahead as fast as you can, so I'll have to think up extra things you must do, to make sure you don't start loafing." She spoke with a fierce and tender intensity which delighted him.

When school opened, one of the extra tasks she set him was to read the *Journal* every week. He had told her he read all the interesting parts to his father, but she bade him read it all, interesting or not; and he tried to do so. Evan Towers, from Sycamore Hill, was killed by a train robber on his way to New York on business. Mr. David Powell of the Lloyd and Powell Clothing Emporium on Broad Street, bound for New York and Boston to buy stock for the store, was on the same train; and the robber took his pocketbook containing more than a hundred dollars and some valuable papers. Owen heard a word-of-mouth account of that robbery; for Jane Lloyd, whose father was Mr. Powell's partner, was in Miss Williams's class and told them all about it. Alba Hayward and his Peerless Company of Comedians appeared for three nights at the Rink. Thirty-nine Hardiston people went on an excursion to Washington; and on September 20 an apple tree in Roger Attlebury's orchard showed eleven blossoms.

Miss Williams, like Mr. Beecham, advised Owen to pay attention to politics; so when, weeks before the election, the *Journal* printed a sample ballot, Owen studied it intently. The Republican ticket was headed by an engraving of an Eagle, the Democratic by a Rooster, the Prohibition by a White Rose, and the People's Party by a Plow and Hammer; but the names of the candidates, except "William McKinley, Jr." and a man named Seitz, were strange to him. He remembered Mr. Seitz because in the Labor Day parade there had been a wagon full of boys who kept blowing horns and shouting, "Hurrah for Seitz." One of them was Tom Powell, who was in the sixth grade with Owen; and when Owen asked him next day who Mr. Seitz was, Tom said loftily:

"Why, he's the People's Party candidate for Governor." Tom produced a quarter, showed it proudly. "Mr. Vesper paid us two bits apiece to ride in the wagon and cheer for him."

The People's Party sounded as though it might be all right, and that night Owen asked Tom Glen whether he would vote for Mr. Seitz.

"No, wouldn't think of it."

"Why not, papa? I know you think the miners and farmers ought to have a party of their own; and this is the same thing."

"Seitz is all right, but he hasn't got a chance to win," Tom explained. "And I won't waste a vote. I'll vote for Major McKinley."

Owen was puzzled by this point of view. "But papa, if all the people like you, who really want to have Mr. Seitz elected, would vote for him, maybe he'd win."

Tom shook a fretful head. "Leave be, Owen," he said angrily. "Time enough for politics after you're dry behind the ears."

This was the first time Owen had ever felt sure his father was wrong; but then he realized that his father knew himself wrong, and that this was why he was angry. In sympathetic understanding, he abandoned the point. "Want me to read the paper to you?"

"Yes. Yes, go on."

The *Journal* reported a squib factory just opened at Sycamore Hill. When miners blasted down the coal on the face of the vein, squibs were their fuses. The squibs often failed, or seemed to fail; and not infrequently the miner was injured or killed by a delayed explosion. This squib which would be manufactured at Sycamore Hill was of a new design, but when Owen read the description, Tom said scornfully:

"I don't go for new-fangled things. Our squibs work if you cut off the end right; and if you don't, that's your own fault."

Owen remembered what Miss Williams had said, that some pupils were brighter than others; and he thought that if some miners were not as skillful as his father, they might prefer squibs easier and safer to use. He knew his father was superior to other men; but that seemed to him no reason for scorning an innovation, no matter how new-fangled, which would help men less wise and careful. Owen wished to suggest this, but he was unwilling to provoke his father again; yet it was stimulating and exciting to discover that Tom Glen might sometimes be wrong.

His intensive reading of the *Journal* led Owen this fall to an increased interest in many matters. In Glendale, a baby was born by something called a "Caesarean Section." "This operation," BB wrote, "is named after Julius Caesar, the first baby born in this way. It is performed by cutting into the abdominal cavity and into the womb and removing the child." Once, in a pasture down near Adams Furnace, Owen had discovered a dead ewe with all four feet of a lamb protruding from her body. The paper said this Caesarian Section had been performed, "because it was impossible for the child to be born in any other manner." Perhaps the ewe's lamb could have been born in the same way.

The word "womb" was not itself strange to Owen, but he realized

that he did not know exactly what a womb was, so he turned to the
dictionary. "Womb" led him to "uterus" and "vagina" and "placenta"
and into a maze of unfamiliar words through which he groped like
a blindfolded man feeling his way toward the light vaguely sensed
ahead. He had happened upon a trail with many ramifications,
and in spite of his secret feeling that these were things he was not
old enough to know about, he followed on and on. He came to
blind alleys and fumbled his way out of them. The fact that a
word was in the Bible and also in the dictionary gave it, surely, a
measure of respectability; and he remembered other Biblical words,
long familiar, whose meaning he had never sought to know. "Cir-
cumcize," for instance, was in the Bible; to read its definition was
to face new puzzles.

To read the *Journal* began to be as exciting as to walk through
a forest after a fresh snow; for just as the fresh snow was laced with
the trails of wild creatures, so was the *Journal* dotted with strange
words, each of which was the beginning of a mysteriously exciting
trail. There were many such words in the patent medicine advertisements, and in the advertisements of doctors who regularly came
to Hardiston to treat "private diseases." Some of these mysteries
the dictionary solved for him; some, for lack of a key word, remained
obscure.

He began to read every advertisement in the *Journal*, and thus
to live in a world rich with promise. The advertised medicines
were guaranteed to cure almost everything; but Owen could not
put them to the test. Doctor Haines's Golden Specific would cure
the liquor habit; it could be administered in tea or coffee without
the knowledge of the person taking it, and "thousands think they
stopped of their own free will"; but Tom Glen never touched liquor.
Edmund Keros of 2704½ Union Avenue, Chicago, wrote to the
Journal that he had been one mass of scales, afflicted for three years
by dreadful skin and blood disease accompanied by intense pain
and loss of hair, till he began to use Cuticura Remedies; but Tom
Glen's shock of black hair, touched with gray, showed no sign of
falling out, and he was not a mass of scales. There was a standing
reward of $100 for any case of catarrh that Hall's Catarrh Cure
would not cure. Catarrh, according to the dictionary, was something like Tom Glen's trouble in ridding his nose and throat of the
black phlegm that coal dust produced; but Doctor Hall could not

prevent a miner's breathing coal dust. Electric Bitters would convert Dispepsy into Upepsy, but Owen and his father and mother all had excellent digestions. Doctor Fenner's Golden Relief and his Arnica Salve would banish pain in from two to eight minutes, and that might help his father's rheumatism, while Doctor France's Olive Blossom was guaranteed to cure Women's Ills and might be good for his mother when she complained of being all dragged out. Owen considered suggesting these remedies to them, but decided against doing so.

In his new appetite for information he spent much time at the dictionary in the *Journal* office. He persisted until one day, after seeking out the definitions of neuralgia, palpitations, amenorrhea, dsymenorrhea, leucorrhea, debility, ganglia, and a dozen others, he came at the end of Doctor Reynolds's advertisement to a category called "private diseases." He looked up stricture, gleet, gonorrhea, and syphilis, and fell to shivering and shuddering; and this ended for a time his curious delving.

4

When Major McKinley came to speak at the Fair Grounds in Hardiston, Miss Williams suggested that the class might like to hear him. "But I want each of you to write a composition about the speech and bring it to school tomorrow morning." They went to the Fair Grounds together, and Owen threaded the crowd till his chin was almost resting on the floor of the speaker's platform. That night, he worked on his composition till long after his father and mother were asleep. He wrote, in a conscious attempt to imitate Mr. Beecham:

McKINLEY IN HARDISTON

Thursday, October 1st, 1891, will be a day long remembered in Hardiston. The weather was pretty good. Major McKinley was here from ten o'clock on, till he went up the creek to make another speech in Belton. There was a fire alarm when he got up to speak and a lot of the people went to the fire, but there was not any fire only some hay. Men picked some men's pockets and got money in the crowd.

Major McKinley said he was specially glad to speak here because most everybody in the crowd worked and some of them had been in the army with him at that matchless surrender at Appomatox Court House which declared the imperishable unity of the best nation on the face of the earth. He talked about tariff on wire nails because the factory makes them in Hardiston. He talked a long time, and everyone cheered. I would vote for him if I were a man.

BB's account in next week's *Journal* was longer, and full of names. Owen had thought his composition long enough, but probably the people whose names were in the paper would think Mr. Beecham's piece was better.

That glimpse of Major McKinley had made Owen more interested in the coming election. He read BB's column-long explanation of how to vote the new secret ballot patterned after the Australian method, and tried to understand it. The week before election, BB wrote:

Republicans who cannot read or write need not ask the assistance of the Judges in making out their ballots. On looking at the ballot they will see the picture of an eagle in the upper left-hand corner of the picture. Let them make a cross mark (X) in that little square. Let no one stay away from the election because he cannot read.

Owen wondered why Mr. Beecham did not tell people who wanted to vote for the Democrats, or the Prohibitionists, or the People's Party, how to do so; but then he realized that Mr. Beecham was a Republican, so naturally he would not want to help people vote any other way. Then it occurred to him to suggest to Miss Williams that they have an election in school. Miss Williams was delighted, and Owen asked Will Davis to strike off some proofs of the sample ballot which the *Journal* printed every week. On the morning of election day, the boys in the room marked these ballots — girls of course could not vote — and McKinley got seven votes out of the ten.

Owen voted for Mr. McKinley; but with a feeling that to do this showed an attempt at thoughtful discrimination, he distributed his votes for other offices among the four tickets. Major McKinley was elected Governor, and Owen felt himself a part of the triumphant majority; but he was embarrassed, a day or two later, when Miss Williams told him he had marked his ballot improperly.

"You marked so many names that sometimes you voted for two candidates for the same office," she explained. "My Uncle Isaac was an election judge, and I showed him your ballot, and he said it would have been thrown out."

"How did you know it was mine?"

She smiled. "The others all voted the straight ticket, Republican or Democratic; but I saw you make a lot of marks on yours. Did you really have opinions about all the different candidates?"

"Well, no, but I thought there were bound to be some good candidates besides just the Republicans."

"I'm sure there are." She smiled. "BB would say our government is based on parties, and that you only need to vote for the party you prefer; but when women begin to vote, I expect they'll pick and choose just as you did. But Owen, when a man has an opinion and wants to express it, he must know how to express it properly. It isn't enough to think clearly; you must be able to say what you think in such a way that people will understand you."

That was like Mr. Beecham's advice to learn a lot of words and how to use them. "I guess most people vote a straight ticket, maybe just because it's easy," he hazarded.

"Yes," she agreed. "Most men do what's easiest. But if a man — or a boy — wants to follow his own path, he must learn how."

5

Miss Williams, as a teacher, was in almost every way different from Miss Dine. Miss Dine had been lavish with easy praise, but Miss Williams was as quick to reproach poor work as to praise the good. To be kept after school by her was not — as it had been under Miss Dine — a pleasant opportunity to see more of teacher.

But like Miss Dine, Miss Williams seated her pupils in such a way that, as far as was possible boys and girls alternated. Also, the better students were placed in the rear rows, the poorer ones in front. "This is so I can keep my eye on those who need most help," Miss Williams explained. "And also on those who have to be watched. A boy in the front row who wants to throw a paper wad or a spit ball has to turn around to do it, so it's easier for me to catch him." They laughed with her at this, as they often did laugh at her pleasant way of saying things. She had the gift of keeping them interested and attentive; and even when she was at the blackboard with her back to the class, there were few disturbances.

She had more often to discipline girls than boys. The girls were forever passing notes to one another, the missives going from hand to hand till they reached the intended recipient. This had to be done when Miss Williams's back was turned; and usually it required a whispered word of instruction. Miss Williams seemed to have keen ears; she heard the faintest whispers, and thus intercepted many a note in its progress. When she did so, she was apt to require the person who had written the note, or the one who received it, to read it aloud to them all; and this regularly led to guffaws from the class and embarrassment on the part of the culprits.

On one of these occasions, Owen was an indirect victim. The girl on his left, Jane Lloyd, was a year or so older than he, with heavy dark hair that was almost black, and blue eyes; and she was so pretty that Owen liked to watch her, when she was looking elsewhere so that she would not know he was doing so. This day, Miss Williams at the blackboard was diagramming a sentence with some structural complications. "Cheered by the news, of which they had long despaired, the defenders with one accord rushed to the ramparts." Owen was paying strict attention when Jane reached across and laid on his desk a folded slip of paper. He looked at her, and she pointed insistently at the paper, and he saw printed on it: "To Molly."

There was only one Molly in the room. Molly Moury sat three seats toward the front, and across the aisle. Owen obediently passed the note to Janet Frye, his right-hand neighbor; and Janet reached over the shoulder of Morgan Williams, seated in front of her. But Morgan was startled by Janet's hand thus suddenly appearing before his eyes, and he made a sound. Janet dropped the note, and Miss Williams turned around in time to see it flutter to the floor in the aisle beside Morgan's seat.

"Bring it here, Morgan," she directed.

Morgan picked up the note and stumped down the aisle. Miss Williams asked: "Is it yours?"

"No'm."

Miss Williams looked at it. "I see. Molly, it's for you. Take your seat, Morgan." Morgan, glad to escape, dove for his seat; and Miss Williams said: "Molly, come here. Now Molly, I don't like to read other people's mail, but since this note to you has interrupted our class, we'd all like to know what's in it."

Molly took the note and uneasily unfolded it; but when she saw the few words inside, she giggled so that it was some time before she could obey; and she read at last in spasms and explosions: " 'I am going — to invite — Owen — to my party — Jane.' "

Molly was so funny that everyone laughed, at her as much as at the note, and Jane squirmed, and Owen was at the same time frozen with astonishment and red with delicious embarrassment. Miss Williams said gently: "Well, Jane, I'm sure it will be a nice party, and I know you'll all have a good time; but let's plan our parties during recess, not during lessons. Molly, go to your seat." Molly, convulsed with mirth, flung herself down the aisle. She was a roly-poly, fat as butter, and the least excuse was always enough to throw her into paroxysms. Her father was the undertaker who had managed Willie Tutson's funeral; and Owen wondered whether Molly went to funerals, and whether she giggled at them.

Miss Williams said crisply: "Quiet now. We'll go on." That sobered Molly, but till school let out, Owen dared not look at anyone. Probably Jane had not meant what she wrote, or probably she would change her mind; and even if she did invite him, he would not go! The thought of going to any party filled him with fearful longing, but with terror, too. Besides, even if Jane did invite him, he had only his Sunday suit to wear; and it was too short in the sleeves, and the coat was too tight to button, and the pants ended two inches above his knees and they were as snug as the tights worn by acrobats in the circus.

So he could not go to the party, even if he wanted to. He was sure Jane would not invite him; but when the school day ended, and they marched out and broke ranks in the hall, she came to him — everyone watching — and said: "Owen, will you come to my birthday party a week from Saturday night?"

Owen dared not say "yes"; he would not say "no." "I guess so, if I can," he told her.

She smiled beautifully, and whirled to link arms with Molly and march triumphantly away. Owen hurried uptown to the *Journal* office and his work there, feeling light-headed and happily confused and frightened and yet stubborn too.

Before he went home to supper, he had come to a decision. His wages he delivered every week to his mother. The money went into the family purse, where it helped bridge the gap between what Tom Glen earned and what they needed to spend. Tom was a good miner, and he was paid seventy cents a ton for the coal he mined, and he might get out three or four tons a day. But the mine did not work every day, and out of his wages he must buy his tools and equipment and the oil for his lamp, and his powder and squibs, and he must pay for having his tools sharpened. With powder at $2.25 per keg, oil at seventy cents a gallon — Tom's lamp burned about a pint a day — and sharpening tools costing seventy-five cents a month, Tom's net earnings were well below his gross. In an exceptionally good month he earned as much as fifty dollars; but his average — though this was in part the result of his rheumatism — was less than half that figure. The garden helped in summer, Mrs. Glen's chickens helped, the pig they butchered every fall helped, and the money Owen earned in the *Journal* office or by mowing lawns and doing odd jobs helped a great deal.

But Owen's decision today was to ask his mother if he could keep, for a while, the money he earned, and with it buy a new suit of clothes, with long pants! Then the next time he needed a new suit, he would have one. Before he went home, he stopped in Lloyd and Powell's Clothing Emporium to investigate prices. For the suit he liked best, the price was $6.49. He could pay for that, said Mr. Powell, at the rate of a dollar a week. Owen went home nursing the memory of that suit, and for fear his courage would fail, he spoke at once to his mother and told her what he wished to do.

He knew there were no bounds to her love; but he had feared, even if she consented, to see the frown of worry knit her brows. Instead, she smiled in obvious great happiness. "Yes, you can buy a new suit, Owen," she said. "But you won't have to wait to pay. I've been saving up for you, saving a quarter almost every week, every week I could, out of what you brought home." Her eyes suddenly were wet. "For a surprise, sonny. Because you're a real good boy."

She brought down from the shelf behind the stove the huge ball of twine upon which she wound every piece of string which came into the house. It was a big ball, four or five inches in diameter.

"I knew nobody would ever look for it here," she explained, and she began to unwind string from the ball. "You keep the part I unwind straight, Owen," she directed. "So I can wind it back on again." He brought a stick of firewood to serve as a spool, and wound as she unwound. Almost at once he saw a glint of silver between the strands. "I've had to unwind it many a time, and wind it up again, to hide them," she happily explained. "There've been times I've had to borrow from the ball, but I always paid it back soon's I could."

Owen watched in trembling delight as first one quarter, and then another, and then two or three at a time, appeared from the unwinding ball. She piled the quarters in fours. "So there's a dollar in each pile. How'd you happen to decide to get you a new suit, Owen?"

He told her about Jane and the party. "And I'm going, too!"

She looked at him proudly. "Is she nice, Owen?" He nodded, coloring. "Pretty?" He nodded again, and she smiled and paid attention to the twine she was unwinding. "There's twenty-four quarters; that's six dollars," she said. "Almost enough. But you'll want a new shirt, and a tie, and shoes. I'll knit you a pair of socks. And it's her birthday, so you'll want to take her a nice little present. So you'll need a little more."

Owen said conscientiously: "Mama, hadn't you ought to keep this money? Don't you need it? I don't have to go to her old party, or get a new suit, or anything."

She shook her head. "We'll get along. Your father says the United Mine Workers man is coming to talk to operators in Hardiston County, and maybe they'll raise wages; and anyway there's always plenty of work in the winter, long as the rheumatism doesn't lay your father up. No, it's yours, Owen, and you can have it."

As she added another quarter and another till she had seven piles of four each on the table, Owen remembered that he would have two more paydays before the party, and reminded her of this. Since school began, he did not work all day Wednesday, so he earned now only a dollar a week; but two weeks would be two dollars. Six dollars and forty-nine cents for the suit, and a dollar and a quarter for shoes, and fifty cents for a shirt and ten cents for a nice new necktie, and maybe a quarter for a present for Jane; less than nine dollars would be enough, and with two paydays to come, they needed only the seven dollars in quarters already on the table.

When he pointed this out, she rewound the ball of twine. As she finished, Tom Glen came in, and saw the quarters; and Owen felt a quick alarm, but his mother said reassuringly: "Why, papa has helped me save it, Owen! He loves you, same as I do. He wants you to have things." She told her husband: "Owen needs a new suit, Tom."

Tom Glen said amiably: "Guess he's earned it."

So Owen forgot to be dignified, and kissed them both, dancing with happiness, and Mrs. Glen's tears flowed and she wiped her eyes and said: "Well, there, I don't know when I've had a happier time."

Owen bought the new suit next day. The material was a brown, pepper-and-salt pattern; coat, vest, and his first long pants. He decided that to appear in this new guise for the first time at Jane's party might occasion some remark, so next morning he wore the new suit to school. His mother wondered if he had not better keep it for best, but Owen said: "Oh, mama, I can't wear long pants part of the time and short pants part of the time. Besides, I have to sort of get used to it."

He wore it to school that day and the next, and provoked no more than a pleasant amount of laughing comment, and Saturday morning he wore it to work. That was a cold morning, and Owen jog-trotted most of the way to the *Journal* office. It was still half-dark when he got there; and he built roaring fires in the stoves. Will Davis arrived, flapping his arms for warmth; and Owen and Will stood by the pot-bellied stove in the pressroom, now red-hot, putting one foot and then the other up on the fender to warm them. They talked of the weather and of the day's work about to begin, and then Owen smelled something burning and looked down and saw that the right leg of his trousers — his right foot was on the fender, bringing his trousers near the red-hot stove — was black and smoking for several inches below the knee.

He struck at this black spot with his hand and out of the charred trouser leg a section six or seven inches long and three inches wide vanished in dark ashes, leaving Owen's long underwear exposed to view.

In that moment of tragic discovery, BB came in, and saw the damage, and saw Owen's woeful face. "Well, now that's too bad," he exclaimed. "But we can fix it. Will, you lend Owen a pair of your overalls, and I'll take those pants and have them mended."

Owen, white with despair, submitted hopelessly. Obviously, the trousers were ruined beyond repair, and he could not waste money buying new ones. Wearing Will's second-best overalls, the legs turned up, he saw BB fold the trousers over his arm and go out; and he went about his tasks in a stunned wretchedness. Not even the joy of feeding the big press that afternoon could compensate for the morning's catastrophe.

But just before time to go home, BB brought back the trousers. "Mr. Powell's tailor did a good job," he told Owen, showing him the pant leg. "He matched the material, and put one side of the patch right in the crease where it doesn't show, and the other side in the seam. Unless you looked for the patch you'd never notice it."

Owen, reluctant to believe his eyes, saw that this was true; and joy flowed into him again. The new trousers, having suffered and survived, were dearer than before; and also, they were certainly no longer painfully new! He could wear them to the party or anywhere and not feel strange and queer.

6

Except for such relatively dull occasions as Church Sociables or Bean Suppers, where there were more adults than children, this was Owen's first party. The guests were invited for supper, but Owen was not sure what Jane's supper time might be, so he waited across the street from her house and a block away till he saw school-mates by ones and twos begin to arrive. Then he moved nearer, and timed his advance to meet two other boys at the gate. They greeted each other in gruff tones — "H'lo, Bill." "H'lo, Owen." "H'lo, Ed." — and went up the walk together. Bill Myers knocked, and Jane was in the hall to greet them, with her mother and some-one whom Jane called "Aunt May." Jane introduced the boys to Mrs. Lloyd and Aunt May, and they went into the parlor already half-filled with children while Jane opened the door to later arrivals.

Owen had brought Jane a small book of poems, no more than two inches one way and three the other, bound in what looked almost like leather. Miss Williams, at his blushing request for advice, had suggested his choice. The name on the cover was *Sonnets from the Portuguese*.

"They're very beautiful sonnets," Miss Williams had assured him.

"And if Jane isn't quite grown up enough to enjoy them now, she will some day. Or at least she ought to!"

Owen had read two or three of them. They seemed to be about love, and he found them embarrassing, but Miss Williams must know what was right. He saw that Bill and Ed had packages in their hands, so he held fast to his; and he and the other children sat stiffly waiting for things to begin to happen. Two of the girls whispered together and giggled; and then a sudden startled hush fell on them all. Looking cautiously around to discover the cause, Owen saw that Hetty Jenkins, who was the oldest girl in Miss Williams's room and the most mature, and whose mother this year had let down her dresses, had now crossed her legs. Her left ankle rested on her other knee, so her right leg was in full view. The other girls in the room were still in short dresses, and their legs embarrassed no one; but Hetty's legs, since her skirts had been let down, were no longer supposed to be seen.

The shocked silence continued, Hetty apparently unconscious of the cause, till Mrs. Lloyd came in from the hall and said cheerfully: "Now, children, I think it would be nice if we collected all the little gifts you were so nice to bring and kept them for Jane to open after supper."

Everyone was relieved to be rid of these burdens. For supper there was a big table flanked by two small ones, and cards on which their names were neatly written told everyone where to sit. Owen was next to Jane, with Molly on his other side; and when they were seated, Mrs. Lloyd and Aunt May brought in plates heaped with fried chicken and potatoes and beans, and there were hot biscuits and jelly, and after that came frozen custard and an angel-food birthday cake with thirteen candles. Jane, her dark hair tossing, her color high, cut the cake; and they passed their plates, and Mrs. Lloyd and Aunt May watched happily from the doorway.

When dessert was done and the dishes cleared away, Jane opened her presents. Most of the parcels were unmarked, so Jane, unwrapping each one, exclaiming, "Oh how wonderful!" "Oh how nice!" "Oh how sweet!" might ask: "Whose is this? Whose is this?" When she opened Owen's package — he recognized it and waited breathlessly — she cried: "Oh, a book! Poetry! What a cute little book! Who brought it?"

For a moment no one answered, and then Owen, at once proud and miserable, blurted:

"I did!"

"Why, Owen, it's wonderful! Thank you so much!" She passed on to the next gift, and Owen filled his lungs with deep relief. But a moment later Jane's mother came beside her and picked up the book and looked at it and then at Owen and then took it to show Aunt May in the doorway; and Owen felt their eyes upon him, and without looking directly at them he saw Mrs. Lloyd toss her head in the way his mother tossed her head when she was about to say a disapproving: "Well!" He felt perspiration bead his brow. Maybe Miss Williams had been wrong!

After supper, Mrs. Lloyd pinned on the wall a sheet on which was roughly drawn the silhouette of a tail-less donkey; and Morgan Williams, blindfolded, had to take a piece of rope ravelled out like a tail and pin it on the donkey. His hilarious misplacement of the tail, and the equally absurd results of other trials, put them all at ease. Owen saw Mrs. Lloyd and Aunt May nod together as though satisfied with the way things were going and depart to do the dishes.

The game with the donkey's tail somehow turned into *Blind Man's Buff*, whoever was "It" groping around the parlor with outstretched hands, the others scrambling over chairs and sofa and dodging around the table to escape capture; and there were squeals and whispers and sudden shouts when someone was caught. Then they played *Drop the Handkerchief*, and Owen, though he had never played this game, quickly understood the rules. Bill Myers dropped the handkerchief behind Hetty Jenkins, who whirled and caught him and kissed him roundly; and Hetty dropped the handkerchief behind Morgan Williams. He clumsily failed to catch her, and was jeered for his failure. Morgan in turn chose Jane, and she caught Morgan and pecked him on the ear.

Then she started around the circle, and as she passed behind Owen, from the corner of his eye he saw the handkerchief fall to the floor. He snatched up the handkerchief and leaped in pursuit. The parlor floor was covered with matting, on which lay small rugs; and Jane, trying to round the circle, stepped on one of these rugs. It slid under her and she fell, and Owen, too close on her heels to check himself, fell over her. They rolled together in a tangled heap, legs and arms somehow entwined, her hair in his face; and something hot and violent swept through him. When he kissed her, her laughing lips met his.

At the same instant a hand caught his arm in an iron clasp and half-dragged him to his feet, and Owen faced Jane's mother. Jane scrambled up and smoothed her skirts and brushed back her hair, and — still laughing — said: "We fell down, mother."

Mrs. Lloyd held her voice under control. "I think you'd better play some quieter games, Jane. And go fix your hair!" Jane, with a little grimace, dashed away up the stairs; and Mrs. Lloyd looked at Owen and seemed about to speak but changed her mind. "Suppose you all play *Jenkins Up*," she suggested, trying to smile. "Jane will be down in a minute!"

No one else dared speak, but Molly Moury protested: "We can't all sit down at the table, Mrs. Lloyd."

"Well, then — " Mrs. Lloyd looked faintly desperate. "Well, play *Button, Button, Who's Got the Button.*" She saw their silent scorn, and wrung her hands and considered *Tiddledy Winks*, and decided these children were too old for that. "Play something quiet, anyway," she urged. "Something you can play sitting down."

Jane reappeared. "Can we play *Wink*, mama?"

"Oh, Jane, don't you think kissing games are a little silly?"

"No, I think they're fun!" Jane retorted in open defiance.

Mrs. Lloyd looked at her severely. "Well, unless you can think of something sensible to play, I'll have to send you all home. Make up your minds."

She walked stiffly away toward the kitchen; and Jane saw Owen still trembling and shaken, and she came toward him.

"It wasn't your fault, Owen. Don't feel bad."

He nodded, unable to speak, and Molly said: "Jane, I know a game . . ."

So they became stiffly decorous again. They sat in a circle and played Molly's game. This began by someone whispering something into the nearest ear, and the whisper progressed around the circle to the beginning again, and the joke was to see how much the original sentence had changed in its whispered progress. But that soon bored them, and the fun lagged, and after a while Bill Myers said he guessed it was time to go home; and suddenly they were all saying polite goodnights to Mrs. Lloyd and Aunt May, who appeared in time to receive these stiffly formal farewells.

They all went out together, separating at the gate into two groups. Owen was in the group that turned to the right, and from

behind him he heard a teasing sing-song of many young voices.
"Jane's Owen's gir-rul!" "Jane's Owen's gir-rul!" He stuck his hands
in his pockets, grinning happily in the darkness. The boys and girls
in the group with him were politely silent; but as presently by ones
and twos they took their separate ways, from each departure the
sing-song came softly back to him. "Jane's Owen's gir-rul!" Morgan
Williams and Janet Frye were the last; they lived almost next door
to one another, and at Milton Street they turned aside together,
their teasing voices soft in the night, and he took his homeward
course alone. He strolled slowly, kicking at pebbles in the way,
scuffing his feet, warm with content.

Monday morning, a block from school, someone had written on
the sidewalk with a stub of carbon from the arc lights: "Jane's
Owen's girl." He did not care! He had brought an apple, and he
gave it to Jane, and she smiled in beauty and thanked him grate-
fully.

7

After that night of Jane's party, Owen lived in a new world; but
Hardiston went on its customary way. The De Pauw Quartette
gave a concert at the Rink; and a week later came a comedy called
The Two Dans, and the week after, May Smith Robbins in *Little
Trixie,* with an extraordinary versatility, played five different parts.
The fourth-class postmasters in the county voted to ask for higher
pay, work began on the new Masonic Temple, and *Ten Nights in a
Bar Room,* which the advertisements called a pure, moral drama,
played at the Rink.

At home Mrs. Glen was making apple butter, with Allie Jenkins
to help her through the day, keeping the long paddle steadily in
motion, while at night Tom and Owen took their turns. Then came
hog-killing time and Owen helped not only his father but Will
Davis too. Will and Evan Harned killed their hogs together; and
when the pigs were stuck, little Lulu Harned wailed in sympathy,
till Owen took her in his arms for comforting, and her sobs and the
squeals of the pigs ceased together. With hog-killing, spareribs
came in season, and the pork that could not be salted must be eaten
before it spoiled. Owen, after doing his duty to a big rib-roast of

pork baked in beans, was pretty sure that late fall was the best time of the year.

Early in December, Indiana miners struck, and every miner in Hardiston County was asked to give twenty-five cents a week to help support the families of the strikers. Owen contributed to that fund, though his mother said there was no sense in his doing this. "You're not a coal miner, Owen, and if I have any say about it, you never will be."

"I'm working," he insisted. "We're all workingmen, and anything that helps one of us helps all of us."

Tom Glen supported him. "Let him give what he's a mind to, Annie. The miners out in Indiana need help now; but it will be our turn to need help some other time."

Mrs. Glen came down that week with a touch of *La Grippe,* but she refused to stay in bed or to have a doctor and was soon herself again. Others were less fortunate. The *Journal* reported there were over five hundred cases in Hardiston, and a number of elderly people died.

The old year ended. A miner in Slacktown, up the creek, murdered a man in a quarrel over a woman. At recess on the day school began again after Christmas vacation, Freddie Ames pulled one of Jane's pigtails so hard he made her cry. Freddie's father was David Ames, who had proved such slow pay when Owen cut his lawn; and Freddie himself was a gangling youngster two or three years older than Owen, who should have been a class or two ahead. He had twice failed of promotion, so his sister Celia, a full two years younger, had caught up with him and did not let him forget it. Today at recess her sarcastic sneers — she and Freddie were in a group which included Owen and Jane and two or three others — goaded him to a blind frenzy; but if he laid hands on his sister, it meant a licking at home. Lacking any other outlet for his rage, Freddie grabbed Jane's braid and yanked so hard she fell.

Owen, too late to protect her, sprang at Freddie and beat him down in such a raging fury that Freddie, more frightened than hurt, roared aloud. Mr. Atkinson came running out to stop the fight and took them up to the office and paddled them both. He disposed of Freddie first, and sent him snivelling back to his room, and then paddled Owen; but having done so, while Owen submitted in a stony silence, he said severely:

"You'll have to control that temper of yours, Owen. If you don't, one of these days you'll kill someone, like that miner up the creek last week. If I hadn't pulled you off him, you might have killed Freddie."

"I wanted to!" Owen retorted, and for that he was paddled again. He submitted almost indifferently, recognizing that Mr. Atkinson had to do such things as a part of his job.

Early in January, Amy had another baby, a girl; and a week later Dave came to Hardiston to tell them the news. "She's named for you, grandma," he said. "So you'd better come back with me and see her, and I'll put you on the train at Sycamore Hill tomorrow." Mrs. Glen hurried into her best clothes and went with him, leaving Owen and his father to take care of themselves overnight; and she came home next day beaming with happy pride.

The short winter days passed swiftly, the evenings were long. Owen every week read the *Journal* to himself or to his father. BB was urging the nomination of James G. Blaine for President, and of Foraker for Senator. The county last year had paid farmers $996.77 for sheep killed by dogs, and the *Journal* said all dogs running at large should be shot. A sleet storm damaged the orchards in the county, and Governor McKinley spoke at the United Mine Workers' Convention in Columbus, and congratulated the organization on ending the Indiana strike. By the first of February, coal business up the creek was booming. Some operators were advertising for men to mine the needed coal, and Erie Mine was busy too.

Late that month, Owen went one Sunday afternoon for a walk with BB; and they stopped to talk with a farmer named Dean, two of whose children had been bitten by a dog. "I got a madstone," Mr. Dean told BB. "Got it from Elijah Peters, lives up the road a piece. His son sent it to him from Texas, got it from the Indians. I put it on the bite on Dave's leg and it stuck for an hour and twenty minutes; and on little Sal's arm it stuck for an hour and thirty-five minutes, and they was as well as ever, next day."

"Was the dog mad?"

"Certain. I shot it."

"I never heard of a mad dog in February."

"Well this one was. Dogs is no good anyway. There's three or four bands of wild dogs right around here. There've been twenty·

four sheep killed in three miles of my place here, and over sixty more all bit and tore."

"Can't you shoot the dogs?"

"Shot two, but it's easier to just collect from the county."

BB asked in a curious tone: "Why should the county pay for sheep that are killed by dogs, and not for chickens?"

Mr. Dean spat. "Dunno, but long as I keep sheep I hope they do."

As they walked on, BB reminded Owen of this remark. "What did you think of it?"

"How do you mean?"

"Whenever you see a man who expects the county to take care of him, you can be sure he'll never amount to much. Wild dogs destroy sheep, but so do worms destroy apples, and potato bugs destroy potatoes, and lightning destroys houses, and skunks kill chickens. Dean would collect from the county for all those losses if he could. I like to see men help themselves. Look yonder, for instance. There's Evan Foster's new house. Evan's helping himself."

They were approaching the Frisby Mine, and Owen saw two men and a woman nailing flattened powder tins like shingles on the roof of a small house built of new boards. BB stopped to speak to them, and Evan slid to the ground. "Hate to work on Sunday, Mr. Beecham," he said with a smile, "but the mine's running every day, now, and it's all the time I get."

"Better the day, the better the deed, Evan. When a man builds himself a home, it's a sign he's a good citizen and will prosper. You'll be able to make a garden here, too; that will add one third to your income." BB added: "I saw you in Columbus, the day McKinley spoke to the convention."

"Yes, I was a delegate."

"Your new president, Mr. McBride, is an able man."

"Guess he is," Evan agreed. "He was State Commissioner of Labor Statistics till he resigned to take the place."

When BB and Owen presently went on, Owen asked: "Did you go to the United Mine Workers' Convention, Mr. Beecham?"

"Yes, to two sessions. The delegates were a fine lot of men — and every man in the room seemed to know Cushing's *Manual* by heart! By the way, your neighbor, Charles Morgan, took the chair for a

few minutes at one of the sessions. They tell me he's an authority
on parliamentary procedure."

"What does that mean?"

"Well, a parliament is an assemblage of men gathered to discuss
matters in which they have a common interest. You've heard of
parleys?" Owen had not, and BB said: "A parley is a talking-over,
a discussion; and a parliament is a big parley. The British Empire's legislative body is called a parliament, and the French too.
Our Congress is a parliament, and so is our state legislature.

"But when a hundred or two hundred or five hundred men get
together to talk things over, they can't all talk at once; so there
are rules about how such discussions shall be conducted. Ever
hear your father speak of Cushing's *Manual,* or of Robert's *Rules
of Order?*"

"No sir."

"I expect he's studied one or the other, or maybe both. If he
hasn't, Charles Morgan has. Borrow it. Study it. You're old
enough to learn how meetings are run, to learn the rules."

Owen took Mr. Beecham's advice. Tom Glen had once owned
Cushing's *Manual.* "But I lent it to someone and that was the last
of it." So Owen went to Mr. Morgan, who heard his request with
a quizzical half-smile.

"What are you up to, Owen? Going to have a debating team in
school?"

"No sir. I just want to know about meetings and things."

"It's pretty complicated stuff for a boy — or for a man either,
come to that. How old are you, anyway?"

"Twelve and a half."

Mr. Morgan looked at him with thoughtful eyes. "Well, I wish
a few older men would get the same idea." He went to his desk.
"Here, here's Robert's *Rules of Order.* I'll make you a present of it.
If you get stuck, come ask me questions, any time."

During the next weeks, Owen read the small, red-bound book
from cover to cover. In the back, he found advertisements of other
books. One was *The World on Wheels.* There were a dozen high-
wheeled bicycles in Hardiston, and a few of the new safeties.
Morgan Williams's big brother David had a Sterling, "built like a
watch," and as shiny as a sharp knife blade.

Another advertisement described a book called *Masters of the*

Situation; or Some Secrets of Success and Power, and a third advised everyone to read *On in the World; or Hints on Success in Life.* Owen decided that some day he would study all those books; but in the meantime he set himself to read and to memorize and digest this one small volume. It was small enough to fit into his pocket, and yet packed with mysterious precepts. Even the table of Rules Relating to Motions was two pages long, and there was another page of Rules Relating to the Table itself, before you reached the Preface and the Introduction. Owen's mind was for a while a jumble of phrases: Main Motions; Motions and Their Order of Preference; Questions of Privilege; Lie on the Table; Previous Question; Motion to Commit; Questions of Order; Motions to Adjourn. Slowly and painfully he memorized one phrase, and then another, and another, which he believed he understood; and one March afternoon, on his way home to supper, he said aloud to the post which supported the arc light at the corner of Ridge Street: "Mr. Chairman, I move to adjourn!"

The sound of his own voice startled him, and he looked hurriedly all around, relieved to find that there had been no one to hear.

8

That spring was for Owen a procession of bright days. In school from Monday through Friday, Jane sat just across the aisle from him; he could look at her whenever he chose, and without looking at her at all he could feel her gentle presence there. More than once he went after supper to walk past her house, and sometimes he saw her through the window, studying or reading by the lighted lamp. Once when in school they all sang *Juanita,* he looked at her as he sang the tender words, and her eyes met his and she smiled and they sang together: "Lean thou on my heart."

His was a completely undemanding devotion, and it was wholly of the present. Even in his most secret thoughts his adoration did not look into the future. He never dreamed of telling her his love, of hearing words of love from her; certainly he never looked ahead to the time when they would both be grown up, never thought: "Some day we will be married." Twice or thrice he brought her apples, once a stick of candy, and once in March a small bouquet of arbutus; but he usually delivered these gifts secretly, taking care to reach his desk before she reached hers, watching his chance to lift the lid of her desk and drop his gift into the space below where she kept her pencils and books and pads. When she came to her desk he waited, hardly breathing, till the moment when she lifted the lid and found his gift; he listened for her soft happy whisper: "Thank you, Owen," and met her eyes and her smile. The day he brought the arbutus, she sniffed its fragrance in delight, and pinned the little cluster of flowers on her dress and wore it proudly.

His hours in the *Journal* office were equally contenting, except for one circumstance. Nellie Tutson sometimes came there, pretending that she came to see her cousin Edna; but if Owen were setting type in the loft, she always tried to talk to him, leaning against the type case beside him, picking up pieces of type and putting them back in the wrong boxes, getting in his way, pressing against him, plaguing him. "I don't ever get to see you since I quit going to school, unless I come here. You don't ever come past the house any more, or down to the mine."

"I'm too busy." He spoke sullenly, pretending industry. "Move over. Your arm's in my way."

"I have to stay home, mostly. Papa's been awful upset since he killed Willie, and if mama can't handle him sometimes I can help."

He did not want to talk to her, but he remembered wondering at the funeral how Mr. Tutson felt about killing his little boy, and fearful interest prompted him. "What does he do?"

"Oh, acts kind of crazy. Seems like taking a strap to me does him more good than anything; but when I see that coming, I get out of the house. I hide in Willie's cave. Papa's scared to go there." She smiled teasingly. "Same as you are. It's bigger now. You come down some day and let me show you."

"What's he scared of?"

"Scared Willie'll be there."

Owen grunted scornfully; but he felt the prickling of his back hair.

Nellie came to the office one day with John Carver. They climbed the outside stairs to the loft, and John began at once to talk in low tones to Edna, while Nellie stood beside Owen, putting her arm across his shoulders, laughing when he squirmed away. "Ain't you

glad to see me, Owen? I guess I'm about the oldest friend you've
got in Hardiston. Remember?" He pretended not to hear, his eyes
on his copy, working steadily; but he felt his cheeks burn, and
hated Nellie for reminding him of that day in the barn. "Remember, Owen?" she insisted.

He laid down his stick and slid from his stool and fled to the
pressroom, where she could not — or at least did not — follow him;
but she came on other days, and often, when Erie Mine did not
work, John Carver came with her. Bets, who was always so good-
natured with everyone else, seemed to be angry whenever John
came to talk with Edna, and Edna obviously did not like John. She
continued to work all the time he was there, giving him an occasional brief word. Owen wondered why a man as nice as John
had anything to do with her.

One Saturday morning, Owen was putting a new tympan on the
job press when he saw John pass through the alley toward the outside stair and go up to the loft. For a while, he heard an occasional word from Edna and the faint murmur of John's voice, till
at last Edna said in a louder, sharply angry tone:

"I'm not your girl!" John murmured something Owen could not
hear, and Edna exclaimed: "Well, I'm not any more!"

After a few minutes, while Owen was washing his hands and
preparing to go to dinner, John went through the alley to the street;
and when Owen started home, he saw John standing on the corner
outside the Flagg House, half a block ahead. As Owen came
nearer, John walked out into the middle of the street where Main
and Broad intersected and stood waiting for a farmer's wagon to
pass. When it was gone, he suddenly knelt down there in the
middle of the street, still muddy from the passage of the sprinkling
cart. Owen thought he must be drunk, but then John drew something shiny out of his pocket and put it against his head; and just
as Owen realized that the shiny thing was a revolver, he heard the
shot. John fell over on his side in the muddy street, and people
ran toward him from all directions.

Owen ran, too, and a crowd pressed quickly around, everyone
asking why, why, why? Marshal Henson, summoned from his
barbershop, came to take charge; and he and two other men carried
John's body down to Mr. Moury's undertaking parlors. Owen and
other boys and men crowded in after them, and the Marshal began
to take everything out of John's pockets.

Among these things was a cheap watch, and when Bob Henson opened the case, it was to reveal a little curl of brown hair. That set everyone talking again. "Who?" "Who?" "Why?"

Owen was as bewildered as the others and the mystery was still a mystery Monday. Then on their way to school, Owen and Morgan Williams and Bill Myers were talking about it. Owen was half a hero because he had seen the tragedy, and he had seen that lock of hair.

"But nobody knows whose it was," he said. "Or why John did it or anything."

Someone behind him said gloatingly: "I know!" He turned and saw Nellie Tutson. "I know whose it was!"

Morgan Williams told her scornfully: "I bet you don't!"

"I bet I do!" Nellie was all triumphant. "It was mine! He thought it was Edna's. He was in love with her, and he asked me to get him some of her hair and he'd pay me a dollar. I gave him some of mine, instead, and he didn't know the difference!"

They were startled into silence, and she giggled and walked away, her hips swinging, her hand touching her hair. Then the school bell rang to call them in. Owen, without knowing why, felt stained and unclean, as though he had fallen into mire. When Jane came to her seat across from him, he did not look at her but sat with lowered eyes, miserable and ashamed.

VI

March 1892 — *Christmas* 1892

F OR A YEAR or two, since the night Amy was married and he heard
Pete Radford's leering word, Owen had tried to shut his mind to
the fact that adults were moved by mysterious impulses to mysterious actions. Familiar as a country-reared child must be with
the physical behavior of animals, he had revolted at Pete's suggestion that Amy and Dave might act in like ways, but he would not
have hated Pete so much had he not secretly realized that the other
was right.

Yet this was a knowledge he fought against accepting, even
while he began to observe in himself evidences that it was true.
He remembered from his babyhood the warm happiness of being in
his mother's arms, of sleeping with Amy and even of sleeping in the
same room where Amy and Miss Williams were in bed together.
To see Miss Dine's pretty leg produced in him a sensation pleasantly akin to that baby pleasure; and he was ashamed of this, thinking that he must be disgracefully different from other boys. When
his glimpse of Nellie Tutson that day in the haymow affected him
in the same way, this seemed to him to prove that he was right to
be ashamed.

As he grew older, he found that this feeling in himself might be
provoked in strange, unrelated ways. Once a theatrical company
came to town and posted on the billboard at the hotel corner a
lithograph of a beautiful woman, and someone spat tobacco juice
on the bare shoulders of the woman in the picture. When he saw
that stain, Owen felt this same mysterious provocation. To wrestle
with Morgan Williams or some other boy, to hear from Mr. Atkinson's office the smack of the paddle as the Superintendent punished
some unfortunate and the culprit's cries, to see Bets clap her hand

against Edna's hip as she passed the other's high stool, to feel the roughness of the blanket under which he slept in winter, to see men marching in steady rhythm, to be near a church when the bell suddenly began to ring close overhead — there were dozens of these stimuli, any one of which might thus affect him. That moment when, playing *Drop the Handkerchief*, he fell over Jane Lloyd and kissed her remained pure beauty in his memories; but there was a similarity in all these secret emotions, proving they were akin. His mind and body, during these years of adolescence, were so intensely alive that every sight or sound or touch or thought was in one way or another an excitation. This extreme sensitivity was almost painful; it made him wish to shout, to run, to laugh, to sing, to stand on his head, to do something new and spectacular and violent which would let out all the exuberance within him.

When John Carver shot himself, and Owen knew it was because of Edna, he recognized that this tragedy, like the disgrace of Miss Dine and Mr. Freeland, was a part of the same universal mystery; and he began to admit in himself a tremendous and overwhelming curiosity. His mother kept a few chickens to supplement their meagre table; and long ago he had observed that roosters sometimes chased hens and held them down on the ground, and had asked his mother why. She said they were fighting; but now Owen began to be sure this was not so, and that what the rooster did to the hen was like what a bull did to cows. One day when his mother had gone to spend an hour or so with Mrs. Lewis, he caught a rooster, and later a hen, and examined them in an unsuccessful attempt to find out what they had been doing, and how. When he read in the *Journal* that Ben Willis, Jr., the well-known stallion, would make this season of 1892 at the home of Neil Palmer, a mile or two out the Pike, he haunted the spot till one day he watched the stallion brought to a mare. Mr. Palmer saw him watching and called to him to come nearer, but at the summons he fled in guilty terror.

To watch the stallion revived in him his interest in horses and in stables. Tom Lovering's livery stable was on an alley through which he could go from school to the *Journal* office; and he began to take that route, lingering as he passed the wide doors to see what was happening inside, or to catch fragments of conversation among the men idling there and try to understand.

At recess, boys his age and older and younger might gather in the enclosure surrounded by a high board fence where the school privies were, and even though he understood little of their snickering talk, to listen was exciting, making him tremble and grow hot and go uneasily back into school.

Sometimes these boys spoke of Nellie Tutson — though they called her Nell — and they often talked about other girls whom Owen knew only by name, girls in higher classes in the school. Their talk clung so closely to a single theme that Owen could not fail in the end to understand them; yet in his understanding there were many gaps, and he turned to the dictionary in the *Journal* office. Sometimes he gathered thus a grain of fact, but more often the word he sought was not in the dictionary, or if it were there it did not mean what the boys seemed to mean. There was, for instance, no such word as "hore," and "hoar" just meant "gray," or it was a kind of frost; so Owen could not understand why they referred to Nellie, or to any other girl, as a hoar.

He was hungry for knowledge, but he could not bring himself to question the other boys; and obviously, he could not ask questions of Mr. Beecham, who probably did not even know about such shameful matters. Mr. Beecham was interested in more important things, such as the proposal to build a streetcar line from Belton through Glendale and Slacktown to Hardiston, or when a coal miner at Glendale was killed by the delayed explosion of a powder charge, or when a Belton boy was run over by a train, or when little Mattie Owens tried to climb through a window into the Long Branch schoolhouse and the sash fell on her neck and held her hanging till she was dead. BB was forever reminding his readers in the *Journal* that silver was down to eighty-six cents an ounce; the Free Silver advocates, he said, were trying to make everyone accept a dollar which wasn't worth a dollar. Owen felt sure that a man whose thoughts centered on such presumably important things as these could not be expected to answer questions about what profane men said in stables, and what no-account boys talked about in privies.

In May, his mind found new matter on which to feed, for the *Journal* began to publish each week installments of a novel called *The Scarlet Letter*. Owen read the first passages in a puzzled absorption. He understood that the letter on Hester Prynne's dress was a mark of shame and, in some fashion not at once clear to him, so was the baby in her arms. When in the next week's *Journal* she refused to name the baby's father, Owen guessed that the father was the minister, Arthur Dimmesdale. But if they were married, why did she not say so? A week later it turned out that they were not married, for her husband, Roger Chillingworth, came on the scene. Theirs, said the novel, had been a loveless marriage, and this seemed to mean that Mr. Chillingworth was not the baby's father. Owen wondered if people had to love each other in order to have a baby. Was it possible that love was what the stallion, Ben Willis, Jr., did to the mare? Had the minister thus loved Hester Prynne?

Whatever the minister had done, the interminable chapters of the novel made clear that it was wrong; but, and this was most confusing, the man who wrote about Hester obviously thought she was good, and blamed the people who punished her, and did not blame her for the baby.

The novel became increasingly tedious, and eventually Owen stopped reading it; but he thought about it for a long time. He imagined Hester Prynne sometimes as looking like Miss Dine, and sometimes as looking like Nellie Tutson. Mr. Dimmesdale certainly was not like Mr. Freeland, but perhaps he was like John Carver. Owen remembered that Mr. Dine said Mr. Freeland had got Miss Dine in trouble. Did that mean Miss Dine had a baby? Must she always wear the letter "A" on her dress?

And why that particular letter, why "A"?

Once he dreamed about Miss Dine, with a baby in her arms and the letter "A" on her dress; and in his dream she was kneeling in the middle of the muddy street, and suddenly she was John Carver holding a revolver, and Owen shouted to John; and he woke to his mother's call from the next room.

"Owen! Owen, wake up! You're having a nightmare."

Because John had killed himself on her account, Edna Tutson acquired in Owen's eye a new character. He had always disliked her, but now he became afraid of her as well, and his thoughts were full of fearful questions. Was she a witch, one of those women his mother used to tell him about when he was a little boy, women in the old country who could turn themselves into rabbits, and who ran about making cows and sheep sick, and led men to their deaths in horrid bogs? Unless she were a witch, how could she make a

fine man like John Carver give up his great dreams of becoming a
school teacher, and of going to college, and of learning to be a lawyer,
and shoot himself in the middle of the muddy street. When, setting
type, Owen perched on the high stool beside hers, he was intensely
conscious of her there so near him. Somewhere in her lay danger,
a danger he could not understand.

He thought Bets was afraid of Edna, too, for Bets was suddenly
gentle to the other girl, and sometimes she brought flowers and set
them in a glass where Edna could see them as she worked; and once
Owen, coming upstairs a moment after they had arrived for work —
his bare feet were soundless on the treads — found them embracing.
He had never thought Edna liked Bets, yet she was hugging Bets
hard and tight.

Then Bets saw him on the stairs and pushed Edna away and
said angrily: "Owen, after this, you cough when you sneak upstairs, or I'll box your big ears for you." She was flushed and hot,
and he thought she was frightened too. Grown people did many
things he could not understand.

One day on his way to the *Journal* office after school, he overtook
and passed Adelina Fortune, that bedizened little old woman who
met the down train every afternoon and who always walked alone.
As he passed her, she was talking to herself; and he caught the
words:

"Dear John."

He stopped and turned to face her, astonished and inquiring.
"John Carver, ma'am?"

"Dear John went to Cincinnati," she said. "But he'll be back on
the afternoon train. I must be ready for him." She went on past
Owen, nodding and whispering, and he followed, wondering about
her.

At the office he found BB alone; and he asked: "Mr. Beecham,
what makes Adelina Fortune the way she is?"

BB hesitated; he said in a sympathetic tone: "Not many people
know this, Owen, and you'd better not repeat it. John Fortune was
a Hardiston man; he went to the war, and brought home a Southern
bride. I've been told she was a lovely girl. When their baby was
born, it was a Negro. Fortune took it away, two or three days after
it was born, and he never came back. No one knew why he had
gone, no one knew the baby was a Negro, no one but the doctor
and the woman who helped the doctor when the baby was born.

Mrs. Fortune told everyone he had gone to Cincinnati on business, and she began to meet the afternoon train — he would come home on that train if he ever came — and she's been the way she is now for over twenty years."

John Carver killed himself because he loved Edna, and poor Mrs. Fortune went crazy because her beloved husband left her. Love was a dangerous and deadly thing.

2

The coal trade was slack that spring, and not many Hardiston County mines ran as much as half-time; but as long as Union Furnace was in blast, work at Erie was more regular than elsewhere. When one Monday evening in May Tom Glen announced that he would not work next day, Mrs. Glen asked sharply:

"And why not? Won't the mine run?"

"Yes. But John Nugent's called a mass meeting in Slacktown, and I'm going."

"John Nugent? Wasn't it him that said you were under scale last year? And you called him every name you could curl your tongue around?"

"He's state president now," Tom told her. "He's come to organize a sub-district. I'm secretary of Erie local, so it's my job to go and report what they do."

"Oh it is, is it? And who pays your train fare? Not the local, I'll be bound. And who mines your coal while you're gone. There's three dollars and fifteen cents we owe Mr. McAuliffe down 't the store. You might just stop in and pay that on your way to the train."

"Now, Annie, be easy," he said, mild yet firm. "It's my job and I'll do it, talk all you want."

"Talk, is it? You're a fine one to talk about talking. I suppose you'll talk yourself out of a job again before you're done." She rose and began to clear the table, fuming in an undertone; and Tom got up and went to her and put his arm around her, chuckling.

"Sputter, sputter, sputter, mama!" He kissed her cheek, and Owen saw her for a moment yield and press against him. "If you were a teakettle you'd keep the lid dancing!"

"Go on with you." She freed herself. "I ought to know by now it's no good trying to stop you when you're set on doing something."

Tom went next day to Slacktown, and Wednesday he took the train to Belton to attend the convention called by President Nugent. Owen that week saw his father in a new character. For one thing, Tom wore his Sunday suit, and for him to be thus soberly clad on a weekday was strange enough; but also he carried his head higher, with a more alert eye and a different tone in his voice, and he came home Tuesday and again on Wednesday a little flushed, talking more loudly and more rapidly than usual.

He told them all that had happened. The convention set up a sub-district to include Hardiston and Clinton Counties and a part of another. "Thomas Jones will be president," he explained. "Eben Howell — he lives in Belton — is vice-president; and old Matthew Price is secretary-treasurer. You've seen him at church, mama."

"That old man! He don't look strong enough to hold a pen, much less a pick."

"He's not a miner now, too feeble; but he was for fifty years. Tom Jones is a Clinton County man."

Owen was interested in these matters, not for their own sake, but because of his father's interest; but he, too, had news to report; and when Tom Glen had told all there was to tell, Owen had his chance. "Papa, the circus is coming Monday, and Mr. Beecham gave me three tickets for all of us."

"Guess I'll be working Monday, son," Tom said, with a sidelong glance at Mrs. Glen.

"Oh, the tickets are for the night," Owen explained. "I knew you couldn't go in the afternoon."

"I don't know as you ought to stay up all hours of the night that way, Owen," his mother said doubtfully; but Tom Glen protested:

"Sho, once won't hurt him. We'll all go."

And they did. Owen was absorbed, but once or twice he heard his mother utter an angry ejaculation, and say to his father: "Hussies! Might as well be nekkid!" So he understood that she was shocked because some of the lady riders and acrobats wore tights; but till then he had hardly noticed this fact, and he wondered why it was that till his mother spoke of them he had not thought about the legs of the circus ladies.

May was a stormy month. A heavy rain gullied the streets, and a wind and rain storm with thunder and lightning blew down some trees and branches and damaged roofs and chimneys. Mr. Beecham took the gullied streets as text for a full column urging that Main and Broad Streets be paved with fire brick; he printed letters from nearby cities quoting the cost of such paving. What the *Journal* described as "part of a baby's body" was found in a disused well in Belton, and Owen asked Mr. Beecham how it got there. BB said: "I'm afraid its mother didn't want it, Owen." His tone discouraged any further question, but Owen added this incident to the mosaic of enigmas which slowly fell into a pattern in his mind. School closed, and at the Commencement Exercises in the Rink, there were fourteen graduates. All but two were girls, for while the lower classes in Hardiston schools might include twenty-five or thirty children, most boys stopped before High School. At the Commencement, while one of the girls was reciting a composition, older boys in the gallery whistled and laughed; and BB in his account of the exercises said the "young savages" in the gallery should in the future be excluded. Owen knew why those boys made a noise while that particular girl was speaking. Her name was Jen England, and he had heard them talk about her in the enclosure around the school privies; but he did not enlighten Mr. Beecham. Madame Goff, seventh daughter of a seventh son, and who had been born under a caul, spent a week at the Flagg House telling fortunes and teaching hand-painting and embroidery; and June days sped. President Harrison was renominated at Minneapolis.

At the end of June, BB took Mrs. Beecham and the children to visit relatives in West Virginia. They had all gone to Mississippi last winter to spend Christmas with Mrs. Beecham's family there; and BB often went to Columbus or to Cincinnati for a day or two at a time. Hardiston people liked to travel. In the *Journal* almost every week there were items reporting that So-and-So had gone to New York, or to Boston, or to St. Louis, or to San Francisco, or even to Europe. Owen read these paragraphs with an envious longing, wishing he, too, might go to faraway cities; and once he had confessed this to Mr. Beecham, and the editor said:

"That's a good ambition to hold on to, Owen. Make it come true when you can. A man's mind is enlarged by travel. To live narrowly, in a narrow sphere, confines the mind just as the skull confines the brain. Of course, too many Americans go to Europe when they travel, instead of learning more about their own country.

They're like children always wanting to go over in someone else's yard to play, instead of enjoying their own yard. But that's because this is still a young country. As countries go, you know, the United States is no older than you are."

"I'll be thirteen in November."

"Exactly!" BB chuckled. "As nations go, the United States is just about thirteen."

During Mr. Beecham's brief absences, Will was editor as well as foreman; and this time, since school was over for the year, Owen spent every day in the office. BB returned from West Virginia the Friday after the Fourth, stopping at the office before going home, and Owen listened while Will reported all that had happened during the editor's absence. When business was out of the way, Will said:

"We expected you back Tuesday."

"I stayed longer than I expected. I went to Homestead."

"Did you so?" Will's tone was quick with interest. "See the battle?"

"I saw a good many things."

Owen asked: "What battle, Mr. Beecham?"

"You don't read the dailies?"

"No sir."

"You'd better," BB said. "Every day is history, you know; and the dailies record that history. Here." There was on his desk an accumulated pile of exchanges, and he sorted out half a dozen Columbus and Cincinnati papers. "Take them home with you." And he explained, talking rather to Owen than to Will: "There's a strike in the Homestead Mills, the Carnegie Steel Company. The company has been making a lot of money, but here two or three weeks ago they decided to reduce wages, and the men refused to accept the reduction. So Mr. Frick — he's the man who runs the company — closed the plant and sent for three hundred Pinkertons. They . . ."

Owen interrupted. "What are Pinkertons?"

"Men employed by the Pinkerton Detective Agency. They're like policemen, except that instead of working for towns and cities, they work for private individuals." He caught Will's eye and smiled faintly. "Ask your father about them."

"He'll admire to tell you," Will dryly predicted, and Mr. Beecham repeated:

"So Mr. Frick sent for three hundred Pinkertons. He had put up a high wooden fence around the plant, with barbed wire on top of it, and people were calling it 'Fort Frick.' Before the Pinkertons got there, the strikers broke down the fence and took charge of the plant; and when the Pinkertons came down the river, the men fought to keep them from landing."

"And captured the lot of them," Will exclaimed.

Mr. Beecham said in mild reproof: "Will, you know all this, but Owen doesn't. The men had guns, and even a cannon, Owen; and they used dynamite. A good many were killed on both sides, and the Pinkertons finally had to surrender. They were made to run the gantlet of the crowd after they surrendered, and there are about thirty of them in the hospital — as well as several dead."

Owen's blood was racing, his hands and arms and cheeks were tingling. "The men licked them!"

BB nodded slowly. "But the men will be licked in the end. Soldiers will come to guard the plant; and the company can afford to be idle for months, or for years if necessary. The men can't. They'll lose out in the end."

"But they did lick them."

"That was a bad mistake," BB insisted. "It turned public feeling against the men. There was danger for a while of a wholesale massacre."

"I wish they'd killed them!"

BB spoke in gentle tones. "A civilized man doesn't kill another man. Fighting with fists is the sort of thing boys do, just as fighting wars is the sort of thing nations do in the process of growing up; but when boys become intelligent men, they settle differences without violence."

"I'd have killed them, all the same!"

"That's because you're still a boy, Owen."

Owen was silenced; but when he read to his father the accounts of the battle in the papers BB had given him, Tom Glen was as angry as Owen had been, and as near profanity as Owen had ever heard him. "They ought to have killed the last one of them," he cried. "Pinks! They're a lot of thugs and burners and murderers that hire out to murder decent workingmen. They do it for money! Yes, and they make trouble so they'll be hired to stop it. Back here six-seven years ago in the Hocking strike, the operators hired nine hundred Pinks, and then, when they were sure the strike was

beaten, they laid off five hundred of them; but the bloody-handed
Pinks set fire to a car of coal in a Straitsville mine — the mine's
burning yet — just so the ops would have to hire them back to keep
them from setting any more fires! There never was a Pink that the
world wouldn't be better off if he was dead!"

His father's anger, instead of sharpening Owen's, somehow
sobered him. He quoted Mr. Beecham as deploring the battle, but
Tom cried furiously: "Him? He's always saying Blaine's a great
man, but Blaine owned some of those Hocking Valley mines. Mr.
Beecham talks calm enough, but nobody's cutting down his pay and
starving his children!"

Mrs. Glen said sharply: "There, Tom, stop your wild talk and
come to supper. There's pork chops enough so you and Owen
won't starve tonight, anyway!"

Tom at table continued to talk, with no abatement of his anger;
and Owen, listening to his father, realizing that Tom Glen in his
wrath said many things he did not mean, came to agree with Mr.
Beecham and to think his father wrong. Those strikers in Homestead would go hungry, and so would their families, and yet
eventually they must yield. Certainly, if the summer was a slack
season for steelmakers as it was for coal mines, the steel men were
foolish to strike in July. Men who wanted to strike should wait for
a season when their employers needed them. The time to strike was
when you could afford to be idle, and when the men who owned
the mines or the factories where you worked could not.

This was so obvious that when the thought first took shape it
did not much impress him; but after he had gone to bed it recurred.
He could not remember that he had ever heard anyone say anything like it. Men must have said it time and time again, but not
to him; he had thought it up himself. A deep excitement stirred
in him. He had thought of his brain as something with which to
study and to learn and to remember; that it could also be used to
create was like a revelation. He lay long awake, wide-eyed in a
sort of wonder.

3

During BB's absence, Will in his capacity as editor had filled the
paper with matter BB had written in advance, but he added many
items of his own. In his account of the Fourth of July celebration,

he described the bicycle races, the horse races, the baseball game; and he concluded: "Two hundred and fifty kegs of beer were used up during the day, and there were a lot of used-up men."

Saturday, BB came back to the pressroom to laugh with Will and Owen over this, and to add: "You did a good job, Will."

"Well, did the best I could. Owen was a help. He took a pile of work off my hands."

"That's fine, Owen. I'll have to give you a bonus." Something quizzical in his tone BB asked: "Which would you rather have, a twenty-five-cent raise or a two-dollar bonus?"

Owen did not hesitate. In eight weeks he would earn the two-dollar bonus, but the extra quarter would go on forever. BB applauded his choice. "Right. There's an old saying that a bird in the hand is worth two in the bush, but that's not true. If you leave the two birds in the bush to raise a family, they'll provide you with a good many birds in the hand." He looked at Will and laughed. "If voters realized that, they wouldn't be so easily fooled by politicians who make big promises."

Monday morning, Owen went as usual to sweep out the office; and after his morning tasks were done, he walked out to Mr. Beecham's home to mow the lawn. He brought the lawnmower from the shed behind the house and began by going entirely around the house close to the foundation; but when he reached the back porch, BB was there to speak to him.

"You'd better not mow the lawn today. Our little baby's sick, and the noise might bother her." Owen, seeing his reddened eyes and his pale, drawn lips, was full of sympathy for which he found no words. BB added, as though speaking by rote: "She was a little upset Saturday, and she got worse yesterday."

Owen picked up the lawnmower — since to push it would rouse its clattering voice — and carried it back to the shed. He thought Will Davis ought to know about Mr. Beecham's baby, so he returned to the *Journal* office, and told Will the baby was sick, and said he wished he could do something.

"Well, why don't you stay on here and help me?" Will suggested. "The way you did while he was away."

Owen agreed. "But don't tell him I did. He'd think he had to pay me, or give me another raise."

Late that afternoon BB came to the office with a sheaf of manuscript. "I'll have some more ready tomorrow," he promised. So on the way to work next morning, Will stopped at the house. When he reached the office, he told Owen the little girl was still pretty sick.

"BB says she can't hold anything down, getting weaker all the time."

He and Owen went about their work in silence. The *Journal* must go to press tomorrow. BB had given Will a long letter from a farmer who remembered the Morgan raid and who wrote a column and a half about it, an extensive account of Children's Day at the Christian Church signed "Contributor," a printed program of the Hardiston County Fair to be held next week, and a notice about the new time-table on the Ohio Southern. This material would take care of the front page, and the back page would accommodate the correspondence from localities in the southern part of the county. Page four could be filled with boiler plate; but Will was worried about page three, usually given over to editorials. When he left the office that afternoon, he told Owen: "I'll have to see if I can get something from BB for that." Wednesday morning he brought a four-column history of the Methodist Church in Hardiston, written by the Reverend Mr. Drum. "BB was saving it till some time when he had room," he explained. "It will take care of page three; but it'll take the girls all day to set it."

"How's the baby?"

"Worse."

"I can help set this about the church."

"I guess I can do it faster than you. You get the press and the folder ready, and fill the ink trough, and grease the press, and keep an eye on the office while I'm upstairs."

So Owen that morning did double duty. Two or three farmers came in to pay their subscriptions, and a dozen men and women stopped to ask how the baby was. Owen wrote out the occasional items they gave him and sent them up to the type loft: So-and-So is visiting her sister, Mrs. So-and-So; Mr. So-and-So, the well-known farmer of Albion Township, paid us a call last week; Mr. So-and-So of Adams reports heavy showers last Monday in his neighborhood. To put these paragraphs into acceptable form was a simple matter of finding a suitable model in last week's *Journal* and substituting new names for old.

In mid-afternoon, Will came down to make up page four, and

from the composing stone he could keep an eye on the office, so Owen went up to pull proofs and — since BB was not here to do it — to read them for typographical errors. Not till supper time were they ready to go to press, and it was nearly midnight before Will and Owen locked the office and started home.

Will's way led past BB's house, and although to do so meant for him half a mile or more of extra walking, Owen went with Will, hoping to hear good news. As they came near the house, they saw windows still lighted, and at the foot of the steps they paused uncertainly. Then a dark figure, moving slowly, halted at the top of the steps above them; and after a moment, as though answering an unasked question, Will spoke.

"It's me, BB. Me and Owen. The paper's out and all mailed."

BB said huskily: "Thank you, boys." Then he added in a low tone: "Our baby died just about dark." He spoke very carefully, as though his words were important. "Doctor Gorman called it cholera infantum."

Owen gulped hard, and his eyes streamed tears. Will coughed. "Guess you'd better get some sleep, BB."

"I guess so. Goodnight, now."

BB came back to the office Friday. He was always so ready with a smile and a cheerful word that it was hard to see him now grave and silent. Tomorrow, he said, they would take the baby down to Sardis Church. "It's my mother's family's old burying ground," he explained.

So he was away all day Saturday, and Owen and Will between them kept the office and met the many visitors whom Saturday always brought to town. Monday, when BB returned to the office again, things seemed to Owen little changed.

4

Columbus and Cincinnati dailies came every day to the *Journal* office, and with BB's permission Owen that summer regularly took at least one paper home. He read aloud to his father every word that dealt with the Homestead strike. BB rarely mentioned the strike in the *Journal*. "The sooner the men accept defeat, the better," he said, when Owen asked his reason. "By fighting the battle of the sixth of July, they lost the sympathy of law-abiding people; and they forced the Government to take sides against them. I sympathize with them, but they're beaten, and to print anything about their strike will only help prolong the agony."

Owen was accustomed to accept as gospel anything Mr. Beecham said; but now his color rose. "Don't they deserve to win?" he challenged.

"The company can afford to pay them more money, yes; in that sense they deserve to win. But they were wrong to seize possession of the plant, and wrong to fight the Pinkertons; not just morally wrong but also tactically wrong. What they did was not only a crime, it was a blunder. A man named Talleyrand said that, and it's true. When the leaders of the men let violence start, they committed a fatal blunder — and lost the strike."

"Seeing the Pinkertons made them mad, and when you're mad you want to fight."

"It's a poor way to win."

"How can you win if you don't fight?"

"Get the other fellow mad," BB assured him. "Get him mad enough and he'll make the blunder."

So the *Journal* concentrated on local news, reporting the mild smallpox epidemic which came to Hardiston almost every summer, the Street Fair when two alligators escaped and one was later captured in a Hardiston hen yard, the personally conducted excursions to Niagara Falls, the heat wave when the mercury touched 107, the Bean Dinners and Church Socials, the storm of lightning which killed two men and stunned five others, the death of a man — and of another a week later — who sat down on the railroad track near Belton and stayed there till the train hit them.

"Didn't they hear it coming?" Owen asked; and BB said:

"I suppose they were drunk. The saloonkeeper who made them drunk murdered them."

"Why don't they shut up all the saloons? They don't do any good."

BB said thoughtfully: "I'm not so sure. If they were altogether bad, they would have disappeared long ago. I sometimes suspect that the saloon survives because of the good in it."

Bets had a week's vacation that summer, and Edna too; and while each was gone Owen took her place in the office. He set type,

as they did, on space rates; and when BB measured his proofs at the
end of the week of Bets's absence, he said approvingly: "See here,
you're pretty fast. You've earned as much as Edna — yes, twenty
cents more than she did." The week after, when Edna was away,
Owen drove himself to top speed and beat his previous record; but
Bets, though she never seemed to hurry, outstripped him by a
margin of more than a dollar.

Summer took its sultry way. The entry of Erie Mine caved in,
and while no one was hurt, the mine shut down; so Tom Glen was
idle for a while, with more time to think about the Homestead
strike, and to brood and rage. Twice that summer, he and every
worker in Erie Mine had contributed a day's earnings to help the
strikers, and Owen gave a week's wage. When an anarchist shot
and gravely wounded Henry Clay Frick, BB, whose foremost interest was always politics, commented in the *Journal*:

> *No matter where his sympathies lie, every man con-
> demns the murderous attack. But it should be remarked
> that there are no Republicans involved in the Homestead
> strike. Mr. Frick, as well as the commanders of the militia
> there, are democrats.*

Owen that summer read every new dispatch from Homestead;
he was intensely partisan, his youthful zeal nursed and nurtured by
Tom Glen's steady anger. Owen often heard his father discuss the
strike with other miners; he saw that each one felt that the failure
of the strike would be a blow at himself, and once he spoke of this
to his father.

"Aye," Tom Glen agreed. "It's in the heart of every man that
works with his hands, Owen; the knowledge that an injury to one
is the concern of all. When a strike loses, so does every man that
labors."

Owen asked in a thoughtful tone: "Is Mr. Frick a great man?"

"Great?" Tom looked at his son in some surprise. "Great?" He
hesitated, spoke with care. "All men have nobility in them, Owen,
from this Mr. Frick down to the youngest trapper boy in Erie Mine;
but when a man begins to think himself great, the nobility in him
shrinks to the size of a pea. Mr. Frick's greatness is only dollars
he's held back from the earnings of them that work in his mills.

Great?" He chuckled in sudden mirth. "Why, Owen, that man is so little you could put the souls of a thousand like him in the eye of your mother's needle!"

Owen grinned, pleased by his father's laughter. "And papa, he'll have to pass through the eye of a needle to take his money to Heaven, won't he?"

Tom puffed his pipe. "Yes. Owen, I'd rather be a striker out of his mills, starving and watching my children starve, than him. I wouldn't wonder but he's sorry himself, sometimes, that the anarchist man didn't kill him."

More than once that summer, Owen and BB went into the country together; and on a day in late August while they ate lunch, Owen led the editor to talk about the strike now seven weeks old. Mr. Frick had told the Congressional Committee that the mill was worth five or six million dollars, but that it would go bankrupt unless wages were reduced; and when someone appealed to Mr. Carnegie as the owner of the mill to interfere and settle the strike, he said he could not if he would — and would not if he could. Owen asked BB: "Does Mr. Carnegie really own it?"

"I believe so."

"You mean he really owns five or six million dollars?"

"He's a very rich man, Owen."

"How did he earn it all?"

BB said soberly: "Owen, pin this in your hat. No man can honestly earn a million dollars in a lifetime. Nine-tenths of all the things a man does are made possible in the beginning by the muscles and the brains of other men; and this is particularly true about getting money. To accumulate a million dollars by hiring cheap labor isn't earning money, it's stealing it. When a man has to have a job in order to live, you can hire him cheap; but you haven't earned the money that you saved by not paying him more. You've stolen it as truly as if you'd stuck a gun at his head."

Owen frowned, his thoughts taking another turn. "It looks to me, if you want to keep Mr. Frick, men like him, from stealing your money, you have to fix it so you don't have to have a job."

"Not quite. Frick can't make steel alone, all by himself. He has to have men who will work for him. So if all workingmen refused to work unless he raises their wages, they could bring him to time." He went on: "And actually, Owen, when laboring men make their employer pay them more, they're doing him a favor. The employer who keeps wages down when he could afford to raise them robs not only his men and the community; he robs himself, too. Cheap labor is bad for everybody. No man can ever be really well off if his neighbors are poor."

Owen, his eyes intent, said quickly: "It all comes back to an injury to one injures all."

"Exactly. The South with slave labor made a few men rich, but most men — I mean white men — were wretchedly poor. The labor question is more threatening today than the slavery question was in 1840. We have a protective tariff to protect capital; but capital needs no protection, for money can always take care of itself. What we need is protection for labor. The best protection for labor would be a tariff of five hundred dollars a head upon immigrants."

Owen had heard BB say this before, but now he protested. "If they hadn't allowed immigrants, my father and a lot of people in Hardiston County could never have come to this country at all."

"I don't mean people like them. They came here to stay, to live. But no one should be allowed to come here and save his money and take it home with him. He ought to promise to become an American citizen and agree to stay here before he is allowed to come at all. Good Welsh and Scottish and Irish and English stock will always be needed and welcomed; but many of these Homestead strikers don't even speak our language."

"Papa didn't speak our language when he came!"

"No, but he learned it. That should be required."

Owen said stubbornly: "Requiring it won't make them do it, any more than Miss Williams could make pupils learn geography or spelling or something by telling them they have to. Some won't and some just can't."

"No remedies are simple." BB rose. "Well, time to move along. We don't want to hurry, or we'll miss something along the way. Walking's like any other way of travelling; the faster you go, the less you enjoy it."

Summer waned. The Knights of Labor sent the proceeds of their Labor Day celebration to Homestead; but in spite of Owen's hopes, the strike was slowly dying. The dailies reported that by ones and twos and dozens, men were going back to work on the company's terms. In October, the strike leaders were indicted for treason, and

Mr. Frick and others for murder; but BB was sure that they would all be acquitted, strikers and owners too.

News from Homestead began to disappear even from the dailies. The Ohio Southern ran an excursion to Chicago to see the dedicatory ceremonies at the Columbian Exposition. In the week before election day there were five mine accidents in Hardiston County; two men were killed, one lost an arm, three were crushed into hopeless cripples.

The Democrats won the election, and BB commented in the *Journal* that the Republican Party was too much the rich man's party. He named Wanamaker, Elkins, Depew, the Vanderbilts and Carnegie to make his point; and in the next issue of the paper he wrote:

> *The Homestead Strike was called off last week. It cost $6,500,000 and 35 lives, but Carnegie wins at last. Had he been poorer, the men might have won. It was labor's resentment, roused by the strike, that beat the Republicans. The support given the Republicans by rich men was the kiss of death.*

5

Late in November, Tom Glen's rheumatism struck him down, and for several days he stayed at home. When he was better he went back to work; but after a few days he told Owen's mother: "I can't dig enough coal to keep us going, Annie. I can drill my holes, and blow down the coal; but the shovelling it into the car just about breaks my back."

"You'll get better, Tom." They were at supper.

"I can manage all but loading the cars."

Owen said hopefully: "Papa, I could do that for you." But his mother cried in a sort of desperate panic, as though already knowing herself beaten:

"That you can't, and you never will, Owen. You've school to keep you busy."

"I can't earn money in school!"

"You can learn in school, and you earn money at the *Journal* office."

Tom Glen watched them, his eyes turning from one to the other, and Owen felt his father was on his side. "I'll never learn anything much from Miss Means, mama." His teacher in the seventh grade was Mrs. Jenkins's sister, that buxom, acid-tongued spinster whom Betty and the other Jenkins girls called, behind her back, "Aunt Wormwood." She was perhaps fifty years old, addicted to sarcasm, and with a way of flying into sudden petulant rages at any provocation or at none. "She's no good. I hate going to school to her, and four boys in our room have already quit to go to work."

"Oh, son, I don't want you going into the mine. I want you —" Mrs. Glen hesitated, looking apologetically at her husband. "You're a fine good man, Tom; but I want Owen to be something besides a miner."

"What's wrong with coal-mining, Annie?" Tom's tone was mild, and Owen found this reassuring. When his father and mother fell into argument, it was always the one who was wrong who got mad, so his father's mildness now suggested that Tom Glen was right, and knew it. "A lot of people would freeze to death if we didn't dig coal to keep them warm. It's man's work."

But if Tom were not angry, neither was Mrs. Glen. "Well, it's not boy's work, Tom," she urged. "And Owen's just turned thirteen!" His birthday was not a month past.

"He's as strong as many a man." Owen was in fact well grown, three or four inches over five feet tall, with broad shoulders and a massive head under his shock of dark hair. "He can swing a shovel as well as anybody, let him once get the knack of it."

She wrung her hands. "Oh, Tom, Tom, I don't want him to!"

"Well, nor do I," Tom agreed. "I didn't ask him to. It was his idea. But if you say 'no,' Annie, why, 'no' it is."

"I do! I do! I'll still say 'no,' to my dying day."

Tom nodded. "That settles it, then. Owen, you heard your mama." He rose, straightening his creaking back, and went to pat her head. "Never mind, Annie. We'll get along."

Owen was silenced, but not convinced. School under Miss Williams, though it had never held for him the keen exciting fragrance which Miss Dine somehow shed about her, had nevertheless the contentment of work well done. But under Miss Means he lived through hour after hour of fretful or half-sullen resentment at her reasonless petulance. He hated her bigness, and her physical strength. When even the biggest boys provoked her, she might come swooping down upon the offender and grasp his shoulders in hands like the jaws of a vise and shake him till his head seemed about to fly off his shoulders. Owen hated her hoarse voice, and her sarcastic words that could score like a lash. To escape from her would have been a release as welcome as escape from a cruel jailor.

Nevertheless, to please his mother, he tried to please Miss Means. It never occurred to him to be sorry for her, to suspect that her apparent hatred of them all arose from a deep-rooted maternal instinct never satisfied; that she hated the children under her tutelage because they were not her own; that now, when she knew she would never marry and would never bear babies upon whom she could lavish boundless love, her body and her soul alike revolted. He knew nothing of the torment which accompanies in women the lingering death of the reproductive capacity. That Miss Means should fling open every window on a bitter day when they all shivered with the cold seemed to him only a cruel device to make them uncomfortable. She had been a teacher for thirty years, had given her life to the children of other women, and had grudged every hour; but Owen had no comprehension of the torture of that long purgatory. When two years later he heard that she had been sent to the insane asylum at Athens, he felt some faint touch of puzzled pity; but now he wished only to see the last of her, and dreaded each day in school.

But this was not the only reason for his eagerness to go to work in the mines. The Homestead strike, since he read about it every evening to Tom Glen, had drawn Owen and his father close together. At the same time, Tom, whose eyes troubled him more and more, began to use Owen's help in doing the small amount of correspondence and of records and bookkeeping which his post as secretary-treasurer of the Erie local required of him. If there was a letter to be written, he told Owen what to say and Owen wrote it; if there was a meeting of the local to be recorded, he told Owen what had happened and Owen wrote the minutes. The effect was to awaken Owen's interest in the machinery of the Union, and he read the minutes of past years, when the workers in Erie had been members of the Knights of Labor, and felt himself one of that noble company, pledged with them to the conviction that an injury to one was the concern of all.

So in spite of his mother, he wished to become a miner; yet this was in his mind not so much the selection of a way of life as it was enlistment in a crusade. The Homestead strike focused his thoughts in an intense concentration. He agreed with BB that the battle was a blunder; but an even worse blunder, he felt sure, had been to begin the struggle at a slack season when the mill-owners could shut down without suffering heavy loss. He criticized the strike leaders for their mistakes, but he held to a flaming certainty that their cause was just. In the heat of his emotion there began to be forged a purpose. It was still formless and uncertain, but under the hammers of the years, form and certainty would come.

A few days before Christmas, a miners' meeting was held in Belton, and delegates from thirty-eight of the forty-nine larger mines in Hardiston County attended. Tom Glen went as a delegate from Erie Mine, and Owen persuaded his father to let him go along, even though it meant missing a school day, and meant that Will must attend to his chores at the *Journal* office. They rose early, and Mrs. Glen gave them breakfast, and they walked together through the dark streets and the icy cold of the hour before dawn to board the miners' train.

At that meeting Owen watched for the first time the procedures of which he had read in Robert's *Rules of Order,* and this demonstration brought that book to life for him. The meeting had no important business to transact. An old man who seemed to Owen distressingly feeble — Tom Glen explained to Owen's whispered question that this was Matthew Price, secretary-treasurer of the Sub-District — read the statistics of coal mining in Hardiston County for the preceding year. Then someone else made a speech about the defects of the single-entry room and pillar system of mining, as compared with the County of Durham system; and someone replied, agreeing that the County of Durham system might well prolong by one-fifth the productive life of a mine, but urging that the manner of mining was properly a matter for the operators to decide.

Then the chairman introduced the speaker of the day. "You all know him," he began. "So he needs no introduction." Nevertheless, he proceeded at some length, referring to the speaker in the third person until Owen was in an itch of impatience to know the name and hear the man himself. "Born in Scotland, he early interested himself in the problem of mine safety and became an

authority upon the subject. He introduced and fought through the
Ohio Legislature, twenty years ago, the first mine-safety law in the
United States; and from 1874 to 1878 he was chief inspector for the
state. He is not only a miner himself and an expert on safety
measures in mines, but a student and a historian. Every miner in
Ohio, yes, and in the United States, is in his debt.

"Gentlemen I give you a gentleman you all know, the founder of
our neighboring community of Glendale, good neighbor, good
miner, good man — Andrew Dale."

Mr. Dale proved to be stocky and almost fat, rather short than
tall, with a block of a head and white hair and a snow-white beard.
His eyes were grave and weary, one of them half-closed, one eye-
brow cocked; but his voice was strong and clear and moving, and
Owen listened in a steady concentration.

Mr. Dale spoke at first of how mines were being made safer for
the miners, and how they could and would be made safer still.
"For the years bring steady gains," he said. "The whole history of
mines and of mining is one of advancement to better working
conditions, and to better wages.

"By comparison with the past, you who work in the mines of
today are fortunate indeed. Three hundred years ago in Scotland,
miners were legally slaves; the old chronicles say that not only
miners, but often their families, lived and died in the mines and
never saw the day. This is hardly true; but at that time miners
were thought of as subterranean beasts, inhuman, shapeless and
deformed.

"But the time came when more miners were needed, yet no men
would willingly become slaves; so a hundred and twenty years ago
the British Parliament passed a new law that said: 'Because Scotland makes miners live in slavery and bondage, persons are discouraged from becoming miners; so hereafter any man who goes to
work in mines shall continue to be free as other men are, and all
present miners under twenty-one shall be free in seven years, and
all others under thirty-five in ten, and all older than thirty-five
in three.'

"That law ended legal slavery in the mines of Scotland; but the
passage of that law was not an accident. It did not just happen. It
was the result of the upward pressure of your forebears. We know
there must have been attempts to strike, and struggles for a higher

wage, because the law provided that any miner who had ever asked higher pay, or had urged his fellows to strike, should remain in slavery two years more."

An angry murmur ran through the hall, and Mr. Dale went on:

"In those days, women worked in British mines as draft animals, as you use mules today. Two women handled each car. The one in front had a belt around her waist, from which a chain ran between her legs; she crawled on hands and knees, pulling the car. The women behind pushed it. Women were considered by the operators valuable property, and a miner to whose wife a girl child was born was paid harigold money as a reward. As recently as fifty years ago, women in England worked twelve to fourteen hours a day in the mines, often on all fours, often in water inches deep.

"The grievances of men and women then were like your grievances today, only worse. You complain about the screen which now spills out of your carload a considerable amount of coal before it is weighed; but the rule then was that for a short-weight car the miner got no pay at all, and for a car that was overweight he got no extra pay. Since then there have been many changes, forced by law; but whenever any law was proposed to improve conditions in the mines, the owners declared that the new law would close every mine in Britain — just as Mr. Frick, six months ago, after his Homestead Mill had made profits not less than thirty-three per cent the year before, said that unless wages were reduced the company would go bankrupt!"

There was a harsh laughter in the hall, an angry mutter and stir; but the speaker raised his voice and they hushed to listen and he went on. "It was the tragic and terrible accidents in the mines which by awakening public sympathy passed the laws by which you benefit today. In 1862, two hundred and five miners were killed in an accident in Hartley Colliery, in England; and that tragedy led, after a ten-year fight, to the passage of the first safety laws over there.

"Our Ohio law was modelled on that British act. When the law was before your legislature, the operators called it the fruit of irresponsible agitators. I was one of those agitators, and we all stood for a lot of abuse; but we weren't disturbed by hard words. We knew that the tree that bears the most nuts gets the heaviest clubbing." A chuckle ran along the crowded rows. "And the operators swore over and over that if the law were passed, it would close every mine in the state. The same cry had been raised in England, but the English law did not close the mines in Britain. The Ohio law was passed and yet there are seventy mines still working right here in Hardiston County, and hundreds more in Ohio. Knowingly or not, the operators lied."

A sullen murmur ran across the hall, and he went on: "Your great-grandfathers would have thought your lot today a happy one; but your great-grandsons will marvel that you were able to endure what you do endure. From your gains, they will reap the benefits. Remember that a lifetime is a short time, and be patient. Expect many failures, but remember that a small failure may be part of a great success.

"And remember that a little is better than nothing. Gains once made are never wholly lost, and many small gains make one large one.

"If you look only at today, despair is easy; but you can look back with pride, can look forward with high confidence." He was a moment silent, then held up his hands and said in a great voice: "Go on! Press on! Press on!"

When he sat down, Owen wished to leap to his feet, to shout, to cheer; but from the audience came brief, almost perfunctory applause. Owen thought the men were insensible and dull; thought they should be by Mr. Dale's words as exalted as he. Mr. Dale had spoken quietly, with no passion in his utterance; perhaps if he had seemed more excited, the listeners would have become excited too; perhaps a speaker must catch fire before he can inflame his listeners.

Or perhaps it was because Mr. Dale did not look at them. He had not looked at them at all. Owen was sure of this, because Mr. Dale's eyes were fixed on him from beginning to end.

He heard the chairman say a word of thanks, and then add: "The chair will entertain a motion to adjourn." The men moved slowly out into the open air; and Owen, drawn as iron filings are drawn by a magnet, worked through the crowd to overtake Mr. Dale, moving with the others toward the door. Someone spoke his name and he looked around and found Mr. Beecham at his shoulder.

"Oh, hello, Mr. Beecham," he said. "I didn't see you before."

"I came up so I could write a piece about the meeting for the paper. Did you enjoy Mr. Dale's speech?" They were outside the hall, the crowd dissolving.

"Yes sir. He looked straight at me all the time."

BB chuckled. "That's a high compliment to him, Owen. It shows he's a fine speaker. If you ever make a speech, look at your audience. You wouldn't try to shoot without taking aim." Andrew Dale had stopped a few paces off and stood there in talk with the man who had presided at the meeting. "Come along and meet him," he suggested. He led the way and Owen followed. BB greeted Mr. Dale and his companion. "Mr. Dale, this boy would like to shake your hand. He works in the *Journal* office. His father's Tom Glen, the delegate from Erie Mine." As Mr. Dale extended his hand, BB added: "He says you looked straight at him all the time you were talking."

Mr. Dale smiled. "Hello, son." He studied Owen for a moment, thoughtfully. "Are you going to be a miner?"

"Yes sir." Owen was full of emotions for which he could find no words. "Yes, I am."

Mr. Dale caught Mr. Beecham's eye, then glanced at the other man, the man who had presided at the meeting. BB said: "Owen, shake hands with Eben Howell. He's vice-president of the Sub-District."

Owen and Mr. Howell clasped hands, and Owen heard Mr. Dale say in half-amused undertone to Mr. Beecham: "The Holy Grail, BB?"

Owen did not know what that meant, but feeling himself excluded by the obvious understanding between Mr. Dale and Mr. Beecham, he turned away to find his father. Tom was talking with two other men, and Owen stopped near him, waiting; but his eyes followed Mr. Dale and Mr. Howell and Mr. Beecham as they moved away.

VII

January 1893 – August 1893

In January a bill was introduced before the Ohio Legislature providing that coal should be weighed before it was screened, and Owen asked his father's opinion of its justice. "Mr. Beecham says there are two sides to the question," he explained. "But I can't see but one side. If you dig coal, slack or no slack, you ought to get paid for it."

"I'm for it," his father agreed. " 'Course, it won't make a lot of difference to me. A good miner don't make much slack. These winter miners that just come into the mines when there's no farm work to do, they make a lot; and some say this law would throw them out of work, say the operators wouldn't hire them. I don't know about that, but I do know the operators are against the law, and as long as they're against it, I'm for it."

Something like appraisal showed in Owen's eyes. "Is that sensible, papa? The operators are bound to be right sometimes, so if you're always against —"

Tom spoke in resentful surprise. "You're pretty young to be arguing with your father."

Tom Glen's resentment meant that he knew he was in the wrong; and Owen, understanding this, felt for an instant a kindly tolerance that intensified his affection for the older man, and obediently he held his tongue.

The mine was working every day, and coal was up to $3.50 a ton delivered; so this promised to be the most profitable winter in Hardiston County's history. Miners and operators alike were prospering, and Tom calculated that Erie Mine was showing a profit of $150 a day. He was mercifully free from rheumatism, and in the first two weeks of January he mined fifty-one tons of coal. For the

162

first time since Owen had become conscious of money's part in their lives, he and his father were between them earning more than enough to meet the family's needs; and when BB gave Owen three tickets to hear Bill Nye at the Rink in mid-January, Tom insisting that Owen's mother buy a new dress, they all went together.

Owen particularly enjoyed the lecturer's remarks about his dog, which was bald-headed on the end of his tail because he once put his tail into a kettle of boiling water. "When he took it out," said Bill Nye, "which he did —" Next day in school, the memory of those words set Owen laughing so hard he could not stop; and Miss Means pounced on him and shook him till he was afraid his neck would break. She dragged him out of his seat and marched him forward, a hard hand tugging him at his ear, and spun him around to face the school.

"Owen knows something so funny that I'm sure we all want to share it!" she announced. "Now, Owen, tell us what it was! See if you can make us all laugh!"

Owen rubbed his maltreated ear. "I got to thinking about Bill Nye's dog."

"Indeed? And what about Bill Nye's dog? And who is Bill Nye?"

"Why, he lectured at the Rink last night. He said, 'I had a dog —'" Owen, without intending to do so, began to be Bill Nye; his voice changed, he became completely serious, and when the class giggled he put on a look of such comical surprise that they laughed the more. "'I called my dog Entomologist, because he collected so many insects.'" For a moment Owen ceased to be Bill Nye, as he explained: "An entomologist is a man who collects insects. I looked it up in the dictionary."

"Really!" Miss Means's tone made his cheeks burn. "Next thing, you'll be teaching the class, and I'll be one of your pupils."

"Yes'm," Owen agreed, and smothered mirth ran across the room; and then Owen was Bill Nye again. "'My dog Entomologist was easily recognized, because he was bald on the end of his tail. This baldness was acquired one day when Entomologist, while re-arranging some of the insects behind his ear with his right rear foot, inadvertently put the end of his tail in a pan of boiling water. When he took it out — which he did —'"

Their hilarious laughter interrupted him; he looked from one face to the next in wide-eyed surprise, pretending to be not only bewildered but also deeply pained by their mirth, and they laughed harder than ever. He risked a side glance at Miss Means, and she too was laughing; but instantly she changed from a smile to a scowl, and that quieted the children.

"'When he took it out — which he did,'" Owen repeated, "'his tail was bald.'" He wished he could remember what came next; but he had been laughing so hard through that part of the lecture that he only half heard, so he skipped to a part he did remember. "'Entomologist had a fine appetite. He liked to eat, and he spent most of his time doing it. His appetite was his ruin in the end. One day, I borrowed the dish in which I usually fed him and used it to mix a batch of plaster of Paris. I turned away for a moment, and Entomologist ate the entire mixture and licked the bowl clean.

"'When I discovered this, Entomologist was already beginning to have misgivings. He sat looking down at his own stomach in hardening concern.'" Owen had to wait between sentences for mirth to die. "'Entomologist had an excellent digestion, but for once he had taxed it too far.

"'So that was the end of Entomologist; but he lives in my memory, and I keep before my eyes a reminder. On my desks rests an oval white paperweight inscribed with this legend: "Portrait in plaster of Entomologist, my dog. Interior view."'"

A storm of laughter silenced him. He had a sudden intoxicating sense of power, and might have gone on, but Miss Means said sharply:

"That's quite enough, Owen. Take your seat." Owen obeyed, and she spoke to the class. "I had not realized you children were such barbarians as to laugh at the agonies of a dumb animal . . ." Owen, drunk with his success, raised his hand. "What is it, Owen?"

"Bill Nye said Entomologist wasn't dumb, not when he put his tail —"

Laughter rewarded him again, and Miss Means cried: "Silence!" She looked from one to another. "You're all so amused by the agonies of a dumb animal, I think you need to be tormented a little yourselves to teach you sympathy. So you will have no recess today, and you will all stay a half-hour after school. And you, Owen, will stay an hour after school each day this week.

"Now, unless some of you still think this is funny, we will go on with our work."

That was bad, but Owen met Jane Lloyd's eyes, and she smiled reassuringly; and he felt a high content. To have made not only

the children, but even Miss Means, laugh was certainly an achievement of which he could be proud. When the school day was done,
and the rest of the class at the end of their extra half-hour had been
dismissed, he stayed alone with Miss Means, pretending to study,
thinking in triumphant contempt: "Darned fat old maid!" He
imagined how ridiculous she would look if a man ever tried to kiss
her, and the thought made him want to laugh again. No one would
ever try to kiss Miss Means. She looked hard, as though she were
encased in a shell.

His punishment curtailed his after-school time at the *Journal*
office, but when he told Mr. Beecham the reason, BB laughed as
hard as anyone; and when he came to school next morning he met
Jane Lloyd at the gate, and Jane said: "That was awful funny about
the dog, Owen. I went with papa and mama to the lecture, and
you were just as funny as Mr. Nye. You sounded like him. If I
hadn't been looking right at you, I wouldn't have known it was
you."

"I sort of pretended to myself I was him."

"Like an actor. Maybe you'll be an actor when you grow up."

He was happy in her praise, but he said: "No, I'm going to be
a coal miner."

After church on Sunday he and Miss Williams walked together
as far as Belton Street, and she remarked, rather as a question than
chidingly: "Miss Means says you're the most unruly boy in school,
Owen."

"I didn't do anything. Only I got to laughing."

" 'Got to laughing'?" she echoed. "Why not say 'laughed in
class'? Yes, she told me. I don't suppose you did it just to make
trouble."

"I didn't," he agreed. "But then she made me stand up and talk.
That was kind of fun, making them laugh whenever I wanted to."

"Not 'kind of'; just 'fun.' " When Miss Williams thus corrected
him, it was never an irritation. She did it in such a friendly way
that he liked it. "Being able to handle an audience is a real gift.
You must cultivate it."

"I want to." She always made him wish to be strong and fine and
good. He looked at her as he spoke and realized that he was taller
than she, and the abrupt discovery gave him a surprising pleasure.
"I want to learn how to make speeches."

"I suppose the first thing is to have something to say, something that you think is interesting. You had something to say, the other day in school. You were interested; and if you're interested, the people who hear you are sure to be."

"I thought it was funny, too."

"Exactly," she agreed. "And when you feel things yourself, it helps make your listeners feel them. If you feel the right things. Some old Roman said an orator is a good man, skilled in speaking. To be good comes first; then comes the skill in speaking. But that's just learning to think on your feet."

"I like the way you explain things. Miss Means just makes everybody mad."

"Well, I'm glad you like my ways; but in the long run, a man has to teach himself. You'll be through with school one of these days. When they're through school, most people stop trying to learn things; but if you expect to make something of your life, you'll have to go on learning." Listening to her, keeping step with her, Owen felt in himself an extraordinary happiness, a warm and glowing pride, a high desire. She asked: "What do you want to do, Owen? What do you want most of all?"

"I guess I want to take care of papa and mama," he hazarded. "So papa won't have to work when his rheumatism's bad, and mama won't have to work so hard, and — worry all the time." He remembered Andrew Dale's talk to the miners. "And I want to make things easier for coal miners."

They had come to the corner of Belton Street, where their ways parted, and she stopped. "I'll always help you, if I can; so when you don't understand something Miss Means tells you, come and ask me." For a block or two along Pearl Street, church-goers homeward bound came strolling toward them. "I'll wait for the others," she said. Isaac Williams and Charles Morgan were together, Mrs. Williams and Mrs. Morgan a few steps behind; and half a block away Owen saw his father and Evan Jenkins, and then Mrs. Jenkins and his mother, and behind them the three Jenkins girls, Betty with a young man at her side, May and Allie close behind. Marged's uncle and aunt, when they reached the corner, stopped for a further word with Charles and Mrs. Morgan; and Marged and Morgan Williams, with a farewell to Owen, went on their way.

If Owen waited, he would probably have to walk with May and

Allie; so he continued alone, thinking of what Miss Williams had said about learning to make speeches. Mr. Beecham said that to be "skilled in speaking" — Owen liked the phrase — you needed a vocabulary. That meant knowing a lot of words, and Owen took the next opportunity to ask Mr. Beecham whether there was any book about words.

"The dictionary?" BB suggested.

"I look up words in it, but the dictionary doesn't do me any good unless I know what word I want to look up."

"Well, the Bible's full of words. Do you read that?"

"Papa reads it aloud, the Welsh Bible, for our prayers; but if his eyes are bad I read the English Bible for him. I read it clear through when I was a boy."

"Read it again," BB suggested. "And then read it again and again. There are lots of words in the Bible. Then perhaps when you're older you'll want to study Latin and Greek. They'll help, and French and German, too. You know, a Welshman can pronounce any language, because his tongue is smooth on both sides!"

"I want to read a book about words," Owen said stubbornly.

"Well, there's a book called *Lavengro*. The man who wrote it was interested in words, and writes about them. I loaned my copy to a gentleman in Mississippi. As soon as he returns it, I'll lend it to you, if you like."

"Will he send it back pretty soon?" There was in Owen the impatience of youth, which seeks to accomplish all in a day, not yet understanding that life takes a long path toward a forever receding goal.

2

Through February the bitter cold continued. It was so cold, said BB in the *Journal,* that rabbits froze to death in their forms. Lloyd Davis killed a wildcat down near Adams Furnace. Forty feet of tapeworm was removed from a boy named Albert Casting, and this made almost five hundred feet of tapeworm which had been removed from Albert in four years. James G. Blaine died, and Mr. Beecham paid him tribute. The Ohio Legislature passed a law making railroad time legal, but Tom Glen and most Hardiston folk

would continue to schedule their lives by sun time. Someone put
out poison baits, and in a single week fourteen dogs were found
dead. BB advocated the annexation of Hawaii, and advised that it
be used as a penal colony for life convicts; that capital punishment
be abolished in favor of banishment to Hawaii; that convicts be
settled there on small farms. A horse at a grade crossing down near
Sycamore Hill, frightened by an approaching train, ran away up the
tracks; and the train killed the horse and the two men in the buggy.
A hoist in a Slacktown mine, bringing men to the surface, banged
into the top of the shaft; seven men were thrown clear, but three
fell back down the shaft and were killed. In mid-April, the Ohio
Senate voted down the bill requiring that coal be weighed before it
was screened; Herbert Canter, who owned more Hardiston County
mines than any other one man, led the fight which beat the bill;
Senator Phillips voted against it, and BB predicted that Hardiston
County miners would defeat Senator Phillips at the next election.

On the first of May, with a demand for an increased basic wage
and as a protest against the defeat of the anti-screen law, Ohio
miners struck. The mines were running full time, the miners had
been able during the winter to accumulate some savings, the omens
of victory seemed bright; but for once, Tom Glen was opposed to
striking.

"There's hard times coming," he said gloomily. "The coal trade's
all right, but furnaces are shutting down. Summer'll kill the coal
business anyway. If it was me, I'd stick to the job and save all I
could."

Mrs. Glen said sharply: "Now you're talking sense, Tom. Why
don't you?"

But Tom Glen shook his head. "Oh, if there's a strike, I'll come
out. I'm no scab."

Owen, having gone barefoot all summer since he could remember, and having suffered the normal youthful quota of cuts and
abrasions, knew what a scab was; but this clearly was not what his
father meant.

"What's a scab, papa?"

"A man that hires on to take another man's job in a struck mine."

"Why do they call them that?"

"Because they're about the lowest kind of man there is, Owen.
Scab's as good a name for them as any other." And to Mrs. Glen:

"No, Annie, this is one time I wasn't for a strike. The United Mine Workers ordered it, and I'll stay out with the others, but it's a bad time for it."

Tom Glen used his free time to put in a garden, but May was warm and dry, so the garden had a poor start. Amy bore a boy baby, and she and Dave named it David, like their first who died. Hardiston, heretofore officially a village, passed the five thousand mark in population and was reorganized as a city. BB in the *Journal* urged respect for the Sabbath. "Even church-goers, although they attend the morning and evening services, may be seen riding in carriages or on bicycles on Sunday afternoon."

In spite of dry weather, grass began to grow, and Owen used his noon hours to mow lawns. Mrs. Paxley, when he knocked at her door for the first time that spring, said in surprise: "Why, Owen, how you've grown! You're taller than I am! Let's stand back to back." She caught his hand. "Come in here to the mirror where we can see." Owen, in some embarrassment, allowed himself to be led into the hall where they stood with their backs together and looked sidewise at their reflected images. "There, you see!" she cried. "If it weren't for my pompadour, you'd be half an inch taller. You're not a boy any longer, you're a young man." And, meeting his eyes in the mirror, she smiled: "And a mighty good-looking one, too!"

He moved uneasily away from her, and as she followed him out on the porch he backed away. "I just came to see if you wanted me to cut your lawn."

"I certainly do. Every week. Keep the grass short. And I'll always have some lemonade for you."

He was glad to be out-of-doors again. "I'll come tomorrow," he said, looking up at her where she stood on the top steps.

"Yes, do," she agreed. He looked back from the gate and she was still watching him; he felt her eyes follow him as he crossed the street and went toward school.

Next day, during the morning recess, Betty Myers spoke to Owen, inviting him to a picnic at Panter's Caves on the Saturday after school let out. Owen knew the spot, for though the caves were a fair ten miles from town, he and BB had sometimes walked that far. At the head of a wooded gulch, the soft puddingstone had through centuries eroded, leaving an overhanging shelf; and under

this overhang, pock-marked with many small craters by the drip
of water through the porous conglomerate, lay a crescent of sloping
sand. The stream made, even in a dry season, a slender trickle,
widening into pleasant knee-deep pools. "We're going in Mr.
Lovering's big carryall," Betty explained. Tom Lovering owned
the livery stable. "And mama's going to take two freezers of ice
cream, and cake, and fried chicken and everything."

Owen said doubtfully: "I work all day Saturdays."

"Oh, please come, Owen," Betty urged. "Jane's coming! Everybody's coming."

"The whole room?"

"Well, not everybody," Betty admitted. "But Morgan, and Tom,
and — oh, you know what I mean."

Owen wondered whether Will Davis could spare him for the day.
"We have to run off the inside, Saturdays."

"What's that?"

"The inside of the paper. It comes in a big sheet, and we print
four pages — that's the inside — Saturdays, and the other side
Wednesdays."

"Why don't you ever take anyone to see the paper printed,
Owen? I know Jane's dying to, and so am I."

It was not unusual to have visitors in the pressroom on Wednesdays. If the paper was late going to press, Mrs. Beecham sometimes
came after supper, and she might bring a friend or two; and sometimes out-of-town visitors were brought to watch the press and the
folder in operation. To go to see the furnace cast — a brilliant display
when the molten iron flowed out of the stack and into the molds —
and to come to see the paper printed were the most interesting
spectacles Hardiston had to offer. Owen, warmed by Betty's flattering tones, said: "Well, I guess you could come Wednesday night,
if you want to."

"Oh, we do! And you will come to my picnic, won't you?"

"If I can, I will." Remembering Jane's party, he asked: "Is it your
birthday?"

"Oh, no, you don't have to bring presents or anything." The bell
rang for the end of recess and she begged smilingly: "Please, Owen?
Do come."

He said, gruff with embarrassment, that he would see. On the
steps, Jane joined them, and she and Betty made him confirm his

promise to take them to see the paper printed; so after school on Wednesday they all went together to the office. They were in time to see Will make up the last form, and Owen showed them how to read type upside down, and told them the names of things: the stone, the composing rule which Will used so dexterously, the form, boiler plate, the quoins. Then he and Will carried the locked forms to lay them on the bed of the press and secure them there; and they braced themselves to push the folder into place, sliding it along tracks of rounded strap iron.

The inside, which had been printed Saturday, lay in a neat pile a foot thick on the low table in the file room. Owen lifted off the wide boards that served to hold the sheets flat; he folded the top inch or two of the pile a third of the way in from one end and from the other, and lifted the flat roll thus formed and carried it in and opened it flat again on the feed board of the press. Will brought another batch to add to it.

"That's enough to begin with," he said. "You start. I'll chunk up the fire."

Owen, big with pride, prepared to feed the big press, with Jane and Betty to see and to admire. Power came from a steam engine in the shed built against the back wall of the pressroom. Will went to add fuel to the fire and to throw in the gears; Owen climbed up on the platform, and as the belt began to move and to slat on its pulleys, trying to look calm and competent, he slid a sheet of paper down against the guides and thrust the lever that threw the moving belt into its proper position. The press began to turn.

Owen from the corner of his eye saw Will talking to Betty and Jane, and he heard their voices raised above the rumble of the press. If a folder tape should break, he must throw off the belt so that the press would stop before too many papers were spoiled, and he hoped this would happen so Jane could see how quickly he met the emergency. Bets and Edna in the file room arranged their paste pots and the long yellow slips on which the addresses of subscribers were printed, and made ready to wrap the papers and address them. BB came from the office to speak to Jane and Betty, and Will climbed up beside Owen with a nod which meant he would take over.

Owen joined Jane and Betty, and as he did so Betty cried: "Oh Mr. Beecham, will you let Owen have Saturday off so he can come to my picnic? We're all going down to Panter's Caves."

BB said cheerfully: "Yes, indeed. Owen's worked hard. He's entitled to a day off."

Betty exclaimed in thanks, and Owen said: "I didn't know whether you could get along without me."

"Well," BB said gravely, "I guess we can manage for once."

He went back through the file room to the office. When to watch the big press at its monotonous task lost its novelty, Owen's guests began to look for other interests. Owen showed them the job press. It had been made ready to run off a flyer advertising a sale of shoes at Mormon's Clothing Store. The type was in place, and Owen brought a sheet of newsprint and folded it and trimmed it down to size in the cutter. The girls were deliciously impressed by the long, heavy, keen blade.

"It would take your finger right off, wouldn't it?" Jane asked in a shivering tone, and Owen agreed that it would. He printed half a dozen flyers for the girls to take home as souvenirs, and Betty, watching the jaws of the press open and close, made a small sound of wondering terror.

"Doesn't it ever shut on your hand and mash it?"

Owen shook his head. "You can stop it with the treadle," he explained. "You catch it on the rise, just before the press closes. Like this, see!"

He put his hand, flat, the fingers spread, into the closing press; but he stopped the treadle just too late. The press touched his hand and he felt for an instant the brief, relentless pressure. When the jaws of the press opened, on the fresh tympan were five small spurts of blood expelled from beneath his nails; his fingertips and his thumbtip were red.

Betty screamed, and Jane cried woefully: "Oh, Owen!" Will heard Betty, and saw what had happened, and stopped the big press and bounded toward them.

Owen was so ashamed of his own awkwardness that he scarce felt the pain. He shook his hand, scattering drops of blood. "It don't hurt," he muttered. "Joke on me, Will."

Will did not laugh. "It's no joke. I've had it happen to me." Owen, sure that Will would never have been guilty of such folly, loved the man for that lie. Bets and Edna stopped their work to

come and sympathize, and then BB appeared, and Will — busy
getting warm water, and tearing a clean towel into strips for
bandages — told Mr. Beecham: "It's not bad. He might not even
lose a nail."

Owen dipped his hand in the basin, and with Betty and Jane
standing solicitously by, Will dried the hand and tried to bandage
the fingertips; but he was clumsy, and Jane said: "Let me. I know
a way to do it."

So she ministered to Owen, looking up at him while she worked,
asking: "Too tight? Does it hurt, Owen?"

"Naw," he assured her, and grinned to prove his word; and Betty
said, appealing to them all:

"Isn't he the bravest thing? If it was me, I'd simply die!"

BB approved Jane's bandages. "But Owen, you won't be able to
do much with that hand. Better take the rest of the week off." He
loked at Betty, smiling. "And have a good time at the picnic." He
added a warning. "But if that hand doesn't get better, go see
Doctor Gorman."

Owen enjoyed their kindly solicitudes, and the touch of Jane's
fingers as she bandaged his hurts was delicious. Jane and Betty
walked with him as far as the corner of Pearl Street, and offered to
go all the way. "Are you sure you're all right alone?" Jane asked.
"Don't you feel faint or anything?"

Owen said he felt fine. At home, his mother took him briskly in
hand. He was forever stepping barefoot on broken glass or on unseen nails, or somehow acquiring a stone bruise; his father often
came home with abraded knuckles, or with barked shins. For these
injuries to her menfolk Mrs. Glen had a sovereign remedy. From a
crock on the shelves she selected now a crust of bread, blue with
mold, and over this she poured enough hot milk to convert it into
a firm mush. She put this bread poultice on Owen's fingers and
thumb, the four fingers wrapped together, the thumb separately.

"There, sonny, they'll be as good as ever in the morning." She
kissed him. "Hurt, does it?"

"Some," he admitted, unwilling to confess how much those
crushed finger-ends actually did hurt.

She said in smiling tenderness: "I expect you think you're too
big a boy now to sit on my lap."

He grinned and said he wanted to, and she chose the low rocking chair and he sat on her knees, his head towering above hers till she made him curl down and put his head on her bosom; and she held him tight, rocking him, singing a soothing little tune, patting him in time to her song.

Owen felt like a small, beloved child again; yet there was a difference. As a child he had always delighted in her softness, but now there was something exciting about it too. Half-asleep, his thoughts drifted; embraces were a part of that adult experience about which his speculative conjectures now so often centered. Drowsing in his mother's arms he loved her more than all the world, his thoughts half-thoughts, half-dreams.

3

The morning of the picnic dawned cloudy, but when Owen set out for Betty's house the sun was breaking through, the promise fine. He found Tom Lovering's carryall already at the gate. Dan Davis, Will's brother, was the driver; and he had tied the horses' reins to an iron weight half as big as a teakettle, while he helped Mr. Myers load the picnic fare. Owen joined the other boys in carrying out pillows and blankets and all the miscellaneous odds and ends which Mrs. Myers considered necessary for the success of the day. Mrs. Lloyd, Jane's mother, was helping; and Mrs. Myers's younger sister — she was married to Doctor Lewis, the dentist — was doing something to her baby, which lay in a slat basket on the front porch, when Miss Williams appeared.

Owen wondered whether she were going to the picnic, and hoped she was. She had heard of his accident, and offered sympathy, and he said his fingers didn't hurt much. "But two of my nails are coming off," he told her proudly.

"They'll grow back again," she assured him; and went up on the porch to admire the baby, and Owen realized that she and the dentist's pretty wife were probably about the same age; but he thought Miss Williams looked somehow different from Mrs. Lewis. Having babies probably changed the way ladies looked.

The carryall, drawn by two horses, had seats running lengthwise from behind the driver's seat to the rear, where steps made it easy to climb in. Its top, supported by iron standards, was fringed along the sides; and rolled-up curtains could in case of rain be lowered and secured. Under Mrs. Myers's directions, Dan Davis and the boys packed into the vehicle behind the driver's seat the ice-cream freezers, a clothes basket full of food, many parcels and blankets and pillows, and the baby in its basket.

As soon as they were well on the way, Miss Williams started them singing songs; and between songs they played games, some familiar, some invented for the occasion. *Jenkins Up* under these circumstances was novel and delightful. Passing a quarter from hand to hand with no table-top to conceal your hands while you did so meant that you could hold your neighbors' hands for brief delightful moments. At "Jenkins Up" or "Jenkins Down," someone was forever dropping the quarter, because you had to slap your hands down on your knees. That meant a scrambling search on the floor of the barge, and if the quarter fell out, Dan had to stop while it was recovered.

When they tired of that, they practiced *Pease Porridge Hot*, each with the person opposite, chanting the traditional formula faster and faster till someone missed and they all collapsed in laughter.

Before they reached their destination, Mrs. Lewis's baby began to cry. She took it out of the basket and held it in her arms, but it cried harder than ever; and Mrs. Myers said something to her in a whisper and Mrs. Lewis blushed and laughed, and the baby continued to cry as the horses turned off the highroad and followed the byway up through the woods toward the Caves. When the carryall stopped, everyone got out; and Mrs. Lewis and Miss Williams hurried away, taking the baby with them. Almost as soon as they were out of sight among the trees, the baby's cries abruptly ceased.

The children showed a tendency to scatter in all directions, but Mrs. Myers and Mrs. Lloyd kept them busy, spreading tablecloths, laying out knives and forks, distributing plates of fried chicken and potato chips and bread and butter. Before they were done, Mrs. Lewis and Miss Williams came back, the baby quiet. Mrs. Myers asked: "Happy now, is he?"

"Sound asleep. He was just hungry, that's all."

Owen watched pretty little Mrs. Lewis thereafter with a profound interest, but whenever she looked toward him he was careful to avert his eyes.

After they had eaten their fill, Mrs. Myers said briskly: "Now you boys go start exploring. The girls must stay and help us clean up. It won't take a minute."

"We can help, ma'am," Owen suggested; but Mrs. Myers bade him go along, and he wondered why she and Mrs. Lloyd looked at each other and smiled. He ran to overtake the other boys, and as they reached the foot of the waterfall, Morgan shouted:

"Last one to the top's a nigger baby!"

They scrambled up the slippery, broken crevice down which the brook cascaded and came to the wooded level above the over-hanging ledge. There, when they had all achieved the heights, Tom Powell, apt to be the leader in any game, gave them a sing-song challenge:

"Y'don't dast follow me! Y'don't dast follow me!"

He ran to the brink of the overhang and walked precariously along the edge. Owen could see the ground sickeningly far below them, and fear was a cold bubbling in his stomach; but he followed Tom, and the others followed him, holding fast to trees or bushes, their feet within inches of empty space.

Then they heard the girls approaching below them, and called: "Hi, Betty! Hi, Janet! Hi, Molly! Hi, Jane! Look where we are!" Squeals of terror were their applause, and a frightened chorus demanded they come down, and Tom led them to the lip of a deep cleft and down that rift to the sand below. The girls told them how brave they were and how foolish; and they began to investigate the sandy slope under the overhang. In a dry spot Jane discovered small cone-shaped hollows, and she called:

"Oh, here are some doodlebug holes." With her fingertip she gently disturbed the sand in the small crater, chanting the mystic summons: "Doodle up! Doodle up! Doodle up!" In the bottom of the little crater something moved, and a small squat shape briefly showed itself and then disappeared again into the sand.

"That's an ant lion," Owen told her.

"No, it isn't, Owen. It's a doodlebug," Betty protested, kneeling beside Jane.

"Well, Mr. Beecham says they're ant lions. They dig these holes for traps, and ants fall into them, and the ant lions eat them."

Morgan Williams proposed that to test this they catch some ants, but Jane said that would be cruel. Then Betty suggested playing hide, and they counted out and Tom Powell was It. He buried his face in his arms against a huge oak tree and counted a thousand by tens, while the others raced for hiding places; but he counted so quickly that when he opened his eyes Jane and Betty were still in sight. Betty demanded that he start over and count a thousand by fives, and he good-humoredly agreed. After the count, he found Betty first, and one by one the others, sometimes winning and some-time losing the headlong race for home, till Hetty and Jim Tower were the only ones still out; so everybody shouted to them to come in free. Jim came down from the shelf above the caves, Hetty from across the brook; and they agreed that the brook, the caves, the lunch ground and the road should be bounds. Betty was It, and she began to count, and Hetty seized Owen's hand, whispering:

"I know a dandy place, Owen."

He did not want to go with her, but she held fast to his hand, and he could not free himself without a tussle; so he ran beside her, and she led him to a knoll above the brook where two huge rocks leaned close together, with a narrow crevice between. She crawled into this crevice, beckoning him to follow. The space was narrow, and they were pressed close, lying on their stomachs, side by side. She whispered:

"Isn't this dandy, Owen?"

"M-hm."

Their faces were scant inches apart. She said softly: "I like you." Her lips touched his cheek, and her arm lay across his shoulder, and for a moment he was filled with dismay and yet with a trembling excitement.

But in that moment they heard a laughing voice that seemed startlingly near. Bushes a few inches from their heads masked the end of the cleft in which they lay, and Hetty inched forward and cautiously parted the leaves to look through. She giggled, and crooked her finger at Owen, and he squirmed up beside her to see what she saw.

Below them, the little stream widened into a sandy pool, and in the pool Mrs. Lewis and Miss Williams were wading, their skirts bundled up above their knees. Mrs. Myers, the baby in her arms, sat with Mrs. Lloyd on the further bank, laughing at something someone had just said; and Miss Williams, knee-deep in the creek, cried: "Oh, I know another." Then she recited:

"A charming young lady named Mabel
Once danced a skirt dance on a table,
    Till a man in the crowd
    Cried out good and loud,
Just look at the legs on the table!"

They laughed again at that, and Hetty was convulsed, pressing her hand over her mouth to silence her mirth. Then Owen heard from a distance Jane calling. "Owen! Owen! Hetty! In free-e-e!"

He started to wriggle backward out of the cleft, but Hetty caught his arm, holding him, whispering: "Wait! Wait!" He was afraid Miss Williams would hear her. "Let's stay here! They'll never find us!"

In a half-panic, he broke free, backed away, scrambled to his feet; and he started toward the big oak that was home. Sulkily she followed him. "All right for you, Owen Glen." But he did not pause. Something like fear hurried his feet. He remembered that Hetty was one of the girls whom older boys sometimes talked about. This year, among the boys in the room over which Miss Means held sway, Owen had heard more of that talk than ever before. Jane and Betty and Molly Moury and Celia Ames and Janet Frye were the only girls in Miss Means's room whom it spared. Celia was not here today, but the other four were. And Hetty.

He was glad to get back to the oak, and glad Jane had not heard Miss Williams recite that poem. Hetty had giggled, but it would have bothered Jane. He had never imagined that grown people made jokes among themselves about legs and things. Boys did; they wrote dirty poems in chalk on privy walls, and drew or carved dirty pictures and signs. Of course the poem Miss Williams had recited was not as bad as the poems on the privy walls; but it was about legs!

Yet Jane's mother, and Mrs. Myers too, had laughed when she recited it; so they certainly were not shocked. Yet his mother had been shocked by the legs of the lady performers in the circus. There was here a distinction he could not understand. It might have something to do with the fact that seeing their legs today was not at all like the day he saw Miss Dine's.

When Owen and Hetty rejoined the others, Morgan Williams had found, in a cleft of the rocks, a dark cave with two strange birds in it, and they all went to see. The birds, covered with white down, were as big as spring chickens, and they stood on shaky legs and clacked their beaks. The nest smelled of rotten meat, and Owen guessed these were young turkey buzzards, and looked up through the trees to see whether the old birds were circling overhead; and Betty went to fetch her mother and the others to see this wonder.

So presently it was time to start for home. On the long ride back to town, most of them were tired and sleepy, and Owen's drowsy thoughts were a tumbling confusion; Miss Williams's white legs in the clear water, and that rhyme she recited, and her laugh; Hetty pressing against him; Mrs. Lewis feeding her baby just as a mare feeds her colt; the day itself, the secret forest all around, the solitude which seemed to press them together, the shared withdrawal from the world — all these seen in retrospect were like a warm bright color in his eyes.

As they came into town, they dropped people off at corners convenient to their homes. Owen and Miss Williams alighted together; and she asked: "Was it fun, Owen?"

"Yes'm."

"I thought everybody had a real good time."

"I guess so." Usually, with her, he was at ease, feeling in her friendliness and liking; but now because he had seen her knees and heard her recite a wicked poem she was a stranger.

She may have sensed this, for she asked: "Did your hand hurt you?"

"Not much, no'm."

She looked at him with puzzled eyes, then half-smiled, shook her head. "Well, goodnight now." They parted and he took his homeward way.

4

The strike which began on the first of May ran a dwindling course. Since there was a steady demand for coal, operators hired men where they could. There were a few fisticuffs between miners and strike-breakers; and up the creek the Home Guard was called out and armed with cudgels to prevent violence. By the middle of May, the men one by one and two by two were already drifting back to the mines.

But Tom Glen, though he had never favored the strike, would not return to work until Union Headquarters said the word. Mrs. Glen called him stubborn as a mule. "If other men go back, why can't you? Do you have to be so high and mighty all the time?"

"The man that goes back before he's told to is a deserter, Annie. They shoot deserters in the army — and the Union's an army; but we'll never win a fight if men desert. I'd like to see us slower to start a fight, and a good sight slower to give up, once we've started. That's the only way the Union will ever get anywhere."

"Think a little more about me, and less about your Union! The Union don't cook for you, and wash and mend and sweep and scrub for you."

"You'd not want me doing a thing I'd be ashamed of!"

"Ashamed of working? You'd better be ashamed of loafing at home!"

Owen sympathized with his father, for surely without loyalty from the men the Union would never be strong; but he knew his mother must grieve to see the little they had saved steadily slip away. He and his father earned the money, but it was she who made each dollar do the work of two. It was for her sake he spoke. "Papa, I think mama's right. I — "

His father swung sharply toward him. "Be still. Shut your mouth."

Owen, though he knew Tom Glen's anger was a confession, felt wrath in him to answer his father's ire. "I've got a right to say what I think! I'm the only one bringing any money home. Mr. Beecham says if you don't work when you can, there'll be a day when you can't."

Tom Glen looked at him for what seemed to Owen a long time. He shook a weary head. "No need of hot words, Owen, between me and you. Nor between you and me, Annie. Let me do what I must." He added firmly: "For I will!"

He stood his ground against all their persuasions; and Isaac Williams, head of Tom's local at Erie Mine, was of the same mind. After church that Sunday, Owen heard them, homeward bound, talk together. "I saw Herbert Canter yesterday," Mr. Williams told Tom Glen. "He says the wage question is closed, says eighty per cent of the miners are satisfied with the way things are."

Tom Glen made a rumbling, angry sound. "Satisfied with poverty? Starvation? Slavery? The pay is slave pay! The day men get a dollar and a half at the best, and the rest of us seventy cents a ton, with a lot of the coal not three feet thick, and half of it nut and slack to sift through the screen."

"There's talk of a committee to investigate."

"Investigate? What's there to investigate?"

"What it costs to mine coal; wages, all that."

Tom shook his head. "Wages don't matter now. Nothing matters now except not running away from a fight after we started it."

Isaac nodded. "I'm with you, Tom. But there's not many of us that are."

The agreement to select an investigating committee marked the end of the strike; and since through May the demand for coal continued, there was at first work enough. But Tom had been three or four weeks idle, so the money Owen earned in the *Journal* office and by mowing lawns was welcome at home. Yet such work was scarce. Some rain had come to ease the drought, but not enough. Mrs. Paxley's yard grew faster than most, and she never turned Owen away; but she and Mr. Beecham were his only regular customers.

The week after school let out, when he went to Mrs. Paxley's and brought the lawnmower from the shed, Nellie Tutson came to the kitchen door. "H'lo, Owen." He had seen her now and then during the winter and spring, either by accident on the street or when she came to the office to speak to Edna, and he knew that except for drinking heavily and steadily, Mr. Tutson had recovered from the grief of having killed Willie; but her friendliness always made Owen uncomfortable.

"What are you doing around here?" he demanded.

"Working for Mrs. Paxley."

"What doing?"

"Hired girl."

He grunted. "I mow the lawn."

"I can do that."

He knew this was true, and the thought that she might do it, and thus rob him of a source of income, was alarming. "Where is she?"

"Uptown."

"Well, I'm supposed to do it, so I might's well go ahead."

She said amiably, "I'm not stopping you." But when he began, she walked beside him, trying to talk to him above the racket; and she was still with him when Mrs. Paxley returned.

Mrs. Paxley spoke sharply: "Nellie, is your work all done?"

"Pretty near."

"Well, you'd better get at it and stop bothering Owen."

"I wasn't bothering him."

"Go in the house at once!" Nellie, with a half-smile at Owen, obeyed, and Mrs. Paxley asked: "Owen, are you and she old friends?"

"I guess so."

"You mustn't keep her away from her work."

"I didn't want her around!"

She laughed, touched his shoulder approvingly. "Of course you didn't! I'll tell you what! She isn't here Tuesday afternoons: so after this you come Tuesday, and she won't be here to bother you." He was relieved to be able thus easily to avoid Nellie. "I'm going to meet Mr. Paxley in Cincinnati tonight," Mrs. Paxley continued. "And we're going to Chicago, to the Exposition; but I'll be back when you come next week. I'll tell you all about it."

Owen was not sure he wanted to hear all about the World's Fair. Dan Davis, Will's brother, who had driven the carryall the day of the picnic, had since then gone on an excursion to the Fair; and Owen heard some of the things he told Will after his return. Dan had a good deal to say about statues of naked women, and about pictures of girls with nothing on but a veil; he assured Will that they were as bad as any saloon pictures he ever saw, and he said the crowds were full of women painted up like dolls, and ready for anything. He spoke of a place named the Midway, and of something which he called a Hoochie-Coochie. Owen's impression — he only half-understood Dan's allusions — was that the World's Fair must be one of the seductive anterooms of Hell; and he was afraid Mrs. Paxley might tell him similar shameful things.

But he only said, "Yes'm," and she went into the house and he continued with his work. Before he finished, Dan Davis drove Tom Lovering's hack up to the gate, and she called from an upstairs window:

"Be right down, Dan."

"Want me to come up?" Dan winked at Owen. "Plenty of time."

"Oh, Dan, you stop!" Owen wondered why she giggled. She disappeared from the window, and a moment later she came out of the front door in hat and cape and with a small bag in her hand. "Here's your quarter, Owen. I'll see you a week from Tuesday." She climbed into the hack and drove away. Owen decided she was catching the up train to Hamden. Maybe some day he would go to places like Cincinnati, and Chicago.

Will's wife had a baby that Friday, a boy. Will, when he came to the office Saturday morning, walked like a man seven feet tall, shouting his news to Owen who was sweeping the file room when he came in; and he pumped Owen's hand, and kept saying over and over: "And she's fine, and he's a real buster. Nine pounds. We're going to call him Joe. You ought to see him. She's fine. He's nine pounds. Joe's his name. Say, he's a buster. Come over and see him tomorrow. She's fine, and so's he. What a pair of lungs! Boy, he's a buster." Owen began to chuckle and then to laugh, and Will laughed at himself and they laughed together like hysterical schoolgirls, till Will suddenly stopped and mopped his brow and said in a shaken voice: "God, but I was scared! She was all night, from yesterday afternoon till half-past four this morning." He sat down weakly, his color drained away, staring at Owen, nodding. "But she's all right." He kept nodding. "She's all right. She's fine."

Before the girls arrived, Will was himself again. Bets clapped him on the shoulder and told him he was quite a man; but Edna kissed him, her arm around his neck while his hung limp at his sides. When she released him, he looked unhappily at Owen, and when she was gone, Will said in a low tone: "I'd like to get BB to fire her, but I guess she needs the job."

Owen went next day with Will to see the new baby. Will's was a small, neat white house with a lawn and two flower beds in front, and a garden behind; and inside, the house was so clean it made Owen want to walk tiptoe. Will's other two children — Annie was five and Bill was three — greeted them in the front yard when they arrived. Lulu Harned, now almost ten, with golden curls and tremendous brown eyes, was with them. "Mr. Davis likes me to keep an eye on them," she told Owen, with the composure of an adult, while Will went in to clear the way. "They're so little, they're always getting into trouble, if somebody doesn't."

Owen asked whether she had seen the new baby, and she had; and then Will called them in. The baby was asleep, but Mrs. Davis was awake and smiled proudly up at Owen, while the children peered over the foot of the bed at her and at the baby in the curl of her arm. Owen thought she was certainly the prettiest woman in the world.

When after a few minutes they came out and sat on the porch, Will began to laugh again, to laugh at nothing; and suddenly he put his face in his hands, leaning far over, and then he sat up again, laughing, tears streaming out of his eyes. "I guess you think I'm a fool, crying now."

"I guess you naturally would," Owen said. "Just being glad from getting over being scared."

5

Tuesday afternoon when he pulled the lawnmower out of Mrs. Paxley's shed, she came to the kitchen door to speak to him. "I'm going to lie down, Owen — I'm trying to cure a headache — but there'll be lemonade on the kitchen table when you finish. Help yourself, won't you."

But when half an hour later his task was done and he came into the kitchen, he found neither the promised lemonade nor his money. Instead, there was a note.

> *Dear Owen, I was thirsty myself, so I took the pitcher upstairs. Come up and get your quarter and I'll give you a glass.*

The suggestion was vaguely alarming, and the lemonade alone would not have persuaded him; but he wanted his quarter. He went through the house to the front hall, but at the foot of the stair he hesitated. She must have heard him, for she called:

"Come on up, Owen." Reluctantly, he obeyed; and when he reached the head of the stairs she added: "In here!"

He crossed to the open door, but when he saw her he stopped still. Mrs. Paxley was lying on the couch, and she wore a wrapper like the one his mother sometimes wore while she was getting breakfast for him and his father, except that this was pink and it was silk, while his mother's was gray flannel. The wrapper was disarranged so that he could see Mrs. Paxley's bare shoulder and a long stockinged leg. The pitcher of lemonade stood on the table beside her.

When he stopped in the door she said: "Come in, Owen. It's so hot today, I just had to do something to keep cool. Come in." She sat up, reaching for the pitcher. "Here!" She filled a glass and held it out to him.

Owen crossed uncertainly to take it, careful not to look at her for fear she would be embarrassed. He gulped half of the lemonade before he realized that it had a taste he did not know. She said: "Sit down. You must be tired. Rest and cool off."

"I've got to go along."

"Oh, do sit down. I just got back yesterday from Chicago. Don't you want me to tell you about it?"

Remembering Dan Davis, Owen shook his head. It was bad enough to be here alone with her, and her not dressed, without having to hear things like that. "I've got to go," he insisted.

"Oh, not till you finish your lemonade, anyway."

The glass was still in his hand, and he took another gulp, wondering why the lemonade tasted that way, and she laughed teasingly. "I think you're embarrassed, Owen. You're as red as a beet." She drew her wrapper more closely around her body. "Nellie says you're awfully shy. She told me about the day she surprised you in the haymow, when you ran away. But you needn't be embarrassed at me, you nice boy." Owen tasted the lemonade again and made a face. "Don't you like it?" She rose and poured a glass for herself and drank deep. "Why, it's delicious," she insisted.

He could smell her perfume. "I'm not thirsty, I guess."

"You must be. You look hot!" She touched his head and his cheek with the backs of her fingers. "You're as hot as a stove, Owen."

"I've got to go," he mumbled. "I finished the lawn. I just came up for my quarter."

She laughed teasingly. "Suppose I haven't got a quarter?"

"Well I can come and get it tomorrow." He edged toward the door.

"Oh, I've got one somewhere." She picked up a purse from the table, fumbling in it, humming a little tune to herself; and suddenly she asked: "How old are you?"

"Thirteen, going on fourteen." He blinked, because something was the matter with his eyes. The window behind her and all that side of the room seemed to be moving as he looked at it.

She laughed. "Thirteen? I might have known. You're really still just a little boy, aren't you. Big as you are." She came toward him. "Here's your quarter, little boy."

She extended her hand, the quarter in her palm, but when he reached for it she cried: "Boo!" He recoiled, leaping backward in scrambling haste; and she laughed and tossed the quarter toward him. "There! I'm not going to bite you!" When he leaned over to pick up the coin, he lost his balance and almost fell. "But one of these days, you'll wish you had stayed."

He ran down the stairs and out through the kitchen, but then he went more carefully. There was something wrong with his eyes; trees blurred before him, and he bumped into one. As his shortest way home, he cut through the yard of the schoolhouse; but he was terribly sleepy. Under the shade of a maple by the alley fence he sat down, and then lay down; and when he looked up, the leaves of the maple seemed to flow past between him and the sky. He shut his eyes, and he lay there for a long time before he felt like walking home. Before he got up, he decided he would never mow Mrs. Paxley's lawn again.

6

Many Hardiston people went to the World's Fair that summer, and Miss Williams was among them. On her return, she stopped over Sunday with her Uncle Isaac before going on to her father's home at Adams Furnace, and walking home from church she told Owen some of the wonders she had seen. "I wish you could go, Owen. It would be a real education."

He had no desire to see the things of which Dan Davis had boasted. Was it possible that she felt as Dan did about them? After all, she had recited that poem about legs. He asked no questions, but she talked without prompting. Apparently there were other sights at the Fair besides those which had inflamed Dan. Miss Williams, like Dan, spoke of the Palace of Fine Arts; but to her the paintings and the statues which Dan remembered with such disquieting gusto had seemed beautiful. Yet Dan had

said there were pictures and statues of women with no clothes on!
Owen could not imagine Miss Williams looking at such pictures.

He trudged silently beside her, eyes on the ground. "And they
had models — they were really full size — of Christopher Columbus's
ships," she explained. "The *Nina* and the *Pinta* and the *Santa Maria*.
The Queen of Spain had them made and sent them to the Fair.
They're so small you can't imagine men crossing the ocean in them.
Then there were models of the *Teutonic* and the *Majestic*, the
biggest ships in the world. And models of old railroad trains and
modern trains and Pullman cars."

The Court of Honor, Miss Williams thought, must be the most
beautiful spot in the world. "And you'd have wanted to see the
huge Krupp gun, and you'd have spent days in Machinery Hall,
and the Electrical Building." She spoke of bicycles by the score,
and beautiful carriages, and the Ferris Wheel — Owen required
her to describe that at length — and of dresses made of glass. Owen
did not understand how anyone could make a dress out of glass,
but Miss Williams said she had brought home some glass thread,
so he went with her to her uncle's house to see it. The thread was
disappointing. It was in short lengths only a few inches long, all
tied together like a shock of wheat.

"You couldn't make a dress out of that! You couldn't even sew
with it," he protested; and when Miss Williams reminded him that
she had actually seen beautiful gowns fashioned from cloth woven
of just such thread, he replied: "Well, I'll bet the ends would stick
into you!"

She laughed at his refusal to be convinced. "I do wish you could
go and see for yourself!"

"I wish so too," he admitted. But there was no chance of that
at all.

The day after he saw Miss Williams, Owen went to cut BB's
lawn, trundling the lawnmower from the shed and proceeding to
the task. Four-year-old Bertie, BB's son, came out on the back
porch with Aunt Jane, and Owen paused to speak to him. Bertie
was dressed in an extraordinary fashion. He had long yellow curls,
and he wore a wide-collared white blouse loosely tucked into black
velvet knee pants, and a black velvet coat with no buttons, dec-
orated around the edges with a fringe of black things shaped like
acorns. Wide white cuffs were turned up over the sleeves of this

coat. Owen said: "H'lo, Bertie. What you got on clothes like that for?"

Aunt Jane said: "It's his Lord Fauntleroy suit!" And Bertie added: "I'm going to Eddie Arthur's party."

Owen saw Aunt Jane's pride. Probably she and Mrs. Beecham had made these extraordinary garments. "Well, those are pretty fancy clothes, all right. You look fine."

Aunt Jane said: "Now, Bertie, you stay on the porch till I get ready. Don't go on the grass, or you'll fall down and get grass stains on your knees. You watch him, will you, Owen?"

So Owen and the little boy sat sedately side by side, and Owen made conversation. "What are you going to do at the party, Bertie?"

"Eat it up."

Owen grinned. "I guess you will, at that. You'll come home fat as a pig."

"I will not!"

"You will be if you go eating up parties all over the place."

Bertie abandoned the argument. "I've got a marble gun," he announced.

"Is that so? Let me shoot it sometime."

"I will if you don't break it. And I'm going to get a baby sister." Owen wondered whether this was why he had not seen Mrs. Beecham all summer. Bertie added, in matter-of-fact tones: "I had one, but her soul flew away to Heaven. I saw it. So I'm going to get another one."

"You can't see a soul!"

"Well, I saw a picture of it."

"What did it look like?"

"Like papa's telescope all folded up, and white, with wings. Aunt Jane showed it to me in the Bible book, on the page where you write about people dying."

Owen knew what he meant. "Oh, that's a scroll!"

Before Bertie could argue the point, Aunt Jane called the youngster. "All right, Bertie; I'll take you up to Eddie's now."

After Bertie's revelation, Owen was not surprised when ten days later Mr. Beecham came proudly to tell them that he and Mrs. Beecham had another little girl. Owen noticed that in that week's Family Record, instead of emphasizing the announcement by italics, the editor printed this wonderful news like that of any other birth:

"Beecham, July 20, a daughter, to Mr. and Mrs. B. Bertram Beecham, of Hardiston." Perhaps he was afraid it had been bad luck to reveal to the world his happy pride upon the birth of the other little girl, the baby who died. Owen's father and mother, like most Welsh people, felt it was tempting fortune to be too happy over anything.

But though BB in print restrained himself, Owen thought his happiness was like a bright garment upon the man.

7

Before summer was well begun, the demand for coal dwindled till there was little work for any man. Erie Mine, supplying Union Furnace, ran with some regularity; but other mines cut to three days a week, or two. "Some folks are bad off," Tom told Mrs. Glen one night at supper. "Evan Foster was down to see John Powell today." Owen and Mr. Beecham had stopped to talk with Evan Foster one day a year ago last January, when Evan and his brother and Mrs. Foster were roofing their new house out by Frisby Mine. "He says Frisby's worked just six days in June, and he only earned a little over twelve dollars. He was thinking John might take him on. They built a new house last year, and had a baby, and his wife's sick."

"Yes, and like as not he was one that was hot to strike." Owen's mother spoke in hopeless anger. "But she's the one to suffer for it now."

"I wouldn't wonder but a man feels worse when his wife's sick than she does." Tom's voice softened. "Don't you go getting sick on me, Annie."

"Go on with you, Tom." She pushed her hand at him as one pushes a horse in the stall. It always made Owen warmly happy when they were like this together.

The strike which began on the first of May had ended with the agreement to investigate mining costs throughout the state, but the investigation came to nothing. Representatives of the miners objected to the interpretation put upon the May agreement by the operators, and adjourned the proceedings. Herbert Canter, who was one of the operators on the committee, wrote a letter to John

McBride, president of the United Mine Workers, which Mr. Beecham printed in the *Journal*; but it was all about depreciation of mine property, and about whether it cost more to mine coal with machines than with men. His father could not explain to Owen what depreciation was, so he asked Mr. Beecham.

"Depreciation?" BB echoed. "In what connection?"

"Here in Mr. Canter's letter."

"I see. Well, in that sense, Owen, 'depreciation' is a pretense. It's a way the operators can claim it costs more than it actually does to mine coal. To avoid taxes, they value their coal in the ground at two cents a ton. Then they pay your father seventy cents a ton to mine that two-cent coal. By the time they dump the coal into a railroad car it has cost them about two dollars. They sell it — as the market is today — at something over three dollars. That's over two dollars profit. You'd think they'd be satisfied. But here comes the depreciation. They've used up a ton of two-cent coal, so their coal in the ground is worth two cents less than it was; but they'll claim their property has depreciated fifty cents, or a dollar, or maybe two dollars."

Owen was puzzled. "But Mr. Beecham —" He was sure there was something wrong with Mr. Beecham's figures. "That don't sound right. It don't make sense." BB was watching him, and suddenly Owen leaned forward. "I know! Papa can't just go and dig coal. Before he can do that, the operators have to hire a lot of other men to open up the mine, and to build the tipple, and lay the tracks, and timber the entries and — all sorts of things. It costs the operators a lot more than the seventy cents a ton they pay papa."

BB chuckled. "Good boy! I wondered if you'd figure that out. I talked the way —" It was his turn to hesitate. "Well, I talked the way an ignorant miner would talk. Of course, some of your leaders realize that the operators have their problems — and some operators are beginning to see that your Union is their best friend. Now depreciation, as Mr. Canter uses it in that letter —" BB nodded toward the *Journal* in Owen's hand. "It's a bookkeeping term, meaning loss due to wear and tear, or to the disappearance of value. Like the silver dollar. The silver in it used to be worth a dollar, but here two or three weeks ago, India quit coining silver. Before that happened, silver was worth sixty-seven cents; next day it was worth less than sixty, and it's worth less all the time. Your silver dollar today has depreciated in value till it's only worth forty-eight cents." He added: "That's why business is bad. The Free Silver men want to make us accept that forty-eight cents as a dollar; so everyone is scared, and times are hard — and will be worse."

Times were worse for Tom Glen a few days later, for on the first of August, Union Furnace blew out. BB headed the paragraph reporting this news, "Union Furnace Goes Democratic," and re-minded his readers that the democratic victory last fall was respon-sible for the spreading panic. The closing down of Union Furnace meant that Erie Mine would also close. Tom was near despair. Mrs. Glen tried to reassure him.

"We can get along, Tom, till the mine opens again."

"I doubt it ever will," Tom predicted. "I talked to John Powell today. He says they're like as not shut down for good and all."

"We'll manage, man dear." And she said reassuringly: "There was good work all winter till the strike, Tom, and I put something by. We won't starve yet awhile."

Her tone was light, but Owen saw how she fought to hearten his father. Next day was Saturday, so he went to the *Journal* office; but Sunday he was at home, and after dinner Tom Glen sat in gloom, slumped in his chair, his hands dangling limp between his knees until Mrs. Glen drove him to move.

"Get up with you, man. Get out from underfoot. I'm sick and tired of you sitting there with your face a foot long. Go on, get out of here."

He rose wearily. "No place to go, Annie!"

"Well, get out of my sight, anyway. Go pour ashes on your head, if you're bound to be a mourner. Go hoe the garden. Go anywhere. Go on."

Tom went out-of-doors, and Owen was sorry for him, and was about to follow and to comfort his father, till his mother without a word walked into their bedroom and closed the door. After a moment he heard the protest of the squeaky springs on their bed, and then silence, and then a sound and another. He crossed softly to the door to listen.

His mother was crying; he heard low racking sobs, and then a muffled wail, and then an angry cry. He opened the door, but she did not hear him. She lay across the bed, face down, her back

toward him; but her head was lifted, she was propped upon her
elbows, her fists beat the coverlet, and with each blow she uttered
a terrible little grunting sound as though she cried: "No! No!
No!" But then her head fell into her arms, and after a moment her
shoulders heaved in a long inhalation and she lay still.

He closed the door — if she heard, she made no move — and left
her there.

Through the weeks that followed, except on Wednesday and on
Saturday when, as he had done last year and the year before, he
worked in the *Journal* office, he stayed much at home with her; and
he saw how she struggled to lift Tom Glen to confidence again.
Each day she sent him away from the house "Does you no good
to sit here and count your troubles. Go talk to someone, see some
men. The house is no place for a man anyway."

Owen thought she was wise to do this, for certainly his father
was always, when he came home, more like himself; and one
morning after Tom Glen was gone, Owen said admiringly: "You
know how to handle him, don't you, mama?"

She looked at him with a strange glance. "Handle him? I don't
know, Owen." She left the dishpan and sat down in her low rocker
by the door, drying her hands in her apron, looking out through
the open door. "Do I handle him? Did I ever handle him, I
wonder?" Her eyes shadowed; she half-smiled. "I wanted him the
first minute I saw him, Owen. That was before he went to the War.
When he came back in his fine uniform —" She nodded, tender
amusement in her eyes. "Well, you might say I handled him then.
Someone had to tell the man his mind. So we were married, and off
he went, and then Tom was born that the slate caught when you
were a baby, and my Tom came back from the War." She rocked
slowly, sadly. "Maybe I could have handled him. Maybe I did.
But if I did, it was poor handling. We might have had a good
farm in Gallia to this day; but it was off to Illinois for us, and
shenanigans with Knights of Labor, and talk big talk, and strike,
and away to Indiana, and the same all over again, and back to
Ohio. And here."

She no longer rocked; she was a woman of stone, staring through
the open door at the slack pile down the run. Owen sat on the
doorstep at her feet. For a long time she did not move, but at last,
with a faint start, she looked down and met his eyes and shook her

head. "No, sonny, I've never handled him. I've just loved him close and dear, and he's loved me. And if you ask me why I picked him to love, I'll never know." She laughed in a sudden, warm fashion and leaned forward to towsle Owen's hair. "There've been times I could have killed him, sonny, but I've always loved him, just the same."

Her face had lighted, it settled now in dark shadowed lines again; and Owen said softly: "You're awful worried, aren't you, mama?"

She nodded, and wearily she rose. "Yes, I'm worried. I can't remember the day I wasn't." She returned to the dishpan. "If he had a job, I worried for fear he'd lose it; and if he hadn't, I worried for fear he couldn't find one." Her back was toward Owen, her hands among the dishes. "Yes, I'm worried all the time."

Tom came home at noon that day with a fine free-swinging stride and a high head and good news. Moses Evans was opening up a second entry at Miss Ellen, his big mine up the creek; John Powell, who had been mine boss at Erie, would go to Miss Ellen. "They'll need more men," Tom explained. "And John's taking some of us with him. We'll start in a couple of weeks."

When he began to speak, Mrs. Glen sat down, rocking quietly; but Owen saw her color drain away and then return, and he saw her great relief. He saw his father's, too. With maturing understanding, he saw them for the first time clearly. He had till now thought of them as grownups, of himself as a child; but in this hour of revelation he realized that they were not just grownups; they were old and tired and fearful.

But he was young, in stature almost a man, able to rescue them from secret fears. He went that afternoon to see John Powell, at his home out Peach Street beyond where Will Davis lived. Owen had known the mine boss only from a distance, seeing him at the mine when he went there to wait for his father. Approaching the house, he saw Mr. Powell pulling weeds in the garden, so he went through the gate and around the house. Powell heard his steps and looked up and said: "Hello, there! You look like Tom Glen's son."

"Yes sir, I am."

"My Tom says you're the smartest boy in his room." The man came along the row with extended hand. "Glad to see you. Looking for Tom?"

"No sir, I'm looking for you."

Powell eyed him for a questioning moment. "Well, we don't have to stand here in the sun," he said amiably. "Come up on the porch." Owen followed him to the back porch, and the mine boss said: "All right, what can I do for you?" So Owen explained, and at more length than he had intended, and Mr. Powell said at last: "You'd do better to stick to school, Owen. I'm keeping Tom at it, yes, and sending him to college too. You'll have time enough to work, later on."

"I want to start now. I can't stand it to have them worrying all the time. I work at the *Journal* office some, every morning and afternoon, and Wednesday and Saturdays in the summer; and I earn two dollars a week there, and some mowing lawns. But I could earn more in the mine."

"Talked to your folks?"

"Not yet. I didn't see the sense, unless I had a job."

"How old are you, son?"

"Fourteen in November."

"You're big for your age, all right." Powell scratched his head. "Well, I can pay trapper boys sixty cents a day. But we won't run every day."

"When the mine doesn't run, I can work in the *Journal* office Saturdays, and Wednesdays, too."

The mine boss nodded. "Well," he said, "if it suits your folks, it suits me."

So Owen went proudly home. When he told them, his mother fought herself into helpless tears; but she could not shake him, and Tom Glen took his side. "Let him try it, mama," he urged. "Even if it's only for a spell, long enough so's we can get our heads above water and maybe put a little by." Mrs. Glen, in bitter grief, had at last to yield.

VIII

August–September 1893

TOM AND OWEN would not be wanted at Miss Ellen till September; but Owen's decision drew him and his father once more close to one another as they had been three years ago, when in the last days before Amy was married they spent long days by the creekside, while Tom told old tales or drilled the boy in the speech he was to deliver at last day of school. There had been times of late when Owen thought his father mistaken, or stubborn, or stupid; but now that was no longer true. His father was a high priest of the craft to which he proposed to devote himself; as a neophyte, he was attentive to Tom Glen's every word.

When first they were alone together after Mrs. Glen's protests had been beaten down — it was next morning and they were off toward town — Tom dropped his arm across Owen's shoulder, and that awkward caress stirred Owen close to happy tears. "But I'll tell you one thing, son," said Tom, as though continuing a conversation already begun. "You'll be no trapper boy." This had been John Powell's proposal. "You're too near man's size for that. We won't tell mama, not now, anyway; but you'll come into my room and help me."

Owen's pulse leaped; but then, fearfully, he remembered that Mr. Harned and his son had worked a room together, and died together under twenty tons of slate. Owen thought his mother, when she heard he was in the same room with his father, would remember that double tragedy and dread a like end for them. "I sure want to work with you, papa; but it will upset mama, won't it?"

"No, no. She'll be easier in her mind to know I've got an eye on you."

Owen was bound for the *Journal* office, but Tom turned aside
at Belton Street to see Isaac Williams. "I want to find out if he's
going along to Miss Ellen," he explained, and Owen went on
alone. This was Wednesday, so he would be all day in the *Journal*
office. As he finished sweeping the file room, Will came in, and
then Edna. She paused at the foot of the stairs to look across at
Will, just putting on the short apron which protected his garments
during the day. He was having trouble knotting the strings, reaching around behind his back, and she laughed and came close to
him, saying:

"Here, honey, let me!"

But Will backed away. "Look out, there. You'll get your fingers
burnt!"

"I wouldn't mind, if you burned them."

Owen, angry for no reason he could have named, brushed against
her as he went to stand his broom in the corner behind where she
stood, and she spoke in sharp resentment; but then Bets and Dan
Davis, Will's brother, came in together, and Bets and Edna went
upstairs.

Dan looked after them with an appraising eye. "I'd take the thin
one, if it was me," he remarked.

Will drawled: "You didn't come for that. How much do you
want?"

Dan spoke in hurt surprise. "Want? I don't want a thing, Will.
I just came in to pass the time of day." He spoke to Owen. "Hi,
kid! How you and Sadie Paxley getting along?"

Owen flushed, turned away. "I used to cut her grass, that's all."

"I'd say keeping her grass cut was a man's job," Dan commented,
with a grin; and he asked: "Know her, Will? Her father used to run
a hotel out in Iowa, and they say that by the time she was eighteen,
she'd slept in every bed in the hotel. Then this Paxley inherited
some money, so she married him." He lounged nearer Will, who
was putting the stone in order, clearing the forms. "And speaking
of money, Will, I could use a couple of dollars till Saturday."

Will laughed shortly. "I don't know how you do it, Dan, but you
always pay me on the nose. If you ever miss — "

"Oh, I won't miss, Will. Can't afford to. Thanks."

Dan drifted away through the file room, and Will returned to his
task. Without looking at Owen, he said after a while: "Dan won't

ever amount to anything, Owen. Don't let him bother you."

"I don't like him."

"A dirty man can lay a dirty tongue on anyone. It don't prove anything. Dan's a liar from way back — where women are concerned." He looked up the stairs, returned his attention to his work again. "If he ever tells a lie about me that gets home to her, I'll likely kill him."

"She wouldn't believe it."

"It would bother her, all the same. I won't have her bothered." His tone was gentle enough, yet Owen was for a moment afraid of him; he came pressing near Will's side to watch what the foreman was doing, and Will grinned. "Looking for type lice, Owen?" They laughed together, and the day was fine.

2

The paper went to press that afternoon, and at BB's suggestion, he and Owen next day walked the long ten miles to Sardis Church and on past the furnace to Sycamore Hill to catch the up train. With a shortage of rain all summer, the fields were dry, the corn crop badly stunted; and every farmer with whom they spoke was full of complaints. Two or three miles south of Hardiston, they passed Ira Skilling's farm. BB had been the principal speaker at a Bean Dinner in the hilltop grove on Ira's place the preceding Saturday, and he referred to this, adding:

"Old Ira died in his sleep Sunday night. Maybe it was the heat Saturday that killed him. His death notice is in this week's *Journal*. That's the hard part of the life of a country editor, Owen. Tom Cordingley, who founded the *Journal*, once told me he had written over three thousand death notices of people he knew personally. The day of the Bean Dinner, it was as hot as I want to see. There were twelve hundred people there. Ira had hauled up a barrel of water, but they drank it all, and by the time I came to speak, there wasn't a drop of drinking water in the grove. I was spitting cotton."

"I want to make speeches some day."

"Why?"

"I just want to."

"Well, the first step is to have something to talk about."

Owen nodded, and as though in response he said: "I'm going to work in a week or two. In Miss Ellen, up the creek."

BB had not known this plan; he asked questions and Owen answered them. "That's one of Mr. Evans's mines," BB remarked at last. "You know him, don't you?"

"Yes sir, papa rents our house from him."

"He and Herbert Canter between them beat the Anti-Screen Bill. They're against anything the miners want. I notice the Glendale miners had a mass meeting ten days ago to cuss out Senator Phillips because he voted against it. If the miners are going to vote against him, Phillips will be a load on the ticket this fall."

Owen said nothing; politics was of small interest to him. The road wound around the flank of the hill, and BB remarked that it followed an old Indian trace. "The lowland down there was a bog till the farmers tiled it," he explained. "So the trace came along this hillside, through the hardwoods, where the going was easier. If Hardiston ever decides to put in waterworks, a few wells down there will find plenty of water." The day was hot, and he mopped his brow. BB always wore stiff-fronted shirts and a round collar; but today he had left coat and collar at home, and his shirt bosom was soft with perspiration. He chuckled at his own thoughts. "Why do you suppose 'perspire' is more elegant than 'sweat'? I suppose because 'perspire' is from the Latin, and 'sweat' is Anglo-Saxon. In the old days, only learned folk spoke Latin; so they 'perspired,' while serfs 'sweated.' Snobbery has deep roots, hasn't it?"

"What's 'snobbery'?"

"Well, 'snob' comes from the Latin, too, like 'perspire.' In the old days, when a census was taken, noblemen put their titles after their names on the rolls; but a commoner, an ordinary man was 'John Smith, s. nob.' — which meant 'without nobility.' But it's ignoble to pretend to think you're better than others, so when anyone does that nowadays, we say he's a snob; that is, 'without nobility.' See?"

They walked for minutes in silence. Once BB said: "Hullo, there's a mockingbird." The bird, with a flicker of white tail feathers, crossed the road ahead of them and alighted in a thorn tree, from which another bird at once departed. "And that was a shrike that flew off," BB said. "A butcher bird. They kill grasshoppers and mice

and sometimes small birds and hang them on the thorns to eat later.
Let's see if that thorn bush is the shrike's pantry." So they climbed
the fence and inspected the tree, but found nothing. "I've seen
mice and things in thorn trees in winter," BB said. "But it's hard
to see them when the leaves are on."

Back in the road again they strode more briskly. "We'll eat our
lunch at a spring down below the cabin where I was born," BB
promised, but presently his pace slowed. "Let's stop in at this
house," he suggested. "You'll see something you're not likely to see
again. These people have twenty-three living children."

The house was sagging toward disintegration, so that in profile it
suggested a swaybacked horse; it was weathered gray except where
here and there a few flakes of dirty white paint still clung; there
were broken panes in the windows, and half of one chimney had
toppled over, so that some of the bricks still lay spattered on the
curled cedar shakes. The front gate was broken, sections of the
fence around the yard had fallen down, and the yard was knee-high
in grass and weeds except where the chickens wandering everywhere had eaten it down to baked, bare ground.

As they came into the yard, Owen saw a boy and two girls
digging a hole by the fence; and a boy sat in the shade of the barn.
When BB knocked, someone called an invitation, and BB pushed
open the door. The kitchen seemed to Owen to be full of people,
boys and girls, men and women; but no one rose or spoke till BB
said cheerfully: "Well, it's a fine day, Mr. Skeele."

A lanky man of no particular age, with a shock of black hair and
a black beard, sitting tipped back in a chair facing the stove, spat
a brown stream into the grate. "Howdy, BB. Hot, though."

"Good many years since I used to board up at Uncle Josh's," BB
remarked. "But none of your children ever came to Redfern School."

"Too fur. I don't hold much with school, anyhow."

No one suggested that they come in. Owen, under the fixed stare
of many eyes, was uncomfortable; but BB seemed at ease. He and
Owen stood on the wide stone that served as doorstep, and BB tried
to lead Mr. Skeele into conversation; but the task proved too difficult and at length they said goodbye. On the road again, BB for
a while did not speak; then, seeming to remember he was not alone,
he said: "Well, Owen, you saw most of the family. They have nine
sons old enough to vote — that's ten votes, counting Mr. Skeele's

— and five more boys growing up. All Republicans, I'm glad to say." But he did not sound glad, and he held silence so long that Owen became concerned.

"What's the matter?" he asked.

BB seemed to rouse. "Oh — I was just doing a little addition — and subtraction. My great-grandfather Beecham had eleven children and raised five. He was an English barrister of high repute. As nearly as I can count, he has twenty-one great-grandchildren living, nine of them males. Those whom I know, or know about, are respectable, reasonably educated, hard-working men and women; they're the sort of people we call 'good stock.'

"But Ed Skeele's family can outvote — today — all my great-grandfather's great-grandchildren. Think what will happen when Ed Skeele's great-grandchildren come along. It isn't the meek who inherit the earth, Owen; it's the breeders." Almost without a pause he added, in an easier tone: "I used to gather hickory nuts off that tree ahead when I was a boy. We're coming to the house where I was born. You can see the roof of it now. A log cabin. See."

When they were at ease beside the spring, the cabin, to which a frame wing had been added, stood fifty yards above them, and twice Owen saw the faces of children at the windows; but none came out to speak to them, and BB did not knock at the door. "The farm's run down now," he remarked. "All gone to briars and sumac; but it was a good farm when I was a boy. Three of my sisters died in that house in one week, Owen. They had diphtheria, and so did I. The doctor came and took a steel rod dipped in castor oil and stuck it down their throats to clear the phlegm; but when it was my turn, I bolted through the door and out into the snow, barefooted, and I wouldn't come back till father promised not to let the doctor do that to me. They all died, but I got well." Owen thought Mr. Beecham said this with a certain pride, as though he believed his superior wisdom had saved his life.

Lunch was always a pleasant interlude. Owen enjoyed watching Mr. Beecham relish his victuals. The editor ate with a fine gusto, and with many approving comments. "M-m, m-m, but that's a tasty sandwich!" "Did you ever taste a finer stuffed egg than that one?" "There's the sweetest early apple in the world!" "A piece of pie like that gives a man good dreams."

Half an hour after their stop for lunch, they came to where Dave and Amy lived with Dave's father and mother. The whole household was in the yard admiring a two-seated spring wagon drawn by two horses and glistening with new paint; and Amy ran to Owen to hug and to be hugged.

"Come along and see Dave's new express," she invited. "He just brought it back from Sycamore Hill. New harness and everything."

She held Owen's hand, leading him, beckoning BB, and they followed her. Owen had not seen her since they came to little David's funeral two years before. Then she was in tears, or her eyes were red with grief; but today she was bright with happiness, buxom and pretty. Little Annie, a year and a half old, begged Dave to lift her into the fine new wagon. The baby sprawled on a blanket on the ground, three months old and so fat that he pivoted on his stomach as he tried to crawl, revolving like a turtle as it prepares to drop off a log. BB went to the porch with Dave's father to talk with Mrs. Lewis, who suffered from dropsy and seldom left her chair. Dave climbed into the express and Owen lifted Annie up to him and Dave drove the horses at a sedate walk around the farmyard, while Amy and Owen watched, and she gave him many messages for her mother and Tom Glen.

She tried to keep them here, but they had miles to go. As he and BB went on, Owen remembered how he had grieved at Amy's wedding, and he told BB, and pointed up toward the woods where he had hidden after the wedding supper.

"I was awful homesick for her. I thought I'd never see her again, and I thought I'd just stay there and die." He grinned at his own folly. "Then a crowd came to give them a belling, and I had a fight with Pete Radford, and Bobby Roberts took me home."

"Radford? Isn't he the boy who was sent to the Reform School for robbing a store in Sycamore Hill?"

"Yes. It was in the *Journal*."

"What did you fight about?"

"He talked dirty about Amy. I bloodied his nose. He was bigger than me, too."

BB smiled. " 'Thrice is he armed that hath his quarrel just.' " Owen looked at him inquiringly. "Or in other words, every dog fights best in his own yard." He pointed across the valley to a white house a mile or more away. "That's Uncle Joshua's, on the other

road. I boarded there when I taught at Redfern School. There's a
path up over that hill, a short cut. It used to be dark by the time I
got home, and I often sat down on a stump on that hill to rest. One
night there was a skunk on the stump, and I didn't see him till I
sat on him. I had to bury my best suit of clothes. That was a real
tragedy. You remember how you felt when you burned a hole in
your first long pants?"

Owen grinned absently. To remember Pete Radford had turned
his thoughts into another channel. After a silence that lasted twenty
paces, he asked suddenly, blurting out the question: "Mr. Beecham,
what's 'secret practices'?" He felt BB's surprise, and not looking
up, his cheeks hot, he explained: "It's in Doctor France's advertisements in the *Journal*." And he quoted: "They 'sweep to an
untimely grave thousands of young men of exalted talent and
brilliant intellect.'"

BB cleared his throat: "You read those advertisements, do you?"

"Yes sir. And they" — BB guessed he was quoting again —
"'blight young men's most radiant hopes, making marriage
impossible.'"

It was a moment before BB spoke. "I don't read those ads. They
come in boiler plate, so I don't even read proof on them." His tone
changed, he was almost chuckling. "In fact, I never read any
medical advertisements. They always make me think I've got the
diseases they promise to cure. The way to keep healthy is to avoid
thinking that maybe you're sick. People who run to the doctors all
the time make invalids of themselves."

Owen had guessed the advertisements concerned matters he was
too young to know about, and Mr. Beecham's manner confirmed this
conjecture; but when the editor presently began to talk again, Owen
had an uncertain feeling that in an oblique way the older man was
answering his question.

"I told you one day," BB remarked, "that you're about the same
age as the United States. Neither one of you is grown up yet, but
you're both on the doorstep of early maturity." He hesitated. "The
United States is a lusty, healthy, growing boy. It still thinks of
itself as a boy in a man's world. It's shy, and easily embarrassed;
and it brags as a boy brags, not to impress others but to convince
itself that it's getting to be a big boy now." He walked a few steps

in silence. "We — the United States — keeps trying to find out more about itself, trying to measure its own powers, testing the capacities it's just beginning to suspect. For instance, we kill Indians to prove to ourselves that we're brave and strong, but fifty years from now we'll be ashamed of the way we treated the Indians."

He looked at Owen, but the boy's eyes were on the road, and BB went on: "That's the great advantage of being young. Youth has such a wealth of resources that to waste them does no permanent harm. The mistakes of youth are a lot less important than preachers of fire and brimstone try to make us believe. Remember how glad his parents were to forgive the prodigal son?" He added, half to himself: "But I don't suppose the fatted calf was ever killed for a prodigal daughter."

At Sardis Church they turned into the churchyard and came to where little Anne Beecham was buried, and BB cleared away some weeds that grew across the grave. "We're placing a stone here as soon as we can," he said. Owen had thought of Mr. Beecham as a rich man; a sudden deeper affection made him warm. They went on past the furnace, idle now, with pig iron that could not be sold stacked across the flat. Even the store was closed, and the small houses on the flat were deserted; but Owen pointed out to Mr. Beecham the one in which he had lived.

"I guess no one will ever live here any more," he hazarded.

BB said cheerfully: "Don't be too sure. Old Adams Furnace isn't dead yet, Owen. My Uncle Josh was one of the original stock-holders — they had a rule that none but Welshmen could own stock — but the stock was never worth much till the Civil War." He and Owen had stopped to rest, sitting on the steps of the store. "They used to tell about an early meeting of the furnace company. They had bought a bull to improve their cattle. The treasurer reported that the furnace was losing money, and the furnace store was just about breaking even, but the bull had showed a profit. Uncle Josh moved to shut down the furnace and the store, and proceed to operate the bull!"

Owen laughed with him. "But I guess they'll never sell all that iron out there unless there's another war or something."

BB's eyes narrowed. "Another war," he murmured. "Yes, I suppose that would revive the furnace. In the Sixties, iron hit ninety dollars a ton." He added reflectively: "Three hundred and forty-five men and boys from this township went to the Civil War, and thirty-six were killed or died.

"But war or no war, the furnace will start up again, one of these days. Of course, they're not paying dividends now, but I hear Ed Williams is buying every share of stock that's for sale, and Ed doesn't throw money away." Mr. Williams was by reputation almost as rich as Herbert Canter. He and his father owned Union Furnace, which meant that they owned Erie Mine, and other mines up the creek. BB added: "Hardiston County iron is fine for some special purposes. Silvery iron, they call it. You'll see our furnaces prospering long after the last coal in the county has been dug."

Owen looked at him in surprise. "Will they ever dig it all?"

BB smiled, rising. "They used to say our coal was inexhaustible; but twenty-five years from now, the end will be in sight. Well, we've got to move. A hot day like this, I could sit here for hours. Ever notice how heat wilts our consciences as well as our collars. In winter it's easy to be good."

When they came to Marged's father's farm, Marged was sitting in a hammock under the trees, Bobby Roberts on the ground beside her; and at BB's hail she came running to greet them and to ask them in. "Papa and Aunt Molly are gone to town, but I'll make you some lemonade." Marged's mother seldom left her bed. Something mysteriously incapacitating had happened when Marged was born; and Aunt Molly, ever since, had lived with them and cared for them.

To Marged's invitation, BB admitted he was thirsty; so they sat on the shaded porch while she disappeared toward the kitchen. Back at the furnace, Owen had seen the house where Bobby used to live now closed and shuttered, and he spoke of this; and Bobby said he had saved enough to pay something down on the old Evan Morgan farm on Hermit's Fork. "So mama and I live there now. I'm getting it in good shape, and I'll soon have a real farm."

Marged came back with a dewy pitcher and four glasses, and after a moment BB told her Owen's news. "He's going to work in Miss Ellen, up the creek."

Marged cried out in disappointment. "Oh, Owen, really? You're giving up school? Do you have to?"

He said honestly: "I don't have to, but I want to. I'm too old to go to school."

"Why, you'll be going to school all your life, Owen! You'll never stop learning things!"

"I can learn faster not going to school."

"It's hard, studying all alone."

"I can learn all I want to." Miss Means last year had, he was sure, hindered more than she helped; but he did not say so, thinking Miss Williams might defend her.

"You can if you will," she agreed; then suddenly her eyes lighted. "Oh, Owen, remember before you got the double promotion we studied together, and you really did a year's work in five or six weeks. Mr. Atkinson says I'm going to teach first-year High School this year, so I'll be studying myself this winter. Maybe we can study together again!"

Owen hesitated. His father always came home from the mine black-faced and grimy, his clothes saturated with coal dust, his feet plastered with mud. "I'll probably be pretty tired every night."

"Nonsense!" She laughed affectionately. "You won't be tired, not after you're used to it." Then, as she saw his doubts: "But you can't decide yet. You'll have to learn a lot about the work in the mine first, anyway. We'll talk about it again when I come to town, shall we?"

On the way to Sycamore Hill, Owen, thinking of what Miss Williams had said, remembered how happy he had been when they worked together, till BB remarked: "Miss Williams is a fine young woman, isn't she? It's a wonder some young man hasn't married her before now."

Owen looked at him in sharp surprise. He had never imagined that Miss Williams would presently get married; but after all, she was as old as Amy, and Amy had had three babies! He remembered when Miss Williams used to spend the night with Amy, and she and Amy slept together a few feet from where he lay on his pallet on the floor. The memory roused in him that stirring like a hunger which he had learned to recognize, and which so many and such different things awakened. To think that Miss Williams might some day marry someone made him now as wretched as he had been when Amy married Dave.

Riding home to Hardiston on the train, feeling the stiff-fibered plush through his thin shirt, he sat sidewise, his back half-turned to Mr. Beecham, pretending to be absorbed in the passing countryside.

3

Any old clothes would do for Owen to wear to the mine; but Tom Glen said he would need brogans, and a cap and lamp, and a dinner pail. "The cap and lamp you can get at the company store," he advised; and privately, to Owen, he added: "You'll need some tools, too, but we won't tell mama yet."

On the Sunday night before he was to go to work with his father, Owen lay long awake, wondering whether he would be frightened in the deeps of the mine, groping through a cloud of ignorance into the unknown future. The roar of Star Furnace, far away at the other end of town, came through the night like the growl of some great beast. Familiar with the throbbing beat of Adams Furnace, he had when he first came to Hardiston hardly noticed the deeper note of the furnaces here; but tonight, though Union Furnace was shut down, the roar of Star was loud in his ears; and though his bedroom was on the side of the house away from town, he could see a brightness outside his windows when the bell was tipped and the flames leaped high against the sky.

He slept at last, and his father waked him. "Rouse up, son. It's half-past four."

Half-asleep, he stumbled out of bed. He saw through the open door his mother by the kitchen stove, making coffee, frying bacon. His sleepy fingers fumbled with his clothes, struggled with the stiff laces of his new brogans; and when he was dressed he went drowsily into the kitchen. His mother looked over her shoulder and said in a strange, angry tone:

"Up are you?" Well, wash the sleep out of your eyes."

In sudden maturity of understanding he knew that she was cross because she was worried and frightened and sad, and he went to her and put his arm around her, pulled her head nearer, kissed her cheek. "Now, mama, I'll be fine."

"Wash your dirty face," she said crossly, but she returned his kiss. "There, hurry. Breakfast's ready."

He felt older than she, old and wise and tender. He scrubbed face and hands in the tin basin, and sat down at the table; and Tom Glen came through from the shed, carrying his picks and drill and tamper, and his shovel and coal fork and all his tools. He leaned them against the wall just inside the door, and Mrs. Glen protested: "Now look at you! I've told you often enough, Tom Glen, to keep the dirt off my floor! I'll be on my knees all morning scrubbing up that mess."

"There's no dirt on them, mama. I cleaned them before I put them away, yes, and greased them to keep the rust off."

"Grease is worse than dirt! Put 'em outside."

Tom obeyed, and Owen laughed, and repeated a familiar bit of doggerel:

> "Mama's mad, and I am glad
> And I know what will please her,
> A bottle of ink to make her stink
> And Tommy Glen to squeeze her."

She laid a heaping plate in front of him. "Hush up and eat your vittles." Tom Glen, having removed the offending tools, came to sit opposite Owen. They ate in an earnest silence, sipping the scalding coffee with strong sucking sounds, sopping up the last grease in their plates, the last stain of egg yolk. While they ate, she filled their lunch pails; fried egg sandwiches, pork sandwiches, half a pie in each pail, and in each a bottle of sweetened coffee thick with cream. Tom looked at his silver watch.

"Quarter-past five," he said. "Plenty of time yet." He began to cut tobacco from a plug and fill his pipe. "Well, Owen, by tonight you'll be a coal miner."

Mrs. Glen sniffed resentfully; and Owen, guessing that she would feel better after they were gone, said: "We don't want to miss the train, papa. And there's a lot to carry."

"No hurry," Tom persisted. At the prospect of going back to work again, he was in an easy humor. Nevertheless, when his pipe was going, he rose; and a moment later Owen was in his mother's arms, and she was hugging him and kissing him, and crying too.

When he kissed her, he smelled her tears; and her face was hot and moist from the stove. He wanted to cry with her, but that would make her worse.

"There, mama! There, you'll feel better now. Have plenty of supper for us. We'll be hungry!"

"As if I didn't know!" The new sun was burning away horizon mists, so she blew out the lamp and came to stand in the doorway. Owen and his father shouldered the tools and went up the path to the road; and Owen, looking back, could see her standing, watching, a pale silhouette against the dark doorway. When she was out of sight behind them, he faced the increasing brightness of the east, stretching his legs to match his father's unhurried stride.

Beyond the run, approaching the corner of Ridge Street, they saw Charles Morgan come out of his house on the corner and go on ahead of them; and at other intersecting streets, men by ones and twos appeared, to precede them or to follow them. All were bound, as they were, for the station and the six-o'clock train and the mines up the creek.

The train was in the station when they arrived, the engine with steam up sighing like a monster snoring in its sleep. Owen had been here many times by light of day; but now in the hush of early morning, broken only by the clumping pound of heavy feet and the hissing sigh of the engine, and with the steaming smoke-fouled air stinging his nostrils, the place was strange and wonderful. On the platform Tom said, to one man and another: "This is my boy, going to start in helping me." Owen felt the grip of calloused hands, heard the kindly word.

When they climbed the steps, the cars were already well filled. Owen, leading, would have turned into the rear car; but Tom Glen said: "No, that's for the operators, and school teachers working up the creek, and ordinary passengers. That way, they don't have to sit on dirty seats."

So Owen turned into the forward car, where the seats were grimed with coal dust. After a day in the mine, men had no chance to change their clothes before boarding the train to ride home; so the plush was matted and dark, the sour smell of stale pipe smoke weighted the air, and the floor was stained and grimy.

Owen sat between his father and the window, watching others come aboard; Mr. Powell, and Isaac Williams, and little Mat Steel and big Ed Thorne. Obviously Mr. Powell was taking a number of Erie men with him to Miss Ellen. He saw two boys he knew, Dan Evans and Louie Peters. They had quit school long ago. Dan was a dullard, silent, grinning vacuously; but Louie was of livelier mold. Owen remembered the day when they were in Miss Dine's room together and Louie flipped a bent pin on a rubber band so shrewdly that it stuck in Tommy Morgan's scalp. Louie had been the loudest talker in the enclosure around the privies, with a boastful, bawdy tongue. When they came into the car, Louie stopped beside Owen's seat.

"H'lo, Owen. Going to work?"

"M-hm."

"Where?"

"Miss Ellen."

"Dan and me get off this side of Slacktown, John Thomas Number Three." Mines up the creek were often designated by the name of the operator, the number of the mine. "Wish we'd be together."

Owen did not share this wish, but he said: "Maybe, sometime."

When the engine's bell began to ring and the train to move, Owen saw two miners approaching the station, and not fifty yards away. He expected them to run, but instead they slowed and stopped; and he pointed them out to his father. "Look, papa. Why don't they run? They could catch it."

"Bad luck to run for the train, Owen. They'll go back home."

"Bad luck?"

"The worst kind. I've known three men to do it, and the slate smashed them all. Another thing, if the train runs right by your mine, don't ever go into the entry till the train's gone."

"Oh, papa, that's just superstition. Like witches!"

"Call it so if you want. A lot of things happen in the world that we don't know why. Don't ever laugh at what another man believes, Owen. He might be right and you be wrong." He added with a mirthful sound: "And if you was right and he knew you were, he wouldn't like it, anyway."

It was a seven- or eight-mile run to Belton, but the train would be more than half an hour on the way, for it stopped at every tipple and every siding. At each stop, men by threes and fours alighted and tramped off to the mine where they were employed; and sometimes a young woman got off with them, to teach the nearby school, to return to Hardiston that afternoon on this same train. If men were the only passengers alighting, the train did not always come to a full stop, but only slowed to a crawl, so that they could swing down with a farewell wave of the hand to the conductor or to the engineer. Owen, receptive as a sponge, observed everything and remembered everything.

It was after they had passed through Slacktown — a considerable huddle of flimsy, black-sooted homes and store buildings — and through the smaller village of Glendale, that Tom Glen rose. "Next is ours, Owen," he said. The train had not yet begun to slacken speed, but all the length of the car men were rising, crowding into the aisle, pressing toward the doors.

There were so many to alight that the train came to a full stop. As he dropped to the levelled cinders beside the track, Owen saw, alighting from the operators' car, Moses Evans, and with him young Sammy Howell, whose father had kept the store at Adams Furnace. When the train pulled away, Sammy spoke to him. "H'lo, Owen. Gosh, you've grown! Where you going?"

"So've you!" This was pure politeness on Owen's part. He thought Sammy had not grown at all; if anything, he had shrunk a little. "I work in Miss Ellen." He liked the sound of that present tense.

"I'm teaching Evans School," Sammy said; he added honestly: "Starting today."

"This is my first day, too."

"This is my first school. But it's only little kids." Sammy was sixteen. "I can handle them."

They followed the men up the siding toward the tipple half a mile away, till Sammy turned off to climb to the small schoolhouse on the slope above the tracks. Owen looked after him with mild envy, thinking he too might have become a school teacher; but school teachers only earned thirty or forty dollars a month in the county schools, and a miner could earn more than that.

"Besides," Owen reminded himself, hurrying to overtake his father, "I'd rather be a miner."

A trestle ran out from the mine to reach the siding; and along the siding and along the muddy little stream that threaded the valley, scattered houses stood at odd angles above and below the tipple. The slack pile sprawled along the hillside, rising almost to the level of the trestle. With Moses Evans and John Powell leading the way, the men followed a beaten path which zigzagged up the steep side of the slack pile. Iron tracks coming off the trestle led Owen's eyes to the dark mouth of the entry; and along the tracks and along the dusty road which scarfed the hillside, a few buildings were all alike the color of coal dust and of soot. Moses Evans unlocked one of these buildings and went in, and Owen guessed that was his office; and Tom said to the mine boss:

"Owen needs to get some things from the store. And me too."

Powell took them into the store, where a man in his shirt sleeves, with garters to hold up his sleeves and a short-bitten stub of a pipe in his mouth was busy at a desk. "Mike," said the mine boss, "this is Tom Glen, and his son Owen. Put them on the books. They want some things."

Mike — it was weeks before Owen learned that his name was Ryan — made a note on a sheet of ruled paper; then he clumped to his feet and Owen saw that he had a peg leg, his own leg gone above the knee, so that he walked with a swaggering, pivoting gait. He emptied his pipe in his palm, rubbed the ashes on the leg of his overalls, polished the bowl of the pipe against his nose and asked cheerfully:

"So what'll it be?"

Tom Glen considered. "Well, I've got my picks, but Owen better have his own so he won't bust mine. And give him a shovel and a coal fork. Oh, first thing, he needs a cap and a lamp." Owen, trying on the black box-shaped cap with a leather socket at the front into which his lamp hook would fit, trembled with delight. "Then I'll need a keg of powder, and some squibs, and a can of oil."

"Some of the men like to mix carbon oil and black jack," Mike suggested in a tentative fashion. "I wouldn't go to say they're right nor they're wrong."

"I'll stick to lard oil. I'm used to it."

"A wise man ye be."

Tom scratched his head, to stimulate thought. "Owen won't be needing an auger yet, but give him a scraper and a tamper." Owen handled the tools with delighted pride. The scraper was six feet long, with one end turned at right angles to the handle and flattened like the blade of a shallow spoon. The iron tamper had a copper tip that was grooved on one side, and a steel bit on the other end. Tom explained: "That groove's for the needle to go through. You'll see by'n by. And the steel bit is so if your auger hits lime, or sulphur, or anything it can't cut, you can use the tamper for a churn drill." He spoke to the storekeeper. "Better give us a six-foot needle, too. Mine's only three-foot. Erie's all thin vein." The needle was a slender, pointed rod with one end sharpened to a point, and a ring at the other.

When every need was filled, Tom shouldered the keg of powder, and Mike handed him half a dozen brass discs, each numbered 19. Tom said: "Nineteen? Much obliged. Owen, we hang one of these on any car we load, so the checker'll know who mined the car. Oh, Mike, got an old newspaper?" Mike gave him one, first folding it carefully; and Tom, still balancing the keg, put the paper under his free arm. "All right, Owen. We're ready."

While they were in the store, other men had come up from the houses in the valley below. On the track outside the entry stood two trains of empty cars, each drawn by a flop-eared mule that seemed to be half-asleep. Men were already sitting in some of the cars, others joining them. John Powell beckoned and called:

"Here's your car, Tom."

They deposited in the car the tools, the powder, a gallon can of oil, their lunch pails. "Watch your heads," Powell reminded them. "Low roof." He called to the driver: "All aboard!" The mule put the train in motion and they rolled toward the entry of the mine.

In the cut as they approached the entry Tom lighted his lamp, and Owen tried to light his, but the wick was dry. He knew a sudden panic at the prospect of being in the dark without a lamp; but his father said: "You can fill it when we get to our room."

Then they rolled into the entry, and behind them men and cars were silhouettes against the disappearing daylight. The roof of the entry was so low that the mule's nodding ears brushed the timbers overhead. At first Owen could see the slanting posts that supported the roof timbers, the lagging laid horizontally to hold back the dirt and rock on either side; then daylight disappeared, but Tom Glen's lamp gave enough light so Owen marked where the lagging gave way at first to bare clay and then, as the entry became a tunnel through the vein, to the gleaming blackness of the coal. Owen, looking up at the slate roof close above his head, feeling crushed by the weight of the hill into whose heart they penetrated, gritted his teeth to keep them from chattering, and bowed his head in his arms.

Good-humored voices from ahead of them and behind called casually to and fro. At intervals the mules paused while the rearmost car was uncoupled and left behind; at intervals a door opened to let them through, and the trap boy on duty there exchanged some word with drivers or with miners. They approached and passed something that made a clanking sound — the pump, Tom Glen said, keeping the sump clear of water — and they passed a small fire built on a brick hearth in a niche in the entry wall. Owen's father explained that above the fire a shaft led up to open air; the up-draft drew fresh air into the mine.

When theirs was the last car in the train and the mule stopped, Tom stepped out, and Owen hurriedly followed him. They uncoupled their car and the mule drew the others on, deeper into the mine. The lamps on the caps of the men dwindled in distance, and back along the way they had come Owen saw a lamp, and another beyond that, disappear, melting into the entry wall. He whispered to his father:

"Their lamps went out."

"No, no. They've gone into their rooms, so you can't see 'em." Tom added mirthfully: "You don't have to whisper, son. Now let's fill your lamp."

Owen's hands were shaking so that his fingers would not function; he took off his cap to unhook the lamp, and dropped cap and lamp, and Tom picked them up.

"You won't mind it, half an hour from now," he said gently. Owen wanted to cling to him; his father was a black figure dimly seen, face hidden by the shadow of his visor, the flame of his lamp shedding shadows downward like an umbrella around him.

Tom filled and lighted Owen's lamp, and Owen put his cap on, and his lamp illumined their surroundings. He saw a black oblong of darkness in the wall of the entry just ahead of the car. Tom, bending over, entered this blackness, and Owen stooped to follow him. They came into a forest of bank props, set to support the roof after the jack slate was down. Tom took off his cap and on his knees went forward, holding his lamp high enough so that the flame touched the rock inches above his head. Owen watched him, pressed into silence by his consciousness of the hill's mass waiting to come ponderously down and crush them; he wished to scream, to cling to his father, to run, to bolt out through the neck into the entry and away to blessed day.

"I'm looking for fire damp," Tom Glen explained. "We don't have it much around here, but some mines have enough gas so they need double ventilation. No harm in looking." And he said, like an instructor: "There's fire damp, that burns; and there's black damp, that puts your lamp out; and there's cold damp, comes sometimes after your shots, that puts you to sleep for good."

"Can you see fire damp?"

"You can tell if it's here by the way the lamp burns." Tom finished exploring the room. "None here. Now we'll try the jack slate." Crouching, he moved along the face, striking the roof beyond the last prop with the flat of his pick. "If it's loose, you can tell; it gives a kind of hollow sound." And when he was content: "Guess it hasn't started. All right, we'll clean this up." He touched with his foot some broken fragments, apparently fallen from the roof, which lay along the face. "Then we'll post her up to the face and go to work."

"Is that slate?" Owen asked, pointing to the fragments on the floor. His voice was hushed in a sort of awe, for slate was the miner's deadly enemy.

"Yes. There's six-seven inches of jack slate on top of the vein. If you don't prop it, come two or three days after you take the coal out, and sometimes it loosens and falls. If it does, you clear it away and put in bank props up to the face." He said reflectively: "Well, we won't fill our car today, with all there is to do; but we'll get it in out of the way so they can get past outside."

They returned to the entry and manhandled the car, swinging it off the iron rails onto the stub switch and along two-by-fours laid as a track from the entry through the neck into their room. "We'll leave it here in the neck for now," Tom said. "It'll be out of the way. You shovel that loose slate back in the gob."

Owen brought a shovel. "What's the gob?"

"All that." Tom pointed to a heap of dirt and rock in the back of the room. "Gob's any trash you don't want. I'll post her up to the face. Whoever worked this room last didn't do it. Mostly you do it soon's you've loaded your coal."

Owen began to work, but the room was so low he could not stand erect; and he soon discovered that to shovel in a stooped position was incredibly difficult. Each time he swung the shovel, he instinctively straightened up; each time he straightened up, he bumped his head. After a few minutes, Tom Glen remarked: "Mostly I kneel down to shovel, Owen. It goes easier for me."

Owen found the advice good, but his knees were soon bruised and sore, his back ached, and his hands were raw; yet he finished in time to help his father set the last props, and with wedges already sawed to the right angle, fit them to their task.

"That's that," Tom said at last. "Now we'll make a bearing in."

"Do those posts hold the hill up, papa?"

Tom Glen chuckled. "It'd take more than that, Owen. No, the way of it is, you leave pillars of solid coal, say twenty-five feet one way and twenty the other, between the entry and your room; and mostly your room won't be only maybe twenty-five feet wide, so the pillars are as big as your rooms. It's them that holds things up. About all the props do is to let you know if the hill starts to settle. They'll begin to crack and split. Now here we go."

He selected a light pick, one end sharpened to a needle point, the other flattened to a narrow chisel edge. "You watch me, and you can do the way I do. Here's the vein, see. It's good and thick. What we do is undercut the vein, bear in for maybe three feet, and then shoot down the coal above that." At first on his hands and knees, and then lying on his left side, he began to strike the pick into the coal at the bottom of the vein.

He talked as he worked. "Good dry floor here. Where it's wet and muddy you have to have a board to lie on. If there's water, you can prop one end of the board against the coal and that holds you up out of the water pretty good."

Owen watched for a while, then brought his new pick from the car and attacked the coal at the other end of the face. His father had made the work appear to be easy, but Owen found that to swing the pick while lying on his side was incredibly difficult. It was astonishing to find how heavy, in this position, the pick after a few minutes came to be. He tried doggedly to match his father's tireless strokes, but fatigue soon forced him to pause.

"Wears you down, don't it," Tom said kindly. "You'll toughen to it pretty quick. For today you just take off a foot or so, and I'll go in the rest of the way."

Owen rested a moment, again attacked the task. It had never occurred to him that coal was hard, since at home a lump seemed so easily shattered; but this coal was so tough and brittle that even the needle-sharp point of the pick, without force behind it, did not easily penetrate. He worked for a while on hands and knees, and presently again lay on his side. To change positions was, briefly, a relief. When he needed further respite, he paused to scrape away the cuttings he had dislodged. His father came close behind him, deepening his excavation by a full two feet. At every stroke of their picks, coal dust and splinters flew; the dust hung glittering in the air.

After a time Tom called a halt while they filled their lamps. "They burn out if you forget them," he said. "They don't last much over a couple of hours, mostly less." Owen thought his father must be joking, for surely this torment had endured longer than two hours. Tom added: "Don't ever forget your lamp." Then, chuckling at the joke on himself: "I've seen the time, working in a wet mine, when I forgot my lamp and it went out and my matches were wet." He lighted his pipe. "It's mighty quiet in a room in the dark," he reflected. "All you hear is the noise you make yourself, or maybe a prop cracks when the roof settles a mite, or you hear water dripping. I went and borrowed some matches in a hurry." Owen, sweating from his labors and chilled now from inaction, shivered and tightened his teeth; and his father asked: "Hungry?"

"I guess so." Owen was too tired to know.

Tom looked at his watch. "We might as well eat. It's past nine o'clock."

Owen brought their dinner pails from the car. He had not realized his hunger till he bit into the first of the sandwiches his mother had prepared. He ate with ferocious haste; and without knowing it, he made as he ate a low, ravening sound. His father presently spoke of this, quietly amused. "You're growling like a dog at a bone."

Owen grinned, feeling his body and his courage revive with the hearty food. Tom ate more slowly, talking with a full mouth.

"Well, this is coal-mining, Owen. Tomorrow, we'll start by shovelling up the coal we shoot down today. The last man here cleaned up the coal before he went out, but he forgot to post up; so we had to do that." A ruminative pause. "We've got a good room here, good and dry. Working in water starts up my rheumatism. And this is a good thick vein. You get a vein around two feet, like Erie, and you have to dig up a foot or two of floor to fix it so you can work it at all; or else the day men shoot it up for you. The Hardiston County veins are mostly four feet or under. Some places, up north and east, they'll be five, six, ten feet. That's one reason Hardiston County pay is high. A thin vein, a man can't dig so much in a day."

He sighed with content. "Et all your lunch, have you? Go ahead and finish mine, but leave me some of the pie." Owen needed no urging, and Tom lighted his pipe, sitting at ease on the floor, his back against a pillar. "Yes, we're fixed good here. The mines ain't all as dry as this. Water was running down the entry to that sump we heard the pump working, but we're dry here. We'll get out a lot of coal tomorrow, once we get straightened out to it."

Owen was sated, gorged; a sense of well-being stole upon him. "What happens if we dig all the coal out of this room?"

"Why, we'll draw the pillars, so's not to lose the coal that's in them, and then we'll neck in another room, along a ways, and start all over again."

That meant going deeper into the hill. "What if the entry caved in behind us, the way it did at Erie Mine?"

"There's ladderways in some of the air shafts," Tom Glen said reassuringly. "We'd climb out. There has to be more than one way in and out. That's the law."

"Papa, you said the man that worked here before didn't post the roof; but I thought the day men did that."

Tom shook his head. "No, they drive the entry, and clean up the jack slate, and lay the tracks outside, but we have to lay our tracks in here, and do all's done in our room."

"Do we get paid for it?"

"We're paid for the coal we dig, that's all. And we buy our own powder and tools and oil, and pay to have tools sharpened." His pipe was burned out, and he cleared the dottle and put his foot on it. "Nor we don't get paid for setting here," he said cheerfully, and moved toward the face. "Hands sore?" he asked.

"Some."

"Keep the handle of your pick clean as you can. That helps." Owen wondered how anyone could keep anything clean in this battle with the coal that threw clouds of black dust at every touch. "And your hands will toughen up fast."

He lifted his pick, and Owen, without direction, likewise resumed his labors. The pauses to fill their lamps tolled off the slow passing hours. When they stopped for the third time, they had undercut the coal across the whole face of the room. Owen's hands were blistered raw, the skin rubbed away; he could see lighter spots against the blackness of his hands where grime was not yet thoroughly ground into his tender, freshly exposed underskin. Owen did enough work mowing lawns, hoeing the garden, doing odd jobs, so that his hands were reasonably tough and hard; but the pick handle had found spots lacking protective calluses.

"Now," Tom announced, "we'll get ready to shoot. Let's roll the car up and unload it." They pushed the car near the face, and Tom lifted out the keg of powder and the rest of their gear and laid everything in orderly array. As he did so, a man came stooping through the neck into the room.

"How's it going?" he asked. By his voice Owen recognized Mr. Powell.

"'Bout ready to start our holes. I had to prop her, took time."

"Owen catching on pretty well?" The mine boss was a cheerful, kindly man.

"Certain. He'll be a master hand in no time."

"You'll need six or eight cars a day, when he really gets started." Owen guessed that they knew how tired he was, how sore his hands, and they were jesting to hearten him.

"Oh, he'll have a room of his own, first thing you know."

Mr. Powell went on his way, and Tom said: "Take the fork, Owen, and load the cuttings." He pointed to the litter of small lumps and slack left from the bearing in. "Mostly we'd leave it till we start loading tomorrow, but you can be learning the knack of it. You lift it on the fork like this." He demonstrated, on his knees. "And you shake it to shake out the slack. And you don't throw it into the car; you slide it in easy, like this." The rear end of the car was open. "And keep it clean. Don't go shovelling slate and dry mud in with the coal."

Owen, ignoring his sore hands, attacked the task. The fork, like a big shovel with tines instead of a scoop, held a lot of coal. In his first zeal he scooped up more than he could easily handle, and Tom said wisely: "Three little ones is easier than one big one, Owen." The boy fought the work. To fill the fork was easy enough, but the rest was bitter hard. He could never stand erect, and he tried kneeling as his father did; but to shake the fork or to slide the coal into the car from that posture was incredibly wearying. He tried standing, in a bowed posture unnatural and tormenting, but despite all precautions he was forever bumping his head against the roof. Sometimes, when this happened, he spilled the coal. He wanted to cry with rage and pain; but he thought suddenly of Tom Glen's rheumatism, thought what torture it must be to work all day with bent back when your back was all one blaze of agony; and deep tender love for this tall man filled him like a healing draught.

When the immediate task was done, Tom said approvingly: "Good enough, son. We'll fill our lamps again, and after that you can watch me, the rest of it. Likely you're tired."

"I'm all right."

"You're a good boy. Fetch the oil can. I'll bring a bottle to-morrow. It's easier to pour out of." And when the lamps were full: "Now I'll put in some holes. You set and watch."

Owen was glad to obey. He sat at first in the open end of the car, his elbows on his knees; but the lamp on his cap was near the roof and its flame occasionally blurred against the slate, making it hard for him to see; so he sat on the floor, his back resting against the side of the car, limp and utterly relaxed, watching his father's steady progress.

Tom took the auger, braced it against a post and began to bore into the face of the coal. The sharp steel cut easily; a trickle of coal dust spilled out of the hole as the auger penetrated. Presently Tom paused and removed the auger and used the scraper; he cleaned the hole, inserted the auger once more; he repeated the process again and again.

When he had finished the last hole to his satisfaction, they refilled their lamps. "Now I have to make the ca'tridges," Tom said. He tore off a sheet of the newspaper which he had brought from the store, folded it double, selected one of the picks, stood it on end, and wrapped the doubled paper around the pick handle to make a cylinder eight or ten inches long. Owen observed that the handle of this pick was round and of an even diameter toward the end, and he asked:

"Do you have that pick special for this, papa?"

"Yes. Some have a ca'tridge stick they use, but this pick stands up handy."

"How much powder do you put in?"

"Why, as much as I need. Sometimes a lot, sometimes not so much. Depends on how deep your hole is, and how thick the vein is, and how the face shapes up. Now."

He rewound the cylinder of paper and lapped one end; he took the cap off the powder keg and lifted the keg across his knees; then, leaning down to see more clearly, he poured a black stream of powder into the open end of the cartridge and crimped the end.

"There," he said. "There's one." He laid the cartridge aside. "We'll need six," he said.

"What if your lamp fell off into the powder while you were pouring it?"

Tom looked at him in dry amusement. "Time you start worrying about that, it'll be too late to worry," he said, and filled another cartridge; and when the last was done: "Now we're going to need some filling. Some of that clay from the bearing in is handy." With Owen attentive at his elbow, he took a cartridge and the needle to the left-hand hole. He thrust the end of the needle three or four inches into the cartridge, then carefully fitted the cartridge into the hole, and with the needle pushed it in as far as it would go.

"Fetch me a shovelful of that clay, Owen," he directed; and without removing the needle he began to fill the hole. "Now the tamper, son." Owen brought it, and Tom explained: "This end's copper so there won't be any risk of a spark in the hole." He fitted the grooved head of the tamper over the needle, and rammed the clay lightly home. Removing the tamper, he packed in more filling and tamped that in turn; he repeated the process till the hole was full.

"Now I'll draw the needle. Got to be careful, so's to leave the hole open all the way to the ca'tridge." And when the needle was clear, "Now get me a squib." Owen brought it, and Tom inserted it into the hole, the end protruding.

"All right, son, we're ready to shoot. I'll touch off this squib and it'll squirt fire into the powder. You go on out in the entry and I'll touch her off."

"Where will you be?"

Tom chuckled. "Right out there with you. Go on."

Owen obeyed, peering in to watch as his father struck a match. Then Tom came swiftly toward him, through the neck into the entry. "Fire in the hole," he bawled, and a muffled shout answered him, and then the shot went off, and some small fragments flew out through the neck to spatter against the opposite wall of the entry.

"All right, there's one," said Tom. He led the way back into the room, now filled with smoke that rose and drifted along the ceiling. Working with swift precision he loaded the other holes as he had the first, fired each in turn.

"Can't you shoot them all at once?" Owen asked. "Then you wouldn't have to work in this smoke."

"Not with squibs. Can't touch them off fast enough to get the last one lighted before the first one goes; and even if I did, the first one would shake up the filling in the others, block the holes so the fire couldn't get to the powder. No, one at a time's the only way."

When the last shot had been fired, Tom said: "Well, there, we're done for today. I'll tag the car." He hung one of the brass tags Mike had given him on a nail on the side of the car; and he put the tools in an orderly pile at the back of the room. "You take the dinner pails, Owen. And take this pick. It needs sharpening."

Owen looked at what had been the face of the vein, now shattered by the shots. In the loose coal thrust out by the blasts were two enormous lumps, the height of the vein and as wide as they were high.

"We can't get lumps like that into the car tomorrow, papa."

"Guess not. That one there'll weigh a ton or better. No, we'll have to break it up with a hammer and wedges before we can load it; yes, and that other big one too."

Tom led the way, Owen on his heels. Once at a warning cry from a room ahead of them they halted while a shot sounded in that room. Other miners joined them, and presently they saw the light of day framed in the portal ahead.

Owen was surprised to see it so soon; he had thought they were deep in the heart of the hill. They came out into a bright glare of sunshine, blinding and hurting their eyes, and Tom Glen took off his cap to blow out his lamp, and Owen did the same.

Tom and the other miners crossed to the wash room, and Owen followed them, to scrub his face and hands with soft soap that seemed to have sand in it, and to snuffle warm water up out of his palms to clear his nose. Afterward his father and the other miners sat along the steps of the store, and Owen saw they meant to stay awhile. His legs were weak with fatigue, his hands were sore; he was so desperately tired. He lay down on the weedy slope beside the portal and closed his eyes against the sun, and by and by his father shook him out of heavy sleep.

"Rouse up, Owen. Time to start for the train."

Owen rubbed gritty eyes, creaked to his feet. When he went to sleep, the portal and the trestle had been almost deserted; now there were men all around, and cars along the track all heaped with coal. He followed his father down the path to the siding and away toward the railroad. His nose was stopped up, his mouth felt dry, his throat was full. He blew his nose with his fingers, stooping to wipe them on the grass beside the tracks; he hawked and spat black phlegm. The others were all spitting, coughing, cleaning their noses and throats. He was one of them, a miner, a man!

But it was good to come home to his mother, good to strip off dirty clothes impregnated with coal dust and go with his father into the shed where, men together, they scoured themselves clean. When he came into the kitchen from the shed room, his mother saw his torn hands. She made him wash them again, in warm soapy water, and she put a bread poultice on his blisters. There were angry tears in her eyes. He thought she must surely guess that no trapper boy ever acquired such blisters, but she offered no comment; and in a moment of understanding he decided that his father had told her what they meant to do.

His bandaged hands made it hard to eat, but he ate ravenously all the same. It was only half-dark when he tumbled into bed, but he slept without a dream.

IX

September 1893—*December* 1893

WHEN THE DAY was fine, the walk home from church on Sunday became a social occasion. Neighbors who did not see each other from one Sunday to the next might stroll for a few blocks together and exchange news and comment. As the congregation came out of church, it moved slowly; the flow was sluggish, and for a while a small crowd massed along the walk and on the sidewalk, till by two and twos the worshippers moved away. The church was on Cherry Street, and when the services were over, a proportion of the congregation went to the left toward Main Street; but the majority turned right to file out Peach or to angle along Sycamore and out Pearl, couples turning aside at every corner. The general pace was slow. Marged and Owen, if they were together, usually drew into the lead.

Sunday after Owen's first week in the mine, Miss Williams saw his bandaged hands. "You're hurt," she said, in quick sympathy.

"I got some blisters at first, but mama put bread poultices on them and they're about well now."

"Is the work hard? Tell me about it."

He was happy at her interest, and glad she had not made a fuss over his blisters. Of them he was a little ashamed. "It wouldn't be hard, only you have to bend over all the time, or kneel down, or else bump your head. The roof is only about four feet above the floor. We sort of lie down, when we're bearing in — "

"What's that?"

"We undercut the seam before we shoot down the solid."

She looked at him with faintly smiling eyes, seeing how proudly

223

he used these new words. "I suppose every sort of work has its special words, like pegs to hang new knowledge on."

He wanted to tell her that he was learning many things besides words; and also, he wanted her to understand, without his telling, how hard the work was. Each night he had come home with new aches and pains. His mother always had hot water ready in the shed room off the kitchen where he and his father bathed, and this eased his aches; but each morning, when first he stepped out of bed, they were worse. Not till he was hot and sweating at his work again did they quite disappear.

But he could not tell Marged this without bragging, so he assured her that the work soon became easy. It was fun to make light of her concern; he felt himself a man talking to an admiring child.

She reminded him that he must continue his studies and urged him to come to her for help and guidance; and Owen said he would do so. "At first I was so tired every night that I'd go to sleep eating supper, and papa had to shove me off to bed; but I'm used to it now." And he added: "Mr. Beecham's going to lend me a book named *Lavengro*. It's all about words." She had not read it, and he said: "He lent it to a man in Mississippi, but he told me yesterday the man has sent it back, so I'm going over to borrow it, this afternoon."

2

After dinner that day, Owen found Mr. and Mrs. Beecham sitting on the shady side of the house, BB comfortable in his shirt sleeves, the new baby in her carriage by Mrs. Beecham's chair. Owen said his howd'ye do to pretty Mrs. Beecham, and he admired the baby because he knew that would please them; and then a sudden outcry made them all run to the back porch. Bertie, trying to climb up the shelves of the cupboard as though it were a ladder, had pulled it over on top of himself. Flat on his back, the cupboard across his legs and lower body, he bawled like a calf wanting its mother. BB released him, and persuaded him he was not hurt, and as they walked back to the chair, BB said mirthfully: "Trouble with Bertie, he's topheavy, so he's always falling down, and he always bumps his head. He has eleven stitches in his scalp already — and he's only four and a half."

Owen told Mr. Beecham his errand, and BB went into the house and brought the book and put it in Owen's hands. "You'll find it slow reading, but stick to it. It's worth it." The book seemed in fact a daunting prospect. It was very long — there were more than five hundred pages of small print — and the only pictures were of castles and things like that.

"I guess I can read it," Owen said doubtfully.

"Once you're well into it, you'll hate to stop." The sun had reached BB's chair, and he moved it into the shade. "Tell me about the mine."

So for a time Owen talked and BB listened, asking an occasional question. "While you're waiting for the train to bring you home, what do the men talk about? Politics? You hear any talk about Senator Phillips?"

"No sir."

"He's the nominee, so I suppose they'll vote for him. It's too bad."

"Why?"

"I mean it's too bad that the miners will vote for a man who voted against them. You remember, he voted against the Anti-Screen Bill."

"I haven't heard any of them talking politics."

"It's too bad they don't," the editor insisted. "Too bad they don't recognize their power and use it. Power unused is worse than lost, it's wasted."

"Poor men can't run things, anyway, can they?"

BB said strongly: "It isn't that the rich men control politics, Owen. The truth is that men who control politics become rich. As soon as poor men recognize this, they'll cease to be poor men. With the secret ballot, every man is free to vote as he wishes; and that freedom is an opportunity, and opportunity properly used is power.

"And power is wealth! Don't ever doubt that." Owen, though he could not always understand Mr. Beecham, listened and tried to remember; and BB, readily articulate, went on: "Last fall, in the states where the People's Party combined with the Democrats, they elected four Senators and eleven Congressmen. That set every rich man in the country shaking in his shoes; but that sort of thing will happen, from now on, with increasing frequency. More and more often, the men elected to office will be those who put the interests of all men above the interests of a few men."

The baby stirred in her carriage, with sounds of waking, and Mrs. Beecham leaned forward and lifted the little girl into her lap. Then Aunt Jane — as though from some vantage indoors she had been watching for the baby to rouse — came out of the house and bundled Sarah away. BB went on as though there had been no interruption. "And then we'll have a great country. When working-men use their votes to get higher pay, just as employers use their political power to get higher profits, then to meet labor's demands and still maintain those profits, capital must increase production; and in doing so, they will create in this country the greatest industrial machine the world has ever seen. Our businessmen and manufacturers have the finest productive minds in the world, but every man needs a spur. Workingmen, by demanding higher and higher wages, will apply that spur."

He paused, and Mrs. Beecham said smilingly: "He's run out of breath, Owen. It's your turn."

Owen frowned at his own thoughts. "You mean coal miners ought to vote against Mr. Phillips because he voted against the Screen Bill?"

"Exactly."

"I know you've been saying in the *Journal* all summer that he ought to get beaten."

"I opposed his nomination, yes; but that was because I thought he'd be a weak candidate."

Owen looked at him in sudden doubt. "You'll vote against him, won't you?"

"No. No, he's the Republican candidate, and I'm a Republican. I believe in parties." BB smiled, rose. "There, I've talked your ears off. Take *Lavengro* and read it. Take your time to it. But study politics, Owen. Corrupt it as you choose, politics is just the art of making and keeping friends. The difference between the United States and other countries is that in the United States the workingman, without violence, can seize political power if he is wise enough to do so; if he is wise enough, and finds wise leaders." He added with a smile, extending his hand: "Who knows, Owen; you may be one of them."

3

The day Owen went to work in the mine, he grew older, but he was not himself conscious of this fact. It was only in retrospect, long afterward, that he could clearly see this sharp division between his childhood and his boyhood. From the moment he entered the mine, to meet those who had been his mates in school — Morgan Williams, Bill Myers, Tom Powell — was like meeting half-strangers. He had been one of them, concerned as they were with books and lessons, obeying the bells that summoned them to school, that released them for recess, that called them back again and finally let them go. They still lived by that routine, but now he had gone ahead, while they stayed behind.

He was no longer a child, but he had still to become a man; and though at Mr. Beecham's advice, on the train and at the mine, he listened more intently to the talk between his father and other men, he listened in silence. Someone named Hoke Smith had done something as a result of which some pensions were being stopped. Owen knew Mr. Beecham thought ill of Mr. Smith; and an occasional phrase from the *Journal* lingered in his mind. "Are you getting a $6 pension? Hoke Smith is after you." "Hoke Smith is after Republicans, but has any democrat lost a pension?" "Hoke Smith was burned in effigy" — that word sent Owen to the dictionary — "last week in Adams County."

The talk which Owen heard was touched with anger, for someone in Hardiston or Slacktown or Belton had played informer. "If a man works for a living, they hear about it and his pension is stopped." The speaker was a man Owen did not know. "That happened to Bob Lewis in Belton. He cut off his thumb and finger, chopping wood, the year after the War; but the agent says if he can still work, no pension."

Tom Glen nodded angrily. "Like as not they'll stop mine, next. My eyes begun to go bad before I got home from the War, and they been getting worse ever since; but now the Democrats claim if you wasn't hit by a bullet, you don't get a pension."

Clearly, pensions had something to do with politics; but though the men swore at Hoke Smith, it was in the hopeless tone of those who accept their own futility. Owen wished to suggest that if they voted against Hoke Smith, it might help; yet to do so might make them laugh at him, or scornfully bid him to silence, so he did not speak.

But a few days later he found his voice. The first payday after he and his father went to work in Miss Ellen Mine was to have fallen on the fourteenth; but before that day, Moses Evans and the other operators in the county, pointing to the hard times, the shrinking demand for coal, and the increasing delays in collecting for coal actually marketed, proposed to postpone payday long enough to allow their collections to meet their payroll. A miners' meeting was called to consider this proposal, and Owen with his father went to Belton to attend. The hall was crowded, the men sullen and angry. Owen recognized on the platform Eben Howell, whom he had met the day Andrew Dale spoke in this same hall. Mr. Howell was talking with old Mr. Price, who lived in Hardiston and came to the Welsh church; and Owen remembered that Mr. Howell was vice-president of the Sub-District; Matthew Price, the secretary. Thomas Jones of Clinton County was president; but apparently he could not be here today, for it was Mr. Howell who called the meeting to order and directed Matthew Price to read the notice from the operators.

They proposed to pay on September 30 for work done in the first two weeks of the month, and in the same way to defer each subsequent payment. The question was opened for discussion, and after two or three others had spoken, Tom Glen caught the eye of the chair.

"Mr. Chairman," he said quietly, and Owen was trembling with pride beside him. "My son and I have only been working at Miss Ellen since the first of the month; and the coal we've mined won't any more than pay what we owe for our outfits and all. So it don't much matter to me, this time, what they do about payday.

"But the way I look at it, the operators have money in the bank, and if they want to sell coal on credit, they can afford to. But I can't afford to work on credit, and neither can any of us. We've mined their coal for them, and they've sold it, and we're entitled to our pay —" His voice hardened. "And I don't aim to work after the fourteenth unless I get it. Mr. President, I move we reject this proposition."

There was a second to the motion, and then a long discussion. Owen was astonished at the mildness of the speakers. His father had spoken gently, and most of them professed sympathy for the operators and an appreciation of their problem.

"But when hard times come," said one young man, not much more than a boy, "it's always the miners that get hit first!" Owen wished to shout his approval. He stirred restlessly in his seat; and then another man rose, a man Owen did not know.

"Mr. Chairman!" And when he was recognized, the man said: "This here's Mose Evans's doing, the whole of it. I live in one of his houses up't Miss Ellen. His store there sells beef at twelve cents, eggs twenty for a quarter, bacon thirteen cents, short ribs eight, coffee thirty, sugar thirteen. Anyone wants to can walk to Glendale, or up here to Belton, and get beef for nine cents, three dozen eggs for a quarter, and so on, but that means paying cash. Mr. Evans wants to put off paying cash so we'll have to trade at his store and pay him in his scrip. That way, even if the mine don't make money, the store will." His tones had been level and calm, but now they rang hotly. "Well, I'll starve first, for one!"

A grumble of agreement and approval answered him. Owen, in a fever, touched his father's arm. "Papa, can I say something?"

Tom hesitated, then rose and addressed the chair. "Mr. Chairman, my son Owen — he'll be fourteen in November, and he'll be paying his first tax to the local out of his first pay, when he gets it — asks permission to say a word on this matter."

The general murmur was consent enough; but Eben Howell said formally: "The chair recognizes Owen Glen."

Tom touched Owen's arm, and Owen's heart stopped; but he rose and stood for a moment, trembling and speechless, feeling his cheeks burn. Many of the men had come direct from the mines, so he looked around into blackened faces, pale eye-sockets from which friendly eyes looked back at him.

"Mr. Chairman," he squeaked, and then, more angry at himself than at the smiles he saw, he forced a deeper tone. "Mister Chairman, the Bible says: 'Muzzle not the ox that treadeth out the grain!' Well, I'm no ox." A roar of laughter startled him, but white-faced he went on. "But I've worked in Miss Ellen Mine nine days. My back is sore and my hands are blistered. There's coal dust in my nose and throat, it's gritted into my blisters, it's like sand in my teeth, it's crusted in around my eyes and in my hair.

"There've been times I thought I'd die, but I was proud to stick to it, and proud when papa said I was doing good. I didn't mind how tired I got, or how sore my hands were, long as I was helping him earn money.

"But if I wasn't earning money, I'd never go into a mine again. But if I was — I want my pay!"

He had not meant to stop there, but the thundering roar that his words evoked was so frightening that he slipped down into his seat. When he realized that the men were cheering, to his own shamed astonishment he wanted to cry, and gulped hard to swallow sobs. He scarce heard the roll call of delegates as the operators' proposition was voted down.

At home that night, Tom Glen told Owen's mother what had happened. "And he talked good, mama," he said. "As good as I could have done myself; yes, and better. Time he got through, it was settled."

"Guess he takes after you, Tom. You were always a talker." But Owen felt the high pride in her, and when, passing behind his chair, she touched his head, he shivered with happiness.

They returned Monday to Miss Ellen; and Tom found a message that all delegates were to meet the District Executive Board of the United Mine Workers in Belton that afternoon. When he and Owen, their day done, emerged from the mine, a notice on the wall of the store drew them that way.

TO ALL MINERS
Any coal shot down today, Monday, should be loaded
Tuesday morning; but no shots Tuesday afternoon. Miss
Ellen will shut down till the present dispute is decided.
MOSES EVANS

When they had read it, Tom said in a dry tone: "Well, Owen, you're out of a job so soon."

"Can I go to the meeting with you?"

"No, this is just delegates from the locals. I'll meet you on the train."

After Tom and Isaac Williams and Charles Morgan, who was president of the Miss Ellen local, had tramped away toward Belton, Owen returned to read the notice again. A group of men were clustered there, and one spoke to him. "Hello, Glen. I'm Ernie Vought. I heard you at the meeting."

The other was an inch shorter than Owen, and a year or two older than himself, sturdy and compact. Owen said: "I guess talking didn't do much good."

"I wish I could get up and talk like that. Minute I get up, I forget what I was going to say." Ernie glanced at the notice again. "Well, looks like we're out of work for a spell."

Owen felt a strong stir of liking for the older boy, and they stood for a while in talk together. Vought, it developed, lived in Belton, a short walk from the mine; it was a fair three hours before Owen's train; the mid-September day was fine, and neither was in a hurry. When they parted at last, Owen felt in himself a deep content. Ernie was the sort of man he would always want to know.

Aboard the train for Hardiston, Owen found his father sitting with Isaac Williams, so he sat behind. Not till they reached Hardiston and he and Tom Glen started home together could he ask what had happened at the meeting.

"The operators made a new proposal," Tom explained. "But it was as bad as the other one, so we voted it down. The meeting last Saturday — maybe it was you making the speech that did it" — Owen heard the pride in his tone — "there was only twelve votes for giving in, out of over twenty-three hundred. Today there was a hundred and seventy-four that voted to give in; but we voted it down by over two thousand votes. By day after tomorrow there won't be hardly a mine working in the county."

Owen was puzzled by these figures. "There weren't twenty-three hundred miners there Saturday, papa."

"It's the delegates that vote," Tom explained: "You see, each mine is a local, only they have to have ten men to make a local. Some wagon mines don't have that many, so they get some other little mines in with them, till they've got enough to get up a local. Then all the locals have delegates. Meetings like this one today, and the one Saturday that you went to, a delegate votes for all the men in his local. I'm delegate from Erie local."

"What's going to happen now?"

"Well, we left it up to the Executive Board to talk to the operators. We won't have any more meetings till the Board says."

"The Board in Columbus?"

"No, I mean the Executive Board of the Sub-District. The way it works, after the locals, there's Sub-Districts, and then there's Districts. There's Hardiston and Clinton County in our Sub-District, and the whole State's the District."

Next morning Owen stayed home. "All I'll do is load what we shot down yesterday," Tom explained. "It won't take me long." To face an idle day left Owen at a loss. His mother, too, was unhappy; she had hidden from Tom her grief at this abrupt end to the new job, but when he was gone she went into her own room and shut the door and did not come out till Owen called:

"You all right in there, mama?"

She was a moment in answering. "I'm all right, yes. I'll be out in a minute."

When she joined him, he stayed with her awhile, watching her busy with the dishes; he milked the cow and offered to feed the chickens, but she said: "I've give 'em the last corn we had. They'll have to pick for themselves. We'll be eating the old hens now right along, before they get too thin."

"The pig's fat."

"We'll keep him till cold weather, long as we've milk enough." The cow, dry during spring and early summer, had calved two months ago; they vealed the calf when it was a month old, and the milk they did not use went to fatten the pig.

Owen was restless. "I guess I'll go uptown. Maybe I can help on the *Journal* till the mine opens up again."

"You can go back to school."

But there was no real hope in her tone, and he shook his head. "I'm too old to go to school." Tamely to take his place among children again would be a humiliation beyond endurance. School was behind him forever.

4

While the strike continued, with surprisingly little disturbance, life resumed its normal course. The *Journal* supported Senator Phillips for re-election. A Xenia man asked a franchise to build waterworks in Hardiston. Thirty-seven Hardiston people went on an excursion to the World's Fair. A Slacktown man sat down on the railroad tracks to rest and a train killed him. Mr. Evan Forbes and Mr. and Mrs. Thomas Watson were gone to New York to buy stock for Mr. Watson's clothing store. A seventeen-year-old girl, arrested in Belton for stealing, took morphine and died. The Christian Missionary Society had a sociable. Lloyd Thorne, hunting quail, shot and killed himself when he dragged his gun, muzzle first, over a rail fence. Mr. Beecham urged that a "Kid Bell" be rung at eight o'clock every night, after which no children under fourteen should be allowed on the streets except with their parents. With furnaces and mines shut down, hundreds of Hardiston men were out of work. Young Phillip Fremont — whom Owen knew only by name — was appointed to Annapolis. A play called *Editha's Burglar* visited the Opera House.

Owen saw Miss Williams at church each Sunday, but he avoided her, hurrying away when the services ended. If he waited, she would want him to come and study with her, and he had no time for that now. He had begun to read *Lavengro*, and it absorbed him completely. It was written by a boy — though Owen soon began to suspect that the boy was grown up when he wrote it — and the Preface said it was about a Scholar, a Gypsy and a Priest, but Owen had not come to them, nor to the "brave old soldier and his helpmate, the ancient gentlewoman who sold apples, and the strange kind of wandering man and his wife." The book was all about the boy himself, things he did and people he met and things he thought; and it was crammed full of words which Owen had to look up in the dictionary in the *Journal* office. He came to "plebeian" and "posthumous" before he had finished the first page. The book spoke of a man named Big Ben Brain, who to Owen's disappointment died in the same paragraph in which he first appeared. Owen wondered whether BB Beecham's name was Ben. Words and words came pelting at him; "vouchsafed" and "lustrous" and "loutishness" and many more. The boy in the book had an ape and a dog for playmates, and he wrote holy letters in the dust and scared a Jew who had said something about "pedlary"; and when he was six or seven years old he was given a book about a man dressed in the skins of animals who was frightened when he found the print of a naked foot in the sand. Owen decided that after he had read *Lavengro*, he would ask Mr. Beecham if there really was such a book as that, and read it too. The boy in *Lavengro* read it over and over for months. Once he caught a "viper" — that turned out to be a snake — in his hands, and he met an old man who caught snakes for a living and who had seen the King of the Vipers. Some people called the boy in the book a *sap-engro,* which was not in the dictionary. The book was in fact full of words not in the dictionary, but sometimes Mr. Beecham was able to tell Owen what they meant, and sometimes by reading carefully and thinking hard he could guess their meaning.

To read *Lavengro* and try to understand it became a passion, filling every empty hour. Sometimes while he read, when he was most intent and absorbed, the words he read sent his thoughts racing off into strange paths. To read of an old woman whose long hair fell down about her shoulders; to read how the boy in the book learned to ride a cob — a cob, clearly, was some sort of horse; to read how Bagg fought Jerry Grant with buffets and falls; these scenes and many others awoke in Owen that dry-throated hunger, that eager stir of pulses, that thudding pound and tension which he had come to recognize. The boy in the book said his first ride on the cob was like first love; and he talked about flush and triumph and glorious sweat as though they had something to do with first love. The woman with hair falling around her shoulders, and the ride, and the fight all made Owen think of the night at Jane Lloyd's house when they played *Drop the Handkerchief* and he chased Jane and fell over her and kissed her. To remember made him warmly happy, so one day he passed the schoolhouse just as school let out, and came up behind Jane and spoke to her.

"Hello, Jane."

Betty Myers was with her; they turned, and Jane said: "Oh, hello, Owen." They all walked on together and Jane asked: "Why aren't you at the mine?"

"We're shut down because Mr. Evans don't want to pay us." Owen kicked a rock off the sidewalk. "We had a meeting and voted not to work till he did. I made a speech."

"Oh, Owen! Honest? I'll bet it was a good one."

Betty said giggling: " 'Member when Miss Means made you make a speech about the dog?"

Owen grinned. "About when he took his tail out of the water — which he did!" They laughed delightedly and Betty said:

"You were awful funny."

"Well, I was trying to be." He watched Jane sidewise. Her hair did not hang loose around her shoulders like that of the old woman in *Lavengro,* but it was a thick glossy braid down her back with a bow of black ribbon on the end. He wished he dared touch it. She asked:

"Are you a trapper, Owen? Jim Tower's a trapper."

"Naw!" With mild scorn. "All trapper boys do is open and shut doors. I help papa mine coal. He's going to let me make cartridges pretty soon."

"What for?" Before he could answer, someone across the street called: "Yoo-hoo, Owen!" He looked and saw Nellie Tutson, sweeping Mrs. Paxley's front porch; and Mrs. Paxley appeared in the doorway behind her. It was the first time he had seen Mrs. Paxley since that day last summer when he fled from her as he had once run away from Nellie. To see them now together, these two, made his cheeks burn and his heart pound. With only a hurried glance that way, he lifted his hand in a dismissing gesture and walked faster.

Betty Myers turned in at her own gate, and Jane asked again: "What are the cartridges for?"

"To shoot the coal down. You roll a newspaper around a pick handle and fill it with powder and that's a cartridge. Then you drill holes in the coal and put the cartridge in and explode it with a squib. Papa says I'll be a regular miner in another year."

"I wish you were still in school, Owen."

"I'm too old for school."

They crossed the street toward her gate, and she said: "I don't think you're too old for school. Some boys go clear through high school."

"Well, I have to help papa."

She looked at him shyly, the gate between them. "If I have another party sometime, will you come to it?"

"I will if I can."

"I'll see if mama'll let me." She hesitated. "Well, goodbye."

He waited at the gate, watching her go up the walk and up the steps; she paused then and turned and waved her hand, and he waved his, but as she went into the house he became conscious that Nellie and Mrs. Paxley were watching from her veranda, a few doors away. With a mysterious sense of guilt, an inexplicable apprehension, he turned his back and, fighting the instinct to hurry, walked steadily away.

But he soon forgot Mrs. Paxley, and Nellie too, in remembering his few minutes with Jane. Except for casual encounters, he had not seen her since the picnic. He thought she was prettier than ever, but perhaps that was because her skirts were longer, so that she was now more like a young lady than a little girl. For a moment he regretted that he was no longer in her room at school, would no longer see her every school day.

Sunday, Miss Williams spoke of her. "I saw you and Jane Lloyd walking home the other day. Jane's a nice girl."

"I guess so."

She smiled. "Guess so? You know very well you think so."

"She's all right." He felt her eyes upon him, and knew his cheeks were red, and grinned wretchedly.

"Well, you needn't be ashamed of liking her," Miss Williams protested, laughing at him. "I'm sure she likes you, too."

He decided next day that everybody in town must have seen him with Jane, for Will Davis spoke of it. Owen was helping fold the winter's programs for the Women's Literary Club. You took one sheet, held the edges exactly together, and with the bone handle of a toothbrush from which the bristles had been removed, you creased the fold. While Owen folded, Will arranged the folded sheets in order and stapled them, and once he asked: "How you and Jane getting along?"

Owen felt his ears burn. "Jane who?"

Will laughed. "That pretty little girl you brought here one day last summer, the one that bandaged your smashed fingers. Wasn't her name Jane?"

"Oh, her. Yes, that was Jane Lloyd."

"Seen her lately?"

Will's tone was dry, and Owen grinned and shook his head. "You can't get a rise out of me."

But it was fun to be teased about Jane, and on Thursday he once more made a point of passing the schoolhouse just as school let out at noon.

Jane saw him this time as he approached; she hesitated, and seemed about to turn her back. He said Hello, and she answered with some wordless sound. He asked quickly: "What's the matter?"

"You can't walk home with me."

"Huh? Why not?"

"Because we'd have to pass Mrs. Paxley's, and she saw us last time and came and told mama." Owen stared at her, unable even to shape a question; and Jane said: "Mama says I mustn't have anything to do with you." He was red and wretched, and Jane said gently: "It's not my fault, Owen. I like you, honest I do."

"What did I do?" He managed that much.

"Well, all I know is Mrs. Paxley told mama that when you used to cut her grass you were always telling lies about her, and she said you were a nasty boy."

Owen jammed his hands deep in his pockets; that seemed somehow to help. "I never told her any lies. And I never told any lies about her. I didn't do anything."

"I know it, Owen; but I have to do what mama says. Don't I?" He made an angry sound. "So — please don't walk home with me. Will you?"

"Well, all right, if you don't want me to!"

"But I do like you, Owen."

"Sure, I guess so."

She hurried away, and after a moment he turned through the alley beside the schoolhouse, feeling as though there were many eyes upon him, kicking absently at stones in the dusty alley. He felt himself wronged, knew a profound self-pity. Grown people ought not to go around telling lies about children.

Yet he was helpless, for if he denied having lied they would probably just think he was lying again! He was so indignant at this slanderous charge of lying that for a while he forgot Mrs. Paxley's other accusation. She had called him a nasty boy. To remember that made him for some reason more frightened than angry. What did she mean? Was it something he did not himself know, something grown people could tell by looking at you? Maybe she meant he was like the young men in Doctor France's advertisements? He decided to read the next one, to seek enlightenment; but there was none in that week's *Journal*, and when he looked back through recent issues he could not find one. Saturday, while Will was making up the inside, Owen saw a gap on page five that was just about the size of one of those advertisements, two columns wide and a half column deep; and Will went to the plate box and began to saw out plate to fit, and Owen — trying to keep his tone casual — asked:

"Doesn't that doctor's ad go there?"

"BB don't print them any more."

"Why not?"

"Said the doc was a quack. He was, all right; but he paid good money for his ads."

"Did you ever go to him?"

Will grinned. "Me? What for? Them's fighting words, Owen." He fitted the plate and locked the form, and Owen helped him lift it on the bed of the press. He wondered why Mr. Beecham had stopped printing those advertisements.

But that was a minor mystery compared to this riddle of Mrs. Paxley. He was afraid of her, of what she might say about him, of what she might already have said not only to Jane's mother but to other people. He dreaded meeting her, and he began to dread meeting anyone, stayed much at home. His mother asked him why.

"What's the matter with you, moping around the house all the time?"

"Nothing."

"Let me see your tongue?"

"I ain't sick. I mean, I'm not sick." But he bared his tongue for her inspection.

"Hm! Looks all right, but I'll give you calomel to be on the safe side."

"Oh, mama, there's nothing the matter with me."

She ignored him, crossing to the shelf, returning with a pill and a glass of water. "Here!"

"I don't need any —"

"I can still hold your nose and push it down your throat if I have to, big as you are."

So he surrendered, but when she later brought the second pill he balked. "No. I'm not going to take it."

"Why, son, you have to, now. If you start and then stop, calomel will salivate you every time. You don't want that, I can tell you. I've had it happen to me."

"I'll risk it."

She threw up her hands. "All right, have it your way. But for goodness' sake get out from underfoot. Go on, take a walk, get some fresh air, do something."

He obeyed her, sorry for himself thus driven from home with no place to go. Even mama did not want him around.

5

Early in October, after the miners had been five or six weeks idle,
the operators made a new proposal; they would pay, on October 25,
half the wages that had been earned before the middle of October;
they would pay on November 10 for all other work done in October,
and there would be a payday November 25 and December 10.
After December 20, regular paydays would be resumed.

The complications of this offer confused Owen, but since his
father was opposed to accepting it, so was he. Hardiston miners
voted against it, a hundred and nineteen to four; but Slacktown and
Glendale and Belton were overwhelmingly in favor of accepting,
so the men returned to work, Tom and Owen among them. Owen's
muscles were soft from weeks of idleness, and for the first few days
he came home at night almost too tired to stay awake.

With the election only two or three weeks away, Tom Glen —
and the other men at the mine — were suddenly interested in
politics, and on the train, or while they waited at the siding in the
afternoon, they talked of nothing else. Isaac Williams, who was
calm enough about most things, took his politics seriously. He was
older than Tom Glen by ten or a dozen years, and he wore his years
with a ponderous gravity, as though they laid upon him an obligation to be wise. Long before Owen learned that Mr. Williams
was head of the Erie local, he had felt for the dignified old man
respect touched with awe. Tom Glen was the first man in Owen's
world; yet the boy knew there were men who in the general scheme
of things bulked larger than his father. Mr. Beecham, certainly, was
one, and Isaac Williams was another.

So when now, in the late afternoon while they waited for the
train, Mr. Williams took the floor, Owen listened as to an oracle.
The old man was a McKinley partisan. "I went to war with the
Major," he liked to say. "And he's been my commanding officer ever
since."

He needed no cue to sing the other's praises; and one day some
hint of criticism of McKinley's labor record led him to relate an
anecdote. "The Major was always a friend to miners." Mr. Williams

never failed to give McKinley his military title. "I remember back
fifteen-twenty years ago, 1875 it was, I was working in the Warmington Mine, up south of Massillon. That was the time of the big
strike in the Tuscarawas Valley. It was the Miners' National Association then, before ever the United Mine Workers was thought of;
and John Siney was our man. Mark Hanna was one of the
operators.

"What started the trouble, we'd been getting ninety cents a ton,
and they wanted to cut us to seventy."

Someone echoed in surprise: "Ninety cents?" Seventy cents was
the rate in Hardiston County today.

"Ninety, yes. So we had an arbitration, but it went against us,
so we struck. They brought in strike-breakers, and that started a
riot, and Mr. Warmington pulled a pistol, and the men took it
away from him and near killed him!" Owen saw the sparkle in the
old man's eyes.

"But then came the militia, and then one night a lot of the
strikers blacked their faces and set fire to all the mines the company
owned. So they arrested a lot of the men that did it, thirty or forty
of them, and some of us went and got Major McKinley to defend
them. That was an exciting trial. Mark Hanna came every day to
listen. Major McKinley did a fine job, but three or four of them
were sent to the Pen in spite of him.

"Well, then we didn't have any money to pay him, but the
Knights of Labor took up a collection and raised around a thousand
dollars. The Major wouldn't take it, but he made them use it to
help the families of the men that got sent up, and then he went to
Mark Hanna and got him to help get the men pardoned." He
finished, with emphasis: "Yessirree, and Mark Hanna's been a good
friend to miners ever since. The Major too. The both of them are."

"Mark Hanna's an operator, all the same," Tom Glen objected;
but Isaac Williams shook his head.

"Not tarred with same brush as the most of them, he's not.
There's never been a time since that trial that the Union, yes, or any
man alone, couldn't go to Hanna and talk reasonable."

That tale, carrying as it did the flavor of the past, of the golden
days when miners were paid ninety cents a ton, of the brave days
when a drawn revolver was more a challenge than a threat, of the
reckless days when masked by night and by artifice desperate men

did desperate deeds; that tale of weak men in peril defended by a brave young hero, of valiant rescue and gracious forgiveness, entered into Owen and became a part of him. He relived it in his thoughts, and when on election day Major McKinley was again the victor, Owen agreed with Mr. Beecham's prediction in the *Journal* that the next step was the Presidency.

His only other interest in the results at the polls centered in the fact that Senator Phillips had been re-elected, and by a larger majority than in 1891. Obviously, most of the miners in the county had voted for him; yet certainly Senator Phillips had proved he was a friend not of the men but of the operators. Owen asked his father: "Papa, did you vote for Senator Phillips?"

"Yes; yes, I did."

"He's against the miners, isn't he?"

"Well, I wanted to vote for McKinley, and I always vote a straight ticket. If you don't, you have to go marking all the names separate, and that takes so long that everyone watching you knows you've scratched. Straight ticket's safest."

Owen remembered the mock election in Miss Williams's room in school, when she had noticed he took a long time to mark his ballot and so was able to identify it; so obviously his father was right, and the secret ballot was not so secret after all. But he resented with a certain anger the thought that his father might prefer the safe way.

"Well, papa, I guess you're not scared to vote the way you want to."

Tom looked at his son with dry eyes. "No, I'm not scared, just sensible. I used to go rooting and tooting around, shaking my horns and bellering; but now mostly I go with the crowd. I'm too old to want to be blacklisted again."

A fortnight after the election, politics was forgotten in the news that Moses Evans was desperately ill. Since he owned not only the house they lived in, but the mine where they earned their living, this fact came nearer home than the fate of any officeholder. They heard it first at church, when the minister in prayer called on God to "be merciful to our brother and Thy servant, now on the threshold of Thy house of many mansions. We pray Thee to withhold Thy summons, that he may tarry yet a while with us."

All around the church, when heads were raised after the prayer,

eyes consulted; but till after church was over, few knew who the
minister meant. Then, suddenly, everyone knew that Mr. Evans
lay at death's door. Some said heart failure, some said a stroke; all
agreed that he was in dreadful case. Each Sunday thereafter, the
weekly prayers were like bulletins from his bedside; pleas for
mercy, then thanks for the hopeful promise of recovery, then jubilation at its certainty.

Owen would have been more concerned about Mr. Evans if he
had not been so absorbed in *Lavengro*. The boy in the book was
in Ireland, learning the language and having adventures with
strange men and huge dogs in bogs. Owen was with him — except
in the flesh — and he begrudged the evening hours when he must
read to his father; but Tom Glen was hungry for every word. That
fall, Terence Powderly, Master Workman of the Knights of Labor,
resigned; and Tom mourned as at a hero's death. Since before the
strike ended, Tom had looked to the future with increasing pessi-
mism. When they went back to work, he said: "Aye, we'll work
while we can, but it won't be for long, with factories shutting down
everywhere, and men out of work. A shut-down factory don't need
coal, and men out of work can't buy it. There's a hard winter
coming for us all." Thereafter he found dark, ominous presages
in news which seemed to Owen innocent enough; and Mr.
Powderley's resignation seemed to him a final blow.

Time proved his fears just. In the Pittsburgh District, the rate
per ton was reduced from seventy-nine cents to fifty cents; and early
in December, Union Headquarters in Columbus called a special
convention, to meet January 9 in Worthwein Hall and seek some
remedy for the deplorable condition of the coal trade.

On the way home from church Sunday morning, Isaac Williams
and Tom Glen walked together, discussing this, and Owen walked
beside them. "We'll have to do something," Isaac said soberly.
"Or every operator in the state will be bankrupt."

Owen's father hooted in scorn. "Operators? Since when does the
Union have to help the operators? It's us miners they're supposed
to look out for."

"If the operators can't make money, they can't pay our wages,"
Isaac insisted. "You can't get blood out of a turnip."

Owen, listening, watching one and then the other, had for a
moment something like a vision. He seemed to see clearly and with

more than human comprehension that operators and miners were harnessed to the same tremendous wheel, hauling it up an incline so that it forever threatened to roll backward and drag them with it. United, they ruled the wheel; but unless they worked with a single mind and without dissension, the wheel would master them. Owen remembered an engraving in the big Welsh Bible, an engraving in which thousands of slaves under the lash of the overseers pulled a vast stone toward an unfinished pyramid. In that engraving, the overseers wielded the lash; but in Owen's vision the operators were not overseers, they were slaves equally with the men.

Unless operators and men worked in harmony together, then all equally would fail. This seemed to Owen so obviously true that he thought it must be equally clear to everyone. Yet, when they reached the corner of Belton Street and paused till the others should come up with them, Tom Glen was still insisting that operators and men were inevitably enemies. Faith in his father's wisdom blurred that vision of Owen's, and made it fog and fade; but it would return.

As the days passed, Tom's steady predictions of disaster began to frighten Owen, and when in December his father's small pension was stopped, the boy shared the impact of that catastrophe. The week before Christmas, an item in the *Journal* revealed to him the flavor of despair. An old man down in Gallia County, a cousin of Tom Glen's, having been arrested because under pressure of poverty he raised a postal money order from thirty-five cents to forty-five cents in order to buy a sack of flour, tore a strip from his blanket and hanged himself in his cell.

When Owen that evening read this item to his father, Tom Glen banged the table with his flat hand and cried in bitter grief: "Hear that, Annie? That's what we're coming to."

Owen asked, in pale bewilderment: "But papa, why did he hang himself?"

"He'd robbed the gov'ment, and he knew he'd go to the Pen for it, and he couldn't stand the shame."

That was a sorry Christmas for them all.

X

December 1893 — *April* 1894

Before Christmas, the demand for coal steadily decreasing, Moses Evans reduced the working week at Miss Ellen to three days. This cut their combined income back to what Tom had used to earn alone; and before the first of the year, a mild attack of rheumatism limited Tom's activities. He could make cartridges and load the holes and fire the shots; but drilling the holes, and all the pick and shovel work fell on Owen. The result was to reduce their output, but to accelerate Owen's education as a miner. He learned how to anticipate the loosening of the jack slate and how to set bank-props and wedge them; and, also, working at home with sand instead of powder and under Tom Glen's eye, he learned the knack of making cartridges. One day his father told him: "Son, you can handle a room by yourself any time, the way you're coming along."

Owen grinned with pride, not quite believing, yet pleased in spite of his doubts. But when in January, Tom came down with *La Grippe,* and they knew it would be a long time before he could work again, Owen accepted the challenge and went to the mine alone. His mother would have had him stay at home; she was afraid he might make a mistake for which his life would pay. But Tom reassured her, and Owen said:

"Besides, mama, Mr. Beecham says every man who has a job had better hang on to it, so I'll hold papa's for him if I can."

"Oh, son," she protested. "You can't. You're just a little boy."

He laughed, hugging her affectionately, pressing his chin down on top of her head. "Not as little as all that, mama. I'm a head taller than you!"

He was in fact six or seven inches over five feet, and strong enough so that the actual labor was within his strength; but he found there were many things about mining which he did not yet know. How to place your holes in order to shoot down a maximum amount of coal without making your next day's work unnecessarily awkward; how much powder to a cartridge under varying circumstances; how deep the holes; how firmly to tamp the clay down upon your cartridge for a heavy shot, and for a light one; under what circumstances your holes should slant down, or up, or across the face of the vein: to all these questions and to many more, since Tom Glen was not there to answer them, Owen had to learn the answers as he could. When he was hopelessly at a loss, little Mat Steel in the room next to his could advise him, or if necessary come and demonstrate, and John Powell looked in two or three times each day, and at night Owen put many questions to his father.

But chiefly he learned by doing, and his daily production at last began to increase. When first he mined two tons of coal in a day, he went home with a high head.

December had been relatively mild, and January began gently; but the hard times grew worse. The operators, competing with one another for the vanishing market, beat down the price till coal sold in Cincinnati at $2.00 the ton. This, said BB in the *Journal*, was the lowest price on record. Seventy-three railroads had gone into receivership last year. The biggest mine in Slacktown shut down, adding a hundred and twenty men to the large number already without work; and Isaac Williams estimated that Hardiston County mines had cut production to one third. At Belton Number 1, for the first week of January, the men averaged to earn $4 — and they were better off than most. There was a proposal to compel railroads to reduce their rates; and the United Mine Workers at the special meeting in January discussed reducing their own wages, in order to help the operators meet the competition of Pennsylvania and West Virginia mines. Of the delegates at the meeting, ten voted for the reduction, forty-four opposed it, and nineteen were in doubt; but they agreed to submit it to the districts to decide.

Tom Glen, still sick at home, raged at that suggestion. "It's all this new Union they've got us into. The Noble Order would never do that. Call themselves United Mine Workers, do they? United Friends o' the Operators, I call 'em! Tell the ops to go to thunder, I say."

But Owen remembered that moment when he had seemed to see so clearly operators and miners all harnessed together to a common task. "If we don't help them, they can't help us," he urged. "As long as the operators can work the mines and make a little money, they will; but they don't have to, not if they're losing money. The coal in the ground will stay there. They don't have to let us dig it, but we have to dig it to earn enough to feed us. I'd rather mine coal at ten cents a ton than not mine it at all!"

He had spoken mildly, feeling his way, not quite sure of his own thought until he put it into words; and Tom said with an angry laugh: "Ten cents a ton wouldn't feed you, Owen; not when you can't dig two tons in a day."

Owen flushed. "How much coal I can dig doesn't have anything to do with what I think."

"The man that digs four or five tons a day knows more about mining than the one that digs two tons!"

Owen stood his ground. "Maybe he doesn't! A man with no legs and no arms could still know all about coal-mining. It doesn't take arms and legs to know things; it takes brains." He was so intent upon his point that he failed to note the warning signs, till his father burst out in a storm of furious wrath. Mrs. Glen hastily summoned Owen away, led him out-of-doors.

"Leave him alone, Owen," she protested. "Don't argue with him."

"But he's wrong, mama!"

"Well, and if he is, you don't have to be the one to tell him so! Remember the Bible: Honor thy father and thy mother."

"I do, mama. It isn't that! But papa's been striking and trying to start strikes all his life, and look what it's got him!"

Instantly her eyes flamed and she boxed his ears, her hands clapping home so hard his head rang with the sound of many bells. "Hush! You hear me! If you're ever half the man your father is, it'll be time enough for you to talk. Now you leave him alone!"

She turned into the house, closing the door behind her; and he wiped a knuckle across his eyes. Surely, since he was for a while the bread-winner, he had a right to hold opinions, and to express them.

He found that the men at the mine outwardly agreed with his

father; yet he thought the very violence of their opposition to the reduced wage, and their empty threats, were evidence that they knew they were wrong. He wished to persuade them of this, and he remembered Mr. Beecham's suggestion, made so long ago, that asking questions might be a form of persuasion.

One day, walking from the tipple down to the siding with Isaac Williams, he began to experiment. He asked the old man how long he had been a miner, and Mr. Williams answered him at length. Like many another, he at first worked only in the winter, tramping to the mine from his father's farm near Massillon. When his father died, he continued farming and mining too, till the growth of the nearby city made it possible to sell the farm for building lots. He came then to Hardiston and bought a home. His savings gave him a modest income; he made a garden, and kept a cow and a pig or two; and though he had worked in Erie Mine and now in Miss Ellen, it was more from choice than necessity.

That first question had proved so fruitful that Owen tried another one. "I guess you know pretty much everything there is to know about coal-mining, don't you?"

Isaac nodded, with his habitual grave dignity. "As much as most men, I expect."

"Well, what happens to coal if we don't mine it?"

The old man looked faintly startled. "Why, nothing, Owen. What d'you suppose?"

"Does it just — stay in the ground?"

"What do you expect it to do, sprout like seeds?"

"Who owns it? Who owns the coal in the ground?"

"The operators, of course. Like Mr. Evans owns Miss Ellen."

Owen was frowning as though with an effort to understand. "Is it like — well, like money in the bank, that a man doesn't have to spend unless he wants to?"

Mr. Williams puffed his lips. "I suppose you could say so, but Mr. Evans can't turn it into money till he sells it, and he can't sell it till we mine it for him."

"Just the way he can't spend money in the bank till he draws it out?"

"Why, yes."

Owen persisted, a secret excitement in him, his eyes on the cross-
ties, spacing his steps upon them. "Does he have to mine it if he
doesn't want to?"

The other, elaborately tolerant of such stupidity, said patiently:
"No, there's no one to make him. No, he can block up the entry and
leave the coal there for good and all if he's a mind! But he'd never
make any money out of his coal that way."

"Then is that why he hires us to mine it; so he can sell it and
make money out of it?"

"Why, yes, of course." Mr. Williams looked at him in a sudden
attention. "That's why we're only running three days a week. If
we mined more coal, he couldn't sell it without cutting the price."
He added thoughtfully: "And with coal as cheap as it is, he can't
make any money even if he sells it."

"But then — isn't he sort of foolish to pay us seventy cents a ton
to dig his coal, and then sell it and lose money on it, when he could
just keep it in the ground?"

The old man chuckled. "Well, Owen, you've got me in a corner,
kind of. I don't know but he is. Maybe Headquarters is right, wanting us to take a cut to fifty cents."

"Wouldn't you rather mine coal for fifty cents than not mine it
at all?"

Isaac Williams laid a hand on Owen's shoulder, still half-laughing.
"Don't push an old man too hard, son. You get at things in a back-
handed kind of way, but — well, I always liked coal-mining. If it
comes to saying yes or no, I'll like as not take the cut, I guess."

Owen treasured his memory of that conversation. Of course, Mr.
Williams was not an ordinary miner. He had money enough so he
did not have to work; yet Owen thought even the bitterest opponent
of the wage reduction, if he were honest, would have answered
these questions just as Mr. Williams had answered them. He tried
the experiment, always cautiously, on other men, men with whom
he chanced to sit on the train or with whom he walked up from the
station. The results were always much the same.

Before the local met to vote upon the proposed reduction, excited
by what seemed to him a great discovery, Owen nerved himself to
put it to the test. Tom Glen, still weak from his attack of *La Grippe*,
could not attend the meeting, so Owen went alone; and during the

discussion he rose and addressed the chair and secured the floor.

"Mr. Chairman," he said, "I'm just starting in to mine coal, so there are a lot of things I don't know, and a lot of questions I'd like to ask, so I'll understand better." He paused. "Maybe someone can tell me what happens to the coal if we don't mine it."

A murmur of amusement answered him; but Owen, his heart pounding, did not wait for an answer. "Does it just stay in the ground? Do the operators own it, as long as it stays in the ground? Is it just like they had money in the bank? Do they hire us to mine it just so they can sell it?"

He realized that he was talking too fast, giving them no time to think; so he began to pause between questions, looking from one man to the next, letting each man find his own answers.

"Does it do the operators any good to mine it and sell it if they don't make any money selling it?

"If they lose money selling it, wouldn't they be smarter to just leave it in the ground?

"If I paid a dollar and a quarter for a pair of shoes, wouldn't I be foolish to sell them brand new for a dollar?

"If it costs the operator seventy cents a ton to have us mine it, and a dollar and a half to get it to market, and then all he can sell it for is two dollars, wouldn't he be smarter to just leave it in the ground till he could have us mine it and make some money out of it?"

He paused and waited, then added quietly: "I don't know the answers, any better than you do. But I do know I'd rather mine coal at fifty cents a ton than not have a job at all."

He sat down, and there was an uneasy stir across the hall and for a moment no one spoke. Then three or four men were on their feet at once. They were angry, but Owen thought they were angry not at his questions but at their own unspoken answers to those questions. They were recognized in turn, and others after them. The speakers each began by denouncing the proposal to reduce wages, but each man, before he was done, faltered and stammered, as though his own thoughts confuted his arguments. Owen became conscious that Charles Morgan, who as president of Miss Ellen local had the chair, was watching him with a thoughtful eye.

When the question was put, a scant majority accepted the proposed reduction. Owen, after the adjournment, found himself surrounded by older men, resentfully trying to make him see the error of his ways. John Powell, the mine boss at Miss Ellen, was on the fringe of the group, saying nothing; but when the men drifted away, he touched Owen's arm.

"Walk along with me," he suggested; and when they were clear of the dissolving crowd he said: "Quite a line of talk you put up, there."

"I just asked some questions."

"I know. You made them convince themselves. And you didn't go down to them; you made them reach up to you. You didn't undershoot your audience." Powell spat. "Owen, Miss Ellen is cutting down to two days a week. They'll likely cut to one day, or shut down altogether, if things keep on the way they are."

That was bad news. Owen did not speak, for there was nothing to say; but then Mr. Powell went on: "I heard yesterday that Union Furnace is going into blast again. That means they'll need coal from Erie; not much, but some. They want me back there, but for the coal they want, I'll only need about forty men. Isaac Williams is coming back with me, and Evan Harned, and some of the others; Mat Steel, Ed Thorne. You and Tom can come back if you want. We'll run four days a week to begin with, anyway. We'll start up on the twenty-second."

Owen went home with that good word to cheer his father, and he reported the vote of the meeting. "I made a speech, too," he said in a shy pride, forgetting Tom's opposition to the wage cut. "Or, anyway, I asked some questions."

"What questions?" Tom's heavy tone made the words like a blow; and while Owen answered, Tom watched him with angry eyes. When he spoke, it was as though he were passing sentence. "I wouldn't wonder if you changed some votes."

"I guess I did," Owen admitted, like a confession.

"So you've cut our wages." Owen felt his face burn. "Well, we'll have to dig more coal to make up for it; but maybe that's the way you want things to be."

Owen had come home proud and happy; his father's anger was a lash across his cheek.

2

Tom Glen's convalescence from *La Grippe* was slow; he was left with obscure aches and ugly fleeting pains which he could neither locate nor define. At the least exertion he perspired profusely, and he was so weak that to walk across the room left him breathless. Mrs. Glen, distracted with worry, concealed her concern behind a sharp and scolding tongue; and Owen, though he as often as his father was her target, understood, and felt for her the tolerant sympathy a child may feel for the weaknesses of its elders.

On the Thursday before Erie Mine reopened, Mr. Beecham stopped at the house to ask whether Owen cared for a day in the hills. Tom Glen, a blanket around his shoulders, huddled by the stove, and the editor said sympathetically: "I'm sorry to see you laid up."

Tom Glen spoke in a twisted irony. "I picked a good time. There's no work; and not working I don't get hungry, so we save on victuals."

BB said reassuringly: "You'll be up and around pretty soon." Men in good health are easily optimistic about the illnesses of others. He added: "But times are hard, sure enough. A year ago, every well man had a job; now there are three men for every job, everywhere. That's what the Democrats have done to the country."

"Them and the United Mine Workers, cutting our own wages to fifty cents a ton."

"I hear wages may have to come even lower. But the man who can keep a pig and raise chickens and turkeys and geese and make a garden and keep a cow will always get along. The wise man, nowadays, will move to an abandoned farm, buy one or rent one."

"That's easy saying, hard doing. You can't buy a farm — no, nor rent one either — without you've got money."

"I suppose not." BB turned. "Owen, I expect you'll want to stay with your father."

"I'm reading the *Journal* to him," Owen assented, hoping his father would bid him go along; but Tom said nothing and BB departed and Owen read on. A company had at last been incorporated to build an electric railway between Hardiston and Belton, and the

Hardiston City Council had voted to grant a franchise for the use of streets where the cars would run. The *Journal* suggested that some hundreds might find employment building the railway. *Philip Phillips's Peerless Pilgrimage*, a series of three lectures, would be given at the Rink next week; the lectures were illustrated with a limelight photo-opticon. Hardiston County operators a year ago were advertising for miners; now most miners were working less than one-third of the time. By proposing the annexation of Hawaii, the democrats had launched the United States on a program of imperialism, greatly to be deplored. Tramps were becoming increasingly numerous; one who committed a burglary said when arrested that he did it in order to get sent to jail, to a comfortable lodging and enough to eat.

Owen read without attention, his thoughts elsewhere. His father seemed asleep, his eyes closed, the shawl tight around his bent shoulders. Since that angry explosion when Owen came home from the meeting that voted to accept the wage cut, Tom had held toward his son an accusing silence, and Owen suffered under the burden of unspoken blame. Half an hour after Mr. Beecham departed, he finished the *Journal*. "That's all there is that amounts to anything, papa."

Tom grunted and stirred in his chair; and Mrs. Glen, knitting in her low rocker, looked at him and then at Owen, some concern in her eyes. "Oh. All right," said Tom, as though he had been asleep and now was waking. "All right. Where you going?"

"Nowhere. Unless you want something."

"No." Tom closed his eyes again. "No."

Owen met his mother's glance, and she nodded reassuringly, and her lips seemed to move. He knew she was telling him not to worry, that everything would be all right; and when he now went out-of-doors she followed him, closing the door behind her. He came near her, and she said: "Don't feel bad, Owen."

"I wish he wasn't mad at me."

"He'll get over it. Don't feel bad."

Sunday was fine, and Tom insisted on going to church. He walked home as far as Belton Street with Isaac Williams; and that afternoon he dictated to Owen a notice of a meeting the following Saturday to reorganize the Erie local. "You post it up at the mine tomorrow, son," he directed.

Monday, Owen's first day in Erie Mine, was in some ways as

adventurous as his first day in Miss Ellen. He had never before been in Erie, and conditions were markedly different from those in Miss Ellen. Erie was a shallow vein, not three feet thick; and this meant the roof of the room was lower, the work correspondingly more cramped and awkward, and the amount of coal a man could dig was definitely less.

Yet by the end of his fourth day at Erie, the strangeness had passed and he began to be at home. Tom was still too weak to work; but he came with Owen to the meeting Saturday. They sat together, and Tom whispered to his son:

"You keep track of things, so you can write up the minutes for me afterward."

Owen nodded assent, wondering why his father did not sit at the secretary's table. Isaac Williams took the chair and called for order. The first business was to choose officers, and Isaac was duly re-elected president, Evan Harned vice-president.

Then Mr. Williams, from the chair, said: "The next business is electing a secretary-treasurer. Thomas Glen formerly held that office; but he has suggested as his successor his son, Owen Glen. Tom's eyes are giving him trouble, and he tells me Owen was doing most of his work for him before Erie shut down. Do I hear a motion?"

Owen, frightened and trembling, caught at his father's arm. "Oh, papa, no!" he whispered. "Please don't!"

But Tom Glen looked at him and winked, and he put his arm around Owen's shoulders; and Owen forgot everything except that his father was not angry with him, that his father was proud of him and trusted him. Then he heard Mr. Williams say: "The ayes have it, and Owen Glen is unanimously elected secretary-treasurer. Owen, come to the table."

So Owen rose and obeyed the summons. He was two months more than fourteen years old.

3

The happy knowledge that his father had arranged his election was at first foremost in Owen's mind; but after the meeting, while he and Tom Glen and Isaac Williams walked together as far as the corner where Charles Morgan lived, he began to have misgivings.

That little red book which Mr. Morgan had given him, *Robert's Rules of Order,* devoted almost four pages to the duties of the secretary, the "clerk or secretary"; and as many more were given to the duties of the treasurer. But Owen was both secretary and treasurer, and according to the book, the duties of the treasurer "vary in different societies" while those of the secretary were decidedly elastic. So when he and his father were alone, he asked helplessly: "Do you think I can do it, papa?"

Tom assured him. "It's easy enough, son. You just write down what happens at meetings, and keep track of who pays their tax, and all like that."

"Don't everyone pay it?" Erie local had voted today a tax of five cents a month; at Miss Ellen the tax was ten cents.

"It ain't everybody that can. The Union Constitution says locals pay twenty cents a month for every member, but not many do it. If you collect a dollar a month in taxes, you'll do good." They turned off the Pike down the path toward the house, and Tom said: "Come along in and tell your mama. She'll be tickled pink."

Mrs. Glen listened in smiling gladness, her eyes shining. "Was it your doing, Tom?" she asked, when Owen's tale was told.

"I told Isaac Williams my eyes ain't up to the job any more, and he asked who'd be a good man, and I told him Owen. He will, too."

"He will so," Mrs. Glen agreed. "He can do anything he's a mind to."

Next day after church, Miss Williams hurried to him, smiling and taking his hand. "Congratulations, Owen. I should think you'd be so proud." The congregation was still coming out of church; and she looked over her shoulder: "Here's an old friend of yours. Remember Bobby Roberts? He came up to spend Sunday. I hurried out ahead to catch you before you got away."

Bobby's hand gripped Owen's firmly. "Glad to see you again, Owen. And congratulations. Marged told me your news."

"It doesn't amount to anything."

"It amounts to men respecting you. You can be proud of that."

Marged said happily: "They do, Bobby. Owen has made speeches at union meetings, good ones. Uncle Isaac says half the miners in the county know about him."

Owen grinned with embarrassment, and Bobby said: "That's all right if they know the right things about him." They laughed together; and Owen expected Bobby would say goodbye, but he did not do so. Miss Williams looked at Bobby and then at Owen.

"Come along with us, Owen," she suggested.

By that invitation, Owen felt himself excluded. It was his right to walk with her, not Bobby's to walk with them; not the other way around! The hurt was keen. He blurted out an answer.

"I have to wait for mama and papa."

That afternoon he lost himself in *Lavengro*. He read with dreaming eyes the chapter about a poet, a Welshman named Ab Gwilym, who loved a woman named Morffyd. The boy in the book said Morffyd was wife to a man named Bwa Bach, and he said Ab Gwilym's poems were all really letters to beg her to meet him in the woods. Owen's pulses thudded as he read, and his eyes clouded and his vision blurred. At supper time, he put the book away, but he imagined Ab Gwilym and Morffyd meeting beside some bright dancing forest stream, embracing gloriously. He wished some of Ab Gwilym's poems were in *Lavengro*, but they were not.

After supper he turned to the book again, reading why the boy who wrote the book was called Lavengro, and reading about Tawno Chikno, a man so beautiful that the most beautiful women — yes, even an earl's daughter — embraced his feet, begging him to make her his wife "or anything else." Owen pondered that phrase, so mysteriously provocative; but when he went to bed, it was Morffyd who filled his half-dreams. She met Ab Gwilym in the forest, but sometimes a thunder shower made her leave him, and once a fox frightened her away, and always something happened, so that Ab Gwilym was forever denied. Owen felt himself equally cheated and denied. He drifted at last into hot disordered sleep, and dreamed of Morffyd, and woke weary and hard worn.

4

The mild winter, said BB in the *Journal*, was kind to the poor. The Hardiston laundry caught fire, and when the fire engine got there the cistern was dry, so they put the hose down a crawfish hole; but the water in the hole was soon exhausted and the laundry burned down. Three hundred and sixty-five people from Hardiston County had visited the World's Fair last summer. BB thought Hardiston young women should refuse to accept the attentions of young men who did not respect themselves; and Owen remembered that Jane Lloyd's mother had said Jane must not speak to him. Probably that meant she thought Owen did not respect himself; but BB said young men who did not respect themselves drank, and swore, and smoked in the presence of ladies, and Owen knew that of these vices he was innocent.

Additional Locals: Down in Adams County a murderer was lynched; but the last murderer arrested there, said BB, had been tried three times, at a cost of over four thousand dollars, so the lynching was not to be wondered at. Corbett and Mitchell, since their prize fight, should be indicted for assault with intent to kill. The winter was so mild that a farmer near Slacktown killed a blacksnake. John Temple Graves in his lecture at the Rink said the only good thing about Abraham Lincoln was that he was born in Kentucky. Few Hardiston County mines were running more than two days a week; the average miner earned not over $4.50 in a week. Fifty cents a ton for shallow vein mining was a starvation wage. A boy in Belton was killed when he tried to board a moving train and fell under the wheels. A wealthy New York man thought Hardiston County coal so admirable that he had ordered a carload. Several Hardiston County churches held revivals, and the number of people converted had reached two hundred before the end of January. Revivals were always a success when times were hard. Senator Phillips refrained from voting on the bill for an investigation of the sufferings of the poor; his vote would have passed the bill, and those who had hoped he would abandon his stand against all labor measures were disappointed. One Hardiston County operator, when told that the miners were starving, said he hoped to see them so hungry they would eat their own children. To protect him from violence, his name was kept secret. The Presbyterian Church established a "Barrel" to receive contributions for suffering poor. *The Fast Mail* played at the Rink, but the audience was small. The total of converts at the various revivals up to February 21 was over seven hundred. John de Witt Miller would lecture at the Rink February 27 on *The Uses of Ugliness*. A new minister was installed at the Presbyterian Church. Moses Evans, after two months in bed, was able to be about again. To eat a raw onion every day would keep off colds. It was as important to exer-

cise the brain as the body; and next to eating, the most profitable
habit was reading. When the Brady House caught fire, the fire
apparatus reached the hotel in four and a half minutes after the
alarm. The Young People's Society for Christian Endeavor held
their convention in Sycamore Hill. The Milkmaids gave a benefit
March 17 at Y Hall to raise money to help a lame boy whom they
had made their charge. Leland Powers, lecturer and impersonator,
would appear in Hardiston March 28 under the auspices of the
Ladies' Aid Society of the Methodist Church; the lecture would
not begin till 8:15, so everyone could attend prayer meeting beforehand. The Legislature passed a law forbidding the use of air guns
in streets and alleys in any city or town. Scientific temperance
instruction would be established in Hardiston schools. In the April
elections, the Republicans were victorious almost everywhere in
the state. Of 1765 convicts in the Ohio Penitentiary, 63 admitted
that they were drunk when they committed their crimes, 768 had
attended Sunday School, 833 used tobacco; only 295 were married.
Dogs in 1893 killed 320 sheep in Hardiston County. The seventeen-
year-locusts were due this year, but they would do less damage
than the democratic party had already done.

5

When Tom Glen was able to return to work, he took a room of
his own, and Owen continued to work alone. Tom, though he never
seemed to hurry and though he was forever complaining of his
back, usually produced well over three tons in a day, and sometimes better than four; but Owen had not yet learned the many
wise devices which to Tom were so nearly second nature that it
never occurred to him to explain them. The boy, zealous to equal
or exceed his father's production, drove himself to the utmost; but
two tons remained for him a big day's work.

He was spurred not only by his ambition to match his father, but
also by their need for money. The wage cut had reduced their
earnings by twenty cents a ton; and he tried by greater efforts to
make up this loss, but the gap between what he and his father
earned and what they needed grew wider all the time.

In March the cow sickened and died and they could not buy

another; yet to be without a cow meant that they would have no milk for a pig this summer, and no pork next winter. Tom spoke of this, but Mrs. Glen said crisply:

"Next winter's a long time off. Let it take care of itself. What I don't see is what we're going to eat right now, till the garden comes along."

But spring was always a time of hope, and the occasional hot April days were finely seductive, making Owen restless and desirous. Sometimes after work, he went with other boys and men from the mine to a pool in Erie Creek. The pool, though it was nowhere more than three feet deep and only twelve or fourteen feet long, was called "the swimming hole." It was pleasant to scrub the black coal dust off your face and body and out of your hair and then dry yourself in the baking sun; but Owen, rather than resume his grimy clothes, sometimes brought another pair of pants and a shirt, wrapped in newspaper, and after his bath dressed in them.

There was a pagan joy in these hours by the muddy water of the creek, half a dozen boys and young men soaping and lathering their naked bodies equally begrimed which presently gleamed white and clean. Owen, at first shy about undressing before the eyes of the others, soon became used to it; his furtive interest in what he saw about him gave way to a matter-of-fact acceptance of masculine nudity. The rough talk, the good-humored laughter at Owen's revealed immaturity, the battles when they pelted one another with balls of mud, all combined to make a jolly interlude. On hot afternoons they might stay an hour or more, reluctant to depart. When someone, dry after a few minutes in the sun, decided to put on his clothes, the others rubbed him with mud so that he had to go into the creek to wash himself again and wait to dry once more. Thus they delayed their own departures.

The creek was bordered by willows and lesser bushes, and the swimming hole was screened by a considerable thicket, an old field gone back to weeds and sumac and young saplings through which a path wound to the waterside. One day four of them took this path together. Except for Owen, Chet Masters was the youngest of the four, two or three years older than Owen, two inches taller, twenty pounds heavier. Mat Steel and Ed Thorne were the others. Owen liked these two. They were always good-humored, and while they enjoyed a joke as well as anyone, their jests were kindly, and their tongues were clean.

But Chet was cut from a different pattern; there was malice in him, and he regularly made Owen, in little ways, his butt. He lived near the mine and not far from the Tutsons, and once or twice he guyed Owen about Nellie. "She says you always run away from her, kid. When you going to grow up?" Owen disliked him, sometimes hated him.

Owen today as usual deposited his newspaper-wrapped bundle of clean clothes between the roots of a willow by the creek. When after his bath he went to get them, the newspaper was wet; he unrolled the bundle and found the sleeves of his shirt and the legs of his pants knotted tight. Worse, the knots had been soaked in the muddy creek water and were all begrimed.

He turned, holding his shirt in his hand. "Who did this?" he demanded, red with anger. Mat and Ed faced him gravely, but Chet grinned in a way that admitted guilt. "Did you, Chet?" Owen demanded.

"What do you want to make of it?"

Owen felt rage fill his throat; he wished to get his hands on Chet, but the other was already dressed, and he was near the path that led through the thicket. Owen, naked as an egg, could not pursue him through the thicket and out into the sight of the world. If he jumped at Chet now, the other would just laugh and run away.

Yet guile might serve. "All right for you," he said morosely. He plucked at one of the knots in his shirt, moving forward as though to go down to the creek bank to wash the dirt away. Chet stood casually, off his guard; and when Owen passed within three paces, he dropped the shirt and sprang. The older boy tried to run, but Owen caught him.

They wrestled and went down, Chet uppermost; and he laughed amiably. "Easy, kid. Don't get your dander up!" Sitting on Owen's chest, his knees on Owen's arms, he reached behind him, tickling Owen's stomach. "Cute little feller!"

Owen's outraged twist threw Chet off balance, and Owen freed an arm and flung it around the other's neck and hauled him down; but Chet rolled over and they scrambled to their feet, and Chet was angry now. He charged in, and Owen's flying fist struck his jaw on the left side.

To Owen's astonished terror, Chet lurched forward on his face and lay still. Owen had seen steers butchered; he had seen them drop in just that way, every muscle letting go, when the sledge struck home between their eyes. He looked helplessly at the older men. "Is he dead?"

Mat Steel turned Chet over. "Out cold," he said, and he looked at Owen with surprised interest.

"Is he dead?" Owen repeated, mumbling with fright.

"Huh-uh! Be all right in a minute. Say, you hit him a good one!"

Chet stirred, and gasped back to consciousness. Owen hastily untied the knots in his clothes, and he was dressed by the time Chet sat up, turning his head in a vacant way, his eyes not yet focusing. "What happened?"

Ed Thorne said: "Owen caught you a lick in the jaw."

"Gosh!" Chet looked at Owen, his eyes steadying, and Ed helped him to his feet.

"I got mad." Owen's word was half-apology. Fright had chilled his rage.

Chet touched his bruised chin. "I guess you did!"

"You all right?"

Chet managed a grin. "I'll never be the same." He said in subdued protest, "I was just having fun."

"I didn't go to hurt you."

Ed Thorne said: "You kids better shake hands."

"Sure." Chet extended his hand and Owen took it. "No hard feelings, Owen?"

"All right."

The tension ended, and Mat Steel laughed. "Owen, if you ever get mad at me, give me a chance to run, will you?" Mat was neither so tall nor so heavy as Owen. Owen grinned; and they went single file along the path, separated, took their several ways.

Nellie Tutson's home, though not on Owen's direct road to and from the mine, was on the most convenient route from the swimming hole; but since she now worked for Mrs. Paxley every day except Wednesday, it was months since he had seen her. Today she was in the yard, but Owen, trembling with excitement and intoxicated by the sudden discovery of his own fistic prowess, did not know this till she spoke to him.

"H'lo, Owen."

"Oh! H'lo." He walked steadily on.

"Where you been?"

"Swimming."

She was keeping pace with him inside the fence. "Where'bouts."

"Down't the swimming hole."

"What's your hurry?"

"Got to go home."

"Oh, you've always got to go home — or somewhere."

He hesitated. Nellie had told Chet he was always running away from her! Well, he was not afraid of her, nor of anyone else; not now, not after today! He stopped, turned to face her. "I don't have to hurry."

She laughed in a friendly way, leaning her elbows on the fence between them. She was taller than he remembered, and not fat and dumpy the way she used to be. She asked: "Want me to walk a ways with you?"

He had to remind himself that he was not afraid of her. "All right, if you want to."

She went back to the gate and joined him. "What's that bundle?"

"My work clothes."

"Did you work today? You're all cleaned up."

"We went down to the swimming hole."

"I know where that is! Can you swim?"

"Some, dog-paddle."

"I wish I could. Teach me, sometime?"

Seeing a sudden vivid mental picture of her at the swimming hole with Chet and the others, he flushed to the ears. "No!" His word was almost a shout.

"Why not?"

Her tone was mirthful, and he saw she was teasing him; so he answered curtly: "I won't, that's all."

"You're scared!"

"I am not!"

They had come up Ridge Street to the corner of Peach, half a block from Mr. Beecham's; and she stopped. "I have to go get Mrs. Paxley's supper. Want to walk down with me?"

He welcomed the chance to escape. "I'm going to help papa in the garden."

"Well, anyway, I'm glad you're not afraid of me any more." She was near him, smiling into his eyes.

"I never was afraid of you!" He backed clear. "Well, g'bye."

" 'Bye, Owen."

He hurried his steps; but he decided Nellie was all right, especially when you got over being afraid of her. After licking Chet Masters so soundly, Owen was not afraid of Nellie, nor of anyone else.

Nellie was certainly pretty, too. He had not realized that before.

6

As secretary of the Erie local, Owen received an occasional letter or a notice from State Headquarters. At the January convention in Columbus, President McBride had proposed that the miners suspend work long enough to deplete the supply of coal above ground and thus end throat-cutting competition among operators and restore the coal business to a healthier condition. If this could be done, he urged, then wages might be re-established at their former level. The convention voted such a suspension, and early in April Owen received a copy of the resolution then adopted.

> *Resolved, that on and after Sunday noon, April 21, 1894, no coal shall be mined in that part of the United States and territories governed by our organization until such time as our general officers and national executive board shall order the miners to resume work.*
>
> *Resolved, that we declare it to be the purpose of the general suspension to restore the scale of prices and conditions of employment which prevailed at the beginning of the year.*

With this was enclosed another resolution pledging a full observance of the law, and respect for life and property.

Owen had favored voluntary reduction in wages, because that was designed to help the operators keep the mines running; but this suspension, since it would close the mines, seemed to him a mistake. Surely, in times like these, with work scant, miners would be wiser to work while they could.

But he was not surprised to find that his father approved. "A good thing," Tom said strongly. "The Union will never get anywhere if it keeps babying the operators. The only way to make 'em come to time is to strike."

"It's cutting off our nose to spite our face, papa. This is no time to be throwing ourselves out of a job."

"As good a time as any," Tom insisted. "The garden will keep us going this summer; and come fall, things will be better."

There had been a time when Owen thought his father infallible; but that was no longer true. Surely it was folly, when the chance to work at all was a treasure to be sought after, to throw that chance away. He wished to protest, to argue the point; but if he did, his father would get mad again.

"I'll have to take this notice down to Isaac Williams," he decided, and said no more.

Owen waited till after supper to go to Isaac. When he reached the house, Morgan Williams was mowing the front lawn, and Owen stopped to talk to him. Since Morgan was still in school, Owen's tone held a certain condescension, as though a man spoke to a child.

"Hello, Morgan. How's school?"

"All right. We've got a pretty good teacher."

"How long you going to keep going to school?"

"Through High School, papa says."

"Is he at home? I have to see him." Owen spoke with dignity, feeling the importance of his errand. "Some union business."

"Yes, he's home. He's in the house." Owen relished the respect in Morgan's eyes. Then Miss Williams came out on the porch and called to him, and he went toward her.

"It's mighty nice to see you, Owen. I never do see you now except Sundays."

"Yes'm. I came to see Mr. Williams."

"I'll call him." She went to the door. "Uncle Isaac!" And a rumble from inside, "Owen Glen wants to see you." She told Owen: "He's coming. Won't you sit down?"

"It's union business," he said. "I better go inside." He met her uncle at the door. "I've got some mail to show you, Mr. Williams," he explained.

"Come in to the lamp."

Owen followed the old man into the sitting room and gave him the printed resolutions. Mrs. Williams came through from the kitchen, rubbing some fragrant ointment on her hands; and Owen guessed she and Marged had been washing dishes. She spoke to Owen in habitual friendliness and went out on the porch, and Owen

heard her call: "Morgan, hurry up and finish before it's too dark."
The lawnmower resumed its clatter.

Mr. Williams, having read the resolutions, handed them back to
Owen. "You post them up," he directed. "We'll have to call a
meeting, decide what we'll do."

"I don't see any sense in it," Owen suggested. "A time like this,
if a man has a job, he'd better hold on to it."

"Well, I guess it won't hurt anyone's feelings if we do quit work
for a while. I kind of hate to, though."

"I think when we cut our own wages we did enough to help the
operators! It's time we looked out for ourselves."

Isaac chuckled. "Maybe so. They say the Lord helps them that
help themselves." He rose. "Hot in here. Let's go sit on the porch."

Owen followed him, still rebellious. Mr. Williams and his father
agreed the suspension was a wise maneuver, but Owen thought
them wrong. He was proud of being a miner in his own right.
There was a fine satisfaction in tramping off to the mine with his
father, in greeting his fellows at the portal, in dropping off at the
entry to his room, in loading the coal he had shot down the day
before and then setting props and drilling new holes and charging
them; there was proud content in emerging from the mine, the
day's work done, a man among men. This suspension would end
all that for a while, or — Owen was young enough to nurse despair
— perhaps forever.

On the porch, Isaac filled his pipe and he and Mrs. Williams
rocked peacefully side by side. Morgan and the lawnmower rattled
through the deepening dusk. Owen sat on the steps, trying to
devise some argument to sway Mr. Williams, and Marged came
beside him.

"Still reading *Lavengro*, Owen?" she asked.

"Yes'm. And I've started reading the Bible through again."

"Why?"

"Well, Lavengro — he's a boy, four years older than I am — he
wanted to learn how to read a Danish book, so he got a Danish
Bible and matched it up with his Bible in English and learned
Danish that way." He added honestly: "I get kind of tired of
Lavengro. The Bible's more interesting."

"I never thought of learning other languages out of the Bible,"
Marged reflected. "I suppose the Bible is a universal language, isn't
it? It says the same things to Christians everywhere."

"I like to read it aloud to papa. I like the way the words sound."

She looked at him in quickening interest. "Come inside, Owen. I want to read something to you." She rose, and he hesitated and then followed her into the sitting room. Many small books, small enough to carry in one's pocket, were set together in a rack on the table. She selected one and sat down by the lamp. "If you like the sound of words, listen to this." And she began to read:

> "For once, upon a raw and gusty day,
> The troubled Tiber chafing with her shores,
> Caesar said to me: 'Darest thou, Cassius, now
> Leap in with me into this angry flood
> And swim to yonder point?' Upon the word,
> Accoutred as I was, I plunged in
> And bade him follow; so indeed he did.
> The torrent roared and we did buffet it
> With lusty sinews, throwing it aside
> And stemming it with hearts of controversy — "

She paused, looking at him. "'Hearts of controversy,'" she repeated. "That's a wonderful way to use words, isn't it? You know what a controversy is?"

He said hurriedly: "A fight, or an argument or something. He means they swam as if they were fighting the water. Go on. What happened?"

So she read on, and he listened; she selected another and another of the little books and read lines and passages. Once a line in what she read made him for a moment forget to listen. "'Men have died from time to time, and worms have eaten them — but not for love.'" He thought of John Carver, who had surely died for love of Edna Tutson — with a lock of Nellie's hair treasured in his watch. But John shot himself, and probably that did not count as dying for love.

Once he asked, in the harshly intent tone he had used before: "That you're reading, it's sort of poetry, isn't it?"

"Blank verse, yes."

"What are those books?"

She half smiled under his strict cross-examination. "Plays, by William Shakespeare."

"Plays? What kind of plays? Games, you mean?"

"The things actors and actresses perform in the theater. Comedies, tragedies."

"Oh, like at the Rink?"

"Yes, except that these are better, more interesting, certainly more beautiful. I know you're interested in words. Well, Shakespeare, who wrote these plays, knew and used more different words than any man who ever wrote."

"More than there are in the Bible?"

"I think so. And then, of course, many different men wrote the Bible." He looked at the neat row of little books, and she guessed his thought. "You can come here and read them any time, Owen. I don't want to lend them to you, because Bobby Roberts gave them to me for Christmas; so, of course, I treasure them." Her cheeks were pink. "But you can read them here."

"Can I read one of them now?"

She heard her aunt and uncle stirring on the porch. "I'm afraid it's near our bedtime. Suppose you come Sunday afternoon. We might read one of them together. They're good to read aloud. Come Sunday, if you can."

"I can, all right," he said. "I will, too."

7

Before the called meeting of Erie local, Owen had heard enough of the talk among the men to know they agreed with his father and with Mr. Williams; so he did not speak, unwilling to oppose them in what he knew must be a losing battle. The local voted to obey the strike call, and Isaac Williams instructed Owen as secretary to notify Headquarters.

BB had in the past suggested that Owen keep him posted on union news. When Owen told him Erie men would go out, BB said: "Write it out for me, a line or two."

After an hour of painful effort Owen produced the necessary paragraph.

The United Mine Workers of America will suspend work all over the country April 21 so coal will be used up enough to make business better. Hardiston County miners will stop work. The operators have been notified. The miners will be peaceful and obey the law.

He handed this to Mr. Beecham, watching diffidently while the editor read it. "That's all right," BB said. "I'll put a headline on it." He wrote at the top, "Strike Coming," and gave the sheet of paper to Owen. "Send it upstairs," he said.

Wednesday night when the paper was printed, Owen searched its columns and found his product among the locals on page five. He read it over and over, relishing every word; and he took home extra copies of the paper, and showed his father and mother the paragraph. "I wrote it," he said. "Mr. Beecham asked me to."

Tom Glen bade him read it aloud, and Owen did, and Mrs. Glen decided to send it to Amy and Evan. Sunday, Owen told Miss Williams his achievement. "And Mr. Beecham wants me to write up anything about miners," he said. "I'm going to, too."

She smiled, thinking how often Owen thus firmly announced his decisions and intentions. "I'm sure you will."

The day was too hot to stay indoors, so at her direction Owen carried porch chairs out under the big apple tree beside the house, and she brought *Merchant of Venice* and *Midsummer Night's Dream* and *Hamlet*. They sampled each in turn, reading aloud, their chairs drawn side by side, but facing in opposite directions so that their heads were close and their voices could be hushed almost to a whisper. "Because everyone has naps Sunday afternoons," she reminded him with a smile. "And we don't want to keep Uncle Isaac and Aunt May awake — or even the neighbors."

Sometimes she read, and the low murmur of her voice was like a song, and sometimes she bade him read, coaching him in the art. "Keep thinking about the characters while you read. Keep thinking why they're saying the things they say, and whether they're mad or sad or happy or laughing or worried. Read it the way you think they'd say it."

He tried, sweating with the effort; and sometimes she took the book away from him and herself read the passage to make clear what she meant. "You're so solemn, Owen," she protested, laughing at him. "This isn't solemn. It's exciting, but it's gay and merry and dramatic, too." He went home drunk with words.

The following Sunday, although he saw Bobby Roberts in church with Marged in the morning, he went again to the house; but Mrs. Williams told him Marged and Bobby had gone for a walk together. Remembering Dave and Amy, Owen thought maybe that meant

Miss Williams and Bobby were going to be married; but even if they were, for her to go walking with Bobby when she must have known he was coming to see her made him wretched with hurt and loneliness. He had a defiant impulse to seek Nellie Tutson and take her for a walk!

But as he turned away, Morgan came to the door to tell him that Miss Williams had left word he might read in her Shakespeare books if he wanted to; so Owen forgot Nellie. He read *Merchant of Venice* again that afternoon, sometimes in silence, sometimes mumbling the speeches to himself, puzzling over many words.

He was still there when Miss Williams and Bobby returned. She asked which plays he had read, and when she heard, she protested in amusement:

"But we read that last week, Owen."

"I have to keep reading things over and over till I understand them," he admitted. "I'm pretty slow."

Bobby said approvingly: "Slow and steady won the race, Owen. You'll get there, all right."

That was the Sunday set in the United Mine Workers' resolution. Next day the strike began.

XI

April 1894 — September 1894

C OXEY'S ARMY was moving toward Washington; and BB said in the *Journal* that it was an army of tramps, that they could accomplish nothing, that their march could only lead to disorder and possible bloodshed. Hughie Morgan butchered a steer which weighed 2150 pounds and dressed 1258. The promoters of the electric railway were having trouble securing a right of way. The Reading Room, stocked with magazines and newspapers, would hereafter be open from two to five on Thursday afternoons; but what Hardiston needed was a free library. Seven mortgages were recorded in one day, and no deeds; those mortgages, said BB, were the fault of the democrats. Only a small crowd patronized the Walter Main circus, in spite of the male gorilla, the two-headed cow, the clown-elephants, the woman who allowed herself to be shot out of a gun, and all the other attractions; the democrats had left very few people with enough money to buy tickets. The Pullman Company up in Illinois had reduced wages and the employees were forming a union; the company had not reduced dividends; the employees would suffer, but not the stockholders: in hard times, the poor man suffered first and most. A Boys' Brigade had been formed in the Presbyterian Sunday School. Samuel Llewellyn, after two terms in the Ohio House, had been appointed Deputy Mine Inspector. The Cleveland Administration had already cost the country more than the Civil War. The democratic party ruined the Confederacy in four years, but now they had ruined the United States in fourteen months. If there were no tax on homes, there would be fewer tramps. The strike was proving that Hardiston County had the cleanest set of operators and the most sensible and deserving miners in the state.

2

The strike for weeks filled Owen's world and his mind, excluding every other thought or hope or fear. He woke early Monday morning — Sunday, April 21, marked the official cessation of work — and lay awhile in the darkness, remembering that he could stay abed as long as he chose. He felt himself, in that hour before first dawn, one with hundreds and thousands and scores of thousands of other men who all over the United States must be awake as he was, feeling as he did the strangeness of this morning when they broke away from the normal routine of early rising and a sleepy lamplit breakfast and a trudging journey to their tasks.

He rose at last; but when he stirred, so did his mother, and he heard her kindling the fire. "Mama, you don't have to get up for me," he called, knotting his shoe laces. "I just thought I'd walk over to the mine and see what happens."

"You'll go with some breakfast in you." She spoke in harsh tenderness. "If you went hungry, you'd like as not start some new foolishness."

Owen had forgotten his conviction that the strike was a mistake. If the men wished to strike, then so did he. He came to put his arm around his mother's shoulder. "Now, mama, it's not foolishness. Even the operators think it's sensible, with too much coal already dug and no way to sell it."

She shrugged his arm aside. "Don't come buttering up to me. It's easy enough for you and your father. You don't have to scrape and scrawn to feed two hungry men, and nothing to feed them with. It's fine for you. You've quit work, and you can loaf around the house all you're a mind to; but I have to work harder than ever, more to do and nothing to do with."

"We'll get along." He sat down at the table and Tom Glen came from the bedroom. "I can put in two days a week at the *Journal* office, and cut grass and do odd jobs; and pretty soon we can live off the garden." His spirits were high; he was in haste to be off to the mine. He and his father had brought home their tools and gear, so there was no purpose in his going; but Owen invented a purpose. "I'll have to report to District Headquarters what happens," he said.

His father's morning prayer gave him a sense of dedication. "Smile upon us, your children, dear Lord. Strengthen our hearts to long endurance, and help us to feel ourselves united in a holy bond, loyal each to each. We are Thy humble ones; our only strength is in our common purpose and Thy favor. Teach us and help us to stand fast in solid ranks; let each man forget himself and endure privation for the sake of his fellows. Give us wisdom and kindness and fellowship that we may serve our comrades and serve Thee. For Christ's sake, Amen."

Owen rose from his knees with a high heart, and since Tom Glen would stay at home, he set out alone. At the mine he found a considerable group of men, a dozen or fifteen. They had come, as he had come, because it was strange not to come, because it was hard to stay at home with idle hands; but like Owen they invented reasons for their coming, and when he spoke to one and another they said they had come to fetch away their tools, or to see if other men were working. Owen suspected that if one of them suggested a return to work, most of the others would follow. The men in the clustered groups were each shaken by an equal fear, the fear that is the bedfellow of every wage-earner. "When my pay stops, what will happen to my family?" Some of them supported from their meager pay not only wives and children but sick or aged relatives. Mat Steel and his wife gave a home to his father who had lost both legs on the railroad. Ed Thorne's wife was bedridden, and her sister lived with them and cared for her. Peter Teague's wife had died when their sixth baby was born; his eleven-year-old daughter kept house for him and his five younger children. Most of the men were no more heavily burdened than a healthy family with good appetites burdens any man when times are hard; but not a man of them had for months past earned enough for a living. Now their last savings would spill away.

Watching the men here, Owen's thoughts multiplied them into thousands and ten thousands like them, not only coal miners but laborers of every sort. Surely it was not right that men should live thus precariously, haunted always by the fear of losing their jobs; surely it was not right that the whim of a man's immediate boss might at any moment change him from a decent, self-supporting miner into a helpless pauper. Owen remembered how during his baby years in Indiana his father had walked ten and twenty and thirty miles in a day to ask for jobs that were denied him; to beg the privilege of working from before dawn till dark, deep in the earth, in dampness and dust and muck, in order to earn enough to feed and house his family. His father must remember those bitter times, yet Tom Glen had approved this strike, loyally accepting the decision of the Union at whatever cost; and at the thought Owen's heart filled with love and pride.

Inspired by pride in his father, Owen burned with desire to do some great and worthy deed. Suppose these men decided to go back to work, could he stop them? He could not stop them by force, but perhaps by words? He imagined compelling and persuasive phrases which he might use to hold them firm; he saw them, scores of them, pressing toward the entry, and in their path he saw himself, with upraised hand, bidding them stop, wait, consider. He thought of himself as a small boy in their road. The smallness of that heroic figure facing the pressing throng intensified for him the drama of the scene, and Owen easily forgot that he was in fact as tall as many of the men here, and taller than some, and strong enough to hurl Chet Masters into unconsciousness with a single buffet.

To imagine himself in that dramatic role was deeply contenting; but the opportunity he longed for was denied him. No one proposed going back to work, and before the sun was an hour high, the crowd had thinned till only two or three idlers remained. John Powell and half a dozen of the day men prepared to close the mine, shuttering windows on the weight house and the office, and boarding up the portal. Owen wearied of watching them and turned toward home.

His father was busy in the garden, and Owen helped till dinner time. After dinner he walked past Mr. Beecham's, hoping the grass was tall enough to need mowing. It was not, but because there was today some new alertness in him and a quickened perception, he noticed a fact to which till now he had been blind. In front of Mr. Beecham's, the wide sidewalk of bricks laid in a herringbone pattern was uneven. Some of the bricks were thrust upward by the grass roots between them; and in some places grass formed a mat, covering the bricks themselves. In the street, the traffic of ore wagons and farm wagons and buggies had made a dusty beaten track down the middle, but weeds grew tall between that track and the sidewalk.

Going on toward town, Owen's opened eyes saw everywhere the same slack and slovenly neglect. A boy looking for odd jobs might find here an opportunity. When he reached the *Journal* office, BB was not there; but Owen found paper and pencil and labored for a while.

Then BB appeared, and he asked: "Waiting for me, Owen?"

"Yes sir, I wrote something about the strike." Owen handed BB a sheet of paper, and BB took it; but before he looked at it, he said soberly:

"We had an accident out at the house, kept me awhile. Bertie was playing horse, riding a broomstick up and down the kitchen, and he fell and hit his head on the spout of the oil can. It barely missed his eye, cut his forehead open so that Doctor Gorman had to take three stitches." BB mopped his brow. "The little fellow was badly scared, besides being hurt, with all the blood, and the needle. But we can be thankful it didn't hit his eye."

"He's all right, is he?"

"Oh, yes, all right now." BB looked at the paper in his hand. Owen had written:

> *The coal miners all over the United States stopped work today so people would use up coal already dug and make more work.*

BB read it, and looked up at Owen with quizzical eyes. "Have you been all over the United States today, Owen?"

"No sir."

"Been up the creek?"

"No sir."

"Been to all the mines around Hardiston?"

Owen guessed what was coming, and colored uncomfortably, shaking his head. "I know they stopped work at Erie," he said.

BB handed back the sheet of paper. "Always be sure of your facts before you put anything in the paper, Owen. Many things that are true should not be printed; but nothing should be printed that isn't true. Write this over and just say that at Erie the men came out, and that miners were called out everywhere."

Owen nodded. He hesitated, then handed BB the other sheet, and BB read it.

There is more grass and weeds between the bricks of Hardiston sidewalks, and on both sides of the streets outside the gutters, than in a good farmer's field. Something could be done about it.

BB looked up; he met Owen's eyes. "That's true," he agreed. "We'll print that. But suppose we change that last sentence to a question. 'Can't something be done about this?' Questions make people think."

"They don't have to think about this," Owen said stubbornly. "I could dig out the grass in your sidewalk, and take papa's scythe and keep the weeds down outside your gutters." He added: "If you want me to."

"That's a lot of work. Hard work too. I've tried it."

"I can do it. I've got a lot of time."

"How much would you charge?"

"I don't know what it'd be worth."

"Neither do I." BB nodded. "All right, you go ahead; clean the sidewalk and we'll see how long it takes you." He added: "And if you get any news from Headquarters about how the strike is going, let me know."

Owen hurried home to beg an old kitchen knife from his mother. He worked till dusk that night, trying at first to stoop to the task, or to kneel; but each posture soon wearied him beyond endurance, so he sat down on the pavement. The grass was tough; the knife was too limber, and it was dull. His knuckles, grinding against the edges of the bricks, soon were scraped raw. He made what seemed discouragingly little progress; but when it was almost too dark to see, Mr. and Mrs. Beecham came out to inspect the result, and BB was pleased and Mrs. Beecham was delighted.

Tuesday afternoon, when the task was well begun, David Ames, Mr. Beecham's next-door neighbor, stopped to speak to him. "Good job, young fellow," he said heartily. He looked along his own sidewalk, equally grass-grown. "How'd you like to do mine too?"

Owen hesitated, remembering his single experience with this big man. "Mr. Beecham's going to pay me," he said.

"Pay you?" Mr. Ames laughed. "Don't call that work, do you?" Owen looked at his barked knuckles and the blister on his finger. "All right, what's your price?"

"I'll finish Mr. Beecham's and then make you a price."

"Good. See you do." Mr. Ames moved away.

Mr. Beecham's sidewalk kept Owen hard at work for six full days and part of another. BB paid him five dollars. "It's worth more," he admitted. "But these are hard times for all of us. I couldn't really afford to have it done at all. Is five dollars enough?"

Owen was satisfied, and said so; but when he came two days later to cut Mr. Beecham's lawn, Mrs. Beecham declared that five dollars was by no means enough, and over his protests paid him a dollar more. He had already agreed to do Mr. Ames's sidewalk for five dollars, and told her so. "So you don't have to pay me any extra."

"Has he paid you?"

"No'm. I haven't done the work."

"Well, don't you do a lick till he pays you. And tell him I said so!"

He smiled at the indignant defiance in her tones, agreeing with her obvious dislike of Mr. Ames, and liking her; and he took her advice, and was neither surprised — nor disappointed — when Mr. Ames refused payment in advance. There were other pavements to be cleaned. His enterprise set a fashion, and more than one of the striking miners thus found part-time employment to help them through these straitened days. Others mowed lawns — Owen one day saw Chet Masters working on Mrs. Paxley's, while Mrs. Paxley watched him from the veranda — or did odd bits of carpentry, or any chores at all.

The work of weeding pavements had one aspect which Owen had not foreseen; it widened his acquaintance. Not many people passed him at his task without a word of greeting, and a surprising number of men had time to stop and watch and light a fresh stogie and ask questions. Now and then a man he did not recognize spoke to him, and proved to be some familiar acquaintance whom Owen had never seen except with a coal-masked countenance. Once, while he was clearing Mr. Moury's pavement, he saw Jane pass on the other side of Broad Street, and she waved her hand in a gesture of furtive greeting. Her own home was only a few doors beyond. Mr. Moury's home and his funeral parlors were near the schoolhouse, so during the three days he worked there, Owen saw most of those who had been in his room in school, and each day Miss Williams stopped for a word or two with him.

Before the end of April, he had bulletins from Headquarters

reporting the progress of the strike, and he wrote a paragraph for the *Journal*.

> *Over a hundred thousand miners have stopped work almost everywhere except mostly in West Virginia and Pennsylvania. Only twenty-five thousand miners are working in soft-coal mines anywhere.*

The bulletin had added: "Stand firm and it will not be long until there will not be coal enough left in the general market to boil a kettle, and a complete victory will be yours," but Owen did not quote that in the *Journal*. He had an uncomfortable feeling that it sounded like bragging, sounded as if Headquarters was whistling for courage; and he knew that among the men at Erie Mine and the other mines around Hardiston there were many grumblers, sullenly wishing they could go back to work again. It was not easy to stand firm when you had not enough to eat.

When he gave BB the paragraph he had written, the editor said: "We'll print that, Owen; but if coal does run short, the mines in West Virginia and Pennsylvania will start selling coal in Ohio, cutting into the market here. That will hurt the operators — and your strike is meant to help them."

"It's meant to put the price of coal up, so they can pay us more."

"But coal from West Virginia will keep the price down — and our operators here will lose their markets."

"We had to do something," Owen argued, forgetting his first misgivings.

"Probably very few miners had any money saved."

"They weren't earning enough to live on, much less save up."

"I don't suppose the Union has any money in the treasury, to help them out."

The suggestion that the Union should have money in hand with which to help men on strike was new to Owen. "No sir, I don't think so." Yet how admirable an arrangement that would be! He kept it in his thoughts.

A few days later, in a different form, the question of money again arose. A Headquarters bulletin announced that operators and union delegates would meet in Cleveland on May 15 to seek a settlement; the Sub-District was requested to send delegates to that meeting.

Owen took the bulletin to Isaac Williams. Isaac read it, and he asked: "Enough money in our treasury to pay a delegate's railroad fare to Cleveland, Owen?"

Owen shook his head. "Hardly anyone paid the tax, even when we were working. I've only collected three dollars and forty-five cents altogether, and I've paid that into the Sub-District treasury."

Mr. Williams read the bulletin again. "Cleveland, eh? Good many years since I've been in Cleveland. I used to live up that way. Did I ever tell you about the big strike in the Tuscarawas Valley, when I was working in the Warmington Mine, and we set fire to all the Rhodes Company mines. The time Major McKinley —"

"Yes sir, you told me."

"Oh, did I?" Mr. Williams sounded disappointed. "Well." He handed the bulletin to Owen. "I guess likely Tom Jones will call a meeting of the Sub-District to see if we can raise enough money. You'll get a notice tomorrow, I wouldn't wonder."

The notice came; the miners were called to meet Monday, May 7, in the Park in Hardiston, to select delegates and arrange for their expenses. Owen did not know how much it would cost a delegate to go to Cleveland; but he was eager to help raise the necessary money, and he remembered one of Mr. Beecham's axioms. "The way to win friends is to let people do you favors." If this were true, then men persuaded to contribute to the miners' expenses would hereafter be on their side. Friday, Owen cut Mr. Beecham's lawn — Bertie came proudly to show the red, Y-shaped scar, now well healed, close above his eye — and Saturday morning when the editor paid him a quarter, Owen took from his pocket a sheet of paper at the top of which he had writen: "Contributions to send delegates to Cleveland."

He set down his own name: "Owen Glen, .25." BB asked what he was doing, and Owen said: "We're going to take up a collection from storekeepers and people to pay for our delegates going to Cleveland. If I can get two bits apiece from enough people, it will do it."

"Good enough." BB handed Owen a coin. "Put my name down. Who thought of that, Owen?"

"I did. You said anybody that did the miners a favor would be on their side."

BB chuckled. "Well, don't tell on me!" He offered a suggestion. "Owen, try Moses Evans."

Owen was astonished. "He wouldn't, would he?"

"Try and see."

Owen took that advice. He had seen Mr. Evans in church every Sunday since the other's recovery, but there had been no occasion for them to talk together since a year or so ago, before he started to work in Erie Mine, when he sometimes took the monthly rent to Mr. Evans's office. The old man remembered Owen and spoke to him by name, and Owen told his errand.

Mr. Evans growled something inarticulate. "How much?"

"I gave a quarter. If enough people did, we'd have enough."

Mr. Evans reached laboriously into his pocket, produced a battered old leather purse, opened it, selected a quarter, inspected both sides of the coin and at last handed it to Owen. Owen put his name on the list, and thanked him and started for the door. But the old man called him back.

"Don't be in such a hurry. You and Tom went back to Erie?"

"Yes sir."

"Out on strike now?"

"Yes sir."

Mr. Evans snorted through his nose. "Hope it'll help the price of coal. Good idea, anyway. If West Virginia don't steal our market." He peered at Owen. "What'll you live on?"

"We'll get along."

Mr. Evans snorted in a way that sounded as though he had tried to say "Hump" through his nose. "Tell Tom six dollars is too much rent on that house you're in. Call it four dollars from now on."

Owen felt his neck warm with confused resentment. "You don't have to be sorry for us!"

"Sorry for you! Don't be a fool! You're young, strong, healthy! Ain't you?" Owen nodded, would have spoken; but Mr. Evans repeated, in sad amusement: "Sorry for you?" He shook his head. "No. But times are hard. If you moved out, I couldn't get over four dollars from anyone else. Don't want to lose a tenant. Business, that's all."

"Well — much obliged." Owen turned again; and behind him Mr. Evans said in a curious, hushed voice:

"But you can be sorry for me if you've a mind to."

Owen hesitated, but he did not pause, nor turn, because he did not know what to say. He made that morning a canvass of the stores along Main Street, showing each merchant a list with his own name, and BB's, and that of Mr. Evans at the top; and Monday morning, when he joined Mr. Williams on the way to the Park where the meeting would be held, he reported what he had done.

"I've collected six dollars and a quarter," he said. "I've got all the names. I could get more if we need it, but I didn't know how much we'd need."

Isaac Williams looked at him in approving surprise. "You think up some good ideas, Owen. Put my name on your list, too. Here's a quarter. And when they start talking about raising money at the meeting, you get up and tell them."

Owen followed this advice. When the delegates to go to Cleveland had been chosen, Eben Howell, who was presiding, said: "The next business is raising the money for their expenses. State Headquarters has no money in the treasury, and there's only five dollars and ten cents in the district treasury. These are your delegates. What is your pleasure?"

Owen — the meeting was in the open air, the men standing — called: "Mr. Chairman." And when he was recognized, he said: "Mr. Chairman, Hardiston storekeepers and businessmen have given six dollars and a" — he was about to say "a quarter" when he remembered Mr. Williams's contribution — "and a half for this purpose. I've got the money here, and the list of the ones who gave it." He added: "I expect others will give some, too, if we ask them. I'll give the list and the money to the secretary."

He moved forward; men made way for him, and more than one man clapped him on the shoulder and said an approving word as he went by. Eben Howell said: "Thank you, Glen. Men, I suggest a vote of thanks to the merchants who made this contribution. Do I hear a motion?"

The necessary money was raised, and as the meeting broke off, Owen joined his father and they started home together. Owen expected some word of praise, of proud approval; but after they had walked for a block or two in silence, Tom said thoughtfully:

"You know, Owen, you're getting so a lot of the men know you; but I wouldn't go showing off too much if I was you."

Owen was too astonished, for a moment, to feel the hurt. "Showing off!"

"A cute young one kind of tickles folks for a while; but they

don't like to see him getting too big for his britches." Owen wanted
to cry: he bit back tears, nodded, dared not try to speak, stumbled
at his father's side; and Tom said, like an apology: "I don't mean to
say you are doing it, Owen. But see to't you don't."

Owen looked up at his father, but Tom did not meet his eyes.
Seeing the gray in Tom's stubble beard, the lines at nose and
mouth, the sagging chin, Owen realized for the first time that his
father was an old man; not old in years, for Tom Glen was only
fifty-four, but Owen saw on him today a mark, indescribable but
unmistakable, which he had never seen before.

It was frightening to think of his father as old.

3

The meeting in Cleveland ended in futility. Mr. DeArmitt, of the
Cleveland Gas and Coal Company, whose name Owen heard for
the first time when on their return the delegates reported, had
persuaded many operators to ignore the meeting and to refuse to
discuss a settlement. The miners and a minority group of operators
fixed a new wage scale which would have meant fifty-six cents a
ton in Hardiston; but this rate would only go into effect if all
operators accepted it, and the DeArmitt group would not.

So the strike went on, and through the rest of May coal from
West Virginia and Pennsylvania poured into Ohio to meet the
rising demand. Even in Hardiston, Owen heard angry miners talk
of burning the railroad bridges to prevent that traffic. Then President Cleveland acted to protect the bridges, and in Ohio and
elsewhere the militia was called out to meet any violence which
might occur.

There was no violence, but the miners began here and there to
drift back to work. At the Jordan Mine, west of Hardiston, most
of the men returned to their jobs. Owen, eager to keep the strike
alive, went every day to Erie Mine where men were apt to gather,
and one day he proposed to them a parade to Jordan Mine. "We'll
see if we can't get them to come out again."

The sullen men at Erie welcomed that suggestion. "And if they
don't want to come out, we'll drag 'em out," Ed Thorne shouted;
but Owen said good-naturedly:

"No, no; but we'll have some fun, get somebody to beat a drum for us, have a regular parade." He remembered his mother saying long ago that soldiers marched in step to learn to fight together. A parade, a march, would draw these men closer to one another, would unite them. "We'll muster at the Court House, march out from town," he said. "Maybe we can get the Big Sixteen Band to lead us." In print, the "Sixteen" was always "6teen." "And we'll get men from the other mines to march with us."

The notion took hold. While they considered details, Evan Harned appeared, coming from his home not far away; and after some talk with him, they all tramped off together to see Isaac Williams, to ask his opinion and advice. Thus the project assumed an official character. Tomorow, they decided, should be the day. The men would spread the word, Owen and Evan Harned would get the band or at the least some drummers, they would muster at the Court House in the morning.

They gathered for that first parade two hundred miners, and a bass drum and two snare drums to lead them. The marchers were good-humored, smartly keeping step; and a train of small boys followed them down Broad Street. Adelina Fortune, when they passed her tumbledown house in its weed-grown yard, came out to wave her handkerchief as though she thought them soldiers marching off to war. The powder on her face was cracked, and flakes of it had fallen off. At the sound of the drums, she had not waited to bedeck herself; and for a moment Owen felt sorry for her, but probably she was happy enough in her strange mad world.

They marched down Broad Street three abreast, the drummers in front, then Isaac Williams with Owen on one side and Evan Harned on the other, then the trooping men. Molly Moury and Jane Lloyd from Jane's porch watched them pass, and Nellie waved to them from the gate in front of Mrs. Paxley's. Mrs. Beecham and Aunt Jane and Bertie were on the porch when they tramped up the Peach Street hill, and they went on down past Will Davis's and Evan's, with Mrs. Davis and the children and pretty little Lulu Harned waving them on. They climbed Patterson's Hill and so came down to Jordan Mine.

There was a wait, while the drums kept up their clattering challenge, till by twos and threes the men came out of the mine to face the crowd. Then Isaac Williams silenced the drums, and he turned to Owen.

"You talk to them, son," he said.

Owen was intoxicated with excitement, drunk with the rhythm of the drums. He stepped forward, called a laughing word.

"How do you like our parade, boys? This looked like a good day for a walk, and we wanted to have somewhere to go, so we marched out here. Some of us had gone back to work the same as you; but they didn't want to miss the parade, so they came along. You come along and march with us. We're all coal miners. Here's two hundred, maybe more; and there are four thousand of us in Hardiston County. Four thousand men that stick together can get a lot more done than four thousand men all by themselves. What do you say? You don't want to be the only ones working, a fine day like this, do you?"

One of the Jordan men said sullenly: "There's others working besides us; Morrill Mine, and Tom Jones Number 2, and Frisby."

"All right," Owen agreed. "We'll march around and get them too. It's a fine day for a walk!"

He saw a grin of assent here and there, and someone said: "We'll come if they do."

"They'll come if you do!" Owen countered, and he turned and shouted to the men at his back: "Here we go. Roll those drums!"

The Jordan men, grinning sheepishly, fell in. At each mine the result was the same; Owen's good humor infected them all, and more than four hundred miners eventually marched back into town. The following Monday morning the four hundred, led by the Big 6teen Band, marched to the Ohio Southern station to take the train for Belton, where a meeting of almost three thousand miners elected Morgan Jones to represent them when the National Executive Board met in Columbus the following Saturday.

At that meeting in Columbus, a wage scale which would pay Hardiston County miners sixty cents a ton was proposed and accepted, and the men went back to work; but Owen, without recognizing his own inconsistency, was disappointed. The rate when he went to work at Miss Ellen had been seventy cents; the Union had volunteered a temporary reduction to fifty cents. When the strike began, it was not called a strike but a suspension; its avowed purpose was, by curtailing production, to re-establish the conditions that had existed at the beginning of the year.

But a seventy-cent wage was one of those conditions; the fact that the operators had agreed to sixty cents convinced him that

persistence might have won back the seventy-cent scale, and to
accept half a loaf when they might have had the whole seemed to
him folly.

He said so to his father, but Tom Glen disagreed. It seemed to
Owen that he and his father now seldom agreed about anything; if
one of them expressed a firm opinion the other was almost sure to
differ. Thus now Tom Glen shook his head. "No, it's time we went
back to work. The rate don't matter. I'd rather work for sixty cents,
or even for fifty, than not have a job at all." He added: "I've heard
you say the same yourself."

This was true, and to feel in the wrong made Owen angry.
"Well, that was different," he protested, on the defensive.

"You didn't even want to have this strike," Tom reminded him,
and Owen colored resentfully.

"All right, maybe I didn't. But if I get into a fight, I want to
win it."

"Can't always win. I've found that out. Time was when I'd
strike at the drop of a hat; but I've outgrowed a lot of my cockiness
— and so will you."

Owen had small satisfaction from his father, or from Isaac
Williams. "Sixty cents is better than nothing," Isaac reminded him.
"I don't even know as the operators can pay sixty and make any
money."

"We could have got seventy."

"Not without a fight, and a hard one. I've done my share of
fighting in my time, but I don't know as it ever got me anything
that I couldn't have got full as well without."

Isaac and his father seemed to Owen equally mistaken, and Sunday
afternoon on his way to see Miss Williams, he saw Charles Morgan
taking his ease on the veranda and stopped for a few words. He
felt in this man a hint of greatness, some quality which made him
seem to tower above Tom Glen, and above Isaac Williams too; and
he spoke at once of the matter foremost in his mind, asking Mr.
Morgan's opinion.

"What's yours?" the other countered, and Owen recited his conversations with his father, and with Isaac Williams. As he spoke,
his resentment returned and his voice rose, till at last Mr. Morgan
said gently:

"Take it easy, Owen."

So Owen was silenced, and he waited, and Mr. Morgan knocked the ashes out of his pipe into his palm, and tossed them away. He did not look at Owen, his eyes resting on distances.

"Yes," he repeated. "Yes, Owen, take it easy." He spoke slowly. "Men around here have got in the habit of listening to you. You know how to talk to them; yes, and to lead them.

"But, Owen, in the long run, you'll have to manage to be right, pretty near all the time. The first time you want them to do something they don't want to do, they'll quit listening to you."

He puffed his pipe, he rocked slowly, he rubbed one ankle with the other heel. "You see, the sort of man people call a leader don't really lead at all. He finds out somehow, inside himself, what men really want to do inside themselves. Then he tells them they ought to do it, and they think he's wonderful — and yell, 'Hooray for Owen Glen.'"

Owen blushed with pleasure, and Mr. Morgan said: "Yes, son: but you take it easy. Don't get too far ahead of yourself. Don't get so far ahead of the men you want to come along with you that they can't see where you're going. You take it easy, and I wouldn't wonder but you'll be a real big man some day."

4

In the *Journal* the week after the strike ended, Owen read an editorial which BB had written in protest at a paragraph in the *Commercial Gazette*. The *Gazette* said ninety per cent of the miners were foreigners, not naturalized, and paying no taxes; and BB wrote that the *Gazette's* statements were shameful lies.

> There are four thousand miners in Hardiston County,
> and we know personally more than a thousand of them.
> Ninety per cent of them were either born in this country
> or are naturalized citizens; fully forty per cent pay taxes.
> No miner, working two or three days a week and paying
> out of his wages train fare and other incidentals, is rolling
> in wealth; and a miner who raises a family and educates
> them does well, even if he never saves enough to buy a

home; but we know many miners who have built or bought their own homes, and we know one who owns not only his own home but three other houses, all bought with what he has earned with his pick and shovel.

The Gazette also calls the miners law-breakers; but organized capital violates law as often and with greater impunity than organized labor. The miners' crimes are petty, the crimes of capital strike at the liberties of the people and at the roots of our national institutions. There is no comparison between the crime of a poor man who steals bread to feed his famished family and the crime of the millionaire who steals a railroad.

Owen cut out that clipping and saved it; but while it stirred him, it troubled him too. If, as Mr. Beecham said, there were miners who owned their homes, why did not his father? Certainly Tom Glen worked as hard as any man, except when rheumatism laid him low; certainly there was neither waste nor extravagance in their home. Yet they lived in what was not much more than a patchwork shack, while Isaac Williams, a miner like his father, had a comfortable house and good Sunday clothes and many things which Tom Glen had not.

Owen spoke to Mr. Williams at the mine next day: "Did you read the piece in the *Journal?*" The other — he was eating, his mouth full — nodded. "Did you earn enough digging coal to buy your house?"

Mr. Williams shook his head. "No. No, my father had a farm, and we raised all we needed. He and I were winter miners. We worked in the mines when farm work was slack, and saved most of our pay. Then after he died I sold the farm and came to Hardiston." He added: "A lot of farmers do that, work in the mines in winter, get up early and milk their cows and feed their pigs and get to the mine before daylight and get home in time to do the chores."

"Do you know any miner who owns a house he earned with his pick, the way Mr. Beecham said?"

"Why, yes." Mr. Williams named three or four, and he explained: "Good times, when there's plenty of work, a man can save money if he's careful; and if nobody in his family gets sick, and nothing happens, he can hold on to what he saves. But it needs a good man, and a good wife, and good children, and good sense, and good luck, too."

The answer troubled Owen. His mother sometimes scolded Tom Glen, calling him a talker, a trouble-maker; and talking and trouble-making had twice led to Tom's being black-listed, and each time this meant that he was for weeks out of work. If he had had savings, those weeks of idleness would have whittled them away. Then the moving from Ohio to Illinois, from Illinois to Indiana, from Indiana back to Adams Furnace, and finally to Hardiston; those removals would have cost a lot of money.

For an angry moment, Owen blamed his father for his mother's sake; she tried so hard to stretch every quarter to the utmost, to save even a penny at a time. It was upon her that the heavy burden fell; it was because she worked hard, and managed somehow to make ends meet, that Tom Glen could afford to — talk and be a trouble-maker. Yet if Tom Glen had been more patient, less arrogant and proud, how much better for her!

But then Owen remembered with a wistful sorrow that his father was now more inclined to submission, to be silent, and to work at any wage at all. Even through the few years of his own memories, Owen thought Tom Glen had grown older, weaker. He had a sudden understanding that a man's life spills away through the years; that force goes out of him; that defeat leaves scars which do not heal.

Was it because his father, valorous without a saving wisdom, had fought beyond his strength; say, rather, beyond his means? Suppose Tom Glen had first saved, accumulating a reserve, building up his own capacity for endurance. Owen arrived by slow degrees at an opinion which in time became a conclusion. Rich men, the Carnegie Company at Homestead, the Pullman Company up in Illinois whose men were striking now, the railroads who were fighting that strike; they all had money, so they could endure. But workers who had no money, they could not. To win a strike, the men must have saved enough money to live on till the strike was won.

Yet not all men saved money, even when they could. Someone should save it for them, should take it away from them when they were earning plenty and pay it back to them when they went on strike. Mr. Beecham said politics was power and power was wealth; but wealth, money, they too were power. If the Union had plenty of money to feed the men and their families, it could win strikes.

But there were difficulties in the way. The tax in the Erie local was five cents a month, and it should be more; but although the men were back at work, times were still hard, and the local would not vote to raise the tax; at least, not now. Owen was sure this should be done; but also he was sure now was not the time.

Well, he could wait till the right time came. Certainly, since money was power, the Union — in order to match its strength against the operators — must have money; that money must be collected, a little at a time, from the men, and saved. Union was not necessarily strength; the Union must be armed with thrift and wisdom before it could become strong.

5

Owen read in the *Journal* that Mr. and Mrs. Herbert Canter and Miss Canter had sailed for Europe. It occurred to him that none of the striking miners had gone to spend the summer in Europe; but Mr. Canter, in spite of all the talk about the sad plight of the operators, could afford to go. Mr. and Mrs. Moses Evans went to Mountain Lake Park for a vacation, and Mr. and Mrs. David Davis — he, too, was an operator — were spending a month in Wisconsin. But the miners were back in the mines. At the High School Commencement, eleven girls graduated and only one boy; those boys who had not, like Owen, quit school to go to work had dropped out for lack of interest, or because they could not learn their lessons, or because they had no clothes fit to wear to school. The railroads ran excursions south, on a tour that touched New Orleans in one direction, Richmond in the other. BB said in the *Journal* that it was free trade in coal that broke the strike; free trade was a democratic policy, but protection against West Virginia coal would have let the miners win. The Big 6teen Band gave a concert to raise money to buy new uniforms. A man was shot and killed in a saloon in Belton. If American citizenship had value, said BB, an immigrant should pay for it; $500 when he came into the country, $100 a year till he was naturalized. At Pullman in Chicago

the greatest strike in history ended in defeat for the Pullman employees and for the American Railway Union, whose head was a
man named E. V. Debs. Anti-labor newspapers called the strike
"The Debs Rebellion." President Cleveland had sent United States
troops to Chicago under pretense of protecting the mails; the
militia was called out, and courts issued injunctions intended to
defeat the strikers. There had been some rioting, and some property was destroyed — said BB — by the thug element. Five men had
been killed in the riots. The whole country urged Mr. Pullman to
arbitrate, but he said there was nothing to arbitrate. Mr. Debs
and other leaders of the strike were arrested and would doubtless
be sent to jail; so capital had won again. Three hundred and twenty
Welsh miners were killed in an explosion of fire damp near Pont-y-
Pridd. Twelve Hardiston men and women went on the excursion
to Niagara Falls. If you buy what you don't need, said BB, you
may some day need what you cannot buy. The law for labor
should be the law for capital. John Hayes, a miner in Belton
Number 2, lost an eye when a shot went off accidentally; and Peter
Teague was found in his room in Miss Ellen under seven or eight
hundred pounds of slate. He had been cutting out a shot he had
fired the day before. The roof was smooth and slippery, so he
probably received no warning. Miss Abbie Means, who for thirty-
two years had been a school teacher in Hardiston County, was in
the asylum at Athens for treatment; her friends hoped for her early
recovery. On July 19, the mercury touched 99°. Two boys had been
seen stealing food and cigars from grocery stores; they were known,
said BB, and if they did it again they would be pulled.

6

Owen was reasonably sure that one of these boys was Pete
Radford. On his way home to dinner the preceding Saturday, he
had noticed two boys lounging on the Flagg House corner, smoking
stogies, and as Owen drew near, one of them spoke. "H'lo, Owen."
Owen recognized Pete, but Pete was changed. He had grown
smaller. That night of Amy's wedding, he had been taller than
Owen, but now Owen overtopped him by a full two inches. Owen
remembered that he had vowed to give Pete a licking; but cer-

tainly he could not lay hands of violence upon this thin, pale weakling.

"H'lo, Pete." He hesitated, uncertain what to say. "I thought you were in Reform School."

"Oh, they reformed me and turned me loose." Pete produced another stogie, offered it to Owen. "Have a twofer?" Owen shook his head. "Plenty more where this came from," Pete urged, and when Owen still refused, Pete said cheerfully: "All right. It's your funeral." He put the stogie back in his pocket, and Owen said he guessed he had better be going — and went on his way.

But when he read that paragraph in the *Journal* about the boys stealing cigars, he knew well enough that Pete was one of them.

Miss Williams after school let out went home to spend the summer on her father's farm, and Owen missed their Sunday afternoons together. Union Furnace had blown out during the strike, and would not go into blast again until October, so through the summer Erie Mine ran only two or three days a week, and Owen had time on his hands. The hot spell in mid-July sent him, after each day's work was done, to the swimming hole in Erie Creek. One day, on his way home, freshly scrubbed, in clean garments, with his working clothes wrapped in a newspaper under his arm and full of a fine sense of physical well-being, he passed Nellie's house, and she called his name. He stopped at the gate, and she came running to speak to him. There was a fine excitement in her eyes and he thought she was prettier than he had ever seen her.

"What do you think?" she cried, and without waiting for an answer: "I'm going to work in the *Journal* office, Owen."

He felt a faint alarm. "Have you quit working for Mrs. Paxley?"

Nellie giggled. "She fired me. He was sort of joking with me in the kitchen one day, and she came in and slapped his face and told me to get out." She stepped up on the gate, swinging gently. "So I'm going to learn to set type. Edna's getting married; but she says she'll teach me before she quits, and then I'll take her place."

Owen's first alarm had passed; he decided that to have Nellie in the office every day would be pleasurably exciting. "Well, I guess you can learn," he said. "It's pretty easy."

She glanced at his wet hair. "Been swimming? I know where the swimming hole is. Jenkin Powell showed me." He colored at his own thoughts, and she laughed. "Oh, we didn't go in swimming!

You needn't look so shocked! But I did go once, by myself, in the morning. Nobody ever goes there in the morning." She threw back her head in a peal of laughter. "You ought to see your face!"

He blundered away; and as he walked homeward, he found himself imagining that he was alone at the swimming hole and that Nellie came along the path through the screening bushes. What would he do if she ever came there and caught him with no clothes on? He could keep himself under water; but suppose she just sat on the bank and laughed at him and teased him? Or suppose she took off her clothes and came into the water, chasing him, catching him?

He remembered that she was coming to work in the *Journal* office. He was nearly always there on Saturdays, and often on Wednesday too. To know that she would so often be there was at once exciting and alarming. He wondered why Mr. Beecham had hired her; and when on Saturday morning Will told Owen she had begun her apprenticeship, he asked the question.

"Why, he's giving her a try on my say-so," Will explained. "She's sort of a second cousin of my wife's." Owen remembered that Will and Mrs. Davis had come to Willie's funeral. "She tells me you and she are old friends. I know you used to play with Willie."

"Yes, I did."

"She'll use your case to learn on," Will explained. "But I can keep you busy downstairs." And he added: "I think Nellie will settle down. She's got a good mother, and Nellie's good to her. Tutson isn't much use to either of them since he killed Willie, but he used to be a steady, sober man."

Owen decided Nellie needed friendliness and a helping hand. It was as though Will had appealed to him on her behalf; and at noon that day, as a gesture to testify his good intentions, he waited till she came downstairs before starting home to dinner, and suggested they walk part way together.

7

One August morning — he had been swimming in the muddy creek once or twice a week all summer — Owen woke after a restless night with an uneasy headache. He wished he could stay in bed;

but there was work at the mine, and working days were too precious
to be lost. At breakfast, he had no appetite, but he forced himself
to clean his plate, because his mother always fussed and worried
if he did not do so. On the way to the mine, though nowadays he
was more apt to be a step or two ahead than behind, he found it
hard to keep up with his father; but Tom noticed nothing unusual.
He was indignant that morning because he had read in the *Journal*
that down in Gallipolis, where a reservoir was being built and
town waterworks constructed, the contractor was hiring tramps to
do the work, instead of giving the jobs to Gallipolis men who
needed them.

When Owen reached his room in the mine, to load into the cars
the coal he had shot down the day before took him a weary time;
and when his father called to him from the next room along the
entry to bring his lunch pail — they always ate together — he had
not yet finished setting new props up to the face. Later, Tom
Glen's shots sounded before Owen had finished drilling his holes;
and Tom came in and found him not yet done, and joked him for
his slowness.

Owen walked home on languid legs. Next day he worked again,
but he felt worse, his headache persisting; and again and again he
had to go out to relieve himself in the shallow drain that ran along
the side of the entry, and there was a nagging, barely perceptible
pain every time he did so. To walk home was a long weariness,
and to wash himself in the shed seemed hardly worth the trouble.
After supper, his mother, looking across the table at him, suddenly
exclaimed:

"What's the matter with you, Owen? You're red as a beet."

"Nothing, I guess."

"You feel all right?"

"M-hm."

She came to press her hand against his forehead, and she said in
quick alarm: "Tom Glen, this young one's burning up!" She made
Owen go at once to bed; but four or five times in the night he had
to get up and go out to the privy set on the bank of the little
trickling stream that ran along the foot of the slack pile below the
house. Each time, his mother woke, and each time when he
returned she called to him softly: "You all right, Owen?"

"Yes, mama. Just had to go to the privy."

The last time this happened, toward morning, she lighted the fire and brought him a glass of scalded milk. Usually he hated the taste of it, but this time it tasted good. He was glad to remember that the mine would not work today, so he need not get up, and he slept restlessly till full sun.

Before breakfast, his mother made him stick out his tongue. "It's kind of white, Tom," she reported to Owen's father. "All coated, except it's red down the middle. You suppose he's sick?"

Tom said reassuringly: "I guess the scalded milk will fix him up."

But scalded milk did not fix him up, and though Owen was up and dressed that day and the next, he had not enough energy to stir far, and was too drowsy and indifferent to care. Saturday he was too weak to move, and his mother said helplessly:

"Tom, you've got to go get the doctor."

Tom hesitated, for doctors' calls cost fifty cents and sometimes a dollar; but Owen looked sick, and acted sick. "I guess so," he agreed. He trudged away, and came back to report. "Doctor Gorman's out on a baby case, but Mrs. Gorman said he'd come this afternoon after office hours."

Owen knew Doctor Gorman. During one of the regular smallpox epidemics which came to Hardiston almost every spring and summer — usually, to be sure, the disease took a mild form — Owen and the others in Miss Dine's room in school went to the doctor's office to be vaccinated. Doctor Gorman was a gentle, joking, bearded man. He sat at a little table and the children filed past him. He scratched their arms with a small sharp knife and then patted the scratches with one of a dozen little celluloid paddles that stood in a glass of water beside him, putting each paddle back into the glass after he had used it. Owen's arm developed a satisfactory scab about an inch across, and he was left with a fine deep scar. On some of the children the vaccination did not take at all, but Tommy Morgan's arm swelled up as big as his leg and for weeks afterward he could not come to school.

Doctor Gorman came to see Owen about four o'clock that afternoon, and he took pulse and temperature and looked at Owen's tongue, and then beckoned Tom Glen outside the house to hear his report. Tom came back, his face drawn; and he said in a dull tone:

"Well, mama, he's got typhoid fever. Doctor Gorman says there's seventy-one cases in town, counting Owen here." He hesitated. "He says just you nursing him is all he needs, and scalded milk and milk toast and such slop, mostly, to eat."

"Is he awful sick?"

"Not yet. It takes time. He'll be worse next week, the doctor says, and the week after."

"Is he going to die?"

Owen's father said angrily: "How do I know? He is or he ain't." He added more gently: "Now, mama, we'll take care of him. And the doctor said he'd come by every day, whenever he can."

Owen heard them as though they were far away, unreal people in a world without reality. He had no feeling that they were talking about him. His head was aching; someone kept pounding his head from inside with a padded hammer, and under that steady, muffled pounding his senses blurred. It was pretty dark; night probably, and a thunderstorm coming, like the day when Ab Gwilyn met Morffyd, the wife of Bra Bach, in the woods. Owen could not see Morffyd plainly, but to look at her was like being by a warm fire, by a fine warm stove. She began to look like his mother, and she laid her hand on his brow, and he wished she would touch him all over his body with her cool warm hands. It was time to go to sleep, and he told Morffyd so, and she went away from him into darkness, and Amy and Miss Williams lay down on his bed with him between them and he slept between their warm bodies while they whispered across him to each other.

Sometimes everything was clear and customary. This was usually in the mornings, when his mother fed him; and she had to clean him as though he were a baby, and he was ashamed. I'm sorry, mama. I couldn't help it. I'm awful sorry. And she cradled his head in her arms and he smelled her, the smell of cooking, and of her, and of her tears; and he felt her body twitching against his, and his father was a black shadow in the doorway, and Tom was dead under a piece of black canvas on a board or something, and then everything was strange again till another morning when he knew he was talking a great deal, and remembered mama bidding him hush. Hush, Owen. Hush, sonny! Be quiet, now. Be quiet, darling boy. Be quiet. Please. Please. Please. Then for a while he knew all about everything, knew he was Owen Glen, and knew he was sick, and knew his mother was tending him; but those lucid hours did not last very long, and he was glad of that, because he was being sick when he ought to be collecting their tax from the men, and keeping the minutes of the meeting, and reading the minutes of the previous meeting, and loading his cars and shooting down coal and writing things to put in the *Journal* and making speeches and swimming and Nellie Tutson came into the muddy water with him with no clothes on and she was slippery when he tried to hold her and he kissed her and she was Jane Lloyd and Bobby Roberts saw them and said he would never be a leader among the miners if he was a nasty little boy telling lies said Mrs. Paxley and her legs showed and the sun struck in his eyes and his mother said he must drink the scalded milk and he knew who he was and knew he was sick and mama was so beautiful.

Again and again came these intervals of knowing and then of not knowing, and shame pursued him like his own shadow that dragged behind him on the ground, and syphilis and gleet and gonorrhea and Doctor France had burning eyes that wasted manhood and brought ruin and death and secret vice and Jane Lloyd's mother pointed her finger at him and whittled it like a knife saying nasty little boy and Jane was as sweet as his mother and far away and when he ran toward her he could never come to where she was but she was always fair and fine and beautiful and she was his mother giving him milk toast with jelly on it out of a spoon and the sun shone in his eyes and he was Owen Glen and he was sick and he hurt.

But sooner or later his mother was Morffyd again, fading away from him through the dark rumbling of the storm and he was Tawno Chikno and Jane Lloyd was at his feet embracing his feet washing his feet with her hair begging him to make her his wife — or anything else — and when he tried to pick her up she was Nellie Tutson and Jane was watching him from a great distance far away and Miss Williams held out her hand to lead him to where Jane was and two thousand miners circled around him while he shouted to them that they must march with the drums but they turned their backs and he was alone in a great circle of scornful backs crying aloud, desperately pleading, and his mother said Hush Owen it's all right Owen here's your breakfast and the sun shone in his eyes and it was her face and he knew who he was and knew her and he said carefully:

"I'm Owen Glen, and you're mama."

"Yes, Owen. Yes. Eat this now. Poor lamb, you're dripping. You're sweating like a little pig!"

And his father said: "He's all right, mama. He's passed the crisis. He'll get better now."

His mother bathed him, washing him clean with a warm wet cloth, and he was thirsty and she brought water and he drank deep and slept and did not dream. But after that he always knew who he was, and day by slow day he got well.

XII

September 1894 — *April* 1895

It was late August when Owen fell ill. While he lay lost in delirium, and while he came slowly back to health again, week by week the *Journal* wrote the history of Hardiston that might as truly have been the history of any one of ten thousand other little towns. The lawn social at the Catholic Church raised $24.10 for the Christmas tree fund. Mr. Robert Thomas returned on the *Majestic* from four months in Wales, and Corbett, the prizefighter, was his fellow passenger. A hackmen's war broke out when Tom Lovering and Dan Hardin, whose stables had shared the trade, faced the competition of Charley Buck, a newcomer with a mail contract; there were wrecked hacks and black eyes, and Marshal Henson haled all three men to court. Mrs. B. B. Beecham gave a Progressive Logomachy party to honor Miss Hession, her cousin from Mississippi. A squeeze near the east end of Slacktown Number 1 last week shut off most of the southern entry. At the G.A.R. reunion, the youngest veteran in attendance was forty-eight. The Young People's Society for Christian Endeavor of the Presbyterian Church appointed a committee to try to reduce the amount of loud profanity on Hardiston streets. Owen Glen, son of Thomas Glen, and well known to Hardiston County miners, was ill with typhoid. Tom Jenkins lost a foot when he fell while trying to board a moving freight train. The Niagara River, it was said, would run dry in 7000 years; and BB expected that before the river ran dry, the country would have recovered from the Cleveland Administration. Freeman Lewis, conductor on the Ohio Southern, leaned out of his train to flag the engineer, and a post beside the track hit his head and he was killed. A strange haze — some called it fog, some called it smoke —

blanketed Hardiston for five early September days. In one week two men, Dan Boggus and Irving Wight, at different places lay down on the railroad track to rest, and were run over by trains. The two deaths, said BB, are sad enough without saying a word about the cause. The wheat crop broke all records for the county; Bobby Roberts down in Adams Township raised four hundred and three bushels on ten acres, but other farmers did almost as well. Dan Laban raised some apples that ran 16 to a peck; 40 bushels to one tree. Evan Owens raised a beet that weighed 8 pounds, a cabbage that weighed 16, and several 3-pound tomatoes. Farmers should organize dog hunts to save their sheep. In mid-September, Coxey came to Hardiston and spoke to a crowd of four hundred; BB thought him an ignorant, ungrammatical and dangerous advocate of violence. All friends of Owen Glen would be glad to hear that he was on the road to recovery. Only three deaths had resulted from typhoid during the summer; the wild talk about an "epidemic" was started by the disappointed few who had voted for a town waterworks. In the electric light plant Hardiston already had one white elephant on its hands; why acquire another? The county was cindering the Piketon road; it would soon be one of the best in the whole region. The engineer of the down train on the B & O saw a young man — who turned out to be Peter Radford of Adams Furnace — walking on the track; he whistled, but Mr. Radford paid no attention and was killed. The modern beauty — her face glows with health, her countenance blooms with beauty — when she needs a laxative takes gentle and pleasing Syrup of Figs. Mr. and Mrs. Ed Frost and Mr. and Mrs. Thomas Bogart have gone to New York for a week of sightseeing and theater. Mr. and Mrs. Herbert Canter and Miss Canter have returned to Columbus after three months in Europe. The Methodist Conference in late September brought more than five hundred visitors to Hardiston; next to the Bible, the Methodist minister had done most for Western civilization.

2

September was almost gone before Owen's recovery was sure, but even then Doctor Gorman warned them convalescence would take

time. During the worst of his illness, Mrs. Lewis, who lived down
by the Ohio Southern yards and who was Mrs. Glen's closest friend
in Hardiston, at first came regularly to help as she could; but then
Mr. Lewis was killed — he was the conductor on the Ohio Southern
whose death the *Journal* reported — and thereafter Mrs. Lewis had
her own grief to endure. Owen's mother tended him every hour of
the day, spending her strength with a lavish love; and unconsciously
Owen protracted his convalescence. It was bliss to feel his mother's
sweet solicitudes, her steady attendance like a warm caress; and
he relaxed in an almost sensual content, glad to be helpless since
she was here to serve him. Sometimes, when she came to thump his
pillow and to smooth his sheet, he kept his eyes closed, pretending
sleep, pretending he was a baby again and dependent on her to
meet his smallest need.

Sometimes he tried, groping among confused memories, to recapture these days of his life which delirium had blanketed; and
one day he asked:

"Mama, was I pretty sick?"

"You were awful sick."

"Did you take care of me?"

"Every minute, sonny."

"I made a lot of trouble for you, didn't I? Like a baby, so you had
to wash me, clean up my messes."

"You'll always be my baby, Owen. I couldn't have stood it to
have you so sick if I hadn't had you to do for, just the way I did
when you were really a baby."

So that part of his memories was true. "I couldn't help it, mama."

"Of course you couldn't. I loved every minute, sonny, taking care
of you."

There was another trouble in his mind. "Did I talk an awful lot?"

"Now, Owen, you rest. Don't bother your head about it."

"Did I?"

"Most all the time."

"What about? What did I talk about?" She went away into the
kitchen without answering; and because she did not answer, he
was troubled, trying to remember, trying to guess. What did you
talk about when you were out of your head? What sort of things?
Did you talk sense when you were out of your senses? Did the
things you said make sense to those who heard them? Did you

dress naked thoughts in words for all to see? How much of himself had he betrayed? What did his mother know about him now that he had hoped she would never know?

His mother's voice came from the kitchen. "It was just talk, Owen. I didn't listen. I was too busy worrying about you."

Her evasion frightened him; the fact that she did not answer was more eloquent than any answer. He must have said things she would not let herself remember; and he cringed with shame and wept with sorrow for the hurt he had dealt her. Perhaps his father would chide him, scold him, scorn him; he dreaded being with his father alone. While he stayed in bed he was safe, because his mother was always there, a buffer between them; but when he went back to the mine and to work, he and his father would often be together. He dreaded that day as a day of reckoning, nursed his shamed terror, clung to this fox of fear that gnawed at him.

Tom Glen was working four days a week; the coal business, he told Owen, had begun to pick up with the approach of winter. "There's seven or eight folks in Hardiston that have vapor furnaces, or else hot-air heat, in their houses now; and they have to lay in their coal, and people are filling their coal sheds. Then there's talk that Union Furnace will start up soon. Time you're ready to work, there'll be work for you."

Owen thought it would be a long time before he would be ready for work. When first he got out of bed, he had to learn to walk all over again; his legs were wasted thin, and his arms, too, and his body — as his mother said — was a bundle of bones. But as soon as he began, holding to her arm, to take a step or two, strength rose in him like a flood tide. His bed-sores healed, his legs grew stronger every day, his starved body converted into healthy flesh every ounce of food he ate. He had grown taller during his weeks in bed; his pants were too short, and his sleeves, and his mother told him: "You'll be as big a man as my father before you're through. He was six foot three, and big all over."

During Owen's illness, Will Davis had stopped at the house every Wednesday evening on his way home from the office to ask after Owen and to leave a copy of the *Journal*; and sometimes he came on the way to town with a jar of preserves or a glass of jelly or some other delicacy offered by Mrs. Davis. As Owen's strength returned, Will brought him the news from the office. Edna Tutson was gone, and Nellie had taken her place; but when Owen asked who Edna married, Will did not know.

"She was going to get married in Columbus," he explained. "Some man she met when she was up there visiting Alice Dine. She didn't tell me his name."

"Is Nellie any good?"

"Well, her proofs are a sight. It'd be quicker to set her stuff all over than try to correct it, sometimes; but I guess she'll learn if she wants to." He added, after a moment: "Nellie's kind of boy crazy, same as Edna. I guess that comes from the Tutson side. Ever since he killed Willie, Tutson's been drunk half the time; and he sleeps down in the houses opposite the station more nights than he does at home. So Nellie's had some hills to climb; but I think she'll make it, if folks give her a hand up."

Owen's recovery acquired momentum, but when he spoke of returning to work, his mother said fondly: "You'll not go back till I say. I didn't take care of you like a baby for five weeks to have you go get sick again." She, too, began to be rested now, no longer haggard with fatigue and fear; and Tom Glen looked fine.

Marged came one day to see Owen and to tell him and his mother the news of Amy and Dave. She herself had spent a happy summer on the farm; her father had raised a fine lot of squashes, and some of them would weigh thirty or forty pounds. She promised to bring one to Owen's mother. "They'll keep all winter in a cool place, long as they don't freeze." She told Owen about that fine wheat on Bobby Roberts's farm. "I went to help cook for the men the day they threshed it." Owen had thought she would be married to Bobby by this time; he was pretty sure Bobby wanted to marry her, but he was glad they were not married, not yet, anyway.

She had brought *The Merchant of Venice*. "I'll let you keep it and read it," she said. "As long as you're not coming home every night with black hands."

But Doctor Gorman had advised Owen not to read for a while, and Owen explained this to her. "He says sometimes typhoid fever hurts your eyes, or makes you deaf, or makes your hair fall out."

She laughed. "It hasn't made your hair fall out! Yours is almost as long as mine." He knew that was a joke, because — although he had never seen her hair except in a great knot on the back of her head — he was pretty sure it was long enough to reach her waist, or maybe to her knees. He remembered the day he and Hetty Jenkins had spied on her, wading in the creek at Panter's Caves. He had seen her knees that day when he and Hetty peeped at her through the stems of the bushes from their hiding place between the rocks; and now he was ashamed of having peeped, and ashamed of remembering Miss Williams's white legs and her pretty round knees.

"It hasn't made me deaf, either," he agreed. "But when I try to read, my eyes water."

"I'll read aloud to you awhile," she suggested, and she did so, sitting with him there in the kitchen, his mother busy near them. Owen liked to watch Miss Williams as she read, the way her lips moved, the way the sun through the window beside her touched her hair. He thought it made a sort of halo around her head.

BB stopped in one Thursday morning on his way to the country; and he told Owen some of the things that had happened while he was sick, and some of the things that were going to happen. He asked whether Owen had heard the manner of Pete's death. "I suppose he had been drinking." Owen thought that not unlikely. As always, when an election was approaching, BB talked politics; and it seemed to Owen there was always some sort of election approaching. In the even years, every fourth year brought the contest for President, and every second year Congressmen had to be elected; then in the odd years there were state elections every second year, and it was a dull spring when there were neither county nor city officials to be chosen. Then there were conventions before every election, so for three or four months each year, the *Journal* was full of politics; the announcements of the candidates, editorials, sketches, the accounts of meetings.

BB put almost everything that happened in the country to the credit of the Republicans or to the discredit of the Democrats. Of politics in all its activities and implications he never tired. He told Owen now that the Republicans next month would certainly gain control of Congress, or at least of the House. "The Democratic hard times have turned every laboring man against the party. You coal miners, for instance. Under the Democratic wage scale, a man who can mine two and a half tons a day loses fifty cents every day he works. If he mines four tons, he loses eighty cents. The farmer loses eight cents on every pound of wool. Blame the Democrats!"

BB said construction had not yet started on the electric railway, and this delay, too, was the fault of the Democrats and the hard times they had caused. The program for the Y lectures was out; Robert Morse would lecture on *Dr. Jekyll and Mr. Hyde*, Miss Laura Dainty would give a reading of the sort for which she was famous, Colonel Bain was returning by popular request to give his lecture on *Boys and Girls, Nice and Naughty*, and the Ariel Quartette would be the fourth entertainment. "If you want tickets," BB promised, "I'll save some for you." He stayed an hour in cheerful talk, and Owen listened, thinking Mr. Beecham knew how to say things so you did not forget them. "If you want a job, vote Republican." "Republican victory in November will be a foretaste of '96." "The man who develops himself develops his town." "Every self-respecting new resident is an asset to Hardiston." Probably to say things in the right way helped make people believe you and made them remember what you said, just as everyone remembered things from the Bible and from the plays Shakespeare wrote; things like "The quality of mercy is not strained; it droppeth as the gentle dew from Heaven," or "Long withering out a young man's revenue." Miss Williams had read that passage to Owen the other day, and: "With feigning voice, verses of feigning love." She repeated that line, saying: "See how beautiful that is, Owen? It's called 'alliteration,' repeating all those 'f's' and 'v's.' And see how scornful and angry 'feigning' sounds, instead of 'pretending' or 'imitating' or 'making believe.' You can just fairly snarl 'feigning'!" She snarled it so amusingly that they laughed together.

"Feigning voice" and "feigning love," and "withering out a young man's revenue"; he remembered these and he remembered other lines and phrases. Phrases were like words, you could use them as you used words. If, as Mr. Beecham said, to use a word three times was to make it your own, then to use a phrase even once might make it your own. He imagined himself making a speech and saying "with feigning voice, verses of feigning love." It was hard to think of any reason for saying a thing like that to miners. Certainly you would not talk to them about love; but then Owen decided you could say "feigning," about operators, operators like Mr. Canter, who feigned to be so friendly. Owen practiced snarling out the word, whispering it to himself, till his mother demanded:

"Owen, whatever are you mumbling about?"

He laughed. "I'm feigning I'm making a speech."

"Fainting?" Quick alarm in her eyes.

"No, mama! Feigning. It means pretending." He would have to remember that it was a mistake to use even such fine words as this one if your hearers did not know what you meant.

3

On a warm October day, Owen carried his chair out-of-doors to sit tipped back against the sunny end of the house; and presently a farm wagon came down the road from Ridge Street and stopped at the head of the path, and Owen recognized Bobby Roberts and called a greeting, rising to go to meet the other.

"Just came by to see how you were getting along," Bobby explained; but Owen thought there was some awkward embarrassment in his tone. "I was in town, anyway."

"Sit down and stay awhile," Owen urged, and Bobby left his team standing and came toward the house. Mrs. Glen was scrubbing the kitchen floor, and she warned them not to come in; but she crossed to the door, wiping her hands on her apron, to shake hands with Bobby and to ask for news of Amy and the children and Dave.

Owen, without stepping on the wet floor, reached in to get a chair for Bobby. They sat in the sun and Owen wondered more and more why Bobby had come. Bobby asked strange questions. "How old are you?" "Are you back at work yet? "You going to stick to coal-mining?"

Owen answered him, but he was puzzled, feeling older than Bobby and more composed. He, too, asked questions, about Bobby's farm, and about that famous wheat crop. "Miss Williams told me she helped cook dinner for the threshing crew," he said.

"She thinks you're pretty smart," Bobby volunteered. "She talks a lot about you."

"We read aloud together. She's awful nice."

"She says you work in the *Journal* office."

Owen had a sudden feeling that Bobby was seeking the solution to some mystery. "Why, yes," he assented. "Yes, Wednesdays and Saturdays when the mine don't run."

Bobby blurted another question. "Got a girl?"

"Good Gollies, no!" Owen was astonished into a straightforward question. "What are you getting at?"

"Nothing." Bobby moved uneasily, and he rose. "Well, I've got a long ways to go. I guess you heard about Pete Radford getting killed."

"Mr. Beecham told me."

" 'Member when you licked him, night of Amy's wedding?" Owen nodded, and Bobby said: "He was always bad from the start. His father too. They both took after bad girls." He rubbed his hand across his mouth. "You be a good boy, Owen."

That seemed an astonishing thing for Bobby to say, and Owen stared at him in complete surprise. Bobby went to the kitchen door to bid goodbye to Mrs. Glen and then came back to Owen and they walked up to the wagon together, not speaking till their hands touched in farewell. Bobby said then: "Don't ever get the idea it's smart to — be bad. You're all right, Owen. Stay that way."

"Goodbye, Bobby. Come again." Owen could think of nothing else to say. Bobby turned his horses and drove away, not looking back. Owen went slowly down the path, thinking back over this half-hour, trying to guess what had been in Bobby's mind.

4

Toward the end of October, Owen returned to work in the mine; and when he and his father left the house in the darkness of early morning and started up toward Ridge Street, it was almost the first time they had been alone together since Owen fell ill. Owen had forgotten his fear that his father might have heard some of his delirious ravings, might know they were the fruit of secret shameful dreams; but as soon as he and Tom Glen were alone, this fear returned to him. Tom was silent, and for Owen silence was worse than speech; he said at last:

"Papa, my being sick was pretty bad, the doctor's bills and everything, and not much money coming in."

Tom said passively: "Ah, yes, Owen. We were owing money before, with the strike so long; and now we owe more. But I've been in debt before and paid it off, and everyone knows I will again."

"I'll be earning, too, now."

"Take it slow for a while. Don't get sick again." And as though a mood of talk crept over him, Tom went on: "Only time in my life I ever did have much of anything saved up was before mama and me went to Illinois. That was twenty-five years ago. We'd married in 1863, when I had a furlough and came home. But then I went back to the army, and Tom was born while I was at the war, and Evan in 1866. When I came home to stay, I worked cutting wood for charcoal, and we lived with my folks, so we saved money.

"It took the most of what we'd saved to pay our way to Illinois, but I got work there and we saved a little more; but the other babies came, and died, all except Amy, and doctors and funerals cost money; and then I got black-listed, and time I saw I couldn't get another job, what we'd saved was gone. So I borrowed to move to Indiana. I paid that back, but I had to borrow again to move to Ohio. We save for a while, and then it goes and we run into debt, and then we save and pay off again." He added with a grim mirth in his tones: "It costs money to be poor, Owen. When we had a pig every year, and the cow, and mama's chickens, we got along good; but when times got bad, the cow up and died, and there hasn't been a time we could buy another, and you can't raise a pig without milk. When you was sick we bought milk for you from Evan Jenkins, down the road, and I've chored around some for him, times the mine didn't work, to help pay for it. I'm still owing some, but we'll get along." He added: "Long as I keep my health."

The thought that his father might fall sick chilled Owen. "The Union ought to have money saved up to help miners when they're sick."

"The Noble Order used to," Tom agreed. "And there's some of the Sub-Districts try to have a sick fund now. They make a special tax of two bits a month to keep it up to six or seven hundred dollars, and pay a man something after he's been sick four weeks, and pay him twenty-five dollars if his wife or one of his children dies, and pay his wife fifty dollars if he dies. But the hard times put an end to the most of that."

Owen nodded. He knew how few men, even before the strike last spring, had paid the five-cents-a-month tax; certainly none of them could or would pay five times as much. To build up a sick benefit fund of five or six hundred dollars was for the present completely impossible; but some day, when work was plenty and wages higher, that was a goal at which to aim. Yes, and beyond that rose a higher goal. Until the Union had enough money to protect its members during a strike, cold and hunger would always fight for the operators.

The men at the mine were glad to see him back. Owen at first would help his father, until he was strong enough to work alone; but that first day, he thought he would never have strength enough to be of real use. The second day was worse, for then he was not only weak but stiff and sore; but the third day seemed easier, and the work, requiring at first not only all his strength but all his resolution, grew easier for him day by day. On his fifteenth birthday he began with pick and drill and powder to open a neck leading off the entry, to make a room of his own.

Coal came into seasonal demand, and at Erie the full force of better than a hundred men was put to work again, and six days a week became the rule; so Owen had no time for the *Journal* office. He was soon as strong as ever, and when his eyes ceased to trouble him, he read aloud to his father from the *Journal,* and he read the Bible to his father and mother every night before they all knelt while Tom Glen prayed. On Sunday afternoons he went more and more often to Isaac Williams's home, where he and Miss Williams read Shakespeare together. His retentive memory treasured many passages; and sometimes at her suggestion and under her direction he recited the long speeches, trying to imagine in each case what the character in the play was thinking, trying to use the tone which the character would use; and sometimes he faltered and stumbled, and sometimes he caught the swing and pulse of the eloquent lines and was swept by them into such heat and strength that when he finished, he and Marged looked at each other like children who have rubbed a magic lamp and seen a genie emerge.

To read in Shakespeare was to feel yourself always on the threshold of greatness, to be dazzled by beauty only half-comprehended. Unreality became reality; he and Marged yielded together to the steady beat of fine unbroken rhythms.

But to read to his father and mother from the *Journal* was to come back to reality again. In Washington Court House a mob tried to seize a base criminal — BB did not define his crime beyond these words — and the militia fired a volley that killed five men and wounded men and women and even children. Owen wondered what that base crime was, his imagination offering many answers; but it did not occur to him that the daily papers must have printed the truth, and except when Owen went to the *Journal* office he saw no dailies. There were tragedies enough reported in the *Journal*; a hunter shot himself; a young man in Belton came to blows with his father and bit his father's hand, and the father lost first his arm and then his life from blood poisoning; a Slacktown miner fell a hundred and fourteen feet down the mine shaft to his death; Warren Towne was caught by falling slate while drawing pillars, and attempts were made to free him, but before this could be done another fall crushed him lifeless; a premature shot killed John Temple; Thomas Orne, weigher at Flather Number 3, fell off the tipple and was killed.

Owen while he worked never forgot that death waited in the shadows of his low-roofed room; he never forgot the mass of the hill into whose heart the mine probed, hanging in precarious suspension above him. Lying on his side or crawling or stooping low while he earned his daily bread he was not afraid, but neither was he indifferent to the danger which haunted his days; he could imagine dreadful injury and death, and fear them and yet not flinch! Only the stupid are immune to fear; the brave are those who are most afraid and yet remain by fear unbound.

In December, rheumatism came to cripple Tom Glen, and Owen's mother tended Tom and dosed him with Radam's Microbe Killer, guaranteed to cure rheumatism as well as cancer, consumption, kidney and bladder disease and varicose veins. She ironed Tom's back, and put mustard plasters on his spine, and rubbed with burning hot ointment his knotty joints; and Tom groaned and sweated. Except for Christmas Eve at the church — the children received a treat, but Owen was no longer a child — Christmas was just a day when there was no work in the mine and so no money to be earned. When the mine ran, Owen worked at top speed; and by mid-January, when as work began to slacken Tom struggled back to the mine again, their last debts, even to Doctor Gorman's bill, were paid.

5

While there was steady work in the mine, Owen had no chance
to resume his occasional days in the *Journal* office; but he read the
paper every week. BB predicted that the Republican victory in
November — the Republicans captured the lower House — would
bring better times. The Epworth League musicale a week before
Christmas was the great society event of the year. The Teachers'
Institute, for five days after Christmas, was highly successful. A
masquerade party at the home of Mr. and Mrs. Enoch Roberts was
enjoyed by all. There was an opening in Hardiston, said BB for
someone who could give instruction in the art of playing the Jews'
Harp. Forty-seven Hardiston people went to Columbus to attend
the Eisteddfod there. The B & O water tank at Sycamore Hill
caught fire and was destroyed, even though it was full of water;
and BB was jocosely uncertain whether to say it burned up or
burned down. Contracts were let for grading the right of way for
the new electric railway from Belton to Hardiston. Four Hardiston
men severally advertised their willingness to make loans on good
security. In Hardiston and Gallia Counties, the Welsh Bible
Society had raised $41,000 to send Bibles to heathen in distant
lands; but last May when the miners were out of work, Owen had
seen two little boys stealing a pan of food put out for a pet dog.
Veno, the Wonder Worker, lectured at the Rink every night for a
week, selling his medicines. Despite BB's optimistic prediction,
Erie Mine, by the end of January, was reduced to working only
four days a week. The big operators were cutting prices; they
were selling coal at eighty-five cents a ton wholesale, at a dollar-
ninety retail. This would drive the small operator out of business.
Hardiston miners, having had a few weeks of full time, were better
off than miners up the creek; one man in Belton had worked only
five days in November, five in December, and one day in the first
two weeks of January. R. G. Evans, the photographer, took a
remarkable series of photographs of men at work in Erie Mine,
using flashlight powders, a great new invention.

When work began to slack off, Owen turned to the *Journal* office.
BB and Will agreed that there was a place for him on Saturdays,

and on Wednesdays if he were free. Nellie Tutson, now completely at home in the office, welcomed him. "I haven't seen you since you got sick, not to speak to. My, you've grown, haven't you?"

"I don't know as I have." Owen grinned. "Looks to me you've shrunk." She was mighty pretty, even with a smudge on her forehead. "How you getting on?"

She had slipped down off her stool to greet him. "Pretty good, I guess. But half the time I can't read Mr. Beecham's writing." Bets Tilden climbed the outside stairs and came in. "So I make a lot of mistakes," said Nellie, and smiled confidently. "But now you can help me."

Bets said: "Hello, Owen. Welcome home." She shook his hand. "Nellie needs all the help she can get. Half the time I do her work and mine too." She put her arm around the other girl. "But I don't mind, she's so cute."

Nellie wriggled free. "Take your hands off. I hate you pawing me all the time."

"It's just because I like you, honey." Bets pointed to the composing stick in Nellie's hand. "There, baby, you've got that capital S upside down."

Owen saw Nellie's dislike of the other girl, and spoke of it to Will. "Let them fight it out," Will advised. "Bets and Edna finally got along." He added in an awkward tone: "Might help if you kept away from Nellie. She can't keep her mind on her work with a boy around."

Owen tried to follow that advice, but although he could avoid going up to the type loft, he could not keep his thoughts from turning that way; nor could he prevent Nellie's coming to him for help in deciphering BB's copy, or to ask him to explain the cabalistic signs which BB used in correcting her proofs. She had a flattering way of pressing close to him, of looking up at him with admiring eyes, of saying: "I don't see how you do it!" or "I don't see how you can tell!" or "I don't see how you can remember so many things!" His thoughts were full of her.

Returning to the office after dinner on a February Saturday, he and BB chanced to meet at the corner of Broad and Pearl, and so walked the rest of the way together. Outside Hanson's Cafe, Nellie stood in laughing talk with Louie Peters. Louie was smoking a stogie. Owen had disliked Louie Peters since the days when they were in school together; but at sight of him now he had a sudden and astonishing surge of real wrath. He remembered that incident a few days later when, reading the *Journal* aloud to his father, he came upon an editorial paragraph.

Girls should imitate boys in being careful of the company they keep. A girl will walk with tough boys who spit and smoke cigarettes and swear; but if a girl gets tough, not a boy in town will be seen speaking to her.

He wondered whether BB would say Nellie was "tough," and advise him to avoid her. His thoughts stayed with Nellie while he read on. The Flagg House would run a free hack to and from all trains. Foraker was the best candidate for Senator. Every boy should sign the pledge and keep it. V. K. Emmitt's operatic minstrels would be at the Rink two weeks from now. The new income tax would catch all the editors, for Editor James of the Belton *Sentry* had been named collector; but an income tax was better than the tax on homes. The thieves who had been stealing Charlie Patterson's turkeys were hereby warned that a set-gun had been put in place to protect the birds.

When his father presently began to nod, Mrs. Glen brought the Bible, and Owen read a chapter, and they knelt while Tom Glen prayed, and the day was done.

6

Through February, not only were there fewer working days, but at the same time in Owen's room the vein thinned to a scant two feet, which curtailed his production. Seeking to make up for this, Owen spurred himself to utmost pitch, and he finished each day in a stupor of fatigue. On one such day, while at full stretch he pushed a loaded car out into the entry, straining and with every muscle taut, he felt a sharp blow in the small of his back on the left side.

He thought a falling rock had hit him, and he went down on his knees, gasping with sudden pain. He supposed the hurt would slacken and disappear, and it was presently better; but next morning he had to drive himself to get out of bed, and must fight to conceal his torment from his mother's eyes. The day after, the pain was worse. That day, too, he observed another symptom which so alarmed him that — without telling his father and mother what he intended — he went to see Doctor Gorman. He was a badly frightened boy.

At the doctor's he had to wait, since there were others before him. Doctor Gorman's door presently opened and Lloyd Martin came out, the doctor with him. Lloyd was a brakeman on the miners' train; his hand now was freshly bandaged. Doctor Gorman called another patient, and Owen asked Lloyd:

"What happened to your hand?"

"Caught it, making a coupling. But I was lucky. It just mashed two fingers. Doc trimmed 'em off last week, and they're getting well all right." He asked in turn: "What's the matter with you?"

Owen hesitated, then evaded. "I had typhoid fever, and I have to come to see the doctor every so often."

When it was Owen's turn, Doctor Gorman said cheerfully: "Well, Owen, you've put on some weight since I saw you. Sit down. Now what's the trouble?"

"Why, I've got a kind of a lame back, doctor." Owen reached around to touch the spot.

"Dropped a stitch?"

"I guess so. I was pushing a car of coal. I think a chunk of slate fell and hit me." He hesitated, coloring. "And — a couple of days later — when I went to the privy, it was like there was a little blood in it."

Doctor Gorman nodded in a reassuring way. "Working pretty hard, are you?"

"Sort of. Papa's rheumatism bothers him some, so I've been getting out all the coal I could."

"See if you can use the chamber," Doctor Gorman suggested. "There behind the screen." Owen went to obey, and the doctor looked at the result. "That's all right," he said. "Take off your coat and roll up your shirt." His wise fingers pressed lightly here and there. "All right, fix your clothes." And when Owen had done so: "Sit down. How many tons of coal can you mine in a day, Owen?"

"Well, we're in a thin vein, makes it hard. Two tons, anyway. Twice I've got three."

"Thin vein keeps you bent double most of the time?"

"Yes sir, or lying down. They've shot up the floor. That helps some."

The doctor placed his fingertips together. "How old are you, sixteen? Seventeen?"

"Fifteen."

"Fifteen, eh? You're pretty young for such hard work, haven't got your growth yet. I think you ought to take a rest."

"I can't. We're on short time, anyway, and papa can't do much. I have to work."

"This isn't serious, not yet, but if you don't give yourself a chance to get over it, you may be a sick man all your life."

Owen shook his head, his lips set hard. "I have to work."

Doctor Gorman for a moment did not speak; he seemed to sigh. "I know." He half-smiled, not mirthfully. "The curse of Cain. The sweat of our brow. None of us can ever rest as much as we should. But, Owen, you must rest as much as you can." He opened his bag, took out in turn two or three small vials, and poured from each, upon a sheet of white paper, varying quantities of whitish powder. He mixed these powders thoroughly and then began to fill capsules, opening each one, pressing the ends down into the powder like a woman using a biscuit cutter till each half of the capsule was full, then fitting the ends together. Owen watched, fascinated by the precision of his movements; and Doctor Gorman talked while he worked.

"It's too bad boys your age have to do hard physical labor, Owen; lifting heavy weights, straining, swinging a heavy pick. Your stomach muscles aren't toughened up to it. Most of the ruptures I see among workingmen come from working too hard when they were young. You'll get over this if you're careful, but don't strain at anything, take it easy." He put a dozen capsules into a cardboard box. "Here. Take one every night before you go to bed, and if you don't feel better by the time they're gone, come see me again."

Owen put the box in his pocket, and Doctor Gorman turned toward the door, but Owen did not move. "Doctor," he said uncertainly. The doctor paused, and Owen groped for words. "I didn't — I thought maybe — well, is it anything about my privates, doctor?"

Doctor Gorman rubbed his bearded chin, hearing fear in Owen's tones. "Do you — go with girls, Owen?"

"No sir."

"Good." The doctor hesitated. "I expect you worry about yourself. All boys do. But you're perfectly healthy, son; don't worry. And don't work too hard." He opened the door.

Owen said: "I'll have to bring you the money when I get paid. How much is it?"

"Fifty cents. Don't hurry. Any time will do."

Owen nodded. "Don't tell papa and mama. I don't want to worry them." The doctor nodded, he beckoned to the next patient, and Owen went out into the street.

That was a Friday. Owen went next day, as always on Saturdays when the mine did not run, to help Will Davis in the *Journal* office. He reached the office early, since it was his duty to light the fires and sweep out. Will Davis was usually there by seven, but today he did not appear; and when BB reached the office at quarter of eight he came to find Owen.

"Will's laid up, Owen," he said. "He was taken sick Thursday, a bad cold. He came to work yesterday morning, but I sent him home. Now Doctor Roy thinks he has pneumonia."

Owen's first thought was sympathy and sorrow; but his second was for BB and the *Journal*. The inside was always printed on Saturday. "I can get out the inside, Mr. Beecham." He remembered the heavy forms. "Only for putting the forms on the press. I've got a lame back, can't lift much."

"I could borrow Joe Tinker from the *Star*," BB reflected. "But I hate to be under obligation to them." The *Star* was not only a rival, it was a Democratic paper, and its editor anathema. "But maybe we can manage. I can lift the forms for you, if you can make them up."

Owen, in rising excitement, said: "Yes sir, I can."

BB nodded. "We'll see how we get along."

All that day, big with his new importance, Owen worked in a fine exhilaration; but an accident in the morning — he spilled a double stickful of type when he tried to lift too much into the forms at once — warned him to move slowly, to take utmost pains. To reset the pied type used up an hour of precious time; he must not

make the same mistake again. He remembered to fire up the engine
in the shed behind the pressroom well before it was needed, and by
half-past five the forms were locked and ready. That was two hours
or more behind the usual time; but time did not matter if the job
were done. He reported to BB, and the editor came and put on
Will's apron to protect his clothes and carried the forms to the
press.

Nellie and Bets had finished their day's work and gone before
the press began to turn. BB brought in sandwiches for Owen, each
a fine slice of breaded veal, smeared with catsup and gripped in a
thick bun, and Owen by careful timing could snatch a bite between
revolutions of the press. The work went without mishap or any
interruption; the sheets slid smoothly down into the guides, the clips
led them around the cylinder, the lifter with its long wooden
fingers deposited them flat upon the slowly growing pile.

When at last the task was ended, Owen threw off the belt and
went to draw the fire; he came back and carried the printed sheets,
an armful at a time, into the file room. Then he washed up, preparing to go home; but he was wondering what would happen next
Wednesday when the outside must be printed, what would happen
to the job work which filled Will's days, who would set the ads?
So he was not surprised when in the office BB stopped him, bade
him sit down.

"Owen," he said, "how much do you earn at the mine?"

"About a dollar and a quarter a day, sometimes a dollar and a
half." Owen added honestly: "But this week I couldn't get out as
much coal, with my back hurting. And we only worked three
days."

"Do you think you could take on Will's job here, till he's better?
Would you lose your job in the mine?"

"No sir. I mean, yes. I mean, Mr. Powell would take me back."
Owen's voice trembled.

"I could pay you a dollar a day." BB added apologetically: "I
want to pay Will's wages while he's sick, or I could pay you more."

A dollar a day would be six dollars a week, and this relatively
easy work would give him a rest from the hard toil in the mine.
Doctor Gorman said he needed a rest, and with his back the way
it was, he could never earn six dollars in the mine in a week, any-

way. "Yes sir," he said, no hesitation in his answer.

BB nodded. "Good. We'll see how you get along."

7

Next day Owen, for the first time in his life, wished it were not a sin to work on Sunday; there was job printing in the office waiting to be done, and he itched to be at it. He would have forgotten his usual Sunday afternoon with Miss Williams but for the fact that Saturday's mail brought him the bulletin about the United Mine Workers' Convention in Columbus, and he took that down to Isaac Williams; and of course he told Marged and her uncle his news. Marged was as pleased as he. "It's the first step," she said happily. "I knew you wouldn't always be a miner!"

He was surprised. "Yes, I will. This is just for now."

"But you want to be something better if you can, don't you?"

He colored, half-angry, half-proud. "There isn't anything better. It takes good men to dig coal."

She spoke gently. "You'll always be a miner at heart, Owen. But — well, if you want to help them, you'll have to be more than just a miner. You have to be something else, too." And she said: "Right now, you can do something for them, writing a piece for the *Journal* about the convention. You couldn't do that if you weren't more than just a miner. Do you know any miner who could do it, besides yourself?" And she said: "Write it this afternoon. If I can help you, I will."

"I guess I'd better," he agreed. "But I'll write it myself. It's the only way I'll learn."

"Then do it here and let me read it," she urged, and produced paper and pencil. He worked on the dining room table, Marged leaving him there alone; and at the end of an hour he had produced a long paragraph.

MINERS MEET

The Sixth Annual Convention of the United Mine Workers of America met in Columbus February 12. Ex-President John McBride, president of the American Fed-

*eration of Labor, appeared to answer charges that he gave
Mike Wild $600 to settle the strike of the American Rail-
way Union and to answer A. A. Adams's saying there was
bribery in ending the strike last spring. The convention
acquitted him. The convention instructed President Penna
to try to get the operators to meet the miners this spring.*

Marged thought this too short, thought he should write all about
the convention, thought the Union needed to tell people about
itself; but Owen said the paragraph was long enough. "Not much of
anything happened," he pointed out. "That about Mr. McBride
just says he didn't do what they claimed he did, and the rest is just
something they're going to try to do. They haven't done it yet. If
nothing happened, writing a lot about it doesn't make it amount
to anything."

She laughed delightedly. "Owen, I don't think you know how
sensible you really are."

He flushed with pleasure. "The thing is," he said soberly, "there's
no use stirring up excitement now. The Union can't do anything
but lie low, with times the way they are. They haven't got more
than ten or fifteen thousand members that pay their tax, and about
seven thousand of them are in Ohio, and they can't do anything
just here in Ohio, with Illinois and Indiana and West Virginia and
Pennsylvania not having hardly any members at all. We've got to
wait till we've got more members, and some money in the treasury."

"I see." She watched him happily.

"Brag and blow's no good unless we can back it up. So now's
the time to sing low."

"You're right, of course. I can see it now."

BB approved the paragraph Owen had written. "It's good
because it's short," he said. "It's better to print a lot of short items
worth printing than a lot of drivel no one wants to read. You'll be
able to pick up items from people who come into the office when
I'm not here, too. Always get their names right. People like to see
their names in the paper. Lots of people never do, you know.
Their names never get into print except when they die." And he
said, in Welsh and then translating: "'Os myni glod, bydd farw.'
If you would have fame, die."

So during Will's illness — it would be weeks before he came back to work again — Owen not only handled the mechanical work in the pressroom but occasionally wrote matter for the *Journal*. BB gave him three tickets for *Uncle Tom's Cabin*, and Owen's father and mother went with him to that performance. Owen — copying carefully from the program — wrote next day a paragraph to go among the items of local news. It was the longest of his numerous contributions to the *Journal* during the period of Will's absence.

> *Uncle Tom's Cabin at the Rink last Friday was a success. The Apotheosis; the Ascent of Eva to the Realms of Bliss borne by Angels; the Pearly Gates and Stairway to the House Beyond the Skies; the Ohio River in Mid-Winter by Moonlight; A Southern Paradise at Sunset; Birth of Liberty; Blessing Little Children; The Weird Rocky Pass; and The Cotton Plantation made the most magnificent display of scenic art and mechanical effects ever witnessed. School children were admitted for 15 cents. It was a fine performance but the lights went off at eleven thirty so they had to leave out most of the last act.*

His days in the office were full. He had not only to set up and run off orders for job printing, but to set the ads, to make up the paper, to feed the press; and in addition it was his duty, if BB were not in the office, to meet any callers. There were occasional farmers come to market who stopped to pay their subscriptions and to tell the news of their neighborhoods. Dave Ames dropped in almost every day to sprawl in one of the chairs and smoke an evil-smelling stogie and talk loud talk. One day Nathan Frye, the strapping big farmer with the frail wife and the spinster daughters, whom Owen had met on one of his walks with BB, was there when Mr. Ames came in, chuckling, to tell them the joke on Arthur Paxley. The drummer, in the Post Office that morning, reached into his pocket for a knife to pare his nails and opened the knife and exclaimed, loud enough so that three or four men heard him:

"Say, this isn't my knife. No, and by God, these ain't my pants either!"

Owen thought that incident mysterious, but it did not seem to him funny; yet Nathan Frye and Mr. Ames laughed robustly; and Nathan Frye said:

"Me, I'm always careful where I put my pants."

"Paxley just got home last night." Ames guffawed again. "Says he's sure he had his own pants on when he came home."

Clearly there was in the episode an implication plain to both these men, but not to Owen. He left them laughing together and went back to his work.

There were other more or less regular callers. Mr. Moury, the undertaker, came to whisper with decorous sadness of death and of interment. John Morgan, the drayman, delivering once a week a heavy little box full of plate matter, could report who came and went on every train. Moses Evans often came in to read the dailies, and so did old Charles Williams, principal owner of Union Furnace, who shared Mr. Evans's distaste for buying anything he could borrow. They might sit side by side, each reading one paper and jealously clutching another lest it be twitched away before he was ready to read it. Sometimes Ed Williams came in with his father, and BB liked to provoke them to argument. Charles Williams believed Hardiston iron ore was near exhaustion, that the end of the great days was in sight; but his son had somewhere acquired the notion that small quantities of silvery iron would always be in demand, and that as long as Union Furnace knew how to make such iron, even if it became necessary to import coal and coke and ore from other fields, its future was secure. When Charles denied this, Ed had a standard retort, "I'll give you twenty cents on the dollar for your furnace stock right now." That, Charles always retorted, was nonsense, and Ed was a young fool still wet behind the ears.

At the end of the first week, BB paid Owen seven dollars and a half, instead of the agreed six dollars; and Owen began to feel himself and the *Journal* were one. The Banquet to honor Congressman Bundy, at which both Governor McKinley and former Governor Foraker appeared, seemed to him — though he did not attend — an event great enough to warrant the seven-column account which Mr. Beecham wrote. When BB in an editorial paragraph said, "Congress has adjourned, so the country is safe for a while," Owen felt a fine Republican rage at the Administration; and he agreed with BB's comment: "This Congress has been the cause of more suffering and shame than any other in the nation's history." Once, when BB was not in the office, Superintendent Marbury of

the Infirmary came in to pay his subscription, and Owen after a
few minutes' talk with him wrote:

> *Superintendent Marbury informs us that 122 tramps*
> *have lodged in the Infirmary this winter. The Superin-*
> *tendent has dyed his whiskers.*

When BB read the proof of this, he laughed till he was red in
the face, and called Owen into the office, pointing to the paragraph.
"That's not only a *non sequitur,* Owen," he said. "But it's an
error of tact."

"What's a — whatever that word was?"

"*Non sequitur?* Why, the way you've written this suggests that
Ned Marbury dyed his whiskers because he entertained so many
tramps. '*Non sequitur*' means, 'it doesn't follow.'"

"Oh. What's tact?"

"The art of telling the truth without hurting anyone's feelings."
BB began to laugh again. "But Ned Marbury likes a joke, even on
himself. I'm going to print this."

Owen lived in a steady pride and happiness, and with little hard
physical labor to do, he was presently free from even a lingering
pain. His father was working whenever the mine ran; and with
what Owen earned added to Tom Glen's wages, they were saving
money; the future was bright, the present was contenting.

One day in late March, Owen saw Moses Evans come into the
office and drop wearily into a chair. Since BB was out, Owen went
to ask what Mr. Evans wanted. The old man shook his head.
"Nothing. I just dropped in. Where's BB?"

"Gone to the barbershop. He ought to be back." Mr. Evans
made no move to rise, and Owen, since it was a part of his job to
pick up what news he could, asked:

"Any sign of coal business getting better, Mr. Evans?"

The operator grunted. "We're losing money on every ton we
mine," he said miserably. "We couldn't make money, at the price
coal brings now, even if we only paid forty cents a ton for mining
it."

Owen, to his own surprise, found himself feeling an honest sympathy for Mr. Evans, whom he had once hated; but then came a
cold wind of fear. Forty cents a ton for mining coal, especially

when a man could only work two days a week, was destitution. His work here in the *Journal* office paid well; but for the first time he realized that it was temporary, that pretty soon now Will would come back to work, and then he himself must go into the mine again.

"I hope the rate won't come down any lower than it is," he said.

"I hope so too," Mr. Evans agreed, and then BB came in and Owen left them; but he did not tell his father what Mr. Evans had said. As long as he could take home seven dollars and a half every Saturday, to supplement Tom's earnings, they were all right.

But three days later BB told Owen that Will Davis was up and around, and on the first of April Will returned to work again.

XIII

April 1895 — *June* 1895

D<small>URING</small> W<small>ILL'S</small> <small>ILLNESS</small>, Owen had begun to feel himself a permanency in the office. The physical habit of spending each day there had become so nearly automatic that it was hard to break. But except on Wednesdays and Saturdays there was not enough work to claim two men's time — he thought of himself now as a man — and it never occurred to him to wish to capture Will's job and make it his own.

Nevertheless, the abrupt loss of that fine seven dollars and a half a week was a hard blow; he felt physically hurt, as though he had been kicked in the stomach. He knew, too, that it must be equally hard for his mother, since in her hands rested the task of wise spending, and the infinitely more difficult task of managing without spending, when to do so was necessary. But when he spoke to her of this, he found her not only hopeful but confident. During these weeks of relative prosperity, she had bought from Evan Jenkins down the road a fresh cow and a suckling pig. The cow would provide milk for them and for the pig, which they would butcher in the fall. She had bought, too, two broody hens, and eggs for them to brood. These purchases, which were rather investments than expenditures, would, when coupled with the produce of their summer's garden, go far to feed them until late fall and would contribute to their fare through early winter.

"So we're all right, Owen," she told him reassuringly. "We'll get along fine."

Owen found John Powell, the mine boss at Erie, ready to give him work again; and the men, even though it meant less work for them, seemed to welcome his return. Owen thought there was in

321

this welcome a noble generosity. He had heard his father and other
men talk of mines where when there was little to be done the mine
boss, by assigning a few individuals to full time on the job, condemned the less-favored to poverty and hunger. Certainly, here at
Erie fifty men working six days a week could produce as much
coal as a hundred men working three days; but no one begrudged
his fellows a share in the work and in the pay that could be earned.

The mine seldom ran more than three days a week, and often
only two. On working days, Owen and his father could each
earn close to a dollar and a half a day; when the mine was idle,
Owen sought odd jobs. But odd jobs were hard to find. Not many
people in Hardiston escaped the pinch. Hard times, beginning
slowly, gripped them tight and tighter. Men mowed their own
lawns or they let the grass grow tall and run to weeds. Not since
he quit school had Owen spent so much time prowling the town, as
alert for a chore that needed doing as a hungry fox for possible prey.
Peach Street and Broad and Pearl, lined with homes of the modestly
well-to-do, were his favored hunting ground. More than once he
saw Chet Masters mowing Mrs. Paxley's lawn; and once or twice he
saw Jane, either on her own front porch, or home-coming, or de-
parting, but he rather avoided than contrived these meetings. If
on his way to town or on his way home he saw her ahead, he slowed
his gait in order not to overtake her and force upon her his
company.

To leave school and go to work had been to move from one world
to another. These worlds were separated, not by any social gulf,
but by something less tangible. Thus Owen and Morgan Williams,
though they still saw each other two or three times a week, were
no longer equals; Morgan was still a schoolboy, Owen was a man.

Yet the fact that Owen was working was not alone responsible for
this. Such boys as Louie Peters and Dan Evans and Jim Tower
quit school and went to work, not because they wanted to work,
but because they could not keep up in school. Owen, on the other
hand, had been, if not the best student in Miss Williams's class and
again under Miss Means, at least one of the two or three best. To
fail in your studies and go to work was to descend; to excel in your
studies and still leave school and go to work was to climb. Morgan
was a year older than Owen, and Bill Myers and Tom Powell were

two years older; yet having quit school and gone to work, Owen was as mature as they.

The second Sunday after Will returned to work, Owen walked home from church with Miss Williams, and she led him to talk of his experience in the office. "I didn't have any trouble making up the paper and running it off and all," he told her. "But sometimes I had to figure out what a piece of job work would cost, and that got me all mixed up. And writing pieces for the paper was hard, too."

"You've probably gone rusty on your arithmetic," she suggested. "Any tool gets rusty if you don't use it. Why not let me get you straightened out? We might do some work on grammar too."

"I guess I ought to study something," he admitted, and he said reflectively: "You know, I've noticed a funny thing. I use better grammar when I'm talking to you." She smiled with quick pleasure, and he added: "To you and Mr. Beecham. I never noticed it till I noticed that when I'm talking to Will, or to somebody who comes into the office, or even to mama and papa, I sound different. I think I imitate the people I'm talking to." He grinned. "When I listen to myself talking to you, I sound as if I were making a speech!" She laughed in ready understanding, and he confessed: "But when I try to write something for the paper, I get all stiffened up. At least, my head does, as if my brains were all thumbs!"

"Maybe you're a natural orator, who knows?" Something in her tone or in her eyes made him for a moment forget that she was a grown woman, he still a boy. "Come down after supper any night. I'm never busy."

He said teasingly: "Except when Bobby Roberts is up from the farm."

"I haven't seen Bobby for quite a while." She was suddenly pink. "But he's never here weekdays, anyway."

Thereafter, once or twice a week till school let out, they spent an evening together and she guided his work. In other ways, too, this was for him a time of growth and ripening. The number of people he knew and who knew him steadily increased. During his term of service in the *Journal* office, he had come to emulate Mr. Beecham's friendly interest in every person he encountered. On their walks together Owen had often heard the editor lead a taciturn farmer into conversation, asking many questions while each

answer led to another inquiry. BB might ask about weather, or
about crops past and prospective, or about sheep-killing dogs, or
Indian relics, or birds and beasts and flowers, or about family
affairs or ancestry or kinfolk. In default of other topics he often
spoke of Morgan's Raid; for every farmer who had lived near
Hardiston during the War, now thirty years in the past, remembered
the raid and liked to talk about it. Owen had seen Mr. Beecham
listen over and over again to the same anecdotes, always with what
appeared to be an interest as keen as though he were hearing the
story for the first time.

Once he spoke of this, and BB nodded. "I listen because I may
at any time hear something new, but also because it pleases everyone to have an audience, and I like to please people." And he said:
"Most men and women, especially men and women on the farms,
are lonely; they're glad to find someone to talk to. You ask a man
questions and then listen to his answers and he'll remember you
pleasantly." He added, with a smile: "Every woman knows that
from the day she's born. There's no better flattery than a show of
interest — and everyone enjoys flattery."

Owen remembered, and sometimes, talking with a stranger who
had come into the *Journal* office, or with someone on the street,
listening to his own voice, he thought it might have been Mr.
Beecham speaking.

                                    2

Early in April, a bulletin from headquarters in Columbus sent
Owen to see Isaac Williams. President Penna of the United Mine
Workers had met a few operators from Illinois, Indiana and Ohio
to discuss with them the possibility of calling a joint convention
which would settle upon a wage scale for the coming year; but
operators from the Pittsburgh District refused to agree any such
convention as long as the Ohio wage scale remained nine cents
lower than that in the Pittsburgh District. When Mr. Williams had
read the bulletin, Owen asked:

"What does he want us to do?"

"Nothing, far as I can see. He just says he's met some of the
operators to talk things over, but their talk didn't get anywhere.

They'll never get anywhere as long as the rest of us take wages nine cents under Pittsburgh."

Owen asked thoughtfully: "Why do the operators here pay less than the Pittsburgh District?"

"Always have, late years, anyway."

"But there must be a reason." Owen spoke in faint impatience.

Mr. Williams said vaguely: "Well, they pay different rates in different places, depending on how thick the vein is, and whether it's summer or winter, and all that; but in the long run a miner makes about the same in a day, wherever he works. Where the rate's high, it takes longer to dig a ton, that's all."

"Well, it didn't just start up of itself," Owen argued. "Someone must have started it! Who started it? When did he start it? How did he get men to agree to it?"

"Don't see what difference it makes. But I don't know."

Owen nodded. "I suppose somebody does know. I'll find out. Mr. Williams, if the Union did win a higher wage scale, would all the miners get it, or just union men?"

"Why, the operators pay all their men the same rate, whether they're in the Union or not."

"That's not fair. I mean, if the Union does all the work to get a raise and then the men that didn't do anything get the benefit?"

"It's always been so in my time."

Owen felt a stir of anger at that empty repetition. "How would it be if the operators agreed they wouldn't hire anyone but union men?"

"No operator'd agree to that. If he can get men cheaper, he'll always do it."

"Don't let him!" Owen spoke hotly, provoked by the stubborn lethargy of this old man.

"Times like these, with three or four men for every job, a man can't get up on his high horse about things — Union or no Union."

Owen nodded reluctantly. "I can see how it wouldn't work unless most of the men were in the Union." Mr. Williams puffed on his pipe, not commenting, and Owen went on: "But Gollies, if you could make that the rule, that the operators couldn't hire anyone but a union man, wouldn't that make all the men come into the Union? And then let the operators take the tax out of everybody's pay, the way they do now for what the miner owes the store for powder and oil and all, and hand it over to the Union?"

The older man chuckled. "You're quite a hand to ask questions, Owen. Some day you'll find someone to give you the answers. But it won't be me."

Owen rose, putting the circular from Headquarters back in his pocket. "Then you think I don't need to write anything to them in Columbus."

"Mr. Penna didn't ask anything. No sense in doing anything till you're asked."

Owen walked homeward in a frowning dissatisfaction, in something like sadness. He had at first seen Isaac Williams through Tom Glen's eyes, as one who was great and wise and strong; but if to searching questions as to why, Mr. Williams could only answer, "It's always been that way," then perhaps the old man was less than he had appeared.

Surely no man could understand the present unless he knew the sources from which the present had sprung. Today was the child of yesterday. This nine-cent differential existed; for that existence there must be a reason, and that reason must be more than chance. Perhaps if you knew why the differential existed, you would discover that it should be changed.

He thought of going to Charles Morgan. Surely Mr. Morgan would know the truth. But suppose Mr. Morgan did not know? Owen put off inquiry. For today, one shattered idol was enough. Before this, Owen had begun to suspect that his father was not the giant he had once seemed to be; now Isaac Williams too was unsteady on his pedestal. There was no one to suggest to Owen that his father and Isaac Williams were as they had always been, that it was he who had changed.

3

A fire which began in Basker's livery stable spread to the Merchant's Hotel and burned through the wall of the *Journal* pressroom, but BB and the *Journal* continued to record the current history of the town. John Talcott shot a wild goose in his corn field and the bird weighed nine pounds. R. G. Evans, the photographer, patented a

flashlight machine consisting of eighteen alcohol lamps mounted in
a frame so that the pull of a trigger threw a spray of flash powder on
the flames, producing a brightness as light as day. Taxes are all
paid by the poor; the rich shift their taxes to the poor man's
shoulders. If you have no job, go to work on a farm; town life is a
curse to the idle. The Knights of Pythias organized an excursion
to Boston, and sixty-eight Hardiston men made the trip. Slate
killed Aaron Rich in Hancock Mine, and William Shannon was
killed in Slacktown Number 2 when a shot fired in an adjoining
room blew through the pillar and shattered his skull. The first two
weeks of April saw a record number of marriage licenses issued;
the future of the race depends on marriages for love. The roses
picked by the rich are watered by the tears and fertilized with the
blood of the poor. The Fire Department horses will hereafter be
used to haul the sprinkler wagons as well as the garbage cart. Chief
Black of the Fire Department has asked the City Council to raise his
pay from fifteen dollars a month to twenty-five dollars, and will
resign if this is not done. His pay should be raised, even if it is
necessary to reduce the Mayor's salary to do it. The waterworks, if
built, will hurt the Fire Department; let us wait till the light plant
is a success before trying a new venture. The B & O will run an
excursion train to Chillicothe for the Sells Floto circus.

4

On a Thursday in mid-April, Owen walked into the country with
BB to seek out the early wild flowers and to take note of the many
migrant birds which were here one day and gone the next; and
during the morning he asked BB the question Isaac Williams had
not been able to answer. "Mr. Beecham, why do coal operators here
pay nine cents less than in the Pittsburgh District?"

BB hesitated. "Well, that's a long story, Owen. I can give you
the general picture." And he sought to make the matter plain. "It
works through the Hocking District. Back ten or eleven years ago,
Hocking Valley wages were accepted as the Ohio standard. Operators and miners agreed in that. That was in 1883. Of course,
that was before the United Mine Workers was organized. There

was no Sub-District such as you have now, taking in Clinton County. Hardiston County was all in the Belton District."

"What was the scale then? How much a ton?"

"Seventy cents, I think. Then in 1886, the Belton District miners asked for five cents more than the Hocking figure. That went to arbitration before Judge Alonzo Taft of Cincinnati, and he decided there was no reason for any differential. Since then the wages in the Belton District have been pinned to the Hocking figure."

"I can see some sense to that," Owen admitted. "We're right next door. But why should the pay be nine cents less here than in Pittsburgh?"

"The Hocking District has an agreement with the Pittsburgh thin-vein mines, setting that differential. The theory is that the differential allows coal from the two districts to compete on an even basis in the Chicago market. They say our coal costs more to produce but that with the miners and day men paid less, the price of coal can be held down to a figure which will let it compete."

Owen made a harsh sound. "Do you understand all that?"

BB hesitated. "Well, the differential has lasted long enough so I suppose there must be some sense to it." They were approaching a farmhouse. "I've talked myself dry. Let's stop here and get a drink of water."

It was into Nathan Frye's yard they turned, and when they approached the pump, Mrs. Frye and her two spinster daughters came out in a high excitement. Mrs. Frye was almost toothless, a small withered old woman whose garments were much too big for her, as though she had once been plump and now was shrunken. While she teetered from one foot to the other, the daughters in a sort of antiphony poured out their story. A woman had come to the farm from Hardiston that morning. "In a hired rig from Lovering's," said one daughter. "Driving it herself," added the other. "And drove into the yard and got out — " "And came right into the house — " "Not knocking or anything — " "And a baby over her arm — " "And laid the baby down on the bed — " "Papa and mama's bed — " "And she said, 'There!' and walked out — "

They had protested, they had followed her to the buggy, they had pushed the baby into her arms; but she let her arms hang limp, she would not take it. They argued and threatened and pleaded — Owen could imagine the two sisters, both talking at once — but the woman whipped up the horse and drove away, leaving the baby in their care.

Owen, listening to their chorus, observed that Mrs. Frye said nothing; she stood teetering from one foot to the other, looking at her daughters as each spoke in turn. BB asked whether they knew the woman; they did not. She had told them she came to Hardiston on the down train, but she made no other explanation.

Owen and BB had their drink of water and went on, and Owen asked: "Why do you suppose she did it?"

"Sometimes babies aren't wanted. Their mothers — get rid of them."

"I mean, why would she bring it here and just leave it with them?"

"Well, you know Nathan Frye," BB reminded him. Owen nodded, and BB went on: "I suppose he's fifty, maybe more; but he doesn't look it. He's the youngest-looking member of the family. A lusty-looking man."

He paused, as though he had explained the mystery, but Owen protested: "What's that got to do with it?"

BB met his eyes. "If this woman with the baby came on the down train, she might be from Chillicothe," he suggested. "I know Nate Frye went to the Chillicothe Fair last summer. I expect he had a good time."

Owen, swinging along beside the editor — he was almost as tall as BB's five feet, ten inches — frowned in a puzzled way. "You mean maybe he knew this woman in Chillicothe?"

"Knew her?" BB smiled in an amused relief. "Yes. Remember in the Bible, Owen, every once in a while a man knew his wife and she bore a child?"

Owen had often wondered about that Bible way of saying things. "A man always knows his wife, doesn't he?"

"The Bible means he knew her as a rooster knows a hen, or a stallion a mare, or a bull a cow." Owen felt his cheeks burn, and BB said explicitly, "This woman may have blamed Mr. Frye because she had a baby." Owen was all one scorching flame of embarrassment; he looked sidewise at Mr. Beecham, and BB was red in the face, and for a while neither of them spoke. Then BB said carefully: "You see, when men go with tough women — or boys with tough girls, that way — there's apt to be a baby. Or if not, they may get sick. I expect you've heard boys talk about gonorrhea."

"It was in Doctor France's advertisements, and I looked it up in the dictionary."

"I see. Yes." BB after a moment added: "So — going with tough girls is not only bad, immoral; it's unhealthy, too. Some of those sicknesses, men never get over them. If, afterward, they marry, their wives may catch the disease; and their children may suffer too. The sins of the fathers, remember? In the old Mosaic Laws, a lot of the things Moses told the Jews were sins were unhealthy too; they were sins because they were unhealthy. To keep yourself clean and healthy is a most important part of what we call being good."

Owen asked no further questions, but he remembered, with a sense of escape, some of his thoughts; thoughts about Nellie, when he imagined her surprising him at the swimming hole; thoughts about the day Mrs. Paxley wanted him to stay; thoughts about Hetty Jenkins when they hid together at the picnic and she kissed him. His memories were frightening. He had walked unwarned through dreadful perils; but now he would know these hazards and avoid them.

BB always brought lunch on their tramps together, usually in a compact package; but this morning he carried under his arm a large pasteboard box of the sort in which tailors pack suits, and while they ate — they made their nooning in that hidden gulch which they had visited once before, where now the ground was all carpeted with violets — he explained this. "Mrs. Beecham has the two young ones in Athens, visiting relatives there, and I want to send her some flowers." So after they had lunched, he and Owen packed the suitbox full, with one row of white violets pressed in among the purple blooms, and wet moss around their stems to keep them fresh.

Returning to town, they again passed the Frye house, and there was a buggy at the gate which Owen recognized as Doctor Gorman's, and half a dozen men and women stood in a group in the front yard. They told BB that Mrs. Frye had shot herself, with Mr. Frye's revolver; but she was not dead, and Doctor Gorman was working on her now.

"Is Frye here?" BB asked.

"He went out in the barn, by himself."

BB turned that way, but when Owen came by his side, the editor said: "You'd better stay here, Owen. He may not want to talk to anyone."

So Owen waited, and once or twice he heard from the house a wailing cry of dreadful woe. He thought that must be one of the daughters. After a while Doctor Gorman came out of the house, and the neighbors waiting by the gate crowded around him, and Owen joined them. Doctor Gorman said Mrs. Frye might get well. "She's lost a lot of blood, but the bullet didn't touch her lungs or any vital organ; just broke two or three ribs and came out her side."

BB crossed from the barn to speak to the doctor, and Doctor Gorman went toward the barn while BB turned to the watchers. "The kindest thing you can do is to go on home," he suggested. "Mr. Frye and the girls can take care of her." They moved away, and BB told Owen, "We'll go along too." And as they walked back toward town he said soberly, "When I got out to the barn, Frye was trying to get up courage to hang himself; but I think he's all right now." And he said in a reflective tone: "Strange how often we're cruel to those we love. When Frye came home, Mrs. Frye accused him of being the father of that baby. He denied it, and she called him a liar — so he admitted it in cruel words, and stamped out of their room; and he heard the shot before he reached the bottom of the stairs."

Owen shivered. "I bet he's sorry."

"Of course. But I wouldn't wonder if they were happier, from now on, than they've been for years."

"Are you going to put anything in the paper about it?"

"No. No. Why should I? Everyone in the county will know all about it before next week's *Journal*." They walked a few rods in silence, and BB said, with a half-humorous note in his voice: "Sometimes I wish I could bring out a paper full of pleasant things. 'Mr. and Mrs. So-and-So find themselves more in love with each other every year.' 'Mr. and Mrs. So-and-So are going to have a baby next summer and they're as happy as a couple of spring lambs.' 'Mrs. So-and-So is mighty proud of her husband, and he thinks she's the finest woman in the world.' 'Mr. So-and-So went out of his way to do a kindness yesterday.' 'Mr. So-and-So, who used to be the town drunk, has not tasted liquor for thirteen years and is now one of our leading citizens.'" Mr. Beecham sounded as though he were being funny, but Owen did not feel at all like laughing. "I could fill the *Journal* every week with things like that, Owen; true things. Most people work hard and live happily and are proud of their children and kind to their neighbors — but that's not news. News is something out of the ordinary. When the *Journal* prints a paragraph about someone being hurt, or killed — it's because that's unusual. The real things in the world, the fine things, the things worth while, the simple ordinary lives of self-respecting people, the things that happen every day to everyone — those things don't get into the papers."

Owen thought of his father and his mother. Certainly nothing like this that had happened to Mr. and Mrs. Frye would ever happen to them; and Mr. Beecham's words gave him for a moment a consciousness of the millions of people like them in the world, the millions of lives which were lived in quiet industry and shared helpfulness and self-respect, and which were not news.

5

The strike of a year ago had been settled on the basis of a sixty-nine-cent wage in the Pittsburgh thin-vein region, which meant sixty cents in Hardiston; but when the Pittsburgh field cut wages, that settlement collapsed, and instead of sixty cents, most Hardiston County operators after May 1 paid fifty-one cents. With only two or three working days a week, no man could on that wage support a family; so after President Penna had failed to bring together a wage convention, Michael Ratchford, who was president of District 6, the Ohio District, decided to try his hand. Of eleven thousand taxpaying members of the Union, seven thousand were Ohio miners, so the state could hope to act alone. President Ratchford asked that delegates be sent to a special convention to consider what might be done. The call came opportunely, since the annual meeting of the Sub-District which included Hardiston County was about to be held in Belton; the request could then be brought up for discussion.

When he boarded the train for Belton, Owen joined old Matthew Price, secretary-treasurer of the Sub-District. Mr. Price was so thin that even in the cramped seats on the train he was able to sit with his legs crossed. Nervously stroking the back of one hand with the palm of the other, he asked whether Erie local had any money in the treasury.

"Forty-six cents," Owen told him. "Nobody pays the tax now, or hardly anybody. I did have fifty cents, but I had to buy two stamps."

The old man scratched his chin with a shaky, bony forefinger. "Think we'll send delegates to this special convention?"

"We ought to."

"It won't do any good," Mr. Price predicted. "Waste of money."

"We have to keep the Union going."

"What's the use, till things get better? And they couldn't be worse."

"They could be," Owen assured him. "Mr. Beecham says he wouldn't be surprised if the scale came down to forty."

They pulled into Belton station, and Mr. Price rose so stiffly that Owen half-expected to hear his knees creak. "Forty cents, eh?" The old man uttered a strange, shrill cackle of mirth. "You couldn't feed a chicken on that." He laughed again, the squeaking laugh. Following him off the train, Owen groped for a memory; something about a "shrunk shank," and then the last of it, the childish treble, that "pipes and whistles in his sound." He had meant to look in the dictionary and see what "sound" meant in that quotation, but had never remembered to do so. Yet the sense was clear enough, and as he followed Mr. Price along the platform, dim pity touched him for the frail old man.

President Jones called the meeting to order. Owen, seeing him for the first time, thought he seemed hale and hearty, with a broad bluff beard and a full chest and a wide brow; and neither hair nor beard was more than sprinkled with gray. Yet he had the look of having shrunk. You thought that but for his beard the skin under his jaw would be seen to hang in folds, and the hand that lifted the gavel was thin and palsied.

Mr. Price in his dual function as secretary-treasurer first read the minutes of the previous meeting, then reported income and expenditures, and announced a balance of $53.84 in the treasury. Charles Morgan moved a vote of thanks for this balance, and the motion was carried with a general chuckle.

Before they proceeded to the election of officers, President Jones asked that he be not re-elected. "I'm getting old, men," he ex-

plained. "And I'm not as well as I was. You all know Eben Howell
has had to relieve me of many of my duties." He raised his gavel.
"The chair awaits nominations for president of the Sub-District."

Eben Howell was the inevitable choice; Thomas Egan of Clinton
County was chosen vice-president in Howell's place, and Matthew
Price was re-elected. Someone moved a vote of thanks to the
retiring president, and then the question of sending delegates to
the convention proposed by District President Ratchford was
opened for discussion.

Isaac Williams and two Belton men whom Owen did not know,
one after the other argued that with business as bad as it was, such
a convention would be a waste of time and money. Owen, remembering his father's warning not to be forever showing off, and
Charles Morgan's advice to "take it easy," had not meant to speak;
but he disagreed so violently with Mr. Williams and the others,
just as he had disagreed with Mr. Price on the train, that without
consciously deciding to do so he rose and addressed the chair.

Once on his feet his thoughts began to take form. "Mr. Chairman," he began, and hesitated, looking all around, looking from
man to man, feeling as he always did when he faced an audience
that subtle multiplication of himself, that sense of being suddenly
more than an individual. When he spoke, he heard his own voice
like that of a stranger, paraphrasing familiar words. "It matters
little what we do here today, or what we say here today. Nothing
we do will raise our wages. The coal business is flat on its back; and
operators and miners suffer together."

Again his eyes swung from man to man, but he did not see them;
instead he saw again that picture like a vision; he put it into words.
"Yes, suffer together. We are bent under a heavy burden, toiling
like draft horses in the traces; and not miners alone, nor operators
alone, but all of us together. Somewhere, once, I saw an old steel
engraving. Some of you may have seen it. It showed thousands of
men, each with a harness fastened to his shoulders, each bent in
toil. Inch by inch they moved one of the great stones that went to
make the pyramids. And as I looked at that engraving I knew that
if one man fell, if one man failed, then the huge stone would slide
backward, dragging them all to loss and waste and death.

"The coal trade is the stone we strive to move forward, miners
and operators together; but now for a while the forces which grind

us all equally under the heel of hunger and want are too strong for us. We cannot pour new blood into the flabby veins of the coal industry; we cannot extract more money from the empty purses of the operators.

"But better times will come. Let us make ourselves, our Union, strong to serve in those better days to come. If a miner out of work lies abed all day, his muscles grow soft and weak; and when the call comes, he is unfit to work again. Right now the Union is like that idle miner; it is out of work. If we let it lie abed, if we let it rest inactive, it will grow weaker all the time.

"But if we exercise it, drill it, use it, try to extend it to unite all miners — why, then, when the fine day comes, it will be as sharp as a new pick in a strong man's hands, ready to work for us.

"A wise man uses his idle hours to sharpen his tools and harden his muscles. The Union is our tool. Let's keep its point sharp and its edge keen; let's keep our muscles strong.

"How? I need not tell you, for well you know. It is when we are about to be absent one from another that we beseech God's guidance and guardianship. Alone, we are weak; but we know that together we are strong. To meet together is to grow strong. Each of us draws strength from meeting with our fellows here today.

"So let us meet together, even if only to exercise this Union of ours. A horse stalled too long never won a race. I move you, Mr. President, that three delegates be appointed to the special convention called by District President Ratchford."

There was a reluctant approval in the brief clapping of hard palms, and someone offered a second to the motion. With no further discussion, the president was empowered to name the requested delegates.

The convention met before the month end. On May 8, Owen received a circular from the Executive Board reporting the expected failure.

After four days of continual session and meeting jointly with the operators of Ohio three times, it was impossible to make a scale for mining even at last year's prices. The operators were determined for very low wages. The delegates adopted the following resolution:

"That no work be done in or around the mines until a

settlement was made, except pumping and bailing water."

*This your executive board will endeavor to carry out in
every particular and in order to be successful in securing
the rate of wages demanded, viz: Sixty cents per ton for
pick and 36 cents per ton for machine mining and drilling,
we must have the entire support and co-operation of every
member of our organization. We respectfully request that
every man will do his duty lawfully.*

The following resolution was also adopted:

*"That any and all matters relative to price be referred
to the locals before settlement." This will be done. No
price will be agreed to without the consent of the locals.*

Owen took the circular to Isaac Williams; but his own opinion
was already formed. The proposal to stop work would fail. Men
whose families were already hungry would not give up their
meager wage on the thin chance that a strike might succeed. He
would not urge any man to strike.

But he would himself stop work, and for as long as the Executive
Board directed him to do so. When Mr. Williams, having read the
circular, asked his opinion of it, Owen told him this. "I'll stop."

"All by yourself? Kind of foolish, aren't you? A one-man strike
won't get you anywhere." They were on the front porch. This was
Wednesday evening, and Owen had stopped on his way home
from the *Journal* office. Marged came out to join them, and her
uncle said with a kindly derision in his voice: "Listen here, Marged.
The State Executive Board wants us to strike, and Owen knows the
men won't do it; but he says he's going to quit work and strike all
by himself. Can you make any sense out of that?"

"I expect Owen can," Marged suggested, her eyes turning toward
him.

"I don't know whether I can make sense out of it or not," Owen
admitted. "But the Union will never amount to much unless the
men obey orders." He added in a lower tone: "And I want to see
the Union amount to a lot."

"Of course." Marged turned to her uncle. "That seems sensible to
me, just as sensible as a soldier obeying orders — even when he
knows he'll probably be killed."

"Well, maybe." The old man rose. "You better post up a call for a meeting, Owen. We'll have to vote on it, anyway."

He went into the house, but Owen stayed awhile, and Marged moved to sit beside him. "I'm worried about Uncle Isaac," she said in a low tone, looking over her shoulder at the open door. "He seems so tired all the time."

"I guess a man gets more tired when he's older," Owen suggested; and he told her about old Mr. Price, squeaking and shaking. "I was sorry for him, but I don't know why I should be. He's well off, doesn't work any more."

"Uncle Isaac doesn't have to — but he'd be unhappy if he couldn't."

"Maybe Mr. Price would work if he could." Owen considered that possibility. "Moses Evans told me one day he wanted me to feel sorry for him. That was after he'd been so sick."

"You and I are both pretty young, compared to them, aren't we?"

"I wonder what it's like, being old."

"I suppose it's like climbing a hill — and suddenly knowing you can't climb any higher." Marged hesitated. "It must be hard to know that you're never going to see over the top of the hill ahead of you."

"I wonder if you ever do know." Owen suddenly half-laughed. "My *dadcu*" — he used the Welsh word — "papa's father, down in Gallia County, is still alive. He's been teaching Sunday School sixty-five years, or I guess it's seventy now, because it was five years ago I saw him. He told me he'd read the Bible twelve times, and he'd read the New Testament twenty-seven times and the Psalms twenty-eight, and he was starting the Bible all over again; so I guess he expects to see over the top of the hill."

"He must be a fine man."

Owen grinned in the shadows. "I guess so, but he kept talking about how many times he'd read the Bible till I asked him what 'make broad thy phylacteries' meant. I got a whopper of a licking for that; the last licking I ever got."

She looked at him thoughtfully, the light from the hallway shining across her face; and suddenly she smiled. "Or ever will get. You're not a boy any more, Owen."

"Maybe that's what started us talking about getting old." He rose. "Well, I guess I'd better go home." She rose with him. "Where's Morgan?"

"Gone to Celia Ames's party. Remember her? She was in my room the year you were."

"Yes, I know. I saw her coming out of school the other day. I always hated her because she was so mean to Freddie." He chuckled. "Wonder if she let him come to her party."

She said irrelevantly, "You're not even sixteen, are you?"

"Not till November. Well, goodnight."

The following Monday, the local — as Owen had expected — voted against stopping work; but next day Owen told John Powell what he meant to do, and when he had loaded the coal he had shot down the day before, he took home his tools.

6

Additional Locals: Mr. and Mrs. Herbert Canter have gone to spend six weeks in Europe. Unless the electric railway from Belton to Hardiston is built soon, local capital will take over the project. Girls should be careful about giving away photographs; never let your picture go where you would be sorry to be seen. Every wagon hauling iron ore through our streets hints at returning prosperity. A keg of powder exploded in Miss Ellen Mine last week and Thomas Hughes was so badly burned he is not expected to live. At a revival meeting in the church at Rock Run, Thomas Fortune was hit by a missile fired from a slingshot; he drew a revolver and shot Evan Lloyd in the leg. John Rickson got a broken arm when his horse ran away with him. Wah Sing of St. Louis has come to Hardiston to establish a laundry. *Queen Esther* was presented at the Rink by the Belton Choral Society. Stallion Strader Joe will make the season of 1895 at Tom Lovering's livery stable. The lightning rod is disappearing; so will the silver craze. Tom Merry's horse ran away, ran into a telephone pole, and broke his leg and had to be killed. In the third runaway in a month, Mrs. Robert Horne suffered a severe concussion of the brain. Something should be done to prevent these runaways. Foraker, a friend to silver, but not an enemy of gold, should be our next Senator. Professor, a dog which every day raced the miners' train out of Slacktown, last week tried to run in front of the engine and was killed. A crush in Belton Number 1 last week shut off the west entry; it is now being reopened and timbered. The roof in the new entry of Mary Baker Mine proved so tender that day men are helping the miners to secure it. Chief Black, having been refused a raise in pay, has resigned; this and the projected waterworks will between them destroy the efficiency of the Fire Department. The Ohio Southern Railway has gone into receivership. Arthur Paxley, who returned from a business trip last Monday night, was shot and killed by a burglar whom he surprised in his home.

7

Owen's last day's work at Erie was a Tuesday. It was early afternoon when he reached home, but he worked in the garden till supper, replanting beans killed by Monday night's heavy frost, so he did not hear the news of Mr. Paxley's death till Wednesday morning in the *Journal* office.

"Made some excitement in town, I tell you," Will Davis assured him. "Doctor Mayland had the inquest in the Court House yesterday afternoon, and everyone who could get in was there. I went myself." He gave Owen a straightforward report. "Tom Lloyd was the first one there after it happened." Mr. Lloyd was Jane's father; their home was four doors from the Paxleys'. "He'd been out in his nightshirt and overcoat covering his roses when it turned so cold, and he heard two shots from Paxleys' and he saw someone run out of the house and away along Broad Street, and then he heard Mrs. Paxley yelling. He ran over there and the front door was open and she was on the stairs with a lamp, in her nightgown, and Mr. Paxley dead at the foot of the stairs. So he went and got Bob Henson and Doc Mayland."

"After Mr. Lloyd, Mrs. Paxley took the stand. Mr. Paxley had been shot with his own revolver. Marshal Bob Henson found it, next morning, in a flower bed by the front porch; and Mrs. Paxley recognized it. She testified that her husband came home late, after she was in bed and asleep, and sat on the edge of the bed talking to her, not bothering to light the lamp; and they heard someone downstairs and he went down and then she heard the shots and lighted a lamp and found him dead at the foot of the stairs.

"After she was through, Doctor Mayland said that was all the evidence," Will explained. "But then Adelina Fortune wanted to testify. She was got up the way she always is, flour and paint all over her face, and her hair in the same greasy ringlets, and that old-fashioned bonnet and the lace shawl. She lives just up the street a ways from Paxleys', so Doctor Mayland let her talk, but she just raved on about the time her husband went away and how she'd waited for him and if he came back she'd welcome him and not shoot him. So finally they hushed her up. Mrs. Paxley had gone out by then, after she got through her testifying."

Owen asked in a puzzled tone: "How did Mr. Paxley get home, that time of night? There's no train."

"Mrs. Paxley said sometimes he got to Hamden on the late train and hired a rig to bring him down. The thing that struck BB funny, Paxley had his overcoat on when they found him, and his hat was right on the floor there by him. BB said he couldn't figure a man coming home late and sitting on his wife's bed in the dark with his overcoat and hat on."

Owen asked BB, when the editor reached the office, "What do you think happened, Mr. Beecham?"

BB said quietly: "There's an old New England saying, Owen: 'Take it from whence it comes.' When someone sends me an item for the *Journal* and doesn't sign his name, I never print it. The writer may be prejudiced, one way or another; he may lie, even without knowing it. And of course if I know he is a liar, I don't believe him, anyway." He hesitated. "I take everything I hear 'from whence it comes.'"

"You mean you don't believe her?"

"What she says sounds like a lie."

"Are you going to say so in the *Journal*?"

"No, I shall just quote what she said. Some day we'll know the truth."

But others were not so easily silent. Owen that day had the task of folding and stapling programs for the Chautauqua Circle, which Will had printed on the job press the day before. This kept him at a table just back of the office, so he saw and heard every visitor. Dave Ames came in to tell BB about that day in the Post Office when Mr. Paxley discovered the pants he wore were not his own. "You heard her say he came upstairs in the dark, here Monday night.

Well, my guess is he came upstairs in the dark that other night, and undressed in the dark, and someone was there with his pants off, and whoever it was, he waited till Paxley was asleep and then got the wrong pair of pants and sneaked out." The smell of Mr. Ames's stogie — he always smoked three-fers, three-for-a-nickel, the cheapest sort — was foul and nauseous. "Yes sir," said the big man in trumpeting tones. "I'll bet a dollar Mrs. Paxley knows the name of that burglar."

There were others equally ready with their tongues; and during the days that followed Owen heard many an unkind word about Mrs. Paxley. But after that first week, people stopped talking about her. Without fresh fuel, the fire died; there was no more to say.

8

On the twenty-first of May, President Penna issued a call for a national convention of the United Mine Workers to meet in Columbus on the twenty-ninth. The day after the convention met, Owen went with BB on a tramp into the country; and the editor spoke of the Columbus meeting, about which Owen had written a paragraph for yesterday's *Journal*.

"Will anything be done, do you think?" he asked.

"No sir, not likely. It's just to try to keep the Union alive through hard times."

BB said in a quizzical tone: "I hear you're quite a figure in mining circles. How did it happen Eben Howell didn't name you a delegate?"

Owen grinned. "Well, for one thing, I didn't ask him to."

"Why not? He who bloweth not his own bazoo, for him his bazoo will not be blown. The office doesn't seek the man, the man seeks the office." He said more seriously: "You'll have to study politics, Owen. Some day a purely labor party will develop. You want to be ready."

"I guess there's time enough."

"You'll live to see it! When that time comes, capital will say it's treason for labor to use its political power to better its condition. But capital sees no treason in using its political power to better its condition. Rich men argue that they use their power for the good of the nation; but when they talk about the good of the nation, they mean their own good."

"They don't think that's what they mean," Owen suggested. "Or they think their own good is good for the United States."

"Men tend to think as their class thinks," BB urged. "The income tax would have hit the rich, so rich men thought it was wrong; and the Supreme Court is made up of men who either are themselves rich, or who think as rich men, so the Court decided the tax was unconstitutional."

"I don't understand about it," Owen confessed. "Papa never has to pay any tax, except to the Union."

"It's not the same thing." BB spoke with a chuckle in his tones. "A year ago last winter, Congress put a clause in the tariff bill providing that anyone who earned over four thousand dollars a year had to pay a two per cent tax on his income. So rich men took it to law, claiming it was illegal to tax some incomes and not tax others — and the Supreme Court threw it out." He added: "But if your father, or President Penna of the United Mine Workers, or such men as they, who do not earn four thousand a year, had controlled the Court, they would have thought the tax was a fine thing."

Owen grinned. "I guess it will be a long time before there's a miner on the Supreme Court."

"Maybe not so long as you expect. You see, Owen, the history of the world is the history of the rising political power of the common man. For a thousand years, ever since the English longbowmen shot the knights off their horses and ended the Dark Ages, every great war has been followed by a great emancipation. The longbow ended the power of the man on horseback, armored in iron and steel; the vote will end the power of the man armored in great wealth. I suppose Herbert Canter, in good times, employs maybe five hundred men; but each of those men has one vote — and Mr. Canter has only one. So some day their five hundred votes will outvote Mr. Canter."

"I never saw him. Just his pictures."

"He's a good man. He's a man of great ability, kindly and honest; but I'd never blame a miner who disagreed with him — and used his vote to make the disagreement an effective one." Owen, thinking hard, looking into the future, did not speak; and BB asked:

"Speaking of freedom, have you read anything about the Cuba revolt?"

"No sir."

"You'll find frequent dispatches about it in the dailies. Cuba is owned and ruled by Spain, and they're trying to win their independence."

"Do you think they're going to?"

"Eventually, yes. Just as surely as you coal miners will one day be free. For freedom is a thing every man desires, and the steady pressure of that desire will sooner or later burst every barrier in the way."

9

The National Convention called by President Penna drew sixty-one delegates to Columbus, but all but ten of them were from Ohio. There were no funds in the union treasury, and the Union — and the national officers — were living on borrowed money, so the National Convention accomplished nothing. Under the leadership of President Ratchford, District Number 6, the Ohio District, which included eighty per cent of the Union's total strength, went into conference with Ohio operators; but the only result was an agreement, submitted to Ohio miners for their ratification, to accept the fifty-one-cent wage.

This was in effect a confession of defeat, an admission that the strike call issued early in May — and which at Erie only Owen had obeyed — had been everywhere a failure. On ratification, the miners voted 5091 For, 4351 Against; and the abortive strike was at an end.

Owen was glad to be back at work. June had brought hot weather, but the depths of the mine were always cool and pleasant, a relief from the steaming summer heat. To come out in mid-afternoon and face the hot blast of day was like opening an oven door. He liked his days in the *Journal* office, but he was happier at the mine, loading into the cars the coal he had shot down the day before, testing the jack slate, wedging props to support it, sprawling on his side while he undercut the vein, loading the coal thus loosened, drilling holes and rolling cartridges and tamping home the charges. The first shot filled the room with smoke and

coal dust, and each shot increasingly fouled the air; but a
wet handkerchief across mouth and nose helped a little, and it
was always a relief to fire the last hole and make his way out to the
portal and away to the swimming hole.

One day in late June, while Owen was setting bank props, he
felt a heavy jar through the solid rock under his feet; and instantly
thereafter he heard an inhuman, squalling cry. He leaped out into the
entry and ran toward the sound. That toneless squall, repeated,
made him think of a day long ago by the creek down at Adams
Furnace when he and Sammy Howell, discovering a bull frog on
a log below the bank, dropped a heavy rock upon it. The frog, legs
pinned, forelegs clawing to be free, uttered a croaking sound hor-
ribly like this which drew him now. Other men were running ahead
of him, their lamps flickering; still others came behind him, racing
toward the room from which the outcry came.

It was Chet Masters's room. A mass of jack slate ten feet long,
six or eight inches thick, and three or four feet wide, had fallen; and
Chet was pinned under it. When Owen reached the spot, Chet lay
on his face, the slate covering all of him except his head and one
shoulder and part of his back. Chet's cries were already weaker,
his mouth was open, his tongue protruded.

John Powell, the mine boss, had been among the first to reach
him. Under Powell's direction, the men laid hands on the edge of
the slate and tried to lift it. It rose half an inch, no more. Someone
shouted for a pry; a prop was thrust under the edge of the slate,
with a chunk of rock for fulcrum, and the slate rose a little. They
wedged rock fragments under it to save that small gain, and set
a fresh lever. They worked together in headlong haste, their black
faces illumined by the lamps in each man's cap, their white teeth
and the whites of their eyes catching the light. New levers raised
the slate an inch at a time; but the further edge of the slab, as it
was tilted upward, crushed Chet's feet and leg bones with sharp,
cracking sounds. Chet, his chest relieved of some weight, could
breathe again; he strangled and babbled and wailed.

Owen was one of those who lifted the great slab. When they
dragged Chet's broken body free, his legs trailed like frayed ropes;
and Owen was near to fainting at the sight, and a hideous smell
sickened his nostrils. John Powell said suddenly:

"Easy! Let him lay! His insides are squeezed out!"

Owen turned and stumbled away. In the entry he bowed down, and a bitter stream poured from his mouth; he scooped up water from the drain beside the tracks and splashed it in his face, and staggered toward the portal. Behind him the sounds diminished; he saw daylight ahead and ran to meet it and flung himself along the sunned ground, his face buried in his arms, weeping without tears. Hiccoughs shook him like heavy blows.

The outside workers had run into the mine at the first alarm, so for a while he was alone; but at length he heard men coming out, heard their muttered words.

"He didn't last long."

"He was lucky he didn't, mashed that way."

Owen sat up, and other men appeared, and then a coal car pushed by many hands. Owen's father and Isaac Williams and John Powell were close behind the car which held Chet's body; and Mr. Powell called to the men around him:

"We'll knock off for today, boys. Work tomorrow."

The men stood for a moment in an uncertain group, and one or two started to move away. Mr. Powell sent one of the day men to bring a wagon to take Chet's body home, and Owen remembered that day in his babyhood when his older brother was killed. Then he saw that his father had brought their dinner pails, so they turned homeward together.

After a moment Tom Glen asked: "Were you in there, Owen?"

"At first, yes. But I got sick when they pulled him out, so I came away."

"Didn't hear what he said, then?"

"Only his yelling."

"He killed Mr. Paxley," said Tom Glen. "He was there, in the house, carrying on with her, and he heard Mr. Paxley coming upstairs. He jumped him at the door, and Paxley had the gun, and Chet got his hands on it and got it away from Mr. Paxley. They'd fought halfway down the stairs by then, and Mr. Paxley came at Chet again and Chet killed him." He brushed his mouth with the back of his hand. "Chet got it all out before he died. He acted like he wanted to tell somebody."

Owen strode beside his father, eyes on the ground. Surprised by the realization that he was not surprised, he discovered that without shaping the thought into words, he had long known the truth.

He remembered the day Dan Davis came with the hack to take Mrs. Paxley to the train, and how Dan joked with her, and he remembered Mr. Ames's loud mirth at the episode of Mr. Paxley's pants. Those must have been Chet's pants which Mr. Paxley found himself wearing. He wondered what Mrs. Paxley would do, now that everyone knew the truth; and as though in answer to his thought his father said:

"I guess likely she'll leave town. Good riddance to bad rubbish."

Owen in a sudden cold wave of terror thought that if he had been a little older, that day Mrs. Paxley called him up to her bedroom, he might have been in Chet's place. "Carrying on with her." That was his father's phrase.

Yes, and maybe killing Mr. Paxley. He hoped his father would never remember that he had used to cut Mrs. Paxley's lawn; it seemed to him that by her shame he too was shamed.

XIV

June 1895 — November 1895

ADDITIONAL LOCALS: Miss Marged Williams is taking a summer normal course at Ohio University. The town pump should be replaced; the old wooden pipe is rotted through and much water leaks out and is wasted; the pump is thirty-two years old. Dan Tailor hauled three and fourteen hundredths tons of iron ore to Union Furnace in a single load, the record. The fifty-one-cent wage scale for miners, said BB, proves that the democrats are still in power. Miners' wages should be higher; and teachers' wages should be raised. Poor teachers did irreparable damage to youthful minds. The annual Literary Meeting at Sycamore Hill was well attended. Children's Day at the churches gave inspiration to many boys and girls. Many Hardiston people went on the excursion to the State Christian Endeavor Convention at Springfield. Mrs. Frank Thorne, Miss Edith Thorne and Miss Sadie Porter departed June 19 for two months in Europe. Street loafing by boys and girls should be suppressed. No man who used tobacco should be allowed to teach school, for smoking leads to drinking. All drunkards use tobacco. The residence of Mr. and Mrs. Charles Arthur was destroyed by fire June 21; Fire Department and bucket brigade proved unable to check the flames. A meteorite weighing twelve ounces fell in Mrs. Fred Evans's garden and dug a hole four inches deep. Bonds to finance the building of the electric railway from Belton to Hardiston have been sold and contracts will soon be let. Thomas Shea rode from Hartford, Connecticut, to Hardiston on a bicycle in four days and thirteen hours including stops for rest, sleep and meals; he reached Hardiston June 25. The Methodist Church has voted to employ no minister who smokes. Chester Masters was caught by a fall of

slate in Erie Mine June 24 and died almost at once, but before
he died he confessed killing Arthur Paxley six weeks ago. The
County miners and operators met in a joint conference June 29 to
discuss reducing rents and the price of powder, oil and coal to the
men. A committee was appointed to study the subject. District
President Ratchford of the United Mine Workers was in Belton
July 5 and 6 adjusting a dispute at the Wheelwright Mine, closed
since April 1, and was an interesting caller at this office. Professor
Howe of Cincinnati says belief in the power of the madstone is a
delusion as absurd as belief in the divining rod. Mrs. Arthur Paxley
has removed to Cincinnati. Hardiston should forbid farmers and
others from hitching their horses to trees; it kills the trees. Coxey is
seeking the Populist nomination for Governor; if he is nominated
it will kill the party. A Ross County man hiccoughed himself to
death. The Belton waterworks went dry, and water from Belton
Number 2 was pumped into the mains. Andrew Husted, from whom
in the last ten years ninety-five feet of tapeworm has been removed,
has now been relieved of the last thirty feet, head and all. Rain-
fall, by mid-July, was six inches below normal; unless they boiled
all the water they drank, people would soon be drinking dregs full
of typhoid germs. Twelve hundred men and boys heard Coxey
speak at Slacktown, but he made few if any converts. Three tramps
who turned burglar ended in jail. Thomas Roberts is home from
Wales. Farmers were boycotting Hardiston because the absence of
hitch rails forced them to pay the livery stables to put up their
teams. Two months ago, *Trilby* was all the rage; but now, except
for a few Trilby Hearts dangling from bracelets, the book is forgotten. In Hardiston County for the year ending March 13, 1895,
there were 335 deaths, 853 births; the violent deaths numbered 52.
No deaths were caused by doctors using anaesthetics. Of the
deaths, 88 were babies under one year, and 135 babies died under
three years of age. September had the largest number of deaths,
April the least. The bicycle, bringing people nearer together, will
some day make the whole world kin. The money spent in the
United States on alcohol and tobacco would in ten years build
homes for every man in the United States. There were seven mad-
dog scares in the last ten days of July, and eleven people and four
horses were bitten. The madstone owned by Elijah Peters was sold
at auction to settle his estate. It brought $405, more than its weight

in gold. The charge for its use was a dollar for each hour it adhered to a bite, and it adhered to a bite in little Annie Jenkins's leg for fifteen hours. Several dogs have been shot, and the Mayor has ordered all dogs muzzled. It is strange to see a twenty-five-cent muzzle on a ten-cent dog. Miss Jane Lloyd was the hostess last Saturday on an all-day hay-ride to Hermit's Fork. A good time was had by all.

2

Owen had feared that Chet Masters's confession, by pointing scornful fingers at Mrs. Paxley, would remind people of what she had said about him; but he was to find that when she was discredited, he acquired by a process of reversal a certain credit. He first guessed this when a few days after Chet's death, on his way to town, he heard a call behind him and looked back and saw Jane waving, calling, "Owen, wait for me." He waited, surprised yet happy too, and Jane overtook him. "Going uptown, Owen? I'm going to the store."

"Your mama doesn't want you walking with me." He had forgotten how small Jane was; her head barely reached his shoulder.

"Yes, she does. She says she doesn't believe a word Mrs. Paxley said. Come on." By his side, she added: "And Mr. Beecham told her you're awful smart, and Miss Williams says her uncle says you're going to amount to something." Owen flushed with happiness and also with embarrassment. "But of course," said Jane complacently, "I knew you were nice, all the time. We always liked each other, didn't we?"

"Sure."

They walked together as far as her father's store, and Owen hoped everyone saw them; when they parted he strode on high-headed, and his heels struck hard. Next day in the *Journal* office, Nellie Tutson spoke of this encounter. Bets had gone down to the pressroom, and Nellie was correcting proofs, moving between her case and the galley on the press. "I never will learn to put two e's in 'every,'" she said fretfully.

He was sticking type at the case beyond hers. "You don't make as many mistakes now."

"And I always spell 'social,' s-o-s-h-u-l!" She lifted the word out of the line. "I saw you with Jane Lloyd yesterday. She's your girl, isn't she."

Owen resented that. Nellie was not even good enough to look at Jane, much less talk about her. He grunted, without answering; but after all, Nellie was a lot nicer than she used to be. "Darn it, you made me make a mistake."

"She's awful nice."

"Hush up. I can't work with you talking."

She laughed teasingly. "You're red as a brick." Then, touching his cheek with her finger, she made a hissing sound. "Why, Owen, you're burning up!"

"Leave me alone," he protested. He was no longer at all afraid of Nellie, and usually to talk to her was easy enough; but whenever she came near him, smiling, whispering, the same thing always happened. It was not because she was prettier than she used to be, for certainly she was not as pretty as Jane; but she woke in him a deep excitement of which he was ashamed. He was glad now when Bets came upstairs, so that he and Nellie were no longer alone.

Neither he nor his father went to the meeting of miners and operators in Belton that night, when a rent reduction was discussed. The difficulty of getting home afterward was too great; and also Moses Evans had long ago reduced Tom's rent from six dollars to four, and four dollars was not unfair.

Saturday, Owen was in the type loft when Mr. Beecham called upstairs, summoning him to the front office. Two men were there with BB, and Owen recognized Eben Howell, and greeted him, and then BB said, "And Owen, shake hands with your District President." Owen gulped as though he had been hit in the stomach, but he took the hand the other offered, and BB added: "Mr. Ratchford, when your Executive Board called the men out last May, Erie local voted to go on working; but Owen here staged a one-man strike. He stayed out till the whole state voted to go back to work."

Mr. Ratchford looked at Owen with an interested eye. "Mr. Howell has mentioned you, Glen. Why did you stay out?"

"Well, I don't think the Union can ever get anywhere unless we all take orders." Owen added honestly: "And I could afford to. I earn some money here in the *Journal* office, and I don't have to support a family, and I live with papa and mama. But I don't blame anyone for not striking."

"It's pretty hard for a man to strike when it starves his wife and children," Mr. Ratchford agreed. He said to BB: "But the men at Wheelwright have stuck it out."

Owen drew back, feeling himself dismissed; yet he lingered a moment longer. BB asked: "Did you get a reasonable settlement?"

"I think so. The men go back and the manager agrees to make the changes we want — he has three months to do it in — and to give up his insistence on their doing the dead work, and the rules he wanted them to accept." Owen watched him, scarce hearing what he said, trying to guess what quality in him had set him where he was; but Mr. Ratchford looked much like other men, with plenty of hair and a heavy mustache and a big jaw that seemed soft rather than bony. When the two men rose to go, Owen went back to his work, but he kept Mr. Ratchford's image in his mind.

His pleasant days continued, and it seemed to him there was a new friendliness in everyone. The day Mr. Arthur's home burned, he had been at work in the mine, and he did not see Mrs. Arthur till weeks later, after Chet was killed. Returning home one day past the corner where the house had stood, he saw two men at work cleaning out the cellar hole full of ashes and debris, and Mrs. Arthur was watching them. She came to the fence to speak to him, said with that chirky little smile so natural to her: "Hello, Owen. Well, I won't need my grass cut for a while."

"I'm mighty sorry, Mrs. Arthur."

"Don't be! Not for me! There's nothing like a good fire for a house-cleaning. I've been working my fingers to the bone for five or ten years, taking care of that old house and all the things in it, and I was sick to death of the lot of them all the time. Now the last one of them's gone. I feel like a slave after the Emancipation Proclamation." She was so merry that he decided she meant it, and laughed with her, and she bent to caress the absurd dog at her knee and went on: "Wait till you see our new house! It's going to be pressed brick. I've wanted a house built out of pressed brick ever since I saw Herbert Canter's in Columbus. It's so smooth and red. We'll have a big new lawn for you, too!"

Owen was not sure she was as pleased as she pretended, but

certainly there was in her a warm friendliness he had not seen
before. He had so long felt himself under a shadow that to find
people liked him was an intoxication.

When Jane invited him to her picnic — it would be on the first
Saturday in August — he went to Mr. Beecham to ask whether he
could be spared. The prospective loss of a day's pay did not make
him hesitate, but Will — and BB — should be forewarned. BB
assured him that Will could manage well enough. "Who's going?"
he asked.

"I don't know. Mostly Jane's room in school."

"What year is she?"

"First year high school next fall."

"High school only graduated two boys, this year. What happens
to them?"

"Some of them quit school to go to work, if their families need
the money. And some of them want to earn money, anyway, so
they'll have it to spend."

"I suppose so. And to spend their time loafing on street corners.
They learn to smoke cigarettes, and that stupefies them, dulls their
minds. You don't smoke, do you?"

"I used to smoke catalpa pods, and buggy-whip handles, when I
was a boy. But I don't now."

"One trouble is," BB reflected, "that businessmen hiring boys
don't give a preference to high-school graduates. If businessmen
valued education, more boys would want to be educated. Where is
the picnic to be?"

"Some place called Hermit's Fork."

"Well, you'll have an interesting day. Ever hear how Hermit's
Fork got its name?" Owen had not, and BB told him the story.
Owen sometimes thought Mr. Beecham knew everything that had
ever happened in Hardiston County, and usually he listened with a
lively interest; but today he was anxious to get away so that he
could find Jane and tell her he could go on her picnic.

He wished he could buy a new suit, since his Sunday suit was
too short for him in the arms and legs, and tight around the
shoulders too; but though he knew his mother would consent to the
extravagance, he knew too what it would cost her in worry and contriving. Besides, by losing a day's work he was already making a

sacrifice to go to the picnic at all. Then, too, people would not dress up for a hay-ride; and probably it would be hot, so he would take off his coat, anyway; and while he was sitting in the hay, the fact that his pants were too short would not show, not much.

His mother, when he told her about the picnic, was distressed about his clothes; but Tom Glen said she was making a fuss over nothing. "Any old clothes are good enough for a bunch of young ones riding all day in the dust, Annie. You'd have him all dressed up, coat and pants and shiny shoes and a hat, yes, and like as not his collar too, choking him half to death, till he wouldn't have a good time at all."

She was silenced, but not convinced. The demand for coal for the lake trade, which usually stimulated business during the summer season, this year had little effect. In the last two weeks of June and the whole of July, Erie Mine ran only nine days, and for those six weeks Tom and Owen between them brought home less than thirty dollars. Nevertheless, the day before the picnic, while Tom was in the garden, Mrs. Glen came to Owen with two crumpled bills and some odd silver.

"Here, sonny," she said proudly. "I know you really want a nice new suit, and I've got over twelve dollars saved up, so I can spare this. Here's seven dollars. Mr. Lloyd has some real handsome suits for that."

Owen had long since accepted the necessity of doing without, but this sudden temptation shook him. "Why, I don't need a new suit, mama," he began, in a qualified yielding; but before he could go on, he saw her fingers curl as though to protect her small treasure, saw her lungs fill with deep relief at his rejection of her offer. He bit back the word so nearly spoken, and said instead: "But if you've got all that money to spare, get yourself a nice new dress or something."

She laughed and her closed hand pressed the money against her breast; yet she urged, "You'd look real nice, Owen."

He hugged her, teased her. "Why, I look nice, anyway! Don't I?"

She kissed him, retorting, "Somebody's getting pretty stuck up, seems to me!"

"Got a right to be stuck up, with a mama like you."

"And a fine father, too, Owen!"

"I sure have." Her quick word had held something defensive, as though Tom Glen were under attack; he spoke to reassure her. "He's grand. You both are."

"We're both awful proud of you."

3

It was at Morgan's suggestion that on the day of the picnic he and Owen met at the corner of Belton and Pearl Streets, to go on to Jane's house together. Janet Frye, who lived next door to Morgan, came with him. Tom Powell and Bill Myers were at Jane's before them, helping Mrs. Lloyd bring out on the front porch the clothes basket full of lunch, the ice-cream freezer, and the quilts in which it would be packed to keep off the heat of the sun. Jane made them welcome and set them to help, and Owen found Betty Myers and Molly Moury in the kitchen wrapping sandwiches. Celia Ames arrived alone, with Freddie a block behind her, and Della Jones and Jenkin Powell came together. When the hayrack turned into Broad Street and stopped at the curb, a boy thirteen or fourteen years old, and with the biggest freckles Owen had ever seen, was handling the big farm horses, and a jolly big woman fairly bulging out of her white dress, holding a huge black umbrella as a sunshade, sat beside him. She waved and called: "Hello, Maggie! Hello, Jane!"

The boy pulled up his horses with loud, important whoas, and everyone raced to climb in; but Mrs. Lloyd called the boys back to help load the provender. While this was being done, the girls disposed themselves in the hay, and when everything was loaded, Jane beckoned Owen to sit beside her. The boy who held the reins reached into an open box under the seat and produced two battered tin horns.

"Here!" he said soberly, frowning to control an obvious desire to grin. "You can blow these so folks will know we're coming." He tossed them back into the hay, and Jane caught one.

"He's my Cousin Lew," she told Owen. "And that's Aunt Net. She's his mother."

Mrs. Lloyd brought a dozen wide straw hats and passed them into eager hands. "The sun will be hot, you know. And you'll get sunburned, too." She climbed to the high seat beside Aunt Net, gave a last look around. "Well, I guess we're all here, Lewis. We can start."

Owen counted six girls, six boys — not including Lew; and they had all been in Miss Williams's room with him except Jenkin Powell. He had known Jenkin since before they were pallbearers at Willie's funeral, but only casually, and he had never forgotten that it was Jenkin who spied on Miss Dine and Mr. Freeland and betrayed her to the world. Certainly, too, Nellie Tutson and Jenkin had done shameful things together. Perhaps Mrs. Lloyd did not know the sort of boy Jenkin was. Owen was surprised, too, that Freddie Ames was in the party, and under cover of the blare of the horns, he asked Jane: "How'd you happen to invite Freddie?"

"Celia's so mean to him that I kind of like him."

"Well, what did you invite her for, then?"

"Oh, she always says such mean things about people, you have to."

Their progress out of town was a noisy one; they shouted greetings to everyone they passed, and blew horns, and sang. In the well-shaded streets, where the sprinkling wagon had laid the dust, they laughed and squirmed and shifted the hay to make more comfortable seats; and some of the boys sat with their feet dangling outside the wagon bed, letting the slowly revolving wheels rub against the soles of their shoes. Owen did not do this. Shoes wore out fast enough without any help.

For half an hour after the start, they were a lively crowd, and Aunt Net had as much fun as any of them, forever turning around — at risk of crowding Jane's mother off the seat — to scream something to them all and shriek with laughter. But then the sun and the dust stirred up by the horses and by the wheels began to take toll. The big umbrella gave some shade to Mrs. Lloyd and Aunt Net, who like a squeezed sponge was leaking through the shoulders of her white dress; and the straw hats Mrs. Lloyd had provided each found a wearer. Some were too large, and some too small, and there were many exchanges in the effort to achieve a better fit. Owen's large head was a problem till he borrowed Tom Powell's knife and made slits in the sides of the hat to allow it to expand. That set a fashion, and one boy after another cut holes in the crown of his hat to keep his head cool. Tom trimmed away the whole top of his hat, keeping only the wide brim to shade his face, and Betty Myers begged him to fix hers the same way, and he did so.

Their experiments with the hats filled another half-hour. By that time they were fairly baked, sweat streaking their dusty faces. At the watering trough in the valley beyond Dixon's hill, everyone got out to drink the water that came down from a hillside spring in a wooden pipe, and they washed their faces so that they were for the moment damply clean from hair to jawline.

They went on, the heavy horses reluctantly managing an occasional short trot. Boys jumped out of the rear end of the wagon and walked behind, or they lagged till the hayrack had gone fifty yards or so and then raced to overtake it. The hay stuck to wet hands and faces and necks; the dust settled in a pale yellow-brown shadow on their hair and their garments; they gasped for air, sitting with mouths open like hens in the shade on a hot day; and everyone — except possibly Mrs. Lloyd — had a wonderful time.

After three hours on the road, Lew turned the horses through a gate — Jenkin Powell foresaw that gate and ran ahead to open and to close it, and Owen wished he had been the one to do this — and down across a meadow where the hay had been harvested, to a knoll shaded by four good maple trees and a straggly, lyre-shaped elm. Around the foot of the knoll meandered a muddy little creek, and the hayrack had hardly stopped before every boy except Lew, discarding shoes and socks and with trousers rolled high, waded into the cool water. The girls alighted more demurely, and Bill Myers called from the creek:

"Come on in, girls. The water's fine!"

Jane asked: "Can we, mama?"

Mrs. Lloyd, still perched on high, said crisply: "Hush, Jane! Not now. After we've had our picnic, we'll go up around the bend and you can wade there. Here, help me down!"

Jane reached up, and then Lew and Jane helped Aunt Net, who reached the ground with a shriek of mirth and a cry: "Heaven help me, I've bust a gusset!" Lew blushed for his mother's indelicacy and with the dignity demanded by his importance as the man in charge, he unhitched the horses and stood on tiptoe to pull their bridles off and turn them loose to graze.

Mrs. Lloyd took command, calling to the waders in the creek: "Boys, clean out the spring, please, so it will clear."

The spring, a trickle of surprisingly cold water, flowed out of the knoll a foot or two above the level of the stream. It was full of dead leaves, and a frog lived there; but at their approach he removed his residence to the creek below. They scooped out the leaves and the muck with their hands, finding that the spring was walled with flat stones. The water at first was yellow with mud, but then a thread of clear water showed in the yellow, and the mud began to settle, and presently the spring was clear. Jane brought a tin cup, and they dipped and drank, and Mrs. Lloyd produced basin and soap and towel so they could wash dusty faces and hands.

Owen, remembering what BB had told him, said to Jane: "Old Mr. Hermit walled up this spring, when he came here to live."

"Oh, was there really a Mr. Hermit?" She looked around, up and down the meadow. "Where's his fork?" The picnic was spread, a big tablecloth on the ground well covered with plates of fried chicken, potato salad, pickles, cucumbers, tomatoes, bread-and-butter sandwiches, glasses of jelly, jars of jam.

"That's the name of the creek," Owen explained. "It runs into another creek named Black Fork, and that runs into Grassy Fork and makes Symmes Creek."

Mrs. Lloyd heard him. "Do you know about Mr. Hermit, Owen?"

"Yes, ma'am. Mr. Beecham told me, when he knew we were coming down here."

"You must tell us about him while we eat our picnic," she suggested. "Now, children, everybody help themselves. There's plenty, so don't hold back. Betty, pass the potato salad." They settled themselves cross-legged, facing the tablecloth, the girls careful to adjust their skirts. "Go on, Owen," Mrs. Lloyd directed. "Now everyone listen. Owen's going to tell us about an old, old man named Hermit who used to live right here on this spot. He was a real hermit, too, wasn't he, Owen? You tell us all about him."

Owen was hungry, and so were the others; but he talked while he ate, swallowing hurriedly between sentences. "He was the first white man ever settled in the county," he said. "He got into trouble in Virginia and came here. Virginia was bigger then than it is now. Right here was part of it. Of Virginia, I mean. He dug a hole in the side of this knoll and roofed it over with sticks and mud for a house, and he put the rocks in the spring, to wall it up."

Lew asked: "Did he farm here?"

Owen, his mouth full, shook his head. "It was all trees then, and lots of animals, deer and bears and buffaloes, I guess, and not many Indians."

"When did he come here?"

"Around a hundred years ago, Mr. Beecham says. And then some more settlers came; but when there weren't any deer left so he couldn't kill them to eat, he started stealing the settlers' hogs. Or anyway, they claimed he did, and a man had him arrested, but he couldn't prove anything on Mr. Hermit, so they turned Mr. Hermit loose and whipped the other man for saying he'd stolen his hogs.

"But before that, his twin brother had come here, and the Indians killed him, and after that when they saw Mr. Hermit, they thought he was his brother's ghost, so they didn't bother him. But after it got settled around here, Mr. Hermit moved to Pike County it is now, and lived in a cave till he died."

Betty shivered. "Br-r-r! I hope his brother's ghost isn't around here now. Wouldn't you hate to be here at night?"

Tom Powell winked at Owen and moved away toward the spring, and Jane said: "I don't believe in ghosts!"

Molly Moury said: "Neither do I. There's no such thing!" Bill Myers declared that he had once seen a haunted house and at night you could hear ghosts in it, and Jane and Molly and Janet Frye agreed he was being silly. Then from the direction of the spring came a hollow, hooting groan: "Hoooooo!" Betty clutched Morgan's arm and clung to him.

"What's that?"

"Ghost, sure as shooting," Morgan told her. "Hold on tight. I won't let him grab you!"

But Jane said loftily: "It's nobody but Tom Powell." She called: "Tom, you stop! You're scaring Betty."

Tom came back, grinning; and Betty pretended to be furious with him. Then the boys began to tell ghost stories, taking turns, speaking in sepulchral tones. As their hunger eased, Mrs. Powell said it was time for ice cream and cake; and when they had emptied the freezer, she told Owen they ought to try to find the hole that had been Mr. Hermit's home. Jane reminded her of the promise that the girls might go wading, but she said it was too soon after eating.

They circled the knoll looking for a trace of Mr. Hermit's dugout, but found nothing that seemed likely; so they trooped away down the creek. At the fence, the stream entered a woodlot where cows were pastured, and not far beyond the fence it widened out into a shallow pool that reminded Owen of the swimming hole by Erie Mine. The girls refused to go into the pasture with all those cows, so the boys climbed the fence to drive the cows away, shouting and throwing clods; and Betty called, over and over:

"Come back! Please come back! They'll hook you."

The boys drove the cows two or three hundred yards, and returned like heroes; but the girls still would not venture through the fence, so they all drifted back toward the knoll, pausing to throw lumps of dirt at a green frog on the bank. Halfway to the knoll the boys proposed to build a dam, and they waded into the brook and worked at that awhile, till Jane led the girls away, bidding the boys stay here.

"Because we're going wading," she reminded them, and the girls departed. The boys, at Owen's suggestion, went back down into the the woods to see if the water in that pool was deep enough to swim in. It proved to be almost waist-deep, and they splashed and shouted and threw mud balls and raced along the bank, naked bodies shining in the sun. Owen was the only one among them who could swim at all; he managed a few strokes from knee-deep to knee-deep, swimming dog-paddle, hands and feet splashing to their envious applause.

When they came back to the knoll with sleek wet hair, and wet spots showing on their shirts from dressing before their bodies were dry, the girls were there. Mrs. Lloyd said they had all better stay in the shade and keep cool awhile for a change; so they sat or sprawled, and Tom Powell and Bill Myers started a game of Mumblepeg, and Lew and then Owen and Morgan Williams and Jenkin Powell joined the game, plucking the grass short where the knife would strike. The girls were spectators; and Owen, between throws, watched Jane, and sometimes her eyes met his and she smiled. He was the second to go out, and Jenkin Powell was last. Bill Myers, first out, made the peg and had first licks at it, but he missed it completely. Owen in turn took pains to hit it not only squarely but hard; he drove it flush with the ground, and had a shout of applause, and a humorous groan from Jenkin. When the others had taken their licks, the peg was completely out of sight, but Jenkin shouted "Noseys," so he was allowed to dig a hole for his nose; and then he lay down and plunged his face into the earth and came up with a fine mouthful of dirt and with the peg triumphantly between his teeth, and everyone applauded. Owen decided Jenkin might be all right, after all. He wondered if he would have taken defeat as amiably. But then Jenkin went down to the spring to wash away the mud, and Jane ran to get a tin cup and pour water for him, and Jenkin spluttered and blew and made a great show, and Jane and everyone laughed at him and Owen decided Jenkin was a Smart Aleck, always showing off. He wondered how Jane happened to invite him, how she happened to know him at all; and when they came back from the spring and she sat beside him, he found a chance to ask her.

It turned out that Jenkin was in her room in school. "And he's loads of fun when he gets started," Jane declared.

Owen grudgingly admitted to himself — and then to Jane — that this was true. "I guess so. He used to be a trapper boy at Erie. His uncle's the mine boss. I thought he lived on a farm."

"He does, but after his father died, his mother wanted him to finish school. Jenkin does most of the farm work, too. He isn't going to high school." Next year they would all be in high school together, with Miss Williams again as their teacher. "He's going to stay at home and work the farm."

The Mumblepeg game did not continue, and everyone was drowsy from much food, so for a while they were idle in the shade. Mrs. Lloyd had decided they would wait till it was cooler before starting home, and the sun was low before Lew caught up the horses. Once under way, Owen sat between Jane and Betty; and when the sun set, Mrs. Lloyd thought they must all be hungry, so they gnawed left-over fried chicken and ate dry bread-and-butter sandwiches. As dusk came, they spoke more softly, and they lay down in the soft hay, pushing it into mounds for pillows. Owen's hand touched Jane's, and she patted his hand, and he turned his to clasp hers. They lay side by side, and he was full of a rich, gentle happiness, tired and sleepy and drowsily content. She whispered, her lips close to his ear: "It's been fun, hasn't it, Owen."

"Best fun I ever had."

"I'm glad we're friends again."

"So'm I."

"You were wonderful, telling about Mr. Hermit."

"I'll bet he had fun, living there."

"I'd have been scared. Wouldn't you?"

"I guess so. But I'd have had fun too."

Silence for a space, looking up into the deeps of the darkening sky. "Look! There's a star. Star light, star bright, grant the wish I wish tonight."

"What did you wish?"

"If you tell, it won't come true."

"I made a wish too."

Her hand pressed his. "Maybe we wished the same thing, Owen."

Mrs. Lloyd spoke, from her high seat above them. "Are you all asleep back there? Why don't you sing something?"

So they roused, and they came back into Hardiston at last, the horns blowing, their young voices blending in the night.

                                    4

Additional Locals: There was a wreck on the Ohio Southern; the bridge across Paint Creek collapsed, the engine went into the water, the engineer was drowned. A small tornado swept Hardiston; the wind blew freight cars off the B & O siding onto the main line. Wiley Marshall died after an operation to remove the vermiform appendix; this was a useless, worm-shaped thing — it was called "vermiform," said BB, because it was worm-shaped; and he quoted the Latin — that grew out of the intestines. Sometimes a grape seed or other small hard object lodged in it, and unless the appendix was removed you died. The operation had been successfully performed several times elsewhere in the United States. Hardiston County last year produced 1,499,287 tons of coal, leading the state in total production. Mr. and Mrs. Theodore Mason returned from a trip to California. Mrs. Adelina Fortune, who came to Hardiston in 1866 as the bride of Charles Fortune, died August 24 at her home on Broad Street; her body was not discovered till two days later; a two-gallon kettle half-full of moldy boiled cabbage was found on the stove. There was no other food in the house, and Doctor Mayland, the coroner, said she died of ptomaine poisoning. The Christian Endeavor musicale at the Presbyterian Church

was a success, and so was the Bean Dinner at the Fair Grounds,
where a thousand people ate, at BB's guess, three hundred thousand
beans. Since the Republicans carried the House of Representatives
in 1894, times had been a little better. This year, BB predicted, they
will win the Senate, next year they will elect a President; then all
will be well. A prominent actress — a sketch of her appeared in the
Journal and Owen was fascinated by the opulence of the bosom
which her extremely low-cut gown revealed — wrote a letter to
Lydia Pinkham, saying that her nervous system was shattered and
her health ruined by womb trouble till by following Mrs. Pinkham's
advice and taking her Vegetable Compound she achieved a complete recovery. Owen thought she certainly looked healthy enough
in that picture, deliciously beautiful. A son was born September 9
to Mr. and Mrs. B. Bertram Beecham; thus calmly the *Journal* reported the great event, but BB was jubilant with love and pride.
The last four tracts of land necessary for the electric railway right
of way had been condemned. The Y lecture course would this
winter bring to Hardiston the Royal English Bell Ringers, Mr.
George R. Wendling who would lecture on *Unseen Realities*,
William Colledge who would discuss *Second Fiddles*, and Mr.
Charles T. Quilley who would give some humorous readings. The
Cleveland Administration had been without profit and with very
little honor. On October 8, Bushnell and Foraker spoke in Belton
to two thousand cheering men. A mine tipple in Slacktown burned
and two hundred men were thrown temporarily out of work. By the
end of October, five miles of track on the electric railway had been
laid. The Belton waterworks were a failure, and were for sale. A
merry group of his friends gave Owen Glen a surprise party on his
sixteenth birthday.

5

The late summer and early fall were for Owen and his father and
mother a hard and weary time. A few days after Jane's picnic,
Amy's little Davy, who was just over two years old, died of cholera
morbus. They all went down to the funeral, and because Amy's
fourth baby was expected daily, Mrs. Glen stayed on for another
week. The baby proved to be a boy, and against Mrs. Glen's protests, they named it David, too.

"I told them it was tempting Providence," she said when she came home to Hardiston. "They named their first David, and it lived seven months; and they named their third the same, and now he's dead and gone. But Amy says she's going to give her Dave a son named after him if she has to have twenty young ones to do it. She will, too. Amy's real set in her ways."

"Long as she gets comfort out of it, that's the main thing," Tom said, his arm around her. "Be easy, mama. You're tired out."

"I guess I always will be," she assented, weary in her chair. "Did you and Owen make out all right with me gone?" So she settled again into the hard rule of the days.

A boiler explosion at Erie Mine — which fortunately injured no one — wrecked the tipple; the mine shut down, and since the vein was thinner all the time, Tom thought it might never run again. He and Owen sought work up the creek, but the industry was so nearly stagnant that there was no place for them. After weeks of enforced idleness, during which Owen helped with the harvest on the nearer farms, Tom found a place on the construction crews which were building the electric railway. His task was to cut brush and to help level the right of way; and the work in the open air made him feel young and vigorous again.

The shutting down of Erie Mine for the time dissolved the local; but occasional circulars from Headquarters still came to Owen. President Penna persuaded operators in the Pittsburgh District to advance the mining rate from fifty-nine to sixty-four cents a ton, to take effect October 1; and Hardiston County operators followed suit with an advance to fifty-five cents. Since there was little work, the gain was moral rather than actual; but even this was lost when the Cleveland Gas and Coal Company refused to agree to the higher scale. That was Mr. DeArmitt's company. He refused to make any wage agreement with the miners, and with equal stubbornness he refused to agree with other operators in the Pittsburgh District. When Pittsburgh operators entered into any compact, it was always on condition that the Cleveland Gas and Coal Company would join them; but Mr. DeArmitt would never do so. The man came to personify, in Owen's mind, stupid and malignant greed; but when he said this one day to Isaac Williams, Marged's uncle shook his head.

"He's right by his lights, Owen. George Pullman, Henry Frick, Andrew Carnegie; there's many a rich man thinks he has a right to run his own business his own way. I wouldn't wonder, if you owned a coal mine, you'd feel the same as they do."

Owen was sure this was not true. "I might not want my miners to tell me what I could do," he admitted. "I can see that. But if most of the other owners agreed to something, I'd go in with them. If I was an operator, I'd likely stick with the operators." He added passionately: "But the operators and the miners are all in this business together. They've got to work together, not let one man like Mr. DeArmitt run things."

The older man said in friendly condescension: "A lot of the time, Owen, you sound like the things BB writes in the *Journal*. He's got some good ideas, but he's still pretty young. He's always so dead sure. When you get to be my age there's mighty few things you're real sure of."

"The old men dream dreams, the young men see visions. I know. It's the young men who feel sure. So they're willing to fight, and sometimes they win." Owen asked abruptly: "You know President Ratchford?"

Mr. Williams nodded. "He worked around Massillon when I did. Did I ever tell you about the big strike there in the Valley in 1875, when the men burned the mines, and Major McKinley — "

"Yes, I remember," Owen said quickly, and with a faint sense of guilt remembered Mr. Beecham's statement that no gentleman had ever heard a story before; but it was too late now to recall his word. "He's not very old. President Ratchford. He's young enough to see visions. He called us out last May when there wasn't much work, even if we'd stayed in."

"He didn't win anything by it. There wasn't any sense to it. When you get older, you get so you know, and knowing saves you wasting a lot of energy."

"I hope I never get that old!" Owen's voice was scornful.

"You will if you live long enough." The old man said gently: "And when you're my age — I hope you won't have to take too much lip from some young squirt."

Owen was instantly contrite and ashamed. "Oh, I didn't mean — Well, I didn't — it's just that I get worked up about things."

Mr. Williams chuckled. "All right, son. But I began to think you thought I was Mr. DeArmitt."

Owen when he started for home was still regretful; but though

his affection for Marged's uncle remained unshaken, his respect for
the old man's opinions was no longer blind.

6

Mid-October brought a slight increase in the demand for coal,
and Owen and his father found work at Miss Ellen. When Tom
gave up his job on the construction gang, Owen's mother protested,
urging him to stick to the steady job and steady pay; but he said
hotly: "Steady, my foot. Come Christmas, the railroad will be built
and I'll be out of work. And anyway, Annie, I'm a coal miner, and
likely I always will be."

"Yes, till you're so crippled up with rheumatism you can't swing
a pick! Then I suppose we'll move out to the poor farm."

"It won't come to that yet awhile!"

"It'll come sooner than you think, if you ask me."

Owen hated to hear hot angry words between these two who
were his world; but he thought Tom Glen was right. He said
quietly: "It won't come to that while I'm around, mama."

She brushed her knuckles across her eyes. "Oh, I know, I know.
You're a good boy, Owen." And to her husband, tenderly relenting:
"And you're a good man, Tom. You'll have to let me fuss and scold,
sometimes. It gets the worry out of my system. Let me go ahead
and talk. I know you always do the way seems best to you."

So they returned to Miss Ellen, at first for two days a week, and
then for three. Owen, relieved of the torment of idleness, the
tedium of weary days when he hunted work and found none,
relished the hard toil. His production began to increase; three tons
a day was no longer a distant and almost unattainable goal, and
one day he loaded four cars and heaped the last so high that he
weighed in a few pounds better than four tons; but that was an
achievement he did not soon repeat.

The return to Miss Ellen had numerous indirect results. He re-
newed acquaintance with Ernie Vought, for whom even on their
first encounter he had felt a quick liking which persisted. They
came to be close friends; so close that Owen sometimes thought of
David and Jonathan. It seemed to him Ernie was the sort of man
for whom you could feel real love; the other had so many kindly

traits, so many inconspicuously thoughtful ways. To sit in quiet talk with Ernie was a pleasure as keen as he had ever known; yet the things of which they spoke were simple enough. Ernie's interest in the Union, in mining, in the rights and wrongs of life, was slight. When Owen talked himself into a blaze of indignation at something or other, Ernie listened politely; but when Owen finished and fell silent, Ernie was apt to call attention to a towering white cloud, or to a distant bird song, or he might speak of someone he particularly liked, or of some fine quiet deed. The two were as different as possible. Ernie had the trust and the unquestioning faith of a child; to Owen, every aspect of the world and all its works was open to challenge.

Another incidental result of Owen's return to Miss Ellen was to bring him into more frequent contact with Charles Morgan. Though they were neighbors, their homes only a few hundred yards apart, there had been little to draw them together; but now they rode to and fro on the same train, and occasionally, on the train or on the walk from the siding to the mine, they fell into conversation.

Usually Owen was the questioner; but the man found in the boy much to provoke his curiosity. He felt the impact of that seeking, questing mind, and one day he asked:

"Owen, do you know about the International Correspondence Schools?" And when Owen admitted ignorance, Mr. Morgan said: "You might want to take some of their courses. They'll teach you anything you want to know about mining. I'll give you the address."

The result was that Owen wrote to Box 940, Scranton, Pennsylvania, for the mining circular, and he read it hungrily. There were courses in arithmetic, in drawing, in mine-surveying and mapping and in higher mathematics; there were courses that dealt with the gases found in mines, with mine ventilation, with prospecting, with opening shafts and slopes and drifts, with working methods. The very names of the subjects were like glimpses through a briefly opened door, revealing a rich and fruitful land. Mechanics, steam boilers and engines, air pumps, haulage, hoists and hoisting, mine machinery, percussive and rotary boring — even to read the catalogue made Owen's eyes shine with gluttonous appetite.

But the tuition was two dollars a month for each course, and that was a staggering sum, half as much as the rent of their home. They lived so close to want that two dollars could not be lightly spent, and certainly not now. This dream must wait awhile.

7

Owen gave no thought to his approaching birthday. Beyond one of her rare kisses from his mother, and a clap on the shoulder from his father, these anniversaries had never been marked by any particular observance. Birthdays came and were gone, often completely unremarked.

But since the picnic at Hermit's Fork he had been increasingly conscious that he was growing out of his clothes; that when he stood beside Mr. Beecham he could look down upon the editor. One day, secretly, he measured himself against the door jamb, laying a stick across the top of his head, then twisting out from under it and marking the spot where it had touched the jamb and bringing his mother's tape measure from the cigar box in which she kept her needles and thread. The mark on the jamb was a fraction of an inch more than six feet above the floor; he had grown a full three inches since spring.

He wondered that no one else had noticed, but on the Monday night before his birthday, when he and his father came home from the mine, his mother after supper and before she began to do the dishes, suddenly remarked, "Owen, I've made up my mind." He watched in surprise as she rose and went to reach up to the shelf above the stove for the baking-powder can which stood there. From it she drew a one-dollar bill, and another, and then poured into her palm many pieces of silver. She laid the money on the table in front of him.

"There!" she said in a vigorous tone. "There's five dollars and ninety-one cents." She did not need to count the coins. "You've shot up like a weed this summer, till you're popping out of your clothes. There's a sale at Mr. Lloyd's store, seven- and eight-dollar suits for five dollars and forty-eight cents. You go get you one!"

Owen stared at the money, not daring to look up at her. Four months ago she had offered him seven dollars for a suit; and he remembered how thankfully, when he refused it, she took it back again. But that seven dollars had been only a part of her savings; he suspected the baking-powder can on the shelf was empty now.

"It's all you've got, isn't it, mama?"

"Well, what if it is? You and papa get your pay tomorrow."

"I don't need a suit."

"If you don't, no one ever will! Every time I looked at you last Sunday, I like to died! I told you I've made up my mind. Now hush up and do as you're told!"

Owen wanted to cry; he gulped and looked at his father. Tom was watching him with proud, smiling eyes, and his mother looked happier than he had seen her for a long time, and Owen remembered something Mr. Beecham had once said. "The way to make people happy is to let them do things for you." Certainly his mother and his father were happy now; so he rose to kiss his mother and tried to say something, and choked and could not, and they all began to laugh together, and all talked at once.

"But I'll be working tomorrow, and maybe Wednesday, too. So I can't get it till Thursday."

"Well, the sale's all this week," his mother assured him. "You get it Wednesday if you don't work, and get it Thursday, anyway. They'll likely have to alter it, but make them do it for you that day. The Williamses want us to come to supper Thursday night."

Owen was astonished, for except to go to church socials, they never went to supper anywhere, and no one ever came here. "Come to supper? What for?" he asked stupidly.

"Why, no reason except they asked us. Mrs. Williams and Marged came to see me today." She said with pride, "I guess likely it's because you're there so much, and they like you. So you get that suit. I want you to look nice."

The prospective new suit was excitement enough; but that was not all. Wednesday afternoon on the miners' train, his father said casually: "Owen, you've got some long black hairs straggling around your chin. 'Bout time you shaved them off. I've got an extra razor you can use."

Owen rubbed his hand over his chin. It was true, he felt a few hairs there. He had not been conscious of their existence; for though he always looked into the small and patchy mirror hung beside the kitchen door to part his hair, he and his father sharing the comb which lay on the shelf below, he had never paid much attention to his face. He tried to keep his voice as casual as his father's. "Guess I'd better," he agreed.

He plucked at one of the hairs and felt the prick of pain and

wondered whether Jane had noticed them. He had seen her several
times since the hay-ride, encountering her on Broad Street or on
Main, walking with her as long as their ways coincided. Once she
asked:

"Why don't you ever come down to our house, Owen?" It had
never occurred to him to do so, and his heart thumped. "We sit in
the porch hammock after supper sometimes, and Betty comes over,
and Molly, and sometimes some boys."

"Well, maybe I will," he said huskily; and twice or thrice in
September and once on a warm October night he had walked past
her house in the early dark; but there had been no one on the
porch, and he lacked the courage to knock and ask for Jane.

To think now that Jane might have noticed his hairy chin made
him hot and ashamed. Thursday morning after breakfast his father
brought out the razor, and his mug and brush. Tom usually shaved
only on Saturdays. "But I guess I'd better shave today," he explained. "Long as we're going to the Williamses for supper. You
can watch me and see how to do it."

The razor he gave Owen seemed to be brand new. Tom's own
was old, with a blade worn thin by many honings. Owen watched
his father; and he wondered why his mother sang as she worked.
It was a long time since he had heard her sing.

Then he remembered that this was his birthday, and he started
to tell them that it was about the best birthday he had ever had; but to
say that might remind them that they had forgotten, so he held
his tongue. He realized that he did not even know when their
birthdays came. Probably grownup people did not pay any attention to such things. It was just children who had birthday parties,
like the time he went to Jane's, and they played *Drop the Handkerchief,* and he kissed Jane.

When he had shaved, cutting himself not even once, for his skin
was smooth and clear, he went to town to buy the new suit. Mr.
Lloyd came to wait upon him, and helped him make a selection,
advising him on the quality of the material and the suitability of
the various colors. Blue, Mr. Lloyd admitted, was in the long run
the most serviceable. "But it shows spots and lint. Now this dark
gray pepper-and-salt — "

Owen looked at the price tags, but they were marked with letters
instead of numbers. "I want one that's in the sale for five dollars

and forty-eight cents," he explained; and Mr. Lloyd assured him that the gray pepper-and-salt was in the sale. The coat fitted him across the shoulders, but the sleeves were too long. Mr. Lloyd said they could easily be fixed.

"Today? I want to wear it tonight."

"Today, yes. That looks well on you, Owen. Suppose you try on the pants."

The pants, too, were overlong; but Owen, surveying himself in the mirror, felt an honest pleasure in his own appearance. He sighed in slow decision. "All right," he said.

Mr. Lloyd nodded. "Then I'll have the sleeves and the pants shortened right away." With pins and a flat piece of chalk he marked the coat sleeves and the trouser legs. "It will be ready this afternoon," he promised.

"I'll come get it," Owen agreed. He felt that the waiting would be long, and he went to the *Journal* office, thinking he might tell Mr. Beecham about his purchase. BB was away in the country for the day, but Owen told Will Davis, and Will showed a flattering interest.

"But don't go burning the leg out of it, the way you did your first long pants."

Owen grinned. "I should say not!"

He wandered aimlessly down Broad Street past Jane's house. Of course, Jane was in school, but with a fine new dark gray pepper-and-salt suit, he could come and see her any time. Yes, or go anywhere else he wanted to. He planned to come, maybe tomorrow night, and surprise Jane; but then he remembered that her father would tell her about the suit, so she would not be surprised.

But Miss Williams would be surprised tonight at supper, all right. Owen wondered what Miss Williams would say, and then he thought maybe she would not like the suit; and he remembered in sudden doubt that his mother had warned him to take the suit outside the store and see it in the daylight before he decided. His first thought was to hurry to the store and remedy this oversight, but then he realized that by this time the legs and the sleeves had been cut off, so it was too late! The purchase was irrevocable, and he had miserable fears; but even if the suit was awful, he must pretend it was all right, and wear it, anyway. It would be a long time before he could buy another.

He went gloomily home to dinner, but he answered his mother's questions with a careful enthusiasm. "Just wait till you see it, mama; you just wait, that's all."

When he returned to the store, late that afternoon, Mr. Lloyd made him try the suit on. "To be sure it fits," he explained. Owen took the opportunity to step out-of-doors. It looked all right; but the day was dark and sunless, so he could not be sure. Mr. Lloyd packed the suit in a box for him, and he hurried home and opened the box for them there, and his mother said it was beautiful, and his father pinched the material between thumb and forefinger and said approvingly:

"Good goods, Owen. It'll wear like iron."

So they all dressed in their best and set out for the Williamses, and Owen towered above them both. His mother held fast to his arm, laughing in a high, happy excitement, and Owen wished it were daylight so people could see him. When they reached the house, Mrs. Williams and Marged noticed the suit as soon as Owen came into the lamplight; and Marged made him turn around and turn around, crying:

"Let me look at you! Let me look at you!" Owen obeyed, miserably happy. "It's wonderful," Marged assured him, and Mrs. Williams said:

"You look real nice, Owen."

Even Mr. Williams agreed that the suit looked all right. Owen wanted Morgan to admire it, but Morgan did not appear, and when Owen asked where he was, Miss Williams said he was having supper at Jim Tower's house. If Owen had not been so pleased with the new suit, he might have thought Morgan's absence queer.

Supper would have been a little constrained but for Marged, who allowed no silences and somehow kept them all talking without talking all the time herself. Owen had never seen his mother look so pretty, laughing and happy, her cheeks pink and her eyes bright. Tom Glen and Mr. Williams more than once laughed out loud. Supper was thick onion soup in which were laid slices of dry bread, a wide platter of fried steak beaten tender, a bowl of boiled onions and another of mashed potatoes white as snow, a fragrant flood of gravy, hot home-made bread and butter, grape jelly and gooseberry jam. Owen and his father and mother had lived so long on garden stuff and pork and milk and eggs that they were ravenous at the mere sight of this fine fare.

"I declare," Mrs. Glen confessed, "it's good to eat something you didn't cook yourself, for a change." She and Tom Glen did full justice to the victuals, and Owen, too, though he was handicapped by the necessity of taking care not to spill anything on his new suit.

When they had eaten to full content, Marged bade them all sit while she cleared the table and brought in the pumpkin pies. She went to and fro between kitchen and dining room, refusing any help; and somehow everyone stopped talking, and Owen discovered they were all watching him, and wondered why. Then Miss Williams came from the kitchen with a pie in each hand; and Owen heard other footfalls behind her, and a whisper of low laughter.

And then, pressing past Miss Williams, a dozen people burst into the room — Jane and Betty and Morgan and Jim Tower and all the rest — and they were all laughing and shouting:

"Surprise, surprise! Surprise, Owen! Surprise!"

They crowded around him, laughing and clapping him on the shoulder, and then they waited for him to say something. He was trembling and wanting to cry, and helpless in his chair.

"Aw, Gollies!" he said, and laughed unsteadily and brushed his hand across his eyes.

XV

November 1895 — April 1896

THE SURPRISE PARTY was on Thursday night. Saturday, BB called Owen into the office. "Sit down," he suggested, and he asked, "Is work still slack at the mine?"

"We get in three days, right along; sometimes four."

"Can you dig as much coal as your father?"

"No sir, not very often. I dug four tons one day, since we started at Miss Ellen, but it's mostly about three, or maybe three and a half."

"At how much a ton?"

"Fifty-one cents."

"How does that work out by the week?"

"Well, last payday, I got ten dollars and fifteen cents, even after they took out for my powder and oil and all; but that's for two weeks. I'd worked seven days. There was one payday I got over twelve dollars."

BB nodded, he said in a new tone: "Owen, Mrs. Beecham and I are leaving Thursday for Mississippi, taking the children. I'll come back soon after Christmas, or right after New Year's at the latest. Do you think you could run the office while I'm gone?"

Owen, not understanding, said honestly, "Will doesn't need me, except Wednesdays and Saturdays."

"I mean the front office." BB smiled. "I mean, be the editor." Owen stared at him, and BB said reassuringly: "I know you can take care of the callers all right, find out what they want, get some locals from them." And, seeing that Owen was speechless, he went on: "I'll send out the December bills before I go, and the January bills after I come back, so you won't have to worry about that. As the bills are paid, you put the money in the bank. You'll want to keep a record of what comes in from subscriptions and paid bills, and give receipts for it. I'll tell Mr. Vaughn at the bank to give you the money to pay the girls and Will and yourself. You'll have to measure the girls' work and figure out what's due them. They get twenty cents a thousand, and I call ten inches a thousand ems." He was talking quietly, but perhaps he saw Owen's confused alarm, for he said: "Don't try to remember all this. I'll write it out for you, show you how to keep the books, all that. I'll leave enough copy to keep you going, and you and Will can pick up locals." He hesitated. "Well, how does that strike you?"

"Gosh, Mr. Beecham, I couldn't do all that."

BB smiled. "You wouldn't be doing 'all that' all at once, Owen; you'd only be doing one thing at a time. Any undertaking, seen as a whole, appears impossible; to build a temple, to write a book, to bail the ocean dry. But you build the temple a brick at a time, you write the book a word at a time, you'd bail out the ocean — if you had anywhere to pour the water — a bucketful at a time; and any-one can lay one brick, or write one word, or dip up one pail full of water. You can do it. I'll pay you seven-fifty a week, as I did when you took Will's place; and if you do well, I'll give you some-thing extra when I come home." Owen agreed to try, and BB said: "Good. You'd better start Monday morning; then I can show you everything before I go."

Owen went home between fear and pride. At supper, keeping his tone severely matter-of-fact, he said: "I'm going to lay off from the mine for a month or so, papa."

His mother, serving them, asked quickly: "What for? Sonny, are you all right?"

"Yes, sure; but Mr. Beecham's going to be away till New Year's, and he wants me to run the paper for him while he's gone."

She looked puzzled. "What's the matter with Will Davis? Is he sick?"

"Oh, I don't mean printing and setting type and all that. He wants me to be the editor, do everything he does, write pieces and collect money and pay bills and everything!"

"Well, I never!" His mother dropped into her chair and sat staring; and Tom Glen grunted in doubtful scorn.

"Better stick to your job, Owen. There'll be coal miners after all the editors are dead and gone."

"This is just till January, papa. And I'll be learning a lot."

"You'll be writing pieces, and — doing the business, and every-thing?" When Owen nodded, his father said in a curiously humble pride: "BB must think well of you, son."

Church on Sunday gave Owen an opportunity to tell Miss Williams his news, and she was as happily excited as he. "Can I help you any way at all?"

"I don't think so. I guess I can handle it."

"Well, if you need me, ask me, won't you? I could come after school, maybe help keep the books straight, write things for you."

"You can do that!" he agreed in pleased inspiration. "I mean, write out any items you hear, and bring them in, or give them to me. You know, the 'Additional Locals.'"

"Of course I can! And I certainly will." She looked at him upon a sudden thought. "BB often puts little editorials in among them, says what he thinks about things. Are you going to do that?"

"I don't know whether I'd want to or not. Or have anything to say. I'll ask him tomorrow."

BB, when next day Owen put the question, seemed a little startled; but then he relaxed, chuckled. "Well, an editor takes his chances, Owen. If what you write makes someone mad, you'll have to take the blame." That day and Tuesday and Wednesday he drilled Owen in all he would need to know. He showed the boy the account books in the safe — it was never locked, the combination long since forgotten and the lock jammed and useless — and taught him how to make out receipts and how to record expenditures. Each day, under his eye, Owen made necessary entries. By the time the paper went to press Wednesday afternoon, Owen's fears had given way to a high anticipation; but when BB, on the way to the station Thursday morning, stopped to say goodbye, Owen had to brace himself against a rising panic.

Yet from the first, the work ran with a deceptive smoothness. To fill the paper was easy enough. BB had left a mass of copy; a dozen letters from readers, a score or so of editorial paragraphs to be used as fillers when needed, and a series of six articles dealing with the origin of the alphabet and the development of words. Business houses which carried displays in the *Journal* sent in "readers," short paragraphs of advertising matter which were always printed in the "Additional Locals." Marged came after school almost every after-noon with a grist of items. Correspondents from small communities

in the southern part of the county contributed three or four columns
a week, and there was a steady flow of letters from BB. The first
was a detailed account of the journey to Mississippi, and Owen
decided Mr. Beecham had not intended this for publication, but he
was himself deeply interested in the experiences of the travellers.
BB had written:

DEAR OWEN: *Well, here's the record of our Odyssey. We
rose at 3:30 A.M., for preparations. Our train left at 5:10
A.M. Andrew McAuliffe of Pearl Street, with wife and
daughter Pomona, were fellow passengers; and at Beaver-
town General Preston of Chillicothe boarded the train.
All these friends left us at Glen Jean, and we reached
Thrifton without further incident. The Chillicothe accommodation was thirty minutes late. The ride to Cincinnati
was uneventful except that we passed the remains of a
wreck near Midland. We reached Cincinnati at 11:15 and
boarded the L & N transfer. The car was crowded, and
hot as August. A five-mile ride brought us to Milldale,
Kentucky, where we boarded the regular train for Louis-
ville. There we changed into the Memphis sleeper, on the
same train, and rode to Humboldt, Tennessee. From
Milldale to Humboldt, 400 miles. The sleeper conductor
overcharged me a dollar, and explained it off by showing
me an old rate schedule. My mistake was in giving him
a five-dollar bill to pay four dollars fare. I will make
change myself hereafter in paying a Pullman Pirate. We
reached Humboldt at 2:50 A.M., thirty minutes late. The
expense of our day's travelling was only $6.40. The dis-
tance was 538 miles, but our mileage, $32.30, cost us noth-
ing. I took my family to the hotel and then went to the
M and O station to inquire for my mileage book. I found
a thousand-mile book each for my wife and myself. I then
went to the hotel, paid my bill, $1.50, an extortion, left a
call for 4:45 and retired. Our train came on time, 5:07 A.M.,
and we reached our destination at 1:40 P.M., 743 miles in
all, amounting to $44.60 for railroad fare. This cost us
nothing, our expenses being only $11.00. Mrs. Beecham,
Bertie and Sarah arrived well, but Robert and I had
contracted colds.*

Owen was puzzled by BB's reference to something called mileage; but he showed the letter to Will, who was able to explain. "Newspaper editors always get free travelling on the railroads. The railroads like to keep on their good sides." That impressed Owen. To be an editor, with the privilege of riding free on railroads anywhere, was like being handed a key to the promised land; certainly an editor had this advantage over a miner.

And editing the *Journal* was surprisingly easy. Owen found big John Morgan, the drayman, a fruitful news source; Mr. Moury knew when anyone died; the Court House recorded births and marriages, and Will and Owen garnered many a paragraph from men or women who called at the office.

Mr. Ames dropped in almost every day, sprawling in one of the chairs, reading the dailies which came to BB as exchanges. "Can't see any sense in buying papers," he told Owen. "When BB gets them all and I can read 'em free." He listened openly to Owen's conversations with callers. He was there Tuesday morning when a tall farmer came in to pay his subscription, and Owen asked his name.

"Charlie Patterson," the farmer said; and Owen, writing out the receipt, asked:

"Have any more turkeys stolen after you put out that set-gun, Mr. Patterson?"

"Eh? Oh, you mean last winter. No, that fixed 'em."

A few minutes later, another caller said his name was Taller, Fred Taller. "Ever have any trouble with that dog-bite?" Owen inquired.

"Who, me?" The man stared in surprise; and then: "Oh, you mean here three-four years ago? When I hired 'Lijah Peters's madstone? Hell, no!"

After Taller was gone, Mr. Ames said: "See here, young fellow, how do you know so much? I was in here Saturday, and Neil Palmer came in, and you asked him about that stallion he used to have, Ben Willis, Jr. I've heard you do the same sort of thing before, too. You know every Tom, Dick, and Harry in the county, do you?"

"I've read their names in the paper, that's all."

"And then you remember 'em? Say, you ought to go into politics, if you can remember names like that."

Owen, considering the matter, thought Mr. Ames might be right.

Certainly it was true that during the weeks while he was in charge
of the office, he again and again heard himself make some personal
remark to a caller. Old Aaron Rich had lost a son of the same
name, killed by a fall of slate a few months before. Hugh Barnum
had held exclusive rights to sell *In Darkest Africa* in Hardiston
County, and had advertised for canvassers. Andrew Husted had
some trouble with a tapeworm. John Talcott once shot a wild
goose. William Moore had installed, a year or two ago, the first
vapor furnace in Hardiston. Dan Laban's was the finest orchard in
the county. Again and again, when a visitor gave his name, it
awoke in Owen some association; he saw that men were pleased
thus to be remembered, and recognized in his memory an asset
which might one day prove valuable.

As Mr. Beecham had advised, he tried to read the exchanges, the
weeklies and semi-weeklies and the dailies too; and he cut and
pasted up and printed every paragraph that referred to Hardiston
people. When a former Hardiston man died of hydrophobia in
Columbus, he clipped the whole story, a column long, and headed
it, "Where Was the Madstone?" The man had been bitten in the
cheek weeks before; the wound readily healed, and the victim had
no warning of his impending agony and death until a few days
before he died. In a Cincinnati paper Owen found an interview
with Mr. Mills, chief promoter of the electric railway between
Hardiston and Belton which would connect with the railroad at
the junction beyond Belton. Mr. Mills predicted that the electric
cars would be running by Christmas, and Owen printed that interview in full. When in mid-December, President Cleveland sent a
message to Congress protesting England's attitude on the boundary
dispute between British Guiana and Venezuela, and saying that it
might be necessary for the United States to act under the Monroe
Doctrine, the dailies displayed the message under big headlines,
predicting war with England. Owen wondered whether Mr.
Beecham would want him to print anything about that; but he was
relieved of the decision, for before that week's *Journal* went to
press, a letter from BB enclosed a long editorial paragraph about
the Cleveland message.

The United States can act no nobler part than to protect
the weak. The regular army should be increased at once
to 100,000 men. President Cleveland's Venezuela message

*shows that the elections of '91, '93, and '95 have made him
an American. Toledo, Cleveland and all other American
cities on our frontier facing the Great Lakes should
organize volunteer naval reserves, since in case of war
with England the United States may be attacked from the
Lakes. President Cleveland has the backing of every
American.*

BB's letter had been mailed in Atlanta, Georgia. The editor
wrote that he and Mrs. Beecham were attending the Exposition
there, and he enclosed a column or two of notes with the names of
five Hardiston people he had met at the Exposition.

2

The daily excitement of his work had not made Owen forget that
Christmas was coming, and the fact that each payday put seven
dollars and a half in his pocket made him feel lavishly generous.
His birthday surprise party had been more than an empty gesture,
for everyone brought him presents. Jane's was a beautiful two-
bladed knife with a pearl handle, in a chamois case. He used it to
cut clippings from the exchanges, running the keen blade down the
column rule as he had seen Mr. Beecham do. The knife was his
pride and pleasure, but there were other gifts: a fat book from
Miss Williams containing, in small print, all of Shakespeare's plays;
a slingshot from Morgan Williams — though Owen felt he was too
old to play with slingshots; a necktie from Betty Myers, and a pair
of dress-up shoes from his father and mother; a key ring, three
handkerchiefs, two puzzles, a Logomachy set, a parcheesi board, a
Jews' harp, a set of Authors. Owen was delighted with this treasure-
trove, and as Christmas approached, he wanted to give every giver
something in return.

But that was obviously impossible. To do so would have meant
spending six or seven dollars, and although in his openhanded zeal
he would have done so, he knew too well the thinness of the family
purse. The money he earned he gave to his mother, each payday;
but surely, if he asked her, she would let him keep a little to buy a
Christmas present for Jane; and he wanted to get something for
his father and mother, and for Miss Williams.

He decided at last upon a subterfuge; the week before Christmas, instead of giving his pay to his mother, he waited to see whether she would ask for it. He was prepared to evade the question, to suggest that Mr. Beecham would pay that week's wage when he came back from Mississippi; but she asked no questions, so with seven dollars and a half in his pocket, he felt rich and free.

He knew what he wished to give Jane. She wore a bracelet from which dangled a Trilby Heart and a dozen lesser charms. In the windows of Mr. Jewell's jewelry store — the legend in all the store's advertisements read, "Go to Jewell for a jewel!" — there was a tray of charms. One of them, like a small locket, was of gold, set with an infinitesimal blue stone the color of Jane's eyes, and Owen mustered courage to go in and ask the price.

The charm was twenty-five cents; and his first relief at learning he could afford it gave way to an uneasy feeling that it was too cheap. "Is it gold?" he asked.

"Not solid," Mr. Jewell admitted. "But it will stay bright for quite a while." Owen turned the charm uncertainly in his hands, and Mr. Jewell asked: "Were you getting it for a young lady?"

"Yes sir."

"These charms are a fad now," the jeweller suggested. "But fads come and go. You might want to give her something that won't go out of style."

Owen looked along the showcase. "What?" he asked.

"Well, a spoon is always nice. You might give her a spoon, to start her silver."

"Silver?" Mr. Beecham regularly pointed out in the *Journal* that silver was cheap, and Owen did not want to give Jane anything that looked cheap. "Do they have gold spoons?"

Mr. Jewell chuckled. "I've never heard of one, except the kind rich people's babies have in their mouths when they're born." Owen resented the other's amusement, and Mr. Jewell saw this and added gravely: "They do, yes; but silver is much more suitable for the table. Now here." He produced a velvet-lined tray on which a dozen spoons of different patterns were displayed. "These are handsome."

Owen silently agreed that they were beautiful. "I guess they cost a lot, don't they?"

"Some are two dollars, some two and a half."

That was startling; but Owen surrendered to a reckless prodigality. He wetted his lips. "Well, all right."

"Good. Now which one do you like? Mr. and Mrs. Beecham get one every year for little Bertie's birthday, so when he's twelve years old he'll have a dozen." Mr. Jewell selected a spoon. "This is the kind they gave him this year. Do you like it?" If Mr. and Mrs. Beecham liked that pattern, it must be all right, and Owen was about to assent; but Mr. Jewell added: "They give him a different kind every year."

Owen's eyes blurred with excitement. He was intoxicated by his own lavish generosity; but to choose was beyond his strength. "I like that one," he said, eager to end this ordeal.

"Very well. Now, do you want it marked?"

"What does that mean?"

"Engraved. Her initials, perhaps; or hers and yours. I'll show you." Mr. Jewell went behind the screen and brought out a large serving spoon, engraved in flowing script, "V.E.T." "Mr. Towne is giving this to Mrs. Towne for Christmas; those are her initials."

"How much does it cost to have it marked?"

"Nothing. We always do that."

"Mark it 'J.L.,'" Owen said decisively.

"Perhaps you'd like it 'J.L. from O.G.'?"

"No. She might not want me in it. Just 'J.L.'"

Mr. Jewell produced a card with sample lettering. "Which style?" he asked. "These are script, and these are monograms, and these are block letters."

"Block letters! Those, there!" Owen touched the card with his fingertip. "The others are too fancy."

"I feel the same way myself," Mr. Jewell agreed. "But some people like them fancy. I'll have the spoon ready tomorrow."

Owen left the store, divided between delight in his own audacity, relief that the matter was decided, and fear that Jane would not like her gift. He went on to make other purchases. His mother's teakettle was old and battered, leaks had been soldered in half a dozen places, and the wooden part of the handle had split and fallen off; so now only the rivet remained, and Mrs. Glen, to lift the lid, must first raise the rivet with a knife or a spoon or her fingernail.

So in Humphrey's Hardware, Owen bought his mother a new teakettle, for a dollar forty-eight, and while he waited for his change his eye fell on a large mirror in a yellow oak frame. There was only one mirror in the house at home, and that had lost some of the mercury off the back, and it was so small that Mrs. Glen complained she could not see to put her bonnet on straight. Owen asked the price of the mirror — it was ninety-eight cents — and bought it; and at Lloyd and Powell's he bought a new black tie for his father to wear to church. Miss Williams was a problem, till he remembered — the memory was like an inspiration — that once long ago when she spent the night with Amy while they still lived down at Adams Furnace, she had come down to breakfast with her hair in a braid and tied with a wide blue ribbon, as though she were a little girl. She seemed to him that morning so pretty that he stared at her in rapture, so now he bought for her a yard of ribbon, of that remembered blue.

Christmas fell on a Wednesday, and the *Journal* went to press at noon on Tuesday so that Owen and Will and the girls might have a free Christmas Eve. The Christmas number did not satisfy Owen; there were too many sad things in it. The miners' train struck a man named McCall on the railroad track near Slacktown, and strewed portions of his body for two miles along the rails. A woman who took her husband's dinner pail to him in Tom Darwin Number 3 was killed by a fall of slate; and a fifteen-year-old boy named John Bender threw a switch on the Ohio Southern and derailed an engine. He told Marshal Henson that he had read a dime novel about a wreck, and wanted to see the engine bump along the ties. Miners and operators, meeting in Columbus, reached an agreement. The new scale provided for a raise of six cents, beginning March 1; but if the Cleveland Gas and Coal Company refused to pay the advance, neither would the other operators.

Owen wished there were some way to make the *Journal* look more like Christmas, and sound more like Christmas; but he did not know how to do so. It went to press, and when he and Will had delivered the papers to the Post Office, they locked up the office and started home. They walked together down Broad Street as far as Jane's house. There, Will went on, and Owen crossed the street and turned in at Jane's gate.

Mr. Lloyd answered his knock, and Owen thrust the little packet into his hand. "Christmas present for Jane," he said hurriedly.

"Oh, I'll call her."

"Huh-uh! I've got to go home." He turned away.

"Merry Christmas, then."

"Merry Christmas, yes sir." Owen escaped, stumbling over a dislodged brick in the walk to the gate. Behind him the door closed.

He left the ribbon for Miss Williams. "Marged's gone home for Christmas," Mrs. Williams told him. "But she's coming back the day after for the Teachers' Institute. I'll give it to her then."

"Much obliged." He added, "Merry Christmas," and hurried away.

He decided to wait and surprise his mother and father tomorrow morning, so he hid their presents overnight in the shed, brought them in to the breakfast table. His father's thanks and his mother's delight were all that he had dreamed. They had a fine new cap and a pair of suspenders for him.

3

Big headlines and page upon page of news and conjecture in the dailies had made it clear to Owen that President Cleveland's message to England was important; but full comprehension came only as he listened to the excited talk on the streets. Every caller at the office wanted to discuss the probable war with England. No one seemed at all frightened at the prospect; they were pleasantly excited, and they seemed for some reason proud, as though each one of them had done something brave and wise. The question was, Would England fight? Or would she back down? There were constant arguments, and Owen noticed that the disputants were as likely as not to change sides from day to day.

Marged came up from her home the Saturday after Christmas, to attend the Teachers' Institute which would open on Monday, and Sunday she took the opportunity to thank Owen for his Christmas present. "It's perfectly beautiful," she assured him. "And of course, it's my color! Did you know we all have our particular colors? Ladies, I mean."

"Sort of — colors that you like?"

"Yes, and that look well on us. How did you know this was my special blue?"

"Well —" He hesitated, feeling his cheeks hot; then went on: "Well, you were staying all night with Amy once, and you ate breakfast with your hair in a braid, tied with a blue ribbon like that."

She looked up at him, and she seemed so serious that he was startled. "But that must have been years ago!" she murmured.

"Well, I remember it. You looked so pretty." Her eyes fell as though she were sad. "I thought you'd like it."

"I do." She nodded. "I do, Owen." Her tone changed to a laughing question. "Well, how did the editor of the *Journal* get along while I was away?"

"All right, I guess. Everybody's talking about the war, wanting to know what BB thinks about it."

"What does he think?"

"I don't know."

He saw nothing particularly amusing in that reply, but she laughed so merrily that he grinned with her; yet he asked, "What's so funny?"

"Oh, not funny really." Her eyes met his. "I guess I'm just laughing because I feel like it. Don't you know the way I mean?"

"I guess so."

In the office, questions were still persistent, so it was a relief to Owen when a letter from BB announced that he would return the Friday after New Year's, and enclosed another editorial.

THERE WILL BE NO WAR

Great Britain will not make war on the United States. She cannot afford to. A war with us on account of Venezuela would force her to fight all North and South America except Canada. She would lose one half her commerce, and that she cannot risk.

If she waged war upon us it could only be upon our seaports, but they contain so many British subjects that she cannot afford to bombard them or to levy tribute. Her subjects would suffer from any bombardment, and their property would be seized to pay any tribute demanded.

If she entered into war against us, the nations of Europe would cut up Turkey; she would lose Suez and her road to India, Russia would move into India and we would annex Canada. Her own subjects, Irish, Welsh and Scotch, would volunteer in our armies to wipe out old scores.

The end of it all would be the disruption of the Empire and the annexation of the British Isles as a territory of the United States.

There will be no war.

Owen and Will agreed that BB was right. "Maybe all those things he talks about wouldn't happen," Will commented. "But he's right when he says there won't be any war. That's the main thing. He's right, I'll bet on it."

"The dailies are all talking about our whipping England if we have to."

"We won't have to. They're talking through their hats."

There were enclosed in BB's letter other brief editorial paragraphs.

Hair will grow on the dead, even in the grave, so the democratic party may still accomplish something.

The Cubans seem likely to achieve independence. Let President Cleveland permit free intercourse between Florida and Cuba for thirty days and the deed will be done.

If a shoe factory employing 1500 young men and women were established in Hardiston, our young people could earn a million dollars a year.

Friday, as he had promised, BB came home. Mrs. Beecham and the children, he told Owen, would stay in Mississippi till March 4.

"Bertie's in the first room in school there," he said, and he added in a mirthful tone: "You know that Y-shaped scar on his forehead where he fell on the oil can? The Mississippi boys tease him about it. They say he's branded Y for Yankee." He chuckled, reaching into his pocket. "He wrote us a letter while we were in Atlanta. See if you can read it." And as Owen puzzled over the scrawled lines: "Isn't that quite a letter for a six-year-old?"

"I should say so."

Thus they came to matters of business. "Well, I judge you got along all right without me. Let's go over things."

BB was so well satisfied with Owen's meticulously kept accounts and his orderly records that he paid an extra week's salary as bonus, and Owen went proudly home. But with BB once more in charge, he would not be needed in the office. Monday, with a fine lift of spirit at returning to old familiar ways, he went with his father to board the miners' train.

4

The new agreement between miners and operators was published in full in the *Journal* for January 8, and Owen read it aloud to his father that evening after supper. The agreement provided for a wage scale of fifty-five cents a ton in the Hocking District; and for the abandonment of the long ton in favor of a ton of two thousand pounds; but the coal was still to be screened before it was weighed, the screen six feet by twelve and with bars an inch and a quarter apart.

Since he began to work in the mines, this requirement had become for Owen a personal grievance on which there could be only one opinion. He read that clause and cried: "It's about time the Union put a stop to that, papa! If the operators sell the slack and the little stuff that falls through the screen, then we ought to get paid for it."

But Tom Glen demurred. "I don't know about that."

"You always were against the screens!"

"Well, in a way I was; but you take a miner knows his business, and there's mighty little slack in his coal. A good miner shakes out the little stuff, and he picks out the slate. A ton of coal with him is a ton of coal. But the winter miner that's too lazy to do it right, what he calls a ton may turn out to be fifteen-eighteen hundred pounds of coal and the rest trash. My ton has more coal in it than his. Why would he want to be paid the same as me?

"I wish you'd make up your mind," Owen said half-angrily. "I've heard you get as mad about the screens as anybody. They can't be right part of the time and wrong the rest of the time."

"Yes, and they can," Tom Glen insisted. "Clean coal, my coal, it don't need to be screened; but the sort of trash some men put in their cars ain't coal at all till it's screened and picked over." He said, in what was meant for praise: "You're learning fast, Owen;

but one of my cars will outweigh yours a hundred pounds after they're screened."

Owen was too resentful to speak, yet he knew this was true. Although he was inches taller, and pounds heavier than his father, the older man under good conditions mined four or five tons in a day, while he had never but once mined a full four tons; yet Tom never seemed to hurry. After a moment, Owen said grudgingly:

"I guess so. And you get out more coal than I do. I don't see how."

"You'll learn the knack of it, Owen; how to use your auger, and how deep to make your holes, and how much powder to use. Too deep a hole, you bust out lumps it takes half a day to break up, and if the hole ain't deep enough, or you use too much powder, you bust the coal up too fine. You'll learn, son; you're learning all the time." Tom wagged his head, said again: "But once you get rid of the screens, the man that does a bad job can earn as much as the man that does a good one."

Owen knew a reluctant respect for the pride of men like his father, pride in their craft, pride in their skills. "But not every man can learn to do it right," he urged. "They do the best they can, and it's just as much work to shovel dirt and trash as it is to shovel clean coal." He said hotly: "And anyway, even the poorest kind of miner ought to be paid enough to live on."

"Then a good man ought to be paid more than a bad one," Tom Glen retorted.

Owen reddened, feeling himself in the wrong. "The good men get along all right, but we ought to help out the men that don't have the know-how! And besides, a bad man in a good seam will get out more coal than a good man in a bad seam; and you have to take the room the boss puts you in. John Powell could put you where you couldn't earn much, papa; and he could put me where I could earn more than you."

"He wouldn't do that! He wants good men where they can do good work."

Owen frowned, not with anger but with concentration, trying to see clearly and to put in words an idea just come to him; he forgot his resentment. "Look, papa," he cried. "As long as the operators keep us all trying to beat each other, we'll never stick together. I think every man ought to be paid the same, whether he digs one ton

or five. If the Union could make the operators do that, everybody'd
be for the Union."

"A good man's worth more than a poor one!" Tom Glen was
angry in his turn. "He ought to be paid more."

"No sir!" Owen was so absorbed in his idea that he spoke curtly.
"No sir. Everybody ought to be paid the same."

"Whether he digs five tons a day, or one? Stop talking like a
fool!"

The word was a slap in the face. Owen reddened. "Stop treating
me like a child!"

Mrs. Glen had been making beds and cleaning up their room
and Owen's. She came to the open door. "Owen, mind how you
talk to your father, or big as you are, I'll handle you."

Owen felt the bitterness of the wronged. Why did she always
take his father's side? What was there in Tom Glen which made
her hold him high? What had Tom ever brought her but grief and
sorrow and toil and desperate privation? Where would they be
if he did not earn money and bring it home to her? He remembered
her tender love through the years of his babyhood; and he wished
to be in her arms, close to her, feeling her arms around him. But
she had crossed to where his father sat, and now leaned down
to press her cheek against his father's, and her eyes on Owen were
hard and stern.

Tom Glen said gently: "We're just talking union business, mama.
Owen was reading me the new agreement. Go on, son, read the rest
of it."

Owen obeyed him, feeling lost and alone. The clauses dealt with
the size of cars, the dates that should be paydays, payment in
scrip, deductions from a man's pay, operators were forbidden to
discriminate against a man for refusing to trade at the company
store, and there was a provision for arbitration. Owen read to the
end without comment, nor did Tom Glen interrupt him. Mrs. Glen
had gone back to her bedmaking; and when Owen finished, his
father said:

"Well, that's pretty good, all the way."

Owen made an angry sound. "It doesn't amount to a hoot, papa!
Listen." He read again a sentence in the first paragraph.

If the general price paid for mining in the thin veins of
the Pittsburgh District shall increase or decline, the nine

cents per ton differential shall be adhered to, and all mines in Ohio shall occupy the relative position which now exists.

Tom nodded. "That's always been so, Owen."

"Oh — you sound like Mr. Williams! That clause makes me mad enough to spit! It means that if Mr. DeArmitt, hiring immigrants that can't even speak English, cuts wages, then the other operators in the Pittsburgh District and then here in Ohio will do the same. We don't work for Mr. DeArmitt! He doesn't pay us! But any time he takes the notion, he can cut our pay five or ten cents a ton. That's not right, papa!"

"Well, Owen, a lot of things in the world are so that ain't right. Mr. Evans can't sell coal higher than DeArmitt does, or people won't buy it. When DeArmitt cuts wages, he cuts the price of coal; and Mr. Evans — and every other operator — has to do the same. So they have to cut our wages. It ain't right, but I don't know how we'll ever get around it, things the way they are."

"We will, somehow."

"And anyway, Owen, you're crying before you're hurt. DeArmitt's paying sixty-four cents now, so we go up to fifty-five cents, anyway."

"Not till the first of March."

"I know. But Isaac Williams thinks by that time things will be even better so we'll go to seventy cents Pittsburgh, sixty-one here."

"What does Mr. Williams know about it?"

"Well, he's an old man, Owen." An old man, yes; but age need not bring wisdom. Owen put a bridle on his tongue; and his father said, almost like a plea: "Besides, if business keeps on, pretty soon we'll be getting in five days a week, and maybe six. As long as we can work, we'll get along."

Get along! Get along! Tom Glen's passivity, his willingness to endure no matter what mistreatment as long as they could get along, seemed to Owen abject and craven; but he held his tongue. "Guess I'll take a walk," he said, and rose, and put on cap and reefer and opened the door. His mother called:

"It's bedtime, Owen."

"I'll be back pretty soon." He shut the door behind him and strode away, his angry thoughts churning. Why were old men always so sure they were right? Why did his mother always take

his father's side? He felt himself cast out from their close community. Suppose he did not go back to the house; suppose he went
away and left them to each other. He knew he would not do so,
yet he was young enough to find a bitter content in pretending
that he might, in imagining their sorrow and their longing for him
to return. The night was cold, and he turned up the collar of his
reefer and walked faster, relishing the warm blood-beat through
his body, the iced wind on his cheek. He tramped the length of
town and back, and so came home more at ease, and loving them.
Their light was out when he came in, but the lamp turned low in
the kitchen and the warm stove welcomed him, and his mother
called to him softly through the open door. Owen went in to touch
her head, and her hand clasped his, while Tom Glen, on his back
beside her, snored and snorted. She whispered something, and he
bent to hear.

"You weren't here for prayers, Owen?"

"I'll read a little now, and you pray with me."

She touched his cheek, and in the kitchen he turned up the lamp
and opened the Bible and read in First Samuel of the calling in the
Temple. When he knelt, he saw her watching him; his head bowed
and their prayers joined.

5

Additional Locals: Tickets on the miners' train have been reduced
to $2.00 for fifty-four rides. It was proposed to establish Judea as a
refuge for persecuted Jews from Russia and Germany, and BB said
the time was ripe for this to be done. Utah on January 4 became
the forty-fifth state in the Union. Let the eagle scream! The proposal to raise the tax on saloons to $500 would put the poor men
among the saloonkeepers out of business, allow the rich saloonkeepers to make their places more attractive, and thus increase
drinking. If good reading matter were brought within reach of all,
the dime novel would soon disappear; Hardiston should have a free
public library. This was Leap Year, but the intelligent girl would
only propose to a man if she knew not only him but his parents,
and only if he were older than she — because in twenty years that
would make a lot of difference — and only if he were blue-eyed —

because blue-eyed men lived longer — and only if he had strong healthy teeth and a good breath. *The Prodigal Father* delighted a large audience at the Rink. Forty-six Hardiston men went to Governor Bushnell's inauguration. Foraker was elected to the Senate. On January 21, the rails of the electric railway, which would be called the Belton-Hardiston Belt Railway, crossed the Hardiston corporation line. Doctor Williams's Pink Pills for Pale People had proved a Godsend to many women. *A Thoroughbred,* coming soon to the Rink, was not in the least like Ibsen; it was true dramatic art. Hardiston County in 1895 paid $1009.92 for sheep killed by dogs; but why not kill the dogs and give the money to indigent old soldiers? The United States should end the Turkish massacre of Armenians if it took the last dollar and the last man. Cuba should be free, and if given the chance enough Americans would volunteer to make it free. A tumor weighing 97¾ pounds was removed from a Scioto County woman who weighed 175 pounds; she then died. A committee would investigate the question of building city waterworks; it would be necessary to avoid failures like the waterworks in Belton and Chillicothe and Portsmouth. Banks were failing, factories were closing all over the country; keep Hardiston sound. Every miner should plant a garden next summer; a two-acre garden will yield $100 worth of food. Every farmer should raise sheep for their meat; mutton was medicine. Onions and pineapples were cheaper than doctor's bills. The man who starves his wife should face the whipping post, tar and feathers, and a ride on a rail; and certain men in Hardiston would profit by remembering this. The Sunol, the Hercules and the Stella were the three best bicycles on the market. The banquet February 13 to welcome the Belt Railway to Hardiston was a great success; but President C. C. Waite of the Hocking Valley, the principal guest, fell ill next day with a congestive chill and died a week later. Mrs. Madison Vane was hostess at a delightful progressive Crokinole party. The new Belt Railway fare from Belton to Hardiston would be fifteen cents. Cars would leave Hardiston at 5:45 A.M., 6:00, 6:15 and hourly thereafter till 3:30; then half-hourly till 6, then hourly till 10:00 P.M. The schedule from Belton to Hardiston would correspond. February 21, the mercury touched 9° below zero. On February 26, the first electric car ran a trial trip with a distinguished group of guests. In Hardiston more than

2000 people inspected the interior of the car. March 4, there were
27 persons in the county jail, the largest number on record. Mrs.
B. Bertram Beecham and three children returned March 20 from
Mississippi, where they had spent the winter with relatives. Miss
Fan Minor, a cousin, came with them. Miss Minor was the guest
of honor at a trolley party March 29. The guests went to Belton in
a special car to attend the Presbyterian Church Social there, and
returned at midnight. The Belt Railway, making it easier to come
and go, will increase crime in Hardiston, and all law officers
should be on their guard. On a car a few nights ago, the engineer
had trouble with four Belton toughs. He had all four men on the
floor at one time. William Tutson was the first man killed by the
electric cars. He fell asleep on the track April 20 and was run over.
His daughter Eleanor is a valued employee of the *Journal*. Congressman Fenton, in a stirring speech in the House of Representatives on Cuba's fight for independence, said in part:

> *I favor the resolutions touching the recognition of the
> belligerent rights of the struggling Cuban patriots. I
> take it that to do so is no infraction of international law;
> but even if it were, international law is largely the product
> of monarchical governments, formulated with a view to
> their interests. But there is a higher law which demands
> intervention when the iron heel of tyranny seeks to de-
> stroy the inherent rights of man. Even though interna-
> tional law seems to legalize the butchery of helpless
> human beings made slaves by a relentless despotism, there
> should be no delay in thrusting it aside to succor the
> heroic and long-suffering people of Cuba.*
>
> *To withhold our protest against this revival of the
> modes of warfare practiced in the Dark Ages would be
> either a confession of weakness on our part, or a tacit ap-
> proval of the war of extermination practiced by General
> Weyler and his hordes. Let us send the greeting of 70,-
> 000,000 freedmen from the oldest and greatest Republic
> in existence, to the newest, the beautiful Queen of the
> Antilles.*

6

Nellie's father was killed late Saturday night, at the corner down near the railway station where the electric cars turned up Elm Street to Main. When the car approached, he was lying on the track just around the curve, so that the headlights — swinging as the car turned — did not reveal his body till too late. Owen heard of his death on the way home from church next day, and he decided to go see Nellie and her mother and tell them he was sorry.

After dinner he set out, and thinking Will and perhaps Mrs. Davis might want to go with him, he stopped at Will's home; but seven-year-old Annie told him: "Papa and mama are over at Mr. Tutson's. He's dead." Lulu Harned was with Annie on the front porch, and the two little girls were cutting out paper dolls.

"Where's Bill?" Owen asked. Bill was the five-year-old, a rowdy youngster always ready for rough tumbling play, and Owen and he were friends.

"Lulu put him to bed to have his nap," Annie explained. "Mama told us to do whatever she said."

Owen thought Lulu was going to be a mighty pretty girl, with her fair hair and deep brown eyes. In fact she was already pretty, though she couldn't be more than twelve or thirteen. "Bill mind you, does he?" he asked, in a jolly tone.

"He does when I pretend I'm his mama!"

"I'm too old to have naps," Annie boasted.

"You're pretty grown up, all right," Owen agreed. He was smiling as he went on toward the Tutsons'; but then, remembering his errand, he ceased to smile. He found Mrs. Tutson and Nellie sitting with a small circle of friends. Mrs. Lewis was among them, though Owen had not known these two knew each other. Will's wife, sitting next to Mrs. Tutson, smiled at him in that beautiful, gentle way she had; and he spoke to Mrs. Tutson and to Nellie, feeling large and awkward because there were only ladies in this room, the menfolk all in the back room with the coffin, or in the kitchen. Mrs. Tutson said much obliged, and Nellie thanked him and he saw her lip tremble, and a great tenderness filled him. He wished to take her in his arms and comfort and caress her; he could not do this under so many eyes, yet the impulse persisted.

Next day he went to Mr. Tutson's funeral, walking the long two miles, remembering Willie's funeral four years ago. But on the day of Willie's funeral it rained; today was fine, the sort of day only April can provide. Nellie was taller than her mother, supporting Mrs. Tutson on her arm as they walked from the grave back to their carriage; but when they passed near Owen, he was reminded that though she towered over her mother, she was actually very small herself. She met his eyes, and hers warmed with friendliness so that she seemed to smile; and his impulse to tenderness was strong. Wednesday in the *Journal* office he came beside her stool and put his arm around her shoulders and gave her a fine hug; and if she had looked toward him he would have kissed her, but she only said: "Hello, Owen; thanks," and went on setting type. He did not feel rebuffed; his gesture had been a clumsy attempt to express his sympathy and he knew she understood.

Except for his brief sympathetic sadness for Nellie's grief, that was a happy winter and spring for Owen. After Christmas, Jane wrote him a note to thank him for her spoon; and Mrs. Lloyd, when they met on Main Street by the Post Office, said approvingly: "Such a thoughtful thing to do, Owen; to give her something nice which she can always keep. Not many boys would have thought of it."

"It was Mr. Jewell," Owen admitted. "He said it would be nice."

"It is, but many boys would have insisted on some worthless trinket." She nodded a pleasant farewell. "You must come and see us. Jane has homework every night except Friday and Saturday, but come either of those nights, whenever you can."

A few days after that encounter with her mother, he met Jane and Betty Myers — they were almost inseparable — and Jane thanked him again for the spoon. "I've put it away safe," she said. "And I'm going to keep it till I" — she hesitated, her cheeks bright — "till I'm grown up."

Betty giggled, and Owen knew what Jane had been about to say; and he realized that Jane was as old as Amy had been when she and Dave were married. Of course, he was not as old as Dave had been; but he soon would be; just three or four years. He dreamed some blissful dreams, till he read in the *Journal* what Mr. Beecham said about Leap Year and about the tests a girl should apply to choose a husband. He did not measure up to Mr. Beecham's qualifications, except perhaps the one about having good teeth; for Jane was a year older than he, and instead of blue eyes his were so dark as to be almost black. That depressed him; but maybe Mr. Beecham was wrong.

The day the first electric car came to Hardiston, he met Jane and Betty in the throng, and together they climbed into the car, moving with the flowing stream of sightseers. They tried the seats, waved at friends through the windows, and inspected the controls and rang the bells. Betty and Jane decided on the spot that they would organize a trolley-ride for some Saturday after warm weather came, and take a picnic and get off at some station up the creek and spend the day. They said Owen must come, and he nodded hopefully.

March was mild, and April brought warm growing weather; and Jane and Betty organized the trolley picnic up the creek. Owen, although the picnic was to be on Saturday, expected to go, and discussed with them their plans, suggesting that they leave the trolley at the Miss Ellen stop and walk up to the head of the valley. They decided upon this; but the day before, Will Davis went to bed with a heavy cold that threatened pneumonia; and BB asked Owen to fill Will's place on Saturday.

He agreed, and went to tell Jane he could not go with them, and she was disappointed. "But you come to our house tomorrow night and hear all about it. Mama says we must be home before dark, so you be sure to come."

Owen promised to do so; and next evening as he approached the house, the sound of many voices on the porch gave him courage. He found them all gathered in the shadows on the veranda, to live over again their happy day. They had followed the siding as far as Miss Ellen, and then the road that dwindled to a path along the creek bank. At the head of the valley, they climbed out to picnic above the falls where the creek trickled over a conglomerate shelf; and afterward they picked flowers which soon wilted, and they climbed the hill to look out to the south and west over other hills bright in spring greenery, and then raced headlong down the hill to the falls again.

Thus sped the afternoon, and they relived it now, laughing at remembered incidents, and Owen laughed with them. This was to be the first of many occasions when Owen spent the evening on Jane's porch. Sometimes others were there, but not always. One evening, when he came before any others and they heard voices approaching, Jane caught his hand and led him around the corner of the house to the side yard. There a peculiar tree with branches that hung low, almost touching the ground, had been converted by Mr. Lloyd into a shaded retreat for hot summer days, with a circular seat built around the tree.

"I used to play house here when I was a little girl," Jane whispered to Owen, that first time she took him there. "Betty knows about it, but I made her promise not to tell. We'll keep quiet and they'll never find us."

Owen had a delightful sense of a secret shared, of something intimate and excitingly clandestine about their hiding place. When calls sounded from the sidewalk in front of the house, she held his hand to warn him to silence till the visitors went away. After that first occasion there were others, equally intoxicating. In that retreat, they always talked in whispers, and this brought their heads close together. One night, to his amazed delight, and almost by accident, he kissed her. They were whispering and he leaned nearer, and she bent her head and turned it half-away, and without premeditation his lips touched her smooth cheek.

She murmured: "No, Owen, we mustn't," and he said he was sorry; but that was not their last kiss. Their evenings in the arbor were always short, because at half-past eight Mrs. Lloyd called Jane in; but these hours together left him drunk with happiness. Usually he and Jane held hands, talking gravely about matters completely impersonal, each pretending not to know that their fingers intertwined; but twice more after that first time, he kissed her, and once when her mother called her — they had been talking gravely and solemnly about God, and about being good, and working hard, and always aiming high — she swiftly kissed his cheek before she went to answer her mother's call.

Owen decided that he and Jane were in love. Theirs was a holy love, grave and restrained and undemanding. He had never heard of Sir Galahad, but he determined for Jane's sake to devote himself to a lifetime of selfless endeavor. He would do fine Christlike deeds for her; and he imagined himself as a bearded man with gentle, kindly eyes, wise and just and full of good works. His love for her made him grieve for his past wickednesses; but he believed profoundly in repentance and the forgiveness of sin, if you took care to sin no more.

Yet the sins of the fathers were visited upon their children. Would his sins, even after they were forgiven, be visited upon his children? He put the frightening thought aside, because it was wrong to think about having children; yet though he accepted this dogma as true, he perceived a contradiction. One way to be good was never to think about having children, but babies were things fathers and mothers were proud of, so surely they were not the fruits of sin.

Maybe babies came to people who loved each other just because they loved each other, and not for the same reason that colts and calves and little pigs were born. The Bible said babies came when a man knew a woman, and he remembered that Dave and Amy had used to walk together to learn to know each other. He contrived occasions when he could walk with Jane. It was too bad they did not go to the same church. Walking home from church was certainly a way to know each other. He and Miss Williams so often did this that he knew her better than he knew anybody; there was between them a quick eager reaching of mind to mind which no one else provoked in him. When his father, or Isaac Williams, said something with which he disagreed, he felt a mysterious resentment at their ignorant stupidity; but if he and Miss Williams thought differently about anything, it somehow made him like her better, even while he tried to help her understand why she was wrong.

This fine closeness between him and Miss Williams probably resulted from their walks together; and realizing this made him feel that by liking Miss Williams he was wronging Jane. So he made every possible occasion to walk with Jane; and when they were together, he, shortening his steps to match hers, felt the bond of the shared rhythm drawing them close together, felt himself strong for any task and capable of any greatness.

Once he spoke to Mr. Beecham about this mystery, this fact that walking together drew people closer. They were off to the country, and though he was taller than Mr. Beecham, they were both long-bodied, their legs short in proportion to their height; so it was natural for them to keep step. It happened they were silent for a while, marching like soldiers; and Owen remembered what his mother had said long ago, that soldiers marched in step to learn how to fight together, and spoke of it.

"Is that true?" he asked. "Is that the reason?"

"It's one of the reasons," BB agreed. "Of course, a principal reason is to give them exercise, strengthen their legs so they can march long distances; but marching in step helps weld them into a unit."

Thinking of soldiers prompted Owen to ask, "Do you still think there won't be any war?"

"You're remembering that editorial I sent you from Mississippi last winter?"

"Yes sir."

"I've regretted that, more than once." Owen looked at him in surprise. "That was the sort of editorial a twelve-year-old boy might have written. I should have known better."

Owen hesitated. "I didn't see how we could ever annex England the way you said we would," he admitted. "But it sounded to me as if you were right about there not being a war."

"Yes, I was right about that; there'll be no war. England won't go to war over anything as little important as a few square miles of Venezuela jungle. We talked mighty biggity, but that was because we're still pretty young, and like to carry a chip on our shoulder. Boys fight, but grown men — really grown men — settle their disagreements in peaceable ways."

"I haven't had a fight for a long time."

"I know. You're growing up. A hen a year old is pretty well grown up, or a two-year-old dog, or a three-year-old horse, or a twenty-year-old man, or a thirty-year-old elephant, or a hundred-year-old alligator, or a five-hundred-year-old nation. The United States is still a boy." He laughed in sudden amusement. "And when I write a Tom-fool editorial like that one, so am I."

They left the Pike to turn cross country, following a stump fence that divided a woodlot from plowed land. "How long does it take a country to grow up?"

"Some never do, just as some boys never do. Growing up isn't as automatic as it seems to be. Of course, for a while, nations — and boys — grow up fast, they learn fast. A baby learns faster than a man because its head is a third of its body, and man's head is only an eighth of his. Boy babies learn to walk, and to talk, and to fight with other boys; and then they begin to feel a new kind of strength, the beginning of physical manhood. They begin to feel differently about girls."

Owen, since between the fence and the broken ground there was only a narrow path, walked behind Mr. Beecham yet close enough to hear. The editor continued: "A boy begins to realize he can do something he couldn't do before, but he doesn't comprehend the consequences which may follow if he does it. Vice, you know, is not a single hound, but a pack. He doesn't guess that he may get sick, or that because of him some girl may have a baby for whose life he is responsible, or that he may find himself married to the wrong kind of girl and his whole life ruined."

"I guess it's pretty important who you marry."

"It's the most important thing a man ever does. The important thing is to marry a woman who loves you — because, after all, you can't build a fire with icicles. And marry a woman who is smarter than you, more intelligent than you, with a headstart on you in some respect, if not in all ways. Then she can help you up to her level. That's particularly true of the uneducated man. The function of education is to anticipate the lessons of experience; so an uneducated man should marry an educated woman, so she can share with him the lessons she has learned.

"But I was talking about boys and nations. They're much alike. When they're young and strong, they don't realize that if they use their strength, incalculable consequences may result."

"What's 'incalculable'?"

"Something you can't plan on, or foresee. Every action has results, though we don't always know it. Because a blacksmith was careless, a nail came out, the shoe came off, the horse went lame, the messenger riding the horse was late, the battle was lost, the war was lost and a great empire fell — and all because of a careless blacksmith. Everything matters. If a strong young man strikes an old man, he may cripple the old man for life — and have to support him and take care of him from then on. Getting back to that silly editorial of mine, if we went to war with England and beat her and annexed the British Isles, we'd have to protect her and take care of her forever; so actually, we would lose more than she. It's the victor who always pays; the beaten nation can't. The loser has nothing left with which to pay. The only thing more costly than defeat is victory."

He chuckled at himself. "I can see all these things clearly enough when I'm talking with you, quietly, out here in the country; but writing at my desk, led astray by my own thoughts, I can be as absurd as I was in that editorial. Someone said, 'Oh, that mine enemy would write a book.' That was because a man can say a thing and then deny he said it, or insist he didn't mean it; but when a man writes a book or a newspaper editorial, and it's printed, he can never take it back. It can always be thrown up to him. Writing is a dangerous profession. I've heard that you make good speeches, Owen. Take my advice. Make all the speeches you like; but don't ever write a book."

7

Through those spring months, though Jane filled his dreams, Owen had other things to think about. Under the December agreement, the new wage scale of fifty-five cents a ton was scheduled to go into effect on the first of March. The operators not only anticipated that date and began to pay the higher rate before the agreement bound them to do so; but on the thirty-first of March they advanced the rate per ton to sixty-one cents, and the Pittsburgh rate went up to seventy cents.

But, alone among Pittsburgh operators, DeArmitt's Cleveland Gas and Coal Company refused thus to raise the wages of its men, and this seemed likely to force the whole Pittsburgh District, and the Hardiston County operators, to return to the lower scale. The miners began to discuss among themselves whether if that happened they would strike, and the officers of the Sub-District called a meeting to consider the situation.

Erie Mine, idle for weeks after the boiler explosion wrecked the tipple, had before this resumed operation, but with a reduced work force; so Tom Glen and Owen and Isaac Williams and some others stayed on with John Powell at Miss Ellen. They became members of Miss Ellen local, which included not only the Miss Ellen but three other Moses Evans mines, and was the largest in the Sub-District. At Erie, Owen as secretary-treasurer had felt

himself a person of some importance. In Miss Ellen, he was am-
bitious to achieve distinction, and he took every opportunity to
talk with his fellow workers, asking questions and listening to their
answers, remembering their names and small details of their personal affairs, seeking friendships everywhere.

When the call for a meeting was issued, Owen went to Moses
Evans at his home in Hardiston. He had long since learned to
respect the operator who once had seemed to him so heartless, and
even to feel for him a certain affection.

"Everybody's scared, Mr. Evans," he explained. "They think
DeArmitt's apt to make you all go back to the old rate, and some
are saying we ought to strike if you do. I wanted to find out what
you think about it."

The old man rubbed his hand across his bearded chin. "As
long as the Pittsburgh District doesn't cut its scale down to meet
DeArmitt, we're all right to go on paying sixty-one," he said. "I
want to pay it, and I guess most Hardiston County operators feel
the same. I know Mr. Canter does. But warm weather's coming,
business is bad and getting worse, there won't be much market for
coal except the Lake trade — and we'll have to meet Pittsburgh
prices to get any of that. If they cut the scale, we'll be hard put to
it. But I'll pay sixty-one cents as long as I can still do it and make
money."

"Will Mr. Canter?"

"Yes, as long as he can."

"Can I tell Mr. Morgan that?" Charles Morgan was president of
the Miss Ellen local.

"Certain. It's true."

At the station waiting for the miners' train next morning, Owen
found Mr. Morgan, and they sat together on the train while Owen
reported this conversation. The other asked curiously: "How'd you
happen to go to him?"

"I thought it might help us decide what to do if we knew how
he felt."

"Know him well enough to go to him like that?"

"We rent our house from him. And he's been all right to us."

"Mose has changed," the older man commented, in a reflective
tone. "I've known him since I was a boy. My father owned all that
land where you live now, all down the other side of the grove and
along where the slack pile is, and on down to the tracks. He

opened up the Morgan Mine there, and before he died, he sold out to Moses Evans. I worked there till the vein played out. There was a ventilating shaft used to come up in what's my back yard now. And I've worked in one of Mose's mines ever since." He smiled faintly. "Mose always did talk hard, but he never was as hard as he talked; and since he had heart failure, he don't talk as hard as he did." Mr. Morgan looked at Owen thoughtfully. "You want to get ahead, don't you?"

Owen's jaw set, he said through tight lips, "I'm going to." He hesitated. "But I want to get ahead by making things better for all of us, not just for me."

"I was a Knights of Labor man myself, but the Union is all right. Ever read the Preamble to the Union Constitution, Owen?"

"Yes sir. I just about know it by heart."

"Me too. Better wages, paid in money, paid every week; safer mines; honest weights; no Pinkertons; no children working; an eight-hour day. That's the whole story. That's not very much to ask."

"I couldn't have gone to work when I did," Owen reflected. "If they didn't let children work under fourteen. I wasn't fourteen till about two months after."

"I started at thirteen, too. Plenty do. But that clause is like the eight-hour day, Owen. Its real purpose is to spread the work around."

"How do you mean?"

"Why, the more children work, the less work there is for men. And the longer one man works, the less there is for other men to do."

Owen spoke in thoughtful understanding. "I see. I wondered why they wanted a shorter day. I'd just as soon work longer, only the smoke after your shots drives you out."

"So would lots of men. There's some now that go back into the mine at night, after the smoke clears and shoot down some more coal. Night-hawkers, we call them. That ought to be stopped, too. And an eight-hour day will spread the work, give work to men that need it. Four men can do in ten hours what it takes five men to do in eight."

"The Preamble says they want an eight-hour day because it's too hard on men to work long hours in a mine."

"Maybe. But there's plenty want to do it, ten hours, and longer, too. No, the real reason is to make work for more men." The train slowed for the Miss Ellen siding and they rose to alight. "You'd better go to the meeting Saturday," Mr. Morgan suggested. "Tell them what Mr. Evans said."

Owen did so; he quoted what Mr. Evans had said about his own plans, and about Mr. Canter's. "And therefore, Mr. Chairman," he said, "I move you that a committee be appointed to meet the operators and talk things over. They want to keep running, and we want them to keep running. If we put them out of business, we put ourselves out of work. Strikes hurt us all, so let's not talk strike till we have to."

The motion was carried; the operators agreed to maintain the sixty-one-cent rate as long as they could sell coal at a profit, and in that precarious balance conditions rested for a while. But Owen had again attracted attention and respect. The fact that during BB's absence he had acted as editor of the *Journal* gave him additional prestige; and when Enoch Madison, the secretary-treasurer of the Miss Ellen local, was killed by a fall from the loading chute while weighing coal, Charles Morgan named Owen to fill his place until the next meeting, and at that meeting Owen was elected in due form.

XVI

May 1, 1896 — September 1896

I n HARDISTON, the campaign of 1896 was formally opened by the Republican County Convention, and BB advised Owen to attend. "This will be the most important election since 1865," he explained. "We've had two Democratic Administrations since the War; the first was a failure, and the second has been a catastrophe. If the Democrats win in November, we'll have a panic from which the United States may never recover; so the next six months will decide what sort of country you will live in when you're a man."

"Just a county convention won't make any difference," Owen objected. "And anyway, I can't vote this year, nor even four years from now. I've got time enough."

"'Time Enough' lost the race. And the county conventions are the foundations of the whole political structure."

The convention opened on May Day, when the mine did not run; so Owen, though reluctantly, took Mr. Beecham's advice, and at one o'clock he was in his seat in the Court House. The proceedings followed the pattern set down in *Robert's Rules of Order*. First came the reports of committees: on Credentials, on Rules, on Delegates, and finally on Resolutions. The Resolutions, adopted without debate, congratulated the Legislature on electing Foraker to the Senate; they endorsed Bushnell for Governor, Van Pelt and Crandall for State Representative and State Senator, Congressman Felton for re-election, and Major McKinley for President.

The only business remaining before the convention was the nomination of candidates for Sheriff and Infirmary Director. For Sheriff, ten names were presented. On the first ballot, no man received more than 26 votes, nor less than 14. As the balloting proceeded, the contestants remained for a long time on almost even terms, and Owen felt a rising excitement. He forgot to go home for supper, and when after the fortieth ballot no agreement had been reached and a motion to recess was put to a vote he wanted to shout: "No, no, no."

The motion was beaten, and after the fifty-first ballot another motion to recess was lost. Not till five o'clock in the morning, and on the 191st ballot, was Mr. Drake nominated. His speech of acceptance had a riotous reception.

It was the first time Owen had stayed up all night, and the intoxication of this experience had kept him from realizing he was sleepy; but now, in the reaction after long attention, he stumbled toward the door. Behind him he heard the first nominations for Infirmary Director, and he hesitated, thinking he might stay; but weariness overwhelmed him and he trudged homeward through the early dawn.

He found his mother awake and so nearly frantic with fear that when he came down to the house she ran to meet him and reached up and boxed his ears, crying: "Wherever have you been? What have you been up to?"

He caught her close and she struggled to be free. "I went to the convention, mama. I told you I was going to."

"Conventions don't last all night!" She was raging in relief from terror, and he laughed in reassurance, drew her close again.

"This one did."

She began to cry. "I thought you were dead, or something!"

"Papa could have found out where I was."

"Oh, he said you were all right. He wouldn't go hunt."

When her tears were dry, she would have bidden him off to bed; but he refused to go. "I'm not tired, just hungry. I'll have to be at the *Journal* office by seven. No time to sleep."

At breakfast she and Tom Glen agreed that it was nonsense for two or three hundred men to sit up all night making fools of themselves like that. Owen tried to make them understand the excitement he had felt. "It was like watching a race, or a baseball game or something. One of them would be ahead for a while and then another and then another. Mr. Beecham stayed there all night too."

"More fool he! With all his brains, staying up all night to listen

to a pack of blathering men." But Owen laughed at her heat, and
Tom Glen chuckled.

"'Twon't be the last time Owen's out all night, mama. You might
full as well get used to it. Been times enough in the old days when
I didn't get home till day."

"Yes, with that dratted Knights of Labor. I know! Thank goodness that's over, anyway. The Union has sense enough to meet
by the light of day. Now set, Owen, and I'll give you breakfast."

Owen reached the *Journal* office promptly at seven, but not till
afternoon did BB appear. When Owen asked what he thought
of the convention, BB laughed. "Foolish waste of time. It took
three hundred delegates twenty-four hours to nominate candidates
for Sheriff and for Infirmary Director. The offices aren't worth it."
He added in a sober tone: "If the Republicans can't learn to
manage things better than that, the Democrats will beat them in
the fall. Here are some editorial paragraphs. Send them up to the
girls, will you?"

Owen, since Will at the moment had no task for him, set these
paragraphs himself.

> *No good American is an enemy to silver. Silver pro-
> ducers are entitled to the protection given other busi-
> nesses, but only American silver should be coined.*

> *Money in circulation in the United States amounts
> today to $22.00 per capita. There should be more.*

Owen thought those paragraphs had a new sound. Mr. Beecham
in the past had persistently ridiculed the Free Silver men, and
opposed their proposals. That afternoon while the press was
running, BB came into the pressroom, and Owen spoke of this.
"It sounded as if you thought coining silver might be all right,
after all."

BB nodded. "The only good politics is winning politics, Owen.
It won't help the country for the Republicans to insist on a gold
coinage, if by doing so they lose the election. The poor man knows
that if there were more money in circulation, his share would be
larger; so he's as strong for Free Silver as the rich man is strong
against it. And I don't want to see the Republicans alienate all the
Free Silver votes."

"What is Free Silver, anyway? What does it mean?"

BB said thoughtfully: "I'm not sure I understand, myself, but I'll try to give you an idea. The thing to remember about money is that it's of no use till you spend it, so its value to you is what you can buy with it.

"Money is based on faith. Anything in which people have faith will do for money. The reason we have faith in paper money is because we can buy things with it; but the reason you can buy things with it is because you can always get gold for it.

"But the Free Silver men want to fix it so that instead of gold, you'll get silver — worth half as much."

Owen interrupted: "Mr. Beecham, no one wants to buy gold with a paper dollar; they want to buy — shoes or something."

"It's knowing they can get gold if they want to that gives them faith, and faith makes sound money."

"Suppose the government just said a dollar was a dollar, and everybody had faith in the government? Wouldn't that work?"

"It's been tried, but it has never worked. Thirty years ago, during the War, the government printed paper money. Greenbacks, they were called; and there was no promise to pay for them in gold or in silver or in anything else. They were just dollars. So people lost faith in them, and instead of buying a pair of shoes for — say — two dollars, you had to pay four.

"But at last the government took in all those greenbacks and destroyed them; and now your paper dollars are worth gold." And BB said strongly: "Men have faith in gold, and it's faith that fixes prices, Owen. The more faith — where money is concerned — the lower the price."

Owen said insistently: "I still don't see why the other way wouldn't work if people had faith in the government."

"Nobody would have faith in a government that said paper money was as good as gold."

"What would happen?"

"Prices would rise. The pound of beef that costs you eight cents now would cost — well, say half a dollar. A dozen eggs might cost sixty or seventy cents. A suit of clothes might be twenty-five, thirty, forty dollars, depending on quality. Everything would cost more. How would you get along mining coal at fifty-five or sixty cents a ton if a quart of milk cost, say, ten cents?"

"I'd keep a cow!" They laughed together, and Owen added:

"And the operators would have to raise my wages."

"How much?"

"Well, Gollies, I don't know. Enough so I could buy some milk."

"And all the other things you needed," BB reminded him. "No one trusts money that's backed only by the government's word. Good money keeps prices down, but bad money puts prices up. There's no escape from it."

Owen frowned again. "But Mr. Beecham, in some of your editorials you talk as if Free Silver was all right. If you believe it's so terrible, I should think you'd say what you think."

"It's not a question of what I believe; it's a question of what I can lead others to believe. A leader can only lead people along the way they want to go; and a successful leader believes in certain principles, and tries to further them by acquiring followers; but the politician without principles just looks out for his interests. Now I wonder whether that's a pun, or an epigram."

Before Owen could ask another question, Will called him to feed the job press. While he did so, his hands performing their function without any conscious direction from his mind, he puzzled over BB's words. Mr. Beecham must be right, of course; but it seemed to Owen that as long as you could buy things with it, a dollar was a dollar — gold or no gold.

2

Hardiston County teachers, said BB in the *Journal*, should organize and demand a forty-dollar minimum wage. McKinley was a certain victor in the race for the Presidential nomination. There had been three burglaries in two weeks in Hardiston, so the crime wave which the *Journal* had predicted would follow the coming of the Belt Railway had begun. A hundred and eight coal mines between Belton and Hardiston paid their men, in good times, $75,000 every two weeks. A graphophone, the first seen and heard in Hardiston, was played at the Methodist Episcopal Church before a large audience; the musical instruments were distinct, but the vocalists were not loud enough to be audible in the rear of the large auditorium. On May 30, two locomotives, each hauling four cars of coal, and starting a mile and a half apart, would be allowed to collide on a specially built track at Buckeye Park; excursions would be run to Columbus from all over the state to witness the spectacle, and forty thousand spectators were expected. Six children died of diphtheria in Slacktown. Two girls, conspicuous on the streets of Hardiston, should be run out of town; they were doing more harm than all the saloons put together. A Hercules bicycle could now be bought for $60. Ten boys and seventeen girls received diplomas at the twentieth High School Commencement; to see so many boys graduating was a promise for the future. The road scraper has revolutionized road-making in Hardiston County. The man with a grievance is never satisfied; success puts his teeth on edge. A man who would not put his colt in a poor pasture will hire a poor teacher for his child. The *Gymanfa* at Sycamore Hill was enjoyed by all. Thomas Wales fired two charges of birdshot at boys who climbed his mulberry tree, and inflicted painful injuries; he was arrested. Congress adjourned, early in June, having appropriated $500,000,000; that did not sound like hard times. Mr. Robert Roberts of Adams Township and Miss Betty Howell of Hardiston were married Sunday, June 14, at Sardis Church.

3

Betty Howell had been one of the older girls in Redfern School when Owen was a beginner there. She was Sammy's sister; and when the furnace shut down, her father, who had kept the furnace store, moved to Hardiston and went into partnership with his brother, the shoe man. She and Marged became close friends, although Marged was a year or two the older, and Owen had sometimes seen her at Isaac Williams's home or at church; but though Bobby Roberts sometimes came to spend Sunday with Marged and to go to church with her, Owen had never seen Bobby and Betty together. He had believed Bobby and Miss Williams would some day be married, so this news in the *Journal* surprised him, and he wondered whether Miss Williams felt badly about it. He did not expect to see her till fall, since she would go to normal school in Athens this summer as she had last, and in the meantime she was at home on the farm between the furnace and Sycamore

Hill; but she was in church the Sunday after the wedding, and
when the service ended he hurried to meet her at the door and
walk homeward with her. He asked at once:

"Did you go to the wedding?"

"I certainly did," she assured him. "I stood up with Betty."
She was smiling, and she sounded happy, so he was sure she did
not mind Bobby's marrying someone else.

"Why didn't she get married up here? They live here now."

"Grandma Howell is pretty feeble, too feeble to come this far.
And Mr. and Mrs. Howell were married in Sardis Church, so
Betty wanted to be."

"I always thought you and Bobby would probably get married
some day; I mean when he used to come up here Sundays."

"Oh, that was a long time ago." Her cheeks caught the sun and
were bright with sudden color.

"I guess it was," he agreed.

"He and I will always be friends." He thought she sounded
self-conscious about something. "We talked it all over."

"It's funny you haven't married somebody." And in sudden
desire to make her happy: "You're mighty nice!"

"Do you think so? I'm glad, Owen. But I'll probably turn out
to be an old maid."

"Don't you want to get married?"

"Not unless the right man comes along." And she asked, "How's
Jane?"

It was his turn to color. "Oh, she's fine."

"She's a sweet girl, isn't she?"

"Yes'm." They came to her corner and he asked awkwardly, "Are
you going to be home this afternoon?"

"No, I'm going up on the cars and on to Athens."

He nodded, deeply relieved. He liked being with her, but her
gentle insistence on his studying all the time sometimes made him
uneasy. Also, he had other hopes for the afternoon.

"Well, goodbye, then." After they parted, walking home alone,
he thought she was in some ways as nice as Jane; but that afternoon he and Jane took a walk together, and Janet Frye and Morgan
Williams joined them, and remembering how Amy and Dave liked
to walk together before they were married, Owen was happy with

fine dreams. Some day, when there was more work in the mine and he could save up some money, he would buy a house, or build one, or something, and then — and then — He thought fleetingly that he might get steady work in the *Journal* office, and buy a nice little house like Will Davis's; but he put that thought aside. He would always be a coal miner.

But maybe he would some day get to be an officer in the Union, and have a salary, and live in Columbus; he and Jane. He had never been in Columbus. Some day he would go on an excursion or something and see what Columbus was like, and see where he would want to live.

They had supper at Jane's house, and Owen wished Morgan would take Janet home so he and Jane could sit in the arbor in the back yard; but Janet and Morgan stayed till Mrs. Lloyd said it was time they said goodnight, so Owen and Jane were not alone at all.

4

The Republicans nominated Major McKinley for President; the nomination was on the first ballot. Garrett A. Hobart was the nominee for Vice-President; and the *Journal* printed the platform in full. BB advised Owen to read it.

Owen tried to follow that advice, but the platform seemed to him long-winded and dull. It said the Democrats were no good, but probably the Democrats would say as bad or worse about Republicans. There was a clause about having a National Board of Arbitration; but no arbitrator had ever decided in favor of Ohio miners, so that did not amount to anything. The Republicans said they would agree to make money out of silver, if all the other countries would, and if silver were "maintained at parity with gold." Owen asked BB what that meant.

"Well, practically, it means that a silver dollar would have to be worth a dollar in gold; but with silver as cheap as it is now, that would mean a silver dollar so thick and heavy it would wear holes in our pockets."

Owen, though he thought the Republican platform dull, was glad Major McKinley had been nominated; but in mid-July the first page of the *Journal* was dominated by the account of the Democratic Convention at the Coliseum in Chicago. Even the headlines made Owen's pulse quicken.

BRYAN OF NEBRASKA

The Boy Orator of the Platte Wins the Nomination by His Oratory

The Youngest Man Ever So Honored

He was sent to the Convention as a Delegate; his speech in answer to the gold men touched the right chord and he was made the nominee.

The story that followed recited the convention proceedings; but Owen skimmed down the column till he came again to Bryan's name.

> *After the committee on resolutions reported, a minority report touched off the greatest fight of the convention. Tillman pitchforked the gold bugs and Hill answered. The greatest speech was that of Bryan of Nebraska. He closed with these words:*
>
> *"You shall not press down upon the brow of labor this crown of thorns; you shall not crucify mankind upon a cross of gold."*
>
> *His speech electrified the convention and he was given the greatest personal tribute ever seen. For over fifteen minutes the Coliseum was a pandemonium, and next day he was made the nominee.*

Until that day politics had been for Owen a tedious business which older folk insisted he must try to understand; but Bryan's triumph was high drama, and inspiration too. If, by just making a speech, an almost unknown young man could seize the leadershlp of one of the two great parties, then nothing was impossible, no task too difficult, no goal too distant.

The *Journal's* long account of the convention and of that great oration was too short to content him; he read the dailies too. Even the Republican papers praised Bryan's speech in unmeasured terms; they described Mr. Bryan, his gestures, his voice, his delivery. The fact that he was only thirty-six years old, barely old enough to be President, seemed to Owen wonderful. In less than twenty years, he himself would be thirty-six. If Bryan could do it, so some day could he.

The convention after that speech had wished to change the order of business and nominate Bryan at once; but the young man forbade their doing so. Tomorrow would be time enough! That fine, confident gesture delighted Owen. He read every printed line about the convention itself, and then all he could find about Bryan's early life. Perhaps he could pattern his own life upon this man's. Bryan saw his first political rally when he was twelve, and made his first speech then; but Owen was almost fourteen when he spoke to the miners' meeting in Belton, so Bryan had a two-year start on him. To read that Bryan went to an academy and then to college, and that he became a lawyer, was discouraging; but Owen decided to study hard, and save money, and some day go to college and maybe become a lawyer too. Bryan was elected to the House of Representatives, and two years ago he ran for United States Senator, and now he would run for President!

Owen, reading the record through, was sobered; but he was not discouraged. He had nineteen years in which to rise as high as Bryan had risen; but if Bryan could do it, then so could he. The first thing was to study; to work and to save money and to study. To work, he must find more work to do. To save? Till now he had with rare exceptions given his earnings to his mother; but he knew that if he wished, she would let him keep as much as she could spare. Probably he could put money in the bank, a dollar or two at a time. Mr. Beecham would tell him how to do that.

And he could study. Till Miss Williams came back from Athens, he must study alone; but next winter she could help, could lead and guide him.

Bryan's triumph was inspiring, but the Democratic platform was dull and empty. The Democrats, denouncing the "Crime of 1873, which caused the rise in the price of gold and the fall in other prices, increased debt, enriched the rich and impoverished the poor," uttered no more than a pale echo of Bryan's ringing phrases. Owen did not think of himself as a Republican or as a Democrat.

He was for Bryan; he thought he would always be.

But BB seemed to think the Democratic platform was all right. He wrote in the *Journal:*

> *Cleveland has caused the country more woe than any other man in the history. But the democratic platform is on most points sound. Last year 263,700 foreigners landed in the United States, throwing out of work 150,000 Americans. The democrats would restrict immigration to help labor; they favor a constitutional amendment allowing incomes to be taxed; they would enforce arbitration of labor disputes through the Interstate Commerce clause in the Constitution. These are all good things. The democratic platform deserves respect, and has ours.*

Owen read this, and he spoke to Mr. Beecham about it. "You sound as though you might turn Democratic."

"No. No, I'll never do that. Unless the Republicans win in November, the country will go from bad to worse. A month ago, I thought a Republican victory was sure; but Bryan has changed all that. We'll have a fight on our hands. Every man in the country who is out of work, every farmer who can't get a fair price for his crops, they'll all vote for him. We'll have to fight, and we'll have to have some luck, too, or William J. Bryan will be the next President of the United States."

"I hope he is!"

BB looked at him thoughtfully. "I expect you do! He's a dramatic figure, captures the imagination. But so does a Will-o'-the-Wisp! I'd rather try to get warm at a good coal fire than at a skyrocket's tail."

5

Through that summer, as an undercurrent to the Presidential campaign, coal miners everywhere were weary and near despair. The great disaster near Pittston late in June seemed to many to epitomize the general catastrophe which threatened all. In a small local strike near Cleveland, a miner named William Rettger was killed, and a hundred thousand men and women and children marched to his funeral. BB in the *Journal* week by week conducted a catechism designed to make clear to his readers the silver question; but Owen found that at Miss Ellen and among miners everywhere, no one cared whether dollars were of silver or of gold. Men were jealous of their jobs, of every ton of coal they were allowed to dig. Stories were current of mines where work went by favor, where a mine boss might give one man all the work he could do and give another nothing. Night-hawking became more and more common. Mike Ryan, the one-legged storekeeper, who lived on the side hill opposite Miss Ellen, told Owen: "A still night, if you're awake, you'll hear them shooting from the solid. There's five or six does it right along. That way they get out two-three extra tons a day."

"I don't know as I blame them."

"Trouble is, it makes that much less work for the rest of you, the extra coal they weigh in."

John Powell presently put a stop to night-hawking at Miss Ellen; heavy doors were installed at each entry, and closed and locked at night. Owen, walking with him toward the siding at the day's end, asked, "Did Mr. Evans tell you do that?"

"He said I could. It was my notion. I like to see every man have an even chance."

An even chance? Owen glanced at Mr. Powell in some surprise. The Declaration of Independence said all men were created equal, but long ago at Redfern School Owen had found that was not true. "How can they have an even chance when everybody's different?"

Powell looked over his shoulder, as though in fear of being overheard. "They don't have to be as different as they are. The way the world's fixed now — " He grinned. "Well, them as has, gits! But that'll change by and by."

Owen asked curiously, "Are you for the Democrats?"

The mine boss said with sudden vehemence: "I'm for men. I'm for people. No one will ever see the day he can put a tag on me, Democrat or Republican or anything else, and put me away on a shelf like a glass of jelly." His tone changed. "I've kept my eye on you, Owen. You're all right — or you will be, when you get your growth — but don't ever let any man think he's got you. You keep changing your mind any time you think you should, and first thing you know, you've got him."

"If I could vote, I'd vote for Mr. Bryan."

"He's all right," John Powell assented. "But he can only see out of one eye. The Democrats have some good ideas, but I'm for people. I'm for the People's Party. You read their platform, did you?"

"No. But I read the other platforms."

"Get anything out of them? Any ideas?"

"Well, there was a lot I didn't understand."

Powell laughed shortly. "That's how they fool you. The only thing in either of their platforms that amounts to a hoot is the income tax! The Democrats are for that, and so am I. But — listen, do you save your money?"

"No, I give it to mama."

"Good boy. But you're going to start saving, some day, a dime here and a quarter there. You'll wait till you've got enough to put in the bank, twenty dollars, or ten, or five — and before you get that much, you've spent it. But how'd you like it if when you wanted to save money all you had to do was to go to the Post Office and buy a stamp and stick it in a book!"

"If I saved any money, I'd put it in a bank."

"You wouldn't bother a bank about a dollar, or two bits, or a dime. But you could buy a stamp for a penny! If you could save even a penny a day, figure out how much you'd have, time you was your father's age. Postal savings, they call it. The People's Party's for that.

"And they're for letting all of us vote for the President and the Vice-President and the Senators, instead of just leaving it to electors, and legislators. And they want to stop rich men from getting out injunctions to stop strikes. And they've got another idea. Take it times like these with people hunting jobs, they'd have the government hire men that were out of work and put them to work."

They were approaching the siding where others waited, and Powell suddenly was silent, and Owen said in wonder, "I never heard you talk this much before."

John Powell grinned. "Well, I got started." He laid a hand on Owen's arm, checking him. "But listen, Owen. I'm for people. I've watched you, and you're for people, too. But let me tell you something. People, take 'em by and large, are as crazy as the Gadarene swine. They'll fight you every time you go to help them, the way a drowning man will try to drown anyone that tries to help him. You'll do a lot to help miners before you're through, but you can make up your mind to it right now, you'll have to club 'em over the head to do it." He coughed and spat sooty phlegm. "There, I've talked myself dry. Come along."

"The People's Party is mostly farmers and laborers, isn't it?"

"It's mostly men," Powell told him stoutly. "The Republicans — yes, and Democrats, too — all they think of is business, and cities. But a coal miner's just as much a businessman as the operator that hires him; and as for your cities, you burn them down and the farmers will build 'em again, but if you wipe out your farmers, where'll the city be?"

"Mr. Bryan said that in his speech. 'The miners who go down a thousand feet in the earth' . . ."

"I know, I know." Powell lowered his voice as they reached the siding. "Bryan's a good man. You and me and Bryan, there's three of us." His hand linked comradely in Owen's arm.

Before July ended, the Pennsylvania coal operators who had signed and lived up to the December agreement, and who were paying seventy cents, demanded that the United Mine Workers strike the DeArmitt mines, which were paying fifty-four cents a ton and refused to raise that figure. The Union had been unable to gain a sufficient foothold in the DeArmitt mines to strike and force compliance; but President Penna undertook to secure by persuasion what he had not the strength to compel. For the time, the operators of the Pittsburgh District waited to see whether he would succeed; but throughout the Central Competitive District — Illinois, Indiana, and Ohio as well as West Virginia and Pennsylvania — everyone knew that DeArmitt would not yield, that the question of accepting a reduction must soon be faced.

It was a matter of daily debate wherever two miners came together. Owen found himself on the minority side. He believed that when it became necessary, the reduction should be accepted; and more than once, either at meetings of the local, or where fifteen or twenty men waited around the tipple in the morning or at the siding, he voiced his views. At home, he and his father argued endlessly and sometimes angrily; they went over and over the same ground.

"We're bound to take the cut," said Owen. "We promised in

December that we'd take it unless DeArmitt raised his men. We gave our word."

"Whose word?" Tom demanded. "Not mine. I made no such promise."

"The Union did for you!"

"The Union! What Union? The Knights of Labor was one thing, but this nuzzling up to the operators, like a calf to its mother's tits; that don't go for me! It's the Union's job to take care of me, not to take care of the operators. If the Union don't take care of me — I'll take care of myself."

"Don't get all stirred up! It isn't as important as all that, anyway. It's only — "

"Don't tell me what's important, and what's not!"

"It's only six cents a ton, two bits a day. But if we put the operators out of business — "

Tom rose to storm across the room, and Owen's mother, knitting in the low rocker, said wearily: "Talk, talk, talk, and nothing done! D'ye never get tired of your own clacking tongue, Tom? Aye, and Owen, you're worse than your father, with your sauce and your impudence."

"You always take his side!"

"Aye, like as not," she agreed. "We've gone along side by side for thirty-three years now — and I'm too old to change."

Owen went out-of-doors and swung away, alone and lonely as he always was when his mother thus made her fondness plain. There were hours when he hated his father, hated Tom Glen's slow-witted stubbornness, hated his prating about the Knights of Labor, hated his refusal — or his inability — to see points of wise policy, or even of honor, which to Owen seemed so plain. He walked down to Jane's, sure of a friendly welcome there; but Jane was not at home. She was spending a week, Mrs. Lloyd said, at her Aunt Net's out in the country; so Owen could not see her, and Miss Williams was in Athens, and his mother — he told himself — did not want him hanging around the house.

He decided to go up to the *Journal* office. This was Thursday, so Mr. Beecham would probably be away in the country or somewhere; but Will and the girls would be there.

Will was attending to callers in the office, so Owen went back through the file room and up to the type loft. Nellie was there alone; she said Bets was at home with a cold. Owen took some copy from the hook and fell to work at the case beside hers. Because he was in a dark and lonely humor, he watched Nellie with sidelong glances, letting his thoughts take their course. It was a long time since he had felt afraid of her, or embarrassed by her. Since she came to work here, she was certainly a lot nicer than she used to be; and since her father's death she was more changed than ever. She and her mother still lived in the small house down near the furnace. He asked:

"How's your mother?"

"All right." Her hand did not break its rhythm.

"You folks getting along all right?" She nodded; and he said, "I guess I'll go swimming down there tomorrow."

She did not speak, intent upon her copy; but though he pretended to work, he was thinking of her, wishing somehow to come close to her. "I might go for a swim tonight," he said. "There's a moon!" She did not answer nor seem to hear. "You could see all right, even after dark." She filled her stick, and went to lift the type into the galley; and he asked, "Did you ever go over to the swimming hole at night?"

She smiled, returning to her stool. "No, and neither did you."

"I dare go tonight!"

She laughed. "I can just see you!" Already she was at work again. "You're about as likely to as I am."

"I'll show you!" Why, when he talked to Nellie, did he always feel like a little boy? He never felt so with Miss Williams, nor with his mother, nor even with Jane. With them he was a man, a potential protector; but Nellie always made him feel as though he were about ten years old. "I dast go tonight," he insisted. "Soon's it's good and dark."

"No one's stopping you!"

"I'll be there, all right." She made no reply, and he heard Will in the pressroom below. "Well, guess I'll go pass the time of day with Will. Goodbye."

She gave him a brief, teasing smile. "G'bye, Owen. Have a good swim!"

"I'm going to. You wait and see."

But he did not go to the swimming hole that night, telling himself it was too cold, or too far, or too late, refusing to admit even in his own thoughts his fear that if he went she might join him there.

6

Through August, diphtheria was epidemic in Hardiston; there were many cases, some deaths. It would be wise, said BB, to abandon all public gatherings, to keep your children at home, to sprinkle copperas and lime around the privies. Business was everywhere prostrate; times had not been so hard since 1859. McKinley's front-porch speeches were gems. A fall of slate killed a miner in Belton. A joke on a man is no good unless he can laugh at it himself. The silver dollar should be worth a dollar in gold. The McKinley Barbecue on September 26 would be the greatest occasion in the county's history. The McKinley spider, its webs in every meadow bearing McKinley's autograph for all to read, was an omen of Republican victory. Vote for more work and more wages. Stop immigration. If there is one day's work to be done and sixteen men to do it, wages will be low; but if there is sixteen days' work to be done and only one man to do it, wages will climb. That's the 16 to 1 for which McKinley stands; sixteen times as much work as one man can do. The treasurer of Pike County has vanished, leaving a shortage of $6358.39; Gallia County is short $5675.77, secured by sureties; Scioto County has a $4000 deficit. Hard times turn honest men into criminals. Free trade and free silver equally degrade American workers. The farmers who planted wheat this year have gold mines on their farms; there was a bumper crop and prices are high. Bryan reached his peak with the Cross of Gold speech; now the skyrocket was fizzling. Bryan was a boy orator, yes; he had never grown up. The Boy Orator of the Platte? Yes, but as Senator Foraker said, that was the river which was a mile wide and an inch deep. Silver was worth less every day, but wheat was as good as gold. Gold production in the world this year would be almost twice what it was in 1890; with plenty of gold, silver would be worth less and less. Senator Foraker would be the speaker of the day at the Barbecue. Local operators feared that the pay for mining a ton of coal must come down to forty-five cents, the lowest rate in history, in Ohio mines. Ohio miners would meet in convention in Columbus, October 7, to discuss the situation and decide what should be done. J. W. Hampton has a pumpkin vine eight hundred and eighty feet long. School will reopen Monday, September 28. There have been twelve deaths from diphtheria in the county since September 1.

7

Owen, in spite of the derisive paragraphs about Bryan with which BB salted the *Journal* every week, did not forget the high resolves which Mr. Bryan's sudden rise had inspired; and when Marged Williams, returning from Normal School, spent a Sunday with her uncle and his family, Owen saw her at church and as the service ended hastened to her side.

"I'm glad you're back," he told her almost breathlessly. "Because I've decided I want to learn a lot of things I can't just learn by reading about them." He hesitated, unwilling to confess the fullness of his dreams. "I might want to go to college for a while some day. If you can help me some, this winter, I'd be mighty glad."

She did not let him see her swift happiness; her tone was level, and it held some doubt. "I don't know, Owen. In some ways, you're way ahead of your old class; but you don't know anything about algebra, or Latin."

"Do I have to?"

"Well, to get into college, yes." She added: "And you've always been interested in words. There's nothing better than Latin to help you with words."

He hesitated. "Could I get to be a lawyer without going to college?"

"A lawyer?" She looked at him in astonishment, but he stared straight ahead, and she said: "Why, yes, I suppose so. I know some people read law, in a lawyer's office." She was watching him in puzzled wonder. "You've changed, this summer, Owen."

"Well — I'll be seventeen years old in November."

"I know." She waited, but since he did not speak, she asked, "How's Jane?"

"Fine."

"You and she like each other, don't you?"

"Yes."

They were silent for a dozen paces, and then she said, half to herself: "She's a year older than you." She laughed suddenly, as though at her own thoughts. They came to her corner, and paused, and he asked:

"Are you going to be here from now on?"

"No, I'll go home tomorrow, come back in time for the Barbecue. I expect you'll go to that, won't you?"

Owen shook his head; the Barbecue would fall on a Saturday. "I'll be working in the *Journal* office."

"Oh, I'm sure Mr. Beecham will close the office that day. But anyway, I'll be here right along after that, and I'll lay out work for you to do."

Her prediction that BB would close the office for the day of the Barbecue proved sound. He proposed to Will and Owen that they run off the inside on Friday. "I'd like to shut up shop and spend all day at the Fair Grounds, and I expect you would too."

Owen welcomed this arrangement. The Barbecue was for Republicans, and he thought of himself as a Bryan man; but he could not vote this year, so his politics did not matter. And the plans for the Barbecue — the *Journal* had printed them in detail — made his mouth water. To feed the multitude would require seven thousand loaves of bread. Fifty-five oxen and sheep and hogs had been or would be slaughtered. There were in readiness five thousand tin cups and spoons, and thirty thousand paper plates. Thirty cooks and a hundred waiters would serve the throng.

Saturday morning, Owen was awake before the cannonade at five o'clock ushered in the day. Heavy frosts for three nights had cleared the air, and this morning was bright and promised to be warm. Before he was done with breakfast, farm wagons began to pass along the Pike on their way into town; and he heard the whistle of excursion trains on the Ohio Southern half a mile away.

He went uptown at once after breakfast, and took his stand at the Court House to be ready to watch the parade. When the time came, he counted eight brass bands and six drum corps and seven different glee clubs. After the parade had passed, he raced for the Fair Grounds, down beyond Peach Street on the edge of Erie Flats, where the crowd already ran to thousands and grew larger hour by hour.

When Owen came there, the air was rich with the smell of roasting beef. A majestic figure — Owen did not know till he read the next week's *Journal* that this was Colonel Gus Lambert of Kentucky — seemed to be in charge of the cooking, stalking up and down the trench in which the slow fires burned. The trench was almost a hundred feet long, three feet wide and half again as deep; it was a third full of glowing hickory coals, and as grease dropped from the meat spread on the grills above, small flames played and spurted everywhere. There were quarters of beef, well browned and dripping succulence, halves of hogs spreading a delicious aroma, whole sheep split and bubbling fat as water bubbles from a squeezed sponge.

Owen, finding himself for a moment beside Colonel Lambert, dared a question. "How soon will they be done, sir?"

"They're prime now, m'lad," the Colonel assured him. "The fires were lighted at eight o'clock last night, and since then, fifteen cords of hickory have gone into that trench. The beef went on first. It takes nine hours to cook a quarter properly, and these went on the grills at midnight; the hogs and sheep in their season. They now await your general pleasure." A group had clustered near, and the Colonel made an expansive gesture. "But the Burgoo makes the feast, gentlemen; therein lies the artistry. That's been cooking all night; and the longer you cook it, the better the flavor."

Someone prompted him. "What do you put in it?"

The Colonel cleared his throat. "Ha-hum! The proportions must be exact, but apportioned to the whole. Note down these instructions. For twelve hundred gallons, take two bushels of onions, seventeen bushels of potatoes, fifteen bushels of tomatoes, the leg bones of fifteen beeves, one and a quarter pounds of Cayenne pepper, forty-five dozen ears of corn, a bushel of salt, three pounds of black pepper. Taste at intervals and add what the palate prescribes. Cook till the essence floating in the air so whets the appetite it cannot longer be restrained."

A woman said sharply: "All that Cayenne, it sounds hot enough to burn the rafters out of your mouth!"

"Madam," said the Colonel in severe yet deeply wounded tones, "in thirty-five years of experience I have never had a complaint." He lifted his hat and moved with dignity away.

When the hour struck, Owen was among the first to be served; but as he burrowed back through the crowd pressing toward the

long tables, he came face to face with Jane and Betty, and Morgan
Williams was with them. Owen, hungry and eager, felt a moment's
dismay; for clearly he must give up his plate to them. Jane protested prettily, but when he insisted, she said she and Betty would
share it, and he and Morgan could bring some more. They appointed a tree in the grove to serve as rendezvous, and then Owen
and Morgan pressed into the crowd again to fight their way to the
feast. Small boys slid and wriggled past them, and Owen wished
he could do the same; but he was taller than most of the men
around them, so they had to move with the crowd.

They came back at last to Jane and Betty, each with two heaped
plates, and a cup of Burgoo on each plate; and when those plates
were empty, Owen returned once more to the serving table. Such
delicious fare was outside all his experience. He had occasionally
eaten steak, cut thin and well-pounded, but never such rich rare
beef as this. Half a hog, broiled over coals, offered a flavor wholly
different from that of fried chops or ham; the mutton carried a
savor of its own; the Burgoo distilled all that was most delightful
to the tongue into a single taste. Also, to cap the whole, never
before had Owen known the delight of eating to repletion. When
now he reached the servers, he saw that the quarters of beef had
shrunk, and the carcasses of hogs and sheep were reduced to
skeletons. The long table of rough boards ran with bright juices
which dripped through the cracks to the ground, and beneath the
table, sniffing, lapping dogs shared the bounty.

By mid-afternoon, when the Columbus Glee Club of fifty voices
ascended the stage and began to sing, he and the others were
pleasantly gorged; and Owen was so sleepy that even being with
Jane was not enough to keep him awake. Jane and Betty sat with
their shoulders propped against the trunk of a spreading oak,
Owen and Morgan cross-legged and facing them; and for a while
the two girls kept the conversation at a pitch of determined
vivacity. But presently Morgan and then Owen sprawled at
length, and Owen fought to keep his eyes open. Once or twice
he slept, though only for an instant; once, when he woke, to prove
he was not asleep, he said drowsily:

"There's another parade at half-past six. Senator Foraker is
going to make a speech."

"Parades are awful dusty," Jane commented, and Betty added:

"Yes, and who wants to listen to Senator Foraker? I certainly don't."

Morgan agreed with her. Owen thought guiltily that he ought to wait for the speechmaking; but if he lay here much longer, he would go to sleep and stay asleep, so he lurched to his feet and they all stood together, wondering what to do. Owen led them down to see the trench where the fires still smouldered; and he gave them from memory Colonel Lambert's Burgoo recipe. People by that time were asleep all through the grove; and the four wandered from group to group, counting the ones who snored, the crying babies, the men who slept with their mouths open.

Then Owen saw two men staggering helplessly, and another and another; clearly, they were drunk, and against such sights Jane should be protected.

"Jane, let's go up to your house," he proposed. "There's nothing else here till the speeches."

So they left the Barbecue to its own devices. Mrs. Lloyd asked them to stay for supper. They all agreed that they wanted nothing more to eat for a while; but Mrs. Lloyd said they would soon be hungry, so as a compromise Jane made taffy and they pulled it. Jane's and Betty's turned out as white as snow, Owen's and Morgan's pale gray; and they laughed as they always did at that familiar phenomenon, and after much tasting and counter-tasting they agreed that the gray taffy tasted just as well as the white. Betty was staying all night with Jane, so Morgan and Owen walked together as far as Morgan's corner on the homeward way. Walking home alone after they parted, Owen realized with some surprise that he was a little hungry, so he drank a glass of milk and ate a slice of bread and butter and jelly before he went to bed.

He did not know till next day that the Columbus Glee Club, after the evening program, marched up Peach Street to serenade Mr. Beecham, and BB made a speech to them. Will Davis had heard it. "Good old rock-ribbed Republican doctrine!" he told Owen, with a laugh in his voice. "And he didn't leave Bryan a leg to stand on."

"If I could vote, I'd vote for Bryan all the same."

Will winked. "Well, Owen, there's a lot that can — and will."

8

Thirteen thousand people, said the *Journal* Wednesday, came to the Barbecue on various excursion trains, and seven thousand by carriage and team over the roads. With the five thousand inhabitants of Hardiston, BB estimated that twenty-five thousand people enjoyed the event. Pickpockets, he reported, harvested thirty dollars from one man, five dollars from another; and probably still other victims kept their losses to themselves. There was much drinking, but few got drunk. Yellow seemed to be the favorite color in the dresses of the ladies.

9

On the twenty-fifth of September, the day before the Barbecue, Ohio operators voted to reduce the wage scale from fifty-four cents a ton to forty-five. Mr. DeArmitt, despite President Penna's persuasions, had continued to pay his men fifty-four cents — as against the seventy cents paid by the other operators in the District. In mid-September, the Pittsburgh operators reduced wages to the figure he was paying; and under the nine-cent differential, fifty-four cents in Pittsburgh meant forty-five cents in Ohio.

Sunday afternoon, the day after the Barbecue, Owen went to see Moses Evans, to discuss with him this situation; and on the way home he stopped to report to Charles Morgan. "Mr. Evans says he and the other operators can afford to pay sixty-one cents," he explained. "And they're willing to do it, all over the Sub-District, as long as they can."

"That won't be for long. The Pittsburgh operators will cut the price of coal pretty soon, and the operators here will have to meet the cut."

"Things might get better," Owen urged. "And anyway, we don't have to strike till they do lower the scale."

"Yes, that's so." Mr. Morgan sat in thoughtful silence for a moment. "Why don't you go see Eben Howell, tell him what Mose says. He might want to call a meeting." Eben Howell was president of the Sub-District.

Owen agreed, and next afternoon when his shots had been fired, he tramped down to the siding and across the railroad to the Belt Line tracks beyond the creek, and caught a car to Belton. Matthew Price, as secretary-treasurer of the Sub-District had an office there, and Eben Howell was in the office with old Mr. Price when Owen climbed the stairs. The two men looked up at Owen's entrance. The one small window gave not much light, and they were to Owen only shadowed silhouettes, but Howell said at once:

"Hello, Glen. Come in." He crossed to shake Owen's hand. "I haven't seen you since that day with Mike Ratchford in the *Journal* office."

"Yes sir." Owen shook hands with Mat Price. "I see Mr. Price on the train sometimes."

"He told me you were coming in today. Charles Morgan sent word. Sit down." Seated, facing Owen, Mr. Howell waited; and old Mr. Price tipped in his squeaky swivel chair and watched in silence, and Owen felt his heart's quick pound.

"Well, Mr. Morgan wanted me to tell you about — " He hesitated. "I had a talk with Moses Evans, and he — " He wetted his lips. "Well, the thing is, the operators want to go on paying sixty-one cents. As long as they can, anyway."

Howell said mildly: "Start at the beginning. Tell us about it." There was friendly amusement in his tones. "Don't get excited; just pretend you're speaking at a meeting."

Owen grinned. "I guess I think better standing up."

"Stand up, then."

But Owen, at ease now with the other's friendliness, did not do so. He repeated his conversation with Mr. Evans, and he and Eben Howell stayed in talk awhile. The Belt Line cars passed along the street just below the window, and as one went by, Mat Price at last rose. "That car'll be back in four-five minutes, headed for Hardiston, Glen. Come along with me?"

So Owen too rose, and Eben Howell; and Mat Price locked the door behind them and they went down to the sidewalk. There Howell said: "Glen, Mike Ratchford is calling a District Convention to go over this thing. I want you to be one of our delegates. All right with you?"

Owen felt a swelling in his breast, a high and shaking pride. "Yes sir. Yes, it's all right with me."

XVII

October 1896 — January 13, 1897

Eᴀʀʟʏ ɪɴ Oᴄᴛᴏʙᴇʀ came the notice which Eben Howell had predicted. Miners' delegates were summoned to Columbus to meet
the operators; and Owen was one of eight delegates from Hardiston
County.

He was tremendously proud of that distinction, even though he
and the other Hardiston County delegates went under strict instructions to refuse to accept any reduction. This seemed to Owen
a mistake, and in discussing the point with Charles Morgan, he
said so. "If there's only one way we can vote, what's the sense of
sending us, paying for our tickets on the train and everything. It
would be cheaper to just write 'No' on eight sheets of paper and
mail them."

Mr. Morgan smiled at his violence. "If you don't want to go,
I guess Eben Howell will let you stay home."

"Oh, I want to go."

"I know. I know." The older man spoke kindly. "You're in an
itch to do something. You'll be wanting to make a speech and I
don't know what all. It won't do you a bit of harm to sit and listen,
Owen. Sit and watch and listen, and next time you go to a convention, you'll know what to expect; but this time — well, hold your
water, Owen. Let the others handle things."

So Owen was silenced, but before they took the train for
Columbus, he went again to see Moses Evans. "I'm going to be
a delegate," he explained. "So I like to know how the operators
feel about things."

"A delegate, are you?" Mr. Evans looked at Owen for a long
time with shadowed eyes. "Yes, I sh'd judge you would be," he said
at last. "Want to know about the operators, do you?" And before

428

Owen could reply, he said: "You know, Owen, you're getting old enough so you ought to learn to see the inside of some things."

"I want to, Mr. Evans."

"All right, then listen. Pittsburgh has cut the scale from seventy cents to fifty-four cents. That means forty-five cents here in Hardiston County — and your Executive Board recommends you accept that cut. Isn't that so?"

"Yes sir."

"So actually, your own Executive Board is working with the operators in the Pittsburgh District to reduce your wages. You know that, but you don't know why."

"Yes, I do, Mr. Evans. They're doing it so the Pittsburgh operators can compete with Mr. DeArmitt and finally make him pay the same wages they do."

"That's where you're mistaken, Owen. You know I've always talked straight to you. Well, I'm talking straight now. This whole thing isn't aimed at DeArmitt. It was rigged up between the Pittsburgh and Hocking Valley operators and your Executive Board to force low wages here, and in all the thin-vein districts. If they can put the operators here out of business, then the Hocking District and Pittsburgh can take over the whole trade."

Owen puzzled over this. "I don't see the sense of that, Mr. Evans."

"Doesn't seem sensible, does it? But look at it this way. Your Union and the operators say they're doing all this to compete with DeArmitt. Well, DeArmitt can't supply the whole coal trade; so that claim don't stand up. But here's your own Union says you ought to take forty-five cents, when we're ready and willing to pay you sixty-one cents — and so are the heft of the operators in the Pittsburgh District. I tell you, it's all to starve you out — and to put us out of business."

"Are you sending anyone to Columbus?"

"What's the use? We can pay sixty-one cents as long as business holds up, and as long as other Ohio mines pay it. But if they cut the scale, we'll have to. It's out of our hands — so there's no point in our going to Columbus."

Owen sat with bowed head, staring at his fists, thinking hard; he said at last: "Well, Mr. Evans, I guess I'll never believe the Union is trying to starve us out, down here. But even if we starve, there's another thing. We agreed last December that if DeArmitt

or anybody else wouldn't pay the scale, the other operators didn't
have to pay it. The operators have played fair. They kept their
agreement. They waited till the middle of last month to see if we
could make DeArmitt pay the scale, and we couldn't do it. I think
they've done their part. We ought to do ours."

Mr. Evans watched him for a moment with blank eyes. "Sounds
all right," he admitted at last. "Pretty high-minded. I wish everybody was the same."

2

In Columbus, Owen and the other Hardiston County men stayed
at the Neil House, and Owen filled eyes and ears with many new
sights and sounds. In the bus that brought them from the station,
his head was forever turning right and left, and he was forever
twisting in his seat, trying to see everything that passed; but the
cumulative impression was one of indescribable confusion, thousands of men and women, thousands of wagons and drays and
buggies and carriages and bicycles. Election Day was only a
month away and there were signs and banners everywhere, and
when they alighted from the 'bus he saw campaign buttons in
every lapel. Most of them bore portraits of McKinley, or of both
McKinley and Hobart; and when he saw the rare Bryan button to
match the one in his own buttonhole, it was like seeing a familiar
countenance in a hostile crowd.

He did see one — or, rather, two — familiar faces, on the day of
his arrival. He had gone into the dining room with three other
delegates from Hardiston County. Evan Harned, vice-president of
the Erie local, was one of them; and Evan Foster, whom Owen and
BB had talked with on a day long ago while Evan was roofing his
new house, and a man named Tailor were the others. Owen asked
Tailor whether he was related to the Dan Tailor who one day
hauled almost four tons of ore to Union Furnace in one load, and
it developed that they were brothers. Owen spoke to Evan Foster
about the home he had built; and these men were pleased, as men
always were pleased, to find that he knew a little of their lives.

It was after they were settled at their table and had been served
that Owen saw Miss Dine and Edna Tutson come into the dining
room. They were escorted by two men much older than they, and

as they came in they were laughing over their shoulders at the men, and talking so loudly that their voices carried and attracted attention. After they were seated at a table diagonally across the dining room, Owen could still catch an occasional glimpse of them through the shifting heads of other diners, and he watched them with a furtive interest. They were certainly the prettiest ladies in the dining room, though till now he had never thought of Edna Tutson as pretty at all. Miss Dine was prettier than she had ever been. Yet something about them made him uncomfortable, and he took care they should not see him watching them, quickly averting his eyes if either seemed about to look in his direction. When it was time to leave the dining room, he put his companions between him and their table and thus escaped unseen.

Yet abed that night — he and Evan Harned shared the same room and the same bed — he lay awake long after Harned slept, thinking about them, wondering and guessing. Suppose he had gone to speak to them? What then? Who were the men with them? Where did they live? Would they have been glad to see him? Half-awake, he dreamed blood-stirring dreams.

But after that evening, the business which brought him to Columbus occupied his thoughts and his time so completely that he forgot them; and even his acute consciousness of the strangeness of city scenes was dulled. He found among the delegates others as young as he; but like him they were for the most part silent listeners to the proceedings. The meetings were held in Worthwein Hall on South High Street. The first day, the delegates voted 121 to 13 to retain the current wage scale, but most of the delegates, like Owen, were under instructions and not free to vote as they believed. When a second and third day saw no decisive change in the vote, it was resolved that the question should be referred back to the miners themselves. The locals would vote before October 17 and report to Headquarters; until then, operators must maintain the current rate of pay, or work would stop everywhere.

Back in Hardiston, Owen was selected by the delegates to report to the Sub-District what had happened. When he rose, he knew that not one in four of the men he faced agreed with his opinions. Mr. Beecham had said that the wise leader discovers what men think before they are sure of it themselves and then puts their thoughts into words and they agree. Owen knew what these men

thought, but his own contrary convictions were so strong that he
spoke straightforwardly. He had brought home a copy of the
resolutions adopted in Columbus, and might have been content to
read this to the meeting; but he elected to speak as though of his
own motion, paraphrasing the text of the resolutions when to do so
promised to be effective.

"Mr. Chairman," he said crisply, "I have to report the proceedings
in Columbus. The convention was three days in session; the
instructed delegates voted ten to one to insist on the present wage
scale." A murmur of approval ran across the hall as he went on.
"But Mr. Chairman, many of the delegates — of whom I was one —
voted that way only because we were instructed to do so. It was in
the hope that Ohio miners would overrule their own instructions
that the question was referred back to the locals for a final vote.

"Your Executive Board believes that we are bound in honor to
accept the reduction to forty-five cents a ton." He heard the angry
whispers, felt the minds of the men set hard against him; but
opposition, instead of checking, spurred him on. "Oh, I know some
of you feel we are being betrayed, victims of a conspiracy between
Pennsylvania operators and our own officers. I, too, have heard the
operators, with feigning voice, speaking words of feigned love —"
The savage anger in his tones brought a stir of laughter. "I've heard
them explaining how we are deceived."

"And I know, too, that forty-five cents is a starvation wage. We
all know what it means to dig a ton of coal. We've all done it.
Drill a hole three or four or five or six feet into the seam; drill
another and maybe another. Do it while you're working under a
roof so low that even on your knees you can't hold up your head.
Your back aches, and your knees grow calluses, and the coal dust
gets into your eyes and nose and throat; but you drill your holes
and shoot down the solid and come back next day and — on your
knees, keeping your head down so you won't bump it — you take
your coal fork, shake out the slack and slide the coal into your car.
When it's full, you push your car into the entry. Well, I say you've
earned your forty-five cents!"

Some laughter answered him; he held up his hands. "But if
forty-five cents isn't enough, neither is fifty or sixty or seventy.
Some day I expect to see us paid a dollar a ton." An incredulous
chuckle ran across the hall, and he said cheerfully: "Why not?
Let's set our sights high. I'd as soon drown in a big pond as a small

one." The laughter rose again, and he hushed it, spoke in somber tones.

"Mr. President, we all know that Ohio operators cannot maintain the scale against blackleg competition from non-union miners in Pennsylvania. The way to beat that blackleg competition is to fight them with their own weapons; to work for less — allowing for the differential — than they can work for. This seemed to your officers in Columbus the only chance to avoid a fruitless struggle, long idleness and stark starvation.

"Bound by your ironclad instructions, I and many other delegates voted against accepting this reduction; yet your contract of last December pledges you to accept this reduction if your operators keep faith — which they have done.

"To keep faith is a matter of principle. The man without principles tries to look out for his own interests; but it is to every man's best interests to live by his principles. This reduction must seem to you like a step backward; but don't forget that a small defeat may be part of a great victory. To come to court with clean hands is more than half the battle. No miner comes from his work with clean hands; the coal sees to that. But his hands bear no stains that soap and water will not remove. The stain of a broken pledge is not so easily scrubbed away."

The words of the Board's circular came to his lips. "Your officers recommend that you accept this reduction in your wages. This advice is not given with any degree of pleasure. It is the advice of honest men, not of demagogues who would raise false hopes, and give you false encouragement and advice opposed to your best interests. They are prepared — and I am proud to stand with them — they are prepared to endure abuse and denunciation and temporary disfavor; but they hope for the support of all intelligent and loyal men.

"Your union has tried for years to bring the Pittsburgh District miners to our way of thinking. Thus far we have failed. Now your leaders have determined to use against them their own weapons, and — once for all — to put an end to their blackleg practices. Let us rank ourselves behind our leaders, accept this sacrifice like men, and so march on to victory."

Owen paused and felt their hostile silence, and knew that he had failed to win them. Clearly, a vote taken now would be adverse. He spoke more quietly. "Mr. Chairman, this decision is a grave

one, not to be made heedlessly. Every man will want to consult his
family — and his God. Mr. Chairman, our operators have not yet
asked us to accept this reduction. When they do, it will be time
enough for our decision. I move that no action be taken on these
recommendations at this time."

He sat down, and there was a stir and then a second to the
motion, and an indifferent chorus of ayes accepted it. Owen realized that he was dripping with perspiration, the palms of his hands
moist, his pulse racing, his fingers trembling. When the meeting
adjourned, he moved stumblingly out of the hall, wishing to escape,
wanting no word with any man.

But outside the hall Isaac Williams spoke to him, and others, too,
in disagreement and in anger. He saw his father stalk sullenly
away; but he stayed, forcing himself to speak evenly, meeting their
wrath with composure, their hot words with cool reason. Charles
Morgan, he knew, was on his side; there must be others too. Before
the vote came to be taken, many might be persuaded.

Elsewhere in the state the miners for the most part accepted the
advice of the Union leaders and took a cut to forty-five cents; but
in Hardiston County and in some other districts, the operators did
not attempt to put that reduction into effect. Hocking Valley miners,
when their pay was cut, struck, and they were still out as Election
Day approached. But when they surrendered and returned to work
at forty-five cents, Hardiston County operators felt compelled to
reduce the miners' pay to the same figure. Matthew Price took their
notification to Eben Howell, and on the last day of October notices
went to every mine in the Sub-District.

> *Your board was notified by the Hardiston County oper-
> ators last night that they must have the Hocking Valley
> rate for mining, namely 45 cents. We therefore call a
> special convention to meet in Belton on Friday, the 6th
> day of November, at 8 o'clock* A.M. *in G.A.R. Hall. We
> request locals to send delegates which they have perfect
> confidence in, uninstructed. We also request all miners
> to continue at work up till and including Friday the 6th
> of November, as the 61 cent rate will prevail until that
> time.*

That notice was posted the Saturday before election. There was
no doubt in Owen's mind that the men would vote to strike, and

for him that fact overshadowed anything that happened at the polls. Bryan's defeat, which might once have seemed to him a bitter blow, was as though it had happened to someone else; and the men beside whom day by day he worked were as little interested as he.

He went to Belton early Friday morning by electric car, and the car was crowded and the talk was all of strike. At the meeting he spoke, but only briefly. "You men know I feel we are bound by our promise to accept this reduction, but after today I shall never remind you of my position. When you vote to strike, I go with you, win or lose. If it is to defeat, I will taste defeat with you. Some day we will together taste victory."

After the vote, Owen walked with his father and Charles Morgan in the straggling line of men trooping back to Miss Ellen Mine. Tom Glen was jubilant and boastful, as proud of the strike as though it were already won; but Owen and Charles Morgan were equally silent. At the mine they loaded the coal shot down the day before, then with shouldered tools they tramped away to the car line and so home.

3

Additional Locals: The average wage of our miners on an annual basis is 77 cents a day. The miners' only hope is in the ballot; its proper use will bring results. Vote right on November 3. McKinley is making new friends daily; his front-porch speeches are the most effective form of campaigning. Leg-o'-mutton sleeves have captured the country; but why wear a cape over sleeves as big as a cape? The Woman's Literary Club met at the home of Mrs. Doctor Gorman; Washington Irving was the subject of the discussion. Guests of Mr. and Mrs. Charles Arthur spent a pleasant evening at Logomachy and Cinque. Pond's Extract instantly relieves burns, wounds, abrasions and lameness. The Republican Party stands for honest money and a chance to earn it. Free Silver does not mean you can get silver dollars free; nothing worth having is free except air, rain, and sunshine. Learn how to mark your own ballot; the judges are not allowed to assist you. You need only put a cross underneath the Eagle. Edward Skeele of Adams Township and his ten oldest sons will all vote Republican.

Joy! The Eagle soars and screams, and Old Glory waves. Grover must move out of the White House in March and a disgusted people will then let him fish all he wants. It was a landslide. Four complete sets of scenery were used in *Old Farmer Hopkins* at the Rink. Hardiston County miners, refusing to accept reduced wages, came out November 7. Every mine in the county is shut down. The democratic vote on November 3 was the largest ever cast in the county and larger than any previous Republican vote, but not large enough. The democratic gain was 1819, the Republican, 854. Hostetter's Stomach Bitters is the finest diuretic and tonic known to modern times. The Slacktown Coal Company has put 100 men to work at sixty-six cents a ton; but every other large mine in the county remains idle. The demand for coal is everywhere heavy, and almost every miner in the United States is now at work except in the Hardiston field. The Massillon and Coshocton fields are still working at the sixty-one-cent rate. The Hardiston County strike against the reduction to forty-five cents has been endorsed by the Ohio Executive Board. A forty-five-cent wage in Hardiston means starvation. A man can dig six tons a day, but he cannot keep it up; four tons is a big day; many miners do not average two tons. Hardiston County miners were well prepared for this strike, for it had been a good season for gardens; but some are already in want, some will have to go to the Poor Farm, and at least forty miners have gone to seek work in other fields. There has been no disorder, no violence of any kind.

Many hogs are dying in the county of a mysterious and fatal disease. Wheat reached $1.00 in New York. The Republicans can claim no credit for that, but the rising price of wheat helped beat Bryan. There is too much talk of raising taxes, not enough of reducing the cost of government. The trouble with the labor market is that hundreds of thousands of immigrants came to this country this year, and all got jobs. Between 1880 and 1890, five million Italians, Poles, Hungarians and Russians came to the United States, and most of them were either paupers or criminals.

On December 7, the B & O mail train made the 44 miles from Portsmouth to Hardiston in one hour and nine minutes, with nineteen stops; a remarkable record. The Ohio Southern is in bankruptcy; the shutdown of coal mines here in the county forced it to default on its mortgage bonds. Is someone prolonging the shutdown in order to get the railroad cheap?

4

The miners walked out on November 7, and at first Owen welcomed the relief from steady toil. He had found his life this fall suddenly so crowded that the days sped fast. His resolution to begin a regular course of study meant that two or three times a week he went after supper to talk with Miss Williams; and when he did not go to her he worked at home, sitting at the kitchen table with the lamp at his elbow till long after his father and mother were asleep. He saw Jane less often than during the summer. Then they could sometimes be together under the arbor in the back yard, but now even when she had no homework to do, it was too cold to sit out-of-doors; and to spend an evening, or a part of an evening, with Jane and Mr. and Mrs. Lloyd was not particularly attractive. Even before colder weather drove them indoors, Owen had begun to weary. The delicate kisses which they had exchanged, lips barely touching cheek, were an intoxicatingly fragrant novelty; but after a time he began to feel that in such kisses there was something lacking. He and Jane had long exhausted every ordinary topic of conversation. Jane was not interested in mines and unions; she said the very thought of going into a coal mine just gave her nightmares, and as for unions, what was the sense of them? If a man didn't like his job, couldn't he just quit?

Those three days in Columbus had widened not only Owen's physical but his mental horizons; and also they had brought him into personal contact with the Union's higher officers. He met President Penna, he had a word of recognition from District President Ratchford, and he felt in them and in others a long vision and a strength of purpose which made his own forming opinions seem to him childish and immature; but without suspecting that he did so, he had made himself remembered by some of these men. Communications from Headquarters which came to him as secretary of Miss Ellen local were apt to have a personal word scribbled across the top and addressed to him alone.

At the same time, his influence with the miners themselves somehow increased. His opposition to the strike provoked some men to anger, and made a few enemies; but on the whole he rather gained than lost. Men who voted against him could still respect his courage in opposing them. In discussion he was never violent. He could be positive and at the same time humble; and his faculty for remembering not only a man's name but whether he was married, his deeds, his abilities and disabilities, made each one feel a personal relationship.

But at home this was not true. Owen's opposition to the strike awoke and fed in Tom Glen anger which he did not always control. Owen, for his mother's sake, tried to avoid arguments; but his father forced them, forever gnawing at the same bone, growling like an angry dog. Mrs. Glen, listening to the interchange of increasingly hot words, was torn between these two whom she loved; but when Tom Glen, unable to meet reason with reason, turned to epithet instead of argument, and Owen answered in kind, she was instantly Tom's champion. At such times his mother seemed to Owen as unreasonable as his father; and once, when Tom Glen had gone out and away, he told her so.

"You always take papa's side; but you didn't want this strike any more than I did."

"Your father's wrong oftener than he's right," she admitted. "And he's been so all his life, and many's the time I've told him so. But he's my husband and your father, and I'll not have you calling him a stubborn old fool and all the like of that."

"He calls me names enough!"

She laughed and reached up to pinch his cheek. "Pooh! Sticks and stones may break your bones, but names will never hurt you. As for who's right and who's wrong — there's nobody knows which from which. Men go by their lights, and your father's always done that. Maybe you're smarter than he is, and wiser than he ever was or will be; and maybe you'll go far, and that's something he's never done." Her eyes suddenly were filled. "But that's all the more reason you should love him and honor him, Owen."

To please her, he tried to avoid the discussions which always drew his temper taut as a wire; but there were times when his fists clenched, when it would have been blazing happiness to drive his fist into his father's face. His mother at such moments might sign to Owen to go out-of-doors, anywhere beyond range of his father's tongue; or if it were after supper when their voices rose, she would go to her room and call: "Tom, man, come on to bed."

Tom would yield and obey that summons, and Owen, fetching

his books and settling to his studies by the lamp, could hear their
low voices in the next room and hear the springs creak as Tom lay
down beside her; and knowing his father turned to the tender
haven of her arms, he gritted his teeth with hatred of the stubborn
man.

As the weeks drifted by, he more than once thought of escape.
He might go to West Virginia and find work in the Pittsburgh
thin-vein district, and make friends there. Perhaps he could
stiffen those miners to resist the wage cuts which were inevitably
passed on to Ohio. He thought of going to Cleveland, finding a job
in the DeArmitt mines. Even an imagined meeting with the man
who seemed to Owen the blackest villain in the world, filching
pennies not only from the pockets of his own miners, but from
every miner in the United States, made his blood race and his
muscles knot. Probably it would be better if they never met, for
if he met DeArmitt, he would strike him into the dust. That day
when by the swimming hole his blow laid Chet Masters senseless
hung in the background of Owen's thoughts; he knew his own
strength — but the knowledge was a warning. He had never since
struck anyone in anger, and would never do so; for might not death
lie in the buffets he could deal? Yet death was no more than the
due of men like DeArmitt.

At home, these weeks of late fall and early winter were for Owen
dark and troubled; but he found some release in the studies Miss
Williams prescribed. Latin at once confused and delighted him.
For the grammar of that dead tongue he had no taste, but to encounter in the text many words whose relationship to familiar
English words was instantly apparent gave him each time a quick
pleasure. The Latin dictionary which at Miss Williams's instruction he bought proved a treasure over which he pored for hours;
but when she protested at his indifference to declensions and con-
jugations and such technicalities, he said cheerfully:

"I don't have to know about them to speak English. If I want to
say 'a man bought a horse' I don't have to know a noun from a
verb! I just say it."

"Oh, you make me so mad, sometimes!" He laughed at her
indignation till she laughed with him. "But you do!" she insisted.
"How can I teach you anything when you won't let me act like a
school teacher?"

"I'll bet you don't really care anything about grammar. Besides,

I don't want to speak Latin, or to write it either. I'm just after words, a vocabulary."

"You'll never be able to go to college without Latin grammar."

He chuckled teasingly. "I don't need college with you to teach me."

"Well — all right! If grammar bores you, let it alone. Doctor Johnson said a man ought to read the books that interest him. If a Latin grammar doesn't interest you, and a Latin dictionary does, by all means read the dictionary!"

His hours with her were an escape from the sorrow of watching his friends, idle now while their savings leaked away. He hated the folly of this strike foredoomed to fail, but he had accepted the decision of the men. If they had been wrong while he was right, they would one day remember this with no reminder from him. Not even to Mr. Beecham, with whom during these idle weeks he sometimes spent a day among the hills, did he reiterate his first opinions; he had said his say, it was a time for silence now.

BB never opened the subject. Even after the election, his mind was busy with political matters; and when Owen expressed surprise, suggesting that the election had ended politics for a while, BB, his head on one side, said sagely: "No, you're wrong there, Owen. The real finagling has just begun. I'll give you an example." Three weeks after the election, he and Mrs. Beecham had gone to Cincinnati to see Joseph Jefferson in *Rip Van Winkle;* and this led to a meeting with Senator Foraker. "We had a lengthy conversation," said BB. "And by the way, the Senator spoke of your strike here in Hardiston County, and he said he and Major McKinley had discussed the industrial situation."

"What are they going to do about things?"

"Whatever they can, when McKinley takes office. But what I was going to tell you — just to show you that politics never stops — was this. Senator Foraker told me that Major McKinley urged him to go as a delegate to the St. Louis Convention — where McKinley was nominated. He quoted McKinley as saying: 'If we work together, I in the White House and you in the Senate and as leader of the party in Ohio dispensing the patronage, we can place the party on such a sound footing that it will control the state for twenty-five years!' "

Owen looked at him in surprise. "Can they? How can they?"

"A party's a machine," BB explained. "It's just as strong as its parts, and the parts are the political appointees. Proper use of the appointing power can build a smooth machine.

"So that was the plan — and the promise. Foraker went to St. Louis, and McKinley was nominated; but now — according to Foraker — McKinley has backed out on his promise of patronage. He says Congressmen will control the local appointments, and all Foraker gets is the state, the collectorship and so on."

To Owen, the conception of politics as a machine was new; and BB's words awoke his first real interest in the subject. "But can they do it? I mean, control Ohio for twenty-five years? The Congressmen and Senator Foraker and Mr. McKinley?"

BB cocked his head. "We-e-ll, twenty-five years is a long time." He hesitated. "Don't repeat what I've been telling you, Owen."

"No sir."

"I don't believe you will. Here's something else Foraker told me. Mark Hanna wants to be Senator, so if Governor Bushnell promises to appoint Hanna to serve out Senator Sherman's term, McKinley will take Sherman into his cabinet."

Owen felt something like a shiver touch his spine. "I always thought — you've always told me — that it was the way men voted that decided things."

"In the long run, it is," BB assured him. "But in our government, things are decided through parties, not just through candidates.

"But I'm just telling you all this to show you why I'm interested in politics, in season and out. Politics is to the country what your blood is to your body; it's everywhere — and it never stops."

"It makes me mad to think of Mr. McKinley being so sure he can run things! I wish Mr. Bryan was going to be President. I think he's a great man."

"He is a great man," BB assented. "He has great capacities, yet I think he lacks depth, Owen; and certainly he lacks political wisdom. He backed free silver at a time when gold production was already beginning to solve the currency problem. He captured the Democratic Party, and he'll be nominated again and again, but he'll never be elected. Silver is dead, and with McKinley in office, prosperity will return — and Bryan will have to find a new issue and start all over again."

"I guess you know Senator Foraker pretty well, don't you?"

"Why, yes. I've always admired him, and supported him. We're on familiar terms."

"Last week you printed that speech he made where he said we ought to stop the doings in Cuba, even if we had to fight Spain to do it. And you thought he was right."

"Yes, I think he was. War is terrible, but there are worse things than war. Spain is worse than the unspeakable Turk. If we drive her off the North American continent, the world will applaud.

"Yet we may not need to go to war. Give them time and the blood of her people will make Cuba free."

Owen said mildly: "Cubans getting killed won't make Cuba free. They'll have to kill Spaniards to do that."

BB chuckled: "Of course. I was talking through my hat. The way to free Cuba is to get within shooting range of some Spanish soldiers — and start shooting."

"Wouldn't being free mean more to the Cubans if they did it themselves, instead of us doing it for them?"

"They can't free themselves. They haven't the strength."

"Oh, any man can be free. Only, he can't be free and have everything else too. A miner's free to strike, but he can't strike and still have a job. Maybe in Cuba he can't be free and even live. But anyone can be free."

BB looked at him for a silent moment. "You're running into metaphysics, aren't you? What you say is true, of course; but it isn't practical." He added strongly: "But conditions in Cuba are a disgrace to civilization."

"I guess so," Owen assented. "But there are children — yes, and grownups, too — right here in Hardiston that don't get enough to eat. I call that a disgrace to Hardiston civilization! I can't get excited about the Cubans, when things are so bad here at home."

"We're slow to cast the beam out of our own eye," BB admitted. "Yes, that's true. But everyone feels more virtuous trying to improve his neighbors than trying to improve himself."

5

Early in December, John Powell came to the house. Owen and his father and mother were together, and at Tom Glen's invitation John sat down, twisting his hat between his knees; but after some idle talk the mine boss asked:

"Can I have a word with you, Owen?"

Owen was surprised, but he rose and took hat and coat, and they moved outside together. "Mr. Evans wanted me to see you," Powell said at once, tone and eyes expressionless.

"Wants me to go see him?"

"No. No, that's why he sent me. He wants you to pass the word around that any of the men that come back to work will get fifty-one cents. He says the ops all say the same."

Owen's eyes narrowed. "What's the big idea?" The other lifted his shoulders. "Why didn't he write Mat Price a letter?" Owen insisted. "Mat's the Sub-District secretary."

Powell wiped his mouth with his hand. "Guess they don't want to make it too official."

Owen studied the other's blank countenance. "What do you think about it?"

Powell hesitated. "Well, everybody knows the operators can pay better than forty-five cents. They know it themselves. Mose told me today it was a question of principle, with the operators; but I told him from all I heard around, with the miners it was a question of bread and butter." He spat. "I guess the operators figure a lot of men will go back to work for fifty-one cents without the Union's say so?"

"They won't!"

Powell whittled a corner of tobacco. "Well, I'll tell him I told you."

He strolled away, and Owen returned indoors. Tom Glen had moved his chair; he sat now with feet propped against the stove, puffing his pipe. Owen hung up his hat and coat, expecting questions; but Tom did not look toward him. His mother kept her eyes on her knitting, yet after a moment she said in a low tone: "Tell your father what Mr. Powell wanted, Owen."

Tom dropped his feet to the floor with a bang. "No, he don't! He don't have to tell me anything! Not if Powell and him have business that's so all-fired secret and important!"

Owen flushed. "Mr. Evans sent Powell," he said. "Anybody that goes back to work will get fifty-one cents. They want me to pass the word."

Tom grunted. " Well, you've passed it to me. I'll give it back to you."

"I won't pass it to anyone. They're just trying to win men away from the Union."

Yet he did tell Charles Morgan, but the president of Miss Ellen agreed that no one else need know, and on Saturday, John Powell came to the *Journal* office and withdrew the offer.

"They take it all back, Owen," he said with a cheerful grin. "They don't want any men coming to work, not yet. They're going to wait till the first of the year, and then post up notices at the mines and leave the Union out of it altogether."

"What are they so down on the Union for, all of a sudden?"

"Well, you take a man that's mean enough," Powell suggested. "And that's hated another man long enough; you take a real mean man and let him see the man he hates right flat on his back — well, he ain't going to help him up. He's going to stomp him into the ground."

"The Union's not flat on its back!"

"It's near enough to it. Phil Penna's had a bellyful of being president. He's going to quit; and the talk I hear, the Union'll have some trouble getting anyone to take the job." He moved to lean against the mailing table. "Come here, Owen; let me give you some ideas. I know you. You're like me. You're for people. You'll go a long ways. But you need to know what you're up against." He said in a low tone: "They're trying out machines, Owen. They tried one at Belton Number 2 last week. If the machines all work as good as that one did, that's the end of pick mining."

"They'll have to have men to run the machines."

"They'll need one man where now they need four. That means that pretty soon they'll make the men an offer, and if they don't take it, in go the machines — and three thousand miners right here in Hardiston County will be looking for jobs. Herbert Canter and some of the other operators are over in West Virginia right now, watching the machines work."

Owen stepped back a little, unconsciously lifting his shoulders. "Men and machines together can do a lot more than men alone."

"Men alone are already mining more coal than the country can use."

Owen's jaw set in a hard anger, he flung out a clenched fist. "No, by Gollies! I don't know the answer, Mr. Powell; but I do know that nobody's mining too much coal, not as long as there are people can't keep warm in winter! That's common sense."

"There's coal enough mined if they had money to buy it."

"Then mine more and it'll be cheaper and then they can buy it!"
Owen was in an incoherent wrath, seeking words to express the
thought that seemed to him so clear. "Let's dig so much coal they
can give it away! Let's dig too much! Let the country raise too much
beef and wheat, and make too many shoes and clothes, too much
of everything. I want to see that day! Too much! I've never had
enough of anything yet! By Gollies, Mr. Powell, don't talk to me
about too much, not till there's enough of everything to go
around."

6

Additional Locals: Christmas was quiet in Hardiston; salt pork
replaced turkey on many a miner's table. The performance of the
Edison Vitascope and Concert Company at the Rink was an eye-
opener for the large audience. Eggs are seventeen cents a dozen.
The state convention of the Ohio Mine Workers, held in Columbus
on December 28, was the largest in many years; resolutions pointed
out that business was better, and delegates to the approaching
national convention were instructed to work for a restoration of the
wage scale in effect in 1893 for pick mining. A rate three-fifths
the scale for pick mining was proposed as fair for mining with
machines. The convention voted to levy three cents per dollar
earned on every Union miner in the State to help Hardiston
County miners win their strike. William E. Farms is the new district president, succeeding Michael Ratchford, who will in turn
succeed Philip Penna as national president. Hardiston will welcome the proposed glass factory. The Woman's Literary Club met
January 4 with Mrs. Judge Hayes. Judges should be elected, and
for short terms, to keep them in touch with the people; when
judges cease to represent the people, the wonder is that there are
not more lynchings. The American Federation of Labor proposes
a general demand for an eight-hour day. Unless Republican leaders
are wise, this agitation may elect a democrat President in 1900.
The coming of the bicycle means the doom of the novel. The man
with no enemies has no real friends. Keep a pig next summer and

he will keep you next winter. The sure way to help yourself is to help others. A wise and loving marriage is the best investment you can make. The laborer's dinner pail measures the country's prosperity. The thermometer at the Post Office registered 60° New Year's Day. Mayor Heather of Chillicothe says that James Young's *Hamlet,* which comes to the Rink January 13, is better than Booth's. London *Truth* says "stink" is the word for motor wagons, and adds: "They vibrate so much that if the people in them were cream, they would soon be butter." The prolonged strike menaces the Republican Party in Hardiston County; the shut-down is costing the people of the county $60,000 a week. District President Farms and Vice-President Haskins were in the county last week, encouraging the strikers. At a sub-district convention held in Belton January 6, twenty-three delegates were chosen to attend the national convention which meets January 12. The London *Spectator* says: "The United States will not be allowed to order Spain out of her colony without a remonstrance from Con-tinental Europe, which might be followed by the action of the combined fleets of the Five Powers, and the landing of armies in Cuba." Spain will be ordered out of Cuba, remonstrance or no remonstrance; perhaps not this year, nor this decade, but some-time. And there will be no war. Our manifest destiny is to become the arbiter of the destiny of all mankind. The talker is a bore, the listener is charming. When Mrs. Tom Thumb and her company of Lilliputians come to the Rink, an outstanding feature of the entertainment will be a three-round boxing match between the Magic brothers, the smallest mature pugilists in the world. Ladies of the Pleasant Hour Club spent a delightful evening at the home of Mrs. Charles Arthur. Ohio has 650,000 men fit for military duty; no wonder England agreed to arbitrate the Venezuela affair. In Ohio, liquor licenses are prohibited by the Constitution; but anyone who wants to sell liquor pays a tax of $250 and gives bond to obey the rules. This is perhaps the most perfect and the best administered system in the United States; but it would be a good thing for humanity if there were no liquor tax. The national tax alone has taken $3,000,000,000 from the drinking public, and this impoverishes many and is a fruitful cause of indigence and pauperism.

7

This winter of 1896–1897 was for Owen bitter fare. When the
strike began, he had turned again to the *Journal* office, working
there on Wednesdays and Saturdays as in the past; but the two
dollars he took home each week, no matter how far Mrs. Glen
stretched it, was never quite enough for their necessities.

But Owen had not only to watch his mother's straining and
contriving, and to see her grow thinner every day; he had also to
face hostility among men he had counted his friends. He had
hoped to be sent as a delegate to the state convention, and when
this hope failed, he looked forward to possible selection as a delegate to the national convention. In anticipation of the sub-district
convention which would choose the delegates, Owen asked Charles
Morgan to propose his name.

"I will if you want," the old man told him. "And I know plenty
would second you, but you'd be beaten. You were against this
strike. At first the men didn't hold it against you; but now they
know they're going to lose the strike, so they blame you for being
right when they were wrong. So you'd better wait. Next time
they'll want you for their man."

Owen was young enough to despair. His dreams of leadership
and helpfulness seemed ended forever. His hold upon the men
was lost, as surely as the strike was lost; but if that were true,
into what new channel should he shape his life? To educate himself, to go to college, to become a lawyer and finally, like Bryan, to
burst upon the world, was a fine dream; but as a preliminary, he
must save money, and now there was no money to be saved. His
mother managed as she could; but before the end of the year,
they were again reduced to credit at Mr. McAuliffe's store. Amy
sent Dave from the farm with potatoes and beets and pumpkins
and jars of loose sausage and a supply of side meat; but that was
charity, and Owen rebelled against it. He blamed his father. That
old argument about the folly of this strike was revived; they had
words, on Tom Glen's part angry, on Owen's sullen. One day he
said harshly:

"We might as well move out to the Poor Farm and be done
with it."

His mother, busy at the stove, spoke without turning her head.
"If your home don't suit you, Owen, you can always leave it. Papa
and me have got along for over thirty years, and we can again."

He considered going away, but such thoughts were more pretense and play-acting than serious. Though Owen was in some
ways a man, he was in others still a boy. To think of leaving
home, of leaving the familiar for the unknown and the untried,
was frightening. Then, too, he knew that in the pinch he could
not leave his father and mother. There were occasions when in a
surprising fashion Tom Glen sought his opinion and advice. Owen
began to understand that his father leaned on him and drew
strength from him; to go away would be to rob Tom Glen of something which was his due. As for leaving his mother, Owen thought
he could more easily and with a higher heart cut off his hand and
throw it into the nearest pit. To remove himself from her would
be an amputation. There were bitter nights when he tossed in his
lonely bed, wishing he might go to their room as though he were
still a child of two or three years, and pillow his head against his
mother's breast and smell the smell of her and thus drown in
healing slumber. Once when he had sat late with the Latin dictionary and *Caesar's Commentaries* open on the table before him,
on the way to his room he paused at their door to look in on them.
They were asleep, his father on his back snoring mightily; and his
mother's head was on his father's shoulder and her hands clasped
his father's hand. Owen went on to his bed alone and lonely,
woeful because his father was her love and they were complete
without him.

They were complete without him; and yet he saw that not only
his mother but his father too thought of him first, and last of themselves. He saw how strictly she gave his father and himself the
best of what food they had, the biggest pats of sausage, the thickest
slices of side meat — while she herself grew gaunt, cheekbones
protruding, facial bones conspicuous as those of a skull. He tried
to eat less, till he ached with hunger; but when he left something
on his plate, instead of eating it herself she gave it to his father.
Worse, one day when Owen came late to table, he saw Tom Glen
secretly pass a pat of sausage from his plate to his son's. This proof

of what he had always known, that his father as well as his mother stinted themselves for his sake, was bitter in his mouth. They loved him and he loved them; but they were each helpless to help the others.

Knowing himself the beneficiary of their devotion, he came to be intensely sensitive, till he began to feel that the money Mr. Beecham paid him was charity. He remembered that when the mine was working and he could not come to the *Journal* office, the *Journal* still went to press on time; it was as packed with reading matter and with ads.

Mr. Beecham had first hired him, long ago, to help him buy those schoolbooks which Miss Dine required. That, certainly, was pure kindness; but then, so was all that had followed! Owen convinced himself he was not needed, and one day he said to Mr. Beecham:

"You'd get along all right without me. You're just letting me come here so you can pay me money."

BB looked at him for a moment, his head a little on one side. "Why, yes, Owen, we could get along without you. The world can get along without anyone. If I dropped dead tomorrow, the *Journal* would come out next Wednesday just the same. If Mr. McKinley died the day after he's inaugurated, the United States wouldn't go out of business. We can get along without you.

"But you're worth what I pay you, and maybe a little more." He hesitated. "Just a minute," he said, and he called Will Davis from the pressroom. "Will," he said, "Owen may be leaving us. Can you manage all right without him?"

If any sign passed between them, Owen did not see it. "Well, I could for a while," Will said thoughtfully. "But you'd have to get someone to help me out press days, or else I'll have to slow down on the job work. I can handle a lot more jobs when Owen's coming in two days a week."

BB nodded. "Thanks. Owen and I were just talking it over." Will departed, and BB said seriously: "You've earned more money than I've ever paid you, Owen. See here, suppose you take the last four *Journals* and measure the type you've set; see what you'd have earned if I paid you by the thousand ems, the way I pay the girls."

"Oh, I just do that in my spare time."

"Measure it. I'd like to know."

Owen did so, and he was surprised to find that in the four weeks, in addition to running the job press, feeding the big press, building fires, sweeping out, and doing odd chores of every kind, he had set enough type to earn five dollars and forty cents. Yet his pay amounted to only eight dollars for those four weeks! He had thought himself an object of charity; instead he was ridiculously underpaid! When he reported the figures to BB he added: "So maybe I'd better hit you for a raise."

BB thought he was joking; he threw up both hands, laughed. "Don't shoot! Not till after McKinley's been inaugurated, anyway! Maybe I can give you a raise then. Things should be better."

Owen grinned, but his words had not been altogether jest. An hour ago he had thought Mr. Beecham was charitable to pay him anything; now he decided that BB was parsimonious not to pay him more. He did his work that day in a morose and gloomy silence, scowling and resentful.

He had long ago begun to avoid Jane. If he saw her on the street, he turned away, or crossed to the other side. When chance brought them face to face, she was friendly as in the past, seeking to hold him in conversation, asking pleasant questions; but he answered with brief evasions and went on his way. He was equally careful to avoid men who had been his fellow workers. Since every man felt the harsh abrasion of long idleness and the pangs of poverty and debt, he knew they must resent the fact that he had been right when they were wrong. With Marged he could forget his loneliness as long as they spoke only of the books she bade him study, of his progress and his failure to progress, of his victories and his defeats; but in early January she said to him one evening:

"Owen, when are the men going to end this strike?"

"I don't know."

"Why don't you make them end it?" He looked at her in surprise. Her cheeks were bright with something like anger.

"I tried to get them not to strike in the first place."

"I know. Uncle Isaac told me. He says he knew they were bound to go out, so he didn't try to help you. Men are always so afraid of being beaten! But he thinks you could get them to go back to work now."

"They can go back to work any time they want to — for fifty-one cents."

"Why don't they?" There was a hint of tears in her tone. "Oh, Owen, their families — I see little children sneaking around, peeking into slop pails. Can't anyone do something? Can't you?"

A sense of guilt hardened his tone. "It's their strike! They started it! Let them end it."

She hesitated, watching him doubtfully. "So you're mad at them? Won't help them? Aren't you cutting off your nose to spite your face? If you ended the strike, you'd make a lot of new friends."

"I haven't even got any old friends now."

"Don't act like a child! Just because they sulk doesn't mean you have to. They won't admit they were wrong, for fear you'd gloat over them."

"I'm not sulking. But if they want me to do anything, they can say so."

Her eyes were dancing. "Achilles in his tent?" Owen did not understand, and she told him the ancient tale. "He acted like a boy, of course. Most men do, most of the time. It takes courage to come out of your tent and act like a man."

Because, despite his denial, he suspected she was right, he resented her advice, and he decided to stay away from her, too. His mother and his father, Jane, Mr. Beecham, now Miss Williams — they had all turned against him; the world was all against him.

With one exception. Nellie Tutson was as she had always been. She and her mother, since her father's death, had sold the small house in the flats; they now rented rooms from Mrs. Lewis, who had long been a friend of Owen's mother and who after her husband's death was left alone in the house down by the Ohio Southern tracks. The result had been that Mrs. Lewis and Mrs. Tutson and Owen's mother sometimes spent the afternoon together, and Owen's mother liked Nellie, said she was a nice girl, and real pretty, and took good care of her mother.

Owen saw Nellie regularly in the office. On press nights, she and Bets addressed the papers for mailing. The names of all subscribers were printed on strips of yellow paper, each as long as a newspaper column. The girls' tools were a pastepot, and a small piece of wood which was shod with a brass plate an inch wide and two inches long and had a loop on top through which a finger could be thrust. On each yellow strip there were fifteen or twenty names and addresses. To smear paste on the reverse side of these strips, flip them over, and with the brass plate press down and tear off each address in turn upon a copy of the *Journal* was for Bets and Nellie a mechanical routine, deft and accurate. All the papers for any one post office — Sycamore Hill, Slacktown, Glendale, Belton or the smaller offices throughout the county — were thus marked with the names of the subscribers, then packed in bundles for mailing. Single copies were wrapped separately.

Wednesday night, January 13, Will Davis had a cold, so after the paper had been run off — it was delayed in going to press — Owen told him to go along home. "I'll stay and see them mailed." Before the last papers were addressed, it was late evening. The girls prepared to depart, and they all left the office together. Bets lived at the foot of Main Street, down near Union Furnace, while Nellie went in the other direction. Main Street, except for the arc light at the corner of Broad and the lights in the Post Office and in the *Journal* office, was dark. Owen took the last bundles of papers to the Post Office, said goodnight to Bets, then returned to put out the lamps and lock up. He blew out the lamp in the front office — it was suspended from the ceiling with an ingenious counterweight — pulling it down for the purpose, pushing it up again; but another lamp still burned in the file room, and as he reached it, he heard someone coming down from the type loft.

It was Nellie. "I forgot my purse," she explained. "I had to come back."

Owen blew out the lamp, and they started toward the door that led through the front office to the street. For a moment they were blind in the dark. Owen knew there was a table, the corner of which was near his path, and he reached out, feeling for it to avoid it. In the darkness his hand met Nellie's.

She uttered a low startled word and laughed and would have drawn her hand away; but without any intention to do so, Owen clasped it, held it fast. He began to tremble.

She tugged at her hand. "Let go, Owen!"

His world — that world in which of late he moved alone with none he could call friend — was whirling emptiness, himself the center. But here, in the center, in the darkness, in the warm darkness warmed by the cooling stoves, her hand in his, was Nellie. He groped for her other hand, drawing her nearer while she sought to draw away; he held her fast with one hand, his free hand groped up her arm to her shoulder and then to her neck and cupped her nape. He pulled her roughly against himself, leaning down to kiss her.

Her lips, and even her cheek evaded him. "Don't! Don't! Let go!" she whispered, twisting her head down and away so that her hat was against his face. He fought awkwardly to hold her, and she wrenched away, but he caught her arm. "No, Owen!" she cried, no longer whispering. "Don't!"

Darkness loosed all bonds. He forced her against the table, pressing her backward, holding her face in his hands while she plucked at his wrists, finding her with his lips; and she put her hands against his face and pushed his head away, crying in hushed insistence: "No, Owen! No!" And when he did not release her, "I'll scratch you!"

He grappled her hands, suddenly angry. "You're a fine one to talk!"

"Don't, Owen! You're hurting me!"

"Quit fighting." He held her, pinned.

"Don't! You're too nice to do this."

For a moment he was frozen, then his hands relaxed. She stood up, facing him; he could see her, dimly, in the darkness. "Oh, all right." His voice was sullen, bitter.

She touched his arm. "Come, Owen. It's time I was home."

He went through the office and she followed him; he locked the door behind them. At the Flagg House, their ways diverged, but he did not turn. "I'll take you home," he said.

"I wish you would."

They walked the long half-mile down past the station, and on to the foot of Ridge Street and so to Mrs. Lewis's. On the way, neither spoke; but at the gate she paused, turning to him, waiting.

"Goodnight," she said. "You always were a nice boy, Owen." She rose on tiptoes to kiss his cheek. "Goodnight."

He walked home in angry humiliation. A nice boy? Well, that was what he was, all right! He repeated the words aloud, a sneer in his tone. Sure. A nice boy! Probably she was back there now laughing to herself, laughing at him.

By Gollies, next time she had better look out! He would not let her make a fool of him again.

XVIII

January 13, 1897 — June 12, 1897

T HEIR RENT was due on the fifteenth of each month. Tom Glen had taken the money to Moses Evans in December, but the fifteenth of January found them with only a little more than two dollars in the house. When Owen's mother, at breakfast Friday morning, confessed this and asked what they would do, Tom said harshly:

"Mose Evans can wait. He's waited before."

Owen looked at his mother. "I'll get paid tomorrow, mama. You give me two dollars, and I'll take my two dollars and that will pay him."

She agreed, and next day Owen asked BB if he could have his pay at noon. "I want to take the rent to Mr. Evans before he goes home," he explained. He found Moses Evans in his office and alone, standing at the window, looking out. The old man turned without speaking.

"Here's the rent, Mr. Evans." Owen laid the money on the desk.

The operator nodded. "Sit down." Owen did so, and Mr. Evans took the chair facing him. "How you getting along?"

"Better than most, I guess."

"What good does it all do?" Owen did not speak, and Mr. Evans said ruefully: "Nine or ten weeks you've all been out. You've lost right around a third of a million dollars in pay, among you."

"Mr. Beecham said the strike was costing the county sixty thousand dollars a week."

"Maybe so, if he counted what the operators have lost in profits."

"You can end the strike any time," Owen reminded him. "You can all afford to pay decent wages."

"I know. I don't know but we ought to. But we've always paid

454

the same as the Hocking Valley. Now they've gone up to fifty-one cents, and so have we. But the men don't come back."

Owen, after a moment, said: "Why don't you ask them to?"

"We did!" Mr. Evans was surprised and half-resentful. "We put up notices at the mines, the first of the year."

Owen shook his head. "You have to work through the Union. The Union voted to walk out; they'll have to vote to come back."

"The men and the Union are the same thing."

"Not by a mile, Mr. Evans." And Owen said gravely: "It's not just Hardiston County you're fighting, you know; not just the men who work your mines. It's all the union miners in Ohio, and in the United States, too."

"Somebody's got to give in."

"It won't be the Union." Owen came to his feet in a strong surge of feeling. "Why should they? What good does it do us to surrender? You wouldn't pay enough to live on, if we did. We've got nothing to lose. We're starving already." He strode across the room, turned to face the operator. "But Mr. Evans, we've got the Union to hang on to. It's a sort of dream, maybe; but there's a promise in it somewhere. Every man that pays his tax thinks maybe some day, somehow, if not for him then for his children, the United Mine Workers will do something, do some good. As long as he's got that hope, he's not going to give up his Union. But if you made a proposition to the Union, and gave in enough so the men could think they had won something, you might get somewhere."

"Think so?"

"Well, there's no harm to try."

Mr. Evans's eyes clouded with long thought. "I'm going to Columbus, anyway," he said at last. "I'll see Mr. Canter, see what he thinks."

Mail had played a minor part in Owen's life, and in the lives of his father and mother. First as secretary of Erie local and then of Miss Ellen, he had received bulletins and circulars from Headquarters; but they reached him in casual ways, by the hand of some neighbor to whom the postmaster had committed them, or through Will Davis, or BB, till rural free delivery last year brought a carrier along the Pike past their door.

It was on Saturday that Owen saw Mr. Evans. Tuesday, the

carrier stopped with a letter from the operator, mailed in Columbus the day before.

> DEAR MR. GLEN — *Pursuant to our conversation I met with Mr. Canter and the Executive Committee of the Operators' Association. It was agreed to reopen the mines on a minimum rate of fifty-one cents per ton, and to pay fifty-six cents in the Slacktown District. This is the Hocking Valley scale from which we can make no differential. I write for the Executive Committee, and request you put this letter before the officers of your local and of the Sub-District for their consideration, and whatever action they deem appropriate.*
>
> > Yours truly,
> > MOSES EVANS

Owen's first reaction was anger. This offer, though it might sound like a concession, was not; also, it was addressed to him as an individual rather than as an officer of the Union. He was tempted to destroy the letter, but then came doubt. If the proposal led to negotiations, a settlement might follow.

Yet the proposal should go to the Union heads, and after dinner Owen walked uptown and went to Mr. Evans's office to tell him so; but the door was locked. Presumably, the operator had not yet returned from Columbus.

Owen crossed to the *Journal* office and found pen and paper and an envelope; and he wrote:

> DEAR MR. EVANS,
> The enclosed proposal should be addressed to Matthew Price, Hardiston. He is secretary of the Sub-District.
>
> > Yours truly,
> > OWEN GLEN

He enclosed his letter and that from Mr. Evans in an envelope, and wrote on it Mr. Evans's address, and then remembered that he had no money for a stamp. He could not bring himself to appeal to Mr. Beecham, nor to Will; so he walked home and confessed his need to his mother. She looked at him for a moment, and he saw her eyes fill before she turned away.

"Who's the letter to, Owen?" she asked, reaching up for the baking-powder tin.

"Moses Evans."

She whirled upon him. "Moses Evans!" Her cry was almost a
scream. "Are you crazy! Spending money for a stamp with him
right here in Hardiston! I thought you had more sense!" She
banged the baking-powder tin back on the shelf, with a thin jangle
of coins. "If you've got to write him letters, take 'em and give 'em
to him!"

He could not move nor speak. This was someone never seen
before, this raging, red-faced, furious scolding woman. She met
his eyes and for a moment tried to stare him down, and then her
hands began to toss at her sides as though she were being shaken
up and down, and her head turned this way and that, and he saw
her lower lip caught between her teeth, and a thin red spurt of
blood. She flung on her knees beside the table, her head in her
arms, wailing aloud, and Owen came to her in terror, touched her.
She flamed at him. "Get out of here! Get away from me! Get out!
Get out! Get out!" He backed away, and she tried to rise to come
after him, and tripped over her own skirts and fell on her face
across the floor.

He came a step nearer, and she began to cry aloud, and he knelt
and then sat beside her and drew her in his arms, and she clung
to him with thin arms like wires, and her face wet with tears
pressed into his neck, and he murmured tenderness and comforting
and they stayed like lovers close entwined until her weeping yielded
to deep sobs and then to sighs — and then to laughter. She sat up,
pushing back her hair; and Owen faced her, and she said, in thin
mirth near hysteria:

"Lord o' mercy, what a fuss about a stamp! There's enough
money there . . ." she hesitated, pointing to the tin on the shelf,
calculating. "Enough to buy thirty-eight stamps! Help yourself,
Owen." She extended a hand. "Here, help me up."

He did so. "Are you all right, mama."

"Of course I am. I'm all right, Owen. I'm just fine."

2

Mr. Evans took Owen's advice; he wrote to Matthew Price, and
the Executive Board of the Sub-District met the operators Wednes-

day night, the twentieth; next day they issued a notice to the miners.

> *Gentlemen — Your board met the operators last night.
> The operators agreed that we could resume work on
> former conditions, and that no one would be victimized
> for any part he may have taken in this struggle. We re-
> quest all locals to call a meeting and vote on whether they
> will work at Hocking Valley prices or continue the
> struggle. Record your vote and send it with a delegate
> to be counted next Sunday afternoon.*

The vote was against surrender, and Owen heard some angry talk of continuing the strike to establish a differential against the Hocking Valley field; but he heard, too, that scores and hundreds of miners were going back to work on the operators' terms. He was not surprised when on Tuesday Eben Howell and the Executive Board issued a notice ending the strike.

> *Whereas after the results of the last vote, which gave a
> large majority to continue the struggle, we find miners
> returning to work regardless of their decision to stay out,
> your board, after carefully considering the situation, and
> consulting our most intelligent miners, deem it proper and
> wise and the only thing we can do intelligently, to declare
> the strike at an end. We advise all miners to return to
> work at once.*

Owen worked in the *Journal* office Wednesday, but Thursday morning he returned with his father to the mine. During the next few days he found to his surprise that in the eyes of his fellows he had acquired an increased stature. Moses Evans told John Powell, and Powell told many men, that Owen had set the spark which led the operators to open negotiations and hence contributed to the settlement. Owen's original opposition to the strike was not forgotten, and its failure made many men willing to agree that he had been right in the beginning. Since November 7, every man had lost, in wages he might have earned, even at forty-five cents a ton, some six or seven dollars a week. Now February was upon them, and there were level heads ready to point out that with the spring lull coming on, it would take a long time to make up for that pay they had not earned.

So except for a few who were moved more by emotion than by reason — Tom Glen was one of these — the men decided their strike had been a mistake. That Owen had opposed it won him a new respect.

But not from his father. "You're all swelled up like a poisoned pup," Tom said rancorously. "You need a taking down."

"I haven't said anything."

"You don't have to say anything! I see you, whenever someone slaps you on the back or tells you how smart you are; you look like a cat lapping cream."

"I thought the strike was a mistake, but I walked out with the rest of you — and stayed out, till Eben Howell gave the word."

"Yes, and spent your time hanging around Mose Evans. You'd better stick with your own bread and butter."

Owen's anger broke bounds. "I've earned my own bread and butter for quite a while now — yes, and yours, too, while you polished a chair with your pants here at home."

He would have said more, but his mother hushed him. "That's no way to talk to papa." There were tears in her eyes, and for her sake he was silent, while Tom berated him with many words. In their first hour alone together, his mother said: "Don't mind papa, Owen! He don't mean the half of what he says."

"Why does he say it, then?"

"Part of it's because he's so proud of you. He comes home every night telling me fine things men have said to him about you, pretending it's all foolishness; but he's awful proud underneath. That's part of it, Owen; but the other part is, he's getting old. He's almost sixty. He's an old man and he knows it. It scares him, and he don't want to admit it, and so he hates to let on that you're a grown man. You let him talk, Owen. Don't talk back to him." She smiled and touched his arm. "You'll have an uppity son of your own, some day; then you'll know how he feels. As long as a young one keeps on acting like a fool young one, grownups can laugh at him; but it's hard for a man when he knows, inside himself, that his boy is a better man already than he ever was. You let papa talk. He'll talk big to you about how no good you are; but you ought to hear him brag you up to me."

Owen laughed, and he hugged her hard. "I don't feel grownup," he said. "But I think grown men are awful babies a lot of the time."

"I know. I know. Men never do grow up, none of 'em. If they did, women wouldn't love them. Women love babies, and that's what keeps the world going. We love babies and little boys, and our menfolk always stay little boys to us. You'll never be anything but my little boy, to me. You nor papa either."

"I wish he was the way you are."

She shook her head. "He never will be. Fathers and sons always do fuss at each other. You'll see the same thing in roosters, and rams, and bulls, and all the animals; and that means men! The big bull butts the little one, son or no son; and the little one keeps out of the way till he's big enough to butt his pa!

"But don't make any mistake about it, Owen; no matter what papa says, he's mighty proud of you."

3

Additional Locals: The Young Women's Christian Temperance Union library, containing three hundred and seventy-five books, would hereafter be open to ticket holders every Saturday afternoon from two till four-thirty. Yearly tickets were a quarter, and a book could be kept for four weeks. A revolving holder for hotel registers had been patented by Thomas Martin and would be manufactured in Hardiston. Let every laborer provide himself with an acre of garden, a pig and some poultry.

Only twenty-eight more days of Grover; let the people rejoice!

No man can earn $25,000 a year. When he is paid that much, his salary comes out of other men's pockets. Two boys exploring an abandoned mine near Slacktown were lost for nine hours.

Twenty-one more days of Grover; sing hosannas!

James Stillman was killed by the miners' train near Slacktown, and Charles Day was killed when the fuel hoist gear at Moon Furnace let go. Three men were badly burned when the hearth at Gallia Furnace let go above the tuyeres, spilling molten metal.

Fourteen more days of Grover; strike up the band!

Rains Saturday and Sunday raised Salt Creek eighteen inches above the highest mark recorded in thirty years, and probably higher than in the great flood of 1847. In the glacial era, the Ohio River flowed north. The Edison Vitascope delighted a large audience at the Rink Friday. Walter Himes, a brakeman, was killed coupling cars at Waverly last Thursday.

Seven more days of Grover!

The Hocking Valley Railway is in receivership. Engineers propose to supply the whole state of Ohio with water from Lake Erie.

The People's Edict: Cleveland, March Fo(u)rth!

Americans who wish to commit suicide should get themselves into a Havana prison; the Spaniards will do the rest.

McKinley, Hobart, Bushnell, Hanna and Foraker took office under a fair sky and a bright sun. Hanna was appointed to succeed Senator John Sherman, who became Secretary of State. The era of prosperity has begun.

4

To go back to work after long idleness lifted Owen out of the slough through which all winter he had labored. Life acquired a new savor. His evenings with Marged, even though sometimes for an hour at a time the only sound in the room was the scratching of his pencil, or of hers, wore a new contenting richness.

Also, with spring at hand, he turned back to Jane; but she seemed now to him disappointingly young and immature. If he spoke of the affairs which filled his thoughts, the mine, the Union, the desperate privation which the long winter strike had laid upon so many, she listened till he paused, and said: "Oh, how awful!" or "Oh, how sweet!" or "Isn't that just terrible?" or "Isn't that grand?" But these exclamations left him empty; he wished he could slap them away as one slaps at irritating flies, or buzzing gnats. He blamed himself for being irritated or bored by her; he tried to recapture something forever lost, but when he kissed her, her cool lips were a child's, as empty of emotion as her soft words were empty of intelligence. He tried to define the change in her, but he could never put a name to it, not wise enough to suspect that the change was less in her than in himself. She seemed years younger than he; Miss Williams, on the other hand, now seemed hardly any older.

There was a difference, too, in his feeling toward Nellie Tutson. He felt toward her a certain gratitude — in which there was a

trace of condescension. After all, that night in the file room, if he
had persisted, she was not strong enough to resist him; but she had
prevented his making a fool of himself and he was glad she had
done so. Owen had no illusions about Nellie; he had known her
too long, not only through his own encounters with her but by the
report of other boys. But whatever she had used to be, Nellie was
all right now. Since, although the strike was ended, work soon
slacked off, Owen was often in the *Journal* office and often worked
side by side with her, and found it pleasant to do so.

In mid-March, spring on the flood, Owen and BB went into the
country together; and there was a singing in the air and Owen
thought there was a singing in his blood. Their road passed Nate
Frye's, and when they came there Nate and Mrs. Frye were sitting
out-of-doors in a sun-warmed corner, Mrs. Frye knitting and Mr.
Frye bouncing a baby on his knee. BB called a greeting and Nate
bade them in, but BB said: "Not today. We've a long tramp
ahead." When they had passed out of hearing he told Owen:
"Nate's the proudest father you ever saw."

"Is that the baby the woman left here?"

"Yes. A funny thing, Mrs. Frye's as proud as he. And I don't suppose they were ever really happy before. Forgiveness leads sometimes to a lot of happiness."

For this noon hour BB led the way up Dale's Gulch toward a
spring they had used before. At the edge of the creek, where the
trickle from the spring had built a little fan of fine white sand, BB
checked and pointed; and Owen saw the print of a woman's bare
foot.

"Now what do you make of that?" BB challenged. Instinctively,
Owen looked all around, and BB saw, and smiled. "She's gone," he
said. "Whoever she was. What are you thinking?"

"About Lavengro and Ab Gwilym, and when Morffyd used to
meet him in the woods."

"I know. A woman's naked footprint in the forest will always
thrill a man. That thrill must date back to primeval times." He
knelt, began to break twigs for a fire. "This sex instinct in us is a
strange medley, isn't it? And after all, it's the saving instinct of
the race." He scratched a match. "Whoever left that footprint here
was not an ordinary woman. There was a wild strain in her, which
the forest awakened. It tempted her to wade in the creek, and

probably she would have bathed in it, if it had been deep enough."

"Someone might have seen her."

"Probably she was not alone." BB chuckled. "And if she was, half her fun would have come from being afraid someone really would surprise her."

Owen nodded, recognizing truth. Bathing in the creek near Erie Mine derived an added charm from the fact that Nellie – or someone – might come upon them there. "Who do you suppose it was?"

BB, biting into his sandwich, frowned in an amused way. "More interesting not to know," he suggested. "Then we can think of her as young and beautiful."

They walked, before that day was done, a long twenty miles, talking of many things; and they came home by the Chillicothe turnpike and BB said the country needed more such roads. He added, thinking aloud. "Means new taxes, but the taxes will come out of the pockets of property owners – and the poor will enjoy the turnpikes." After a moment he added: "In any community, you find a few very rich men, and a great many poor ones. High taxes – yes, and corrupt government – are better for poor people. A corrupt government spends a lot of money on public improvements, so they can steal a part of the money that's spent and not be caught at it; but at the same time the city gets better streets and fine public buildings. What would Rome be but for the extravagance of the corrupt Emperors? If Egypt had been a Republic, who would have built the pyramids? The world is full of enduring architectural beauty which has been created for their own profit by greedy and corrupt rulers of men – but the poor man can enjoy that beauty free."

"People in Hardiston County right now would a lot rather have something to eat than a building to look at."

"Did you read that letter signed 'Cuba Libre' in this week's paper? The one I reprinted from the *Mine Workers Journal*, about the suffering among the miners and their families?"

"Yes. Why did he sign it that way?"

"Irony, perhaps. To remind us that while we're all weeping with sympathy for the poor Cubans, there are hundreds of children right here in the county who have no shoes, no decent clothes, no decent home, not enough to eat." He added, like a question, looking at

Owen: "I suppose the conditions he described do exist, up the creek, and elsewhere in Ohio."

"I guess up the creek is as bad as anywhere. The strike this winter used up everything anybody had saved."

"Strikes are losing their influence," BB remarked. "The percentage of failures is steadily increasing. Of course, little strikes are always bound to lose, because immigrant labor replaces the striking Americans. But labor's real weapon is not the strike but the ballot box. Strike with ballots; that's the only sure way."

"Our strike this winter was a failure," Owen agreed. "We can't ever beat the operators unless we have money to live on when we strike. It was crying babies at home that made the men give up and go back to work." He spoke quietly, without heat, as though discussing some problem in mathematics. "I'd like to see every man in the Union put a dollar a month into a big fund till we had plenty."

"You're young and you're not married," BB reminded him. "Last year the miners in Ohio averaged to earn less than two hundred and twenty dollars apiece, for the whole year. If you had four or five children at home, and only earned two hundred and twenty dollars a year, a dollar a month would seem like a lot of money to you."

"The trouble is — " Owen frowned, trying to see clearly. "Well, I know if I had anything to say about it, I'd never strike if business was bad."

"You have something to say about it. No one will stop you from saying what you choose."

"I know. I tried to keep them from striking last November; but I didn't say the right things, or say them the right way, or something. A miner's queer. When there's plenty of work, and he could save something, he won't; and when work's short, and he couldn't save even if he wanted to — he'll strike and starve!"

"His own worst enemy?"

Owen's eyes were on the road. "Well, isn't every man? Outside of getting killed, or hurt, or something, nothing ever happens to a man as bad as the things he does to himself."

"I'd never thought of that," BB confessed, and they were silent for a while, and so came back to town.

5

It was that talk with BB, and a second reading of the letter signed "Cuba Libre" which had been printed in the *Journal*, that decided Owen a few days later to see for himself conditions elsewhere in the county. In Hardiston, the coal deposits were so nearly worked out that the iron furnaces and lesser industries were now the economic life blood of the town. Belton, at the other end of the car line, had once been ranked by the Cincinnati *Enquirer* with Cripple Creek in Colorado, and with Sisterville in West Virginia, as the three wickedest towns in the United States; but in Belton, too, coal had ceased to be the leading business interest. But in Slacktown and in Glendale, every man except those who kept stores or restaurants or saloons worked in the mines; so it was to one of these towns that Owen elected to go.

He went on the electric cars, and alighted at Slacktown. This was Friday, so few or no mines were working. The men were on the streets, talking in little groups, clustering near the saloons. Many of them Owen knew by sight, sometimes only as familiar faces, frequently as faces to which he could put a name. Many more of them, having heard him speak or as secretary make his reports at the miners' meetings, knew Owen. He joined a group of four men. Evan Lloyd and Joe Riley and Moses Dean he knew; they named the fourth, Dan Boggus. The fight at Carson City in which Fitzsimmons beat Jim Corbett, who had only a few years before beaten the great John L. Sullivan, was only a fortnight in the past; they spoke of this, of the mighty punch of the freckled little man and of the solar plexus where the punch landed, and Dan cried:

"Solar plexus, is it? I never knew I had one, till I read it in the paper."

He hiccoughed slightly, and Owen remembered reading in the *Journal*, years ago, of another Dan Boggus, who might have been father to this one and who fell asleep on the railroad track and was run over by a train. He ventured to speak of this.

"That was my old man, yes," Dan agreed, pleased. "He was on

the way home from Tom's Place, over across there, and he laid down to rest a piece." He brushed that subject aside, returning to the prize fight. "Tom got the fight, round by round, by telegraph to his Place." He chuckled cheerfully. "There was more fighting that day in Tom's Place than in the ring out at Carson City. Every time a fight started here, they'd be tossed out-of-doors to go at it, and that made the more room for them still inside. When the knockout came, Tom was stakeholder, and he had well on to a hundred dollars in bets to pay."

When the group dissolved, Dan proposed that he and Owen stop at Tom's Place; but Owen declined. "I'm just walking around to see the town. The strike must have been pretty hard on you all here."

Dan wiped his mouth with the back of his hand in a thirsty way. "Oh, aye, it was hard enough, the cold weather. Three of my young ones had to take turns with one pair of shoes to go to the privy. But it was never as hard here as it was in Glendale, on Red Row, say, or along Ada Bend. We've got a fine warm house. Come along to my place and you'll see."

Owen went with him. Dan was a cheerful small man, and it was clear that he knew everyone and everyone knew him. Children followed him for a taste of his simple friendliness, and he had a word and a laugh for each. His house, when they came to it, was the last of a row of shanties and houses all much alike. His was of two rooms, with loose boards laid on the earth for a floor, and upright planks nailed to sill and plate for walls. The planks were papered with newspapers to hinder the wind. The attic had rough slabs with the bark side down for a floor; the roof was flattened powder tins nailed on poles.

"Now there's as fine a house as you could rent anywhere for four dollars a month," said Dan proudly. "And I built it myself! It cost me, say, ten dollars for lumber — and what I could pick up on a dark night in my travels, a board here and a board there — and a couple of pounds of nails, and there's no rent to pay at all. Mind the door; it's low for a tall man."

Dan's wife was as cheerful as he, neat and brisk and bright. The inside of the hut was all in order, the old stove fresh-blacked, newspapers with scalloped edges laid on the shelves, a touch of curtain at the windows; the red and blue tablecloth was patched but clean. Owen said admiringly: "You surely keep everything nice, Mrs. Boggus. You're as good as my mother."

"It's more of a trouble when the flies get bad," she admitted. "Then I have to keep newspapers spread over everything. But Dan's going to get me some cheesecloth and make me some screens." She asked her husband, "Did you fetch the bit pork, Danny?"

"There, now!" he cried. "I clean forgot, talking with Mr. Glen." He reached in his pocket. "Aye, and here's worse: If I haven't gone and lost the two bits you gave me, too. Wherever could it be?"

She cuffed him lightly. "You! Fine tales! Tom's Place is paved with quarters you've lost so. No matter, I've dug a fine dish of dandelions, and with salt enough on them, you'll not miss the pork."

The children were in and out, in and out. "How many?" Owen asked and Dan said cheerfully:

"Why, seven I made it, last count." He added with a chuckle: "It's not a thing I'd swear to. There's all of fifty children from here to the corner, and if they're the same size you can't tell any two of 'em apart till they get their faces washed."

Owen through the door looked along the rutted street. There were in fact a score or so of children in sight. "A lot of them, all right."

"Aye, it's a fine neighborhood," said Dan Boggus proudly. "If you're ever on Ada Bend up in Glendale you'll see the difference."

"You got through the winter all right here?"

"Well enough. If there wasn't enough to eat on your own table, you were welcome at your neighbor's. There's not but four or five pairs of shoes from here to the corner — children's size, I mean — so if it was cold, or snow on the ground, they couldn't go outdoors. But we could pick up enough dead sticks and wood down along the creek to keep a little fire, and stay close around it. If it was too cold, the young ones stayed in bed. You get four-five in a bed and the ones on the inside are warm, and they'd keep changing. Yes, one way and another, we were all right. But places in Glendale, I hear they had it hard."

Owen did not go to Glendale to see for himself; he had seen enough. He had sometimes thought of his father and mother as poor; but they had a floor and walls and a roof that kept out the weather, and real beds and chairs and tables instead of the rude rough-lumber products of Dan's unskillful carpentry. Compared to Dan Boggus, Tom Glen was rich; but Dan was complacently proud of his quarters, fine compared with the huts and shanties in Glendale. Probably there were places worse than Glendale, too.

Back in Hardiston, Owen's thoughts led him past the home of Moses Evans, and then of Mr. Beecham. They were each one story high, with pleasant wide verandas and a well-trimmed lawn; and compared to Tom Glen's home, they were palaces. At Mr. Beecham's, Owen turned and retraced his steps till he came to the house where — on the rare occasions when he was in Hardiston — Herbert Canter made his home. The house was two stories and a half, of brick, with iron balconies and balustrades, and ornamental fretwork under the sloping timbers at the gable ends. Owen thought it had probably cost thousands of dollars. Now it stood empty, while Mr. Canter was away in Columbus, or in New York, or in Europe.

Dan Boggus worked in one of Mr. Canter's mines, yet Owen could not rouse himself to any honest indignation. The contrast between their homes was not the only contrast between the two men. Mr. Canter, if Mrs. Canter gave him a quarter to buy pork for their dinner, would not spend it for drink and go emptyhanded home. Suppose you took all Mr. Canter's money away from him and gave it to Dan Boggus? That would make Dan Boggus in the long run neither happier nor richer; it would make Mr. Canter neither unhappy nor a pauper.

Money was nothing. Yes, it was something; but what? Perhaps money's value to you depended upon how you got it. To give Dan Boggus a lot of money would certainly be no kindness; but suppose Dan had a chance to earn two dollars a day, and three, and perhaps even four dollars in a day, if such a thing were possible! Certainly Dan would then be a lot better off, and a proud man he would be. Surely there was no better road to self-respect than earning money; not merely enough to live on, but enough and some to spare.

6

Additional Locals: The man with the dinner pail carries the future of the Republic in his hands. Of 4282 miners in the county, 1282 should go back to the farm, for machines will soon do all the mining. Now is the time to buy a pig and spade up an acre of garden. Street loafing is the vice that leads to all others. If you passed a law to prohibit young men going to church, every pew would be filled. Hardiston County peaches will in time pay better than Hardiston County coal ever did. Reckless bicycle riding leads to serious accidents. The Union Temperance meeting at the Presbyterian Church Sunday evening was well attended. Mrs. Evan Williams of Adams Township, whose daughter Miss Marged Williams teaches in Hardiston High School, died Monday, April 12; she was buried at Sardis Church. Floods this year made the Mississippi River the largest body of fresh water on earth. Humphrey's Hardware advertises a $35 bicycle that is a beauty. Why color your own Easter eggs when you can buy them cheaper at the Egg Social at the Baptist Church? Cows and horses running at large inside the corporation limits should be put in the pound. A committee has been appointed to study the practicability of putting bathrooms in our school buildings. The Sherman Law, by Supreme Court decision, is now a living thing; the complacent plutocrats who cheered the Court when it outlawed the income tax and issued injunctions that defeated Labor are now screaming abuse. The next State Legislature should provide for a few troops of cavalry; for there will be wars as long as Turks, Austrians, Russians, and Spaniards are allowed to rule other people. Hail as big as marbles fell April 25th. The Turks have killed 100,000 Christians in two years, but Turkish bonds are held in Germany, France and England, so those nations will not interfere. The idea of Civil Service originated in China; as a result, in China today every office has its price. Civil Service leads to corruption, laziness and waste. The nation that wants to arbitrate must see a licking ahead. The laborer is always ready to vote for things that raise taxes, even though he pays the taxes in the end. The multiplication of "necessities" makes the poor man poorer. National expenditures per capita were $1.65 in 1840, $10.00 in 1890; no wonder times are hard. To prove your opponent wrong does not prove you are right. People eat hog meat made of corn and slop, yet they scorn horse meat made of corn and hay; but after all, no one since Nebuchadnezzar has eaten hay. If Adam lived 6000 years and saved $100 each weekday, he would today be worth $180,000,000; but the Astors are worth that and they're still alive. One hundred and seventy families own one half of Manhattan Island; ninety per cent of the 2,000,000 residents pay rent. McKinley's message to Congress may lead to war with Spain; he reports Cuban conditions worse every day, with United States citizens suffering and in danger. The Electric Park will open for the summer season next Sunday, May 30. Brains and manure make a farm pay. By espousing the cause of the Armenians, the Greeks and the Cubans, McKinley can win a fame equal to Lincoln's. In May, *Quo Vadis* was the most popular book in the United States. Marshal Henson arrested several disreputable women on the streets of Hardiston Saturday night, and also in some of the houses opposite the B & O station; those who would not promise to leave town are now in jail. Let us have no dealings with an England that makes war on a country as small as the Transvaal. Twelve girls and ten boys graduated from high school; good for you, boys! The Columbus Experiment Station has determined that wide-tired wagons wear out roads less than narrow tires. Jenkin Powell's strawberries are so big that sixteen make a quart; he brought a box to this office Saturday. · Philip Fremont graduated from Annapolis and is home for a vacation before starting off on a two-year cruise.

7

This spring and early summer of 1897 were for Owen empty alike of zeal and of hope. The coal trade had collapsed into almost complete stagnation, and reports from Union Headquarters were steadily discouraging. Less than ten thousand miners were paying the union tax; the treasury was empty; miners throughout the state were reduced to penury, and in many cases they and their families were living on charity. In every mining district, misery and semi-starvation were commonplace.

Yet to Owen it seemed that there was nothing which could be done; for wages meant little when there was no work. In March the Executive Board of the Union issued a circular protesting to the American people against DeArmitt and his methods, but the circular had no result; the Pittsburgh scale was reduced at last to forty-five cents, and Ohio operators outside of Hardiston County cut wages accordingly, in one case to thirty-three and a half cents. Republican prosperity, which Mr. Beecham had so long predicted, was slow in coming.

Owen was saved from absolute despair by the two days each week which he spent in the *Journal* office. He and his father went to Miss Ellen for an occasional rare day or two of work; and for the rest, they tended the garden, and Owen mowed lawns and did odd jobs. Sunday afternoons, or any evening, might find him with Marged at his studies; but he was in no mind for study, weary of waiting for times to change, for the mines to be busy, for work. When he was with Marged, his attention wandered from his books, and he and she might fall into long talk together. It was always of him and his problems that they talked. He spoke of Dan Boggus up the creek, of DeArmitt, of idle mines, of machines and the men they replaced. She was so ready to listen to his concerns that it did not occur to him to be curious about hers. She was busy teaching school, and now that Bobby Roberts had married someone else and no other man seemed to pay her any attention, she would probably go on teaching school as long as she lived. Without consciously shaping this conclusion, he assumed that the pattern of her life was settled. Meanwhile, he liked being with her, not actively nor with any eager anticipation, but with a calm contentment at the time and pleasant memories afterward.

He did not hear of her mother's death till after Marged had gone to Sardis for the funeral. When he knew she had returned, he put on his Sunday suit and went to see her, and told her awkwardly that he was sorry. She nodded. "But mama'd been sick a long time," she reminded him. "She never was really well after I was born." Her eyes suddenly misted. "She always liked to remind me of that," she said, not with any bitterness. "It wasn't my fault." And she added honestly, "Aunt Molly's always been my real mother."

"How's your father?"

"Oh, he's fine. Aunt Molly's there." She met his eyes. "I oughtn't to have said that about mama, Owen."

He thought it must be hard to feel that way about your mother, and he was so sorry for Marged that he wanted to put his arm around her and kiss her and tell her everything would be all right, but of course he did not do so.

He had begun this spring, at his mother's insistence, to keep for himself some of the money he earned. When she made the suggestion and he protested, she said in pretended wrath, "I don't want you running to me every time you want to buy a postage stamp!"

He remembered that day with a sort of horror. "With all the money you bring home, it's a pity if you can't keep some of it."

So he kept what he earned by odd jobs, or by mowing lawns; and when he presently had a sufficient accumulation, he exchanged some small coins for a silver dollar, and showed it to her.

"I'm never going to spend this dollar, either," he said. "Because as long as I have it in my pocket, I'll never be busted."

"You need some more to rattle with it," she reminded him. "Save all you can." Since he rarely spent anything, he was, by the end of May, relatively affluent.

The Electric Park, on the Belt Railway up the creek, attracted crowds to spread their picnic lunches under the trees and to listen to the bands or ride the merry-go-round. The grand gala opening came on Sunday night, the thirtieth of May, and Owen secretly wished to go; but of course that was out of the question. The Sabbath was not meant for pleasuring. But Nellie told him in the office the following Wednesday that she and Jenkin Powell and half a dozen others went to the opening and had a wonderful time.

"And there's a dance every Saturday night," she said. "So I expect we'll go a lot, all summer."

Owen had never even seen anyone dancing. Dancing and playing cards and liquor were devices of the devil. Of course, card games were all right — Authors, and Flinch, and Logomachy; but "playing cards," the sort that included Kings and Queens and Jacks, were pitfalls for the unwary.

Against liquor and playing cards he was secure. He had signed the temperance pledge, not once but three times, as waves of reform agitation swept church and school. He never sipped communion wine, feeling its sweet warmth in his throat, without wondering why his pledge of abstinence was not by this indulgence broken; and if it were true, as the temperance lecturers said, that the first drink was the first step to a drunkard's grave, why did not the communion wine doom them all? As for cards, he had seen men play, slapping down each card with laughter and loud cries while they waited by the siding for the homebound train; but he had no instinct for gaming nor for gambling — he had never even played marbles for keeps — so cards did not attract him.

Yet to spend an evening at Electric Park — with Nellie, or with Jane, or with someone — and perhaps to dance was suddenly the high desire of his heart, till even to think of the possibility made him perspire and made his pulse pound. The Electric Park became for him like Heaven to the followers of Mahomet; a place gay with music, and bright as day with brilliant bulbs, and populated by charming girls, beautiful and friendly, swaying invitation to the embraces of the dance, strolling with you from the light into the shadows, warm in the concealing darkness, soft and kind.

His longing persisted till a Saturday afternoon in June when Louie Peters came to the office to fetch Nellie. Jenkin Powell would meet them at the car. "And why don't you come along, Owen?" Louie suggested. "Maud's going." Maud was his sister. "And Hetty Jenkins, and a friend of hers, and Dave Evans. Jim Tower was going, but he can't. Come along."

They had all been in school together, till Louie, like Owen, quit to go to work. Hetty Jenkins? Owen remembered the day at Panter's Caves when they hid together and she kissed him; but soon after that she went to Columbus to live, and he had almost forgotten her. Maud Peters was completely unexciting, in thick-lensed glasses, with stringy hair, forever giggling. But Hetty? Yes, and Nellie?

Owen felt a pulse in his throat; he set his jaw in hot decision. Probably he ought to go home and put on his Sunday suit, but to do so would provoke his mother's questions, and the clothes he had worn to work were neat enough.

"I'll have to wait till we're through here." The press was rolling, Will feeding it. "Half an hour?"

"We're taking the six-o'clock car. You've got time." Nellie came running down the stairs from the type loft, and Louie told her Owen was to join them. She looked at him in faint hesitation, but only for a moment.

"Oh, that's dandy! See you on the car!"

Owen had in his pocket not only his silver dollar, plus some small change, but also the two dollars that were his week's pay, and a high recklessness began to rise in him. He meant to have a good time tonight, even if he spent it all!

When the inside was printed and his work done, he hurried to the terminus of the Belt Line. The others were already seated in the bay at the end of the car waiting its time. Dave sat with Hetty and another girl on one side, facing the others across the car, and Hetty caught Owen's hand and made room for him between her and the other girl.

"I haven't seen you for a coon's age, Owen. Whatever have you been doing with yourself?"

"Oh, working. I thought you were in Columbus."

"I am. I work in the Neil House, waiting on table, but I've got a week's vacation." She reached across him to tug at the arm of the other girl. "Kit, Kit, meet Owen Glen that I told you about, remember? Owen, meet Miss Peace. Miss Kittie Peace. She came home with me."

Owen shook hands with Miss Peace. He thought she had mighty pink cheeks; but then, so had Hetty. Hetty slipped her hand through his arm. "'Member that picnic at Panter's Caves, when we hid together, Owen? Wasn't that fun?"

Owen remembered, with some disquietude, and yet with a deep stir of excitement, too; and Miss Peace, leaning against his arm, said, "Hetty says you're awful shy."

He felt his cheeks burn. "I am not! But I don't go with girls much."

"You used to go with Jane Lloyd," said Hetty; and to hear Jane's name here made him suddenly uncomfortable. Jane would not be going up to Electric Park like this, with just boys and girls her own age and no grownups along. Hetty leaned across him to tell Miss Peace about Jane, and her light summer dress was low, and loose in front, so Owen looked over her head across the car at Nellie. She was sitting with Jenkin Powell, and Louie and Maud Peters were beside them. Owen wished he was over across the car with Nellie. She never made him uncomfortable and embarrassed as Hetty was doing now, leaning across in front of him; and Miss Peace, on his other side, kept edging closer and closer to him. He began to perspire, and proposed to open a window, but Hetty said: "No, no. It will blow our hair." She smelled of perfume, and so did Miss Peace, and while it was a pleasant fragrance, he felt he was not supposed to smell it; so he sat up straight, and Hetty and her friend talked across him, and Owen saw Nellie watching him with sympathetic amusement in her eyes.

The Electric Park, a tract of eight or ten acres, was set in a grove of oaks on a low ridge a few feet above the tracks, and it was liberally festooned with electric bulbs so that most of it was light

as day. The underbrush had been cleared away up across the top
of the ridge, but down on the further slope a tangled thicket of
young oaks had been allowed to stand. There no bulbs burned.
This shaded secret tract was called the Dell, and it was laced with
many secret, wandering paths. The bandstand and dance floor
were a hundred yards away along the ridge. A merry-go-round and
a Ferris wheel down near the entrance blazed with lights, and the
organ on the merry-go-round filled the air with monotonously
tinkling melody. There were booths for ring-toss, and spin-the-
wheel and all the catchpenny tricks of carnival and street fair; but
these were set along the side of the Park nearest the electric cars.
Up on the higher ground, except for the bandstand and the dance
floor, the grove was open and free of obstructions.

Owen bought his own ticket and Hetty's, and Dave bought one
for Miss Peace, and they all followed Nellie and Jenkin up toward
the dance platform. As they approached, the music and the dancing stopped, but almost at once it began again, and Nellie and
Jenkin joined the dancers. Hetty looked expectantly at Owen, but
he was watching Nellie and Jenkin, and a moment later he and
Maud Peters were alone here together, the others all dancing.
When he looked at Maud, she began to giggle; so he hurriedly
turned his attention once more to the dancers.

He knew, of course, that dancing was wrong. Probably that was
because you put your arm around a girl, and she put hers around
you. But the dancers all seemed to be having a pretty good time —
from which he felt himself excluded and apart. When at the next
change, Kit Peace caught his hand and said, "Come on, you've got
to dance with me," he was at once frightened and tempted.

"I don't know how."

"Oh, you just sort of walk around and keep time to the music,
that's all. I'll teach you." And as the band began to play: "Come
on." She led him up on the platform, caught his right hand, drew
it around her waist, laughed up at him. "Now hold on to me!
Don't be afraid! I won't break!" She took his other hand, pumping
it up and down. "Pom-pom-pom. One-two-three. Now!"

He found himself in motion, and her hand tugged at his, impelling
him to turn and turn and turn. "This is a waltz," she explained.
"It's all just One — Two — Three. A two-step has a kind of a skip
in the middle. Why, you're doing fine, Owen!" She pressed against

him, her knees touching his; she looked up in laughing challenge. "There, isn't that fun?" He nodded. It was fun, even if it was wrong.

Afterward, Hetty made him dance with her, and then Kit again. He wished to dance with Nellie, but lacked courage to suggest it; so unless Kit or Hetty drew him to the floor he remained a spectator. But when Kit danced with him again, driven by the pounding in his veins, he whirled her faster, and held her tighter, till she looked up at him with half-closed eyes.

"I don't think you're so damned shy!"

He had never heard a woman swear before. The shock of it made him stare at her, and then laugh recklessly. "I don't feel shy!"

The dance ended, but she held fast to his hand. "Let's take a walk." Her voice was hoarse and husky. "Isn't there any place we can go?" She led him away through the fringes of the crowd. Along the high ground the lights were bright, but toward the Glen, shadows grew darker into distance. "What's down there?"

"I don't know. I've never been here before."

"Let's go see." She tugged his hand.

They had gone only a few steps when someone called, behind them: "Owen!" He turned, and Nellie and Jenkin Powell were on their heels. "Owen, you haven't danced with me, yet. I wish you would."

Kit, beside him, said something under her breath, something he did not hear, but he freed his hand and took a step toward Nellie. "Sure, I want to," he said.

So they came back to the dance floor together, Jenkin now with Kit. While they danced, Nellie for a while did not speak. She did not dance the way Kit danced; she was not so close to him. He liked her way of dancing. "You're a nice boy, Owen," she said.

"So are you. A nice girl, I mean."

"It's time we all went home. Jenkin and I are going on the next car, and Maud's tired."

"I guess I'll go with you."

"Ask Maud if she doesn't want to go."

XIX

June 12, 1897 — July 26, 1897

The strike that summer came to Owen as a complete surprise. In May and June, not only the *Journal* but also the dailies devoted many columns to the coal industry. Hardiston County had produced in 1895 better than two million tons, more than any other county in the state; but in 1896 it fell to second place, with only a million six hundred thousand tons. This year miners might work more, but they would earn less. Conditions everywhere were bad, but in Hardiston County the strike last winter, ending in complete failure, had left many miners destitute; and since the strike, there had not been enough work to allow them to recuperate.

When Eben Howell as president of the Sub-District called a meeting for June 16 in the G.A.R. Hall in Belton, the announced purpose was to discuss plans for celebrating Labor Day; but at the meeting Mat Price as secretary read a bulletin from President Ratchford at Headquarters in Columbus.

The bulletin began with a statement of union finances as of the first of June.

Income

April 1, 1896, to June 1, 1897, by tax	$8,655.60
Supplies	244.70
Journal	2,105.25
Miscellaneous	262.50
Balance on hand April 7, 1896	166.40
Total	$11,434.45

EXPENDITURES

Salaries and Expenses	$7,967.54
Supplies	1,601.28
Office Expenses	502.21
Telegrams, Postage, etc.	484.20
Miscellaneous	296.29
Balance on hand April 1, 1897	582.93
Total	$11,434.45

The figures spoke for themselves, but President Ratchford went on to discuss the general situation. The Union, he said, was moribund; the coal business was almost at a standstill, and unless it revived, the Union could not survive. Further, machines were fast replacing pick miners. He had appealed to the Executive Board and to the state presidents, by a letter mailed June 7, asking their advice and instructions; but the answers were unsatisfactory, and a meeting seemed to be necessary.

Therefore, he summoned the Board and the state presidents to meet in Columbus on June 26; and since the treasury was almost empty, they must come at their own expense.

The bulletin called for no action by the Sub-District; so after hearing this communication the meeting proceeded to discuss plans for celebrating Labor Day. But Owen paid little attention to this discussion. President Ratchford's suggestion that the Union might not survive this bitter period shocked and confused him. He had assumed, since he was old enough to consider such matters, that he would always be a coal miner; but President Ratchford suggested the possibility that there would soon be no coal miners, nothing but machines.

Then what was he to do; in what direction should his energies turn? On the car, returning from the meeting, he spoke to Charles Morgan, asking his opinion; and Mr. Morgan somewhat reassured him. "Mike Ratchford's too discouraged, Owen. He's a young man, and a young man always sets his hopes too high — or else too low. To a young fellow, life is all peaks and valleys; but when you're my age and look back, you can see that life's no more than a rolling plain, neither heights nor sloughs of dark despond."

"How old is Mr. Ratchford?"

"Thirty-five or so. Mind you, he has good parts, and a high heart; but times have always gone from bad to better in the past, and will again." He chuckled. "Aye, and there'll be men mining coal a thousand years after you and I are gone."

Owen respected this opinion. Nevertheless, he was young enough to share President Ratchford's fears; and he began to watch the dailies for news from Headquarters. The Executive Board met in Columbus on June 26, and stayed in session two days; but it did not occur to Owen that there was even the remote possibility of a strike, so he was astonished to read in the dailies that reporters had asked President Ratchford whether there would be a strike — and more surprised at Mr. Ratchford's answer. He said the consensus of opinion on the Board was against a strike during the period of activity in the coal trade on the Great Lakes; and he added:

"If a strike comes, it will be an act of desperation, a strike against low wages, the shortage of work, generally oppressive conditions."

Marged, although school was over, was still in Hardiston, and Sunday she and Owen walked home from church together. He asked whether she would go to Normal School again this summer, but she said: "No. I'm going to stay home with papa and Aunt Molly." And she asked in turn, in an anxious tone: "Owen — is there going to be another strike?"

"Gollies, I don't think so!"

"Oh, I hope not! Surely things are bad enough already, without that. I hate seeing children go hungry!"

"I don't see how we can have a strike," Owen assured her. "The Union hasn't any money in the treasury, and mighty few miners have any money saved up."

"Mr. Ratchford keeps talking about striking," she reminded him. "Saying 'if a strike comes,' and things like that."

"I guess he's just putting up a bluff."

"Well, he shouldn't!" She was furious. "Suppose someone calls his bluff! Oh, Owen, I hope you don't strike again."

He assured her that President Ratchford would not order a strike; yet her fears waked doubts in him. The possibility of a strike had a curious attraction; he was almost disappointed when on July 2 Mr. Ratchford again reassured reporters. But next day the order was issued. The strike would begin July 4.

Owen, when he read that dispatch, felt his heart quicken. "The

men," said President Ratchford, "are tired of waiting for prosperity
to return. The condition of miners today is so desperate that it
cannot be made worse. In order to prevent any further reduction
in our wages, and to secure a wage that will let us live as Americans
should, with at least the necessities of life within our reach, we will
suspend work until our demands are met."

Owen thought there was in this order to strike, at a time when
the mere chance to work was each man's dearest wish, a high valor,
as though men laughed in the face of hostile gods. He forgot for the
moment his talk with Marged, and his own certainty that a strike
was out of the question. President Ratchford's audacity filled him
with a prickling excitement that made him tingle and walk proudly.
This was a summons, not to swift and easy victory, but to misery
and pain, and perhaps to destruction, and his instant loyalty was
won.

July 4 fell on a Sunday. The thermometer touched 113° in
Gallia County, it was 101° in Columbus, the mid-West panted
under scorching heat; the sunset that evening was an arch of
glowing embers. Under these auspices the strike began.

2

Additional Locals: Several were injured and one man was shot
in a fight on the down train Monday; there should be an arrest.
The ordinance against careless drivers should be enforced, and
runaways prevented. We need a humane society to stop cat-bait-
ing; on a stroll near Sycamore Hill Thursday we saw where boys
had hung a cat. The strike began July 4; it is estimated that 200,000
miners are out. Vegetable gardens will let the miners eat during
the summer; but even if the families of the miners suffer, the
families of the operators will not. Hardiston County operators favor
higher wages and this removes all local bitterness. W. R. Ryan,
national secretary of the United Mine Workers, wrote to Senator
Mason of Illinois: "The stand you have taken in behalf of the
patriots in Cuba deserves commendation, but forty thousand of
your constituents, the coal miners of Illinois, are worse off than the
Cubans." The Pennsylvania investigation proved, what everyone
knows, that the importation of low-priced foreign labor keeps

wages down; but a bill to tax immigrants $100 per head was beaten in the Senate forty-eight to three, to the tune of laughter. This is the most disgraceful episode in American legislative history. Senators give the horse laugh to all measures to aid labor. The statement that there is a diphtheria epidemic in Hardiston is a lie. According to the *United Mine Workers Journal* for July 13, many West Virginia miners are Negroes, brought from Southern plantations on a promise of two or three dollars a week more than they received as plantation hands, and then forced to live in company houses and paid only in scrip. The union paper charges that small West Virginia post offices often "lose" union literature mailed to the miners. Governor Bushnell and the Ohio Board of Arbitration are trying to settle the strike. This has been the longest spell of hot weather on record. July and August are sometimes called dog days, because dogs are supposed to be specially subject to rabies in the hot months. This is not true. Genuine rabies is extremely rare. If a dog bites you, it is a million to one the dog is not mad; but even if he is, *Our Animal Friends* says that vapor baths will eliminate the poison. Except in West Virginia, miners everywhere are out on strike; the strike is the leading topic of the day. The New York *Tribune* says the remedy is less mines and fewer miners, to end cut-throat competition. Pauper labor from Europe has reduced American miners to poverty, degradation, and starvation. Labor suffers more today than slaves ever suffered in the South. Hardiston County is fortunate, for the operators in the county are eager to pay the highest wages the trade will support; a miner here is not a beast of burden but a fellow citizen, a neighbor and a friend. This strike is a rebellion against the European wage standard. The Ladies' Literary Guild met Friday night at the home of Mrs. Thomas Lloyd. A study of miners' earnings in the Sunday Creek Valley section from January through June this year shows an average gross of $5.64 per fortnight; but after deductions the average miner owed the operator $10.14. Last year, the average Hardiston County miner worked 158 days, and he averaged to earn $1.38 per day, $218.93 for the year. Unless he had a garden, a cow, some chickens and a pig, that meant for his family toil, degradation, poverty and death. Andrée, exploring toward the North Pole, proposes to drift across it in a free balloon. There is a report that gold has been discovered in Alaska; doubt-

less many coal miners would prefer to try their fortune there.
Moses Evans, well-known coal operator, announced on July 19
four prizes totalling $75 for the best gardens made by men out on
strike from his mines. Except in New England and New York,
everyone is on the side of the strikers. Hardiston County pikes are
being built of crushed cinders; they will last forever.

3

A week after the strike began, Hardiston County operators
offered to pay those of their men who wished to resume work
sixty and sixty-five cents a ton, pending the settlement of the
strike. Sixty cents was the figure asked by the Union in calling the
strike, so, when Owen as secretary of Miss Ellen received this
notice, his first reaction was a flush of triumph, for surely this was
the beginning of surrender. He must carry this word to Charles
Morgan, president of the local; but passing the *Journal* office he
decided to stop and tell Mr. Beecham the news.

When he went in, BB was talking to a farmer whom Owen did
not know; and he sat down to wait, picking up one of the
Columbus dailies. At once a conspicuous headline caught his eye.

SPAIN AND JAPAN

COMBINE AGAINST

UNITED STATES

The dispatch, from Paris by way of London, said there was a
rumored offensive and defensive alliance between Spain and Japan
"for the mutual protection of Cuba and Hawaii," and that the two
nations had agreed, if the United States persisted in annexing
Hawaii or interfering in Cuba, that Japan and Spain would declare
war and demonstrate against our coasts.

Owen read this with quickening pulse, and when the farmer departed he asked BB: "Did you see this?"

"Yes." BB's tone was casual.

"Isn't it pretty important?"

"Not a word of truth in it. See there!" BB pointed to a paragraph

under a Washington dateline, inconspicuous below the main story
The State Department in Washington commented that the story
was too improbable to discuss. "Some drunken reporter in Paris
met a drunken Spaniard who told him this tale," BB explained.
"He put it on the wire, and the Columbus papers scream it as if it
were true."

"But the headline says it as if it was true!"

"That's the trouble with headlines; they're short, so people read
them, but the headlines can never tell the whole story. Everybody
will read that story, just as you did, and they'll miss the denial, just
as you did; and they'll shiver in their beds tonight dodging
imaginary Spanish and Japanese bullets."

Owen grinned. "It fooled me, all right." He remembered his
errand. "Look, Mr. Beecham." He handed across the notice from
the operators. "I guess we're going to win our strike quick."

BB read the brief note. "Will our miners here in the county
accept this and turn blackleg?"

Owen, prompted by hope, had assumed this would happen; but
Mr. Beecham's question made him hesitate. A blackleg, almost as
bad as a scab, was a miner who continued working when his fellows
were on strike. The definition was enough to make Owen see more
clearly.

"Not if I can help it!"

"Can you help it?"

"I don't know. But I thought you'd want to put this in the paper,
to give the operators' side."

Mr. Beecham said he would do so, and Owen went home, stopping on the way to deliver the notice to Charles Morgan. Mr.
Morgan was not there, but Mrs. Morgan expected him for dinner;
so after his own dinner, Owen returned.

He found not only Mr. Morgan but also Eben Howell. "I met Eben
up town and brought him home," Mr. Morgan explained. They
had heard through Mat Price of the offer made by the operators,
and Owen asked what would be done about it.

"We'll turn it down," Eben Howell said flatly.

"Will you call a meeting of the Sub-District?"

"Don't need to. The executive committee has the right to
decide."

"A meeting might be a good thing, Mr. Howell," Owen suggested.
"It's a good thing for men to get together, to think together and

talk together and — well, just be together. 'Specially when there's something like this strike going on." He urged: "A man alone's like a man waking up in the night. He's awfully easy scared, imagining things; but you give him some company and he's all right. A hundred men are a lot braver than one man. Why don't you call a meeting, anyway? It might do some good — it can't do harm."

"It might do a lot of harm, Owen. I've seen meetings get the bit in their teeth and run like a scared horse. A lot of men together are more likely to act like the worst man in the crowd than like the best one."

Owen said stubbornly: "If they do, that's the fault of the men who ought to be their leaders. It's because they haven't been taught to understand things. And anyway, the way to make the Union strong is to all stick together, and we have to get together before we can stick together! I'd like to see us have a meeting."

Eben Howell chuckled, and he looked across at Charles Morgan. "What do you think, Charles?"

"He's right, I think. That's one thing about Americans, you know, Eben; we learn to get together, do things together. A local that meets once a month, nine times out of ten it's better than one that meets four times a year. I'm for meetings."

Howell nodded, said good-humoredly: "All right, we'll have a meeting; but if the men vote to accept this offer from the operators, I'll take it out of your hides."

Owen said hastily: "They won't. And Mr. Howell, another thing. Mr. Morgan said something about locals. I was thinking this morning, it strikes me we've got too many locals. There must be a hundred in the county, and some of them only have a few members, and a little local without a good man in it to sort of lead the others, it's apt to fly apart, any time. Isaac Williams was president of Erie, and Mr. Morgan's president of Miss Ellen, and they help the members see things straight; but a local that doesn't have a good man in it, you can't tell what it will do. Maybe it would be better if we didn't have so many locals."

"Might be so," Howell assented. "I never thought of it."

"That's one reason I think we ought to have a lot of meetings, while we're on strike." Owen was earnest. "To talk about things like that, about organization, and how to do things better. It will give the men something to think about besides how hungry their children are."

Howell's eyes set hard, reflecting his thoughts; he nodded. "They need something like that," he agreed. "Well, we'll see."

The meeting was held in Belton, and a surprising number of men appeared. The cars and trains from Hardiston brought a quota, picking up scores at every siding, and when President Howell brought the meeting to order the hall was full. Owen and Charles Morgan sat together in the front row. President Howell explained that the meeting had been called to consider an offer from Hardiston County operators; and Matthew Price read the proposal. His voice was as feeble as he was frail, and he coughed often and painfully. Owen thought they should have a secretary who could at least read loudly enough to be heard, and he was on the point of whispering this to Mr. Morgan, but decided that to do so would sound as though he wanted the old man's place.

And on the thought, he knew he did want it! The knowledge was a sharp, bright light striking through his mind. He wanted Mr. Price's job, or Charles Morgan's, or Eben Howell's; yes, or President Ratchford's! Ambition, long germinating in his heart, warming him like an ember of desire, now flowered in a stabbing flame. When, after half a dozen men had talked at random on the question before the meeting, he rose, it was that flame of self-knowledge which flung him to his feet, which fired his tones.

"Mr. Chairman!"

"Mr. Glen."

"Mr. President, are we to play the part of blacklegs? Are we to put into the hands of the operators a club with which they can bloody the heads of our fellow miners throughout the state and the nation? Will we sell them our fists, with which to beat out the brains of our brothers everywhere? This offer, doubtless well meant, is unintended treachery; it is the more dangerous because it is so seductive, because it comes from men who are our friends, who do not realize that they are inviting us to betray our comrades." His voice suddenly rose to a sarcastic squeak. "Eve gave Adam the apple in the Garden, because she thought he would like it. Well, he did, but you know what happened to him, and to her, afterward. I would not call the Hardiston County operators as beautiful as Eve . . ." Laughter roared through the hall, till he stilled it with lifted fists. "But the operators are deceived, as Eve was deceived by the serpent; and if we listen to them we will suffer as did Adam. The operators offer us the poison apple. Theirs is not intentional betrayal, but it is treachery, all the same; it is as dangerous as a deadly poison! Accept it, and you will return to degradation, poverty, starvation, defeat, death. The Devil showed Jesus Christ all the kingdoms of the world, and Christ said: 'Get thee behind me, Satan.' Now the operators show you — sixty cents a ton! Sixty cents if you will betray your fellows! Let us say: 'Get thee behind me, Satan!'

"Mr. Chairman, I move you that the offer of the operators be declined."

Owen sat down, trembling, his palms perspiring, his eyes on the floor, a roaring in his ears; and Charles Morgan, beside him, rose — his hand on Owen's shoulder — to wait till the applause ceased and he could be heard, to second the motion. Eben Howell asked, a chuckle in his tone as though he knew the temper of the men:

"Do you want any further discussion?" A howl of angry laughter swept the hall. "Then those in favor — " There was no need to ask for Nays. "The motion is carried; the offer made by the operators is declined."

He hesitated, and they expected him to invite a motion to adjourn; but instead he said: "Men, we gathered here to attend to this piece of business; but also we're here because it is good to meet one with another, to greet old friends and make new ones, to talk together. There's a young man here, you heard him a minute ago; he has some ideas that might improve our Union. If you're not in a hurry, you might like to hear some of them."

There was a murmur of interested assent, and Mr. Howell looked down at Owen. "The chair recognizes Owen Glen."

Owen, surprised, hesitated; but then he rose and addressed the chair and turned to face the crowded hall.

"Fellow miners," he said mildly. "President Howell was kind enough to say I have some ideas worth thinking over. Well, we all have ideas, and any idea is worth thinking over. Probably I haven't any ideas that you haven't all had. The only difference is that I like to talk about them. My mother says I like to talk just to hear my tongue rattle."

Laughter brushed the nearer faces, and Owen felt these men in his hands, to do with as he chose.

"So I'll talk for a few minutes about an idea or two. I'm not going to ask you to do anything, or to decide anything — just to do a little thinking." There was a chuckle in his tones. "We might as well do some thinking, these days. There's nothing else to do, except keep our gardens weeded, and slop the pig, and tighten our belts as our bellies melt away.

"So let's think awhile; let's dream awhile. Let's pretend, for instance, that when the Union called this strike, they said: 'Boys, you all quit work on the Fourth of July, and stay out till further notice. And every week, go to your local headquarters and draw four dollars a week as long as the strike lasts.' Would that suit you, men?"

Laughter was his answer, but he shook his head. "It's not funny! You can have it that way, next time, if you want it that way." He smiled in his turn. "But it is funny, at that, to be talking about all of us paying a higher tax when most of us haven't got enough money in our pockets to rattle. You're all thinking it's a fine time to talk about higher taxes!

"But it is a fine time! It's a fine time because right now you can all get it into your heads what it would mean. Say to yourselves — 'The next time we strike, the Union will pay us something every week.' The Union will, if we want it that way; but we've got to start wanting it now!

"Remember the seven lean years and the seven fat years? Four or five years ago, you were getting seventy cents a ton. Did you save it? No, you spent it; you thought you couldn't get along on less. Well, you've got along on a lot less, these last four years — because you had to!

"Suppose you'd got along on less in the fat years, not because you had to, but because you wanted to? From 1887 to 1894 — that's seven fat years — there was only five months when you didn't get at least sixty-five cents, and most of the time it was seventy. Say you had paid the Union a quarter a week all that time. If you had, and hadn't used any of it since, the Union could pay you four dollars a week for nineteen weeks right now.

"But if the Union could do that, we wouldn't be on strike; because if the operators knew you could strike without starving — you wouldn't have to strike."

He paused, his eyes swinging all around. "That's one of the things we can be thinking about; whether it wouldn't be kind of pleasant, next time we strike, if the Union paid us something every week. We can't do anything about it now, can't do anything but think and plan. But we can do that.

"And we can plan how to make the Union better. How can we make it better? Well, for one thing, I wonder if we don't have too many locals. Any mine that works twenty-five men can have its own local if it wants to; but do you think maybe we'd have a better Sub-District here if there were just four locals in Hardiston County? They'd run to around a thousand men apiece. Of course, bigness doesn't always have to be goodness; but bigness gets things done. That's just an idea. No harm in thinking about it.

"We can have a fine Union, a wonderful Union; but if we want a fine Union, we've got to buy it, and pay for it. We've got to raise the Union tax, and pay it, and save the money. Right now it's hard for any of us to pay a tax. All right, let's begin now, when it's hard. Let's leave the tax at a nickel a month to start with, but let's every man pay it!

"And another thing, let's decide that anyone can join the Union now; but that after August 1, it costs him five dollars to get in!" He paused, his eyes meeting many eyes. "Do you know why? I'll tell you why. We're going to win this strike! It will be the first strike we've ever won. One of these days, if you live long enough, you will see your Union rich and strong; and do you know the proudest brag a union man will make, when that time comes? Do you know what he'll brag about to his grandsons? I'll tell you." He leaned forward, his voice fell to a whisper. "He'll brag to his grandsons, to his sons, to his friends; he'll brag on the street corners, and he'll give thanks on his knees when he kneels to pray, because he can truthfully say:

"'In 1897, the first time we ever won a strike, I was a paid-up member of the United Mine Workers of America.'"

He sat down abruptly, and for a moment there was no sound. In that silence, President Howell rose. "Well, men, we've got plenty to think about," he said. "Unless someone else wants to say something, a motion to adjourn is in order."

The motion came, it carried; the crowd moved slowly toward the doors. Owen walked with lowered eyes, crushed under this weight of silence; he looked to Charles Morgan for reassurance, tried to grin. "They didn't think much of my ideas," he said.

The other met his eyes, not smilingly. "They're thinking," he replied. "That's what you wanted them to do."

4

On Friday the twenty-third, ten days after that meeting, Owen
received a message from Headquarters.

> DEAR MR. GLEN: *You have been suggested by Eben
> Howell, president of the Sub-District, as a good man to
> work as an organizer in the fields where the strike is not
> yet complete. If you can and will undertake this work,
> please come to Union Headquarters in Columbus at your
> earliest convenience.*
> > *Yours Very Truly,*
> > W. R. RYAN, *Sec'y.*
> > *United Mine Workers of America*

Owen's first proud delight — for surely this letter was an accolade
— did not long persist; misgivings flooded him. He had only once
since babyhood been as far away from home as Columbus; but this
letter would mean going to West Virginia, to Pennsylvania. They
were remote as foreign lands. Besides, what was an organizer supposed to do? How did he go about doing it?

These vague doubts clouded his thoughts while he started home;
it was only as his confusion cleared that he recognized the final
obstacle. The railroad fare to Columbus was a hurdle he could not
overleap.

But as soon as he thought he could not go to Columbus, he was
determined to do so; and when he came to Charles Morgan's and
saw Mr. Morgan sitting on the shaded veranda, he went up the
walk and joined him. Mr. Morgan, like Isaac Williams, had sufficient means so that he need not work unless he chose; he went to
Miss Ellen, not to earn his wages, but to continue to savor the
pleasure of the familiar. Because he had money, he could be useful
now.

When Owen approached, Mr. Morgan had been reading one of
the Cincinnati papers; he dropped it on the floor beside his chair,

said cheerfully: "Well, Owen. Come sit down. Hot, isn't it?"

It was, though Owen had not noticed the fact. "Yes sir," he said; and with no pause he asked, like a demand: "Will you lend me some money?" The older man looked at him in surprise, and Owen drew out the letter from Mr. Ryan. "For this," he explained.

Charles Morgan read the letter, nodding. "Eben Howell said he was going to tell them about you. You could do good work, Owen."

"I want to," Owen agreed. "But I can't even buy a ticket to Columbus."

"The Union would pay your expenses. Since the strike started, they've money coming in, from new members and from old ones — and some outside help too. I know Moses Evans sent them twenty-five dollars." Owen was too absorbed in his own concern to be surprised at this. "I can lend you enough to get you to Columbus, anyway. When do you want to go?"

"Tomorrow, I guess. I'll let you know." Owen went home in a quiet jubilation, carefully controlled. His mother was at the stove; he spoke to her, trying to keep his tone casual. "Mama, I have to go to Columbus. President Ratchford wants me to help organize some of the non-union mines."

She sat down weakly, wiping her hands on her apron. "Owen, you'll be the death of me! I suppose you'll be making speeches and leading parades and fighting Pinkertons all over everywhere, but I don't know as I can stop you! Big as you are! When you going?"

"Tomorrow." And, knowing what her first concern would be, he added: "It won't cost anything. I'll borrow from Charles Morgan to get there; and the Union will pay for it. You and papa can get along."

"Oh, we'll get along, with the garden."

Tom Glen, when he heard the news, said harshly: "Organizer? Thought you didn't believe in strikes! You were dead against 'em last November."

"I believe in the Union."

"It'll never be like the Knights of Labor. There was a noble band."

Owen said placatingly: "Well, I want to help make it as good as we can."

The arrangements for his journey to Columbus were taken out of his hands. That afternoon Eben Howell came to find him.

Eben had had a letter from Mr. Ryan; he would take Owen to Columbus and introduce him to the officers there. "And I'll get the tickets," he said. "I'll meet you in Belton Monday morning. You'd better come up on the miners' train."

"I thought maybe we'd go tomorrow."

"No, President Ratchford will be away till Monday. You come up on the miners' train, and I'll do the rest."

Next day in the *Journal* office, Owen told Will, and Mr. Beecham, and even the girls in the type loft his news. Will drawled: "Don't let any of them Hunyaks organize you with a pick handle, Owen. I hear that's the way they mostly argue."

Owen laughed with him. "I guess I'll be talking to men that can talk English."

"Lots of them can't. Don't be too sure."

Bets, when she heard, offered him a gumdrop, and advised him to carry a bagful in his pockets. "Never saw a man yet that didn't like candy."

Nellie was glad and said so, her eyes honest. "We're all going to be mighty proud of you, some day."

When Owen told BB, the editor for a moment did not speak; then, with something like a start, he exclaimed: "Fine! Fine!" And as though to himself: "I wonder how successful you'll be." And in a new tone: "Well, you'll have a lot to tell us when you come home."

At church next morning, Owen found himself sorry Marged was not there. He wished he might tell her about this great adventure that awaited him. The desire was so strong that he spent much of the afternoon writing her a letter. Writing was so much more difficult than making a speech; your words, on paper, stared back at you. He remembered something BB had said: "Don't ever write a book." Well, he was not likely to write a book. A letter was hard enough. This letter to Marged was not long, but he wrote and rewrote it many times.

DEAR MISS WILLIAMS:

I wish to tell you about my new work. I know you have read in the Journal *about the strike. It came as a surprise to me, because no one had any money saved up, and it looked as if we would just be cutting off our noses to*

*spite our own faces as you say. But when President
Ratchford called the strike I saw it was a brave fine thing
to do. He is a great man, and I would rather strike with
him and lose than win with someone else.*

*Mr. Eben Howell of Belton, president of the Sub-
District, wrote Headquarters about me. I don't know
what he wrote, but I wish I did. I guess everybody likes
to hear when other people say nice things about them,
and he must have, because now they want me to help
organize the mines where there isn't any union, and I'm
going to try, and I hope I can. Mr. Howell is going to
take me to Columbus tomorrow.*

*I will copy off the letter I got from Mr. Ryan for you to
read, and put it in separate.*

*I guess I will be too busy for a while to study much. I
will write you again if anything special happens.*

Your friend,
OWEN GLEN

Even this version did not content him; but he copied Mr. Ryan's
letter and enclosed it. He went early to bed, but sleep was laggard,
and it seemed to him he had hardly slept at all when his mother
roused him to eat breakfast and hurry off to catch the early train.

XX

July 26, 1897 — October 6, 1897

OWEN AND EBEN HOWELL had to wait till late afternoon before President Ratchford found time to see them. When they came into his office, he rose to clasp their hands, motioned them to a seat. Owen thought he seemed older. His hair was only slightly gray, his drooping mustache not gray at all; but there was red weariness in his eyes and a hard set to his heavy jaw.

"I'm sorry you had to wait; but I've been away almost a week, and things had piled up." He said with a sudden light in his eyes, a lift in his tones: "Eben, we're going to double the pressure on DeArmitt." He looked at Owen. "Glen, Eben says you know how to talk to men."

Owen colored, shifting his feet, grinning doubtfully. "I do a lot of talking."

"The thing that hit me," Eben Howell explained, "was that he talked as if being a union man was a privilege to fight for. To hear him, you wouldn't think the Union was asking anything; you'd think the Union was offering, not asking."

Ratchford was watching Owen. "What did you say, in this speech Eben thinks was so good?"

"I told them they'd brag all their lives that they were members of the United Mine Workers in 1897."

"Why would they brag about that?"

"Because this will be the first big strike we've won."

"Ha!" Ratchford half-laughed; he leaned forward, picked up a pipe, filled it. "Well, maybe. We called this strike more from despair than from hope, but we've made progress. One thing,

493

people in Ohio are on our side. That's because we've behaved ourselves, no violence, no fighting, no damage to property. But we've got to get West Virginia. It was coal from those mines that beat us in 1894. Glen, you know who DeArmitt is?"

"Yes sir."

"We've been working on his men, and I'm going to send you up there. If you want to go."

Owen said huskily, "Yes sir. I'd like to beat him."

"Don't like him?"

"Just hearing his name makes me mad."

Mr. Ratchford tipped back in his chair. "No. No, Glen; don't get mad. The way for us to win is to make the other fellow mad. We don't want any fights, anywhere. We don't want any trouble." He turned to Howell. "DeArmitt is trying to get us to start something. You know we've got organizers up there, and our miners from all around are camping out, and holding mass meetings. All of a sudden, a lot of barrels of beer and bottles of whiskey turned up in the camp they call 'Camp Determination'! Nobody knows who sent it. I think DeArmitt, but I don't know. Anyway, there was booze enough to start a war — that was what DeArmitt wanted — but I had it dumped in the ditches."

He turned to Owen again. "Here's the way we work. We hold mass meetings, and get the miners to come, and talk to them. They're nearly all foreigners, so we have interpreters. We tell them what the Union is, and what it's trying to do. A lot of DeArmitt's men have quit work and come in with us. That took courage, because DeArmitt had had them all sign a contract to work for a year, at ten cents a ton below other miners in the district; and in the contract they agreed that if they joined a union, or struck, they'd lose whatever back pay they had coming. And he regularly held back their pay, sometimes for a month or six weeks, so when a man joined us, it cost that man a lot of money.

"But the ones who did, they're our best organizers now.

"Then another thing, DeArmitt got out injunctions prohibiting meetings on his property. Ever been arrested?"

Owen was startled by that abrupt question. "No."

"Well, don't be. Some of our men have gone to jail up there, but you can't do us any good in jail, so keep out of trouble. As

long as you obey the injunctions — that means stay off company
property and don't abuse anyone or threaten anyone — you're all
right." He swung to his desk, said over his shoulder: "We'll pay
your expenses; but don't waste a nickel, because we haven't a
nickel to spare.

"And keep your temper. Don't talk mad, don't get mad, don't hit
anyone, don't threaten anyone, don't even hint a threat. And keep
off company property. I'll send you with Mike Pratt. He'll take
care of you. All right, thanks for coming up. We'll use you."

The days that followed were for Owen a hard training in self-
control. He stayed overnight in Columbus, and Tuesday morning
Mike Pratt led him to the Cleveland train. Thereafter they were
seldom separated; and in tense moments Mike, a little man with
twinkling eye and a long upper lip, soothed Owen like a mother.
His hand on Owen's arm was as reassuring as the hand with
which a trainer gentles a spirited colt. When Owen raged at the
injunctions which hindered them, Mike chuckled reassuringly.

"Easy, lad; easy. They're mad, and the madder they get, the
worse we're hurting them. And the injunctions don't mean all they
say. No assemblies? Why, if you and me meet on the street, we
assemble. No marches? Then if I march myself around the corner
to the restaurant to get myself a dish of stew, I'm open to arrest.
But they don't mean that. It's mostly all threats. They're hurt, hurt
bad, m'boy! So keep a smile on your face and look happy as you
should."

They had been only a few days at Turtle Creek before the
DeArmitt mines were forced to close. Owen, though neither he
nor Mike had made any considerable contribution to that victory,
nevertheless felt a personal triumph. Also, the success went far to
persuade him of the wisdom of good humor and of gentle ways.
Mike and Owen left Turtle Creek, where other organizers would
keep the new recruits in solid ranks, and went to Pittsburgh and
the West Virginia mines. Injunctions hindered them and proclama-
tions by sheriffs here and there threatened to meet with stern
measures any hint of violence; but Mike and Owen and the other
organizers held fast to peaceful methods.

Since marches and assemblies were alike forbidden, they developed a method which proved effective. Singly — since surely one

man alone was not an assembly — they posted themselves along the
public roads, where miners still at work must pass, and greeted
every passer with a good-humored grin and a friendly word.
"Good morning, friend."

It was surprising to see how often the miner would stop and fall
into talk. "Good morning to you." "It's a fine day to stand in the
cool of the shade, now is it not?" "So it is, yes." One word led
easily to another, and passers might stop to listen, so that what had
been one man talking to another became a group of men listening
to one. The fact that few miners spoke English was a handicap,
but Owen made friends with a man, Joe Ceslak, who acted as interpreter. When the deputies broke up these small gatherings on
the streets, someone in the group might invite Owen to his home —
and the others trooped along, so that Owen sometimes faced a
room full of intent listeners. Such gatherings might turn from
serious business to food and drink; the womenfolk came in, the
music began. Owen learned by infection how to laugh and to sing
and to dance as light-heartedly as any of them.

Sometimes Owen and Mike tramped along the highways — once
they hired drummers to go with them, and wished they could afford
a band — and whenever they attracted a sufficient following, one
or the other would make a speech. One night Mike calculated that
they had walked sixteen miles; and on a day when they saw a
horseless carriage surrounded by an attentive crowd, Mike said:
"There's what we should have, Owen, to fetch the men to listen to
us."

"They'd spend their time looking at it, not listening." Owen
pressed nearer. "I'd like to see how it works, myself. Did you ever
see one before?"

"I've had a ride in one. It's like sitting on a bunch of firecrackers
and them going off under you; but I stayed in the thing till it ran
down." The machine they were approaching moved away with a
hiss of steam.

They won friends day by day. The operators announced plans to
employ Pinkertons, armed with Gatling guns, to prevent trespass on
their properties; and President Ratchford sent on for distribution
among the miners a thousand copies of the *Ohio State Journal* with
the headline:

WAR UPON THE DEFENSELESS MINERS

On the twentieth of August, Headquarters in Columbus broadcasted thousands of copies of a circular attacking the tyranny of the injunctions; and Owen and Mike distributed them by the score. To Owen, the circular seemed as sacred as the Bible, as true and as compelling.

> *To organized labor and to all organizations which condemn government by injunction and the use of force to deprive people of their rights as Americans citizens:*
>
> *The great miners' strike has gone beyond a struggle for living wages. All patriotic people must decide whether they will consent to live under an oligarchy of wealth or whether the right to free government, free speech and peaceable public assemblage shall be preserved.*
>
> *The courts, by tyrannical injunctions, have deserted the temple of justice to become the bulwark of confederated capital. They decree that capital is always right and labor always wrong.*
>
> *The present miners' strike originated in poverty and starvation, it was born in the sorrow and destitution of hungry women and children, it was the protest of impoverished and enslaved labor. The philanthropic heart of the nation has responded, and if it were simply a struggle between miners and operators, liberty would triumph over oppression, industry over greed, and right over wrong.*
>
> *But now the courts have volunteered to defend the sordid interests of the rich as against the God-given rights of the poor, and threaten to turn the Gatling guns and Winchesters of criminals and thugs against all who dare protest their despicable restraining orders. The judiciary, prostituted to the bidding of oppressive capital, has discriminated against the many in the interest of the few.*
>
> *The recent injunctions and their application against the lawful rights of the poor, the arrest and incarceration of hundreds of innocent and inoffensive people, the employ-*

ment of armed thugs to overcome and coerce the miners have so exasperated the people that we can no longer be responsible for the public peace.

We appeal to a higher court, the great plain people who have always proven just arbiters; we appeal to them to send delegates to St. Louis, Missouri, to a mass convention to be held Monday, August 30, 1897, the object of which will be not merely to protest against the usurpation and tyranny of the courts, but to compel a return to free government. Our people have suffered all the evils that are endurable; our only alternatives are to submit and entreat our miners to return like cowards to the hovels of misery and shame, or to appeal as we now do to the patriotic hearts of Americans.

The circular was signed by President Ratchford and by the other members of the Executive Board, by Samuel Gompers as president of the American Federation of Labor, and by J. R. Sovereign, General Master Workman of the Knights of Labor. On the twenty-second, two days after the circular appeared, the Pittsburgh operators invited President Ratchford to meet them and end the strike, each state to settle its own disputes by arbitration. President Ratchford came to Pittsburgh, but he rejected that proposal, insisting that any arbitration or other settlement must cover not only Pennsylvania but the whole Central Competitive Field. That night when they called at his hotel, Owen and Mike found him jubilant.

"The strike's as good as won, boys," he told them. "The operators are sick of it, and we'll meet them halfway. You might full as well go home."

2

Back in Hardiston, it seemed to Owen years that he had been away. To meet the same people on the street, to see the same buildings and the same trees was like reliving a dream. It was hard to believe that in the lifetime of his absence there had been so little change.

He reached Hardiston late Wednesday afternoon, and went directly to the *Journal* office. The familiar rumble of the press met him at the door. BB was not in sight, so he went on through the file room where Nellie and Bets left their work to welcome him, Bets with a smacking kiss, Nellie with a friendly word; and Will stopped the press and came to shake his hand. They asked many questions, and Owen answered as he could, and he asked for Mr. Beecham.

"He's out working up the meeting tomorrow," Will told him. "They're fixing to have a big time."

"What meeting?"

"Why, about that circular Ratchford put out. They're getting ready to send a delegate to St. Louis the way he asked them to. I sh'd judge there'd be quite a turnout. Well, I've got my job to do."

He returned to the high platform and threw on the belt; the press began to roll. Owen stayed beside Nellie, watching the swift precision of her work as she applied the paste and affixed the labels. "You're almost as fast as Bets," he said. Bets caught his eye and winked at him, the gumdrop bulging in her cheek. He asked Nellie: "Everything all right? How've you been?" It was fine to see her again, fine to have come home.

He stayed awhile, climbing up to talk to Will or carrying papers from the folder; but Mr. Beecham did not appear, so at last Owen collected copies of the four issues of the *Journal* he had missed, and took a paper just coming off the press, and started home. They would be glad to see him. He began to walk faster, he came home almost at a run.

So there was laughter, and from his mother happy tears, and in his father's voice gruff pride. Supper was garden stuff with a bit of pork for seasoning, and Owen talked while he ate. He told how he and Mike had worked together; he told them of the men he had met, new friends he would remember, Joe Ceslak, and Luke Havitch and Johnny Peteit from Austria, and Big Sam from Memphis, and Daffyd Lewis from Tregaron, and many another. "Luke and Johnny couldn't speak any English, but Johnny took me home, and his boy goes to school and talks as good as anyone. He's got three boys and four girls, and the oldest isn't ten years old yet. His wife's awful nice. They're about the happiest people I ever saw. His name isn't really Johnny, but everybody calls him that.

You ought to see one of their parties! They have a fine time."

His mother for the most part listened without questions, quieter than she had used to be; but as she rose to clear away, she hesitated, half-erect; and her face twisted. He asked: "What's the matter, mama?"

"Just a stitch in my side." She stood straight. "There, it's gone now."

"I'll wipe for you."

"No, no, you sit with papa. I'll listen."

Tom Glen asked if the strike was surely over; and Owen said: "Not yet, but it will be, soon. The operators offered sixty-one cents, and President Ratchford told them sixty-nine and the settlement had to cover the whole Central Competitive Field. He says they'll come part way, says we'll probably settle for sixty-five cents."

"It's about time. Folks are starving here. Well, you had a lively time. Any fights?"

Owen shook his head. "No. No, it was all friendly. Mostly it was talking to men one at a time." He said slowly: "The best part of it was getting to know a lot of men, different kinds of men. I know Mr. Beecham doesn't think much of immigrants, but I've been in their houses and to their parties and dances. I like them fine."

"They'll take the last dollar out of your mouth."

"Not when they know more about things, not when they understand."

When his father and mother had gone to bed, Owen arranged in order the *Journals* he had brought from the office, and scanned them one by one and the history of those weeks unrolled under his eye. In the first, his eye picked out his own name from a column of type: Owen Glen has gone to Columbus to be an organizer for the United Mine Workers. Bogus collectors for miners' relief last week fleeced Governor Bushnell of $100. The Yukon gold excitement has swept the Pacific Coast and men are flocking to Alaska, but coal is gold and nearer home. Clean out your well and keep well. Butter is ten cents a pound, eggs seven cents a dozen. Canovas, who was responsible for the butchery in Cuba, is called a statesman; the man who butchered him is called an anarchist. Evan Jenkins, employed in the electric light plant, was shocked to death by crossed wires last Friday.

Owen, when he read that paragraph came to his feet in sharp grief; he started toward the bedroom door to ask many questions.

But then he checked, for his father and mother were by this time asleep, and — what was there to ask? Returning to his chair, he remembered Miss Means, whom Betty and May and Allie called Aunt Wormwood because she was forever predicting that the whole family would come to some bad end. Miss Means was in the asylum in Athens; but maybe she was right, for Evan was dead. Owen found himself thinking how Evan's Adam's apple pumped up and down when he sang bass in the choir. Probably the girls were still running the farm. They had always done much of the work, since their father was busy at the light plant all day.

He returned to his reading, to the columns of Additional Locals. Governor Bushnell has appealed for contributions to help the miners: flour, cured meats, coffee, tea, sugar, beans, corn meal. One thousand families in Hardiston County need relief. Rule by injunction is tyranny, for the will of one man nullifies not only our laws but the Constitution; Judge Jackson of West Virginia has gone the limit, and miles beyond; he should be thrown off the bench. Wheat stalked across the dollar line Friday, and famine stalks in Hardiston County. There are 157 destitute families listed in Slacktown and Glendale; that means eight hundred hungry people. The strike has been on for seven weeks, but for thirty-five weeks before that, few miners had more than half-time work. In Glendale, after collecting scraps of meat and vegetables from door to door and from the stores, a bountiful soup dinner was served to nine hundred men and women and children. How many weeks must a baby starve in order to win a strike? I wonder whether Judge Jackson of West Virginia was ever really hungry. Government by injunction is despotism and tyranny. Judge Jackson says the operators have a right to induce men to work, but that the strikers have no right to induce them not to work.

Before he slept, Owen decided to go to that meeting BB was arranging for tomorrow; and in the morning he and his father walked uptown together. Drawn by distant strains of music, they joined the crowd which collected in front of the Court House, where Main Street was solidly filled with men and women. Judge Rogan of Belton called for order, and Doctor Roy of Belton made a speech, and so did Daniel Wills of Hardiston, and half a dozen others. They were continually interrupted by cheers and shouts and loud applause, and Tom Glen shouted as loud as anyone.

Owen saw Mr. Beecham on the steps near the speakers, writing steadily in a little notebook, so when with a final roar the meeting ended and the bands began to play and the crowd to dissolve, he moved toward the *Journal* office. BB presently appeared, with Judge Rogan; and he gripped Owen's hand in hearty greeting.

"Will told me you were home. This is Judge Rogan of Belton. Judge, Glen has been working as a union organizer, this last month. Where were you, Owen?"

So Owen had the pleasure of reciting once more the tale of his adventures; and Mr. Rogan, clearing his throat a little self-consciously, remarked that such meetings as this one of which he had had the honor of being chairman certainly helped the miners' cause.

Owen did not agree. The meeting had seemed to him much noise and little meat. "I couldn't hear what they were saying," he said evasively and BB pulled out his notebook.

"Here's the essence. They adopted this resolution." And he read:

> *Resolved, by 3000 citizens of Hardiston County, Ohio, this twenty-sixth of August, 1897, that we send Daniel Wills of Hardiston as a delegate to the St. Louis convention, to urge a Congressional investigation of present conditions and of the powers of the courts.*
>
> *And resolved: That we deem injunctions an extraordinary remedy, not constitutionally applicable to cases like those to which it has been applied in West Virginia and in Pennsylvania.*

He closed his notebook and laid it aside. "Mr. Wills will leave Saturday, on the 12:45. The convention meets in St. Louis Monday."

Owen remembered ringing words and phrases in the circular put out from Headquarters, and this resolution seemed by comparison stodgy and dull; but he did not say so, because he thought Mr. Beecham might have written it. "Do you think very many will go to the convention?" he asked, trying not to sound skeptical.

Judge Rogan — he had a shock of white hair like a plume — cleared his throat. "From all over the country," he predicted. "A spontaneous demonstration! The effect will be tremendous! Wait and see."

"Well, I guess we'll have to," Owen agreed. When Judge Rogan presently took himself away, he met BB's eye. "Pretty fine-looking man," he said warily.

The editor, his head on one side, smiled. "There was some talk, when he was elected judge, of raising money for a testimonial; but Dave Ames said giving Bob Rogan a testimonial was like rubbing a fat goose with grease."

3

The official settlement of the strike came on the fourth of September, when the Union and the operators agreed upon a basic rate of sixty-five cents per ton in Pittsburgh. This meant fifty-six cents in Hardiston County. That was no great gain, but it was victory; and the real victory lay in the fact that the Union had added to its stature. President Ratchford began the strike with only a few hundred dollars in the treasury, and only eleven thousand nominal members; but the organizers drew two hundred thousand men out of the mines, and when the strike ended, the Union listed thirty-three thousand paid-up members and counted more than ten thousand dollars in hand.

The settlement was subject to acceptance by a national convention of miners' delegates, to be elected for that purpose; and until that acceptance, the mines would remain closed. Owen had unconsciously looked forward to the settlement of the strike as the beginning of a new and brighter world. It was disappointing to find that — for a while at least — nothing seemed to be changed. He was impatient to return to work again. They were deep in debt; and the garden would soon fail them.

He felt, too, an increasing concern for his mother. So often when she moved, her lip twitched as though with pain. He asked his father whether she had been sick.

"Sick, no!" Tom told him stoutly. "She's all right. Why wouldn't she be?"

That answer lacked something, and Owen put the direct question to his mother; but she laughed and hugged him and said teasingly: "Worried, sonny? About me? No one ever has to worry about me!"

So he knew she was all right — except for that occasional stitch in her side.

Marged returned to Hardiston in time for the reopening of school, and the first Sunday, walking home from church, Owen told her his experiences. She listened gravely, yet with some unspoken question in her eyes. He spoke of an evening when he and Mike went to dance at Johnny Peteit's daughter's wedding.

"Mike and I were about the only ones in the room who spoke English, except Joe Ceslak. He interpreted for us." He laughed at his own thoughts. "But you didn't need an interpreter that night. Everybody had a fine time, singing, and an accordion going, and dancing, and everybody whirling everybody around, and laughing and sweating and —" He saw she was not smiling. "Well, it was a lot of fun; but I guess it doesn't sound like it."

"Yes, it does." But there was no mirth in her eyes. "I've even danced myself, in Athens last summer, though I'd hate to have the School Board here know about it. But did your parties help toward winning the strike, do you think? You and Mike had a fine time, but there were a good many poor people hungry here at home?"

"Well, that was the way we worked," he explained, trying not to feel himself on the defensive. "Mike's idea was, if we could make them see we had fun being in the Union, they'd want to join. And a lot of them did."

"But you never got mad?"

"We never showed it."

"There was plenty to get mad about," she suggested. "I used to go in to Sycamore Hill every other day with things from the farm. I know eleven families there that had to mortgage their homes; and there were thirty-two families who didn't have enough to eat, even with what I took them, and people like me. They had a commissary giving out bacon and flour and meal and things like that, the same as here in Hardiston. Bread and meat were the scarce things. We brought in plenty of vegetables from the farm."

"Amy and Dave brought things to papa and mama," he agreed. "Or I don't know how they'd have got along."

A slow passion touched her tones. "Did you know little children get fat stomachs when they're starving, Owen? Did you know that when their eyelids turn green on the inside, they're going to die and nothing you can do will save them? Did you know that last week, in Ohio, there were ten thousand children under fourteen who were hungry all the time? And you were laughing and dancing in Pittsburgh! Oh, it's too bad, Owen! It's too bad!"

He saw tears stream down her cheeks; she scrubbed them away and looked up at him, eyes still blazing. He hesitated, said then with a grave maturity, "I didn't feed any babies; but I was trying to help change things so they won't have to starve again."

Her eyes softened. "I know, Owen. I know." Her hand touched his arm. "I wasn't really blaming you. But I get so mad! It seems to me everybody ought to get mad! Don't you ever?"

"I had to learn not to. Mike Pratt taught me not to. If you let yourself get really mad, you choke up and stammer and stumble and can't say anything worth saying. Mike comes from out West, and he knows Mr. Bryan, and he says Mr. Bryan practiced that great speech of his over and over for months, to different crowds. He says you have to do that, and he says if you want to talk to a crowd and get the crowd hot under the collar, you've got to be pretty calm yourself."

"Like Marc Antony," she suggested. "Over Caesar's body. Come down this afternoon and we'll read that speech." Yet as they parted, she called to him: "But I think you ought to feel mad on the inside, even if you don't show it, Owen."

He shook his head; the strike was over; there was no need for rage.

Mr. Wills came back from St. Louis and BB wrote in the *Journal:*

> *There were many delegates, but only 80 had credentials. They denounced the usurpation of power by the judiciary, and summoned all labor leaders to meet in Chicago September 27 to discuss the effective use of the ballot box, and how to end government by injunction.*

Owen read this almost with indifference; he wanted to go back to work, to everyday affairs. He was much more interested in the next paragraph in the *Journal.*

> *Henry Andrews, organist at the Crescent Saloon in Belton, was accidentally killed by a shot fired by W. J. Brown at Stanley Haggerty who was a friend of a man named Trebble whom Brown had knocked down.*

That made Owen smile. It did not sound like Mr. Beecham, and in the office Saturday he asked about it.

"I wrote just one letter of that item," BB explained. "When I read the proof, I put the 'm' in 'whom.' But Owen, look it over. Doesn't it tell the whole story, in a pretty vivid way? Brown and Trebble had an argument, it turned into a fight, Brown knocked Trebble down, Haggerty charged at Brown, Brown shot and missed Haggerty but killed Andrews. Could you tell the whole story in fewer words?"

Owen grinned. "But it doesn't tell what happened to Mr. Brown when Haggerty got to him."

"Ask Bets," BB suggested. "I suspect Haggerty's her beau, from the way she talks about him. She wrote the item."

Owen did so, climbing the stairs to the type loft. "Stanley Haggerty?" he asked. "Works in Slacktown Number 2? A stocky little man?"

To his amusement, Bets was blushing. "Yes, but he's awful strong. He bloodied Whit Brown's nose and took his gun away from him and held him down till the Marshal came."

Owen was glad to find that Bets had a beau. Probably she and Stan would be getting married one of these days, now that the strike was won and the mines would soon reopen. It was hard to imagine anyone wanting to marry Bets, but lots of people seemed to get married right along, and some of them were certainly not as nice as Bets, and no prettier.

Hardiston County miners met September 13 and voted to accept the settlement and to return to work on the sixteenth, Thursday. Owen saw Moses Evans, who said Miss Ellen would work full time for as long as he could foresee; so Wednesday in the *Journal* office, Owen told BB: "I guess this will be my last time here for a while. Mr. Evans says the Miss Ellen is going to run every day, at first, anyway."

"That's fine. By the way, did you know he gave fifty dollars to the commissary to help feed the hungry?"

"I guess he would. He's a good man."

BB nodded. "Most men are. I'm printing the list of contributors to the commissary, but they weren't the only ones who were generous. Some merchants gave so much credit that they're facing bankruptcy."

"We're in debt to Mr. McAuliffe," Owen assented. "But with papa and me both working, we'll catch up pretty quick."

One paragraph in the *Journal* that week came to Owen like an echo from an almost forgotten past. Jane Lloyd had given a Goldenrod party Saturday night. He had not been invited, and he felt a wistful sadness for those long ago days when he had thought Jane so wonderful, and when she liked him too. There was a prize at her party for the first person to make twenty-four words out of "Goldenrod" and the prize was won by Morgan Williams in ten and a half minutes. Owen tried his hand at the task and finished it just under five minutes, and he felt a warming pleasure in this empty victory.

To return next day to the mine again, to rise at first dawn and eat the breakfast his mother cooked for them and tramp off to the station; to greet on the train old friends not seen for weeks of idleness; to alight at the familiar siding, and walk the track up to the tipple, and meet there all your fellows; to ride into the darkness of the mine, pricks of flame from many lamps before you and behind: this was a blissful home-coming. Tools familiar in your hands, the friendly shadows whispering around you, the fine black gleam of the coal: these were sweet and perfect altogether. Muscles long disused might be sore at the day's end, palms might blister, the black phlegm might plague you as in the past, but you were at work again! Oh, work was a good companion for a man.

4

Additional Locals: Fresh oysters will be served daily after October 1 at the Star Cafe. Forbes and Watson advertise a new shipment of Ladies' Capes from $1.98 to $4.98. It required 3768 ballots to nominate Jerry Carpenter of Meigs County for State Senator. A railroad detective named Wallace, chasing tramps off the C H & D freight train near Slacktown, fell between the cars and was killed. Colonel Billy Thompson will display the Veriscape at the Rink tomorrow night, showing pictures of the Corbett-Fitzsimmons fight. Three cats died of diphtheria last week in Chillicothe; children should not be allowed to fondle cats when there is diphtheria around. Agents are wanted to sell the new Eagle Graphophone, priced at $10 and $12. Butter .15, eggs .14, lard .08, chicken 7½ cents a pound, ducks and turkeys 5 cents. George Pullman died October 19, but it is not recorded that any of his employees wept.

Neal Dow died October 17; he hoped to be to the liquor trade what
John Brown was to slavery. At a miners' meeting in Glendale in
the Knights of Labor Hall, Owen Glen of Hardiston described his
experiences as an organizer in West Virginia and Pennsylvania.
He spoke for two hours, and was often interrupted by prolonged
applause.

5

Owen, happily back at work, drove himself to top pitch; he
drilled his holes as deep as the veins permitted, he used his powder
shrewdly, and his production climbed. At their first payday, he and
his father came home together, and each gave Mrs. Glen his envelope and they turned into the shed to bathe. Tom Glen, first done,
went first into the kitchen and while Owen was buttoning his shirt
his mother tapped on the shed door and came in to speak to him.

"Son," she whispered. "You earned more, these two weeks, than
your father."

"Did I? I worked pretty hard."

She reached up to kiss him. "Don't ever tell him, Owen. He's
been the man of the family. Let him always be."

He hugged her gently — if he hugged her hard, nowadays, she
sometimes made a little whistling sound, as though of pain — and
whispered: "Don't worry, mama. He'll always be the man of the
house for me."

The days at the mine were a steady contentment, and in some
ways the best part was seeing Ernie Vought again. Ernie had a
quality which Owen had never felt in any other man. He was
gentle without being weak, with a fine way of seeing beauty in
ordinary things, and of helping others see it. Beyond the fact that
they liked to be together, that they often ate their midday meal
together in the mine, they had no common interests. Ernie went
quietly about his work, never in any way conspicuous, while Owen
had an aggressive friendliness which never rested. They were as
different as two men well could be, and yet Owen looked forward
to seeing Ernie, and remembered happily their hours in company.

There were others whom Owen — with that curious feeling that
he had been a long time away from Hardiston — was glad to see

again, and he enjoyed that Glendale meeting where for two hours he talked of his work in West Virginia. Sometimes his hearers laughed, sometimes they scowled with anger. To play upon them gave him a fine sense of power. He was sure Mr. Beecham would print something about the meeting, so Wednesday afternoon when he came from the mine he stopped at the office to get a *Journal*. At home there was a letter for him, and when he had bathed, while he waited for supper and before looking through the *Journal*, he opened it. The address was in an uncertain hand, and he unfolded the scrawled sheets and looked at the last one and laughed in sudden pleasure.

"Mama, this is from Joe Ceslak. Remember, I told you about him? He was our interpreter." He turned back to the beginning of the letter. "I won't try to read it aloud. Some of it I can't hardly make out."

"Eat your supper first," she advised, and called Tom. "Papa, come on!" Tom Glen had gone to lie down on his bed till supper was ready. He obeyed the summons and sat down at the table and said grace. Owen, while he ate, studied the letter spread beside his plate, puzzling over the scrawled lines.

But suddenly he dropped knife and fork and picked up the topmost sheet. His mother asked sharply: "Owen! What's got into you?"

He tried to speak, waited to swallow, his eyes on the letter. "Joe's brother's been killed. Shot. By the Sheriff. I can't read all of it, but as far as I can make out, a lot of miners, all foreigners, tried to march to one of the mines to hold a meeting, and the Sheriff and his deputies shot them. They killed twenty-eight, Joe says. At a place called Lattimer." He looked toward Tom Glen. "Have you seen anything in the papers about it, papa?"

"I heard about it. That was a long time ago, Owen; a month, anyway. Way off in Pennsylvania."

"Why didn't you tell me?"

"I thought you knew about it. Anyway, you couldn't do anything."

His mother urged: "Now, Owen, go ahead and eat your supper. You can't help what happened a month ago."

"Has the Sheriff a right to shoot men like that, papa?"

"I heard they'd arrested him for it."

Owen pored over Joe's letter, guessing at words he could not read; and when supper was done, he decided to take it to Charles Morgan. Certainly Mr. Morgan could answer some of his questions. But when he got there, the house was dark; and after a moment's hesitation, he went on to Mr. Beecham's.

There Aunt Jane answered his knock. "Why, Owen, come in. Haven't seen you in a coon's age."

"Mr. Beecham at home?"

"Yes." She led the way into the parlor on the right of the hall, where a lamp burned on the marble-topped table. "Sit down. I'll tell him. He's out in the kitchen."

She disappeared, and Bertie in his nightshirt came to the door to say hello, and to add a proud announcement. "We're going to build a new house!"

"You don't say!"

"Yep! And it's going to have the first bathroom in this town, too."

"My, my! When's all this going to happen?"

"Next summer."

BB came through the hall. "Buster, time you were in bed. Give us a hug. M-m! There! One for Owen too." And when Bertie had disappeared: "Well, Owen, glad to see you. Something on your mind?"

"Yes sir." Owen produced the letter from Joe Ceslak. "This is from a man who used to interpret for us while we were in West Virginia. It's from some place in Pennsylvania, and he says his brother and twenty-five or thirty other miners were shot and killed by a sheriff and his men."

"In Lattimer, yes. That happened early in September. The tenth, I think. They killed twenty-five miners, wounded fifty or sixty others."

"After the strike was settled?"

"Yes."

"What did they shoot them for?"

BB hesitated, seeing Owen's controlled anger. "The Sheriff has been arrested, you know," he said. "He and sixty-four of his deputies. They're charged with murder." And he explained: "The men were marching toward the mines to hold a meeting, and the Sheriff ordered them to disperse. He claims they manhandled him — and the shooting started."

"Were they on a public road?"

"Yes. And one of them was carrying an American flag."

Owen grunted. "What do you think of it?" he demanded.

BB hesitated. "This month's *Review of Reviews* has a short piece about it. They say that when men working in the mines around there began to want higher wages, the operators imported these foreign laborers, till there were more men than there were jobs. That brought wages down, so local sentiment was all against the foreigners." He rose. "I'll get the magazine, you can look at it." He left the room, returned a moment later with the magazine opened at the first page.

Owen took it from him. "I know you're against foreigners —"

"I'm against foreigners who work for low wages, and throw Americans out of jobs, and save their money and go back where they came from. I've no quarrel with any foreigner who comes and settles down and stays."

"Joe's naturalized. Here, look at his letter. Joe Ceslak. He can talk English better than he can write it. He's got two children born in this country. I like him. I like all of them. Joe took me to some of their parties, to their houses. They're all right." His tone tightened. "But just because they're foreigners, the Sheriff thought he could kill them!"

BB took the letter, and Owen's eyes fell to the magazine open in his hands. The page was headed: "Progress of the World"; the first paragraph began with "The Massacre at Lattimer." The words were in black-faced type. Owen's eyes ran down the lines, and once or twice he spoke. "A hundred and fifty miners were in the march, and they didn't have any guns or anything. It says that was 'proved by overwhelming testimony.' " And a moment later: "There were more than a hundred deputies, with Winchester rifles and revolvers." And again: "The deputies kept on shooting at the miners after they scattered and were running away. Most of them were shot in the back."

He finished, closed the magazine, looked at BB with blazing eyes. "When will the Sheriff be tried?"

"I don't know. Depends on the courts."

Owen rose, tramped across the room and back again. "I know something about that sort of thing," he said. "I've been working, organizing. The operators call us agitators, but the Union calls us organizers. I've had deputies come up when I was talking with three men on a street corner and tell us to break it up because assemblies were prohibited. Mike Pratt and I have been ordered off a public street because we walked up and down the sidewalk opposite the mine gate. We've had deputies with guns in their hands tell us what to do. We were mad, sure; but we grinned and did what they told us to. But if we couldn't talk English, if we hadn't understood what they were saying to us, I suppose they'd have shot us, the same way!"

His voice had risen till it rang. Somewhere in the house a baby cried; and Owen stopped short, his anger fading. "Say, I'm sorry. Did I wake him up?"

"Oh, Bobby often fusses awhile."

"I guess I got excited. Is he all right?"

"Yes, yes. It's natural for babies to cry. That's just Bobby's way of asking, 'Who's doing all that talking out there?'" They rose together, and BB remarked: "I see a big change in you since you've been away, Owen. You'll be starting a family of your own, pretty soon."

Walking home, Owen found his thoughts circling around Mr. Beecham's remark. Start a family of his own? Once he had imagined that some day he and Jane would be married; but he was sure now that he would never want to marry Jane. He began to think of other girls he had known. Betty Myers was nice, but when you got to know her, she was probably like Jane. Hetty Jenkins? He certainly wouldn't marry her! Molly Moury was too giggly, and Janet Frye was Morgan's girl. Maybe he might wait till Lulu Harned grew up. She was fourteen or fifteen now, and certainly she was about as pretty as anyone he had ever seen; but she would have to grow up. Before he reached home he had decided that he liked Nellie Tutson better than any girl he knew.

He was so absorbed in thinking about Nellie, and how she used to frighten him, and how he used to dislike her, and how pretty she had grown to be, and how nice she was, that at home he went directly to bed, forgetting to look in the *Journal* and find what Mr. Beecham might have said about his speech at the miners' meeting.

He lay awhile awake, thinking about Nellie. He was sure she liked him, and certainly he liked her. Maybe he would marry her.

XXI

October 6, 1897 — *January* 27, 1898

N<small>EXT</small> <small>MORNING</small>, Owen and his father passed Charles Morgan's home just as Mr. Morgan came out to start toward the station. The morning was dull and cloudy with a threat of rain, a raw October day. Mr. Morgan's stocky figure was silhouetted for a moment against the lighted doorway, and they waited at the corner till he joined them.

Owen spoke at once of the Lattimer massacre. "I haven't been reading the papers, not the dailies, lately, and I didn't know anything about it till I had a letter from Joe Ceslak. He interpreted for us in West Virginia, and his brother was one of the men the Sheriff murdered."

"They were all foreigners," Morgan agreed. "I had a letter about it from John Fahey last week."

"Who's he?"

"One of our men. Mike Pratt knows him. He and John Rinn went to that Lehigh and Schuylkill field three or four years ago, to do some organizing, but they hadn't got much farther than some skeleton locals."

Ed Thorne joined them at the corner of Belton Street, and he and Tom Glen walked together, Owen and Mr. Morgan dropping a little behind. Owen asked: "If these men were members of the Union, why were they marching after the strike had been settled? It was settled on the fourth, all but the voting; and this happened on the tenth."

"I don't think they were in the Union, but they were on strike. They worked in Harwood Mines. Harwood Mines and Lattimer Mines were both owned by Pardee Brothers, so these men, strikers

513

from Harwood Mines, started for Lattimer to try to get the men there to come out. That's when the Sheriff butchered them."

"Was Mr. Fahey there?"

"Not when it happened, but right away after. They carried all the dead men and most of them that were wounded into Hazelton, and a big crowd gathered there, pretty mad, ready to go out and really do some damage. It looked like bad trouble coming; but John and some others finally got them quieted down."

"Is anybody doing anything about it?"

"The Sheriff's going to be tried for murder, him and his deputies. What else is there to do?"

"Call a meeting! Raise some money! Send some money to the families of the dead men! Write them a letter, at least. If we want them to join the Union, let's show them we're their friends."

Owen spoke in a hot passion, but the older man said reasonably: "You couldn't raise much money, Owen. Most of us still owe money from the strike. We've nothing to give to people far away, not with our own children as like as not still hungry."

"Some of us can give something! Will you? I'll take up a collection myself."

"I'll give as much as any man!"

Owen said: "I'll hold you to that." And he did. Through the next week he collected thirty-seven dollars and forty cents, in dollars, half-dollars, quarters, dimes, and even nickels; and he sent a money order to Joe Ceslak, and a letter of friendly sympathy.

But after he had done this, the tragedy drifted into the back of his mind. The months of fall and early winter held always for Owen a particular charm. The clear, crisp days, the smell of burning leaves, the brilliant foliage across every hillside, walnuts in their hulls spread on every shed roof to dry, frost-sweet persimmons, huge copper pots set on bricks in every back yard to simmer over the little fires while the long-handled paddles stirred the apple-butter hour by hour — all these sights and sounds and smells and scenes combined to fill him with content and peace. Mrs. Jenkins and the girls, with Evan dead and gone, needed now and then a man's strength at their autumn tasks; and when his day's work was done Owen might go to help them. Sometimes others joined them there, and they sat late around the little fire that kept the kettle simmering and sang old Welsh songs, sad songs and

martial songs and happy songs. Mrs. Jenkins was apt to be quiet,
but May and Betty were ready for mirth, and Allie could never sing
sitting down. She stood swaying, or like a sprite tossing her arms,
or even twirling in a sort of dance around the fire.

During those fine weeks of fall and winter, a new pulse filled
the air. The better times which BB had for so long predicted would
surely follow the election of McKinley at last were here. Factories
reopened their doors, the wheels of industry began to turn, the
furnaces to roar, and from all quarters came the cry for coal, coal,
coal. The demand had begun before the strike; it grew like a
snowball. While good coal was hard to come by, the old slack pile
below Tom Glen's house, its heart long since half-consumed by
gnawing little fires, had for a while become a source of supply.
Tons and tons of the fine black dust were loaded into wagons,
hauled down to the siding and dumped into the cars. During the
strike, this slack brought as much as ninety cents a ton in the car;
yet not so long ago, good coal had sold in Cincinnati for little more
than twice that figure.

When the strike ended and men returned to work, miners from
the counties down along the river flocked to Hardiston County;
and within a few weeks there were not enough coal cars available
to carry away the product of the busy mines. For lack of cars to be
loaded, Owen and Tom and the others at Miss Ellen might sit all
day idle on the gob piles around the entrance, or perched along
the trestle like sea gulls on the ridge of a fish house. On the first
November payday, 4500 miners in the county received more than
$80,000 in pay. Moses Evans had more orders on hand than he
could fill in two months of maximum production.

There was a quickening in the air like the quickening that comes
with spring. Men walked with a lighter step, a higher head; they
laughed easily. Yet though there was work enough, there were
also grievances. Neither wages nor working conditions were
uniform throughout the Sub-District. In some places, miners were
paid for turning rooms, in others they were not. The day men
steadily insisted that they were underpaid. In the Slacktown
mines, pay ran five cents a ton above Belton, although the Belton
miner often worked a thinner vein. Mines in which the vein
might be four or four and a half feet thick — Miss Ellen was one
of them — paid more than other mines with a thin vein where the

floor had to be shot up to make room for the men to work, and
where to load a car was infinitely more difficult. The car could
be rolled close to the thick vein; in the thin vein the coal had to be
rolled or shovelled or dragged to the car.

A mass meeting of the Sub-District in December discussed these
matters, and at that meeting, after consulting Charles Morgan and
Eben Howell, Owen proposed increasing the tax. Mr. Morgan had
been doubtful of the wisdom of the proposal. He urged that the
men were for the most part just now getting out of debt and
would resent any new demand; but in Eben Howell, Owen found
a supporter.

When at the meeting he rose, Owen began in a cheerful vein.
He reminded them again of the parable of the seven lean years and
the seven fat years. "The seven lean years are done — and there
were only five of them, after all. Now the seven fat years lie ahead
— but there may be only five of them; perhaps not so many.

"After a good meal, a man forgets how it felt to be hungry; but
none of us will easily forget the sorrow and hunger and misery of
the lean years.

"Would it be wise to start now to make sure that when lean
years come again they will not be so bitter? We're earning three
and four and five times as much as we earned this time a year ago —
and we'll be earning more. The operators are going to meet with our
National Executive Board in January, to make a new agreement
for next year. Higher pay will be a part of it, be sure.

"So we've good times coming. Would it be well, while we have
the timber, to build the house? For the fat years ahead, you'll have
full pockets; but after the fat years, there'll be lean years again.
But they need not be all lean, all hunger and cold and misery. The
wise man saves some money every payday against the time of need.
Will not a union of wise men do the same? Have you read the
Constitution of your Union, the Constitution of the United Mine
Workers of America? In it I read that each local will pay a tax
of twenty cents per month per member to the national Union.
Have our locals ever done that? Or paid half of that? Or a fourth?
Or anything at all?

"One day a month ago, operators of this district paid out to
forty-five hundred men some eighty thousand dollars. Was there
any man in the forty-five hundred that couldn't spare a dime for
his Union? If there was, I'll lend him the dime myself. A dime

every payday from every man is twenty cents a month per man. Twenty cents per man per month from forty-five hundred miners would amount to nine hundred dollars. A dime isn't much, and one man alone isn't much; he never was, and never will be. But a lot of dimes is a lot of money, and a hundred men together are stronger than a thousand men, each one alone. None of us will ever get rich alone and by himself; but all of us together can make the Union rich.

"And if we make the Union rich, we make ourselves rich, for we are the Union.

"Mr. Chairman, I move that our tax be raised to twenty-five cents per month per man, fifteen cents for the national treasury, and five cents for the district treasury, and five cents for the local."

He sat down, and Eben Howell lifted his gavel. "Do I hear a second?"

Someone called from the side of the hall: "If Glen's got more money than he knows what to do with, why don't he get married?" A general chuckle greeted the jest, but Isaac Williams rose to second the motion.

"But Mr. Chairman," he said, "in seconding this motion, I will say that I expect it to be voted down." His eye swung slowly all around. "I very much doubt if there's enough men here think they can spare a quarter a month to put this motion through. If there is, I'll be a heap surprised."

He sat down, and Eben Powell asked, "Do I hear any discussion?"

For a moment no one moved, and then Dan Boggus rose. "Mister Chairman!" And when he had the floor: "Someone said if Owen Glen had so much money to spare, he ought to get married. Well, as long as it ain't some gal's pappy with a shotgun says it . . ." He waited for their guffaws, then added: "I guess the young fellow will do his own deciding about that.

"Glen can afford the new tax or he wouldn't be for it; and Isaac Williams, we all know he can afford it, too! But I want to say that I can afford it just as good as they can. I'm a rich man! I've got a nice house over in town, good neighbors, good wife, eight or ten mighty fine children." A chuckle ran across the room, and Owen remembered Dan's small wretched hovel; but there was a lift and a lilt in Dan's voice as he went on: "I've got all a sensible man could want, and I don't know as there's anything else I need more than I need this Union. I can afford to put in my quarter every month — and if there's any that can't, I might help 'em out. I'm for the motion. Let her go!"

The roar of affectionate mirth that answered him made Dan, still on his feet, whirl and stare this way and that, till they thought he had more to say, and hushed, and he protested:

"What did I say? I didn't say anything!"

Someone shouted: "Vote!" The word came from all across the hall. Dan sat down, and when the motion was put, the Ayes were overwhelming.

On the vote to adjourn, Eben Howell caught Owen's eye, so Owen waited till as the crowd thinned he could come near the president. When they were alone, Howell said: "Owen, I'm going to put you through as one of the delegates to the January convention. All right?"

Owen held his tone steady. "Why, if you say so."

Howell linked his hand through Owen's arm, and they moved with the crowd toward the door. "You'll go far," said Howell, and Owen raised his head.

"I want to. I want to go far."

He had not seen the little man behind them till Dan Boggus touched his arm. "Go far, did ye say? Well, d'ye know the biggest lie that was ever spoke? I'll tell ye. It's 'He travels the fastest that travels alone.'" He peered up into Owen's face. "Go far? Is that what you want? Then get you a woman, man; mother and wife and lover all in one. Get you a woman, man, or ye'll never amount to a raindrop in the rain."

2

Through those weeks of fall and early winter the *Journal* kept the record. The Ladies' Aid Society of the Methodist Episcopal Church would serve dinner and supper at the church on election day. The Woman's Literary Club met at Mrs. H. A. Jewell's. Hardiston County Coal commands a higher price than other coal, yet there is a nine-cent differential against the men who mine it. The Eisteddfod was a great success; the Venedocia Ladies' Chorus won the grand prize; burglars entered several houses during the evening session, but they were caught, with their loot, in Hamden.

Mark Hanna has been a coal operator for all his mature years, but he never paid a miner in scrip, or ran a "pluck me" store; can his opponent say the same? Six people died of typhoid in the county last week, and many are ill. Typhoid is a foul-water disease; if water in your well is low, or if your well is near a barn or a cesspool, then get your water somewhere else or boil it before drinking it. Bryan spoke here October 29, and special trains and special cars brought the crowd, but Ohio went Republican, in spite of democratic gains nearly everywhere. Bryan was not at his best; the cold air seemed to depress him. Pickpockets robbed forty people in the crowd, and over $500 was taken. Hunters can get excursion rates to Michigan, Wisconsin, and Minnesota. Bushnell won by 28,101; he led his party. Joe Wheeler and Ned Evans bagged 57 quail last Thursday, and lost 8. They had only one dog. Many farmers have posted their land. Don't shoot a farmer's cattle or horses. The miners should receive an advance of five cents a ton on January 1 without asking for it. Hardiston County in October shipped 376,250 tons of coal; the output was about 500 cars a day. The average wage is now fifty-eight cents a ton, but an increase is in order. Miners in the county earned $200,000 in October. November 23 brought the first snowfall. Mrs. BB Beecham with two children has gone to Mississippi to visit her mother. A Hardiston County woman has been living with three children in one room in Portsmouth; she was found when one of the children starved to death. The iniquity of the Civil Service Law is now patent to all; the Republicans should repeal it. The Ohio Southern yard was solidly full of loaded coal cars on the last day of November, a wonderful sight. There will be bad women as long as men crane their necks to look after them. Merry Christmas! The Teachers' Institute which opened Monday had a record attendance. Happy New Year.

3

Through the closing weeks of the old year, Owen, in full flush of physical powers, and because the mine ran almost every day, was mining better than twenty tons a week. Tom's output was less. His eyes troubled him; but his rheumatism did not return. If Mrs. Glen still sometimes winced as though with pain, Owen had come to accept this on her terms, as of no consequence. He had few chances to spend a day at the *Journal* office, and rarely saw BB or Will or Nellie, and the long day's toil left him in no mind to spend an evening with Marged.

But except during her short Christmas vacation — short because she returned to Hardiston on the Sunday after Christmas to attend the Teachers' Institute — he saw her at church every Sunday; and normally they walked together as far as the Belton Street corner, where she turned toward her uncle's home. She shared his pride when he was chosen one of the Sub-District delegates to the National Convention which would meet in Columbus, January 11. Owen and the other Hardiston County men would go up on Monday. The day before, when he met Marged outside church and they moved away together, she asked:

"Owen, do you know about BB's little baby?" And when she saw he did not: "He died this morning down in Mississippi. Mr. Beecham left last night, but he hasn't had time to get there yet."

"Gollies!" Owen remembered Mr. Beecham's bitter grief when little Anne died. "Who told you?"

"I was in the office yesterday afternoon, just after Mr. Beecham had gone home. Will Davis said he had a telegram that Bob was very sick and for him to come. He took the eight-forty-five train last night. I went by the house this morning to see if Aunt Jane had any news — she and Bertie were there; he's in school, so he didn't go to Mississippi — and she'd had a telegram that Bob was dead."

Owen kicked at a pebble in the path. "I guess I'll go over this afternoon, see how they are."

"They're all right. Bertie's only eight, so he doesn't realize things."

"He's certainly been mighty good to me."

She knew it was not of Bertie he spoke. "He's the greatest man in Hardiston County." They walked in silence for a while, and she asked: "Any news with you, Owen?"

He shook his head. "No. Jake Towne got caught by the slate last week. His room was a quarter of a mile from mine."

She looked at him. "Aren't you ever scared?"

"I used to be. I don't know as I am now. You get so you forget it."

"You'll get out of the mines some day."

"I want to. I want to work up in the Union." He hesitated, added: "The president gets a thousand dollars a year, and so does the secretary-treasurer. And the vice-president gets nine hundred."

She looked up at him with a quick glance. "You like the sound of so much money?"

He colored. "A man has to have something to live on. Him and his family."

She smiled. "Thinking of starting a family, Owen?"

"I could. I might. With the mine busy, I'm earning plenty."

Her eyes were straight ahead. "Any — particular girl going to help you? Start a family, I mean?"

"I haven't got that far yet."

They were come to her corner. "Well, when you come home from Columbus, you'll have to tell me all about the convention. Are you going to make a speech?"

He grinned, shook his head. "Guess I'll wait till I'm dry behind the ears."

The convention proceedings were for Owen completely absorbing; yet he was a listener rather than a participant. Mike Pratt was there, and other organizers whom he had met during the strike, and President Ratchford remembered him with a fine word. Mike had heard from Joe Ceslak of the tragedy at Lattimer.

"You know his brother was one of the ones killed?" Owen nodded, and Mike said: "They're going to make a test case out of him, try the Sheriff and the others for killing Mike Ceslak, and see how they come out."

"When does the trial start?"

"February, Joe says. Some of the witnesses are still in the hospital."

"I'd like to be there."

"It will be a long business. Give a bunch of lawyers a chance to make speeches and get paid for it and there's no stopping them."

"Will they hang the Sheriff and the others?"

Mike felt the passion in Owen's tones and he spoke gently. "Hanging them won't bring the miners back to life — or support their families."

"We sent Joe some money for them."

Pratt nodded. "Yes, he said so. So did we."

The proceedings in the convention were tuned to a jubilant pitch. President Ratchford reviewed the strike, and announced that operators and miners would meet next week in Chicago to formulate an agreement covering wages and working conditions for the coming year. He was re-elected president, John Mitchell vice-president; the convention voted to move National Headquarters from Columbus to Indianapolis, and then adjourned.

4

Owen was disappointed that the Columbus papers gave little space to the convention proceedings. Their headlines dealt with the contest in the Legislature, where Mark Hanna, serving in the United States Senate by appointment, now sought election for both the short and the long term. He was elected by a bare majority, and Owen heard more than one sardonic comment on his victory, with the implication that legislators had been bribed.

The day he returned to Hardiston, he stopped at the *Journal* office; yet when BB rose to shake his hand, Owen did not know what best to say. "I heard about Bob," he blurted.

BB turned to arrange some papers on his desk. "Yes." He faced Owen again. "Well, how was the convention? Does the Union expect to accomplish anything in this Chicago meeting?"

"Yes sir. The talk was that the operators were pretty reasonable."

"Herbert Canter dropped in this morning. He says the operators here are agreeable to a ten-cent raise." He sat down. Owen thought he seemed tired.

"Well, I guess I'll say hello to Will," he decided, and went back to the pressroom.

Will was making up the inside, but he had a cheerful word. "Bring home any of that Hanna money? They say it was dropping like leaves in the fall."

"I didn't see any. Do you think all that talk was true?"

"Why, no-o-o," Will assured him in a long drawl. "You don't suppose high-minded men like politicians buy votes — or sell them — do you?"

"You think Hanna did?"

"He's a great man," Will said more seriously. "If he bought McKinley into the White House, it was a good thing for the country." He jerked his head toward the stairs. "Better go up and see our new girl."

"New girl? What for? Who is she?"

"Edith Evans. She came from Adams Township, used to be Edith Blanchard."

"I was in school with her." As so often happened, Owen's memory served him well. "She recited *Sheridan's Ride* the last day of school before we moved to Hardiston."

"She married Dan Evans and they lived in Sycamore Hill; but he died of typhoid fever last summer, so she started setting type on the paper down there. She's going to take Bets's place."

"Where's Bets going? Is she quitting?"

"Yes. She's going to get married, man named Haggerty. Remember the organist that got shot in the Crescent Saloon up at Belton?"

Owen grinned. "I remember, yes. Mr. Brown shot at Haggerty — or someone — and hit the organist, and Haggerty beat up Mr. Brown. Bets getting married, is she? Good for her."

He turned to the stairs. It was pleasant to see Nellie again, and to remind Edith of that recitation, and to tease Bets and see her blush and laugh and reach for another gumdrop. Nellie was prettier than ever, and he wanted to tell her so; but he could not do this with Bets and Edith listening.

"When's the big event, Bets?" he asked.

"Wednesday. This is my last week here."

"Going to invite us all to the wedding?"

Bets, to his surprise, looked almost sad. "I can't, Owen. We have to have it in mama's and my bedroom, and there can't more than three-four people get in there."

"Why do you have to do it that way?"

"So mama can see it. She's been in bed for eleven years, has some kind of rheumatism, can't bend her joints. That's why I go home every noon, to turn her over and sort of take care of her. Haggerty's real good with her. He's rented a bigger house for us, down on Erie Flats, so we'll have two bedrooms; and he's doing good, so I'll stay home with mama."

Owen had never thought of Bets as living a life of devotion and of selfless service. On sudden impulse he put his arm around her shoulder, hugged her closer, kissed her cheek. "Well, if I can't come to the wedding, I can kiss the bride."

She laughed in the familiar, jolly way. "Take another gumdrop, Owen."

"I'll bet being married will agree with you."

"Wouldn't wonder. You'll have to try it sometime."

Walking home, Owen thought everybody seemed to be saying that same thing, or something like it. For weeks now the thought of getting married had lain somewhere in the background of his consciousness. He was earning enough money to be married if he chose, and saving most of it. His mother had suggested this as soon as the last of their debts was paid.

"It's time you had some money of your own, Owen, and not give it all to us. Papa's earning plenty for him and me, so you start and lay some by." And she too had plucked this same familiar string; "You'll be wanting to get married, one of these days, and you'll need money for furniture and things."

After that Owen paid into the family purse two dollars a week for his board. "And that's enough," his mother told him. "If ever we need more, I'll tell you quick enough." She had said one dollar was plenty, but he argued that if he paid so little he would feel he must hold back and not eat much. She laughed at his laughing arguments, but yielded. The arrangement settled into routine; but — this was at her insistence — Owen did not discuss it with his father. "What he don't know won't hurt him," she promised. "Long as he gets a bed and his victuals, he don't let a thing bother him."

Owen's savings went into the bank, but his mother made the deposits for him. On paydays, he and his father each handed her their money; from Owen's, Mrs. Glen kept out the two dollars for board, and gave Owen what he would need for car and train fares and such daily spending. The rest she took to the bank. So Owen had these savings, and his earnings; he could be married if he chose, if he found the girl.

When his thoughts reached this point, there was no question: the girl was Nellie Tutson. He gave no thought to Jane, nor to any other; Nellie was the one. But knowing that he wanted to marry

Nellie was not enough. His only guide in deciding on the next step was his memory of Dave and Amy walking home from church together. Apparently to walk together was a preliminary to marriage; but taking a walk was not much fun now in January, and particularly since they would have to do their walking at night, after his day's work was done, and hers. If she attended the Welsh church, he might walk home with her, instead of with Miss Williams; but she and her mother were Methodists. Their routes to and from church crossed, but at no point did they correspond. Also, the Methodist service was shorter than the Welsh, so Nellie was on her way home before he got out of church at all.

Sunday, walking home with Marged, he was so absorbed in seeking a solution to this problem that she wondered at his silence, said at last:

"Penny for your thoughts, Owen."

He roused with a start, felt his color rise. "Oh, I was just — figuring on something."

"Maybe I can help?"

"I don't guess so." He hesitated. She had helped him with other problems, but he could not well ask her help in this. His own thoughts made his cheeks hot, and Marged asked:

"Do you see much of Jane lately?"

He wondered what made her think of Jane. Probably she had seen him blush and assumed he was thinking about a girl. "No, not much," he said. "I'm working every day."

"You could go see her in the evenings — if you wanted to. And Sunday afternoons."

Her suggestion that he could call on Jane in the evenings applied equally well to Nellie; and while he considered this, he spoke in an abstracted tone. "Sunday afternoon's the only time I can study with you. And read things." He felt her eyes upon him, said recklessly: "I don't care anything about Jane, anyway."

"She's a brilliant girl. She's going to college, you know." They paused at Marged's corner, waiting for the others to come up.

"I heard she was. Can I come this afternoon?"

"Unless there's something you'd rather do."

When he went on toward home he found himself remembering this answer, and he decided there were mighty few things he would rather do than be with her.

The problem of paying court to Nellie continued to perplex him till a paragraph in the *Journal* suggested an expedient. He was reading the locals. Flocks of wild geese flew north over the city Monday. The Pleasant Hour Club met Friday afternoon at Mrs. Freling's. *Daisy, the Missouri Girl,* which would come to the Rink January 25, was a hit in every sense of the word, the most natural play ever presented to the public, a true story of home life.

Like a lightning flash came audacious inspiration. He would take Nellie to the play! He read that item in the *Journal* late Wednesday evening, too late to go to her; but Thursday after supper he picked up hat and reefer. His mother asked where he was going.

"Just take a walk, get some fresh air."

"It's nice and warm out," she agreed; then suddenly: "Oh, Owen, Mrs. Lewis wanted to borrow my extra knitting needles. Can you stop by and give them to her?"

The coincidence seemed to him a happy augury. He took the needles, tied together with a twist of yarn, and put them in his pocket and set out. It was a disappointment, when he reached Mrs. Lewis's house, to discover that Nellie was not there. Mrs. Lewis and Mrs. Tutson were together in the sitting room, and he delivered the needles and had his thanks before he asked for Nellie, asked where she had gone.

"She said she was going to take her present to Bets," Mrs. Tutson explained. "She'd crocheted a nice pair of hushers for her."

"Where does Bets live? I'll go walk Nellie home."

Mrs. Tutson looked at him in surprise. "Didn't you know? Haggerty's rented our old house for them."

Owen thanked her and turned back up Ridge Street, thinking to meet Nellie along the way. He passed a couple, and a man alone, and then as he descended the hill beyond Peach Street he saw another couple approaching and heard Nellie laugh; so when he came face to face with these two he said:

"Hello, Nellie." He added: "It's Owen."

"Oh, hello, Owen." She said hurriedly: "I came over to see Bets, and Jenkin Powell was there, and he said he'd see me home."

"Hello, Jenk?" Owen hesitated. "Your mama told me where you were, Nellie, so I came to keep you company."

A moment's silence held them all; then Nellie said doubtfully: "Why, that's fine, Owen. Jenkin, it saves you all the extra walking."

"I like walking, a nice night like this."

"It's all of three miles, clear to our house and then back to the farm," she reminded him, and she said, in a curious hurried tone: "It's all right, Jenkin. Goodnight."

After a reluctant moment, Jenkin yielded. "Well, all right then. Goodnight."

He turned back down the hill; Owen and Nellie swung the other way. "How'd you happen to be down at Mrs. Lewis's, Owen?" she asked.

"I took some knitting needles down. Mrs. Lewis wanted to borrow them. And I asked where you were and they told me. How's Bets?"

"Fine."

They went on in silence, and Owen felt a pulse beat in his throat. The night was — for late January — warm, but it was not the warm night which made him perspire. He tried to devise an easy conversational approach to what he wished to say, but Nellie set a rapid pace, and they came within a block or two of Mrs. Lewis's before desperation drove him to speech.

"Nellie, want to go see *Daisy, the Missouri Girl* at the Rink Tuesday night?" She did not immediately answer, and he added: "They say it's the most natural play ever written, real good."

She touched his arm as though apologetically. "I can't, Owen."

"Why not?"

She stopped still. "I just can't, that's all."

"Won't your mama let you?" He urged: "Look, Nellie. I wish you would. I've — well, I've been thinking a lot about you lately. Ever since that night in the office. And at Electric Park. You're mighty nice, and pretty, and everything." He hesitated. "Nellie." She stood, her head a little bowed; and he put his hands on her shoulders. "Nellie!"

She looked up at him, her eyes shadows in the pale oval of her face. "Owen, promise not to tell anyone?"

"Tell what?"

"What I tell you."

"You haven't told me anything."

"Owen, Jenkin and I have been married almost a year."

His arms dropped helplessly. "Married? For Gollies sake!"

"We haven't told a soul," she warned him. "Jenkin's mother

doesn't want him ever to get married. She's awful, Owen. She'll
prob'ly live for years and years, but we decided to get married
anyway, and not tell her. She always says she'll kill herself if he
marries anyone. So Owen, please don't tell."

"Gosh! Well, I won't."

"I didn't want to, but Jenkin was bound to. But nobody knows
but you. We went to Portsmouth and did it. Nobody knows here.
So don't tell."

"You'll have to tell sometime."

"I guess so. But not till we have to."

"I bet his mother wouldn't kill herself."

"I don't think she would either, but s'pose she did? And Jenkin
thinks she would."

He scratched his head. "Well, I won't tell." They came slowly
to her gate, and he laughed in rueful mirth. "Joke on me! I
wanted to marry you myself."

"I knew you did; or I knew you would want to, some day." She
hesitated, said in a breathless rush of words: "That's one reason I
married Jenkin."

He stared at her in the darkness. "Why?"

She laughed softly and came nearer and kissed him. "Goodnight Owen. You'll be a great man, but you need a fine wife!
Goodnight."

"Goodnight." He spoke absently, puzzled and half-angry, trying
to laugh at this fine joke on himself; but he was too lonely for
laughter. It is hard to laugh alone. He had a sudden longing to
tell his mother all this new loneliness, to have her comforting.

But of course, when he came home, she and his father were in
bed and asleep; she was his father's.

5

Friday brought a downpour, a deluge of rain which continued
all that day; and when Tom and Owen that afternoon alighted
from the miners' train, there was water across the tracks within a
hundred yards of the station. Unless the rain eased, morning would
see the low ground beyond the station under water. "And if it is,"

Tom predicted, "the trains won't run tomorrow, nor the electric cars can't get through."

Owen consulted the conductor, who agreed that this was true; so when they woke next morning to hear the rain still sluicing on the roof, and looked out and saw the little wet-weather run before their door now a torrent of muddy water ten or fifteen feet wide, they went back to sleep. When Owen woke again, he thought the rain was less. Before noon, the worst of it was past, and after dinner he picked his way through the mud to the road and walked uptown.

The *Journal* office, when he stepped in, was empty, and he would have gone through to the pressroom to find Will; but on the chairs along the wall lay scattered copies of the dailies, and a headline caught his eye: "Riots in Havana." It was a long time since he had had an opportunity to look through the city papers, so he sat down and began to read. This paper was two days old. Consul-General Lee had sent word from Havana to Captain Sigsbee, Commander of the battleship *Maine* in Key West, eighty miles away, that he would forward a cable every day; if no message came through, Sigsbee would know that the cable had been cut and act accordingly. Meanwhile, the Atlantic Fleet had sailed south for maneuvers, and would be able to protect United States citizens if further riots endangered them.

This sounded important and even ominous. BB came in, wearing muddy rubber boots and flushed and perspiring. He greeted Owen with a ready hand.

"Just been down to take a look at the high water," he explained. "Twenty or thirty houses down in the Nail Mill Addition are flooded, and the tracks are all under water."

"Papa and I knew we couldn't get to work," Owen assented, and he said: "It's a long time since I've seen a daily paper. Does this riot in Havana amount to anything?"

"It shouldn't." BB hauled off his muddy boots, drew on his shoes, settled at his desk. "Not if we show a firm hand. I wish every vessel in the Atlantic Squadron were anchored within effective shooting distance of Havana." And he said: "This has been quite a rain, Owen. Horse Creek and Buckeye, and of course Salt Creek, are all out of their banks."

"It's a bad one, all right." Owen thought Mr. Beecham's voice sounded tired. Probably having a baby die was pretty hard.

"I haven't seen you since the convention. How did it feel to be a delegate?"

"I came in the day I got home," Owen reminded him.

"That's right," BB agreed. "I'd forgotten." He brushed his hand across his eyes. "This Chicago meeting means a victory for the miners, doesn't it?"

"Well, I think having a meeting at all is a victory for everybody. If we can meet the operators every year, and all agree on the way things are going to be for the next year, it will stop their cutting prices, cutting each other's throats. It will keep prices where they ought to be — and keep wages where they ought to be. A good thing for everybody."

"I suppose any really good thing is good for everybody, don't you?" BB absently suggested. "If two men make a bargain, and it's a good bargain, they'll both be satisfied. If they're not, then it was a bad bargain — for both sides. What do the miners hope to get?"

"Ten cents a ton more for screened coal, and mine run on a relative scale; and they want to regulate the size of the screen. And they're going to ask for a nine-hour day, if it looks like there's a chance to get it."

"What difference will that make, if you're paid by the ton?"

"Well, in slack times it will spread the work around. The way it is, when times are bad and there isn't much work, some men put in a long day; and sometimes, if they live handy, they go into the mine after supper and shoot down some more coal. Night-hawking, we call that. But if some men dig all the coal the operator wants, other men won't get any work. If a miner's only allowed to work nine hours, then there'll be work for more men." Owen added: "And besides, the tracklayers and bottom cagers and drivers and timbermen and so on, they all work by the day. They work ten hours, and most of them get a dollar thirty-five or a dollar forty. If we can get a nine-hour day, and raise their pay to a dollar and a half, it will help them and help all of us."

"Is there a chance?"

He was sure Mr. Beecham was too tired to talk, so he rose. "From what I hear, not much; not this year. We'll get an eight-hour day, some day; but this year, the raise, and fixing the screens, and signing an agreement to run for twelve months so the coal business will be steadier, those are the main things. If we even got a nine-hour day, that would be just icing on the cake." He turned away. "I'll go say hello to Will."

"Come in again." Owen had heard Mr. Beecham use that familiar phrase a thousand times, but it had now an empty sound.

All day Sunday the wind blew a gale, the waters receded, the sodden earth began to dry; Monday, Owen and his father went back to work. Charles Morgan had heard from Eben Howell, who was in Chicago, that some of the Illinois operators were delaying any settlement of rates for the coming year; but Owen predicted that the miners need only stand their ground. "The operators don't want another strike, not with business good and getting better. We can afford to wait till they give in."

Tuesday afternoon on the train coming home he heard that the *Maine* had been ordered to Havana, that Captain Sigsbee had exchanged calls of courtesy with the port authorities; and in the *Journal* which was waiting for him at home Thursday night, BB commented:

> *This is more than a gesture, and Spain will be wise to understand that fact. The Madrid papers are pouting, calling the visit inopportune, saying it is designed to encourage the insurgents and that it will provoke a conflict. One Madrid editor proposes that the Spanish government send warships to various American ports. That is unnecessary. The* Maine *was sent to Havana to protect the interests of American citizens; the interests of Spanish citizens in American ports are already protected.*

Owen — his father and mother were both abed — was still engrossed in the paper when he heard the sound of footsteps. Someone was coming from the roadside toward the house, and Owen went to the door and opened it.

"Hullo," he called. "Who's there?"

"Charles Morgan." The older man came into the light, and Owen saw that he was beaming. "Had to come and tell you," he exclaimed. "Look here!"

He held out a telegram, but there was not enough light here in the doorway for Owen to read it, so he turned back to the lamp. Tom Glen called from the bedroom: "Owen, who's there?"

Morgan answered him. "Come out here, Tom!" Owen heard
his father stir; but his eyes and his thoughts were fixed on the
telegram, the words written in a flowing hand and with a single
pencil stroke so that each word in a line was connected. It was
from Chicago, from Eben Howell.

> *Tremendous victory. Ten cent increase on screened, run
> of mine relative, size of screen fixed, and an eight-hour
> day. Celebrate.*
>
>   *Howell.*

Owen read this to himself, and then aloud to his father, while
Tom Glen stood gaunt and tall in his union suit, scratching his
head. "Eight-hour day," he echoed. "I never thought they'd get it
down to nine, even."

"No one thought so." Charles Morgan's voice was jubilant.
"We've been dreaming of an eight-hour day for twenty years!"

Tom Glen nodded. "The Knights of Labor worked for it, a long
time ago." He and Charles Morgan looked at one another without
speaking; and Owen, watching them, had a sudden understanding
of what this meant to men their age. It was another upward step.
He remembered Andrew Dale's speech at the miners' meeting up
the creek, years ago. Once upon a time miners had lived in
bondage, had lived underground, had been allowed to exist only
on sufferance of their masters, had no function save to work and
to obey. One by one they had broken their chains; now, like a
bound man to whose members when his cords are loosed strength
begins to return, they were ready to stand erect, to lift their heads,
to move like men set free.

XXII

January 27, 1898–April 20, 1898

ADDITIONAL LOCALS: News of the unspeakable and worse than
heathenish outrage at Belton reached Hardiston Tuesday; little
Lulu Harned, aged fifteen, was seized by a gang of ruffians Saturday night and was recovered Monday morning; Ernest Vought,
who was struck down when he tried to protect her, was fatally
hurt and the little girl is not expected to live. Doctor Murchison,
pastor of the Presbyterian Church, leaves February 5 for a trip to
the Orient. By the eight-hour day in the mines, a great forward step
has been taken. The Hardiston bowling team lost to Gallipolis,
but the local boys have had only a few weeks' practice; they will
come out all right yet. David Morgan was killed Friday by a fall
of slate in Pawnee Mine. A woman leading two children was over-
taken on a trestle near Hooper by an Ohio Southern train Monday;
she was able to lower her children to safety but lost her life.
Edward Davis, the well-known Welsh operator, died January 15
at his home in Wales, aged 45, and left an estate of $20,000,000.
None of his miners has ever earned that much money. Three men
charged with the outrage in Belton have been arrested and bound
over; two were released in $500 bail; the other is in jail. One
Hardiston druggist last month sold 45 gallons of whiskey, most of
it to professed teetotallers. A boy fired at a sparrow with his slingshot and the missile ricocheted and broke a small hole in the plate-
glass window of Mr. Jewell's jewelry store. The boy learned the
lesson that even a starving sparrow has a friend above. Commercial failures decreased 11½% in 1897. The few think and in-
vent; the many profit. We laugh at the farmer rooked by a bunco-
steerer; but the cashier of the greatest bank in the United States
has just resigned because he was rooked out of $393,000 when he

loaned bank money on worthless collateral. Sheriff Martin and
his deputies, who killed twenty-five striking miners at Lattimer
last September, have at last been brought to trial; they are charged
with the murder of one Mike Ceslak; Joe Ceslak, brother of the
murdered man, is a friend of Owen Glen of Hardiston. Miss Alice
Dine, who formerly taught school in Hardiston, died a week ago
in the home of Doctor Samson of Chillicothe, an unlicensed physi-
cian; he is held on a charge of murder and has been threatened
with lynching; a young man in Columbus claims that he wished to
marry her, but her father, formerly a Hardiston resident, forbade
it; the young man sent her to Doctor Samson. President McKinley
was grievously insulted in a letter written by the Spanish Ambassador, who says McKinley is "weak, catering to the rabble, a
low politician trying to stand in with the Jingoes of his party." The
original letter was stolen by a Cuban in Havana and sent to the
Secretary of State. The Ambassador admitted writing the letter,
and his recall was at once demanded, but his Government permitted him to resign. Walker Whiteside will be the Shylock in
The Merchant of Venice at the Rink February 19. Senator Foraker's
great speech urging intervention in Cuba reaches the heights in
the following passage:

> *Conditions in Cuba are unparalleled for brutality, starva-
> tion, murder and all imaginable horrors. Humanity de-
> mands that we intervene and end this atrocious struggle.
> According to the Monroe Doctrine, we can not allow any
> other nation to interfere; the responsibility is therefore
> ours; we must answer for all the pillage, waste, rapine,
> butchery and starvation that may ensue.*

2

The outrage of which little Lulu Harned and Ernie Vought
were the victims awoke in Owen an anger that had no outlet.
The tragedy occurred on the day Evan and Mrs. Harned, who
had taken Lulu into their home when her mother died, moved to
Belton. Their household goods went with them in a wagon followed by John Morgan's dray; but Lulu made the journey in the
electric car, under escort of young Tom Bowles. Tom was himself

only seventeen. When he and Lulu left the car in Belton, it was at a street near the edge of town, and men roistering with drink poured out of a saloon in their path and seized Lulu. While Tommy ran for help, Ernie Vought, passing at the time, tried to interfere. He was struck by a thrown brick and left senseless on the ground and never recovered consciousness.

It was Ernie's death rather than that of the young girl which hurt Owen most keenly. Lulu was a pretty little child, but only a child; Ernie was a man and the gentlest Owen had ever known. He thought there was something Christlike in Ernie's end.

But the tragedy merged into the past, its sharp edge blunted, its outline blurred. Owen's days were full, for they had weeks of steady work. Tom Glen suffered no recurrence of the rheumatism which in the past had sometimes laid him low, and Owen's mother either no longer felt those occasional painful twinges or she had learned to hide them. Tom grumbled because fuses had replaced the squibs with which he had been all his life familiar, but Owen soon came to prefer the fuse. With squibs each hole must be fired separately; with fuses cut to slightly different lengths, so that a man could safely light them all before retreating to the entry, it was possible to shoot all the holes together, and thus shoot down more coal and increase his production and his pay.

To be working every day gave him a fine content which was not easily disturbed. When the Union and the operators agreed upon a ten-cent advance and an eight-hour day, the fact that Ohio operators refused to sign seemed to him unimportant. The agreement would not take effect till April 1; there was time enough.

His attention for a while centered upon Cuba and the troubles there; and when in late January Mr. Beecham printed in the *Journal* a summary history of the insurrection, he clipped it and carried it in his pocketbook.

On February 24, 1895, the cry went forth, "Cuba Libre," and the present struggle for Cuban independence began. The fourth year of war finds them nearer independence than ever before. Callejas, Captain General of Cuba when the war began, was incapable and rapacious. Captain General Campos, who succeeded Callejas, conducted a vigorous but humane war, treating the Cubans as rebels, but also as men. January 18, 1896, Weyler was appointed

to succeed Campas; his barbarous methods horrified the
world. Assassination and official murder became a com-
monplace. He herded neutrals like cattle while they died
of disease and starvation. Blanco succeeded Weyler,
avowedly as the apostle of autonomy; but he substituted
for autonomy a program of oppression and corruption.
The reconcentrados have died — and are dying — by
thousands. It is time to act.

But Owen forgot Cuba when presently Sheriff Martin and his
deputies were brought to trial at Wilkes-Barre. Since the slain
miners were of foreign birth, Austria-Hungary, Germany and Italy,
as well as the United States, kept observers in the courtroom. An
editorial in the *Ohio State Journal* smugly predicted that the jury
would give the Sheriff and his men a fair trial; but after a few days
the testimony began to be so repetitious that even Owen found it
wearying, and dispatches from Wilkes-Barre shrank to a few paragraphs, and then disappeared.

One evening, Will Davis stopped on his way home to leave a
copy of that week's *Journal.* Owen knew that on Wednesday evenings Mrs. Davis always kept supper for Will; but when he met the
foreman at the door and thanked him for the paper, Will seemed in
no hurry to be gone. Owen asked him in, but the other declined.

"Better come in where it's warm," Owen urged.

"No, no; she'll have supper ready." Will asked surprisingly:
"Had your supper?"

"Yes, just finished."

"Walk along with me a ways, keep me company."

Owen was astonished, but he said at once: "Sure. Wait till I
grab a coat." When they reached the Pike, they went up toward
Ridge Street. There was a more direct route through fields and
byways, but snow and wind made it at this season unattractive.
Will did not speak, and when they turned at Charles Morgan's,
Owen asked, "What's on your mind?"

"Oh, nothing. Why?"

"The way you act. Wanting me to walk home with you."

Will hesitated. "I kind of wanted company. Guess I'm scared."
He blurted out the truth. "She's going to have another baby."

"Mrs. Davis?"

"Yes. Sure."

"Well — isn't that all right? She's had three."

"She always has a terrible time. And I'm always scared."

"When's it coming?"

"September. October."

Owen laughed, clapped the other's shoulder. "You started worrying a long time ahead."

"I always do. When we first find out, and then right at the end; those are the worst times for me."

"She'll be all right."

Will tried to laugh. "She always is. She's all right, sure. But I don't know as I can go through it!"

So they laughed together. At the corner of Ridge and Peach, Owen paused. "Think you can make it from here?"

"Sure, I'm all right now. Telling somebody did me a lot of good. Come down and see us sometimes, evenings. It picks her up, having people come in."

Owen promised to do so, but events for a while crowded that promise out of his mind. When he reached home, he read in the *Journal* of the insult to President McKinley in that letter written by the Spanish Ambassador; and next morning at the station he and Tom heard that the *Maine* had been sunk.

The news had come by telegraph to Howie Evans, the station agent and he and the whole train crew were for the time elevated to heroic proportions by the fact that they had first-hand information and would share it. Three telegrams were tacked on the notice board in the waiting room, and men crowded to read. The uppermost was brief.

> The cruiser Maine *was destroyed by an explosion while lying at anchor in Havana Harbor at 9:45 P.M. Many sailors were killed and wounded. Cause of the explosion unknown.*

Owen tried to read this aloud to his father, but there was a press all around them, and many voices. "P.M.? Must be last night." "Cruiser? I thought she was a battleship." "What's the difference?" With everyone talking, Owen had to shout to make his father hear, so he read the other telegrams to himself, remembering fragments and phrases. "Two hundred and fifty dead." "Blown up by a Spanish torpedo." "The correspondent of the Associated Press has been assured by a reliable quarter that Captain Sigsbee is under the impression that the *Maine* was blown up by a floating torpedo." "Mystery." "Investigation necessary."

"Let's get out of the crowd, papa; get on the train," Owen suggested. "I'll tell you what the telegrams say." And when they were seated, he explained: "She was at anchor in Havana, and all of a sudden she blew up and sank. That's all anyone really knows. They think about two hundred and fifty sailors were killed. Nobody knows what happened."

Isaac Williams leaned over from the seat behind them. "Spanish torpedo, Owen," he corrected. "The captain says so."

Owen shook his head. "No, he didn't! That telegram said someone or other 'had been assured' that Captain Sigsbee is 'under the impression.' That's a lot different from saying he said so!"

"It amounts to the same thing. He wouldn't even say he was 'under the impression' unless he was sure."

"It doesn't even say he was 'under the impression,'" Owen insisted. "It just says someone assured somebody that he was."

Tom Glen spoke in anger. "Owen, you standing up for Spain?" Owen looked at him in a sharp astonishment, and Isaac Williams laughed and said:

"No, no, Tom. Owen just likes to argue, that's all."

"I'm not arguing! I'm just telling you what was in the telegram."

"All the same, it was the Spaniards. Just the sort of thing they'd do."

Owen, recognizing the hopelessness of contention, did not reply; and Mr. Williams and Tom Glen went over and over the splinters of fact and rumor as though they were starving men picking last shreds of flesh off splintered bone. It seemed to Owen, during the days that followed, that most of the men he knew had changed overnight from sensible people to obsessed parrots whose minds were closed to reasonable fact, but hungry for any wild rumor. A Belton man named Swagner — after worrying through three sleepless nights about the coming war — shot himself and left a note advising his wife to do the same. The dailies reported the recovery of bodies from the wreck of the *Maine,* and the beginning of an investigation, and said divers would explore the damaged hull. Owen was secretly sure that if the Spaniards had a guilty conscience, they would forbid any investigation of the wreck; but he knew the folly of suggesting this. The Spanish cruiser *Viscaya* visited New York Harbor; and the dailies said: "Every precaution will be taken to prevent a repetition of the *Maine* disaster." Reading that statement at home, Owen laughed aloud, and he read it to his father; but Tom Glen said:

"I don't see anything funny about it."

"You don't? Well, what precautions? What precautions will be taken? Will they hang nets around her to keep any floating torpedoes from hitting her? Or maybe search all visitors to see if they've got two or three thousand pounds of dynamite in their pockets. Papa, I think people are crazy."

Tom said gloomily: "You'd best learn to hold your tongue, Owen. It'll get you in trouble."

"But don't you see how silly this is?"

"Don't sound so to me. Sounds to me right sensible."

"To do what?"

"Well, to take precautions."

"I know. But what precautions? What precautions, papa?"

"How would I know? It says 'every precaution.' That's good enough for me! Trouble with you, you're the only one knows anything! There's other people know a few things, besides you."

Owen caught his mother's eye and saw her warning gesture, so he held his tongue.

3

Wednesday afternoon, instead of coming directly home from the station on his return from work, Owen turned to the *Journal* office. When he arrived, the press was running, the girls already addressing papers to be mailed. Owen lifted a paper out of the folder and opened it.

"Grim-Visaged War," said BB in headlines, "Threatens the Peace of the Great Republic." The sinking of the *Maine* was the greatest horror in the history of navies; circumstantial evidence pointed to Spanish treachery.

Owen folded the paper almost resentfully. The fact that even Mr. Beecham seemed so sure of Spain's guilt made him, like a cat whose tail is pulled, pull the other way. He heard a step and turned and saw Mr. Beecham at his elbow. Here in the pressroom the noise made easy conversation difficult.

"I want to ask you something," he said, shouting to be heard. "Come in the office."

BB nodded and led the way. In the office a man was sitting at ease, reading the *Enquirer*. Something about him was vaguely familiar. Mr. Beecham made no introductions, and Owen sat down beside this gentleman, facing Mr. Beecham at his desk. He unfolded the copy of the *Journal*, tapped it with his finger.

"This sounds like you think we're going to war, Mr. Beecham."

"It seems probable," BB agreed. "The American people aren't anxious for war, but they've been angry at Spain for a long time, and they're really mad now. They won't stand for a cowardly, do-nothing policy in Washington."

"You act pretty sure the Spaniards did it."

"The evidence points that way."

"What evidence?" Owen's tone was challenging; he felt his bristles rise.

"The boilers didn't explode," BB reminded him. "And the deck plates were blown upward."

Owen suddenly grinned. "I don't know why, but it makes me mad to have everyone so sure Spain did it. Who says the boilers didn't blow up? And if the magazines had exploded, wouldn't the deck plates have blown upward?"

"The Court of Inquiry began its sessions Monday," BB reminded him. "They'll find out what really happened. If they find that Spain is responsible, we'll face the gravest decision since Sumter was fired on."

"Do you want us to have a war?"

"Well, Owen, firmness now may save a hundred thousand lives. The Administration has been preparing for war for weeks; navy yards, gun shops, arsenals running day and night. If trouble comes, we're ready to meet it."

Owen looked at his own toes, and he felt an abrupt surprise at himself. Here was he — nothing but a coal miner, his face and hands still grimy from the mine, his garments black and soiled — arguing with Mr. Beecham, who was probably the smartest man in Hardiston.

Yet Mr. Beecham was so surely wrong. The fact that the United States had for months been preparing to fight Spain did not prove that Spain had sunk the *Maine*; and just because you were ready for war did not mean you must start fighting. He spoke in reluctant dissent.

"I don't see any sense in Spain's doing it, sinking the *Maine*. I don't see what she gains by it."

BB, head on one side, urged: "Well, Spain is one of the great powers. She's arrogant, and proud, so she bitterly resents any suggestion that we might interfere with her in Cuba. She probably feels that if we do, she can crush us as easily as a man steps on a worm."

Owen came slowly to his feet, a pulse pounding in his temples. "Crush us? You're crazy! Nobody can beat us! You've told me, many a time, we're just a boy growing up, and we aren't anywhere near grown yet; but we're a lot bigger and stronger than we think we are. Or than anybody else thinks we are. Spain can't beat us! She can't even hurt us!"

BB looked at the other gentleman and smiled. "Youngsters always overrate themselves, Owen. Young men and young nations. Spain couldn't invade the United States, it's true; but she has a great navy. She could levy tribute on our ports, sink our merchant ships, maybe even defeat our fleet. Yes, Owen, it's quite possible that Spain wants war." He shifted in his chair, his tone changed. "But you and I can't settle things, so why get worked up about it. What else have you on your mind?"

Owen sat down again, relaxing. "Nothing. I just came by the office to pick up a paper on the way home."

"By the way, do you know anyone with a house to rent?"

"Don't think so. Why?"

"We're going to build, this summer. They'll saw our present house in two and use part of it for a kitchen, and move the rest to the back of the lot for a shed. So we'll have to move out."

"Bertie told me you were going to build, but I don't know any place you can rent."

BB nodded and Owen moved, about to go home to supper, and BB asked: "Have you seen any of these counterfeit nickels, up at the mine?"

"Don't know anything about them."

"Someone up at Belton is turning them out, using them in slot machines. They're made of Babbitt metal, cast in a plaster of Paris mold by the looks of them. Don't let anyone cheat you with one."

Owen had a curious feeling that BB was making conversation. The editor chuckled. "Another amusing thing; a circular came to the office the other day, offering to write anything from a High School essay, at three dollars and up, to sermons up to twenty-five dollars and political speeches up to thirty. So if you ever run out of speeches, you'll know where to turn. Made any speeches lately?"

"No, we've all been too busy digging coal to hold meetings."

"Anything new in the Union?"

Owen shook his head. "The new agreement goes into effect the first of April."

"Ohio operators haven't signed yet, have they?" Then, as though on sudden thought, BB said: "You know Mr. Canter, don't you?"

Owen looked at the man beside him, solid, neatly dressed, with a comfortable beard; and he knew why the other's face had seemed familiar. "I've seen a sketch of him in the *Journal*, yes." He hesitated, wondering whether to rise and shake hands; but Mr. Canter made no move, and BB's introduction had been completely casual. "We've never met before."

Mr. Canter said in a friendly tone, "I've heard of you, Glen." A faint smile touched his eyes. "Mr. Evans says you feel your Union is a sort of guardian for the operators."

Owen hesitated. "Not quite that, Mr. Canter. But it looks to me as though the operators and the miners were all in the coal business together." That picture like a vision recurred to him. "In a wet mine, if the operators don't put in pumps, and the miners don't keep the pumps working — why, the mine floods. It's all as simple as that. We're all harnessed to the same wheel, and it takes all of us, pulling together, to keep the wheel rolling. If the operators don't do their part, or the miners don't do their part — the wheel starts rolling backward." He looked at BB and said apologetically: "You've got me started making a speech, but you can't start any fight between me and Mr. Canter. The Hardiston County operators are fair, and we've tried to be fair with them."

"They haven't signed the December agreement," BB reminded him, in a quizzical tone.

"There's time enough between now and the first of April." Something like mirth touched Owen's eyes. "We'll explain things to them before that."

Mr. Canter smiled. "I expect they'll be able to look out for themselves."

Owen said doubtfully: "I don't know. If our biggest operator spends half his time in Europe, or New York, or Florida, or Columbus, maybe he needs a guardian to look out for his interests here."

BB chuckled. "That's one on you, Mr. Canter."

Canter nodded, completely good-humored; he said to Owen, "Some of us don't feel the agreement gives us a fair differential against Pittsburgh thin vein."

"You should sign anyway," Owen argued. "It's for your own good to have things settled. If the Union can work with the operators to steady trade conditions, you can plan ahead and know that things aren't going to change without warning. So you'll be a lot better off. An annual agreement will help the operators more than it will the men." He added, "And of course, if you don't sign the agreement, you can have a strike on your hands without half-trying."

Canter said mildly: "We don't like to have you threaten us, Glen."

"I'm not threatening you; I'm just telling you what can happen. The Union's stronger all the time, Mr. Canter; more members, more money in the treasury. And our officers aren't just sitting still. They're planning ahead."

"The officers may be looking ahead, but not the men."

"You mean because we voted down the defense fund?"

Canter nodded. "Your Union will never make real progress till it can finance a strike, keep the men from suffering. The trade unions have already set up such a fund. When you strike, they have cash in the treasury with which they help you; yet here last month two thirds of your membership voted against establishing a fund of your own. As long as you depend on hand-to-mouth contributions, you'll always be weak."

Owen said heartily: "You're right, ten times over. Some of us are preaching that gospel. Our own local did raise the tax to a quarter. The defense fund will come, maybe not in your time or in mine; but the Union — some Union — is bound to live and to grow. Now we're still a baby, just learning to crawl."

"Toward what?"

"Well, right now, toward the meeting in Columbus on the eighth of March to figure out a wage scale for the day men on the eight-hour day."

"A dollar and a half?"

"A dollar seventy-five will be nearer it."

"We're only paying around a dollar thirty or a dollar forty for a ten-hour day. I can't see us paying more money for less work."

Mr. Canter's tones was so mild that Owen felt a certain sympathy for him. "You will see it," he predicted. "It will keep on happening as long as you live — and as long as I live; more pay for less work. You see, Mr. Canter, the December agreement went way ahead of anything we've ever had. Wages went up about eighteen per cent on the average, and the agreement straightened out the screen dispute, and it established fairly uniform conditions all over the Central Competitive Field. And it set up the eight-hour day. From now on, wages will go up and down, as business gets better and worse; but we'll never go back to a ten-hour day — or even to nine hours — and wages will never go down as far as they go up!"

"How about West Virginia? The operators there don't come in on your agreement, and the men there don't belong to your Union; the operators cut wages, and their coal undersells ours."

"We're working on West Virginia, to unionize the mines. The mining rate there is low, the screen is coarse, the hours are long, and the men have to buy at company stores. I think before summer the Executive Board will order a boycott on West Virginia coal."

"It may be a bad time for a boycott, Owen," BB suggested. "If we have a war, the country is going to need a lot of coal."

Owen's jaw set, his tone was firm. "When the country needs coal, the Union has just that much better chance of winning an argument."

"My point was that with us at war you'd have trouble enforcing a boycott."

Owen grinned. "Trouble? When have we ever had anything but trouble?" He spoke again to Mr. Canter. "I've always said the operators couldn't pay us good wages unless they were making money; but it works both ways. When the operators make more money, they've got to pay us higher wages; and when they pay us higher wages, they'll make more money."

BB said seriously: "That's one of the things on which Owen and I agree, Mr. Canter."

Canter rose to go. "I'd like to see the men paid more — if everybody would do it," he assented.

Owen said quickly: "Give us a little time and the Union will

make everybody do it. Then every intelligent operator will count
the Union his best friend. The operator and the miner are partners. The miners know it now; some day, the operators will know
it too."

4

With March, spring began fitfully to come; the days were length-
ening, but the demand for coal slacked off, and Moses Evans,
having filled orders accumulated during the strike, began to reduce
the number of working days. With their gardens to make, the
miners found this no hardship; and Owen enjoyed long hours in
fine sun while he spaded up the plot he and his father would plant,
shaking apart the clods, pulverizing the rich earth, levelling and
raking. To plant a garden gave him a sense of power, of partnership with God in the working of miracles. One put into the earth a
handful of seeds apparently without life; from them arose the
stalks of corn, the climbing peas, the beans, the cabbages and the
twining pumpkin vines and cucumbers. All the bounty of earth, by
the magic of the planted seed, was poured in lavish generosity into
the lap of man.

BB, who in the spring more than at any other season liked to
wander into the country, passed one day and saw them in the
garden and came to stand awhile in talk with them; and Owen
spoke of this miracle of the seeds. "Watching seeds grow makes it
mighty easy to believe in other miracles."

"A seed is dynamite," BB agreed. "Remember Ben Franklin and
the balloon ascension. His companion asked, 'But what use is it?'
and Franklin replied, 'What use is a baby?'" Tom Glen, standing
by, nodded in comprehension, and BB went on: "Every action,
even every thought, is a seed. A man out walking kicks a pebble;
at the next rain the trickle of water which that pebble formerly
diverted takes a new course; the result is that the stream it feeds
is turned from one ocean to another, the climate of a continent is
changed, the character of the men and women who live in that
climate is modified, and the history of the world takes a new course
— all because someone kicked a pebble."

Owen laughed. "I've kicked a lot of them in my time."

"Never can tell what will happen, if you do. Speaking of little things —" BB laughed as he spoke. "Over in Chillicothe last Sunday evening four men went to church, and a nail in the pew where they sat tore a three-cornered rip in the trouser leg of one of them. One of the deacons noticed it when the men came out of church ahead of him. That night, masked, and with revolvers, the men went to a house where a woman named Mag Milton had a number of young women lodgers; and the masked men held up the men callers — as well as the women — and took over a thousand dollars in money and some jewelry.

"But as they left, the deacon who had seen that torn trouser leg saw it again; so he reported to the Sheriff who the men were, and the men were arrested. All because of a loose nail in a church pew."

"I should think the deacon would have been ashamed to admit he was in a place like that."

"The Sheriff had to promise not to reveal his name."

Tom Glen spoke in growling anger. "Hell fire's waiting for the lot of them, the strange woman and all her works. Best rid the world of them."

"I'm not so sure," BB reflected. "Whenever a town drives such women out, you see a big crop of fatherless babies. Most reforms have to come from inside men, you know; not from outside."

"Yet you want us to reform Cuba from the outside," Owen reminded him. "How do you know it would do them any good? Maybe if we drive out the Spaniards, the Cubans will turn villains themselves."

"Well, that's democracy. Every man — and every nation — has an inalienable right to make a fool of itself. To be free is probably the worst possible form of government; a benevolent despotism is certainly the best."

"Trouble is, the despot doesn't stay benevolent," Owen suggested. "Like Sheriff Martin, over in Lattimer. He was a despot, but he wasn't very benevolent."

"The dailies say everyone now admits that the strikers were unarmed. Most of those who were killed and wounded were shot in the back, some of them over a hundred yards from where the trouble started." BB added harshly: "That was just plain deliberate butchery. The Sheriff might have been right in firing into the air, or even in ordering a volley into the mass of strikers to make them disperse; but after they began to run, there was no excuse for any more shooting."

"I can't find anything about the trial in the papers lately."

"No. All the war talk has crowded it out of people's minds — and out of the papers. They'll acquit the Sheriff — and then we'll all forget the whole thing."

"Some of us won't," Owen promised. He asked, "Any news about Cuba?"

"Not much. Spain has asked us to recall Consul-General Lee from Havana; and she accuses us of using our warships to carry supplies to the insurgents." He stirred. "But it's too fine a day to stand talking, and you'll want to get your planting done. Good day to you."

During the fortnight that followed, Cuba, and the shattered *Maine* lying in Havana Harbor, seemed alike to be forgotten. The Court of Inquiry was in secret session, and even the dailies seemed ready to wait for its decision. Philip Fremont of Hardiston, who after his graduation from Annapolis had been assigned to the *Iowa,* wrote from the Dry Tortugas that the ship was at Key West when they heard of the sinking of the *Maine;* and the *Journal* printed the letter because he was a son of Hardiston. Under the familiar heading, Additional Locals, BB recorded that at a meeting of the Modern Priscillas, the young men were required to draw for partners; they drew baby photographs of the ladies present, and their task was to identify the originals. The resulting pleasant confusion was followed by a banquet, a guessing contest, and charades. BB suggested that paupers be put to work on the roads; he remarked that as a result of the growing pension list, the United States was spending more money on war than any other nation except Russia; he expressed the opinion that the plan to build waterworks in Hardiston was on its last legs; he announced that if the $50,000,000 which Congress had appropriated for national defense were all silver, it would fill 59 Ohio Southern coal cars, but he added, "The United States has the money and will not have to borrow it." The first robin arrived March 10, the first blackbird March 13. If you were troubled by pains around your heart, you would be wise to try Hood's Sarsaparilla.

Through March, BB printed much about politics but nothing about the increasing tension between miners and operators. Tremendous rains throughout the state raised creeks and rivers everywhere, and drove even the possibility of war to the inside pages of the dailies; but for Owen, the threat of a new strike was more important than politics, or floods, or the threat of war. The mines, as though the operators were preparing for a work stoppage, resumed full-time operations. The Columbus meeting on the eighth of March agreed on a wage scale for the day men; and as Owen had predicted to Mr. Canter, most categories were to receive $1.75 for the eight-hour day, while tracklayers, timbermen and pipe men were to have $1.90. Ohio operators had signed the agreement, but under protest, and Hardiston County operators offered $1.44.

Owen served on a committee headed by Eben Howell to discuss a settlement, and in these meetings with the operators, it came to be more and more true that he was the spokesman for the Union. He repeated the same argument so frequently, and so nearly in the same words, that Mr. Canter and Moses Evans and Eben Howell and the others were equally amused; and when Owen began, "Operators and men are partners; neither can prosper without the other," Mr. Canter was likely to nod and smile and say:

"Yes, yes, Glen. We know."

Owen argued that in this case it was not only the miners of Hardiston County who were involved. "The December agreement was a promise by the operators to do certain things, and a promise by the Union to do certain things. When the operators promised to pay a certain scale, that implied a promise by the Union not to work for less. If you here in Hardiston County refuse to abide by that scale, you force us to strike in order to keep our promise to other operators."

Canter's beard bristled. "Maybe so, Glen. Maybe so. But it sticks in my craw! From a dollar thirty for ten hours to a dollar seventy-five for eight hours! That's too much for me to swallow!"

"Other operators have swallowed it. If you don't, you'll be taking an unfair advantage of them." And he urged: "You're out of step, Mr. Canter. Badly out of step. You really are."

They arrived at no settlement. The miners would not yield, and while there was a strong group of operators who were willing to do so, Herbert Canter and a few who shared his opinions held the others in line. When the conference ended, Mr. Canter said curtly:

"There's nothing more to discuss. We'll give your points every consideration, and make our decision, and post a notice at the mines. Now I'll bid you good day."

5

....On the twenty-sixth of March, the dailies reported the findings
of the Court of Inquiry. The critical paragraph summarized their
conclusions.

> *In the opinion of the court, the* Maine *was destroyed by
> a submarine mine which caused the partial explosion of
> one or more of her forward magazines.*

In the interval since the tragedy, the first hot clamor had for lack
of fuel died away; but now once more the papers blazed with guess
and prophecy. The fact that a Spanish Court of Inquiry reached
an opposite decision, and insisted that the explosion had been
internal, made no impression on the public mind. On Monday, the
twenty-eighth, President McKinley sent the Court's report to
Congress with a message in which he said:

> *I have directed that a copy of the report be sent to the
> Government of Her Majesty the Queen Regent, and I do
> not permit myself to doubt that the sense of justice of
> the Spanish nation will dictate a course of action suggested
> by honor and the friendly relations between the two Gov-
> ernments.*

Owen read this when on the way home from work he stopped
at the *Journal* office to see the dailies, and he showed the passage
to BB. "That's the craziest kind of talk I ever heard. 'Friendly relations'? We've been calling them butchers and murderers and
everything else for two or three years; and I suppose they've called
us names too."

"This is the language of diplomacy."

"Can't diplomats talk sense?"

BB smiled. "Well, you see, diplomacy was developed by Kings
and Queens, and they were so often cousins of their nation's
enemies that they didn't want to say right out: 'Cousin Jim, you're
a liar and a thief, and if you don't mend your ways, I'll knock your
block off.' So they invented all this bowing and scraping and
general nonsense. If we'd talked turkey to Spain long ago, the
Maine would be afloat today — and there'd be no war."

"Why does President McKinley have to talk that way? He's no diplomat. He's just an Ohio lawyer."

"Oh, this message was written for him by the State Department."

"Senator Sherman? He's Secretary of State, but he's no diplomat either. They're just showing off."

BB smiled. "No, not Secretary Sherman. This was probably written by some clerk in the State Department who's been trained for years till he can spit in a man's face and make it sound like a kiss!" They laughed together, and BB added: "But words don't matter. What McKinley really means is, 'Get down on your knees, you canary-colored murderers, and cry "uncle" before I take a blacksnake whip to you!'"

Owen grinned. "Then why didn't he say so?"

"Maybe he should have. Maybe he should."

Wednesday at the mine Owen learned from Mike Ryan that the operators had decided not to accept the new scale for day men; the notices would be posted Thursday morning. That night Owen and Charles Morgan prepared counter-notices. The men were advised to work through Friday and Saturday. When they had loaded the coal shot down on Friday, their work was done. Monday, the new strike would begin.

Owen and Tom Glen came back to Hardiston, their coal all loaded, early Saturday afternoon; and Owen stopped at the *Journal* office, proposing to write a paragraph about the strike for the *Journal*, but BB shook his head.

"Least said, soonest mended, Owen. Everybody knows about it, or soon will know about it. Let's not rub salt in the sore." He hesitated, said thoughtfully: "I expect the strike will affect the election Tuesday. You think it will last long?"

"I don't know."

"Will the men suffer — and their families?"

"Most of them have some money saved, and gardens coming along; and a lot of the operators are willing to pay the scale, so they may start up their mines."

"I see." BB tipped back in his chair. "Sycamore Hill's planning to furnish a company of volunteers for the Cuban war."

Owen had been so absorbed in union business that he had forgotten Cuba; and BB's remark was like a revealing light shining into dark places. He sat thoughtful for a moment. "If there's a war,

I expect a lot of miners will enlist," he reflected. "Now that they're out of work, anyway."

"The Civil War created a lot of politicians — and of pensions. I suppose this war will do the same." BB smiled in a dry fashion. "A man doesn't get far, running for office in this country, unless he can talk about his old comrades in the ranks."

Owen considered this; he rose, his dinner pail under his arm. "Yes," he agreed, "I expect that's so. If there's going to be a war, I'll have to go."

XXIII

April 2, 1898 — *May* 4, 1898

OWEN WOKE Sunday morning long before day, and he lay half-asleep, wondering why his mother was not busy in the kitchen. Then memory returned. This was Sunday, so he need not get up; nevertheless, he could not sleep. If war came, he would be a soldier. The thought was strange, but it awoke in him no particular fear. His imagination carried him no further than enlistment, a uniform, a gun. Once, when he was nine or ten years old, Bobby Roberts had let him fire a Flobert rifle at a rabbit in its form; but the rabbit leaped away unhurt. Since then he had never fired a gun.

But as a soldier he would have to learn to shoot, have to learn a lot of things. Owen accepted the necessity. He wished to rise in the Union, and he hoped some day to go to Congress, to represent the miners there; but he had never heard a political speech in which the candidate failed to refer, in proud yet modest tones, to his record as a soldier. Therefore, a soldier he must be.

Yet war was folly; or rather, it was a drug which distorted men's thoughts and converted their secret fears into an eager credulity. Because they were afraid, they accepted with an equal appetite the lies that magnified the crimes of the enemy and the other lies that magnified their own virtues. War made men credulous, but it also made them hypocrites. Even President McKinley, after years of mutual abuse and recrimination, could speak of the "friendly relations" between the United States and Spain. That nonsense, that priggish pretense of virtue, was worse than a lie; it was self-deceit.

Owen, coming to full wakefulness, hated the thought of war,

hated the fact that he must take part in it. He wondered whether this hatred arose from fear, whether he hated war because he was afraid of it; yet certainly he felt no fear. If he was afraid, he did not know it.

During the days that followed, union business occupied much of Owen's time. Not all the miners in the country were unionized, but the Union had raised their wages and improved the conditions under which they worked; and to the extent of joining in the strike, they gave it their support. Owen and the other union officers were able to win new members, and Mike Pratt came from National Headquarters to work with them.

Owen took Mike home to dinner, and Mrs. Glen welcomed him, and Tom asked many questions. Afterward Owen and Mike went to see Charles Morgan; and for the week of Mike's stay, he and Owen in a hired rig covered the southern half of the county, talking to miners everywhere. They organized four new locals, added more than two hundred members to the Union.

And they had long hours together. Once Mike asked: "Did ye hear anything from Joe Ceslak?"

"A letter to thank us for the little money we sent is all. Is the trial done yet? It went on so long, till I couldn't find anything about it in the papers."

"Aye, over and done a month gone. They turned 'em loose, the Sheriff and all his deputies."

Owen nodded. "I thought like as not they would."

"I'm going from here to West Virginia, and then on into Pennsylvania. It's a pity you wouldn't come along with me, Owen. There's big work to be done there, and we make a good team."

"I might, some day; but if there's a war, I'll enlist."

Mike laughed. "If it's a fight you want, you don't need to turn soldier. Come along with me and I'll give you a bellyful of fighting."

Their work was not all smooth sailing, and often enough they had to meet discouragement and doubt. "But it's no wonder," Owen pointed out. "This is the third strike in the county in eighteen months, and even men like Charles Morgan and Isaac Williams, men with money in the bank, are beginning to feel the pressure. A lot of miners weren't out of debt when this strike started, so some of the storekeepers have had to go on a cash basis."

"A lot of men tell me they're going to leave, hunt work some-place else, move away."

"Some will," Owen agreed. "And those that can stay, the operators are doing everything they can to make them break away from the Union."

"Any strike's a pull," Mike said thoughtfully. "But this time every operator in the state is against these cut-throats in Hardiston County. We'll bring 'em around."

After Mike had gone on to West Virginia, Charles Morgan one day hailed Owen from his veranda, and Owen went to sit in the big rocking chair beside him. Mr. Morgan foresaw that even when the strike ended, there would be many matters of detail still to be decided. If a day's work was to be eight hours, at what hours should that day begin and end? Did such a day include eating time, or should there be time out for eating. "There'll be all sorts of things coming up," he predicted.

Owen agreed that this was true. "But we can work them out beforehand." And he proposed that they call on Moses Evans. "Say we decide with him how to handle Miss Ellen; then we can go to Eben Howell and start trying to get the other operators to-gether and work out a system for the whole Sub-District."

Moses Evans, persuaded into the strike by Mr. Canter, was anxious to put his mines again to work; but he, too, saw the problems to be solved. Charles Morgan proposed that the eight hours of work should begin when a man reached his room and end when he left it. Some rooms were near the portals, some might be half a mile further; so if time began at the portals, some men would have more working time than others. Since each man wished to dig as much coal as he could, every minute outside his room was wasted. Mr. Evans agreed to this, and he suggested that the men should work from seven to four, with a free hour for eat-ing; but Charles Morgan said if that were the rule, some men would work through much of their dinner hour and thus mine more than their fair share of coal. They agreed that the day should begin at seven; but in the past the men had gone to work by fast time. Moses Evans thought they should now adopt standard time, which was half an hour later. He and Charles differed, too, as to when the day's shots should be fired: half an hour before time to quit, said Charles; at quitting time, said Mr. Evans.

Because of Charles Morgan's long experience, it was he rather than Owen who was the spokesman in these discussions; but when Charles and Moses Evans had summoned all the arguments they could muster, one or the other was apt to turn and ask, "Owen, what do you think?" Owen achieved a position like that of an arbiter between them, and when, as their talks progressed, Mat Price and Eben Howell joined them, and eventually David Davis and other operators, till most of the Sub-District was involved, Owen by waiting till his opinion was asked, and by preserving an impartial tone, maintained himself in this position. Thus, on many issues, he cast the deciding vote.

2

During the strike, not only on Wednesdays and Saturdays but on other days, Owen was often at the *Journal* office. It was pleasant to pass a word with Will, to go up into the type loft and in clouded references tease Nellie about Jenkin, skirting that forbidden subject so closely that her cheek blazed. Once Bets came in while he was there, and she was as jolly as always, and Owen thought her better-looking. It was not that she was no longer fat, though certainly she had lost some weight; there was a difference in her voice, and in her tone, and in her eyes. He was surprised — since these two had used to be so often at odds — to see between her and Nellie now an obvious liking and respect. Perhaps that they were both married created some strong bond between them.

In the office, too, Owen read the dailies and discussed their contents with BB. President McKinley had demanded that Spain put an end to the reign of terror in Cuba; but the more violent friends of Cuba, led by Senator Foraker, demanded intervention and independence. When Owen wondered at what seemed like long inaction, BB said:

"McKinley is preparing an ultimatum."

"What's that?"

"The last word. The ultimate word. He'll demand that Spain do thus and so or take the consequences."

"What consequences?"

"Probably war. The first shot may be fired before our next issue."

"Do you honestly believe that Spain sank the *Maine?*"

"I assume she did; but it doesn't matter, now, whether she did or not. The thing that matters is never the fact; it's what people believe to be the fact. Because they believe Spain sank the *Maine,* most people resent McKinley's waiting so long. They want war."

"Spain doesn't."

"Maybe not, but she has to talk big, so she calls Foraker — and anyone who is friendly to Cuba — a Jingo. And of course the Mugwump press in this country joins that name-calling." He added, in a sardonic tone: "That's the whole art of starting a war, Owen. The first step is to call names. Call the other nation names, and then tell your people that the other nation is calling you names. Then tell your people that the people of the other nation are all liars and murderers, and that they're planning to come and burn your houses and harm your womenfolk. You know you can start a fight in your own neighborhood by telling Bill what John said about him, and then telling John what Bill said about him, till after a while they start saying 'you're another,' and you put a chip on Bill's shoulder, and when it falls off, the fight begins."

Owen looked at him through narrowed eyes. "When we sent the *Maine* into Havana Harbor, wasn't that putting a chip on our shoulder? Daring them to knock it off?"

BB colored. "Well, not quite. I know I thought we ought to protect Americans in Havana."

Owen hesitated; then he asked in a tone that was a challenge: "If you were a Spaniard in Havana, and knew what the United States thought about you, and then a United States battleship sailed into the harbor and said she was going to start shooting any time she wanted to — wouldn't you be kind of mad?"

The editor smiled uncomfortably. "If you start seeing the other fellow's side, Owen, you'll never make up your mind about anything."

Owen frowned with thought. "I think if I were a Spaniard, I'd think Cuba was our island, and I'd think it was just as right for us to kill the Cubans as it was for the United States to kill all those Indians six or seven years ago out in Nebraska."

"The cases aren't the same."

"Don't you think it hurts an Indian to get killed, just as much as it does a Cuban?"

"You're as bad as our Mugwumps." BB smiled. "But then, I suppose I'm a Jingo."

"What's a Mugwump?"

'Well, strictly, a Mugwump is a Republican who doesn't vote for the party candidates. A lot of Mugwumps voted at Tuesday's election. The Democrats carried not only Hardiston County but most of Ohio. You know, your strike affected the result. Some of the defeated candidates here in the county were backed by the operators."

Owen nodded. "We're learning a little about politics. It's easier to get higher wages by voting right than by going on strike."

"Is getting higher wages the noblest aim of man?"

"It's the first step. Until a man has money in his pockets, he hasn't even made a start." Anger touched Owen's eyes. "You heard me talking with Mr. Canter here awhile ago. He's rich and I'm poor; and every time he spoke to me, you could hear him thinking: 'Well, now, it's pretty generous of me, with all my money and all my power, to sit here talking to this pauper as though he were an equal!' "

BB chuckled. "Maybe he felt superior to you, but you didn't sound as though you felt inferior to him."

"I didn't. I felt superior to him. I am, too. He's like a horse in blinders; he can't see all around. He has money — and naturally he wants to keep it. I would in his place. But having money makes him stupid. He can't understand that when other people are better off, so will he be."

"You want higher wages for the miners," BB argued, smiling. "Won't they — after they have more money — be handicapped by their money just as Mr. Canter is by his money now?"

"I don't know." Owen grinned. "But I'd like to try it that way for a while and see."

Sunday, the tenth of April, when Owen and Marged walked home from church together, the world still waited for McKinley's message to Congress. The European powers — Germany, Austria-Hungary, France, Great Britain, Italy and Russia — had sent a joint note to the United States, urging further negotiations in an effort to maintain peace and re-establish order in Cuba. McKinley replied that he appreciated the good will which the note testified, and hoped for an equal appreciation of the efforts of the United

States to "fulfill a debt to humanity by ending a situation, the indefinite prolongation of which has become insufferable."

Marged hoped that from this interchange some good might come, but Owen said: "It won't. They're just snarling at each other."

"Snarling? They sounded polite. And so did Mr. McKinley!"

"That's what BB calls 'the language of diplomacy.'" Owen's tone was scornful. "What they really meant was: 'Look here, young fellow, you'd better pull in your horns or you'll wish you had.' And President McKinley's note meant: 'Oh, go mind your own business.'"

She laughed. "You make them sound like little boys with chips on their shoulders."

"BB and I were talking about that the other day." He paused, thinking that this was the first time he had ever spoken of the editor as anything but "Mr. Beecham," and he wondered whether Marged had noticed; but if she had, she made no comment. He went on: "Any time a country starts making fight talk, it's acting like a little boy." Anger stirred his tones. "We're so self-righteous it makes me sick! We talk about how awful the Spaniards are to kill a lot of Cubans, but we bragged about it when we killed a lot of Indians, thought we were pretty smart." In sudden memory he added: "Yes, and we shot about a hundred coal miners in Lattimer last fall, and killed twenty-five of them, for doing nothing but parade on a public road. That's as bad as anything Spain has done to the Cubans."

"But we arrested the men who shot those miners," she reminded him. "We tried them for murder."

"Tried them, yes; but we found them not guilty! The Sheriff's lawyer said the district attorney had to prove who shot Mike Ceslak, and to prove that whoever did it meant to kill Mike and not just anyone, and to prove that every other man in the posse knew that whoever did it was going to try to kill Mike and agreed to help him do it. That's what we call law. I say Spain can't be any worse."

"Don't you think we ought to go to war with Spain?"

"I don't know," Owen admitted. "I don't know what I do think. When everyone thinks one way, I'm apt to think another. But I do know that any time anyone wants to reform the world, he can find plenty to do, close home. He doesn't have to go to Cuba to make a start."

Marged said thoughtfully: "I remember once when the Welsh churches raised thousands of dollars to send Bibles to the heathen, and children were cold and hungry all around here, and I thought the same thing you just said." She asked, "If we have a war, will you volunteer?"

"Yes. Oh, I'm not doing it to be a hero; but I don't want to have people asking me all my life, 'Why weren't you a soldier?' "

She smiled up at him. "You don't even pretend it's — patriotism, do you?"

"I probably will, twenty years from now," he said mirthfully. "I don't tell everyone the truth, even now. But you're different."

"Does your mother know you're going?"

"No, I haven't said anything to her yet. Of course, we may not have a war."

She said thoughtfully: "One of the boys who went to my school in Glendale is in the Army. George Hebron. And Philip Fremont is in the Navy, on the *Iowa*. Would you rather be in the Army or the Navy?"

"I don't know. I won't do anything yet, anyway."

Next day the dailies reported that Consul-General Lee had left Havana. When he landed in Florida he announced that he hoped to return to Cuba at the head of a division. Spain's Queen Regent proclaimed an armistice in Cuba, and this, seeming to meet President McKinley's demand that hostilities be halted, appeared to Owen a hopeful sign; but BB disagreed:

"There's no stopping things now, Owen. We've talked ourselves into a fighting mood." He added: "I had a wire an hour ago. McKinley's message went to Congress today."

"What did he say?"

"He asked for full powers to end the Cuban war and to establish a stable government on the island; but he opposes Cuban independence. That's going to make the country angry. People have waited patiently; but now they'll take the bit between their teeth."

"What can they do?"

For answer, BB showed Owen a proof. "Here's the *Journal* headline for this week. I think before next week's paper is printed, we'll be at war."

Yet BB was mistaken in this prediction, for that week and part of another passed with no shot fired. Owen, reading the editorials in the paper for April 20 thought BB resented the delay as an almost personal affront.

The United States has deliberated long enough; the time for action is at hand. The world and humanity expects it.

The President recommended intervention but not independence, so Congress is deadlocked.

Did McKinley foresee this? Does he welcome the delay?

Foraker's speech, the greatest the Senate has heard in two decades, held the Senate for independence, 67 to 21. His resolution directs the President to demand and compel Spanish evacuation; it should pass the House.

War was not long delayed. The dailies next morning reported that large army units had been ordered to move, the cavalry and light artillery to Chattanooga, the infantry to New Orleans, Mobile and Tampa. Ambassador Woodford prepared to present the President's ultimatum in Madrid; but Friday, having been denied an audience at which to do so, he asked for his passports. Owen asked BB what that meant.

"It's the diplomatic way of telling Spain we're going to fight her."

"Does that settle it?"

"No. No, under the Constitution, Congress has to declare war; but Congress will do so as soon as McKinley asks them, probably Monday."

"How do you go about enlisting?"

"Well, you can join the Ohio National Guard, or you can go to a recruiting station and volunteer."

"Is there a recruiting station here?"

"No, but I expect there soon will be."

The Sunday papers reported that President McKinley had called for 125,000 volunteers.

3

Owen heard of the President's call first from Marged. They had met outside church, where Owen's father and mother paused to talk with friends, and Marged's uncle and aunt likewise lingered;

and as they moved off together, Marged laid her hand in the ready crook of his arm. "Did you see a Sunday paper?" she asked.

"Not yet. Why?"

"Michael Tooley, lives next door, brought one to Uncle Isaac when he came home from early mass." She hesitated. "President McKinley has called for volunteers."

Owen felt a faint coolness, like a trickle of water, touch his spine. The words had a connotation of commitment, of finality; he was no longer master of his life. "I wonder what mama will say."

"Is she all right, Owen? She looks — tired."

"She works pretty hard. Some day I'm going to earn enough money so she can have a hired girl."

Marged smiled. "I don't think she'd like that, letting some other woman take care of you and your father."

He grinned agreement. "Probably not." Then his brow furrowed. "I don't know whether to tell her now, or wait till it's all settled."

"How will you go about enlisting?"

"Mr. Beecham says they'll probably have a recruiting station here."

"You don't really have to tell her till then, do you?"

"I sort of want to get it over with."

She squeezed his arm. "She'll be so proud of you."

He looked at her in surprise. "Proud of me? I don't think so. She's too sensible."

Marged laughed, removing her light hand from his sleeve. "No one's sensible when there's a war, Owen. You'll see."

When they parted and he went on alone, he overtook Charles Morgan and walked with him as far as the Ridge Street corner; and they spoke of the strike still in progress. There was to be a union mass meeting at Electric Park on Wednesday.

"If the operators don't sign pretty soon, there won't be any miners left in Hardiston County to work for them," Owen predicted.

Mr. Morgan agreed. "I know of over three hundred men who've moved away this last month, gone to work somewhere else."

"You can't blame them, when there's plenty of work everywhere and none here."

"I suppose not. And this whole field is playing out, anyway. The coal here won't last many years."

At home, while Annie Glen went to lay aside her bonnet and

cape and to tuck an apron around her waist so she could warm up
their Sunday dinner, Tom Glen spoke of war and the works of
war. "It's coming again, no stopping it now, not even if anyone
wanted to. I've seen it once, but I never looked to see men turn
into fools again."

"It might not be the same," Owen suggested, remembering some
of the tales he had heard his father tell. "Not so much killing, not
last so long."

"Killing? Oh, there'll be killing enough. But killing's not so bad;
no, nor the battles. They're like a Fourth of July, all fireworks
and parades and cheering." Tom tipped back in his chair, sober
and reflective. "When old soldiers get together and start talking,
it's battles and shooting they mostly talk about; but you might
not have a battle once a month, less than that, maybe none in a
year. The rest is marching till your feet blister and the blisters
break." Passion stirred his tones. "It's sleeping in rain and mud,
it's slapping at mosquitoes and flies, it's being so sick in your insides
you can't get your pants up in time to let 'em down again, it's itch-
ing and scratching and scabbing over; it's eating food that's half-
rotten or all rotten — "

Annie Glen set before him a heaping plate. "Hush up, Tom.
You can eat this and it won't hurt you."

Tom chuckled and set to. "True for you, Annie. True for you."
And he said: "Thanks be, I'm old enough this time to know enough
to tend my own business and let them have their war."

Owen felt his mother's eyes upon him. He looked at her, and as
though he read in her eyes a question, he nodded; but he spoke to
his father. "I'm going to enlist in this one, papa."

Tom Glen's head swung toward his son; he stopped chewing, his
mouth full. "Um?" It was a grunt like a question.

"I'm going to volunteer."

There was a long silence while Tom chewed his food and swallowed it. He did this with a certain deliberation; his fists, with
a knife upturned in one and a fork in the other, rested heel-down on
the table on either side of his plate. Once he raised them a few
inches as though to help him swallow, then banged them down
again. Then he gulped hard and gulped again, and at last his
mouth opened.

"Have I fathered a fool?"

Owen did not speak, and Tom raised his fists again, knife and fork erect, and again banged them down. Mrs. Glen said mildly: "Lower your lightning rods, Tom."

"Eh?" He stared at her, and she pointed to his hands. "Oh!" He laid down knife and fork, and returned to the attack, but now more mildly. "What's got into you, Owen?"

"I told you, I'm going to enlist."

Tom's voice rose a little. "Are you a plumb idjit? What for?"

Owen colored resentfully. "For reasons that suit me."

"Well, then, you'll not!" Tom roared aloud. "You'll do no such thing, so let's hear no more about it."

"It's a long time since you could order me around."

"You're a boy, for all your hulk! Mind your tongue."

"I'll be nineteen in November. I'll do for a man, till one comes along."

"I'm your father, man or boy, whichever you be: and I say you're not to do this. Mind! Honor thy father and thy mother, Owen."

"I'll honor you, papa; but that doesn't mean letting you boss me all my life."

Tom Glen glared at him: he lowered his head long enough to fill his mouth again; he watched Owen in silence till the food was gone. "Ye're needed at home, Owen," he urged. "To take care of your mother; yes, and of me, too, if the rheumatism lays me low. We've tended you from a baby. You'll not leave us lone and lorn, now we're old and tired and you still young and strong."

Owen's mother exploded in sharp exasperation. "Fiddlesticks! Tom Glen, you make me sick. Take care of us, will he? When was the day we couldn't take care of each other?" And to Owen: "Sonny, pay him no heed. If there's a war, then young men must fight it. I'd be ashamed if you didn't, and I'll be proud when you do."

Owen remembered Marged's prediction. Certainly, his mother was proud, or seemed to be. He felt a half-resentful hurt because she whom he loved was so eager for him to go away to danger and perhaps to death. If he were killed, she would remember that she had sent him to that death, and grieve for her folly all her days. Imagining her grief and her self-reproach, he began to be sorry for her — and so to forgive her. But Tom Glen protested: "Annie, you're wrong. What will be left for us, with Owen gone?"

"Why, the mine for you and the house for me, and for each of us the other." She went to press her cheek against his brow. "Be easy, Tom. We'll be fine as can be."

4

That next Sunday, Spain declared war on the United States; next day Congress returned the gesture. To Owen, the formal action by Congress seemed an absurdity, and he said so to BB. "What was the sense? Spain had already declared war on us. If she started shooting, we couldn't just stand there and holler: 'Hey, no fair! We haven't declared war on you.' "

BB laughed with him. "Diplomacy again," he said. "Whenever men find something they enjoy doing, they make a game out of it, make rules about how it shall be played. In the first wars, the winners killed all the men and carried off the women; but men saw that if that went on long enough, there wouldn't be enough of them left to play the game. So to keep the game going, they made a lot of rules."

"Suppose some country didn't wait to declare war, but just started right in fighting?"

"Why, everyone would be scandalized! But it might be a good thing. As long as men can play war like a game, they'll go on having wars. But war's not a game, and rules have no place in it. General Sherman called it Hell, and he did his best to make it Hell, not only for soldiers but for men and women and children. He went a long step back along the road to barbarism, but maybe it was a step in the right direction. Once we see war for what it is — "

He lifted his hands, leaving the sentence unfinished, but Owen finished it for him. " 'A monster of so frightful mien, as to be hated needs but to be seen!' "

"Hullo! Where did you get hold of that?"

"Oh, Miss Williams and I read aloud a lot, Shakespeare and things."

"That's not Shakespeare."

"I know. But he and Mr. Pope both say things so they stick in your mind." He added, "You sort of do that, too."

BB chuckled. "Shakespeare and Pope and me? You've a lot of qualities, Owen; but you'll never be a literary critic. By the way, it's 'such frightful mien.' "

"I don't think so."

"I'm sure of it. Look it up when you get home."

Owen said stubbornly: "You look it up. I know what it is." Then, regretting his own tone, he apologized, smiling. "But I do know, really."

BB chuckled. "You're like a turtle, won't let go till it thunders. Look it up."

Owen had no intention of doing so, but he held his tongue. He went that afternoon to Belton to consult with Eben Howell about the mass meeting to be held on Wednesday. Howell said regretfully:

"I hoped we'd have this strike settled before then, but it don't look so now. We'll call it an organization meeting. There's no real business to be done, but we ought to have a good crowd."

"We could report what we've been working out about how to run an eight-hour day."

"No hurry about that. Lin Varney of the Executive Board is in town, and he'll have something to say, and you be ready to make a speech. I'd like to see two thousand men there — and I think we can do it."

"How about getting some of the operators to come?"

Howell doubted the wisdom of this. "No. No, some of the men will have too much beer, and they might get quarrelsome. If we're going to have any fights, let's keep them private."

Whether there were two thousand miners in the throng at Electric Park that Wednesday, Owen did not know; but certainly there was a tremendous crowd. Before Eben Howell called the meeting to order, Owen had exchanged a word of greeting or a handshake with scores of men. Eben caught his eye and beckoned him to join the group seated on benches on the platform. Mike Pratt was among them, and Mike introduced Owen to Mr. Varney.

Then Eben's banging gavel brought a measure of silence. "Men," he shouted, "come up closer. That beer will wait. We won't keep you here long. We haven't much business. We'll get that out of the way and then we'll have some games and competitions and get better acquainted. Now this is a jubilee meeting to welcome our new members. I have a list here, a list of new members, taxes paid, who have joined us this month. Three hundred and twelve of them! Here they are! Tell them you're glad to have them with us!"

He held the sheets of paper up in both hands for all to see, and roars of cheering and laughter swept the crowd. When he could get silence, he went on: "Three hundred and twelve; that's what we can do when we try! It means we're on our way, men. The waves are rolling in, and we're the foremost wave. Now Lin Varney of the Executive Board has a word for you."

As Varney rose and went forward, Howell caught Owen's eye and nodded meaningly; so Owen began to think what he in his turn would say. Thus he was inattentive to Mr. Varney's remarks, until he began to feel that the other talked for an unnecessarily long time. The men here today were ready for fun, and Owen saw them stir restlessly under Varney's oratory. From this, when he rose, he took his cue.

"Men, Mr. Varney brought us greetings from Headquarters, and Mr. Howell has asked me to respond. Well, Mr. Varney, please take our thanks to President Ratchford and to the Board. We appreciate their backing. We've earned it and we propose to keep on earning it.

"We're proud of our Union. Last year it won a great and terrible strike — and we, its members, won the respect of the whole country for our good behavior during that strike. The Union has established the eight-hour day, the greatest gain in the history of labor from the beginning of time; now it has put the screen bill through the Ohio Legislature, and after next September your coal will be weighed before it has been screened.

"The Union has worked to bring friendly and mutually helpful relations between us and the operators. We're having a little trouble around here right now persuading our operators to let us help them as much as we want to —" A roar of laughter stopped him; he waited with lifted hands. "But they'll see the light.

"Our Union has gathered together in bonds of loyal helpfulness more miners from more states than ever before in history." He waited for a moment, spoke more quietly. "And we have only begun. Our victories thus far are just the first faint glow of coming dawn.

"Well, we shall see that dawn; and one day, with God's help, we will stand together in the full glory of the risen sun."

When he sat down, trembling as always, and with perspiring hands, shouts and cheers of approval beat upon him. He sat with

bent head, glad when Eben Howell quieted them and drew fr
them a motion for adjournment and so let them go.

Afterward, Eben called Owen and Mr. Varney to his side, ai
they had to shake many hands, and talk with many men; but whe
at last they were alone, Eben said: "Owen, come along back t
Belton and have supper with me. Mr. Varney's staying overnight
and you ought to get acquainted with him."

Owen felt his pulse quicken. There was no obvious reason why
this invitation should excite him, yet it did. He agreed, and when
the afternoon was gone and the crowd thinned, they boarded one
of the packed cars. Eben's home was pleasant and well-tended,
and Mrs. Howell seemed to Owen astonishingly young; yet a
daughter named Della, who helped give them supper, was certainly fourteen or fifteen, and Mr. Howell spoke of another
daughter and of a married son. Owen decided Mrs. Howell must
be almost as old as his mother; but her cheeks were plump and
bright, her eyes merry and clear. Watching her made him realize
how wrinkled his mother was, and how tired.

He thought more of her, while they sat at supper, than of the talk
between Eben and Varney; and his thoughts led him at last to a
question. "Mr. Howell, have you been a miner all your life?"

Eben smiled. "Not yet, as the man said." Mrs. Howell laughed
in happy appreciation of her husband's jest, and Owen saw pride
and fondness in her eyes. "But I know what you mean. Yes, I
started when I was sixteen. My father wanted me to finish school,
but I was in a hurry —" He met his wife's warm eyes. "In a hurry
to get married. We were married when I was seventeen, had our
first before I was eighteen."

The question in Owen's mind was still unanswered, but it could
not easily be put in words. "This is a mighty nice house," he
suggested.

Eben and Mrs. Howell exchanged glances. "We started buying
shares in the building loan out of my first week's pay. We were
mighty proud people when we moved in here."

Owen nodded. Here, then, was another miner who had built his
home with his pick, and had kept his wife happy and young.
Owen, watching these two together, remembering his mother's
haggard cheeks and weary eyes, hated his father who had made
her life so hard.

After supper was done, he and the two men sat at table while Mrs. Howell and her daughter cleared away and began to wash dishes; and Owen found himself involved in argument with Mr. Varney over his belief that during good times the tax paid by members should be increased. He thought the other not only stubborn but stupid; and when their talk came to the present strike, and Mr. Varney turned to Eben Howell and said the men might as well go back to work, Owen's opinion of Mr. Varney fell even lower.

But to his surprise he heard Eben Howell agree. "Might as well, yes. A lot of the men will blame it on me, but the operators have never given an inch — and I don't think they will."

"The Pittsburgh business hurt us," Varney reflected. "I mean when our own delegates said the eight-hour law was forced on them."

Eben nodded. "The men — many of them — resent it. There's a lot of night-hawking all over the District. If we stick to our guns now, we'll be idle all summer. We can't keep the men out. We might as well go back. I hear the same story from the locals all over the District; the men — even the day men, the fellows we're trying to help — want to go back." He appealed to Owen. "What do you think, Glen?"

"Why — I don't know. I'm against strikes, if there's any way to help them; but I hate to be licked. I hate to give in."

Mr. Varney nodded approval. "Any strike we lose is a bad strike." He spoke to Howell, and Owen thought his word meaningless. "You're right, Eben," he said. "Couldn't do better." He stood up, and as they all rose, he shook Owen's hand.

Owen stared at him, not understanding, and Eben laid his arm across the young man's shoulder. "I've been telling Mr. Varney, Owen," he explained. "Tom Egan is ailing and failing, so we'll soon be needing a new vice-president for the Sub-District. When we do, you're my man."

Owen felt a faint, incredulous surprise. He had thought Mat Price might presently retire, and had aspired to take Mat's place; but Tom Egan was a relatively young man. "Mr. Egan looks all right," he said doubtfully.

"He's got something wrong with his insides."

Owen was absorbed in his own thoughts. "Another thing, he's from Clinton County. Even if he resigns we ought to put in another Clinton County man, to keep them happy."

Varney laughed in an approving way. "We'll take care of that." He met Eben's eye, and Owen felt himself excluded from some secret which they shared.

Not till he had said goodnight and left them did Owen come to full comprehension of the promise in their words. Riding back to Hardiston in the electric car, he stared out of the window into darkness, grinning at his own reflection in the glass, bursting with pride. He decided he would tell Marged first of all. If he told his mother, she would surely confide in his father; and Tom Glen's tongue could not be trusted. No pledge of secrecy had been required of Owen, but obviously this was not a thing to be talked about.

In Hardiston, he found the streets full of shouting, marching men and the sound of drums; and he followed to see what was happening. The marchers dragged behind them something like a bundle of rags; and in front of the Court House, that bundle was propped up and Owen saw the label on its breast, the name "Weyler," in awkward letters. Then men and boys brought crates and boxes to heap them high, and the flames caught, and General Weyler's effigy, with a mud-soiled Spanish flag wrapped around it, was thrown into the leaping flames.

Owen watched indifferently till the flames began to die. When he started home, he went, past Isaac Williams's house, thinking he might tell Marged tonight but the house was dark. No matter. He would see her Sunday; he could tell her then.

5

In the *Journal*, through that month of April, many columns were devoted to the single, overmastering theme, the war; yet the life of Hardiston went on — and provided Additional Locals. The Reverend L. T. Evans, newly installed minister of the Presbyterian Church, preached his inaugural sermon Sunday night. The Reverend Doctor Murchison, his predecessor in the pulpit, has returned from the Holy Land; he has shaved his beard and looks extremely well. Many Hardiston County men have gone to Alaska, and among them was Howie Evans, son of Howie Evans, Agent. His parents were notified on the ninth that he was killed, with about thirty others, in an avalanche on the Chilcoot Trail. The third Public Rhetoricals of the year at Rio Grande College drew an enthusiastic audience, and the hall was well filled. Sarsaparilla, America's Greatest Medicine, purifies and enriches the blood, and relieves scrofula, rheumatism, salt rheum, hip disease and dyspepsia. Adam found Eve and lost Eden; Noah saved the human race and got drunk; Moses led a nation out of bondage but himself never reached the Promised Land; Alexander conquered the world and died on a spree; Napoleon went from the valley to the peak and then to the valley again: the Republican Party is at the bottom in Hardiston County today because it is run by a gang for private purposes. The Congressional Convention at Portsmouth had cast 1376 ballots through Tuesday April 19, without arriving at a nomination. History in its progress changes the meaning of words: twenty years ago, a humanitarian was one who denied the divinity of Christ; now a humanitarian is one who believes in the brotherhood of man, and McKinley will teach the world the new meaning of the word. The day we declared war, eight Spanish merchantmen were captured; the *Nashville* fired the first shot of the war to halt one of them. There are 40,000 men in the army. The Screen Bill, after ten years of agitation, has passed the Ohio Legislature. It takes effect September 9. The Ohio militia, numbering 7000 men, was called to arms April 25. The Pacific fleet is advancing on Manila in the Philippines, and a Spanish fleet is said to be hovering off the east coast of the United States. There is yellow fever and smallpox in Havana. When war was declared, Secretary of State Sherman resigned. A number of Hardiston County boys are in Ohio National Guard units elsewhere in the state. Stephen Morgan of Hardiston County was nominated for Congress at Portsmouth on the 1477th ballot, and the crowd went wild. Mrs. Herbert Canter and Miss Canter are at the Fifth Avenue Hotel in New York, prepared to sail for Europe.

6

The day after the miners' meeting at Electric Park, Varney and Eben Howell met the operators; and on Monday morning the miners went back to work. Owen heard at the mine the news of Dewey's victory. Until then, he had not comprehended the fact that war was begun.

That day and the next, the dailies clamored the news; but there were many people — not only farmers scattered around the county, but townsfolk too — who got their news only from the *Journal*, and BB knew this, so on Wednesday he reported the battle as thoroughly as though other papers did not exist.

Owen had seen the dailies, but he went to the *Journal* office Wednesday evening and read BB's exultant words with a shared intoxication.

> *A new era has dawned in naval war, and a new dispensation, that of humanitarianism, in the history of mankind. American genius, grit and humanitarianism won their first great triumph on Sunday morning, the first of May. Our only news is from Spanish sources, but they admit we "licked them like sixty" — and that means we really licked them "like two hundred and fifty."*

Owen spread his copy of the *Journal* on the composing stone — clear now, since the forms were on the press — and lifted the lamp near, and read, and wondered. BB had splattered his columns with statistics. The Philippines — till now the very name had been unknown to most Americans — included twelve hundred islands, eight million people, two hundred native tribes; there were one hundred and twenty thousand people in Manila alone; the foreign trade was worth $35,000,000; the islands were a "veritable paradise" of tropical fruits. Forty thousand rebels were in arms there against Spain.

These figures were impressive; but as he read, Owen began to wonder. Were they large enough to justify such jubilation? Perhaps it was the glory of victory, rather than its fruits, which made this success so important; and to see whether this were true, he studied a list of the Spanish ships and of Dewey's, and tallied the guns they carried. To say that eight Spanish ships faced six American vessels sounded as though Dewey had been confronted by a stronger enemy; but the Spanish ships were so small that three of Dewey's vessels outweighed the whole Spanish fleet. As for guns, Dewey's ships carried ten eight-inch cannon, and forty-three others over five inches, while Spain had only thirteen cannon over five inches in her whole fleet, If inches meant anything, Dewey's victory was about as glorious as if ten grown men and forty boys had whipped a dozen boys!

BB was in the front office, and Owen went to speak to him. "This battle doesn't sound like much to me, Mr. Beecham," he confessed. "We had bigger ships than they did, and an awful lot more guns. If we hadn't whipped them, we'd have been ashamed; but whipping them wasn't anything to brag about."

BB tipped back his chair. "You know, you have a useful trait, Owen," he remarked. "You don't accept any statement without question. But you'll have to be careful or you'll find yourself believing things just because everyone else believes the opposite." And when Owen did not speak, he added: "We're celebrating partly because we're excited; we've suddenly realized that we're growing up. A boy of fourteen who is six feet tall and weighs a hundred and seventy-five pounds may still be surprised and delighted to find he can whip a man fifty years old who weighs only a hundred and twenty!

"But don't discount this victory. It will set Admiral Dewey's name among American immortals, next after John Paul Jones. It's the greatest battle ever won by this nation against a foreign foe, it's the first battle between ironclads, and it's the first battle in the history of the world that was fought for humanity. It starts the United States along a path we have never before travelled; and it establishes us in the eyes of the world as one of the great nations of the world.

"So even if the battle had been fought by boys with popguns, it was still a great battle — and a famous victory."

Owen said grudgingly: "You keep talking about humanity. What good does it do humanity for us to sink some Spanish ships and drown a lot of Spanish sailors?"

"It ends Spanish tyranny and misrule in the islands."

"Who will rule them now? Us?"

"Yes — in the name of humanity, and till they're ready to rule themselves."

"Suppose they don't want us to?" Owen tapped the paper in his hand. "You say here that forty thousand of them are fighting against Spain. Suppose when we tell them we've come to rule them in the name of humanity, they start in and fight us?"

"Nonsense! We'll come as their friends!" And BB said in an almost reverent tone: "God has been good to the United States, Owen. He's given us all the riches any nation can desire, so there's no one we need envy, nothing we need covet, no lands we need conquer. Whatever we do can be done, not for our own good, but for mankind."

"Oh, I know what you mean," Owen admitted. "But there are plenty of things in the United States that need fixing before we start running the world for humanity. Take the miners — "

BB laughed, rising. "You're a young man of one idea, but that can be a good thing. You go on fighting for your miners. Every victory you and they win is a victory for all of us. More power to you." He turned toward the pressroom. "A few more victories like Dewey's and no one will have to go to war."

"I've decided to go."

BB paused. "Have you." The words were not a question. "Did you see that Mark Radabaugh is raising a company here in Hardiston?"

"No, is he?"

"He's opened an office in the Flagg House, signed up nineteen the first hour. His company won't go till the second call for volunteers. The National Guard filled Ohio's quota for the first call."

"When will that be? The second call?"

"If the war's over soon, there won't be one."

On the way home, Owen decided not to enlist in Mr. Radabaugh's company, not to wait for that second call. The coal he had shot down today he would load tomorrow, credit it to his father, then go to Columbus or Cincinnati and find a recruiting office where there would be no delay.

XXIV

May 5, 1898 — September 8, 1898

At breakfast next morning, Owen said nothing of his decision. Since the night he supped at Eben Howell's, he had watched his mother, comparing her with Mrs. Howell, seeing how much more hardly life had treated her; and for her gaunt body, her gnarled hands, her hollowed cheeks and deeply sunken eyes, he held Tom Glen to blame. It was her strength and health, not his own, which Tom had wasted in his years of strife; it was she who had paid the price of his defeat.

Thus thinking, Owen came near hatred, and he would not risk any discussion with his father now. To do so might lead to bitter words, and bitterness and anger were memories he did not wish to leave behind. So at breakfast he held his tongue, and on the train and at the mine he said nothing to Tom of his intent. When he finished loading his coal, he trudged out to the portal. Moses Evans was in the store, talking with Mike Ryan, and Owen spoke to him.

"Afternoon, Mr. Evans."

"You're through early."

"I didn't put in any shots." Owen turned to the storekeeper. "Put my cars on papa's tally, will you, Mike." And to Mr. Evans: "I'm going to enlist."

The older man clapped Owen's shoulder. "Good lad! God bless you!" He gripped Owen's black hand, and Mike Ryan flung an arm around Owen, pounding him proudly.

"Give 'em one for me, m'lad! I'd pay a pretty to be going with you."

With their good will to hearten him, Owen tramped away. At home, his mother — she and Mrs. Lewis were knitting sociably

574

together in the kitchen when he opened the door — seemed not surprised to see him. "Well, Owen. Where's papa?"

"I came early."

She looked at the clock on the shelf and nodded. "Why, so you did; but you don't look like a sick man to me!" He thought there was an artificial composure in her tones, that she pretended less surprise than she felt; but then suddenly her eyes widened, her cheeks drained white. "Owen! It's papa!"

"No, no; he's all right. I came home after I'd loaded my coal, didn't shoot down any for tomorrow. I'm going to volunteer."

Mrs. Lewis uttered a reproachful exclamation. "Owen — you're not!" But his mother said calmly:

"Yes, he is, Jane. He told us, days ago. Only I didn't know it would be today."

"I'll go to Columbus," Owen explained. "Enlist there."

"Well, there's a kettle on the stove to warm your tub, and I'll bring your good suit out to you. See if you can scrub the coal dust out of your skin!" She was so brisk and smiling that he wished to take her in his arms, but she gave him the kettle, hustled him away.

When he came back from the shed, clean and clad in his best, Mrs. Lewis was gone. His mother met him in a fashion completely matter-of-fact. "You won't need your best suit, or any suit at all, as far as that goes, not after they find you a uniform; but maybe you'd best wear it just the same. First impressions make a difference. All else you'll need, you can carry in a bundle. I'll wrap it up for you, and you can send it home when you're done with it. You'll not be going tonight?"

"No, I'll take the early train."

"Well, then, you'll be having breakfast with papa, same as always, and it won't be so different." He thought there had been a catch in her voice, but she finished so cheerfully that he decided this was not true.

That day was hers, she ruled its course. When Tom Glen came home, he had heard at the mine what Owen meant to do, and there was a harsh word on his tongue; but she silenced him. "Hush, Tom! Go clean yourself, and come to supper. It's settled, and settled fine, and no talk needed."

She had her way with him. They went early to bed and she roused them before dawn. Owen's train left half an hour before the electric car Tom would take, and she bustled Owen through his breakfast and hurried him away alone.

"Go on with you, now, sonny. Here's goodbye!" She kissed him. "Come home well and fine."

He hesitated, shaken by a wrenching reluctance. "Why don't we all walk to the station?"

"No, papa's not through his breakfast. And anyway, who wants to stretch out anything as bitter as a goodbye longer than he has to." She laughed, and flapped her apron at him as though he were a trespassing hen. "Shoo! Shoo! Be off with you."

So Owen kissed her, and went to shake his father's hand, and returned to kiss his mother again. "Take care of each other. You're the finest people in the world. Goodbye." He carried away with him the memory of them standing side by side, his father's arm around her, their eyes in his.

2

Owen's first letter reached them Monday, and Will Davis brought it to the house on his way home from the office. "It came inside another envelope addressed to BB," he told Mrs. Glen. Tom had not yet returned from his day's work. She thanked him, hugging the unopened letter to her breast; and when he departed, she sat down on the stoop and watched him out of sight before she opened the envelope.

DEAR MAMA AND PAPA:

Well, everyone is excited here because we've heard from Dewey, and he's all right. He killed three hundred Spaniards and wounded four hundred besides; and they didn't kill any of us and only hurt five or six. I guess he did all there was for him to do, but I don't see how it was such a wonderful victory when it was that one-sided.

When I got to Columbus, there was a poster in the station that told me where to enlist so that didn't take long. I've wrapped my suit and things in a bundle to send home. They say we'll probably go to Chickamauga next week.

I'm going to send my letters in care of BB in case the mail carrier doesn't come. I'll do that right along, so they'll be sure to get to you.

Your loving son,
OWEN

She read this slowly, and once her spectacles blurred so that she had to take them off and dry them. Having read each word, she began again, trying to fill by conjecture the many gaps. Where did he go to enlist? Who was there? What did he say to them and they to him? Where did he sleep that night; in a house, a tent, on a bed, on the ground? Was he warm enough? Had he enough to eat? Why did They — already she began to think of They with a capital "T" — why did They send him to Chickamauga?

Her mind was a race of questions, till around her the world began to move in swooping dips and lifts, as though she were on a ship at sea. She raised her eyes from Owen's letter and looked at the black bulk of the slack pile down the run, at the lifted crests of oaks in the grove beyond, at the unclouded sky; she tried to make the world be still, for she knew what this sense of motion, of swooping dips and rises, must portend. It was a relief, when the pain came, to yield to it. There had been so many times when, because Owen and Tom were with her, she must pretend that it was nothing, must bite her lip and smile.

But now there was no one to see, so she let the pain cramp her forward into an anguished crouch. It was as though her spine were being stretched on a rack with twisted cords to the taut snap-point of breaking, and at the same time crushed and crumbled into coals of burning bone. When Tom and Owen were here, her bouts with this cruel enemy within herself were secret, and in them she was always victorious; but when, as now, she was alone, it was bliss to avow her agony by posture and by nail-pierced palm and bitten lip and low keen wailing cries.

Yet after a little she put surrender aside, for Tom would soon be here, and she must be cheerful to face him and give him comfort when he came. She chunked up the fire and filled the kettle, then washed her face and pressed cold water against her swollen lips and taught them again to smile. When Tom arrived, she was feeding the chickens, and she hastened to meet him, and make him sit on the stoop while she read Owen's letter. He listened in silence, and when she was done he grunted sullenly.

"Young jackass! He'll have many a sorry day."

She laughed at him. "Growl all you want, Tom. You don't fool me!"

He grinned. Indoors, she handed him the kettle for his bath; and after supper he asked her to read the letter to him again. Then while she cleared away and washed up, he held it in his hand, his eyes upon it, but she knew that even with his glasses he could not have seen to read it. His eyes did well enough for everything else, but not for reading. Sometimes, pretending to laugh at his infirmity, he said: "I see best in the dark. If my lamp goes out in the mine, like as not I never know."

Owen's letters that summer were not many, but they were looked for, and they were read over and over, and kept as dearest treasures. His mother did not write to him, afraid her secret might reveal itself in shaking hand or unguarded word. He wrote always in BB's care, and sometimes a letter to the editor was enclosed in the same envelope, and thus saw print in the *Journal*. These his mother cut out and kept with the other small possessions which she loved.

It was two months after Owen's departure, the day after the Fourth, when at last she went to Doctor Gorman. That morning, when she had given Tom his breakfast and seen him away to the mine, she surrendered to the naked flame of pain. She watched Tom out of sight, waiting for the hand he always lifted in farewell, then curled on the floor in a moaning, writhing helplessness; but when she could move, she rose and dressed in her best and walked high-headed the long way to Broad Street and to the doctor's office.

He was not there, and when Mrs. Gorman told her he had gone to the country an hour before day, to help Mrs. Travis with her third, and had not yet returned, Mrs. Glen looked right and left in half-panic.

"I don't know what to do. When will he be back?"

"As soon as the baby comes."

She could not face the weary agony of walking home, then walking the long way here again. "Can I just sit and wait?"

"Yes, indeed." Mrs. Gorman hesitated. "You're sick, aren't you? Come in the house and lie down till he gets back."

"I wouldn't put you to all the trouble."

"No trouble, Mrs. Glen. A doctor's wife gets used to taking care of people." She led Owen's mother across the brick wall from office to house. "I'm going to make you lie down," she said cheerfully. "And take a glass of warm milk. Maybe you can have a little nap." Mrs. Glen yielded, abandoning all pretense. Before going to heat the milk, Mrs. Gorman stopped at the doctor's medicine cabinet; and Mrs. Glen, having drunk the milk, drifted easily to sleep.

She was roused by the doctor's hand on hers, and tried to get up, and he said reassuringly: "No, no. Just rest, Mrs. Glen." Mrs. Gorman beside him nodded in smiling reassurance, and Mrs. Glen yielded and lay quietly, while a whisper of pain like the distant voice of an approaching enemy brought her back to wakefulness again. She submitted to the doctor's investigations, too weary to be embarrassed but grateful for Mrs. Gorman's presence; and when he asked questions, she answered them.

"Does Mr. Glen know?"

"No. It would worry the poor man so."

"Owen's gone to war?"

"Yes."

"Did you tell him, before he went?"

"No, I didn't. I was glad he went, so he wouldn't have to be here to see me when I couldn't hide it any longer."

"You've known a long time, yourself, haven't you?"

"Yes, doctor." His eyes met Mrs. Gorman's in one of those glances possible only between husband and wife well and truly wed, and Owen's mother said with a twisted smile: "But I knew nobody could do anything. Only, I had to come today, because I can't hide it any longer when it hurts. I thought maybe you could give me something." And she said apologetically: "I could stand it myself, but Tom would go crazy if he ever saw me the way I am sometimes when I'm alone."

Doctor Gorman nodded. "I can give you something. But you know, you'll have to stop working. You'll have to go to bed pretty soon."

Her head turned on the pillow and her eyes closed. "I know. My mother went the same. I was a young one when she died, but I saw her. I don't want Owen ever to see me look that way, doctor. I don't want him to come home and see me. I don't want him having to remember me the way I remember her." Her throat seemed to fill. "But I want to see him. I don't know. I don't know."

The doctor cleared his throat. "Tom will have to know, pretty soon. And — someone must take care of you. Your daughter?"

Her head moved from side to side. "Amy's got enough to do, with three young ones — the last one's only five months old, and sickly — and Dave, and Dave's mother so big and fat she's as good as chair-bound, so the whole house comes on Amy. But I've told Mrs. Lewis. She's the only one I have told. Mrs. Freeman Lewis. She'll come, and she says Mrs. Tutson, that boards with her, will maybe help when the time comes. They can do for Tom. I can tend to myself."

"I don't see how you've kept going this long."

"I just hung on the best I could. I knew once I take to my bed I won't last long."

"Well, I'll give you something, make it easier. We'll see. We'll see."

3

To Hardiston County, week by week, BB in the *Journal* brought the War. The Spaniards cut the cable at Manila, and that was why no word came direct from Admiral Dewey till a week after the battle. Up till May 10, Spain had captured two American merchantmen, but we had taken twenty-seven of hers. We now control the Philippines, and Senator Foraker says: "Raise the Stars and Stripes there and keep it flying. The sooner this country realizes that it is a power among the nations of the world, and needs colonial possessions, the better." The dailies are full of fakes. During the week after Dewey's victory, and before any direct word came from him, they reported his fleet blown up by mines, and then had him penned in Manila Harbor and four hundred of his men killed. Actually he had none killed, and only eight slightly wounded. As for Sampson, the dailies had him in a battle Sunday, May 1. He sank nine Spanish warships and captured eight, or he was whipped; you could take your choice. Excursion trains took 40,000 people to Columbus Sunday from all over the state to see the soldiers in camp there. One train was wrecked, one killed and six hurt. Thus far, the trains and the mines have killed more Americans than the Spaniards. The trains killed John Sager at Slacktown Monday. A fourteen-pound baby was born in Glendale Monday night. Write Ensign Worth Bagley's name on the honor roll. The *Oregon*, racing home from the Pacific to lend a hand in the coming conflict, is reported safe. She can cope single-handed with Cervera's whole fleet, except perhaps the torpedo boats. She steamed 13,000 miles, a record never equalled in history. Gladstone died May 19; he was the finest Christian statesman the world has ever known. On May 22, at least two Ohio dailies reported that Sampson had sunk twelve Spanish warships; this is the biggest fake of the war up to date. Cervera's fleet is reported to have been in Santiago de Cuba, but whether still there, no one knows. Leiter, the Chicago millionaire, has made over $5,000,000 out of wheat since September of last year. He bought below a dollar, and wheat hit $1.95 in New York May 10. Owen Glen writes from Camp George H. Thomas near Chattanooga:

DEAR MR. BEECHAM:

> It's fine to have the Journal *coming every week, and I'm glad Nellie got the address changed so quick because this week's copy came right on time. We have been here six days now, and they say fifty thousand men will be here by Saturday. We sleep in tents in the woods. I have seen the top of Lookout Mountain, and the Chickamauga National Park with a lot of monuments and cannon and cannon balls to show where the battle was fought, and I went to visit Missionary Ridge. Everybody here thinks we will soon invade Cuba. It looks to me as if the war would cost us a lot of money, with everything the United States will have to buy. One of the men here says that's all right, we'll just invade Spain and make her pay for it; but it's going to cost her as much as it costs us, so how can she pay? I guess we'll do the paying. We are drilling every day now, and marching. It's harder than mining coal.*
>
> > *Your friend,*
> >
> > OWEN GLEN

The war news filled columns every week, but there was always room for Additional Locals. Alice Jenkins, daughter of Mrs. Evan Jenkins, was fatally burned when her dress caught fire while she was boiling clothes in a kettle in the yard; she ran and could not be caught till too late, and she died that night. Burglars broke into two Hardiston houses last week, but the loss was small. A hundred and fifty delegates attended the Young People's Christian Union Convention in Slacktown. President McKinley calls for 75,000 more volunteers. Theodore Roosevelt has organized a regiment called the Rough Riders, but they will fight on foot. May 31 came definite word that Cervera's fleet is in Santiago Harbor; now the problem is to keep him there. Doctor Gorman has brought to this office a sample of smokeless powder; it looks like a piece of wax, about two inches long, and can be bent but not easily broken. It can be lighted with a match and burns readily but with no smoke. Owen Glen writes that he saw three Hardiston boys at Camp Alger; his regiment has been moved to Washington. The month of May was the most eventful in American history since the Civil War.

Cervera is bottled up. In the most gallant deed of the war, Lieutenant Richmond Pearson Hobson on June 3 sank the *Merrimac* across the mouth of the harbor, blocking the channel; he and seven men are prisoners of war, honored even by the Spaniards for their glorious deed. Seven boys and nine girls graduated from High School last week. The most stirring oration was delivered by Herbert Towne; his subject was "America as Liberator." The Reverend Richard Llewellyn, preaching at the Gymanfa in Sycamore Hill, dropped dead in the pulpit. United States marines have seized Guantanamo Bay, where our army will be landed. Spanish warships have been reported off Cape Henry, but as yet no American towns or cities have been bombarded. West Virginia soft coal sold in Philadelphia last week at $1.20, a record low; West Virginia miners are not unionized, so this was scab coal. No friend of labor will buy West Virginia coal. Dewey Day will be celebrated in Columbus next week, and great preparations to honor the hero of Manila are afoot. A part of the *United Mine Workers Journal* is now printed in Slavonian for the benefit of foreign-born miners. Perhaps our most powerful warship, now with the fleet off Santiago, is the *Vesuvius*; she has three enormous pneumatic guns, each 54 feet long and 15 inches in diameter, and fitted with revolving chambers which hold five charges, and she can throw 100 pounds of guncotton a distance of two and a half miles, or 500 pounds one mile; it is believed she can demolish Morrow Castle in an hour; and she may revolutionize naval warfare; Admiral Sampson counts her the most effective vessel in his fleet. June 13, wheat dropped to 90 cents; the big crop broke the price. A resolution annexing

Hawaii passed the House 209–91, after a debate dealing with the sin and disease among the islanders; the resolution now goes to the Senate. Six marines were killed and nineteen wounded at Guantanamo. General Shafter commands the army now being landed in Cuba. John Nevercut of Belton, convicted of making counterfeit nickels, has been sentenced to three years in prison. The B & O has installed electric fans in their sleeping car, which meets with general approval. Sixteen thousand Americans have landed in Cuba. The first dead were reported to have been mutilated by the Spaniards, but Admiral Sampson now denies the charge. War is terrible, but last week in Hardiston County mines one man was instantly killed and another was caught by a fall of slate and died after four hours of agony, while rescuers worked in vain to free him. The Glorious Fourth brought destruction to Cervera's fleet.

4

The day after Mrs. Glen's appeal to Doctor Gorman, Tom Glen brought home a letter from Owen. "I met Will Davis just when I got off the car," he explained. "And he gave me the paper, too." This was Wednesday, press day. "Here's the letter. Paper's in my dinner pail."

She slit the envelope with a hairpin. "Wait while I read it, Tom." He sat on the doorstep, and she pulled her chair near.

FALLS CHURCH, VA., July 1

DEAR MAMA AND PAPA:

This is a day when I want a change. I've seen the sights around here, and I've learned all I'm ever going to learn about being a soldier. Everyone in camp is looking for a call to go to the front, and it cannot come too soon. Everybody tells us we are enlisted for a noble cause, the cause of humanity and to uphold the dignity and honor of our great country and to avenge the 256 brave American sailors treacherously butchered on the Maine; but we want to start doing it.

I have now spent almost two months drilling in a field and sleeping in a tent. Our tents are about ten feet square, with five of us in each one. We make our beds of poles covered with hickory bark laid crosswise. Each man has

*one blanket and a gum blanket called a poncho; and dur-
ing hot weather it is very uncomfortable. Each man has
half a pup tent, knapsack, canteen, tin plate, knife, fork
and spoon, quart cup, clothes, gun, belt and bayonet; a
pretty fair-sized load when we start out on a forced march.
We are all right, no complaints except the meat they give
us smells worse than it tastes. It comes in cans. The meat
or something keeps some of the men sick a lot of the time,
but I'm all right.*

*I received my first wound the other day when we were
all vaccinated except one who had had smallpox. The
wound was done with a sharp pointed bone instrument. It
was like a cat scratch. My arm didn't take, but it did the
other time when I was in school in Hardiston, so it is all
right.*

I saw in the Journal *about Allie Jenkins getting burned
up. That was awful. She was a jolly girl. Miss Means
that she called "Aunt Wormwood" always said there was
a curse on them and it looks like it.*

*It is sprinkling and looks like rain. I will write more
later.*

Your Loving Son
OWEN GLEN

She finished, and looked anxiously at her husband. "He's fret-
ting, Tom. That don't sound like him somehow. You think he's
sick?"

"Not sick, or he wouldn't be writing letters. Will said he wrote
a long one to BB, says it's in the *Journal* I brought home."

He had told her the paper was in his dinner pail, so she picked
up the pail and bade him wait and took out the *Journal*. Owen's
letter was on the first page.

DEAR MR. BEECHAM:

*I will drop you a few lines about our life here. We have
a very healthy camp, the days warm and the nights cool.
There isn't much sickness, except that the food isn't very
good. Sometimes the canned meat is too spoiled to eat.*

*We went on a three-day forced march last week. It was
very hot and dusty. We marched to a little creek called
Difficult because we had such a time getting there, and*

then to the *Great Potomac Falls fifteen miles above Washington. It is a pretty sight. The river on both sides is bordered by high rocky cliffs, a hundred feet or more. The
water falls about fifty feet, and makes mist at the bottom.
A good many of the men crossed on the rocks to the Mary-
land side, but I did not try it. We marched back next day.*

*Monday I got leave and boarded an electric car into
Georgetown, then walked across the bridge into Washington and took a streetcar on Pennsylvania Avenue. That
Avenue leads past the White House and the Congressional
Library Building and ends at the Navy Yard. I got a pass
and went into the Navy Yard and saw many relics that
came from the battleship* Maine. *I got a scale of rust that
came off one of her guns.*

*I then visited the Congressional Library. The dome on
top is covered with leaves of gold. I went to the Capitol
and saw the sights. The paintings in the Capitol building
cost a million dollars. The Library has already cost six
million dollars and isn't done yet. The Treasury Building
is where the United States keeps its money. I saw scads
of it. The Washington monument is 550 feet high and you
can go up 500 feet of it. I saw where paper money and
stamps are printed, but they don't let you see much there.
I saw the Smithsonian Institute and the Zoological Garden. They have a good many animals, and I saw some
coons and some rabbits, the most familiar ones. I guess
this is the greatest country there is, and the richest there
is. Digging coal is small punkins with all the money there
is; but if they didn't have coal where would they be?*

Your friend,
OWEN GLEN

*I guess little things make big ones. Enough blocks of
marble built the Washington Monument, and enough
bricks would build the biggest building here, and enough
miners working for sixty-six cents a ton would earn a
million dollars.*

When she finished, she said in uncertain relief: "He sounds all
right in this one. I guess he's not sick."

Tom rose. "Well, he was bound to go! He's made his bed. If he don't like it where he is, wait till he gets to Cuba. I'll go wash up."

He took the kettle from the stove and went into the shed while she read again the letter in the *Journal*. Tom would be wanting his dinner, but lethargy lay heavily upon her. Doctor Gorman had advised her to use sparingly the capsules he had made up for her, so today she had waited till almost time for Tom's home-coming, and had taken one a few minutes before he appeared. The relief from searing pain made her sleepy; she was reluctant to rise. Her eyes wandered across the columns of the *Journal*. BB, exulting over the destruction of Cervera's fleet, had written:

> *God has turned his face away from Spain until atone-ment has been made for the horrible crime of the* Maine.

God has turned his face away! She repeated the phrase in her thoughts, lifting her eyes to the sky. The brassy heat of the day was not yet much relieved; northwestward a white cloud mass towered gloriously in the guilding blaze of the sun. It's like God with his veil lifted, she thought; and she remembered that to look upon God's uncovered countenance was to die. She would die, yet for Tom's sake she must not; for who would do for him when she was gone. Yet she must die before Owen came home, so that he need not remember through all his days her pain-seared eyes, her anguish-furrowed countenance. She would die, she must not die, she wished to die.

Tom came from the shed and she rose to her tasks and made his supper for him. She herself ate little. Sometimes she wondered that Tom never noticed this; she would not be so lonely if he knew the truth. It was strange that he could be so near her, that he could have shared her bed and her life all these weary years and not guess her agony. She did not wish him to know; but he might at least say she looked badly, or ask how she felt, or — something. Yet till she must, she would never let him know.

He ate and was done and tipped back his chair and filled his pipe. It was time to do the dishes, but she dreaded rising. Any change of posture summoned pain. "I'll read the paper to you," she suggested.

"So do, Annie," he agreed, well-fed content in his tone. "I miss Owen for that. You mind, from the time he was a boy, he used to read to me at night; yes, and then he'd sit over his books long after you and me were abed and asleep."

"You're proud of him as I am, Tom."

"Certain."

"But you always argue and blame, when you talk to him. Why can't you ever let him be? When he was little, when we first moved up here, he all but worshipped you. I can see him now, the first day he went to work, marching off with you to the early train."

He nodded. "A proud boy he was that day, asking a hundred questions, wanting to know about everything." Then, in a different tone, "But it was no time till he was too big for his britches." Resentment edged his words. "Setting out to tell me what was what, as if I was the boy and he the man."

She abandoned the point, for Tom could never be shaken, and argument was weariness. The *Journal* told the story of Cervera's end. The first Spanish vessel came out of harbor at half-past nine; by two o'clock, the last ship had run ashore and surrendered, three hundred Spaniards had been killed or drowned, a hundred and fifty wounded, sixteen hundred captured. When she had read, she asked:

"I wonder why they came out, to be killed like that."

"Might be they hoped to get away."

"It says they couldn't fight back because we had bigger guns and more ships and all. I should think they'd have stayed in the harbor, or just surrendered. They couldn't do any good coming out, and they didn't have to come out and get killed so."

"Maybe it was for glory."

"Glory!" Her tone was contemptuous. "A man might call it glory, but I call it showing off. Been a sight more sensible if they just said they were licked and gave up. But no, they had to have their glory! I never saw a man yet could do something and keep his mouth shut about it. Men are like a pack of young ones, forever yelling: 'Look at me, mama! Look at me!'"

"You're pretty when you get your dander up! What else does the paper say?"

"Well — " Her eyes searched the columns, and she read:

The common people of the world are listening with eager ears for news of our victories, decorating their bare walls with portraits of our heroes, enshrining our national colors in their hearts, and looking forward to the day when the Stars and Stripes shall carry peace and security to

every corner of the world, when men may be men and not
cattle, children be free and not slaves. This is a time to be
proud of our history, our heritage and our destiny. This is
sunrise for the era of freedom for the oppressed all over
the world. Praise God from whom all blessings flow.

Her voice broke as she read, and she said, "Mr. Beecham writes
good, doesn't he?"

But Tom did not answer, and she saw he was asleep, head
drooping on his chest. She watched him for a while with still eyes,
seeing his heavy dark hair grayed and thin on top, his lined cheeks
and jaw now loose and pendent; and she remembered him as a
young man and her sweetheart. Her thoughts, swift as a whiplash
and yet unhurrying, brought marching through her mind the parad-
ing years. She and he had loved each other, and bred children,
and some of their babies died and some lived; they had worked
hard and lived decently, respecting others and respecting themselves. For an instant, she felt the presence of the millions upon
millions of people in the world who were like them, who lived brief
lives and died as she was soon to die. While people lived, they
seemed to themselves to be important; but — what was the importance to the world of herself and of Tom Glen? If they had
never lived, what difference to the world; would there have been
a lack, a gap they were not there to fill?

She closed her eyes, accepting the truth; except to themselves,
she and Tom were of no importance.

But were they not? There were millions like them. Were all
those millions equally of no importance? Suppose none of those
others had lived?

Her head lifted in certainty and pride. Man was important; the
fact that there were men and women was important. She and Tom
shared with all other men and women everywhere the attribute of
life; she had a momentary certainty of her own place and purpose,
a reassuring sense of duty met, of service done.

She had served Tom, and she had served Owen and the other
children, though perhaps Owen had more of her than his share;
certainly between him and her there was a stronger bond. Also,
Evan and Amy already had — or would have — children, and one
day Owen would have children, in each of whom some part of her,

of her blood and muscle and bone, would live and never die. But if she had not lived, neither would they have lived; so to have lived at all was to be immortal. If the generations of men and women had not lived, then there would be no men and women in the world today. She felt herself a part of that river of life, of that miracle which gave her life and by which she passed on the gift of life to others.

If she had not lived, Owen would not be alive. Perhaps for him to live would one day prove to have been important to the world.

Through dreaming eyes she watched her husband's drooping head there across the table, and pride and the courage born of pride flowed through her. She rose and went to his side and leaned down and pressed her cheek to his. "Go on to bed, Tom dear. Go on to bed now, while I get the dishes done. Go on with you."

5

For another month after that night, she kept her feet, and with Doctor Gorman's capsules to help she could be fine and tender for her Tom when he came home. If she were haggard and yellow with the rust of pain, Tom's dim eyes did not see; her voice and the touch of her hand and her arm across him as he slept were her to him.

The day of her surrender, the day when pain keen as an axe cut the roots of her resolution through, it was Will Davis who found her. On the first Thursday in August, he left the office early; and since he had a letter for her, he came past the house. Although the day was sultry, the door was closed; but when he knocked, he heard a low cry, and then a weary moan, and he opened the door.

She was on the floor, too weak to move. He carried her to her bed, and gave her water. It bubbled between her shivering teeth, and she shuddered so that she could not swallow. He left her and ran to Charles Morgan's house and sent Mrs. Morgan to tend her, then hurried to find Doctor Gorman and blurted out his message.

"She was down on the floor, crying, looking awful."

"I know. I've been treating her. I don't know how she's stayed out of bed so long."

"What's the matter with her?"

"Nothing anyone can cure." The doctor closed his bag, ready to start. "I'll go give her what relief I can."

Will did not go back with the doctor. To see Mrs. Glen sick and suffering made him want to hurry home and make sure all there were well. On the way he saw BB appraising progress on the new house, and stopped to tell him Mrs. Glen was ill; and next morning BB, after consulting Doctor Gorman and learning the truth, went to see Owen's mother. She was in bed, Mrs. Lewis tending her; and she exacted his promise not to mention her illness in the *Journal.*

"Because Owen reads it every week, and I don't want him to know."

"Will you be — taken care of?"

Mrs. Lewis answered him. "I'll come every day, or Mrs. Tutson will. And Mrs. Morgan, too."

"Where's Tom?"

"Gone to work." Mrs. Glen smiled faintly. "I told him I'd be as well as ever by tonight, and he believed it, the way men will. They don't like their womenfolks sick, so as long as I tell him I'm all right, he'll think I am."

"Owen will soon be coming home. The war's as good as over."

Her eyes closed. "I hope he won't."

"You'll want to see him."

"I'd want to see him, yes, if he didn't have to see me. You keep it out of the paper about me, won't you please, sir." And BB agreed.

6

Additional Locals: A new committee has been appointed to study the question of bringing waterworks to Hardiston. On July 7, Hawaii was annexed to the United States; westward the course of empire takes its way. President McKinley has called for a day of thanksgiving for our victories. Aguinaldo has proclaimed himself President of the revolutionary Republic of the Philippines. Aguinaldo is all right; Dewey compliments him highly. The Steel brothers are using a steam traction ditcher to tile their land. The

French liner *La Bourgogne*, after a collision off Sable Island, sank
with a loss of 560 lives; the French crew killed many passengers
in battling for possession of the lifeboats, and only one woman was
saved. Santiago surrendered July 17; there was very little yellow
fever in the town. Frederick Ames, son of David Ames of Hardiston, received a slight wound in the fighting in front of the city. A
Hardiston man — we omit his name — fell into a vault while collecting night soil last Friday night and had a thrilling experience
for a few minutes. Owen Glen writes that the food served our soldiers is rotten; cannot something be done about this? Herbert Canter believes the United States should seize and hold Cuba and
Porto Rico and the Philippines, and that we should hold the
Canaries and the Ladrones till Spain has paid our war expenses,
but should not annex any territory in Europe; he says the Monroe
Doctrine works both ways. There are forty-one saloons in the
county. The actors who will open the Twentieth Century are re-
hearsing, and one of them already looms as a giant; McKinley is
an instrument in God's hands, to work His will upon the Spaniards
and perhaps on other dying nations that still canker the earth.
Porto Rico has been seized. Bismarck is dead and Europe is left
without a great man. Mrs. B. B. Beecham and daughter departed
August 1 to visit relatives in Kansas City. The committee recommends that Hardiston have a waterworks if water can be found.

The war is over! Spain has agreed to our terms; she gives up
Cuba and cedes to us Porto Rico and other islands. The treaty will
decide the fate of the Philippines, but meanwhile we will occupy
Manila. The peace commissioners will meet in Paris October 1.
One of the Hawaiian Islands should be set aside for confirmed
criminals. The way to extend our commerce is to annex foreign
markets, but the United States should raise 100 regiments of
Negroes to occupy our tropical colonies. There is much sickness
in our army at Santiago, and seventy-five per cent of our men
there have or have had malaria; this weakens them so that they
are unable to withstand yellow fever or dysentery; on August 7,
3445 were sick, and when the war ended, men were dying at the
rate of ten a day. Owen Glen, according to a letter to his father
from Doctor Thorne, in charge of the Military Hospital at Tampa,
has been seriously ill with food poisoning but is now expected to
recover. Robert Morris of Adams Township wrote from Santiago

to his parents: "I am tired of fighting for these Cubans. I would not give one of our American Negroes for all the Cubans on this island. They are a dirty class of people, the dirtiest I ever saw, and they don't know anything except to shoot and run." Before his letter reached his family, a telegram notified them of his death from yellow fever. James Forbush of Glendale writes from the Klondike that he finds no gold, but the hunting and fishing are wonderful. The ordinance providing for waterworks will be submitted to the people of Hardiston at a special election on September 19. For kidney trouble, Foley's Kidney Cure is guaranteed. The democrats of the county have nominated a painfully weak ticket. Business in Hardiston picked up remarkably in August. A "Welcome Home" banquet will be tendered Lieutenant Fremont during his visit to his parents here next week. Thomas Horton writes from Florida that the soldiers all have great respect for the Spaniards as brave fighters and good fellows, but despise the Cubans; and they say Cuba is not a fit country for a dog to live in, full of fever, rain and rotten food. Adam Mayberry, riding his bicycle down Posey Hill, ran over a chicken; his shoulder was dislocated, his collar bone broken, and his face lacerated in the fall that resulted. President Ratchford of the United Mine Workers has resigned, his resignation taking effect September 1, to accept President McKinley's appointment as a member of the United States Industrial Commission; John Mitchell will act as president during the unexpired term. President Ratchford's new duties made it impossible for him to come to Hardiston for Labor Day as he had planned, and since no national officers appeared to explain last April's fiasco, the miners of Hardiston County feel they have been cruelly ostracized. The New Jersey Supreme Court has awarded $245.68 to Edward W. Reeves because a streetcar frightened his horse, and six cents to Abraham L. Graham because a streetcar killed his four-year-old son; every judge should be a father. Charles Lee was killed by an electric car in Belton Monday. Mrs. B. B. Beecham and daughter have returned from Kansas City. Owen Glen, the first Hardiston County man to be discharged from the army, is coming home on convalescent furlough, and will reach here September 8; he writes that he has lost 26 pounds since enlisting. The Pleasant Hour Club met last week at Mrs. Arthur's. Doctor Talmage's sermon this week, on page 3, will be found unusually inspiring. Enough Hardiston County men enlisted to have formed a company, but no company was organized here. Havana, according to a letter published in the dailies, is a filthy city, the streets littered with dead horses, dogs, cats and chickens, buzzards everywhere. Our flag now flies in two hemispheres: who will haul it down? Who will withdraw from the people over whom it floats its protecting folds?

When this year began, Europe ruled the world and considered the United States a nation of shopkeepers. Spain called us Yankee pigs, France and Germany echoed her. But the sinking of the *Maine* broke the American shell and a new nation emerged; our courage won respect, our chivalry won the love of the oppressed. Now expansion is forced upon us by duty and destiny. The day will come when the Stars and Stripes will wave over every land, over a world with one language, one government, and one religion. Owen Glen arrived in Hardiston last Thursday, the first Hardiston soldier to come home.

XXV

September 8, 1898—*October* 12, 1898

MARGED SPENT that summer of the war at home with her father and Aunt Molly, and sometimes she was oppressed by a sense of guilt because the farm was a happier place with her mother gone. She had never known her father as he was now, beginning each day in high good humor and ending it in calm content. She had become so accustomed to her mother's querulous complaining, her manufactured needs, her elaborately patient submission to what were often imagined or pretended ills, that it was strange to be here now with Aunt Molly's sharp but kindly tongue forever striking amusing sparks and with her father occasionally laughing loud and long, or letting loose his fine big bass in ponderous song.

That was for her a fine summer, till one Saturday in August a buggy paused at the gate and she went to speak to Amy and Dave. Amy, grief in her eyes, said at once: "I've had dreadful bad news, Marged. Mama's awful sick, and I'm going up to do for her." She added: "Dave's taking me in to Sycamore Hill, to catch the up train."

"Oh, I'm sorry, Amy. What's the matter with her?" And, as the most probable: "Typhoid fever?"

"No, I guess it's cancer. Anyway, that's what the doctor says. Mrs. Gorman wrote me a letter. She knew I'd want to know."

Marged bit her lip, clasped Amy's hand. "I'll be in Hardiston Monday. I'll come see how she is." She had had no thought of going to Hardiston till a few days before school opened, but this was Owen's mother, sick and perhaps dying; and Owen was far away.

Dave clucked to his horse and the buggy moved on, but Marged stayed leaning on the gate. Her first thought was to write to Owen. In the three months since his departure, he had written her twice, and she had answered. Certainly she must tell him now that his mother needed him, that he must come home.

But suppose he could not; suppose the army forbade. If he could not come, to wish to come would be a racking and a torment. She decided to wait, to see his mother; then she might send messages from her, fit to comfort and to reassure.

She took the Monday morning train to Hardiston, and went directly to her uncle's home. Her aunt had seen Mrs. Glen. "She's going fast, I think," she told Marged. "Shadows under her eyes as blue as a bluebird's wing, and so weak she can't more than lift her hand. But she's took care of. Mrs. Lewis and Mrs. Tutson, one or the other, is up there every day, and Mrs. Jenkins from out the Pike, and Mrs. Morgan down from the corner. Amy'll go home this week, I wouldn't wonder. She's needed at home full as bad as here."

"How's Mr. Glen?"

"Same as any man. She tells him it's just a little upset, and he believes it, goes off to work every day the mine runs, or tends his garden if he's to home. There's the cow and a pig and no telling how many hens that Mrs. Lewis or someone takes care of."

Marged twisted her fingers together, wanting to help. "Who's there at night?"

"Just her and him. Mrs. Morgan gives him his breakfast with Charles, on his way to the cars; and Mrs. Lewis gets there early as she can, to tend her."

"She oughtn't to be left alone."

Her aunt said gently: "Nothing can happen to her but to die, Marged; and she'll do that anyway. She's ready to." She added: "And a mercy if she did."

Marged shivered in a hard revulsion. There was something wrong with the world when death was mercy, either to the living or to those who died. "Has anybody written to Owen?"

"She won't have it so. Her mother died the same way, all ga'nted to a ghost, and sores on her face; and she don't want Owen to see her like that."

"Is she — that way?"

"No, it's all inside her, but she looks awful, the way they do.

Doctor Gorman keeps her not feeling it, much as he can."

Marged went next morning to see Mrs. Glen, her healthy flesh revolting at the prospect; but imagined horrors were worse than the truth. Owen's mother seemed almost beautiful. Her skin had a limpid clarity, like translucent ivory faintly yellowed by age; the blue crescents beneath her eyes were so sharply defined that her eyes withdrew into deep shadowed caverns, and they were soft as though they swam in a drowsy summer haze or were blurred by heat waves rising from a meadow freshly mowed.

Marged stayed with her all that day, till time for Tom Glen's home-coming. Mrs. Glen gave her Owen's letters to read. "Read them aloud," she said. "I like to read them over and over."

Marged thought as she read how different these were from the two letters she had had from him. She might bring her letters to-morrow and read them to his mother; but that evening, with this in mind, she read them over, and told herself there was little in them that would interest Mrs. Glen. The first was from Chicka-mauga.

DEAR MISS WILLIAMS —

I wish you were here. I'd like to talk to you a while, maybe walk home from church with you. How can a man be lonesome with a regiment or an army of other men touching shoulders with him? There must be another word for the way I feel today. And if I am lonesome — or whatever the word should be — why don't I want to write to mama and papa, or to Mr. Beecham, instead of to you?

Well, what difference does it make why I want to write you? I'm doing it. One reason why may be because I was thinking about you an hour ago when we marched into camp and were dismissed. We all scattered every which way, and for a minute I just stood there, because I hadn't thought ahead to decide what I would do when we were dismissed. The other men moved off and I was alone and all of a sudden I was lonesome. Mama told me a long time ago, that marching together — walking together — made people feel closer to one another. While I was marching with my company, I wasn't lonesome, not till we dismissed. That reminded me of walking home from church with you, like a couple of people keeping company,

when he saw Eben Howell and Mike Pratt coming together to take the train.

Owen rose eagerly to meet them at the door, and for a moment, in the obscurity of the unlighted car, they did not know him; but then Mike Pratt cried out a welcome. "Owen Glen!" And as they struck hands, looking him up and down: "Now what have they been doing to you?"

Owen grinned. "Feeding me rotten canned meat, Mike. Hello, Mr. Howell." The train started with a lurch and they turned back a seat, Owen sitting to face the other two. "I'm glad you're aboard. I went all through the train, looking for someone I knew. What's the news?"

"I don't suppose you've been reading many newspapers."

"Only the Hardiston *Journal*. Mr. Beecham sent that to me every week."

"You know President Ratchford has resigned."

"Resigned?" Owen was startled. "What did he do that for?"

"McKinley appointed him to the United States Industrial Commission. John Mitchell will fill out his term. John's been vice-president."

"I only saw Mr. Mitchell once." Owen looked at Mike Pratt. "We met him in West Virginia last year, remember? But he's pretty young."

Howell and Mike Pratt exchanged smiles. "You don't believe in putting young men in office, is that it?"

Owen grinned. "Well, depends on who it is. Mr. Beecham gave me a speech to learn, about that, once. He said I might need it, some day. It starts out: 'Whether youth can be imputed to any man as a reproach, I will not, sir, assume the province of determining; but surely age becomes justly contemptible, when the opportunities which it brings have passed away without advancement, and vice appears to prevail when the passions have subsided.'"

Eben Howell nodded, a chuckle in his tones. "I just wanted to make sure how you felt. Yes, John Mitchell's only twenty-eight; but he was mining coal when he was thirteen, and joined the Knights of Labor when he was fifteen, and he's been on the State Executive Board, and a national organizer. He's old enough. I've just left him. We've been planning ahead."

Owen asked, "What comes next?"

Mike Pratt answered him. "Now you're on my street. I'm headed for West Virginia. You didn't meet Mother Jones there last year, did you?"

"No, but we heard a lot about her."

Mike grinned. "She makes quite a noise, all right. She'd do us more good if she wasn't in jail so much, but she's done a lot as it is. You know last year when Mitchell and John Walker got to West Virginia, we didn't have four hundred union men in the state organized. Now we're on the way to getting the whole state organized. That's where I'm headed. You'd better come along."

"I'll stay home awhile first."

"We've made a lot of progress, Owen." This was Eben Howell. "Even since you went away. Pat McBryde is the operators' commissioner in Ohio now, and he believes the way you do, that the Union is the operators' best friend."

"Anyone with ordinary sense can see that."

"I never heard anyone make it sound as sensible as you do."

Mike Pratt's was a single-track mind. "We've boycotted West Virginia coal this summer, Owen; made the boycott stick in a lot of places, too. It's scab coal! For coal miners, West Virginia is the back alley of creation. The miners' ton there is twenty-two hundred and forty pounds, but the operators sell two thousand pounds for a ton. Two bits for twenty-two hundred and forty pounds is about the highest wage in the District, and after deductions it runs as low as fifteen cents. Why —"

Owen chuckled, lifting his hands in a gesture of surrender. "Hold on, Mike. You don't have to organize me. I know all about West Virginia. The pay is lower, the screens are bigger, the hours are longer, store prices are higher — and there's an injunction waiting to drop on your neck out of every tree."

"You wouldn't think it was so funny if you worked there." Mike cocked his head in a thoughtful way. "And that might happen, some fine day. Hardiston County coal will play out, give it a few years more." He made a cheerful gesture. "Well, we'll make West Virginia a good place for you to work when the time comes."

At Logan, Mike changed to another train, and Owen moved so that he and Eben sat side by side. At once, Howell said: "Owen, I talked to John Mitchell about you, and I had already talked with

Charles Morgan, and with a lot of others. We've been planning to boost you along in the organization. With Mike Ratchford resigning, they want me at Headquarters more, and around the country to help with organizing; so this will be my last year as president of the Sub-District. We'll put Tom Egan in for a year as a sort of reward, a certificate of merit; but you're going to be his vice-president. You'll have to tell him what to do and help him do it. He'll step out in a year — and you step into his shoes. Owen wetted his lips, not speaking, and Howell added with a smile: "Unless you think you're too young for the job."

"I'll grow up to it. If the men want me."

The older man, watching him, said quietly: "Yes, you'll grow up, Owen. I hope I'll be here to see. And don't worry about the men wanting you. I tell you, I've talked around."

For a time after that, Owen, nearest the window, watched the passing scene; rolling farm lands, scattered woodlots where the oaks as yet showed no fall colors, an occasional meandering and muddy little stream. His eyes were fixed, yet they saw nothing; his thoughts dwelt on what Eben Howell had said.

But they were interrupted at last by a question from the older man. "How's your mother?"

"Mama?" Owen was surprised. "Why, she's all right; fine, I guess." He saw the other's confusion. "Why?"

Eben hesitated. "I thought you knew. Charles Morgan told me she was pretty sick."

"Mama?" Owen's mouth was open.

"That's too bad. Sorry I said anything. But maybe it's just as well you don't walk into it blind. Yes, she's sick abed, not getting any better." Before Owen could speak, Eben added mercifully: "Nor not going to, Owen."

Owen could not breathe; it was as though a band about his chest were tightening. Howell laid his hand on his knee and clasped his leg in a hard grip, thinking as he did so how thin and wasted was the leg under his hand.

Owen asked at last: "What's the matter with her?"

"Cancer."

"Why didn't papa write and tell me? Why didn't someone?" And when Howell did not reply, "Who's taking care of her?"

.

"Mrs. Morgan and the neighbors. She's been looked out for, and Tom too. He's worked right along."

Owen took off his wide-brimmed hat and with it fanned himself; his face was streaming. "I'm so darned weak it doesn't take much to make me sweat."

"You must have been pretty sick."

"I guess so. They said so. It's going to scare mama, seeing me like this."

"She'll be so glad to see you she won't notice."

Except for an occasional empty word they spoke no more, parting at Belton where Howell turned homeward while Owen boarded a Belt Line car. It was late enough in the afternoon so that he thought his father might be waiting at the Miss Ellen siding, and the possibility filled him with dread; but though Isaac Williams and a dozen other men whom Owen knew boarded the car, Tom Glen did not appear.

Owen and Isaac sat together where just inside the door their seat faced other seats across the car; but they were part of a group made up of the men across the car and the men beside them, and Owen's friends had many questions which he must answer, so not till they alighted at the end of the line on Broad Street were he and Isaac alone together. Then Owen asked, "How's mama?"

"The same." Isaac remembered Owen had not been told of her illness. "Where'd you hear about her?"

"Eben Howell was on the train from Columbus."

"She didn't want you to know. Marged's been helping take care of her." Isaac hesitated. "Marged says your mama's scared for fear you'll think she looks bad. That's all she worries over, whether she'll look ugly and awful to you."

Owen wetted his lips, he swallowed hard. "How's papa?"

"All right. He's been getting out a pile of coal." And Isaac said thoughtfully: "I wouldn't wonder if he puts in extra shots, just to keep from getting home early. I expect it's pretty hard for him, seeing it hurt her so."

"Hurt?"

"Yes. Doctor Gorman gives her something that helps; but cancer hurts, Owen."

Owen remembered those occasions when he had seen in his mother's face a twist of pain, and he set his jaw and quickened his pace. When he came up to Ridge Street, Mrs. Morgan appeared on her front porch as though expecting him to stop, but he avoided meeting her eyes and hurried on down toward the small house that was home.

There was no movement at any window, no one threw wide the door. He hesitated for an instant, then turned the latch. His mother was sitting in her low rocking chair across the room, facing the door; and he strode toward her with a happy cry. He knelt to hold her and kiss her, and to lean back and look at her; and then, laughing:

"Why, they told me you were sick! You don't look sick to me! You're as pretty as a girl!"

She held one of his hands with her weak hand. "You've been sick, Owen. You've been sick."

"I'm not now, but I was. They fed us on stuff a pig wouldn't eat, and that got me down, but I'm all right now." He laughed and hugged her gently. "The sight of you would cure me, anyway."

She touched his side with a finger like a claw. "You're thin as a picked bird."

"I was too fat before. Say, mama, you certainly look fine. How's papa?"

"He'll be home soon." She said: "Mrs. Lewis has been doing for me. This is the first day I've been up for quite a while."

Her eyes, as she spoke, had turned across the room, and he saw Mrs. Lewis sitting by the table, her knitting lying in her lap, her eyes streaming. He rose to shake her hand.

"Hello, Mrs. Lewis. How's everyone at your house? How's Nellie?"

"Married and gone," she said. "Married to Jenkin Powell."

Owen nodded. "I know. She told me that, long ago." He remembered that it was because of Jenkin's mother they had kept their secret, and was about to ask what had happened to her; but Mrs. Lewis might say Jenkin's mother was dead, and Owen did not think he could stand that, not now when his own mother was so weary and frail and colorless. "Good for them."

"She's still working at the *Journal* office. Walks all the way to town and back every day. Jenkin's a real good farmer. Mis' Tutson's helped me take care of your mama."

Owen's mother spoke, her voice uncertain. "Marged was here

after dinner, too, Owen. She's been here a lot, but she thought I'd want you to myself for a while." Mrs. Lewis sniffed expressively, and Mrs. Glen made haste to add: "Mrs. Lewis has just done everything for me, Owen. I don't know what I'd have done without her."

"I've been glad to do anything I could, I'm sure." Mrs. Lewis rose, tucking her needles through the sock, pinning it to the ball of yarn. "It's high time I got you back to bed, Annie, before Tom comes home."

In the excitement of expecting Owen, Mrs. Glen had been able to help herself to her chair; but now she could not rise, so he carried her to the bed, laughing down at her in his arms. "You've carried me many's the time, mama. Turn about's just fair." She smiled up at him and tried to put her arm around his neck, lifting it gropingly; but her strength failed, she let it fall again.

While Mrs. Lewis undressed her, Owen went out-of-doors, feeling pent and stifled, wishing he could cry; but no tears came. He walked around the house, deciding the pig would need a lot of fattening before it was ready to be butchered. Probably the cow was dry before now. Then he saw Tom Glen coming down the road from Ridge Street and went to meet him, to clasp hands.

"Well, son, I'm glad you're home. Guess you've seen mama."

"Yes. She's pretty sick."

They moved down toward the house. "Well, she's had a little upset," Tom explained. "She'll be all right by and by."

Owen looked at him in astonishment, and then in sudden swelling anger; but he held his tongue. If Tom still nursed this comforting delusion, let him do so while he could.

3

Owen was weaker than he knew. The excitement of homecoming and then the dreadful shock of revelation at first acted as a stimulant; to know his mother needed his love and his tender comforting gave him a fictitious strength, but that night dreams harassed him, and dawn found him red-eyed and weary to exhaustion. He woke to an uneasy certainty that something was wrong; he and his father should have been up long ago, eating the breakfast his mother prepared, tramping off to take the early car. More fully awake, he knew his mother would never again get breakfast for them; yet since it was full day outside, his father must be gone. He rose and went softly into the kitchen, and from her bed his mother spoke.

"Owen? Good morning, sonny. Better get some clothes on before you take your death of cold."

"Where's papa?"

"Up and gone. Mrs. Morgan gives him his breakfast."

"I'll start the fire, then get dressed."

He moved to the familiar task, but at once he began to know his weakness. He laid the fire and lighted it and put the kettle on, and he asked his mother what he could prepare for her; but when she shook her head, he knew a deep relief. Back in his room, instead of dressing, he lay down on his bed again.

He slept till late forenoon, not waking when Mrs. Lewis came, not till he heard Doctor Gorman's deep tones as he spoke with her in the kitchen. Even then, Owen did not rise. Doctor Gorman looked in on him and saw that he was awake and came to sit on the edge of his bed, studying Owen with quiet eyes, touching his pulse. "You'd better stay in bed, at least for today. You're run down, and pretty tired. We don't want you sick on our hands."

Owen wished to ask questions, but he dreaded the answers. It was easier to imitate his father, to pretend that his mother's illness was "just a little upset." Mrs. Lewis brought him soup for dinner, and he sat up to eat it and then pulled a quilt over his shoulders and went to kiss his mother, to tease her because she was so pretty. "Prettiest girl I ever saw, mama." She smiled so happily that he could not stay with her. Back in his bed, sleep rose like a tide and drowned him. Once when a light shone in his eyes, he half-roused; but he slept again, and woke in the pallid dawn.

This second morning he was stronger. He rose and dressed and went to build the fire in the stove. Tom Glen, stretching and yawning, gaunt in his union suit, came from the bedroom into the kitchen. Owen, in a sudden surge of abhorrence, thought Tom had shared her bed; but looking past his father he saw a mattress and a tumble of quilts on the floor beside the bed, where Tom had lain. He met his mother's eyes and went in to her, drawing the mattress away so he could reach her side; and she said huskily:

"That's papa's bed, so I can touch him if I'm lonesome in the

night. I'd rather have him sleep with me, but I'm so hot he can't
rest if he does."

"I'll make you a cup of tea." Owen brushed his hand across his
mouth.

"You had a fine sleep, son. Marged came yesterday afternoon,
and Mrs. Tutson and Nellie last night, and Will Davis stopped by;
but you slept through them all."

His father was at home that day, and Mrs. Lewis came early.
"I always bathe your mama Saturdays — and Wednesdays too —
so she won't get bed sores," she explained. "It tires her, but afterward she'll take one of her capsules and sleep till she's rested up."

Owen, afraid of being in the way, went out-of-doors; but then,
guessing that Mrs. Lewis might be some time about this task, and
remembering that his mother afterward would sleep and rest, he
returned to get his hat and started for town. He meant to go to the
Journal office, but as he came to the corner of Belton Street he
decided to stop and see Marged on the way.

He approached the house in a pleasant stir of anticipation, but
Marged was not there. Mrs. Williams told him she had gone home
for the day, and she explained: "Marged came up right away when
she knew your mother was sick, and she didn't take time to pack.
She's gone down now to get her trunk before school starts, but she's
coming up on the afternoon train."

Owen was surprisingly disappointed. "Well, I'll see her at church
tomorrow then," he said. "Or I might come down this evening."

When he reached the *Journal* office, Mr. Beecham was out, so he
went through the pressroom and spoke to Will, and Nellie heard
him and came running down the stairs.

"Owen! Oh, I'm glad to see you!" Her eyes were shining, and
she kissed him and hugged him and kissed him again. "There!
But my! you're thin. I heard you were sick."

"I'm all right now."

"Everybody's awful sorry about your mother."

He nodded. "I hear you and Jenkin are living out at his farm
now."

"Yes. His mother —" She caught herself, and he said reassuringly:

"I guess she died. That's all right. Lots of people do, Nellie. I
had two boys die in the next bed to mine, in the hospital. They
just — well just sort of let go and die, like going to sleep. I think

the way it is, when it comes time to die, you don't mind. I'm going to try and have it that way for mama."

Will, here beside them, nodded in assent. "I was there when my father died, and my mother too. They didn't mind. They were ready." Yet his brows contracted with a wrench of anxiety, and Owen looked at Nellie, and she said in mirthful wrath:

"For Heaven's sake, Will, stop worrying! She's going to be just fine!"

"Oh, sure. I know she is. I know."

Owen had forgotten the expected baby. He grinned, and Nellie shook Will's arm. "You Welshmen! You'd rather talk about dying than anything! Owen, come on up and say hello to the others. Barbara Henson's learning, so she can take my place when I —" Her cheeks suddenly glowed; she laughed proudly. "You remember Barbara, Owen. She was in your room in school."

Owen nodded and he and Will went up with her and stayed in talk with the three girls there till the wheel at the head of the stairs whirled, bringing up some fresh copy, and Owen called:

"Hello, Mr. Beecham!"

The editor waited for him at the stair-foot, beaming. "Well, they thinned you down some, Owen. Feeling all right now?"

"Just about."

"Come along." Owen followed him into the front office. David Ames was there, his great bulk sprawling, a leg over the arm of his chair; and Herbert Canter sat beside him. Owen, sorry not to have Mr. Beecham to himself, greeted them, and BB explained: "We've been talking about the future, Owen."

"You mean on account of the war?"

"Yes. Yes, we're a world power now." BB chuckled, and as Owen sat down the editor said to the others: "Owen's heard me say, more than once, that the United States was like a boy coming into his 'teens. This country was born — after a long and painful travail — in 1788, when with New Hampshire's ratification, the Constitution ceased to be a scrap of paper. The mewling, puking infant grew fast. When he was two or three years old — say, two or three decades — he discharged his nurse, ran away from Mother England for good and all. Another three or four years — decades — and he began to steal Mexico's playthings and bully the little boy who lived next door. Then he had a bad attack of indigestion and hasn't fully recovered even now. But now he's been keeping company with a pretty *señorita* — and has to face the consequences. We've been making violent love to Cuba and the Philippines, and now we've got to do right by the poor girls."

Herbert Canter said flatly: "Annex them. That's the way to build up our markets. That's what other nations have done."

"What do you think, Dave?"

Mr. Ames moved to the door to clear his mouth of tobacco. "Well, they're ours if we want 'em; but I wouldn't wonder if it wouldn't cost us more to keep 'em than they're worth."

"Yet perhaps we should pay that price," BB suggested. "We've become the great champions of humanitarianism in the world. That's a proud position, but it carries obligations."

"Hold on to them both," Canter repeated. "We can make a profit out of them and do them some good at the same time, give their people a chance to live decently. That's the humanitarian thing to do."

Owen came slowly to his feet; he crossed to the desk where the ledgers were kept; he set his back to it, resting his elbows on it. "I'm a great believer in humanitarianism," he said. "I'm all for it. But let's be humanitarian to our own people before we go taking care of people all over the world, or we might not have enough humanitarianism to go 'round." He looked thoughtfully at Mr. Canter. "You talk about living decently. I know men who work for you and who live in houses with mud floors and cracks clear through their walls; and they pay you enough rent to buy the house in two years." Canter rose in swift anger, but Owen said: "Don't get hot under the collar, Mr. Canter. I'm not down on you, or any other one man — unless maybe it's someone like Mr. DeArmitt, and I expect even he's got his points, if you knew him. But by Gollies!" He swung toward BB. "Before we start spreading humanitarianism all over the world, I'm going to bring up my dish for a lot of it here at home!"

Mr. Canter said curtly: "We've gone a long way to meet the demands of you and men like you, Glen. Aren't you ever going to be satisfied?"

"Satisfied?" Owen laughed. "Why, Mr. Canter, as soon as any-one's satisfied, he begins to die — and it don't take him long!" His tone changed, became almost accusing. "That's the trouble with this country, Mr. Canter! That's what's holding us back. You, and

men like you, you're too easily satisfied! As soon as you make a lot
of money, you stop trying to find new ways to make more money!"

He repeated the word. "Satisfied? No, I'm never going to be
satisfied! As long as I live — I'm speaking for myself and for as
many miners as will let me speak for them — I'm going to keep
wanting more and more and more. All we've got to work with is
our muscles. We can dig all the coal in the world, but that won't
make the world any better than it is. You, and men like you, you've
got to do that, with your brains. The more money we can make
you pay us, Mr. Canter, the harder you'll have to work; and that's
what this country needs, men like you, working as hard as they can.
You've got money because you've got brains and because you've
used them. Well, we're going to make you keep your brain working, you and Frick and Carnegie and Pullman and the rest. Because the harder you work, the greater country this will be!" He
stopped, suddenly conscious that his voice had risen, that the three
men were watching him with blank eyes. "Well, I guess I got
started," he said.

For a moment no one spoke. Then Mr. Canter grunted, his beard
bristling. "Started? I should say you did! And you'll be a hard man
to stop. Gentlemen, good day!"

4

Owen after supper thought of Marged, but his mother called him
to sit beside her, and she kept him there, her thin fingers clasping his.
For a while she asked questions, till her strength leaked away and
she could only lie looking up at him. As dusk fell, she whispered,
"It's getting so dark I can't see you, Owen." He lighted the lamp,
and she said: "Best have our prayers, son. My capsule makes me
sleep soon." So Tom Glen came from the kitchen, and Owen read
a chapter from the Bible, and he and his father knelt beside the bed
while Tom prayed.

Tom returned to the kitchen and set a match to the lamp there,
and Owen stayed with his mother till she fell asleep. When her
clasp on his hand relaxed, he blew out the lamp and went into the
kitchen. Tom Glen was asleep in his chair, but at Owen's step he
woke and stood up, stretching and yawning. Owen made a sign for

silence, and Tom nodded and took off his outer garments and in his long underwear went to spread his pallet by her bed. When he lay down, light from the lamp in the kitchen touched him, and as though she had roused a little at his coming, Mrs. Glen let her arm hang over the side of the bed to rest on his shoulder, and Owen envied his father her long love.

Mrs. Tutson came next morning to stay with Mrs. Glen while Owen and Tom went to church. As they entered the building, Owen saw Marged with Isaac Williams and Mrs. Williams and Morgan in their accustomed place, and wished to go at once to speak to her, but before they reached their pew, the minister stepped into the pulpit, so that must wait.

Yet during the services Owen found himself watching Marged, four rows in front of him and a little to one side, and remembering how he had watched her long ago in Sardis Church even before she became his teacher at Redfern School. When the service was over, he waited for her on the sidewalk. As she approached, he had an absurd impulse to laugh at nothing, but he controlled it. They shook hands, and as they had done so many times before, moved away together. Tom Glen and Isaac Williams came behind them, and then Mrs. Morgan and Mrs. Williams and all the others whose homeward routes coincided for a while with theirs.

"I was watching you in church," said Owen, "and thinking how I used to watch you in church at Sardis, before I knew who you were or anything."

She looked up at him with smiling eyes. "Seems like a long time ago, doesn't it?"

He nodded. "It is, too," he said seriously. "I wasn't but six or seven years old. It's all of twelve years. That's two thirds of my life. It's a long time to me."

"Your mother's happy, having you home."

"I slept all the first day."

"I know. You were asleep when I was there." She added quietly: "She dreaded having you see her, till I told her you'd been sick. Then she forgot herself, worrying about you. Are you all right now? You're pretty thin."

"I'll put it on again quick, the way I did when I was getting over typhoid. I was really thin, then." He felt a vague dissatisfaction with their conversation. In camp and in the hospital, he had found it pleasant to think about Marged, and to anticipate seeing her again. Without putting his thoughts into words, he had somehow come to great expectations not now fulfilled. Under cover of their almost absent-minded interchanges, he tried to remember what it was he had expected, why this hour now so completely failed to satisfy. He had looked forward to walking home from church with her, and the anticipation had been wonderful; but the reality was nothing. At the corner of Belton Street, they waited till the others came up with them, then parted; that was all.

As his strength returned and he was able to work again, Owen settled easily into routine. He rose early to cook breakfast for his father and himself; then, knowing Mrs. Lewis would soon be here to tend his mother, he and Tom Glen went off to the electric car and to the mine. They came home to find Mrs. Lewis or Mrs. Tutson at the house with Mrs. Glen, and supper well started; and when he had bathed, Owen took over the meal-time tasks while his mother was made ready for the night. On days when the mine did not work, Owen stayed much with her. His father was not so closely by her side; for though winter's forerunners began to touch the rows with frost, Tom still tended the garden and still found out-of-doors small chores to do, not lending himself to the house-keeping tasks to which Owen easily turned.

Yet it was Tom who slept every night on the mattress at her bed-side, within touch of her reaching hand; and sometimes Owen was awakened by the murmur of their voices as they talked together in the night, and he wondered what it was of which they spoke to-gether, and felt himself excluded from that close communion which was the fruit of sweet and heartening habit through the years. He thought his father lucky for having had, so long, her ear to listen to his hurts, her tongue to strengthen him. Owen, because there was in the world no one so close to him as she was to his father, felt himself the loneliest of the lone.

The mine was busy, and his strength was quick to return, and the joy of labor flowed into him and filled him. He found changes. Moses Evans had put in a six-ton motor to haul the cars, and if it proved successful he proposed to abandon the use of mules; but for the present the motor was forever going out of order so that at frequent intervals the mules took up their task again. The Loader, the machine which BB said would end pick mining, had come into use in many other mines, but not here. There was a new pattern of lamp not so smoky as the old.

Except for these small changes, and except that his mother was abed and seemed neither better nor worse from day to day, and except that every evening when he came home he found at the house either Mrs. Lewis or Mrs. Tutson, Owen's world was little changed. Days were chips on the flowing river of time; the future became the present, the present became the past. Will Davis came one morning with a smile that touched his ears; the new baby was a boy, to be named David, and everything was fine. The *Journal* reported the memorial service in Hazelton, Pennsylvania, for the miners shot down at Lattimer a year ago; John Fahey, who had worked as an organizer in the region, was now president of the District and had been the principal speaker. After that first acquittal, all other charges against the Sheriff and his deputies had been abandoned. Jane Lloyd, Betty Myers and Tom Powell were gone off to college in Athens; Morgan Williams was at Oberlin, Janet Frye at Ohio State. Their names came to Owen like the names of strangers.

Normally, he finished his day's work earlier than his father. This was at first because he tired more easily; and later, when his strength had in great degree returned, it was because he liked to come home in good season in order to relieve Mrs. Lewis or help her tend his mother. Since they now travelled to and from Hardiston by the electric cars, which ran at frequent intervals, he had no need to wait for the miners' train.

Owen found that the talk in the cars clung more and more to matters concerning the Union; there was in the men a new unity, a new purpose. Eben Howell was visiting every mine in the District to inspect the screens and make sure they conformed to the new agreement. He found many either out of repair — the story ran that he had thrown his hat through one — or of too large a mesh. These he required to be replaced, under threat of striking the offending mine. The demand for coal was heavy, the mines were busy; yet elsewhere in the state there was idleness. At Jobs, the mines had closed April 1 and thrown eight or nine hundred men out of work; the prediction was that those mines would never be reopened. In Hardiston County the shortage of cars was the only brake on production; but one Sunday afternoon, the mine that day not running, Owen stopped in the *Journal* office and heard from BB a dark prediction.

The day of Ohio as a coal-producing state, BB thought, was

done. "Last year, West Virginia produced more coal than we did — and we'll never catch up with her again."

"Last year it was the strike that cut us down," Owen argued. "The strike didn't hardly touch West Virginia."

"She has more coal than we have," BB insisted. "At the current rate of mining here, the coal in Hardiston County won't last twenty-five years. And actually the current rate will be speeded up by machines."

"And by the night-hawk jaspers," Owen agreed. "Eben Howell gave them fits at the meeting yesterday. He wants the operators to lock up their mines every night, the way we do at Miss Ellen, so the jaspers can't get in. The eight-hour day won't amount to much unless we can stop that sort of thing." He smiled confidently. "But I guess the coal around here will last as long as I do. If it doesn't, I'll go to West Virginia."

"West Virginia is the rock on which your Union will sink or swim," BB predicted. "If you can't organize West Virginia, you're lost. There's coal enough there to break any strike — and the operators have the Southern point of view; they believe labor has no rights."

Owen's eyes narrowed with a warmth of anger. "I wouldn't mind going there to live, to work, to help get the Union established."

BB nodded; he swung his chair and faced his desk, and Owen rose to go. "You haven't been over to see our house," BB suggested. "We're about ready to move in."

"Bertie said last summer you were going to have a bathroom."

"Yes, a tank in the attic, lined with lead; and we'll pump water up from the cistern. And furnace heat. It's the first bathroom in Hardiston, and there aren't more than a dozen vapor furnaces."

"I'll come over some day," Owen agreed, and the other's pride made him remember the day years ago when they stopped to talk to Evan Foster and to admire the house Evan and his wife and his brother had built, and which they were roofing that day with flattened powder tins. Evan had been as proud that day as Mr. Beecham was now; but of course, anyone who could build a house of his own had reason to be proud.

Early in October, Owen began to hear on the cars and at the mine talk of possible trouble in Illinois. Here and there throughout the Central Competitive Field, operators still refused to abide by the agreement reached last December and now almost a year old. In each case, the Union called a strike to force the operators to accept the scale and thus meet their competitors on equal terms. In Illinois the Chicago Virden Coal Company decided to import Negroes from Alabama to take the place of the strikers; they built a stockade around the mine and hired armed guards to protect the Negroes when they should arrive.

The day the Negroes were expected, Owen came home in mid-afternoon. When he reached the house he saw that although the day was cool and almost cold, and the house none too warm, Mrs. Lewis and his mother were perspiring. He suspected his mother had endured a storm of pain, and he sent Mrs. Lewis home and stayed with his mother, delaying any movement to put supper under way, waiting till his father should come home.

But Tom did not come, and it was time for him, and past time; and Owen was grateful because his mother, drowsy with drugs, content to hold his hand and feel him near, asked no fretful questions. The sun had set and darkness began to fall before a knock summoned Owen to the door.

Charles Morgan faced him there. "Come outside," he said softly; and when Owen had done so: "Tom's hurt, Owen. The motor-hauler went out of order today, and they were using mules, and there was one that wasn't broke. It started to act up, and it lifted on Tom, and he fell off the car against the mule's heels and it bucked and kicked him and dragged the car over his legs."

"Is he bad?" Owen did not know his own voice.

"Well, he's alive. We took him to the hospital. They had to cut off one leg up close to the knee, and most of his other foot; but Doctor Roy thinks he'll be all right."

He checked on the word, turning quickly at a sound half-heard; and after a moment someone came through the darkness behind him and spoke. It was Marged. "Have you told Owen, Mr. Morgan?"

"Yes."

"I'll help him take care of Mrs. Glen." She came to Owen's side and he turned with her.

"Much obliged, Mr. Morgan," he said, and he and Marged went indoors.

XXVI

October 12, 1898 — December 31, 1898

WHEN THE DOOR was closed behind them, Marged said quietly: "Sit with your mother, Owen. I'll get you some supper."

Owen, submissive, went to his mother's side; her hand touched his. "Papa come?" she murmured drowsily.

"Right away, mama. He's — " He hesitated. "You better have a capsule." He brought the medicine and a glass of water. Let her sleep, let her sleep.

Doctor Roy thinks he will be all right; that was what Charles Morgan had said. But — all right? With both legs gone? Tom Glen legless and almost blind would not be all right! If his mother died — when his mother died — Owen would be left to tend the father he hated, the man who had bruised her and broken her, who had used her flesh and her strength and her spirit as weapons against every foe. Charles Morgan, Isaac Williams, Eben Howell — these men were as old as his father and their wives were as old as his mother, but their wives were well and jolly and laughing, they were not such weary wasted wraiths as she.

She was so weak that he must lift her head, place the capsule between her lips, hold the glass. She gulped the capsule, sipped the water, let her eyes smile up at him, let them close.

He sat beside her till she surely slept, then went to Marged. "I gave her some medicine. She'll probably sleep all night."

Marged poured coffee for him and for herself; bacon was sizzling on the stove. "And I found some cold potatoes. I'll fry them, with a slice or two of onions. What else would you like, Owen?"

"Nothing. That's enough." His thoughts were not of food; he tried to adjust himself to the world as he must face it now. Perhaps this was his punishment because he hated his father; he bowed

under that guilt, his face in his hands. Marged stood by the stove,
slicing onions into the skillet, slicing the cold potatoes; the bacon
drained on brown paper in the open oven. Her eyes rested on
Owen's bent head, and at last he looked up, and as though he saw
her for the first time he asked:

"Where'd you come from?"

"Uncle Isaac told us about your father when he came home. I
thought you might want — well, might want some company."

He seemed not to hear. "I don't see what I'm going to do." She
waited and he said, in slow fragments: "You think of a million
things — all in a minute. All the times I've — argued with him,
quarrelled with him. When I came home from Tampa and saw the
way mama was — he said it was just a little upset. I got so I hated
him. Other men, they've been coal miners all their — lives, but
their wives aren't worn out. Maybe she wouldn't have got sick if
she hadn't been all the time so tired. That was his fault — anyway,
I thought so — I'd got so I hated him. Maybe that brought it on
him — to have this happen." His slow words slowed and stopped.

"Here." She heaped his plate, then sat down facing him, moving
aside the lamp between them.

"You going to eat anything?"

"We'd had supper before Uncle Isaac came home. He went with
Charles Morgan and Mr. Powell, taking your father to the hospital,
so he was late."

He ate slowly and with care, as though it were something he
had never done before. "The only way I can get along — with him
home — is have Mrs. Lewis here when I'm at the mine. Mama says
Mrs. Lewis won't take any pay. I can't have her if she don't. There
has to be somebody. I can't take care of them and work too."

She let him talk, let him think aloud, let his confused thoughts
take form.

"I'll have to tell her in the morning." He met Marged's eyes.
"Lately, he's slept on a mattress on the floor by her bed, so if she
waked up in the night, and wanted to, she could reach down and
touch him. I'll sleep there tonight. She might reach for him in her
sleep and not feel him and be scared." He ate, tentatively, for a
while. "When she wakes up she'll want to know where he is."

Someone knocked, and Marged went to open the door. Mrs.
Lewis came in. "I just heard about it," she said. "I thought there
might be something I could do."

Owen looked toward his mother's room. "She doesn't know about it yet. I gave her another capsule."

"I had to give her more than I generally do, before you came home. If you gave her another, she'll sleep till morning." Mrs. Lewis took off her cape and went into the bedroom. Marged sat with Owen. He continued, meticulously, to convey food from his plate to his mouth, to chew it and swallow it.

She said: "You'll want to see your father tomorrow."

"Yes. After I'm through at the mine. Before I come home."

Mrs. Lewis returned. "I'll come early in the morning," she said. "So you can get away. And I'll stay all day till you come."

Marged said: "I'll come as soon as school's out."

"The mine won't run Saturday," Owen reflected. This was Wednesday night. "I'll be home all day Saturday and Sunday."

Mrs. Lewis asked: "Want I should stay the night, Owen?"

"No. Much obliged, though. You couldn't do any more for us if we were your own folks."

She looked toward the dark bedroom. "Annie and me got to be real good friends. She was a comfort to me when Freeman was took."

"That was while I had typhoid."

"Yes. I had a son might have been like you. I'm glad I can help out a little now, kind of make it up to her."

She lingered while Marged washed his plate and cup and saucer, and cleaned the skillet and scalded it, and turned it upside down atop the stove to dry. "I'll go straighten out her bedclothes," she said then, and lighted another lamp and she and Marged went into the bedroom together and closed the door. After a time they returned. "She's all right now till I come in the morning," Mrs. Lewis said, and put on her cape, moving to the door. Marged came near him.

"You must get some sleep, Owen."

"Yes." He was already half-asleep, bludgeoned and dull. "Sure. I will."

She stood uncertainly. "Goodnight."

He wished she would stay, dreaded the lonely hours. "Goodnight."

She turned reluctantly, joined Mrs. Lewis, and the door closed behind them.

Owen took the lamp into his mother's room. He unrolled the

mattress by her bedside, spread blankets across it. He undressed, put on his nightshirt, blew out the lamps and lay down on the pallet beside her. The mattress was somewhat hollowed where his father's weight had shaped it; it received him like a kind embrace. To take here his father's place filled him with fierce secret pride, and he reached up to find his mother's hand and clasped it in his own.

He thought that even in her drugged sleep she answered the pressure of his fingers; but if he went to sleep thus holding her hand, his arm would fall of its own weight, and that might wake her. He took his hand away, and thought gently of his father forever maimed and helpless. So sleep received him.

2

Additional Locals: The phone service out of Hardiston has been enlarged, and it is now possible to talk to people in Key West, Denver, St. Paul, and many other large cities. In five years every small town will have the telephone. Frederick Ames, son of Mr. and Mrs. David Ames, who was at home on furlough, was killed by a train in Belton Monday; he was standing on a platform beside the track when a freight train passed, and the platform collapsed and threw him under the cars; he had charged up San Juan Hill, receiving only a slight wound, and then came home to meet his death. At the election September 19, Hardiston voted almost unanimously to construct a city waterworks. A Congressional Committee will sift the charges of criminal neglect of our soldiers in the field; Owen Glen of Hardiston was one of many poisoned by rotten food, but he has recovered his strength. Mrs. Mabel Harrison, deaf and dumb, was killed by the electric cars at Glendale Saturday. The Woman's Literary Club held its first meeting of the season Monday, October 3. We beat Spain in spite of the mistakes of our officers and because of the high quality of our soldiers. Jim Tower and Fred Ford went rabbit hunting Saturday; Jim's gun went off accidentally while he was climbing through a fence, and he was instantly killed. Howard Jones is dead of fever in Florida; he is the third Hardiston County boy to die of disease, but bullets killed no one from this county. Thomas Glen lost both feet October

12 when a loaded mine car ran over him in Miss Ellen Mine; the accident was caused by a half-broken mule; he is reported doing as well as could be expected. Another massacre, as outrageous as that in Lattimer, Pennsylvania, a year ago, occurred last week in Illinois; the United States Navy lost only seventeen men in the war, but fourteen men were shot and killed in a few minutes at the mines of the Chicago-Virden Coal Company; the company imported Negroes from Alabama to take the jobs of striking miners; strikers barred their way into the company stockade; firing started and in a matter of seconds fourteen men fell dead; of the dead, ten were miners, four were guards. It is time our mine-owners ceased to act as though they were Spanish generals and their miners were friendless Cubans. *A Daughter of Cuba,* coming to the Rink Friday, is reported to be a pure, wholesome drama. A goodly host of ministers were in town last week for the United Brethren Conference. Thomas Glen, who lost both feet as a result of a mining accident, will come home next Saturday; his wounds healed by first intention. The Senate Investigating Committee reports that "authorized agents and representatives of Marcus A. Hanna attempted to bribe John C. Otis, a member of the Ohio House of Representatives, to vote for him for United States Senator." The committee's report, a 261-page pamphlet, is mighty interesting reading. Come to the polls November 8 and vote to vindicate Hanna. Patrick Hood of Glendale is the fourth Hardiston County boy to die of fever in Florida. The farce, *A Hired Girl,* will be at the Rink next Monday night.

3

Owen, during the weeks after his father's hurt, tried to escape from thought by working himself each day to the edge of exhaustion. His mother was so much under the influence of drugs that she did not always know him. Once, holding his hand, thinking him his father, she whispered: "Don't weep for me, Tom dear. I'm going to Jesus, and Jesus and I have been loving each other since I was a little girl." When she knew Owen and asked for Tom, Owen told her the truth; but it seemed not to penetrate into the secret world to which her thoughts were now withdrawn, for she nodded in apparent understanding and content. Owen, troubled by this, spoke to Doctor Gorman, and the doctor explained:

"She doesn't really know much that's happening, Owen."

Owen slept every night beside her bed; and Mrs. Lewis often stayed overnight, sleeping in Owen's room where she was within instant call. During the day, Mrs. Morgan frequently came down from her home on the corner to give Mrs. Lewis some relief, or Mrs. Tutson might take her place for a while; and Marged spent each Saturday at the house. But Owen, because work was his best anodyne, asked and receivd John Powell's permission to work on Saturday, even when the mine did not run. He made himself drunk with work; it was escape and solace too.

He went regularly to see his father, taking a northbound car to Bolton after his day in the mine. There was no comfort for Owen in these visits to the older man. Tom Glen vented his black despair in anger at those around him — and at Owen most of all. He was sure that Doctor Roy had neither need nor right nor reason to cut off his legs. The left, he insisted, was only broken; it could have been set. As for the right: "Why, I no more than mashed a couple of toes! Maybe he might have had to trim it up a little, trim off the ragged edges; but no — it's off with the foot for him!" He said Doctor Roy was a butcher, and he was convinced that the nurses and attendants, since he was helpless and at their mercy here, paid him no attention. He was starved, or parched with thirst, or too cold, or too hot, day after day.

Owen at first tried to comfort him, to quiet and appease him, until he began to see that Tom took pleasure in these tirades. It was as though by shouting in a great voice, by issuing commands even when they were not obeyed, by threatening and bluster, he convinced himself that — feet or no feet — he was still a master. With this understanding, Owen learned patience and sympathy; and his words and his tone toward the broken old man became altogether gentle and kind.

Tom never asked how Mrs. Glen was, and Owen at last understood that his father dared not ask, that he knew her illness was much more than "just a little upset." So without waiting for a question, Owen on each visit said some word about his mother. "Mama sent her love." Or: "Mama had a good night." Or: "Mama's about the same." Tom received these bulletins without comment, staring at the wall beyond the foot of the bed, speaking at once of other times.

When the time approached for him to leave the hospital, he was the first to acknowledge difficulties ahead. "I'll be underfoot all the time, and in the way. By the time I get a peg or something fitted onto this stump, I can maybe learn to go on crutches; but it'll be quite a spell. With you gone to work all day, Mrs. Lewis couldn't handle me."

Owen saw the difficulties as clearly as his father, but one evening when he arrived at the hospital he found Tom in high good humor. "Amy was here today," he explained. "She says the thing for me to do is go home with her. She's already got a houseful, and one more won't matter. She's going to have Dave come with the wagon Saturday and carry me down there."

"Don't you want to be at home with mama?"

"You couldn't do for both of us there. You talk it over with mama, see if she don't say the same."

"How'd Amy come up?" Owen spoke absently, weighing and accepting Amy's plan even while he half-resented the fact that she and his father had decided upon it without consulting him.

"Morning train. She says I can stop Saturday and say hello to mama on the way to the farm."

If they were to do that, Owen reflected, he and Dave would have to carry Tom into the house; but though this was easily done, his mother would not know Tom when he came. For days now, Owen himself had been "Tom" to her. "She won't know you, papa," he said. "She's pretty near asleep most of the time."

Tom stared at the wall; he closed his eyes. "I wouldn't want to wake her up. She needs rest, like as not." He added grimly, "I'd as soon she didn't see me like this, anyhow."

Early Sunday morning, Dave stopped at the house to pick up Owen. The bed of the wagon was well stuffed with hay, upon which lay a mattress and a pile of folded quilts and blankets. Owen, tossing into the wagon a bundle containing his father's Sunday clothes and a warm overcoat, climbed into the seat with Dave and they took the Belton road.

The drive seemed to him a long one. He could not remember that he had ever been alone with Dave before. Also, he was embarrassed and ashamed that Dave and Amy must take care of his

father. They would have to do it, because he could not; but this
would mean extra work for both of them, and there was no reason
why Dave should shoulder the burden of his wife's crippled relatives. Besides, Amy had enough to do, with her children and Dave
and his father and the house, and with Dave's mother so bloated
with dropsy that she could only move from bed to chair and from
chair to bed. Thinking these things, Owen could find nothing to
say, and for the two hours or so that they were on the way, the
young men sat in silence broken only by Dave's commands to the
horses and by a rare and empty word.

At the hospital, while Dave and Tom watched him, Owen began
to open the bundle containing his father's clothes. He unfolded
the heavy paper, and then he stopped in a hard embarrassment; for
there on top of the neatly folded suit rested his father's best pair of
shoes.

Owen had packed them unthinkingly; it was too late to hide them
now. He looked at his father, his mouth open, his breath caught;
and Tom Glen stared at the shoes, and his face burned red and
then it paled again. Abruptly he began to laugh, in a quiet, chuckling, secret way. He met Owen's eyes.

"Joke on you, son," he said.

"I forgot, papa."

"You won't have to buy me any more shoes, from now on. Well,
help me set up. You boys'll have to dress me."

On the drive back to Hardiston, Owen sat with his father in the
bed of the wagon. Tom was in a humor almost jolly; but as they
drew near the house, he became silent and his eyes closed. Owen
thought he might be asleep.

They stopped at the roadside above the house, and Owen helped
his father sit up so that he could look at their home. Then Marged
came out of the house and toward them; and Owen saw Mrs. Lewis
in the doorway behind her. Marged climbed on the hub of the
front wheel, leaning in to clasp Tom's hand. "Hello, Mr. Glen.
I'm glad to see you again." She looked down at Owen, standing
now in the road beside her, then back at his father. "Are you
coming in?"

"Is she awake?"

"No. No, she's asleep. She sleeps most of the time, you know."

Tom tugged at her hand, and she shifted her feet on the

hub for greater security, and leaned down near him. He said in a low tone, "Marged, you tell her goodbye for me." She lifted his hand and pressed it to her cheek, not speaking; and Tom Glen lay back and his eyes closed. "You tell her goodbye for me," he repeated. "Dave, let's be getting on."

Marged, her warm tones full of tenderness, cried suddenly: "Wait, Dave. I'll ride down with you, sit with him, keep him company. Wait till I get my cape."

She ran toward the house, and Owen looked after her, wishing wretchedly that she would stay. He turned back to the wagon. "I'll be down to see you, first chance I get, papa. I'll stay with mama now."

His father's eyes did not open, but Tom Glen nodded and moved his hand, and Owen took it. Then Marged returned and climbed into the wagon bed, making herself comfortable beside Tom there, and Dave lifted the reins. The wagon moved away.

4

Mrs. Glen died toward dawn of the day after Owen's nineteenth birthday. There had been rain during the night and a thin drizzle was still falling. Mrs. Lewis had gone a little while before to lie down in the other room, but Owen and Doctor Gorman kept vigil. For three days, since his mother's end came drifting near, Owen had stayed by her side, and he was stupid with fatigue. She died so quietly that he did not know the moment till it had passed, till Doctor Gorman said in a new tone:

"Well, Owen, you might tell Mrs. Lewis. Then you get some sleep."

Owen waked Mrs. Lewis, and he lay down on the bed from which she rose, and slept. When he woke, there was sunshine after rain. Hearing him stir, Mrs. Lewis called to bid him go up to Mrs. Morgan's for his breakfast. He obeyed, and on his return he saw Mr. Moury's black vehicle by the roadside at their path. Mrs. Lewis was in the kitchen. His mother's door was closed, and he heard the low voices of men there.

"I've made your bed up fresh, Owen," Mrs. Lewis said gently. "You go lie down."

He obeyed, submitting passively. She closed his door, and he lay on his back, blank eyes fixed on the ceiling. A leak in the roof had stained the plaster, the plaster which Tom Glen himself had put on when they came here to live eight years ago. The stain was shaped like an enormous foot, and Owen remembered the night when a drip of water woke him, and next morning the stain was there. Little forgotten moments, half-memory, half-dream, came drifting back across the empty sky of his thoughts like meaningless small clouds; they came haphazard, in no orderly array. The party at Johnny Peteit's to which he and Mike Pratt went with Joe Ceslak, where a pretty little bride with rosy cheeks made them all laugh by the way her eyes adored her embarrassed husband; the stale tobacco smell of the tin tags he and Willie Tutson used to collect; the way Miss Williams's cheek moved, if you were watching from a few rows behind her and to one side, when she sang in church; the first time Will Davis let him feed the big press; Nellie running to kiss him when he came home from the war, so happy now and soon to have a baby; Chet Masters squealing like a mashed frog under the heavy slate; the night they played *Drop the Handkerchief* and he kissed Jane; the day his mother unwrapped the quarters from her ball of twine; the day he saw his first lawnmower and was paid a quarter for cutting Mr. Beecham's grass; Morffyd meeting her lover by the forest stream, and her white knees in the clear water; the day his father and Evan brought Tom's body home and he looked up from his mother's arms and saw her tears form and run down her cheeks to fall on his face, and her arms holding him, and how soft she was, and the sweet sharp smell of her; the night a few days before Amy was married when he was wretched at the thought of losing her and climbed down to the kitchen to kiss her, and his mother pinching him to make him stop; the day he and Mr. Beecham saw the print of a woman's bare foot in the sandy margin of the creek: these and many others, memories or dreams, sailed across the valley of his mind.

But then suddenly he knew his mother was dead, and sorrow filled him as poured water fills a jug. A line, echo of some forgotten hour when he and Marged read together, shaped itself in his mind. "Grief fills the room up of my absent child." Well, there was grief enough in the world, to be sure.

His door softly opened, and Marged came in and saw him awake and closed the door behind her; she seated herself on the bed beside him, looking down at him, not speaking. To meet her eyes for some reason loosed his tears; weeping, he turned and buried his face in her lap, and her hand touched his head, his shaking shoulders. His arm around her waist drew her near; he pressed close to her, pressing his face against her breast. Here was warmth and softness like his mother's. He had used to run always to his mother, when hurts brought tears; it was a healing to curl in his mother's lap and press against her, so warm and sweetly soft and fondly tender.

It was a healing to cling to Marged now, and she held him, never speaking.

He did not know he slept, nor for how long. When a sound awakened him and his eyes opened and consciousness returned, his head was in the cradle of her arms, his pillow was her bosom. He sat up, staring at her, listening to the steps of men in the other room who moved slowly as though burdened.

"What's that?" he muttered.

She straightened her back, cramped from sitting motionless so long. "Mr. Moury, Owen."

They were taking his mother away! He started to rise, swinging his feet to the floor; but the sounds had moved into the kitchen. They ceased; the men were gone out of the house with their burden.

So he did not rise; there was no help for him; his mother was dead. He rubbed his head, pressing his temples with his knuckles. "Where's Mrs. Lewis?"

"She's gone."

"I went to sleep."

"Yes." They sat half-facing.

"I felt —" He looked at her. "It was like being in my mother's lap when I was little. I feel better now."

"You needed to let go. Everyone needs to let go, sometimes."

"I've sat in mama's lap when I was about as big as I am now," he remembered. "The time I hurt my hand, feeding the job press. I guess I was quite a load." His eyes were shadowed by his thoughts; they touched hers. "I'm glad it was you here today. Whenever I got lonesome in the army, I'd write to you and feel better." His lips moved, half-smiling. "When I was little, I used to watch your cheek, moving whenever you sang, in church." His eyes fell. "I don't know how it's going to be, coming home here and mama not here."

Marged waited for his thoughts to run their race; he too was silent, thinking. His mother was dead, and Mr. Moury had taken her away, and she would be buried. Where? Well, Sardis. His father and Amy would be near her there. Probably burying people cost a lot of money, and Doctor Gorman would have to be paid, and the hospital, and Doctor Roy, for cutting off his father's legs.

Well, he could pay them all; there was time enough; there was all his life. "I guess mama would want to be buried in Sardis," he said, like a question, and she nodded and he returned to his thoughts again.

But presently he looked at Marged, as though for help. "I'll get along all right, that far," he said. "But when she's buried, and everything is over, I'll be alone. That's going to be queer, for a while." His eyes widened in something like fright. "I'll be alone."

She said simply: "I could be here."

He heard at first without comprehending. "What?" He spoke almost angrily, and she lifted her hands and pressed palms against cheeks suddenly afire. "What are you talking about?" Her eyes were wide, half-fearful; and when she did not speak, he caught her shoulders in hard, hurting hands. "Look here! Do you —"

He did not finish his question, but she nodded, with a faint, venturing smile. "Yes, of course."

His hands fell from her shoulders. "Good Gollies!" he whispered, staring at her; and after a moment, as though this were a puzzle that had long perplexed him: "Then that's why you didn't marry Bobby Roberts!"

His tone was so like an accusation, and his question so surprised her that she almost laughed. "M-hm! But he's the only one I've told. Only, of course, your mother knew without my telling."

Owen stood up, towering, tremendous; he looked at her helplessly, and tried to speak, and his hands sought hers.

She rose, shining, and came into his arms.

5

Additional Locals: Spain cedes to the United States Cuba, the Philippines and Porto Rico, in return for $20,000,000; the islands are dirt cheap at the price, but why pay anything? The Woman's Literary Club met this week at Mrs. B. B. Beecham's. *Lost in New York,* coming to the Rink December 16, is said to be funnier than a farce. Stetson's *Uncle Tom's Cabin* troupe, coming December 23, has the largest bloodhound in the world. The event of the week before Christmas in the Adams Furnace neighborhood was the wedding of Mr. Owen Glen and Miss Marged Williams, at the home of the bride's father. The bride has taught in Hardiston High School; Mr. Glen, well known among miners in Hardiston and throughout the county, is the newly elected vice-president of the Sub-District; their many friends wish them much happiness. The concert at the Methodist Episcopal Church was a success; receipts were $65.00 and that tells the story. It was a Merry Christmas in Hardiston; there were bottles in many a pocket and a smell on many a breath, but maybe the boys will do better next year. Happy New Year to all.

THE END